EMPIRE

STATE OF

MINE$!

ALSO BY NOIRE

G-Spot
Candy Licker
Thug-A-Licious
Baby Brother (with 50 Cent)
Thong On Fire
Hood
From the Streets to the Sheets
Hittin' the Bricks
Maneater (with Mary B. Morrison)
Unzipped
G-Spot 2: The Seven Deadly Sins
Lifestyles of the Rich and Shameless
(with Kiki Swinson)
Natural Born Liar
Sexy Little Liar
Dirty Rotten Liar
Red Hot Liar
Stone Cold Liar
B4 the G-Spot: The Legend of Granite McKay

EMPIRE

STATE OF

MINE$!

The All-In-One Version

A Big Ass Book

Chronicles of Crooklyn
Queen of Diamonds
Money Makin Manhattan
Boogie Down Bronx
Wildin on Staten Island

A NOIRE & REEM RAW JOINT

NOIRE

Urban Erotic Noire Publications
www.AskNoire.com

Empire State of Mine$! is a work of fiction. Names, characters, places, and incidents are the product of the author's imagination or are used fictitiously. Any resemblance to actual events, locales, or persons, living or dead, is entirely coincidental.

Empire State of Mine$!
(A Movie in A Book)
The All-In-One Version

Published by Urban Erotic Noire Publications

First Printing February 2016

ISBN-13: 978-0-9830936-9-5

ISBN-10: 0-9830936-9-5

Printed in the United States of America
10 9 8 7 6 5 4 3 2 1

Visit our websites at:
www.NoireStore.com
www.AskNoire.com

A Note from Noire

Hey fam!

It's about that time to hop a ride on the urban erotic train again as it pulls full force into ya station!

I'm excited to have Reem Raw riding the train with me this trip, and I can't wait for y'all to see what kind of fire this artist is blasting outta his pen! His writing game hits just as hard as his mic game, and I know you're gonna love the way we mixed ink in this urban erotic thriller that I believe is my best banga yet!

My readers are the best in the whole damn game because you're smart enough to #DemandQuality and you know I bring it to you every time the urban erotic train comes charging down the tracks.

So relax for a few and put your feet up. Get comfortable and get ready to be mesmerized by this movie you're about to watch in a book. Travel with me through the five boroughs of the Big Apple, New York City, the heart of the Empire State. Y'all already know it's a state of mind, but I'm about to show you that it's also a state of MINE$!

I lub y'all,
Noire

Sign up for my email contact list at **bit.ly/noiresignup**
Like my Facebook page at **bit.ly/noirefanpage**
Follow me on Twitter at **twitter.com/AskNoire**

A Note from Reem Raw

It's been a long time coming and this is just the beginning. Big shout to all my supporters from Team Noire and the homeys and homegirls from around the way who been rockin with me for forever. I put my all into this and I hope ya'll enjoy this Noire and Reem Raw Joint.

This is dedicated to Capri... Detrae Glover... Carlo Beasley... Albie Cloyd... Jammar Riley... Anthony Garcia... Danny Dan and Mann. Sleep easy. Salute to G.H.F. and N.J.S.

One Love
Reem Raw

Like my Facebook page Empire State of Mines, follow me on Twitter @ReemRaw609, on Instagram @Rawmello609, and on SoundCloud.com/reemraw @ReemRaw609.

EMPIRE STATE OF MINE$!

An Urban Erotic Thriller

WARNING!

This here ain't no romance,
It's an Urban Erotic Thriller
The block is clickin, the plots get thickened
when dealing with straight-up killers!
This the city that never sleeps
The Zip 'em up crew always plays for keeps
Drugs and bosses, slugs and coffins,
lives get lost and pain is deep!
Home of the G's and diamond thieves,
Where crooked police won't let you breathe,
Where the money comes fast and they put you on blast
and the belly of the beast won't let you leave!
A lot of shit goes down in this gunslingers town,
pay ya dues...no rules when they coming for ya crown!
Every borough is thorough and ya life's on the line,
this is NYC, an Empire State of Mine$!

EMPIRE

STATE of MINE$!

(A Movie in a Book)

Episode 1

Chronicles of Crooklyn

A NOIRE & REEM RAW JOINT

There are eight million stories in the naked city of New York.

These five are all the way live.

"Crooklyn niggas get all the loot!

That's because them crazy niggas ain't scared to shoot!"

CHAPTER 1

A Sometimey Muh'fucka!

"Yo, look at Thot McStuffins over there fuckin up them jeans," Black Pearl muttered as he chewed on a toothpick that was sticking outta the corner of his mouth. His lazy eyes were glued to the hips of a glamorous hood chick who was strolling past the project building with her ass high in the air. Mami was a certified and legit bad bitch. Long Brazilian, tiny lil waist, fat titties, and the type of bouncing donk that kept a nigga lickin his lips.

"Fuck that nasty scab!" his boy Dolla spit as they chilled on the porch of building 430. He nodded toward the walkway. "Check out that pigeon-chasin tard-head over there fuckin wit' that watch!"

The tall dude coming toward the porch looked shot out. He was mumbling under his breath and stiff-walking like a two-year-old with a shitty pamper.

Dolla and his four-man crew had just come in from bustin all their traps. Dolla was the baby of the bunch and the cruelest of them all. Short and muscular with a medium-light complexion, he had long dreadlocks and a grimy hood demeanor.

Dolla took a swig off his Corona then passed the bottle to his day-one homey, Ed Mu. His eyes narrowed as he grilled the bum who was shuffling his feet and dangling an old-fashioned pocket-watch from his fingers.

The fourteen-story old folk's building they were holding down was damn near a nursing home. It was quiet and didn't attract no whole lotta attention. It was the perfect spot to establish a fresh drug headquarters, which is why Handgun Goody, Brownsville's most brutal drug kingpin, was trying to find a few empty apartments to pump out of.

Goody had sent Dolla, Black Pearl, Alione, and Ed Mu over to the building to put fear in the hearts of the elderly residents. The other three street soldiers were just following their orders, but intimidating the weak and helpless was right up Dolla's alley.

"Yo, watch this shit," he said. He was amped to clown the bummy-looking cat as soon as dude got up close to the porch. "I'ma fuck homeboy up for that rusty watch."

Dressed in tattered old army clothes, the dude looked like he was off his rocker. He was tall and built real fit, but he moved like he was high or in a daze. He was muttering something under his breath as he checked and rechecked the time on the old pocket watch.

"Man, leave Sometimey alone," Alione waved Dolla's young ass off. Alione was a six-foot-five, tar-black tall drink of water and he didn't waste a whole lotta words. "That shell-shocked muh'fucka don't be botherin nobody but them pigeons up on the roof. You know that nigga's eggs is scrambled. They say he came back from the military all psycho like that."

Dolla grabbed his nuts and bucked at his homey. "Yo I don't give a *fuck* about that nigga's eggs! He don't belong in this old people's building no way. I'ma fuck his retarded ass up."

Stepping over to the edge of the porch, Dolla cupped his hands around his mouth and hollered, "Yo, Sometimey! *Sometimey!* Nigga you hear me callin you! Hur'rup and get up on this goddamn porch! What time is it, bruh?"

The slow-minded veteran looked up like he was confused. His eyebrows dropped low and his lips started moving even faster. He slowed his stroll like he was scared to approach the porch and his stiff little steps became even choppier.

"Come on, fuck-boy! Get your pigeon-pokin ass up here and tell me what time it is!"

"Shut the fuck up Dolla and lee'im alone!" Alione ordered again. "You attracting unnecessary attention, stupid ass! Ain't nothin but old people in this fuckin building, yo. You know they quick to call the cops."

"*Did you hear me, nigga?*" Dolla igged Alione and barked on the bum again. Sometimey stood there shaking like a lil bitch and hiding his watch behind his back. Dolla stepped off the porch and ran down on him real strong. The bum was tall as hell. Dolla's evil glare traveled from his face down to his raggedy army pants and stopped at the toes of his pigeon-shit splattered boots. Then he glanced back up at dude's peasy head that was covered with a stupid little bird cap.

"Yo, I ain't gonna ask you no more. What fuckin time is it, my nigga?"

"I-I-I," the crazy bum parted his lips and whispered as his whole body shook in fear. "I'on't...know."

Dolla yanked his fist back like he was about to cold smash him. Dude ducked low and threw his arms up to cover his head and Dolla busted out laughing.

"Get the fuck outta here you goddamn weirdo!" he hollered as Sometimey jetted across the porch with fear in his eyes.

"Ay, my click 'bout to take over this whole fuckin building, nigga! Nah, these whole fuckin *'jects!* So next time I ask yo dumb ass what time it is..." Dolla rushed behind him and punted the toe of his Timb deep in the crack of dude's ass, "you better fuckin tell me!!!"

The nutcase yelped and grabbed at his ass with both hands. For a second he hopped up and down like a scared lil kid, and then he barreled into the lobby and scampered into the waiting elevator. Trembling, the bum jabbed at the button for the top floor. Then he crouched down low in a pissy corner and covered his face with his hands.

Dolla stood there grilling him. Loud laughter erupted from his homeys on the porch behind him and Dolla's spirits got lifted for the first time all day. He walked back outside and elbowed Ed Mu in his chubby stomach and gave Black Pearl some dap. He cut his eyes at Alione, then he reached for his brewski and cracked up right along with his boyz.

"Man, gimme my goddamn 'Rona!" Dolla snatched the cold bottle from Ed Mu and turned it up for a swig. "Muthafuck that Sometimey muh'fucka!"

$$$$$

Four hours later the sky over the corrupt town of Crooklyn was dark and menacing as the elevator door creaked open in the lobby of building 430. The elderly residents of Van Dyke projects had long ago retreated to the safety of their apartments and the ominous streets were now home to the wicked and the wily.

Dolla was in the staircase getting his meat mauled by a crackhead that he had snatched off the corner for five dollars. The skinny girl with the raggedy weave was on her knees jacking his tiny wiener and slobbering all over his walnuts like her next hit depended on it.

"Nah, don't be shy! Put all this here shit in ya mouth, bitch!" Dolla demanded like he was working with a foot-long dick. "You lucky I don't bang all this wood down your throat and choke ya ass wit' it!"

The desperate fiend put her lip game down on him like a pro. She made her mouth get real wet and let his lil dick go swimming in hot spit as she sucked his miniature nub and squeezed his balls. Dolla groaned deep in his throat and palmed her knotty head. He pumped his joint up into her mouth and gasped with pleasure.

Moments later he let one blast on her, and when she went to let go of his dick he gripped her head firmly between his hands until she swallowed his seed and his shit went soft. Pulling up his pants, he gave her a look of disgust then tossed the five dollar bill at her and kicked open the exit door.

Outside, the other three trap boys were still occupying the porch of the old folks building. With his balls nice and empty, Dolla joined them and they got turnt up and rowdy as they guzzled brew, shot cee-low, and talked cash shit. They gave no fucks about disturbing the peace of the elderly residents and they threatened to pop on anybody who looked out the window and even thought about complaining.

Ed Mu had already made at least three trips to the all-night corner store to restock their supply of Coronas and Remy 1738. He had an overweight thotty on standby at the crib waiting to suck his dick, and after peering into the empty carton he decided to make one last run for the night.

"Yo, a nigga thirsty again," he said as he thrust his hands into the front pockets of his sagging pants. "I'll be right back."

Dolla and Black Pearl were so caught up in shooting a game of cee-low that they barely noticed Ed Mu leaving. Alione noticed, though. He caught up with Ed and they walked off toward the all-night corner store together.

No sooner than they'd disappeared did the elevator door creak open in the building's lobby. A tall, athletic-looking cat stepped out. He was dressed in baggy jeans and his head was covered by an oversized hoody that was blacker than the midnight sky.

He crossed the building's quiet lobby in three deadly strides and yanked the front door open so hard that it crashed back against the wall. The glass panel shattered from the force and glittering shards fell to the ground.

Crouching down as he shook the dice in his palm, Black Pearl looked up and locked eyes with him first.

"Oh *shit* . . ." is all the treacherous young hustla had time to mutter before the barrel of a Tech Nine flashed brightly and hot lead flew at him full force.

Standing three feet away, Dolla was quicker than his boy and lighter on his feet, but not by much. His street instincts kicked in and so did all the alcohol that he had been consuming. Dolla knew he'd just got caught lacking, and he feared he was about to get robbed, or even worse, deaded.

He spun around and rose up outta his crouch like a sprinter coming out the blocks. He had taken about four long strides off the porch, hauling ass super-quick, when the first round caught him in the back of his right thigh.

"*Ahhhh!!!*" he screamed and clutched his torn quadriceps muscle as he broke into a stiff-legged shuffle run. "*Ahhhh!* Muh'fucka you *shot* me!!!"

The second slug ripped through his left calf, hobbling him. The third bullet pierced neatly through his left shoulder. It spun his ass around in a wide circle and slammed him mug-down into the concrete ground.

The hooded gunslinger walked up on him with a cool, steady gait. His footsteps were heavy. His cold face was covered in shadows.

Dolla was gushing red life liquid and shitting in his drawers.

"What the *fuck!*" the tough street-slanga shrieked. Grunting against the pain, he scooted backwards like a crab. "Why you pop on me like that, son? Why you ain't just rob me and take the fuckin stash, yo? Nigga who the fuck is you *anyway*—"

And then he saw the boots.

They were old and scruffy. Army-issued, with the turnt-up toes covered in droplets of dried pigeon shit.

"This *my* muthafuckin buildin!" the gunman spit coldly. "Y'all bum-ass niggas ain't taking over a *goddamn* thing!"

"Oh *shit!*" Dolla shrieked, repeating the very last words of his boy Black Pearl. "Naw, it can't be you! You sometimey *bastard*, you!"

"Yeah," the bum-turned-killer chuckled as he gripped his loaded burner in one hand and slid his precious watch outta his pocket with the other one. "I'm a sometimey muh'fucka alright! You still wanna know what time it is?"

He flipped the rusty timepiece open and laughed mirthlessly into the dark night.

"It's *graveyard* time, pussy!" Slick "Sometimey" Williams growled as his trigger finger jerked and silver death flew from the toolie's chamber. "Nigga it's time to *die!*"

CHAPTER 2

Zippin 'Em Up!

The moon had dipped behind thick clouds that illuminated very little light, lending perfect conditions for the mission that was about to be executed.

On duty and on point, Noodles Baines was focused like fuck. The mute, dreadlocked killer sat motionlessly on a rooftop across from the Tranquil Gardens Gourmet Chinese restaurant. It was located in a renovated butcher shop in Silicon Alley, Brooklyn. Outfitted with the finest weaponry scopes and sniper binoculars that money could buy, Noodles's senses were on high alert.

Down on the street below, two armed security guards were standing outside the restaurant with their eyes in hawk-mode. They had been promised ten grand each for one night's work, and they were about to earn every penny of it.

"Sure are a lot of chinks here tonight," the taller guard said to his partner.

The shorter guard shrugged. "It's a fuckin Chinese restaurant, Billy! What do you expect? Besides, the slant-eyes are making all the money in this town because they've got the computer industry locked up tight." He chuckled. "The chinks out in California have Silicon Valley, and here in Brooklyn our chinks got Silicon *Alley!*"

At exactly ten p.m. a sky-blue 2017 BMW sports coupe sped into view and swerved into the restaurant's parking lot. The driver sideswiped a sweet white Benz that was just being parked by a uniformed valet. The BMW came to a screeching halt and both men jumped outta their vehicles.

The armed guards weren't laughing anymore. They were immediately focused and on edge. Their hands gripped the stocks of their holstered heat, and they were gearing up to let off a few rounds until the insane drama began to unfold.

"What the *fuck!*" the black valet who had been parking the Mercedes popped off. "You trying to get me fired, you fuckin idiot? Look what you did to this goddamn car!"

A brolick young Chinese man dressed in an expensive business suit stood beside his BMW looking crisp and unfazed.

He tossed the black guy the keys to his ninety-thousand-dollar ride and smirked.

"Park my shit and get the hell outta my way or you'll get more than fired, you goddamn ape."

The two white security guards were taken by surprise by the racial slur. They eased up on their guns as they laughed at the throw-down that was about to go down.

"Now this is the type of shit you can only see in Brooklyn," the taller one chuckled. "Bruce Lee versus Bruce *Leroy!*"

The shorter one laughed too. "I got a hundred bucks that says this nigger is about to get Kung Fu'ed by the buff Oriental cat. No, wait. They're paying us pretty good tonight. I got two hundred that says the chink is gonna flying-roundhouse kick that uppity coon right in his throat."

The tall guard was about to seal the bet in favor of the bulky-framed Asian, but then he noticed how strong the black valet was swelling up.

"Yo!" the black dude beefed, looking handsome and muscular in his starched white shirt, burgundy vest, and black dress slacks. "Who the fuck is you calling a monkey? You ching-chong-cholly-wong, general toes, chicken-wonton-soup-sippin, alley-cat-kidnapping *bitch!* Don't let the shiny shoes fool ya, a'ight? Fuck this punk-ass job, I'll slap the sweet and sour spit *sideways* outta ya face!"

The guards roared with laughter as the two suited-up men talked shit and circled each other with their fists balled up. They couldn't wait to see the ass-kicking that one of the men was about to receive.

Surveying the scene from the rooftop, Noodles typed a few words into the small electronic device that would vocalize his commands into the tiny ear-pieces of his crew members below.

Time to move, he typed, and just like that the black valet in the shiny shoes and the hardbody Chinese businessman whirled around in opposite directions until each was facing a security guard. In a calculated movement they both drew short-barreled handguns equipped with deadly silencers and fired once at each guard.

Phewt! Phewt!

The taller guard's Adams apple exploded sideways from his throat as the other guard's brain matter flew from the back of his head. Both men were dead before they hit the ground.

Without making a sound, Slick and his homey Wild Man lowered their weapons and pushed stealthily through the entrance of the Chinese restaurant and disappeared from sight.

Phase One is complete, Noodles typed into his high-tech text-to-talk device that conveyed his message to his team. *Moving on to Phase Two.*

$$$$$

The celebration inside the Tranquil Gardens Gourmet Chinese restaurant was just about at its peak. The main dining room buzzed with excitement and festive sounds. The board of representatives of E-Core Tech Alliance Group was celebrating the hostile takeover of one of New York City's leading firms in the information technology industry.

It was a Chinese-owned company celebrating at a Chinese restaurant, but brilliant minds came in every flavor. There was a mixture of whites and Asians milling about, and several black and Hispanic techies were also on hand.

Seated at a fifty-thousand-dollar table, a clean-cut Caucasian man called Whitey Reynolds watched the happenings up on the stage. His attention was focused on a silver-haired Asian billionaire who sat surrounded by the board of directors and the company's top investors. The billionaire radiated money and power. Whatever he was saying had people grabbing onto his words like he had hundred dollar bills stuck between his teeth.

"Howdy, Mr. Chuong!" Whitey heard a voice shout out in a deep southern accent as a fat little Texas banker pushed his way out of the crowd. Dude waddled over to the edge of the stage then rolled up on his huge belly and climbed up.

Immediately, the security guards on the stage grabbed at their heat and moved to collapse on the greedy little banker but the Asian billionaire waved them off.

"Sorry, I don't mean to intrude," the banker said, extending his hand for a shake. "It's just that I'm in awe. It's not every day a dumb country-boy like me gets to meet a corporate billionaire who's financing the next software breakthrough in the modern world. You high-tech types must be eating deep-fried computer chips in your egg rolls or something."

Posted up near the side doors of the room were two more armed security guards. The older one shot a disapproving look toward the stage guards who had let the banker get up close on the billionaire. Their instructions had been to keep any and every fuckin body away from the wealthy Asian, and they were being paid top dollars to guard the man with their lives.

But the guards on stage were so busy watching the fat country banker that they paid little attention when the front doors opened and a handsome young Chinese man casually strolled in, gun concealed. A black valet was right behind him jiggling a set of car keys in his hand.

Both of their eyes were focused on the two armed security guards who were standing near the side doors of the room. Neither man was their intended target, but nevertheless, both men were going to die tonight.

"Show-time, baby," Whitey muttered under his breath as he sat at the fifty-thousand-dollar table watching the hit about to go down. "Time to get the fireworks popping."

He watched as a beautiful black waitress sashayed in from the kitchen area with her long braided ponytail swinging behind her. Wearing a short white apron tied over a skin-tight black mini skirt, she was shaking her hips and pushing a dinner cart stacked high with covered plates.

The VIP techie guests were ready to be served, and the waitress stopped directly in front of the head table where the Asian billionaire was seated.

She paused for a moment to let the whole room soak up her sexiness. Her lil black skirt was so short and her chocolate body was exploding with so many curves that when she bent over to retrieve a platter from the bottom shelf of the cart, every man in the room took a deep breath hoping to get a whiff of her sweet black pussy.

The silver-haired billionaire's crotch bricked up and his eyes bulged outta his head as he stared at her slim body and thick ass. He was the type of man who could buy any and everything he wanted, but when he reached out like he was gonna run his hand up under her short skirt he got G-checked by the deadly glint in her eyes.

Suddenly she smiled and displayed a row of perfect white teeth. Poking her sculpted ass out and giving all the men a treat, Jewelz Jordan slid her hand discreetly under the cart and gripped something cold and black in her fist.

Turn up, Noodles typed into his device, and simultaneously the Chinese cat and the black dude in the shiny shoes punched bullet holes in the two guards who were posted at the exit doors across the room.

Their movements were so precise and their silencers so effective that the heat rounds crossed the room and hit their targets too fast for the patrons to comprehend what was happening. Both guards dropped to the floor in a bloody heap before the guests seated next to them could even open their mouths to scream.

The beautiful waitress with the thick hunk of ass was completely forgotten as the other two security guards up on the stage saw their partners fall. They drew their weapons and moved in to protect their clients but they failed to notice the waitress pulling a Mac-11 out from under the cart of covered plates.

Her instructions were to take out the entire board of directors and that's exactly what she was gonna do. The sound of thunder erupted from the barrel of her burner, and blood and body fluids splashed the wall behind the stage as she unleashed the sub-machine gun and sprayed left to right, laying the whole table down.

The remaining guards bitched up. They tried to run and take cover but they were met by a hail of hot lava as the 32-shot clip was emptied into their bodies.

The deafening sound of gunfire gave way to the screams of the terrified guests. Terror and chaos blanketed the restaurant like a thick fog. Most patrons were frozen in place and scared to run for fear of being cut down in the random spray of wild bullets.

Only the man they called Whitey remained on chill as he sat quietly in his seat at the fifty-thousand-dollar table. His blue eyes were fearless and colder than ice as pandemonium ripped all around him.

"Kill it," he finally barked into his Bluetooth cufflink, and the entire room went black.

Taking advantage of the cover of darkness, the guests started stampeding like wild cattle. Women screamed, tables were knocked over, wine bottles fell and smashed to the floor, and devoted husbands abandoned their wives and broke for the exit doors.

After what seemed like an eternity, but was actually less than sixty seconds, the lights flickered back on. The scent of blood, death, and gunpowder remained in the bullet-strewn room, but the five contracted gunslingers, also known as the Zip 'em up Crew, had vanished.

CHAPTER 3

Twenty Years Earlier...

A Nightmare in Crooklyn

"How can you *mendddd* my broken *hearttttt...*"

Lil Slick listened to his daddy sing off key as he slow-danced in the living room with his number one baby momma, Kea.

"Damn boy!" Kea laughed as her man grinded his wood up against her coochie and palmed her fluffy ass. She threw her head back as his juicy lips sucked all over her collarbone and he tongued a wet streak all the way up her neck. Kea was young and fine, and she was enjoying every moment of her king's attention. "You know you can't sang for shit baby but I luvs ya anyway."

"If you ain't loving you ain't living, baby!" Big Slick laughed and grinded up on her some more.

Lil Slick's parents, Kea and Big Slick, had grown up together in the same projects. Their families had been real cool with each other, and as far back as either one of them could remember they had always had a love thang going on.

Big Slick Williams was a ladies man though. Very charming and good-looking. He had always wanted to have a big family so Kea got pregnant quickly when she was in her late-teens and gave him three cute babies, damn near back to back.

Even though Kea knew she was Big Slick's favorite woman, she knew she would never be his *only* woman. Kea had long ago made peace with that knowledge because she had something that none of Slick's other bitches could give him: His firstborn son.

Kea had named her baby boy Samir Williams Jr. to create a bond between him and his daddy straight from the jump that could never be severed. And it had worked too. Big Slick was a damn good father who loved the ground their little boy walked on. But when one of his on-the-side tricks pushed out a baby boy of her own, she tried to get clever by naming her son Samir the second.

Kea had hit the fuckin roof. It was one thing to watch some off-brand bitch pushing her man's seed around in a baby stroller, but it was something else to hear everybody calling the outside baby by *her* son's name!

So Kea came up with a nice-ass plan. Fuck a Samir. Niggas in the know called Slick by his street name anyway. She killed all that "Lil Samir" shit and started calling her son Lil Slick, and she made sure everybody else did too.

But name or no name, Big Slick could have a whole damn tribe of sons named after him but none of their mamas would ever have his heart the way Kea did. She had started from the bottom with him. She was Slick's rider, his right-hand, his through thick-and-thin bitch, 25/8. She lived for his slick ass, and she was willing to die for him too.

Like a true trap queen, Kea had helped Big Slick rise to the top of the cocaine market in Brownsville. She had worked right by his side as he schemed, scored, and strategized, yet she still found time to be a freak in the sheets and a damn good mother to their three kids.

Through all the ruthless shit that Big Slick had to endure running the projects while holding it down on the streets and evading the law, what he held most dear, even above the fine bitches and the easy money, was his kids.

Regardless of how any of his baby mommas felt about him, not a damn one of them could ever say he was a bad father or didn't do right by his shorties. Big Slick's seeds were his only weakness, so he kept his business in the street and never brought it back to the house with him.

But on this night, as Big Slick's oldest son watched him squeeze his mother's ass and serenade her with sweet kisses and old-school songs, they had company.

It was Lil Slick's 7th birthday, and Big Slick had brought his two outside-the-house kids over so they could celebrate the occasion together as a family unit.

And in addition to having all of Big Slick's kids present for the festivities, Kea had also invited the pretty little girl who lived next door with her drunk-ass uncle. The six-year-old child called herself having a crush on Lil Slick, and every time Kea looked up the girl was knocking on the door asking if she could come across the hall to play.

Kea felt sorry for the poor lil thing. The girl was usually left in the apartment by herself all day long while her alky uncle ran the streets picking up bottles and chugging Wild Irish Rose. Kea knew the child needed some regular mothering and some decent meals in her stomach, so she invited her to eat breakfast with them on the weekends and to share dinner with them almost every night.

And tonight, in celebration of Lil Slick's birthday, all eight of them had sat around the table together like one big happy family. Kea had burnt up the pots in her firstborn son's honor, and they had stuffed their faces on his favorite meal: barbequed chicken, baked macaroni and cheese, cornbread, and collard greens. Afterwards they sang happy birthday and ate vanilla, chocolate, and strawberry ice cream on top of thick slices of homemade seven-up pound cake. When they were done they chased the whole thing down with big cups of icy red Kool-Aid.

Once the dishes were washed, Kea took the kids into the living room where her and Big Slick turned the music back on again. Lil Slick opened up all his birthday presents and they sang, danced, and enjoyed their time together like close families often do.

After an hour or so of singing and playing with the kids a hard, desperate knock came at the door.

Kea didn't hang out in the streets or have any unannounced company in her house so the bamming on her door caught her off-guard and had her a little concerned.

"I'll get that, baby," Big Slick told her, noticing the look on her face. Lil Slick had noticed the look too, and as young as he was, he didn't like it.

"It's prolly just my brother," Big Slick reassured her as he moved toward the door. "I told him I was gonna be chillin over here with you and the kids and he said he might swing by so he could rap with me about something."

Big Slick answered the door and let his brother in. Hassan Williams, or Crazy Haz as they called him, was Big Slick's little brother, even though he was just as tall as Big Slick, a little bit heavier, and a whole lot meaner.

Growing up, Haz had wanted to be just like his big brother but he wasn't as smooth with his game and he couldn't get the ladies to throw him the pussy the way they tossed it at Slick neither.

Compared to the bull muscles that Slick was packing, Haz was un-athletic and on the pudgy side. They were both street niggas to the bone, but Big Slick was smarter and well respected on the streets while Crazy Haz was feared and had a rep as a grimeball nigga.

Haz was the leader of a crew of stick-up kids who ran around like gladiators in Brownsville, East New York, and Canarsie. They jammed or extorted anybody who looked like they had some money or some product. As a get-money nigga Big Slick was far from a punk himself and he could definitely handle his own. But even the come-up hungry wolves were too leery to test him because they knew how dirty his crazy brother Haz played the game.

"Yo w'sup bro, what's going on wit'chu," Big Slick said as he grinned and gave his little bro a hug and showed him some love.

"Ain't shit, Slick. I'm chillin," Haz responded, sniffing and shifting his eyes back and forth.

Right off the cuff Big Slick smelled the aroma of Kush mixed with burnt cocaine on his brother's clothes. Haz's eyes were bloodshot and slightly glazed over.

"Yo, you smoking them dirties again huh nigga? Got you lookin all crazy in the face and shit. You crazy-dumb for fucking with that shit!" Big Slick said, mad that his brother had showed up around his kids high as a fuckin light bill to try and talk some business.

"Fuck you mean?" Haz bucked, swaying on his feet and looking more fucked up the more he talked. "Yeah, I'm high. So what? I do what the fuck I wanna do nigga! You ain't my pops muh'fucka!"

Big Slick based on him. "Naw nigga I ain't ya raggedy-ass daddy! I'm Big *Bro* that's who the fuck I am! I ain't one of them lil dope heads you be getting dusted with so watch ya tone in my crib nigga! Now let's roll to the kitchen so we can talk, a'ight?"

Haz nodded, then paused to step into the living room for a quick second. "Happy birthday, Lil Slick," he said. He reached down in his pocket and pulled out a twenty, then he gave it to his oldest nephew with a hug and some dap.

As the two men headed towards the kitchen, Kea turned up the music and got out a bag of silver Jax and a rubber ball so she could entertain the kids while their dad and uncle talked in private.

"Yo Slick, I need five ounces of that girl from you, just to show this nigga over in Marcus Garvey that I got the product before I stick his ass. I'll give it right back to you, word is life," Haz pleaded, whispering to his brother in an anxious tone.

Big Slick shook his head. "Hell naw. I ain't fuckin with you like that Haz. Not for nothing. Last time I loaned you some work you was supposed to bring it right back too, nigga. Bad thing is, you didn't even take it and flip it, you just fucked the package up."

"Man, shit happens!" Haz exploded. "I hold you down in these streets, nigga! I keep the wolves offa yo ass, boy! Now when I need a little help right-quick you mister high-and-fuckin-mighty?" screamed Haz, who was trembling with hot rage. The weed mixed with the cocaine fueled his deep-seated jealousy of his brother and allowed him to totally dismiss the fact that he really *had* fucked up the last package that Big Slick had given him.

"Yeah, nigga you *must* be high," Big Slick spit as he scowled at his baby brother. "Who the fuck you think schooled you on this game in the first place? I hold *myself* down out here, little *nigga!* You ain't grinding for yours! You just out there robbing and stealing from niggas who tryna make a lil change to feed they families! I'm a hustla baby, and my gun bang just like yours do! I don't need you for shit, and you ain't getting shit from me. *Period!*"

The verbal lashing from his big brother was too much for Haz to take. In his cocaine-warped mind Big Slick owed it to him, and everybody under the sun who breathed air and owed him *anything* had to pay the fuck up. Brother or no brother.

"Well *fuck you* then nigga, ante-up!" Haz shrieked as he reached in his waistband and pulled out a .38 long-nose and cocked the hammer back. "We mighta came outta the same pussy but I want that *work* nigga, or I'ma dead you up in this bitch!"

Above the sounds of the music Kea heard the commotion and paused with a handful of Jax in her palm. She set them down on the floor and began to focus her attention on the conversation going down in the kitchen.

"I'ma tell you what's gonna happen right now," Big Slick said in a calm, but firm voice. "You gonna put that gun down, apologize to me, and then get the fuck outta my crib right fuckin now before I make you swallow that shit! And you ain't getting so much as a nickel bag from me you ungrateful fuck!"

BANG!!! BANG!!!

Two shots rang out and Big Slick flew backwards against the stove and crashed down hard.

In the living room, Kea shrieked and dove on top of all six kids, covering them with her body.

Crazy Haz stood over Big Slick in the kitchen, wild-eyed and frightened at the sight of what he'd just done. He was in a state of shock and confusion. The drugs had his head spinning and he paced back and forth as he watched the only brother he had gasp desperately for air with two bloody holes slowly darkening his chest.

"I told you to gimme the damn work nigga!" Haz cried out in regret. "Look what the fuck you made me do, Slick! *FUCK!* Why you had to try to play me like that, man? I told you...I told you...I *told* your fuckin ass..." Haz muttered desperately as he watched his brother's life fade away.

"YOU *MOTHAFUCKKAAA!!*" came a roar from the doorway. "I'LL KILL *YOUUU*," Kea screamed as she charged into the kitchen and jumped on Hassan's back. In a rabid frenzy she scratched and clawed and bit at every part of him that she could get a hold of.

Haz twisted and turned violently for a few seconds until he flipped her over and she landed hard on the floor.

"You stupid *bitch!* I ain't never liked your narrow ass anyway!" he spit as he raised his leg in the air and brought his size fourteen boot down square in the middle of Kea's face.

SPLAT!

Kea's nose broke instantly. A stream of blood and snot exploded from her nostrils as she reflexively reached for her face and tried to take cover.

Haz began viciously kicking and punching her around the small kitchen. He bounced her petite frame off the cabinets, the table, and the refrigerator too.

Lil Slick jumped up from the living room floor where his mother had left him and peeked into the kitchen at the carnage that was taking place.

"You fucking slut!" his uncle was screaming as he kicked his mother around like a football. "This shit is all your fault! You turned my brother against me you fuckin tramp! I'ma dead ya dumb ass just like I did him, hoe!"

Haz gripped Kea by the hair and swung her around in an arc. Her head cracked against the kitchen sink like a metal bat slamming a baseball into home-run land. Immediately she went limp and slumped to the floor, blacked completely out.

Kea stayed cloaked in merciful darkness for long, long minutes, and when she awoke she could barely move.

The pain radiating throughout her body was almost unbearable, but somehow she managed to crawl over to a chair and pull herself up to her knees, and then to her feet.

She glanced around in a daze. Blood was smeared all over the kitchen like wet red paint. She looked down and saw Big Slick sprawled out on the floor nearby, bullet holes dotting his chest and his dead eyes opened wide.

Kea's battered face crumpled in grief as she dropped to the floor again and reached toward her man, but a scream from the living room snatched her attention and caused her adrenaline to kick into over-drive.

She climbed to her feet and limped out of the kitchen, holding on to the walls to keep herself upright. When she turned the corner she froze in her tracks and then gasped in breathtaking shock.

All six of the kids lay sprawled out across the living room floor. Blood was splattered everywhere and each of them had multiple stab wounds all over their tiny bodies. Samira, Samille, Samir II, and Samika, were all laying side-by-side, deathly still.

To Kea's horror, Haz was crouching over an injured and struggling Lil Slick, muscling the boy down and jabbing at him with the sharp tip of a butcher knife.

Her heart stopped. She threw her head back and shrieked in pain as she watched Haz extract the blade from her baby's stomach. Lil Slick gasped and tried to fight him off and Haz laughed and plunged the blade deeply into his chest. Kea's nose gushed blood as tears of rage and grief streamed from her eyes.

"Noooo…"

Haz looked up and eyed Kea wobbling with her bruised hands outstretched toward the bloody children.

"*Noooo…*" she moaned again as Lil Slick's small body shuddered and went limp under his uncle's assault. "My babies…*nooooo…not my babies!*"

"Shut up, bitch," Haz muttered with madness in his eyes. "You know the fuckin drill," he spit as he glared down at his bloodied firstborn nephew then dug his fingers in the boy's pocket and took his twenty dollars back. "I'm laying *every* fuckin body down! Lottie-dottie and every fuckin body's gotta go!"

Hassan raised the knife in the air to stab Lil Slick again. Bloodied but unbroken, Kea growled deep in her throat. She glared at him from murderous eyes and her entire body trembled with the vicious rage of a mother bear.

With nothing but her teeth and fingernails to use as a weapon, she crouched down low and made a swift, desperate lunge toward him.

Crazy Haz grinned as he watched his brother's bitch advance on him like a beast. Her arms were extended like hammers. Her fingers were curved and reached for him like claws. She was almost upon him before he drew his heat and cocked the hammer. Still grinning, he pulled the trigger and shot her once. Square between the eyes.

$$$$$

Boom!!!

"Slick! *Slick!* Wake up. You were dreaming, baby. You're safe, honey. It was just a dream!"

Slick's eyes flew open. The haunting sounds of a fading gunshot echoed in his ears and the sight of his mother's dead body swam in his vision.

Right away his fingers flew to his chest, groping and feeling for the knife wounds and the bubbling hot blood. He grimaced and bit back the force of the twenty-year-old screams that were trying to burst from his lips.

Slick struggled to sit up. Every muscle in his body was twisted up tight on a spring, and the blanket underneath him was soaked in hot, terrified sweat.

Jewelz Jordan, the only female member of the Zip 'em up Crew, was crouched down on the sofa beside him. Dressed in a body-hugging sheer white negligee, she pressed her warm hand over the thick scar on his chest as she scooted up closer to him and whispered softly in his ear.

"It's okay, Slick. Calm down. You were dreaming, baby," she said as she kissed the pulse that throbbed in his temple.

Slick's chest heaved up and down and Jewelz continued to soothe him. "It was just a dream," she whispered. "Calm down, baby. It was just a dream."

Slick let out a long deep sigh as he journeyed back to the present. He looked around at the stylish glass-and-marble crib. He was in Money-Making Manhattan. He had come home with Jewelz after the hit last night. She was holding him in her arms and her sweet voice felt like a rope being tossed to a drowning man. He stared up into her beautiful brown eyes and fought against the memories as he tried to pull his shit together.

"C'mon, Slick. Relax, king," Jewelz whispered again as she ran her fingers over the muscles bulging on his chest. She slid them down his hard stomach and under the waistband of his boxers, and she woulda dipped them even lower and gone straight for the dick, but Slick grabbed her hand and squeezed her fingers tight.

Jewelz was a real special chick and she knew him better than most people ever would, but she had that shit wrong. It wasn't just a dream and she knew it. Nah, this shit was his *reality*. It was the story of his fuckin life. The life that murderous monster Crazy Haz had left him with.

Jewelz's hot lips were on his neck now. Sucking up a storm. Her soft tongue teased his ear. She slid her toned thigh across his body and straddled him, her thick meaty ass a nice firm weight pressing down on his groin.

"Lemme help you forget," she whispered as she leaned forward and rocked her hips on top of his. She pressed her stiff nipples to his bare chest and moaned. "I swear I can make all them nightmares disappear and go away in a heartbeat, Slick. I can help you forget everything that happened that day baby. At least for a little while..."

Jewelz's soft body felt like a warm puddle of chocolate goodness in his arms and Slick felt his manhood responding to her frantic thrusts. Pulling her closer, they kissed and humped on each other feverishly as their groins collided and strained to lock. Jewelz stuck out her tongue and left a streak of wetness across his chest as she licked and sucked his nipples. Easing up, she reached between their bodies and gently guided Slick's rigid dick outta the peephole in the front of his boxers. She squeezed the swollen crown and ran her fingers up and down the length of his pretty wood and gripped its thickness as it throbbed in the palm of her hand.

Slick groaned. He slid his hand between her toned legs and swiped at her hot pussy. The fabric of her crotch was soaking wet and a puddle of sweet juice coated his fingers.

Purring like a kitten as she bit down gently on his nipple, Jewelz rotated her hips and grinded her snatch greedily on his hand. Pulling her crotch aside, Slick inserted his middle finger deeply into the hot cave of her pussy, then he quickly withdrew it and rubbed her sweet honey all over her swollen clit.

Jewelz yelped and clamped down hard with her inner muscles as Slick dove back in and finger-fucked her with long strokes. She shivered on top of him as she rocked her hips back and forth in excruciating pleasure.

"Slick!" she panted as she rotated her groin and clenched and flexed her thick ass-cheeks. In a haze of delight she reached up and squeezed her bulging breasts and rubbed and pinched her aching nipples. With his stiff finger plunging in and out of her wetness and her own hands stroking sparks straight outta her nipples, Jewelz knew she could mess around and cum just like that. But she didn't want to. She wanted the whole damn package. She wanted to make love. She wanted to be wrapped in Slick's arms. She wanted to feel him pounding that meat up inside her. She reached between them and grabbed his wrist and thrust her hips to his rhythm and whispered, "Come get this shit, baby. Yeah...this *your* pussy, Slick. This shit is all yours..."

Her voice fell over him like a bucket of cold water. In an instant Slick withdrew his finger from her sucking tunnel. He licked her dripping juices from his hand and then ran his palms over the mounds of her beautiful brown ass and up her slim waist. He thumbed Jewelz's plump breasts and cupped her under her arms, and then he gently lifted her up off of him and set her aside on the couch.

"What's up?" Jewelz panted looking puzzled in the face. Her breath was coming quickly as her chest rose and fell. "What's wrong?"

Slick shook his head and she saw the problem shining right in his eyes.

"Mannnnn!" Jewelz slapped her hand down on her thigh and whined. "C'mon now, Slick!" she spit with mad exasperation. "Every time we get started on a lil something you find a damn reason to stop. Boy look at your *dick!* That shit is bricked up to the max! You can't tell me you don't want none of this!"

Ignoring the disappointment in her eyes, Slick sat up on the sofa and swung his bare feet down to the floor. He stood up looking tall and diesel and sporting thick chocolate wood that was popping veins everywhere.

Guiding his erection back into his drawers, he glanced over his shoulder at Jewelz. She had folded her legs up under her and was perched on the sofa looking like a slender, sexy cat. The two of them went way back. Back to better and worse days. That look of love in her eyes told their whole damn story. It was a story of life and of death. Of pissy projects and of heartbreaking passion. It was a story of guns and a story of roses. It was time for him to go.

"So once again you gonna get me wet and jet, huh?" Jewelz sucked her teeth. "Hold up, don't go nowhere yet. I got some fish sticks in the freezer. You want me to fix you some with a bowl of buttery grits and scrambled eggs before you roll?"

Slick heard the longing in her voice as he let his hungry eyes roam over her cinnamon gorgeousness. She looked fuckin delicious. Jewelz was the perfect piece of chocolate eye candy and some day the right dude was gonna eat her sexy ass straight the fuck up.

Slick put his hand on his dick.

"Nah. I'm good. I gotta break out. Gotta get back to Brooklyn."

Jewelz still looked disappointed but Slick knew she'd get over it. She always did. His shit was raw and complicated. He had never promised no female a tomorrow because a tomorrow wasn't promised to him. The only thing he was built for was that fuck 'em and forget 'em, every-now-and-then type of shit. That's just the way he rolled.

Silently, he strode across the living room in his boxers. His body was brolick and well-formed, and his large muscles flexed as he picked up his bag. He pulled out his traveling clothes; some wrinkled army pants, a raggedy shirt, and a pair of pigeon-shit covered boots, and got dressed.

Crossing the room again, he stuffed last night's work gear, including the burgundy vest and the shiny black valet shoes, deep inside his bag. Without looking back, he pulled his peasy-haired wig and his crazy bird cap down low on his head and dipped.

CHAPTER 4

Oh So Sly!

In the era of street thugs who gave less than a fuck about the lessons of the past, Sly McFly was an Original Gangsta who had reached an age where he had forgotten more than the young'uns of today would ever learn.

Mister McFly, as he liked to be called, puffed on a Cuban cigar as he relaxed in the backseat of his cocaine-white Audi A8 luxury sedan and enjoyed being chauffeured down the harsh urban streets of Jamaica, Queens.

Tall, thin, and light-skinned, Sly was cool and majestic as he gazed outta the window with a look of pride and nostalgia in his eyes.

These were the corners and blocks where he had made his bones at. Not only was he one of the last of the OGs to survive these bitter streets with his throat intact, his name still invoked love, fear, and respect to this very day.

Even as a youngsta Sly McFly had been the perfect blend of sophisticated gent and street nigga, and he had always made calculated moves. He was a flashy cat, but he also knew when to get low. He was far less visible now in his older age, yet his name still rang bells on the city streets. Part of the reason that he had prospered when so many of his peers had perished is because Sly understood that there was a balance to be maintained in the game. There was a time to flex muscle and let yourself be known, and a time to fall back and stay off the radar.

Today was not gonna be one of those days.

"Take a left here and drive real slow. We ain't in no rush," he told his long-time driver, Chimp Charlie.

As different as the neighborhood had become over the years, Sly McFly still loved to run these streets. He loved to soak up the sights and the sounds of his town. Every day he saw something new and interesting. It was like he was a tourist who had never been here before.

He gazed out the window. These blocks held decades of memories and they all flooded Sly's mind as he rode through his hood. His soul was ingrained in the fabric of this ghetto. He had always been in love with these streets, but after more than thirty years in the trenches he was under no illusions that the streets loved him back.

Sly was no longer going full throttle in the hood but he would never be totally legit. He still had a hand in the drug game, but his ever-sticky fingers were also in the diamond game as well. These days, instead of ruling over a major cocaine and heroin empire, he spent most of his time collecting payouts and slanging knowledge down on a beautiful young chick who was trying to tap into a diamond mine at the New York Diamond and Jewelry Exchange.

"We almost there boss, do you want me to circle the block a couple times?" the ape-looking driver with the flat forehead and sloping jaw asked.

"Yeah, that's cool, Charlie. Go 'head around a couple more times then you can park and wait for me," Sly replied as he exhaled a thick cloud of sweet-smelling cigar smoke.

His cell phone vibrated with a special rhythm and Sly rested his cigar in the ashtray and answered it. As always, he spoke freely in the presence of his driver, who was also his friend. Chimp Charlie had been working for him for countless years and they spent a lot of time together riding around Sly's territory picking up extortion payments from the legitimate businesses that he squeezed for protection payments.

"How's Honore?" Chimp Charlie asked when his boss was finished with his call. "She still handling her business down at that jewelry exchange?"

"Hell yeah," Sly responded with a chuckle. "When it comes to stacking paper she stays on her toes. I swear that girl is the apple of my eye, but I ain't never met a chick who chases a dollar the way she does. *Never.* Honore's a natural at this game, my man. Just a fuckin natural."

Chimp Charlie chuckled in return. "That's good, boss. She sure got it honest. I bet they ain't never seen nothing like her at that jewelry place. She keep doing what she's doing and playing her cards right and she could own that whole thing one day. That's how white folks get they money. Dolla by dolla, they steal that shit."

Chimp Charlie pulled up at the walkway that led to the project building eyeballing the scene suspiciously as a group of young-heads loitered and clowned on the porch.

"You want me to walk in with you Sly?" You know these new niggas be acting real tough nowadays."

Sly McFly flashed an OG smile at his driver who was at least ten years younger than him. He climbed from the car and brushed the wrinkles from his expensive white suit that was a perfect match for his imported white leather shoes. He stood tall and regal underneath his white John Bull top hat. His dark wavy hair hung past his shoulders as he clutched his diamond-studded bone-white cane in his fist.

"Nah, I'm straight, Charlie. I been walking up in that building for longer than these young pups been alive, man. I'm just gonna check on my girl Frita and come right on back."

Sly walked toward the building with his trademark pimp swagger and eyed a group of young niggas on the porch who were engaging in a fierce cipher. One dude was up in the other one's face yelling and spitting harsh lyrics with maddening aggression. A gang of spectators had surrounded the two MCs and were cheering loudly for the bars that hit the hardest.

Sly slowed his pace down a little bit to take in what was going on.

"You been a bitch nigga...I can show you how to get rich, nigga!...you my son...you sprung from a seed outta my dick nigga....you snitch, nigga!... fuck around you get clapped up...I'ma run Queens like Sly...Preme...and Black Just!"

The crowd reacted loudly at the mention of the old heads who had come before them. Sly was caught off guard by the props given to his name, and to the names of two of his peers, Supreme and Black Just.

He stared closely at the young'uns. These kids seemed to range in age from about fourteen to twenty-five. Their glorifying words made Sly think about all his old drug hustles and the gunplay that had left a bloody trail throughout these Queens neighborhoods.

It was startling that these young wanna be's were paying homage to the Gs who had come before them because Sly was sure none of these new niggas even knew what he looked like.

"Damn, old head! What the fuck you staring at?" A young curly-haired nigga barked when he noticed how closely Sly was observing the cipher.

Sly grilled the light-skinned, freckle-faced young'un. Back in the day he would have slaughtered his little ass for stepping to him like that. The kid damn near withered under his glare, even though he stood there trying to act like he was thorough.

Yeah, muthafucka, Sly thought coldly. The mouth could lie, but the eyes told it all, and when the little nigga nervously broke his gaze that was all Sly needed to see. He was like Tyson, he took an opponent's heart before the fight even got started.

Sly shook his head. This lil embryo ain't want no problems. He was just showing off in front of his crew. Sly didn't feel the need to check the youngsta any further so he gave him a pass.

I don't understand why these lil niggas be in such a rush to die, he thought, knowing it was only old age that had softened him and kept him from breaking the kid's neck.

Ignoring the rest of the young hoods, Sly kept it moving and entered the building to go see what was up with his lady friend from way back in the good old days.

Frita Jones had been down for Sly long before he was McFly. She had been in his corner when he was just plain old Sylvester Mack, a pretty Cuban nigga who was swinging his way outta the jungle and trying to solidify his name in the streets. Sly had been fucking her younger sister at the time, but that didn't make no whole lotta difference to Frita. A tall redbone with a killer body, Frita was one of the original get-money bitches from Hollis and she didn't give a fuck whose throat she had to step on to get what she wanted. In her prime she had been a Queen Pimp who used to throw extravagant pussy parties for all the big-time willies throughout the boroughs, and she had kept them supplied with a vast selection of the finest trim that money could buy.

Sly and Frita had developed a thing between them that was built on lust and lies, and it had stood the test of time. They were both handsome physical specimens and over the years they had knocked plenty of boots and funked up plenty of sheets. They had dreamed big from the gate and the streets had loved Frita and Sly. When they stepped out together they were just like the black Bonnie and Clyde and they were the perfect compliment to each other's style. They were ambitious, lethal, fabulous, and on the streets of Cop Killa Queens, Sly and Frita were treated like ghetto royalty.

In addition to their love thang, the two of them also shared a deadly bond of secrecy between them. Late one night in a clutch situation, Frita's loyalty to Sly had been put to the test. Frita had never gone very far in school, but that was one test she passed with flying colors. When Sly came banging on her door shaking and covered in blood after murdering a woman that they both loved, Frita had let him in and accepted everything he put in her arms, including his gun. Frita had put her love for Sly ahead of her own family, and neither one of them would ever forget it.

"Hey baby, how's everything going?" Frita said as she opened the door and greeted Sly with a big kiss on the lips. Like him, Frita was getting up in age but she still looked good. In fact, she was beautiful as hell to Sly, and she played an important role in his business operations.

"What's going on, old lady," Sly said as he smiled and slapped her lightly on her ample ass. He felt his dick jump. Frita was wearing a slinky bathrobe, and with her nipples about to poke a hole in the fabric Sly wondered if she was naked underneath.

"Ain't nothing old up in here but you and the furniture," Frita responded playfully as she poked fun at him.

Frita's crib was one of the many stash houses that Sly controlled throughout the city, and he used a small crew of older black women as fronts to hand off cash and drugs between him and his slangas. This is what kept Sly's face off the streets and insulated him from the eyes of the law, who hardly ever suspected older black women of pushing dope in their own neighborhoods.

"So listen, Sly," Frita said as she stirred a pot of beans she had cooking on the stove and then sat down at her kitchen table and sparked up a Virginia Slims. "The reason I called you over here is because that mannish-behind Malice is getting too big for his britches."

Sly frowned. "Is that right?

"Yeah. The other day it was supposed to be business as usual between us. I went to meet Malice like I always do, and he was supposed to give me his weekly deposit just like you told him to. But instead of handing it over he starts asking me where I bank at and how much money I be collecting for you on my runs every day. I told him I wasn't telling him a goddamn thing, so he got mad and grabbed me by my arm and said he wasn't paying me shit.

Sly's eyes narrowed. "That fuckin coward put his hands on you?"

Frita nodded. "Yep. The little fucker manhandled me and accused me of being a thief. Shit, the way he was showing out I thought he was gonna raise up and back slap me."

Sly stared at her for a moment. It was hard to believe one of his young pups was nipping at him like that, but if Frita said Malice was smelling his balls then that lil nigga was definitely smelling his balls.

"Don't worry. I'll handle his ass."

Frita pulled on her cigarette. "I know you will. It's just a shame that these stupid young cats have no respect for wisdom and experience. I started to put my razor to his face for touching me like that, but I knew you would wanna deal with him yourself."

Frita rose from the chair and sashayed over to the sink, her flesh moving deliciously under the slinky bathrobe that hugged her hips and accentuated her meaty ass.

"Don't even worry about it," Sly stood up and repeated. "Same old shit, different toilet tissue. I'ma take care of him," he said as he leaned on his cane and gave her a look like he wanted some of what was under her robe.

Frita had been seeing that look in his eyes for the better part of four decades and she loved it. She giggled like a schoolgirl as Sly came up behind her and squeezed her thick thighs. His breath was warm on her neck as his hands crept upward until his fingers were teasing the stiff nubs of her nipples.

"Go on now old man," Frita teased as she felt herself getting moist. "You ain't take your Viagra this morning, did you?"

Sly chuckled thickly in her ear. He thrust his hips forward so she could see what the fuck he was working with.

"Do I look like I need any goddamn Viagra?" he smirked as he grinded into her fluffy ass and poked her with the tip of his hammer. "I got this dick nice and hard all by myself," he told her. "No medication necessary."

Frita bit her lip in pleasure as Sly lifted up the back of her robe and exposed her naked buttocks. She was heavy in the back but her cakes were still round and firm, just like they'd always been.

Sly got down on his knees like he was as limber as a teenager. He grabbed her smooth ass-cheeks in both hands and lifted them up high and spread them apart.

Frita shuffled her feet to open up her stance and give him easy access. He dove head-first into her na-na from behind, licking her out with the expertise of a professional pussy eater.

"Oh *shit!*" she exclaimed softly as her pussy dripped and her old knees wobbled. All she could do was hold onto the sink as she spread her legs wider and damn near sucked his whole head between her thighs.

Sly was down there sweating like a dog between her legs. He tongued her clit and licked her ass until Frita screamed and cursed and got her nut, then he stripped down naked as she took off her flimsy robe and flung it on the floor.

They stood there staring at each other with mad sexual heat flowing between them. Neither of them had the bodies they had once had in their youths and they accepted that. They had lived long enough to grow older and wiser, but despite the snow on their rooftops there was still a raging fire burning in their ovens.

Moments later, Sly had Frita bent over a kitchen chair as he rammed his joint up in her from the back. She moaned and shivered as he reached around her and squeezed her full breasts and licked his tongue up and down her shoulder.

They fucked real wet and nasty-like, with nothing but fucking on their minds. Wasn't no worrying about getting pregnant, no worries that a jealous husband or a wife might walk in and bust them, no worrying about one of their kids hearing them making all kinds of delicious sex noises. Nope. Sly and Frita fucked with the straight-up goal of giving each other pleasure, and by the time Sly groaned and grunted and busted him a nut, Frita had already gotten herself another one too.

"You almost made me burn my beans," Frita complained as she clutched her lower back and straightened up.

"You almost made me miss my meeting," Sly said, grinning as he eyed her naked fineness.

Frita walked over to the stove and turned off her pot, then grabbed a clean dishrag from a drawer.

"Here." She squirted some Joy dishwashing liquid on it and wet it with hot water. She wiped herself first before handing it to him. "I'm gonna run and get me a shower. Clean yourself up then get on outta here and go handle ya business. I got a couple of things planned for today too. Cucci's taking me shopping. You know baby girl gotta do her mama's wardrobe right at least once a month," Frita said as she smiled at him.

"A'ight. Thanks for that lil snack," Sly said licking his lips. "It was just as sweet and tasty as it always is. I'll handle Malice as soon as I get a chance. I'll give you a call in a couple of days when it's done."

Frita's smile turned into a frown. "You sure I gotta wait that long for you to handle that lil nigga? I can slit his throat my damn self, you know."

"Be easy, baby," Sly said as he wiped off his dick and put his clothes back on. "I got a big job coming up with Honore. There's major money involved so I gotta give it all my attention. I'll take you out to help me celebrate when it's all over."

Frita beamed at the mention of a night on the town. "How's Honore doing?" she asked. "Tell that gal she need to come around here and see her old auntie more often."

Sly nodded. "I'll tell her. Don't worry. I'll call you soon and let you know who the new guy is because Malice is about to get faded," Sly said as he kissed her on the cheek.

Frita eyed him with a hint of worry in her eyes. "Sly, you be careful messing around with them young boys, you hear? You ain't no young lion no more and these kids in the game now are a whole lot stupider than we were back in the day."

"Don't even worry about it," Sly said with a grin as he finished getting dressed and put on his white top hat. "You know how I get down. Didn't I just show you what kinda life I still got left in me? Everything is gonna work out just fine."

$$$$$

Sly McFly exited the elevator in the lobby and saw that the rap battle was still raging on the porch. The crowd had dwindled down some but the energy level was still wired high as the two rappers competed viciously for props.

Sly was making his way past when he heard a harsh young voice address him from the crowd.

"Yo, whattup, old head?" the curly-headed kid said as he grilled Sly McFly. "I thought I told you to kick rocks, grandpa? Limping around here with all that white on! Fuck is you going anyway? Baptism day ain't today my nigga!"

A couple of thugs caught wind of the words and turned their attention away from the rap battle and got ready to catch a few laughs.

Sly almost laughed at the kid's sudden burst of courage too, but instead of reacting he simply waved the kid off.

"Go ahead, young nigga. I ain't here to cause no trouble I'm just trying to be on my way," he said walking around the crowd as he headed off the porch.

"Yeah, faggot! Looking like Snoop Dog's great-granddaddy! You on your way but ya old ass ain't moving fast enough!" the curly-headed chump barked as he ran up behind Sly and kicked him dead in the ass.

Sly stumbled forward but quickly caught his balance in a show of surprising agility. He slid his leg out and stopped his fall, and simultaneously swung his ivory cane in a swift wide arc. The diamond-gripped rod struck the young boy across his knee. The blow buckled his leg and sent him crashing down to the ground.

"*Nigga what!*" Sly was on him in an instant, towering over the boy as he slashed down with his cane and smashed him across his shins. "You dare put your feet on me?" Sly screamed in incredible disbelief. "Your *feet*, nigga? Ya muthafuckin *feet*?"

He cracked the kid on the back of both of his hands, making his fingers go numb. He beat the young'un all in his scrawny chest until the kid moaned and coughed. Then he swung the cane like a bat and hit a homerun with the kid's head.

"*AAARHHHHHGGHHH!!!*" the little curly-haired runt shrieked in pain, unable to hold his cries in even though his homeys were watching.

Sly was on a roll. He popped the young thug all over his head until purple lumps jumped up on his yellow skin. When the boy tried to use his hands to shield his head from the blows, Sly damn near broke his lil fuckin fingers as he hammer-thumped his hands with the end of the cane.

"I bet the next time you'll respect your elders and watch yo mutha...fuckin... *MOUTH!*" Sly raged as he cane-punted the kid in the face, bloodying his nose.

He raised the cane in the air again and bashed the kid in the mouth like he was cracking a whole rack of pool balls. The impact loosened both of the boy's front teeth and he immediately shrieked and grabbed his bleeding mouth.

By now the cipher had ceased and all eyes were on the beat-down that was taking place. Sly McFly was in a rage brought on by the blatant disrespect that the kid had shown him. He continued to wail on his young ass, knowing the boy was broken and defeated, but the killer in him wanted to take the little nigga all the way out.

Knowing a bunch of impressionable young eyes were on him, Sly battled to regain his composure. He raised his cane again and stared down at the frightened little nigga who was now a bloody and petrified mess. He flicked his wrist and clicked a hidden button on the side of his cane, and a long, deadly-looking silver blade shot out of the tip.

"Listen up, you lil pussy-ass bitch!" Sly spit. He breathed fire as he jammed the glistening sharp tip of the knife into the frightened thug's crotch and pierced the fabric of his saggy pants. "If I ever catch you disrespecting any of these OG's who walk the streets out here I will slice your little fuckin nuts clean off, do you hear me?"

"Yeah!" the kid screamed in pain. "I hear you! I fuckin hear you!" Again Sly struggled with himself. He couldn't believe this narrow-assed juvenile had put his goddamn feet on him! Back in the day dude woulda been found chopped up in a Dumpster for some shit like that. Sly thrust the cane's blade even harder against the kid's dick. All it took was one more good jab and everything in his worthless lil nut sack would spill out in his dirty drawers. The little shit-for-brains adolescent could forget about ever fucking a bitch or fathering a kid.

"Yo where the fuck is your daddy at lil nigga?" Sly demanded.

"He...he's dead, sir," the spineless boy responded. "He got killed."

"Yeah? Well I'm probably the wolf who buried his ass! I'm *Sly McFly*, lil nigga! *Mister* McFly to you, and don't you ever in ya lil bitch-ass life disrespect me again!"

Sly flipped his cane over and jabbed the kid hard in his nuts with the handle. "Say my name, muthafucka!"

"Mister McFly!" the teen squeaked and tried to cup his balls.

"Say it again, nigga!" Sly jabbed him in the nuts again.

"*Mister McFly!*" the boy screamed. "*Mister McFly!*"

"Good! Now get the fuck up and move around!"

Sly pushed a button and retracted the blade back into his cane, and the terrified young boy scrambled to his feet and took flight into the building.

All the other thugs on the porch just stood there staring at him in silence. They had all gasped when he revealed his name, and now they looked respectful and bewildered at the living legend who was standing before them in the flesh.

Sly McFly brushed off his suit and nodded at the crowd of young wanna-be's who were silently saluting him. The word would now fly through the projects that Sly McFly didn't miss a fuckin step. The streets were always watching and today it had been his show.

Straightening his top hat, Sly had just turned around to head back to his car when he heard one of the thugs mumble.

"Man, that ain't him! The *real* Sly McFly woulda killed that stupid nigga!"

Sly had to shake his head and chuckle at that one.

These lil niggas gonna think I'm soft now, he thought with a smile.

"Think again, youngbloods," he muttered and went on about his day. "Think again!"

CHAPTER 5

Pebble Beach

There was no place Slick dug more than the rooftop of the fourteen-story project building that he had grown up in. It was usually quiet and deserted up there, but tonight the sight that greeted him as he stepped through the doorway was all ashy ass and swinging balls.

Two crackheads were stretched out on the pebbly tar fucking up a storm. The female was on her back with her thick yellow legs spread wide open. The heels of her crusty feet were pointing straight up at the sky as she moaned out loud and shivered and shook and totally got her fuck on.

Slick could hear her juices sloshing as the old-head who was jammed between her thighs went to town on that pussy. His narrow black ass pumped like a piston as he pounded his meat deep inside her wetness and went all out for his nut.

Slick slammed the rooftop door as hard as shit to announce himself, but the old dude had no fucks to give. He kept right on pumping and grinding as he looked over his shoulder and held one finger up like he was in church. He bit down on his bottom lip for a quick second, then he got right back to work and tried to drill a hole in the chick's back.

Seconds later, the gray-haired nigga gasped and grunted. He moaned out loud and called for Jesus a couple of times, and then he scrambled to his feet and yanked up his silky drawers.

Slick watched quietly as the thick, banana-colored female took her sweet-ass time rolling over on her knees. Naked from the waist down, she stood up and shook her meaty butt around like a dog shaking off water. Her flowery sundress fell down over her bare hips and stopped right above her knees.

"Sorry 'bout that," the old school dope-head said as he bopped proudly past Slick and headed toward the door. "Thanks for waiting, my nigga."

"Fuck outta here," Slick said quietly.

EMPIRE STATE OF MINE$!

The female grinned as she sashayed past him holding her head up high like Slick didn't just see her fat, naked ass. Her dirt-buster house shoes made scraping sounds on the tar and a stream of cum ran down her ashy leg. The smell of funky sex radiated off her in waves as she walked by.

Slick shook his head and glanced around after they were gone. The pebbly rooftops of project buildings were valuable pieces of real estate in the hood. They served as lookouts, meeting spots, fuck pads, and drug dens, and there would always be crackheads, winos, and hoes competing for their piece of the rock.

But the rooftop of building 430 in Van Dyke projects was Slick's territory. He guarded that shit like the king of the castle. It was the headquarters of the Zip 'em up Crew, and home to a fleet of homing pigeons that were Slick's most trusted collaborators.

Most of his birds were what New Yorkers called, "flying rats." They were ordinary pigeons that he had trained to go out to specific locations during the day and then return home to the rooftop at night.

But there were about a dozen birds in particular, his most prized and intelligent messengers, who were the heart of Slick's business operation. These special birds looked just like all the regular clucking and shitting pests, but they were the key to Slick's success with the BBU. They also kept the Feds and the local police from following his trail and fuckin him up the ass.

The BBU, or Body Bags Unlimited, was known on paper as the security firm of Banfield and Baines Unincorporated, but hired guns in the game knew all that fancy shit was just a front. The BBU was actually a conglomerate consisting of high-level officials who held day jobs in law enforcement, politics, and state and federal government. They fronted like public servants, but their real mission was the contracted elimination of targeted human beings in the five boroughs of New York City. Slick and his posse were professional gunslingers who filled up as many body bags for them as possible.

It had taken a lot of careful planning for Slick to select and assemble his highly efficient team of shooters. They were a five-member crew and each of them was responsible for a particular borough in the city of New York. Every gunslinger in his squad had major history with Slick and they operated under a strict set of rules and bylaws.

Slick was tossing a few handfuls of grain to his pigeon when his cell phone vibrated on his waist. He glanced down and saw it was a text message from his right-hand manz, Noodles.

I'm in the elevator coming up, the text message read. *Don't fuck around and spray me when I come through the door a'ight?*

Minutes later the door swung outward and his homeys Noodles and Wild Man stepped out on the roof. While Slick was still dressed in the rags of his alter ego Sometimey, Noodles and Wild Man were draped in their regular gear. Noodles's style was cool and casual, but as usual Wild Man was wearing the white boy tags with the black boy swag. His shit was set from top to bottom in trendy fly gear like Polo, Hollister, and Levi.

Noodles came over to the bird coop and dapped Slick out.

"Yo whattup," Slick said, showing his ace some love.

He turned to Wild Man. "Sup, my nigga!"

Wild Man nodded. He didn't fuck with pigeons like that so he said whattup from a distance.

Slick eyed his boy Noodles. He was the linebacker type. A down-ass cat from the Bronx. Noodles was big and muscular with long dreadlocks, and as usual he wore a high-necked shirt to cover the metal trach tube in his throat. The two men had met in the Army as members of an elite special ops combat team. Slick had been a platoon sergeant and Noodles had been the most loyal and dedicated soldier on his squad.

They had clicked up on the New York City tip and got real tight, and when Noodles got knocked for slumping a fellow soldier, Slick turned himself in and took the rap.

Not a lotta niggas woulda done no wild shit like that, but for Slick it had been an easy decision. He had already come to a crossroad in his life. Everybody that he loved was already dead, and sometimes he had a death wish himself. He had thought that the military training regiment would quiet that reckless urge that his family's murders had opened up in him, but he was wrong. Because on the inside, in his heart where it really mattered, Slick was just as dead as his family members. He was just waiting to get buried.

The cracker that Noodles had murdered was one of them racist skinheads, and him and his KKK friends had ambushed Noodles while he was out on a remote field site. Them redneck soldiers had jumped Noodles and tied a rope around his neck, then dragged him through a muddy swamp until he blacked out.

Noodles had almost died and he'd been scarred for life, but he had survived. He had told the investigators who the cats were, but not one of those cowards had been brought to justice. Not one.

A couple of months later the ringleader of the skinheads was found hanging upside down from a rafter with an American flag stuffed down his throat. Fourteen bones in his body were broken and his throat was sliced open from ear to ear.

It took six hours for the military investigators to arrest Noodles and charge him with murder. The brief trial was a joke, and the moment the conviction came in they snatched Noodles and tossed his ass as deep into the shitty bowels of the brig as they could throw him.

But Noodles had an insane fear of being locked down in small spaces, and when Slick went to visit him his boy was a fuckin wreck. Noodles had been refusing to eat or drink ever since he got there. He was huddled in a corner hearing voices and fighting off invisible enemies, and he had lost a crazy amount of weight off of his six-five frame.

It was obvious that he wasn't gonna make it in the bing. So despite what it was gonna cost him Slick had gone to his military superiors and 'fessed up to the murder. Noodles was let go and Slick became a convict. He ended up serving nine months on a murder bid before his sentence was overturned on appeal and the killing was deemed a justifiable homicide.

It had been a real risky maneuver that could've cost Slick his freedom for the rest of his life, but he had no regrets. His right-hand manz Noodles had spent every day since then showing Slick the utmost loyalty and allegiance. Noodles knew exactly what kind of sacrifice that Slick had made for him, and he woulda laid down his life for him. All he had to do was ask.

But Slick decided he didn't want Noodles's life. He wanted his stealthy surveillance techniques and his eagle-eye sniping skills. So Slick had invited his ace to get down with the Zip 'em up Crew, and promised him he could rake in way more cheese from one job than he had made in six months with the military.

Noodles was wit' it off the rip. His moms was real sick in Guatemala and she needed money for her heart medicine, so he was all the way game. Free to do his thing, Noodles took to the murder game like a fish takes to water, and right off the bat he became one of the most dedicated and proficient members of the team.

"Yo, that was some quality work y'all put in at that Chinese Restaurant last night," Slick said as he eyed Noodles and Wild Man. "But another mission just came down the pipes that we need to talk about. It's coming up quick so I need both of y'all to be ready."

"I was born fuckin ready," Wild Man rocked back on his heels and sneered. Slick knew his cocky Asian brother spoke the truth because he lived up to his street name on a daily fuckin basis.

Just like Slick, Wild Man was a product of the grimy streets of Brooklyn. His family had owned the Wing Luck Chinese restaurant near the train station on Rockaway Avenue since way back in the day. But as a skinny Asian kid living in a crime-ridden all-black hood, Wild Man had grown up in the trenches fighting to prove his manhood almost every single day. He used to get the shit kicked outta him walking back and forth to school until he developed some heavy hand skills and started earning his brutal rep.

Slick used to grub on mad egg rolls at the Wing Luck all the time when he was a juvenile. Him and Wild Man had gotten into their first dust-up when they were both thirteen, and by that time Wild Man was already well on his way to becoming a criminal beast. He was scrambling on the streets with a reckless posse, and they were pulling brutal kick-doors and drug-related kidnappings left and right.

Slick's grandmother was still alive back then and she had him running errands for all the old people in the building. When Wild Man called himself squeezing Slick for the money he was carrying for old lady Johnson's blood pressure pills, Slick had twisted him up on the concrete and jammed a snub-nose deep up under his nuts.

Slick had won that round, but by the time Wild Man turned seventeen he had packed on twenty pounds of muscle and was terrorizing grown men on the streets of Brooklyn. He had fallen in love with martial arts and he carried a razor blade in his mouth and kept something sharp shit in every pocket.

While the majority of trigger-happy hittas preferred to kill niggas from a distance, Wild Man was a junkie for that toe-to-toe up-close combat shit. He was lethal with his bare hands and highly proficient with anything that had a sharp edge on it.

The respect Wild Man earned in the hood was rapid and widespread. Them same cats who used to stomp him like a rat back in the day would scamper to the other side of street if they saw him coming now. They didn't even know how to fuck with a dieseled-up Hulk-lookin Chinese hitta who carried a blade under his tongue and walked outta his house every single day looking for trouble.

But Wild Man's attraction to trouble had put him in a trick bag more than a few times. He had fucked around and caught a charge that coulda put him ass-down in a cell for a good long minute, but the judge was an old Asian cat who took mercy on him. He gave Wild Man the option of either going to jail or joining the Marine Corps, and Wild Man had jumped at the chance to get his hands on a government burner and shoot shit up.

The military regime of the Corps had tried to instill discipline and a code of honor in Wild Man. But as a product of Brownsville he was from a place that had no discipline and he walked amongst beasts who obeyed no code of conduct. After five years in uniform Wild Man had returned home to The Ville, and the only thing he had to show for his service were the skills he got from his combat training: how to hunt, how to survive, and most importantly, how to kill.

Slick had tapped Wild Man for his squad right after he was ejected from the service and it was one of the best decisions he had ever made. Despite their lil bang ups back when they were young'uns, the two of them had become true brothers. Even though Wild Man could be reckless and had a quick temper, Slick knew that when it came time to yank that trigger his Asian-persuasion brother was the Zip 'em up Crew's Most Valuable Player.

Slick got another buzz on his cell phone alerting him that Whitey and Jewelz were on their way up to the rooftop too. He pulled his shit together and got ready to put an appeal out there. He was about to hit his team with a request that was real crucial to him, but had the potential to cause some static at the same time.

So what's poppin with the next job? Noodles typed on his text-to-speech device as soon as all five of them were onsite and their circle was complete. Noodles's vocal cords had been fucked up by his near-lynching, and ever since the night of his assault he had been mute and unable to speak a single word.

Slick reached up under his cap and retrieved a scrap of paper that he had taken off his bird and tucked away. He unfolded it and looked out at his click. "We got a message that says there's a jeweler down on Fulton Street who needs to be pushed off the edge of the fuckin planet. We ain't got a lotta info on this one, though. Matter fact, besides the time and the place, they didn't give up any other details. All I know is we're supposed to hit a monkey holding a red briefcase."

Mad snide comments broke out amongst his crew.

"Hit a monkey? That's all you got?" Wild Man's slanted eyes flashed dangerously under the moonlight. "Them suckers gonna toss out some bogus lil cookie crumbs and they just expect us to walk up on a job with our eyes closed?"

Slick held up the note. "That's it, man. That's what the paper says."

"Yo, but where's the rest of the details at?" Wild Man demanded. "How many heads are they expecting on the scene? What kinda resistance is out there that we might run into? What we gonna do if we bump into any unexpected firepower? What's the rest of the fuckin set-up, yo?"

"I just told you the note don't specify none of that," Slick said. "But they doubling the paper on this one so we taking the job."

"Hold up," Wild Man challenged. "Don't we get to vote on that shit?"

Slick nodded. Son was right. Even though he was the HNIC, the Zip 'em up Crew voted and did shit the democratic way.

He posted up. "A'ight, everybody who's down to take the mission give up the nod. If you ain't feelin it then give up the finger."

Three heads nodded right off the bat. Wild Man's hand moved like he was about to throw up a bird, but then he nodded too.

"A'ight, bet," Slick said. "We taking this shit, and since it's going down right here in Brooklyn I'm calling the shots. But while we voting," he said, keeping his voice cool and steady, "lemme hit y'all with a lil something else I wanna bring to the table."

His eyes swept over the Brooklyn skyline and then he began.

"Ere'body knows my grandmother raised me right here in this building," Slick said. "It's an old folks joint and she had to take the housing authority to court so they would let me stay here after my family was murdered."

Slick's eyes went hard.

"I had a lil static out here the other night," he admitted quietly. "I had to clap a couple of young niggas downstairs on the porch. They fucked with me and I had to put 'em down for a nap."

"Why?" Whitey asked. "Who were they?"

Slick shrugged. "Just some low-level street soldiers. They workin for some new nigga named Handgun Goody. He's fresh outta state boots and him and his brothers done took over the drug scene in Brownsville. There's six of them. Handgun, Ice Pick, Cannonball, Razorblade, Chainsaw, and Hammerhead. They call themselves the Goode Brothers Gang. Handgun is their HNIC. That nigga started out smalltime, but he blew up while he was in the joint. Right now him and his shooters are tryna push up on these elders around here. They just waiting for one of these old ladies to have a heart attack so they can take over her crib and set up a distribution headquarters in the building."

Slick let his eyes grill his posse one by one.

"But I can't let that shit happen. I ain't *gonna* let it happen."

Noodles nodded and typed. *So what you wanna do about it?*

"I wanna hire the team," Slick said. "On an independent contract at my financial expense. I wanna take Handgun Goody and all five of his bitch-ass brothers down and squash them suckas flat out. Straight up."

"Fuck for?" Wild Man was the first to buck. "You ain't gotta live in this building, man. You got a sweet condo in the city and you rolling in doe, my nigga. Let them Goode Brothers have this shit." Wild Man leaned over and spit on top of a pasty mound of bird poop. "I ain't never liked coming up here no way," he shrugged. "Fuck this building. We can find us another spot to conduct our bizz at."

"Yo, there's a bunch of old people living here!" Slick barked. "Old *black* people, nigga! I don't know how y'all get it in over in Chinatown, but around here we don't throw our elders in the trash with the beer cans and the shitty pampers! We look out for them for as long as they drawing breath, my nigga!"

Jewelz and Noodles nodded in agreement and it was Wild Man's turn to get swole. "First of all, I ain't *from* Chinatown, ya dig me? I'm from right muthafuckin *here*, just like you! Second of all, you asking for a *side* hit! We *don't do* side jobs, remember? And we don't do no outside killings neither, and that's a BBU rule. Plus, you talking about the five of us going up against a whole fuckin drug click! Is you serious? C'mon now, slime. We're hit men, not detectives. If them toy cops in the housing authority and the entire 73rd Precinct can't keep Goody and his henchmen from taking over the streets, let alone this building, then how the fuck is we supposed to do it?"

"We do it just like we do everything else, *gunslinger!*" Slick exploded. "We devise us a plan and then we execute that shit! I'm coming outta my pockets for this, yo! I'ma pay y'all niggas lovely for it! Fuck, is you scared or something? These low-level gang pussies got you shook?"

"Nah, son," Wild Man smirked. "Fuck the doe. This ain't no green-lit mission, my man. It sounds like some on-the-side shit to me, and according to our rules that type of thang is off-limits."

"Fuck the rules—"

"Ayo, what's that number one rule you all the time barking about? 'Obey and abide!' And what's the number two rule? 'Never mix bizzness with pleasure' right? Well, the four of us is out here on the assassin grind and you over here tryna be on some crazy vigilante shit!"

"Aw, you just saying that because these old people up in here are *black!*" Jewelz blasted on Wild Man and rolled her eyes. "Somebody better tell this nigga he's Chinese! If this was an Asian neighborhood he would be a hundred percent down for the ride."

Slick gazed at the beautiful chick sitting before him with her lumped up cleavage and curvy thighs. He stared deeply into Jewelz's beautiful eyes, trying hard to remember why he hadn't fucked her lights out in her crib that morning when she had begged him to.

Years earlier he had plucked Jewelz off a local enforcement team where she was holding down some territory for a major Bajan druglord. Jewelz was hot with a pistol, but her specialty on the team was sexual seduction and deadly poisons. The girl seemed to get her shit off on fast acting toxins, nerve agents, blow darts, and lethal herbs and powders. She was an expert at slipping shit in a target's food or drink, and most members of the team were leery about eating anything she cooked. They called her the "Last Supper" because Jewelz could burn you a gourmet meal in the kitchen and snuff you out at the same time.

But Jewelz was also loyalty in the flesh, and Slick knew she had his back in all matters big and small. She reminded him of his mother Kea, a down-ass go hard bitch if he had ever seen one. If he had come out and said he wanted to hijack a fuckin plane, then Jewelz woulda shot the flight attendant and pistol-whipped the pilot.

Slick stared into her pretty eyes as Wild Man blasted on her, "Not for nothin, Jewelz, you can miss me with all that 'black people' bullshit," he warned her. "This ain't gotta be no Chinese neighborhood! It's *my* fuckin neighborhood! Like I said, I was born and raised right here in The Ville, baby. This is *my* fuckin hood too!"

"Then act like it, my nigga!" Slick spit. "Jewelz knows what time it is. The elderly black queens in this building raised me, man. They fed me, they wiped my nose, and they whipped my ass. Fuck you, muh'fucka!" Slick shook his head again. "I ain't leaving them for the wolves to eat. It's family over ere'thang, and they my peeps."

Wild Man nodded right back. "Yo, Slick. I'm your hitta too, fam! I'm ya heathen! Ya number one shooter in the uber, and you know I'm thorough! But we're *hit men*, not DEA! This shit is a problem for One Time, yo! Let them clowns handle it. That's what the fuck they get paid their little bit of cheese to do."

They were a team divided, and Slick knew now was the time to put all his cards on the table.

"Yo what you got to say about it?" Slick turned to the last member of the team, the clean-cut white boy who was dressed in a UPS uniform and sat on the ledge with his feet propped up on an official-looking brown box.

Whitey took a deep breath before responding. As the oldest and the most educated of the group he was the team's Lady Justice. He was the equalizer and the tiebreaker who watched and listened from the sidelines. Hailing from the stellar borough of Staten Island, he was a clean-cut Caucasian with white-collar swag, but he stayed getting his gangsta tested because of his wholesome demeanor and his movie star good looks.

Whitey was the former military defense attorney who had been assigned to work on Slick's appeals at the conclusion of his murder trial. He had known right from the gate that Slick was innocent of the crime he had confessed to, and he had worked damn hard to get the conviction overturned and get him outta the bing.

But Whitey didn't do all that work just because it was his job or because he had a problem with killing human beings. Nah, the squeaky-clean looking white boy actually had no problem with the murder game at all. He just didn't believe in doing that shit for chicken change. With Whitey it was all about the dolla bills, and that fact, combined with his deceptively cold heart and countless disguises, made him a very dangerous and valuable member of the crew.

"We're a team, people," Whitey finally said in his usual logical way. "We get paid top dollars and we're damn good at what we do. That means if one of us rolls then we all gotta roll. No fair ones over here. If one of us starves, then none of us eat. And if one of us burns, then all of our asses go up in smoke."

Whitey grilled the crew with the unconditional authority of a confident white man in his eyes. "Remember, the only reason we've been successful for this long is because we trust each other and we respect the game. That means we think as one, then we vote as one, and then finally we *act* as one."

He looked at his brother Slick, then he looked at his brother Wild Man and said quietly, "Y'all know what time it is. Let's vote."

Slick wasn't surprised when the count came up just like he expected it to. Four nods and one finger. Wild Man's.

His take-down plan to save the elderly residents of his building was DOA. Dead on arrival.

Not a fuckin problem, Slick thought coldly. Didn't no fuckin body sitting up on that rooftop love the people in that building the way he loved them. Didn't nobody owe them what he owed them neither.

"A'ight let's move on to other business," he said, his voice calm and steady as he shook off his rage and went straight into leadership mode. It didn't matter how the fuckin vote had come out, and he gave less than a fuck about the rules. Slick was still gonna take Handgun Goody and his fam out. He'd take all six of them out by himself, if he had to. On his dead mother's grave, them Goode Brothers had to be fuckin erased. Slick was gonna hunt them niggas down and get the drop on ere'last one of them. Even if he had to catch 'em sleeping out there in the darkness, one by one.

CHAPTER 6

Pleasure Above Bizzness

"Yo, Noodles," Slick said, moving on with the meeting as they continued to discuss the bizz at hand. "I need you to do some surveillance for this next job as fast as you can. Make sure our exit corridor is solid and you memorize the layout until you get that shit down-pat. I don't wanna run into no surprises when we burning rubber outta there, you feel me? Whitey can help you find out when the jakes change shifts and what routes they take. The target is gonna be at a jewelry store on Fulton Street in Bed Stuy. We're gonna enter through the back door and we need to hit it hard and fast, and that means everybody gets in and out in two minutes or less."

Noodles nodded in agreement and typed, *I got you my nigga. We gonna sleep-walk whoever's in there and get that bread like we supposed to.*

Slick nodded and gave out his next instructions.

"Whitey, you know what your role is gonna be. Get with some of your connects in the police department and have them sweep the block real good before we arrive on the scene. Tell 'em to bust out a big can of Raid and spray all the roaches they can find, and make sure that shit is nice and clean by the time we roll in, you got it?"

Whitey nodded. Because of his work in the criminal justice system he had formed dirty alliances with moles inside nearly every government agency on the map, and he had major connections in police departments all over the city. "Yep. I'm on it."

"One more thing," Slick told him. "Once we hit the monkey and get that red briefcase, our instructions are to drop it in a locker in midtown Manhattan. You a white boy so I want you to handle the drop personally, you feel me? I was gonna send Noodles to do it, but I don't want no trigger-happy cops fuckin with him at that time of night in the city. Just make sure that briefcase gets in the specified locker safe and sound, you got that?"

Whitey nodded again. "Got it, boss. It's as good as done."

Slick turned to his hotheaded Asian partner who he still loved like a brother even when he pissed him off.

"Yo, Wild Man, make sure you grab the gats and get the gear ready. You need to find some wheels and a dumpsite so we can toss all that shit off when we're done too. Fulton Street is a high-traffic area and we ain't leaving a shred of evidence behind," Slick added.

Wild Man smirked with confidence. "Ain't 'bout nothing. I'ma handle my responsibilities. I'm ready to cash out on this one and get that chicken, man. It sounds like it's gonna be good and easy to me."

"Yo!" Slick whirled around and grilled him hard. "Fuck you talking about *easy*? If you know like I know, ain't no easy jobs in this business," he spit at his dude, "and the only good job is the one where we all make it outta that muthafucka wit'out getting our wigs blown back."

Slick wiped his face on his arm sleeve, careful not to get bird shit in his eye.

"A'ight, my niggas, it's time to make some moves," he said, closing and locking the pigeon coop. "We going up in this bitch blind so it's a must that we have our shit tight. There's a lot that's gotta be done and we only got a small window to get it done in. Remember, *no witnesses, no worries.* Now let's go hard-time my niggas. Get ready to grind, people. Grind!"

$$$$$

Jewelz was the last member of the posse to leave the rooftop and Slick could read the hopeful thoughts in her mind as she eyed him and lingered behind. All he had to do was say the word and she would drop her drawers and jump on his dick right then and there, body and soul. But what the fuck was that gonna cost him?

As strong as Jewelz was, and as much as he knew she could pull her weight and hold her own, there were times when Slick regretted tapping her for the team. He was naturally protective over her and he was more concerned for her safety than he was for his own. Jewelz was also beautiful and sexy as fuck, and he wanted her real bad, but he refused to slip up and smash her. Putting that pleasure above bizzness was a sure recipe for losing focus and getting both of them slumped out there on the streets.

Even still, Slick couldn't help how he felt inside. It just didn't seem right for a chick who had been through all the shit that Jewelz had been through to be living the kind of life that made you confront death on a daily basis.

He remembered the night that he had lucked up and reunited with her. It had been a cold and wet night in the blasphemous borough of the Bronx, and Slick had walked into the Lights Out Mixed Martial Arts Gym a little after midnight with his shades on and wearing a long black overcoat. The gym was crowded with male and female fighters getting their late-night training in. Young up-

and-coming competitors were honing their skills in grappling, striking, and submission techniques in the hopes of one day making it to the big leagues like the UFC.

Slick was highly skilled in the sport but he had a totally different reason for being there that night. He'd come to the gym on behalf of the BBU. They'd sent him to have a conversation with the owner of the establishment known simply as Andy, a smart Bajan cat with major drug connections who had started earning his stain in the streets around the same time that Slick had gone into the military.

Word around the hood was that Andy's family in Barbados was rich and powerful. It was suspected that he got a lot of his start-up money from his people and then invested it in various illegal hustles.

Andy had insulated himself pretty well from the wolves and stick-up kids because he was feeding and funding a lot of his would-be enemies. But he was far from untouchable. Slick had made his way to the rear of the gym where the main office was located. He knocked on the door and a female voice told him to come in. He opened the door and entered the spacious office and saw a beautiful, full-breasted woman sitting at a big oak desk. She was known as Haitian Tisha and she was one of Andy's top captains.

Tisha was what you'd call a boss-ass bitch, and Slick respected her cunning and calculated swagger. Not only was she highly intelligent, but her heart was colder than ice.

"*Sak Pase*, you must be Tisha," Slick said with a slight smirk on his grill. Although caught off guard, the Haitian beauty maintained her poker face like a true professional.

"*Nap Boule*, young stranger. Please have a seat. What can I do for you?" she responded without relaying her sudden heightened sense of awareness.

Haitian Tisha saw a lot of hoods come in off the streets, but she could tell by his demeanor that something was very different about this man. The way he had just walked up in her office made something deep inside her scream that he was threatening and dangerous. Slick took a seat and began to talk.

"I can see that your boss isn't here so I need you to deliver a little message to him."

Slick said this in such a deadly tone that it momentarily froze Tisha's finger as she reached to push the small red button under the desk that would alert her bodyguard in the adjacent room.

"There's a certain young snowball by the name of Lola Berkman that Andy has clucking and sucking for him, and I'm respectfully requesting that he cut her loose and let her go free. Lola comes from a good white family and they're worried about her, therefore she needs to be returned to them no later than six pm tomorrow evening."

Haitian Tisha never batted an eyelash.

"Now," Slick said, still wearing the cold smirk on his face. "Failure to comply with my respectful request will result in my people showing up at that house on Staten Island that Andy just bought for his baby's mother. I'll instruct them to test out her dancing skills to see if she has what it takes to be a top-dollar stripper and dick sucker."

The words weren't even outta his mouth good when the office door busted open. Before Slick could blink, a chick brandishing a chrome .45 handgun was aiming her heat directly at his dome. The sight of her made Tisha's spine relax as she leaned back in her chair and gave Slick a little smirk of her own.

"You must be out of your fucking mind coming through my employer's establishment making threats," Haitian Tisha barked from her pretty lips. "Nigga we running shit up in here, and you obviously don't know who the fuck we are," she snarled and then jumped up outta her chair. "Matter of fact, who the fuck are *you*?"

She flicked her hand in the air. "Never mind. It don't even matter because whoever you are your game is weak. You fucked with the wrong one tonight you fuck-nigga!"

Ignoring the pistol aimed at his dome Slick calmly took off his dark shades and looked into the windows of Tisha's soul as he spoke quietly.

"*Fuck-nigga?*" His laugh was deadly. "You see, the thing is Tisha, I know everything about y'all, and y'all *fuck-niggas* don't know shit about me."

"What the hell are you talking about?"

Slick leaned back in his chair. Even at the end of a gun barrel he exuded a killer's confidence, cooler than the other side of the pillow.

"Listen, I'm not big on explanations or intimidations. I'd rather let my actions speak for me. So if you're as smart as I think you are, then look me in my eyes and tell me what you see. Do I look like the type of amateur *fuck-nigga* who rolls around half-stepping without covering every angle or planning for every scenario?"

His dark eyes sucked at hers, suffocating her in his glare.

"I advise you to tell this bitch over here to tuck her strap because you have a young sister who is very near and dear to you and she gets off her night job up in the Bronx in about fifteen minutes. If this bitch don't drop her heat my people will be mailing your sister's fuckin head to that nursery school right off Fordham Road that her son Tey-Tey attends. So please don't do your precious sister and your cute lil man nephew that way."

A look of shock and horror washed over Haitian Tisha's face.

"Okay, okay!" she pleaded in a negotiating voice, trying to maintain control over a situation when she knew damn well she didn't have any.

"I'll give Andy your message! I'll tell him exactly what you said! Just please don't touch my sister or my nephew because one little stank-pussy white bitch just isn't worth all this trouble!"

She waved frantically at the young woman near the door. "Put the damn gun down! Put it down!"

Slick finally turned to look at the chick who had gotten the drop on him. His cool, calm persona almost crumbled the moment he stared into her big brown eyes.

Their eyes locked and she returned his gaze with a look of confusion and familiarity. When it finally dawned on her who she was looking at, the sudden recognition made her stagger backwards.

What felt like a bone-deep connection of hours had only lasted for a split-second, and Haitian Tisha's impatient voice broke them out of their trance.

"Hurry up! Escort this cocky bastard outta here, Jewelz! And make sure he don't fall and break his neck on the way out the door!"

Slick had wanted to jump outta his skin at the sound of the chick's name, but he played it cool and smoothly put his shades back on as he rose from his seat.

"Thank you for your cooperation, Tisha," Slick said calmly. "Somehow I knew you were a real smart woman, and if your boss has any questions or concerns tell him I'll be contacting him personally if Lola isn't returned to her home address at the specified time. I can guarantee you that."

Without waiting for her response, Slick walked calmly out of the office with Jewelz clocking right behind him. The moment they stepped outside the gym he snatched her into the shadows of a doorway and she flung herself into his chest and wrapped her arms tightly around his neck.

"*Jewelz...*" Slick embraced her closely as she whimpered and cried out and trembled like her very soul ached.

All Slick could do was hold her close. His heart was pounding and his breath was all caught up in his throat.

Tears slid from both their eyes as the painful memories that had been deeply buried so long ago threatened to explode out of their entwined bodies like a blast of dynamite.

Jewelz pulled back first.

"Lil Slick! What the fuck are you doing here?" she whispered in amazement. "Boy is you crazy? Rolling up in Andy's spot like the Gestapo coulda got you shot!" She looked up at him with her teary eyes lit up with joy, pain, and confusion all at once.

Slick chuckled as he used his thumb to wipe the glistening tears from her cheeks. "Nah, what the fuck was *you* doing up in there?" he angled his chin at the gym, "Playing hired heat for them low-level outta town niggas?"

"It's been *years*," Jewelz said, ignoring his question and squeezing his hands tightly. "So many *years* since the last time I seen you! I never knew what happened to you after the funerals and all—"

"*Shhhh....*" Slick pressed his finger to her lips and then ran his sleeve across his damp face and shook his head.

"Look, I gotta make a run, baby girl. I can't talk right now. Lemme get your number."

Jewelz spit out her cell phone number and Slick quickly logged it into his phone.

"Way to keep closed lips back there," he praised her. "You know I wanna get with you, but now ain't the right time. I'll holla. I wanna know what you been up to. I wanna spend some time with you and hear all about your life, Jewelz, but now just ain't the right time."

Slick leaned down and kissed her on the cheek as he struggled to control the painful memories swirling through his mind. Jewelz was like a ghost from his past. From the most horrific part of his childhood. He felt a surge of protectiveness for her and he had a sudden urge to snatch her up and take her with him.

Fighting against his swollen heart, Slick pulled away to leave but Jewelz grabbed him by his coat. She clung to him like a child and she could barely get her words out past her desperate cries.

"No, wait up, Slick! You can't just run off and leave me just like that! Where you staying at? Tell me where I can find you at?"

"I'ma get at you," Slick said and backed away feeling like his heart was about to fall outta his chest.

They stared at each other with intense survivor's guilt shining in both their eyes. Jewelz opened her mouth to protest again, but before she could say a word Slick whirled around and took off around the corner and into a dark alley.

Jewelz was stunned. All she could do was stand there filled with an undying emptiness that just like a vicious stab wound, plunged straight through her heart and deep into the depths of her soul.

CHAPTER 7

Reunited and it Feels So Hood

With her eyes locked on him while her mind played on rewind, Jewelz stood on the rooftop under the moonlight reading Slick's thoughts right outta his head. That night at Bajan Andy's joint had played out for her like a dream come true.

But a whole month had passed before she'd finally heard from Slick. She had thought about him constantly, night and day, and she coulda kicked herself in the ass for not getting his number before he ran off. Or at least finding out where he stayed.

But when his call finally came she was shocked by how cold and distant his conversation was and she couldn't even believe where his head was at. Instead of wanting to get up with her so they could reminisce about their dreams of Paris, Greece, and Switzerland, and all that sweet lil puppy love that they had once shared, the only thing on Slick's mind had been the possibility of forging a lucrative business relationship with her.

"Yo, the reason I'm calling is because I got a proposition for you," Slick had told her straight off the bat. "I wanna make you a job offer, Jewelz. That lil worker-ant shit you doing for Bajan Andy is way beneath you, baby," he said. "Come hook up with my organization and I'll show you how to become a real professional and increase your skill set. Fuck with me and all these lil slanga niggas you clocking will be bowing down in your presence and showing you the utmost respect on these streets."

Jewelz had jumped on the chance for a new grind. Especially since it meant she'd be much closer to Slick and sharing a part of his world. And now, as she stood facing him on the rooftop of his grandmother's building with her deepest feelings shining brightly from her eyes, she realized that even though she saw him practically every day she was no closer to Slick than she had been during all those years when they were apart.

"Look," she told him, sensing his turmoil. "Fuck that vote we took just now, and fuck them stupid-ass rules about side-hits and outside hits too. I'm down to help you take Handgun Goody and his entire crew out. Just tell me the time and the place and I'm there on the job, Slick. That's my word."

"Jewelz," Slick muttered, his mouth suddenly bone dry. He didn't even wanna tell her but he had to. He hated to have to tell her. He just didn't wanna take her back to that dark-ass place that both of them had come from. But he knew he *had* to. He had done his research and he couldn't let her walk up on this shit blind. She needed to know what kinda mix she was getting herself into. He had to tell her.

"Check it out, there's more to this situation than what I let on to the crew," he confessed. "It ain't just about the old people in this building, yo. It's about my people too. It's about getting revenge for me and for you as well, ma."

A brief flash of concern crossed Jewelz's face and suddenly she was all ears as she left the doorway and walked back out to the open area of the roof.

"What are you talking about, Slick? I already said I'd help you murk that nigga. What are you tryna tell me?"

Slick shook his head and placed his hands on her slender shoulders. "Yo, before you sign up for this job I need you to know who you really running up against, a'ight? You need to know that Handgun Goody ain't just some slum nigga fresh outta the joint and running dope all over Brownsville, Jewelz. That nigga used to scramble in our old building back in the day. He was locked down for a good minute, but I looked into his background closely and he's the same nigga who came knocking on the door that day. He's the same nigga who—"

Suddenly all the blood seemed to rush outta Jewelz's body.

Slick pulled her close as her smooth brown skin flushed and beads of sweat broke out on her nose. She took a deep breath and stared up at Slick like he was miles away. His lips were still moving so she knew Slick was talking, but for some reason she couldn't hear a damn thing he was saying.

Instead, what she heard is what her little six-year-old ears had heard on the fateful day that was buried deep in their past. She heard the gunshot and Miss Kea's bloodcurdling screams coming from the kitchen. And then she heard the terrified cries of helpless, innocent children as a butcher knife was plunged deeply into their chests and stomachs by a raging fuckin madman.

"Lil Slick," Jewelz's knees felt weak as she fell against him and called him by his childhood name. She thought about the first time she had met him. How she had knocked on their project door and told his mother that one day she was going to marry her oldest son.

"My name is Diamond-Ruby-Emerald-Amethyst-Moonstone-Sapphire Jordan," she had proudly announced, and Miss Kea couldn't help but bust out laughing.

"Diamond-Ruby-Emerald-Amethyst-Moonstone-Sapphire Jordan?" Kea had held the door open and repeated in surprise. "Well, pleased to meet you, sweetheart. Come on in, baby girl. You're just a beautiful bag of jewelz, now ain't you honey?"

The name Jewelz had stuck, and so had her infatuation with young Slick. That day had been the first of many days and nights that Jewelz had spent in the Williams household playing with Slick and his siblings and being loved on by Kea and Big Slick.

Jewelz remembered the first time that her and Slick had snuck in his mother's closet together and hid behind the clothes way in the back. They didn't hump or kiss or do nothing nasty like most kids do, they just wanted some time alone so they could hold hands real tight and make their plans. Slick's grandmother had given him an Encyclopedia of the World, and they had sat close together in the darkness whispering about all the faraway places that they planned to visit when they grew up. Jewelz had told Slick that she wanted to have lots of babies, and Slick had promised to marry her and take her to Paris, Holland, Greece, and then finally to Switzerland so they could raise their kids there one day.

Jewelz had clung to those sweet memories through a lotta hard days, but she also retained the memory of looking into Slick's eyes as they lay stabbed up on his living room floor with the smell of death in the air and chaos ensuing all around them.

Miss Kea had been shot dead and Lil Slick had practically been gutted, and Jewelz had been severely wounded too. She had heard Crazy Haz as he ransacked the apartment, screaming all kinds of crazy gibberish from the back room as he searched desperately for his brother's stash of drugs.

As weak and bewildered as she was, Jewelz had summoned the strength to do what she always did. Stretched out on her back and staring up at the ceiling, she had inched her battered body painfully across the bloody floor until she was laying close enough to touch her best friend. Their fingers somehow found each other and gratefully intertwined. Her and Lil Slick had lay there wounded together. Staring at each other and holding hands, they had gasped for their last breaths together and waited to die together.

Long moments had passed and Jewelz remembered feeling Slick's hand grow slack in hers. His fingers uncurled from hers and became cooler as she closed her eyes desperately begging Jesus to let her die with him. She wanted God to take her wherever it was that Lil Slick had gone.

And that's when she heard somebody banging on the door.

Instinctively, Jewelz had squeezed Lil Slick's hand tighter. She changed her prayer and asked Jesus to let there be help for them on the other side of that door.

She held her breath and peeked from the narrow slit of her eyes. But when Crazy Haz snatched the door open instead of seeing help standing there, Jewelz had seen Handgun Goody. Or rather Dirty Mike, as he had been known back in his younger, filthier days.

"H-h-hey man," she had heard the fifteen-year-old dope-head stutter. "Is Big Slick home?"

"Get your bitch ass up in here!" Haz had snatched the teenager inside and quickly locked the door. With Lil Slick laying beside her already dead or unconscious, Jewelz had closed her eyes and pretended to be dead too.

"Yo, get in the back and let's find that fuckin dope!" she heard Haz bark the order to the tall, lanky teen. The two men had disappeared into the back room together, and when they finally found what they were looking for Dirty Mike tried to dash outta the apartment with his small cut, but Haz had other plans for him.

"Uh-uh!" he exploded as Dirty Mike froze with his hand on the doorknob. "Fuck you think your dirty ass is going? Get in that living room and pick up that fuckin knife, nigga! Finish them kids off! Finish them lil shits off!"

"But they dead!" Dirty Mike had shrieked as he peered into the blood splattered living room that looked like a battlefield. "They already fuckin dead!"

Crazy Haz's laughter had come from deep in his fat belly. "You want that dope, nigga? Then put your hand on that knife and kill they lil asses again, bitch! Make 'em *deader!*"

The teenaged drug fiend had walked into the carnage of the living room and kneeled down beside seven-year-old Jewelz. He gripped the bloody butcher knife by the handle and started jabbing it deeply into the bottom part of her belly without hesitation. He stabbed at her so hard that he fucked around and punctured her tiny womb and the knife slid through her stomach and straight outta her back. He didn't kill her, but he damn sure killed all her dreams.

Jewelz had swallowed her agony and lay there silently under his assault. If she woulda made one sound or uttered just one sniffling cry, Dirty Mike would have kept stabbing until she was deader than dead, and this she knew deep in her young heart.

So she lay there with her head turned toward her best friend, drawing strength from him and staring at him through glazed eyes as she fought the pain and pretended to be dead in order to stay alive.

Eventually Dirty Mike had gone down the line stabbing all the rest of the kids too, and then he came back for Lil Slick. Jewelz was certain that her friend was already gone, but to her surprise Lil Slick's eyes had fluttered open just as Dirty Mike stuck him. Lil Slick had opened his mouth to cry out in pain, but then he passed out again. Silently.

And that's when Haz took his depravity to another level. Stepping over the bodies of his blood-nieces and nephews, he had unzipped his pants and lifted the hem of Jewelz's purple sundress up high. Fumbling with his fly, he took his fat dick out and started peeing all over her.

"Greedy little bitch!" he laughed and cackled as his urine splashed down in Jewelz's face and hair, further degrading and defiling her. "You ain't even related but your hungry ass be over here eating shit up all the damn time! You shoulda stayed home and ate some pork n' beans tonight, bitch!"

"*Yes,*" grown-woman Jewelz whispered into Slick's neck as the horrible memories flashed before her eyes. For years Jewelz had fantasized about killing the men who had dishonored her body and stolen her dreams. She was already cooking up a couple of side hits on a cat named Donnie Haskell and his manz Chimp Charlie, and now that she knew where Dirty Mike was at, adding his name to her murder-list was gonna be oh, so sweet.

"*Yes,*" she repeated again. "Dirty Mike is as good as fuckin dead!"

"Yo, are you *sure?*" Slick stared deeply into her eyes and asked. "Cause I can go in on my own, Jewelz. I plan on wiping Dirty Mike and his whole fuckin fam off the map, baby! I want that pussy to suffer just like we suffered. I want him to know what it feels like to lose every fuckin body you love. I just don't wanna overstep my bounds and take away nothing you might want for yourself, nah'mean?"

"Yeah. But I want me a piece of your uncle's ass too," Jewelz said quietly as she thought about how that nigga's hot piss had felt raining down in her face. "He hurt us too. I wanna kill Crazy Haz."

"Too late." Slick shook his head. "That nigga is done, baby," he said as the sight of Haz's stabbed-up, bullet-ridden body flashed in his mind. "I swear to God erasing his coward ass gave me the best fuckin rush I ever had in my whole life! As soon as that nigga took his last breath I got reborn and felt brand new. Like I said, I can lay Handgun Goody and his entire bloodline down by myself. But I know what Dirty Mike took away from you. I know how bad he hurt you. I just don't wanna intrude on nothing you might need to do for *you,* you feel me?"

Jewelz just nodded, her breathing shallow, her whole body hyped. "I appreciate that respect, Slick. That nigga's grimy face has been burning in my mind for a long, long time and I gotta be the one to smash him. Matter fact, there's only two things I pray to God for every night, and getting revenge on Dirty Mike is one of them."

Slick nodded. "Cool. You got the green light on this job but you need to know that nigga done changed up a lot. He ain't no small-time dirty-ass dopehead no more. He's Handgun Goody now and he stays tight. He's damn near untouchable unless you on a suicide mission and you wanna die with him. He's never unguarded 'cause he keeps a wall of niggas glocked and cocked and on the ready, 24/7. You're gonna have to fake the funk while we take his family out. We'll save his ass for last, but in order to ice him and get out alive you'll have to get up on him close and personal. You'll have to catch him from the inside, with his thumb in his mouth, sleeping like a baby."

"I got this, Slick," Jewelz insisted quietly. "I can do this shit."

"A'ight, but you gonna have to look straight in that dirty bastard's grill," Slick warned her. "You're gonna have to call him Handgun Goody and skin and grin in his face, be all up in his area and pretend like he didn't—"

"I know what I gotta do!" Jewelz cut him off with a sharp glare. "I'm not a helpless little girl anymore! I can handle that muthafucka! You're right. Haz was your kill, but that dirty nigga Mike took something from me that I can never get back. Something that was priceless! Hell yeah, that nigga's ass is *minez* and I'ma make sure he pays up in full!"

CHAPTER 8

Black Girl Gone Cold

An hour later Jewelz was back in her plush Manhattan apartment with her mind racing a hundred miles a minute. She had been telling the truth when she told Slick that there were only two things she prayed for at night. Killing Dirty Mike was going to fulfill one of her desperate dreams, but was she ever gonna have the opportunity to see her most precious dream come true?

Jewelz stood in front of her mirror and stripped out of her clothes. At one time looking at herself naked had been almost impossible. The scars all over her belly had been too painful a reminder of the horrors that she had endured as a child.

Gazing into the mirror, Jewelz reached up and grasped her long ponytail. She removed the black rubber band and slowly unraveled her double-stranded twist.

She dragged her fingers through her hair from her scalp all the way to the ends, wincing as she felt some of her thick strands snapping free and breaking off at the root. She looked down at the long tendrils of loose hair she held in her hand and her heart quaked in pain. Pretty soon she was gonna have to start wearing a wig.

Tears formed in Jewelz's eyes but she refused to let them fall. Losing her hair wasn't the end of the damn world so she wasn't about to start hosting no pity party. Plenty of people got cancer every day. Some lived and some died. She wasn't the only one in the world who was going through some shit.

Yeah, said a small voice in the back of her mind as she placed the giant ball of hair in an ashtray and sparked it up with a cigarette lighter. *But you got cancer twice! Besides, other sick people have families! They got mad people who love and care about them! You don't have nobody Jewelz! Not even HIM!*

Jewelz gazed into the flame as she watched her hair slowly burn. She reminded herself to keep her chin up. She urged herself to have courage and to stay gully. Didn't nobody have to know she was sick unless she told them. She wasn't scared of dying neither because she put her life on the line every day. Nah, what scared the hell outta Jewelz was dying *alone.*

Who's gonna bury me? she often asked herself when she woke up shaking and sweating in the middle of the night. *Who's gonna pray over me?*

Jewelz had been a lucky survivor of the bloody massacre in Slick's project apartment that long ago day, but her life had spiraled even further downhill after that. Hell, to tell the truth she'd fallen damn near as low as a young girl could fall.

The damage to her womb was so severe that Jewelz had to have an emergency hysterectomy right after she was stabbed, and years later she suffered an even greater cruelty to her body at the hands of two more predatory niggas.

She was barely thirteen and sprouting mad titties and lush ass when she got snatched off the street by a pig-faced hustler named Fat Donnie Hassell, and that nigga had taught her the true meaning of pain.

Fat Donnie had him a money-making pimp-ring going where he lured runaways and troubled young girls into his sticky web of sexual sadism, just like a spider hooked a fly.

It was late at night and Jewelz had just slammed outta her apartment after fighting with her alcoholic uncle. His old ass was starting to get real nasty with her. He had taken to busting up in the bathroom while she was taking a shower like he didn't know she was in there ass-naked. Jewelz had just cursed him out and was heading up to the corner to buy a Newport loosie from the all-night candy store when Fat Donnie rolled outta the shadows and snatched her up.

He had muscled her down and tossed her inside of a dark van with blacked-out windows while she kicked and screamed and bucked for her life. Jewelz had rode in darkness and terror as he took her to a cheap hotel room where five other young girls were chained up and being held captive by a crispy black dude they called Chimp Charlie.

Jewelz was stripped naked and chained up too, and all six of them were beaten from head to toe on a daily basis. 24/7 they were forced to lay on their backs and submit to "dates" with all kinds of sadistic old men who liked to fuck young teenagers.

Doing all that shit was bad enough, but Jewelz had more of a banging, mature body than the other young girls so she could pass for being much older than her real age. The fact that she never got her period was a plus for her captors too, because they could make her lay on her back and fuck like a dog every day of the month.

It wasn't long before Chimp Charlie and Fat Donnie had her stripping in the back room of an underground titty joint. Jewelz was passed around like a prime piece of meat, and no matter how many horny, greasy-faced, stank-breath tricks squeezed her ass, pinched her nipples, or dug their fingers deep up inside her tight pussy and slobbered all down her neck, she never pocketed a dime.

But one night the titty joint got raided by the Feds, and in the chaos Jewelz and two other girls mixed in with the crowd and broke the fuck out. Jewelz was relieved to finally escape that hellish existence, and she had ran up outta that joint determined to do something better with her life.

But by then her uncle had drunk himself into a coma and there was no family left to take care of her. She had a choice to either turn tricks on the street or go into foster care, and after all the trauma she had been through out there in the world, Jewelz chose the state.

She stayed in a group home for a few years and as soon as she turned eighteen she broke outta the system's clutches and struck out on her own. In spite of all the grief and hard times that she had endured, Jewelz was stronger, wiser, and ready for the world.

But unfortunately, nothing the world had in store was destined to come easy to her. Every road in her life had been paved with broken pieces of glass and metal spikes. Her path had been treacherous and bumpy as hell. Especially since she had been forced to walk her whole damn journey in her bare feet.

She had eventually gotten a little receptionist job from a temp agency and she worked real hard at it for a while. Jewelz was a damn good employee, making it her business to be the first one to clock in when they opened and the last one to leave at night.

But even still, when she started getting sick and missing work her stingy-ass bosses had refused to pay her for the missed time. They started cutting back on her hours more and more each week. They even brought in a new receptionist as her replacement and expected Jewelz to train the chick and teach her everything she knew!

Jewelz was down in the dumps and in her feelings, but bad luck wasn't through fucking with her yet. She soon found out that she had a disease in her blood that ran in her family. By the time she got her first cancer diagnosis Jewelz had also lost her job. And with no money coming in and no health insurance either, she was ass-out on finding any decent medical care.

Bitter, scared, and mad at the whole damn world, Jewelz had taken a gig as an enforcer for a kingpin named Bajan Andy. In her warped state of mind she discovered that she enjoyed cracking heads and letting her strap ring off.

Andy paid her enough money to buy vitamins and fresh fruits and vegetables, and Jewelz was able to keep working and go through a complete round of chemotherapy without telling a soul. She fought through the sickness all by herself and depended only upon God to help her put one foot in front of the other each day. After it was all over and her doctors told her that the cancer had gone into remission, Jewelz had dropped down to her knees and finally cried.

Running into Slick that night at Andy's joint had felt like a sign from above. It was like the man upstairs was finally wrapping his arms around her and saying, *You are not alone. I am here with you.*

Sick of being sick, Jewelz had started regaining her strength and her positive outlook on life too. When Slick offered her a spot on his team she had jumped right on it. She was happy as hell to be by the side of the only person in the world that she had ever truly loved.

But she had switched street teams, so crashing on Haitian Tisha's sofa was outta the question. Slick had stepped up and offered to let her chill at his luxury crib until she found someplace to stay, and she had jumped right on that too.

Jewelz couldn't front. She had entertained mad illusions of picking up with him right where they had left off twenty years earlier. In her head and heart she had always belonged to Slick and he had always belonged to her too. But unfortunately Slick didn't see it that way and he wasn't even thinking about the past.

She found that out when she called herself serving the pussy on him in the middle of the night. Jewelz had taken a long hot bath and trimmed her female garden up real nice. She had rubbed her whole body down with lavender scented oil, then slipped into Slick's darkened room ass-naked and crawled up in his bed while he was sleeping.

She had trailed her lips down his rock-hard stomach and gripped his long, pretty dick in her hand. She squeezed and jacked that meat bone until he moaned real deep and started fucking up at her in his sleep. Jewelz had opened her mouth wide and slid his throbbing meat along the length of her steaming wet tongue...and Slick had opened his eyes and stiff-armed the shit outta her.

He caught her with the flat of his palm right in the eye, and Jewelz rolled off the bed screaming and then ran in the bathroom holding her eyeball and crying like a lil baby.

"*Jewelz!*" Slick had pounded on the locked door and hollered for her to come out. "Yo, I'm letting you chill here till you get a place, but you can't be coming at me like that when I'm sleep, girl! I ain't even tryna fuck with you like that!"

"*Why not,* Slick?" she had sobbed through the door, confused as fuck with her eyeball throbbing.

Like a love-sick fool she had told Slick all her secrets. He knew all about the low-down trench life she had lived after their violent tragedy. He knew she had been passed around from man to man and sold for top dollars like a piece of raw meat. He also knew that Dirty Mike's blade had destroyed her womb and robbed her of the honor of ever carrying a child. Of ever carrying *their* child, like both of them had once dreamed she would do. And now that he knew she had rolled around in the gutter and he was up on all the nasty, no-mercy shit that life had thrown at her, he was saying he didn't want her no more?

"Why not?" she had pleaded with him again. "We already been through the worst shit *ever* together, Lil Slick! Don't nobody love you like I do, and can't nobody love *me* like YOU!"

"All that shit was way back then!" Slick had barked on her. "This is *now!*"

"But we used to be so close! We dreamed together! We made promises to each other! We mighta been kids, but we made some serious plans for our life! What about *Switzerland?* We were gonna get married there! Don't you remember that shit? We was supposed to raise all of our babies there! What we went through in your mother's house was real bad, but me and you didn't die that day

Slick, and our dreams don't have to die neither!

"All that dreaming shit is *over!*" he had barked again. "My grandmother taught me how to put that shit in the past and keep living for *today,* Jewelz! Like you said, me and you was the lucky ones! We made it out alive!"

"Well at least you had your grandmother to take care of you!" she shot back at him hard. "I didn't have nobody to hold me in the middle of the night except the next perverted fuckin trick!"

"That life is over, Jewelz," Slick repeated quietly. "Forget all that shit! All of it! It's fuckin *over!*"

Yeah, he had crushed her lil heart real good for her that night, but when she looked back on it Slick had gotten one thing absolutely right. Her life *was* over. Jewelz's blood cancer had recently come back. And even though the doctors thought she had a small chance at survival and they said she should fight it, Jewelz knew in her heart that she was fighting a losing battle this time.

She stared at herself in the mirror and sighed. She'd only been taking the chemo for a little while, and other than her hair loss she didn't look all that sick on the outside. It was her insides that were on fire. And the part of her body that burned the worst was her heart. It burned for revenge.

Jewelz didn't fear death because she knew everybody had to go. Her days in this world might be numbered and coming to an end, but before she left this earth she was gonna bloody-bath all the bastards who had ruined her life! Straight up massacre all of them!

She already had a plan lined up for Chimp Charlie and Fat Donnie. But Dirty Mike aka Handgun Goody? Jewelz grinned and shook her head. That nigga shoulda stabbed her in her heart instead of her uterus. Slick putting her on to him felt like a sweet treat directly from the man upstairs.

Jewelz was still smiling as she pulled a purple silk nightgown over her head and climbed her weary bones in bed. She fluffed her designer pillow and grinned her ass off 'cause she wasn't a helpless little kid laying poked up on the floor no more. She was in her grown-woman pop-a-mothafucka assassin bag now, and she was planning on saving Handgun Goody, the slimiest and the grimiest savage of them all, for last.

CHAPTER 9

A Queen's Wrath

Joel Samuelson, a senior executive at the New York Diamond and Jewelry Exchange, had a rock-hard little boner that just wouldn't quit. He was ass-naked and sprawled on his back on the crisp white sheets of the downtown W. Hotel.

Wrapped in a velvet bag and secured inside of a blood-red briefcase on the floor was a five million-dollar diamond that he'd stolen from the most protected chamber of his company's vault. Joel and his sexy pet monkey had been embezzling company diamonds for more than two years now, but this one was by far the most brilliant stone they'd ever dared to take.

It was a risky move that could have landed Joel in prison for the rest of his days, but the half-million dollar bonus called "sweet money" that he'd been fronted from his underground investors made the gamble well worth the risks.

Besides, him and his little monkey had no worries about their thievery being discovered. A fake, but identical, diamond would soon be hand-crafted to such a degree that not even a highly-trained eye could tell them apart.

The fabricated fake diamond would then be slipped into the vault in the original stone's place. It would be months before the switch was detected and anyone realized the real thing was gone.

But by that time the original diamond would have already been smuggled out of the country and sold for a handsome sum on the international black market. Joel Samuelson would be sipping Chablis on a luxury yacht off the coast of a beautiful island in Thailand.

And his gorgeous pet monkey would be good and dead.

Joel gazed up at the naked monkey who was grunting and grinding as she hovered over his lap with her legs cocked open wide. They made one hell of a diamond-jacking team, and while for her it was strictly business, for him there was lots of freaky pleasure involved in it too.

He ran his fingers over her boldly curved hips and wrapped his hands around her tiny waist. She was honey-colored and gorgeous. Her beautiful hazel eyes and long curly hair were a bonus to the stunning curves on her perfectly proportioned stripper's body. Joel grinned inside. Not only did she have the best piece of heart-shaped ass in the whole universe, she was the key to his financial success.

"Oh, yes! I love your beautiful cock! Fuck me deeper!" the monkey shrieked dramatically as she bucked her hips and rode him like a prime race-horse. "Deeper!" she demanded. "Give it to me deeper!"

Joel knew it was all an act and she was pretending to be a white chick in a porno video, but it was definitely doing the trick. He lifted her off of him and flipped her ass-down on the bed. Spreading her beautiful legs wide apart, Joel buried his face in her hot sticky pussy and licked and sucked her clit until her grunts and moans became real as hell.

"Ah, *yeahhh!*" the monkey purred, dropping her act as her pussy squirted liquid sugar and she gapped her creamy legs open even wider. "Lick my shit out, Daddy! My ass too! Put your whole face up in it!"

Joel gripped her ass with both hands and dug his fingers deep into her booty-meat. He squeezed hard as hell as he sucked the juices right outta her pink pussy like his swirling tongue was a crazy straw. The monkey arched her back and thrust her hips in the air. She gripped his head and held it in place as she grinded her wetness and humped it all over his face.

Withdrawing his head, Joel scrambled to climb on top of her. He shoved his erection into her steaming flesh and arched his fifty-year-old back and gave her every last one of the four inches he was packing.

Her juicy cunt felt like a clenching velvet mitten as her muscles sucked at him and drew him deeper inside her female cave. Joel crooked his neck so he could watch his glistening dick disappearing into her slit. His shit was so wet and bricked up it made his whole body break out in goose bumps.

Joel moaned as she fucked up at him, and in response she gripped his meat tighter between her thighs and twerked her ass and made her full cheeks bounce up and down in a staccato rhythm.

Joel gasped. He had fucked plenty of black chicks before but he had never had a piece of pussy that shook him so deliciously. His asshole puckered and he wheezed and panted through his thin lips while she laid that hot nigger trim on him.

Moments later they switched positions again and she stretched out fully on top of him with her plump breasts pressed up against his chest. She locked her legs tightly together and squeezed his dick in a vice grip. Joel yelped and palmed the fullness of her round ass as she humped fast and hard and milked him with her pussy muscles like he was a prize goat.

Gripping one firm mound in his hand, Joel parted her ass cheeks and in-serted his index finger deeply inside her anus. Feeling the stiffness of his wood just on the other side of her soft membranes, he yelped again and his dick jerked twice as he nutted and spurted a hot load into the condom.

The monkey remained on top of him slowly grinding her hips until he caught his breath. Then she sat up and smiled brightly and Joel smiled back.

She looked majestic. The Queen of Diamonds, sitting on her throne.

He gripped the base of his dick and held the condom firmly in place as she lifted herself up. His shriveled-up little dick fell over on his leg like it had been shot dead.

Still breathing hard, Joel ran his fingers through his thick mass of graying chest hair. He watched the girl walk naked across the room. Not only did she have a perfect frame and a thick round ass, she had the softest skin he had ever touched.

"Okay," she said over her shoulder with a smirk. "So now that we got that lil shit outta the way, are we all set for tonight?" Pausing in the doorway she pinned him with her cold hazel eyes and struck a stunning pose outside the bathroom.

Joel nodded. "Yes, my dear. Everything is in order. You just deliver the briefcase to Hymie's place and I'll handle the rest."

She eyed the green duffle bag that was leaning against the wall. "But what about the sweet money we got from the investors? We're still going fifty-fifty on it, right? You wanna go ahead and split it up so I can take my half right now?"

Joel shook his head quickly. "No, I don't think that's a good idea. I'd be very worried if you walked out of here alone carrying a five million dollar diamond *and* a quarter of a million dollars in cash. That's just asking for trouble, dear. We'll divvy up the sweet money the first thing tomorrow morning. And yes, we're going to split it fifty-fifty, just like I promised. A quarter of a million for you, and a quarter of a million for me. I'll meet you on Fulton Street at the jewelry store at nine, okay?"

The sexy young thing hesitated for a second, and then she nodded and smiled. "Yeah, you right. That's a whole lotta paper to be carrying around in New York City. Plenty of people get popped in the back of the head for way less than that. Okay, cool. I'll just get my cut tomorrow morning at nine then."

Oh, yes, Joel thought smugly as he watched her turn around and walk inside the bathroom. She was a stunning broad and she gave the very best head in the whole wide world. But she was also the greediest, deadliest and most conniving thief he had ever met.

What a gorgeous monkey, he thought as his eyes mentally tattooed the image of a sparkling diamond on her back. He imagined it stretching from one shoulder to the other and ending with its tip disappearing into the crack of her deliciously round ass.

It's a damn shame it has to end this way, Joel thought with a grin. He had pitied the little ghetto bitch when her cousin begged him to hire her. He had taken her under his wing and taught her all sorts of dirty tricks and schemes to get ahead in the diamond industry. But she had been a far better student than he was a teacher. He had helped her make an enormous amount of money under the table, but she had turned into such a treacherous little monkey. The more money she got the more money she had to have, and now she was biting the hand that fed her and getting too big for her cage.

Joel had ordered the monkey's murder through the BBU, a company that was tops in the execution game. It had cost him almost the entire pot of sweet money to pay for it, but Joel was cool with that. Dead monkeys didn't get a share of the profits, and once the five million dollar diamond was sold her portion would go directly into his pocket.

He chuckled under his breath.

In a sick sort of way the beautiful monkey would be paying for her own execution and he'd be destroying a cut-throat rival at the same time. You couldn't get any grimier than that!

Joel remained outstretched in the bed until the bathroom door closed firmly behind her, and as soon as he heard the shower running he reached for his cell phone.

"Hymie?" he whispered when the phone was answered at a jewelry store in Brooklyn. "Yeah. Everything's all set. She'll be heading your way to make the drop-off soon. Leave the security guard at the shop to answer the door, and you and Madeline get the fuck out of there! I'll stop by in the morning as soon as I get the briefcase out of the locker."

Click.

Joel was grinning like a muthafucker as he punched another number into his phone, and this time instead of having a conversation he simply repeated the coded instructions that he had issued to the BBU just a few days earlier.

"The animals are about to escape from the zoo," he said happily. "Hit the monkey carrying the red briefcase."

$$$$$

Fifteen minutes later a stylishly dressed young woman pushed through the rotating doors and exited the W Hotel. Her curves were banging like African drums in her skin-tight teal pants suit, and her polished toenails peeked out from a pair of bright teal-and-red designer heels. Under the wide brim of her floppy red hat, a pair of diamond earrings glinted from her ears and a tiny diamond-crusted cross dangled from a choker at her throat.

From her hand swung an expensive red leather briefcase. There was a bright smile on her gorgeous cornbread-colored face and mad confidence in her step as she sashayed her sexy hips toward the shiny stretch whip that was waiting at the curb.

Watching her from a throne-like chair in the grand lobby of the upscale hotel was a regal older gentleman with slicked-back wavy hair that hung down past his shoulders. Handsome and high-yellow, he was dressed in a pitch-black three-piece suit and wearing an expensive John Bull top hat in the exact same shade.

His snake-eyes were intense as shit as he watched the young woman climb in the backseat of the whip, then he stood up tall and spoke discreetly into the handle of his stylish ivory cane.

"The Queen has left the castle," he said in a deep, gravelly voice. "I'm 'bout to wipe the muthafuckin chessboard clean."

$$$$$

Ten minutes had passed since the door had closed behind the beautiful monkey and Joel Samuelson was still laying in the hotel bed ass-naked. He had peeled off his sticky condom and his shriveled pink meat lay limply between his legs.

A slight grin played on his lips as he sipped from a glass of vintage red wine. He laughed to himself as he thought about the sweet wild thang he had just fucked the shit out of in more ways than one.

She had taken the red briefcase with her and promised to call him as soon as she had placed the diamond inside the safe at Hymie's jewelry store.

The plan was for Hymie to duplicate the stone and then hand the real jewel over to Avi, the international diamond trader from Belgium, who would then sell it overseas and filter the profits back to them.

In a non-criminal world the handsome profits would have been split five ways between:

1) Him,

2) The Jewish investors who had given him the half-million dollars in sweet money,

3) Avi, the international diamond trader,

4) Hymie, the diamond fabricator and Fulton Street jewelry store owner and,

5) The beautiful but conniving monkey who was supposed to get the fifth share of the cut.

Joel laughed mirthlessly. On paper it looked like a pretty good plan, but first of all, the call from that beautiful bitch was never going to come.

And that's because the plan had been changed. Instead, of going to Fulton Street and stashing the diamond in Hymie's safe, the stolen gem was going to be stripped from the monkey's cold dead hands and then placed in a completely different safe. In a locker, really.

And once the diamond had been cloned, its fake identical twin would be returned to the vault at the New York Diamond and Jewelry Exchange as originally planned, and the split would only have to go four ways instead of five.

Never trust a New York Jew, Joel laughed loudly as he congratulated himself on a brilliant double-cross and a job well done. The payout on the sale of the diamond would be a huge windfall for everyone involved. Everyone except the monkey!

Bright green dollar signs were busy dancing through Joel's gluttonous mind when he heard a noise coming from the entrance to the suite. It was the distinctive sound of a door being opened and then firmly closed and locked.

The bitch was back!

"Hon, is that you?" he called out.

Joel set his wine glass on the end table and sat halfway up. He peered toward the open doorway. "What's wrong, darling? Did you forget something?"

"Yeah," answered a male voice that was so cold and deep it made Joel's blood freeze in his veins. "I forgot something alright goddammit..."

That was no monkey! It was a gorilla!

Rushing footsteps sounded and then a tall, stately presence filled the doorway. He smelled of expensive cologne and carried a stylish ivory cane in his hand.

"I forgot to *kill* your fuckin ass!"

Joel yelped and twisted in the bed as he lunged under the pillow reaching for his pistol. Crying out, he swung his arm up and managed to palm the revolver and get his finger on the trigger at the same time.

But that was as far as he got before a slice of sharp metal shot out the end of the cane and stabbed him deep in his shoulder. It deadened his gun-hand as he flung himself backwards against the headboard trying to get away.

"Ahhhh!" he shrieked, grabbing at his pierced, bleeding meat.

The stylishly dressed gentleman moved fast for an old head. Rushing closer, he snatched the sheet off the naked white man, and with a gloved hand he did exactly what he had come there to do.

He grabbed Joel's shriveled up balls and yanked them high in the air. And then he gripped the end of his cane and sliced the man's hairy pink nut sack clean the fuck off.

"Aggrrhhhh!" The jewelry executive screamed and clutched at the stump of his nuts as a pool of blood gushed from his body and soaked the sheets under his ass.

"Who the hell are you? What the fuck did you do this for?" he screeched. His hands were covered in blood as he moaned and rocked back and forth clenching his gaping wound in a vice grip. "Oh my God!" he whimpered as his life-blood spurted through his fingers. "I'm dying..." he whined. "Fuck! Shit! Fuck! I'm *dying!*"

Sly McFly laughed mercilessly before aiming his blade at Joel's throat. Thrusting the cane like a spear, he impaled Joel's fat neck dead to the pillow.

"Then nigga quit all that whining and *die!* Fuck was you thinkin anyway, *white boy?* You ain't got the *balls* to fuck with the Queen of Diamonds!

CHAPTER 10

Ready, Set, Hit!

The Zip 'em up Crew of contracted killers were gearing up to take out their latest target. They'd received very little background information about the job, but that didn't matter. The only thing on their minds was the who, the what, the when, the where, and the how many stacks of cash they were gonna collect as soon as the job was done.

It was a quiet night as the crew prepared to put in work at the jewelry store on Fulton Street. It was late, way after business hours, but a drop was about to be made and the Zip 'em up Crew was there to intercept it.

The plan was to line the vic up sweetly and then blast his ass into the next decade. According to their job sketch, the monkey they were targeting for the hit was delivering a red briefcase to the jewelry store. Slick had been instructed to eliminate the target and take possession of the briefcase, then stash it in a locker at a busy terminal in Manhattan.

Typically, Noodles would have stalked and studied their target's entire schedule inside and out, which was usually very easy to do. The type of people they tracked seldom had a sixth sense about them. They walked through life too wrapped up in their worldly obsessions to realize they were being hunted.

But tonight was different. Their instructions had been vague and brief, and the entire team was going in balls to the walls and ass out.

As Noodles sat hidden in the cut listening to his scanner for unexpected police activity and observing people wandering around on the streets, the rest of the team got into their positions in the alley behind the store. They were dressed in all-black attire with black masks, boots, and bulletproof vests that had F.B.I. stamped on the back in bold white letters. Wild Man, Slick, and Whitey checked and rechecked their heat and waited to receive the go-ahead signal from Noodles in their earpieces.

Jewelz was in the basement of the store scoping out the control panel, ready to dead the power source as soon as Noodles gave the word.

Upstairs, shit was just about to pop off.

"Dammit!" a stunningly beautiful woman barked as she stormed into the store's showroom wearing a floppy red hat and cloaked in a cloud of intoxicating perfume.

Her skin looked like bananas and honey, and her curvy figure was mind-boggling as she stood tall in a teal designer pants suit and a pair of teal Jimmy Choo's with the red bottoms.

An older black man was sitting in a chair wearing some high-water gabardine slacks and a plaid shirt. The beautiful girl strode over to him and snatched a thick textbook from his hands. With her lip turned down in a snarl she hauled off and slapped the shit outta him so hard his glasses flew off.

"You supposed to be watching the goddamn safe, stupid!" She pointed toward a back room. "Ain't nobody paying your old ass to sit around here and *read!*"

The elderly man got up and bent over to scoop his glasses up off the floor. He started mumbling a million apologies as he rose shakily to his feet.

"I-I'm sorry, Miss," he stuttered as he reached out to take his textbook back. He was seventy-four-years old and working night security as a college intern so he could complete his associate's degree during the day.

"I was just about to head back there to the safe. I didn't mean no harm. Honest, I'm really sorry. It's just that I have a big exam coming up and I was just trying to—"

"Damn right you sorry!" the beautiful chick bitched as she slapped the shit outta him again. The old man threw his arm up to protect himself, and then he winced and reached out for his book.

"It's just that I have a test, that's all—"

The young chick clutched the book to her chest and twisted it outta his reach.

"I don't give a shit about you or your damn test!" She thrust her red briefcase out toward him. "Here! Stash this shit in the safe right fuckin now! And you better not take your eyes off it for the rest of the night!"

The poor man nodded and took the briefcase from the beautiful, foul-mouthed girl. He felt highly disrespected. He was old enough to be this young chick's grandfather but he swallowed his pride as he reminded himself how badly he needed the extra money. The community college had helped him land this security job, and with a daughter out there tricking her body in the streets, plus a sick wife and three grandkids at home to feed, every dollar counted.

The old man had just opened his mouth to apologize again when the back door smashed inward and shattered on its frame.

Phewt!

A silenced slug tore through the old man's jaw, taking the lower half of his face with it. He stumbled around in a crazed circle, still gripping the red briefcase as it swung from his hand.

Phewt Phewt!

Two more silent-but-deadly rounds sank into him, from two different guns. One of the slugs skimmed the top of his head and damn near scalped him. The other one was a bulls-eye shot to the chest that made him drop the briefcase as his heart stopped cold. His eyes rolled back in his head and he flopped to the floor like a sack of Idaho's finest taters.

"*Oh my god!*" the girl screeched. She jumped so bad her floppy hat fell off her head. The sharp odor of gunpowder mingled with her perfume as she sank to her knees clutching the textbook in front of her face like it was a shield. "*Please!* Don't shoot me!"

Slick's finger was tightening on the trigger when he hesitated.

He didn't usually blast too many females but he had come damn close to lighting one up just now.

And what a beautiful one she was too.

He could only see the chick's eyes and the top of her head behind the textbook, but even that little bit told him that she was gorgeous. Her frame looked slender but her hips were sweet and broad. Her skin was a heavenly color. Her hair was soft and wavy and pulled back into a long curly ponytail.

But it was those eyes that got to him. They were hazel-colored with long, pretty lashes. They were also petrified and filled with cold, stark terror.

No witnesses, no worries.

Slick felt like he had gone into another zone. It was silent in the room except for his pounding heart and the sounds of her soft cries.

Two other figures emerged from the shadows and joined him. Wild Man and Whitey. Slick knew shit was crucial. His team was so amped up with adrenaline that he could feel the intense heat coming off their bodies.

"Sleep her, bruh." Wild Man nudged him, breaking his trance. "Fuck is you waiting for, man? *Pop* that bitch!"

Slick opened his mouth but no words came out.

The gorgeous chick wearing the tight sexy suit and holding a big book out like it was a bullet-proof shield started whimpering uncontrollably. The book slipped from her shaky grasp and she scooted across the floor on her ass like she was trying to back up and hide in a jewelry case.

"Don't shoot...oh God, Mister please don't shoot me...please...I didn't do nothing. I swear to God I didn't do shit!"

Slick's eyes skimmed the title of the book on the floor as he kept his gun trained on her.

Basic Biology.

"Yo, you in college or something?" he asked quietly. He felt some sort of weird shit gathering in the pit of his stomach. The terror in her eyes evoked something vulnerable inside of him that he usually kept in deep check.

She nodded hard as hell, her head flopping up and down like she was tryna break her own neck.

"Y-y-yes! *Yes!* I'm in *college!*" she licked her lips as her eyes darted around and she eyed the dead man on the floor.

"Please. I-I-I'm just a college student doing an internship here for a couple of weeks! I was just trying to study for my test. Mister please don't kill me!" she shrieked. "I'm just an intern! I don't know nothing about what's going on here. *Please don't kill meeee!*"

"Ayo, *whack* this bitch so we can haul ass outta here!" Wild Man insisted, smacking Slick's shoulder with a hard, heavy hand. "We been in here too long already! *No witnesses, no muthafuckin worries!*"

The chick started crying even harder and Slick felt his stomach cave. His entire face was sweating beneath his mask as he went against every one of his cold killer instincts and lowered his weapon.

"Yo, grab that fuckin briefcase!" he barked at Wild Man.

He pointed at Whitey. "Pat her down and then tie her ass up and throw her in the van with us. And on the way out," he added over his shoulder, "jump on all that jewelry over there, yo! Bag it up! Make sure you pick that whole fuckin display case clean!"

"*Really?*" Jewelz snapped as she stepped fully into the room. She had just shot out the security camera and now she stood there clouding Slick's peripheral vision like she was his dark fuckin conscience. "Nigga is you fuckin kidding me?"

She too was dressed in all-black. A loaded pistol dangled from one hand and her other hand was posed on her sexy round hip. "You mean you tryna take this bitch *with us?*"

Slick whirled on her. "When I say move dammit you move with no feedback! You got that? Now MOVE!"

This job was Slick's baby. He was the head honcho of the crew and the lead on the team. So with no further hesitation the gunslingers followed orders and carried out Slick's peculiar commands.

And less than a minute later, as the old man's bullet-ridden body lay there growing cold on the floor, a nondescript van pulled out of the dark alley and sped off quickly into the black night.

$$$$$

"Yo, what's your name Little Miss Intern?" Slick asked calmly over his shoulder.

Whitey had driven them down a dirt road off the Jamaica Bay side of the Belt Parkway and then pulled over in the darkness somewhere behind an old horse riding stable.

Even with their masks on Slick could read the tension in the air like a weathervane. His team was on one. They were confused as fuck too, because for the first time ever "Mister Perfect" as they called him, had taken a detour off course and strayed way off the plan.

Not one of them understood that shit and Slick didn't understand it neither. All he knew was that right about now he was riding on pure emotion. Emotion that the beautiful chick tied up in the backseat had somehow stirred up in him.

"Ay, I said what's your name?" he barked again, and this time it wasn't a question it was a command.

She still didn't answer.

Slick could feel the fear coming off the girl as she sat behind him, wedged in the middle between Jewelz and Wild Man.

He looked over his shoulder slowly and his voice was ice-cold as he repeated himself for the last time. "I *said* what's your name?"

"Honore," she answered finally.

Slick nodded. "Oh, so you's a Puerto Rican mami, huh?"

She sucked her teeth. "I'm *black*," she said, like he was just too damn ig'nant for words. "Honore ain't even Spanish. It's French."

"Oh so you's a French Fry, huh?"

She cut her eyes and smirked. "No, but whatever."

Slick chuckled inside. The girl was nervous, but she was bold too, he noted. And fine as all hell.

Haaa-chu! Haaa-chu! Haaa-chu!

Slick glanced at Jewelz who was sneezing like crazy and waving her hand back and forth in front of her nose like something back there smelled real shitty.

"Damn!" she sneered at the girl as she yanked off her mask and sneezed into it. "Why your-type bitches always gotta take a bath in that stank-ass Poison perfume?" She waved her hand under her nose some more. "I mean, a little bit is cool, but you poured on too damn *much!*"

Slick frowned in Jewelz's direction. "Yo, put your cover back on and untie her," he ordered.

He watched as Jewelz ignored him and flicked her wrist faster than a striking snake. A 007 switchblade appeared in her hand and she slid the tip between the girl's forearms and expertly sliced through the thick plastic bands.

Slick tossed the chick her small designer purse and then outta nowhere he said coldly, "A'ight, ride over. Rise and fly, sweetie. But first ga'head and grab your cell phone and toss it up here."

She frowned. "You want my phone?"

He nodded. "Yeah. Give it up."

"C'mon now, Mister!" the chick whined as her eyes got wild. "Why you gotta take my phone?" She shook her head. "Uh-uh. I can't let you leave me way out here in the middle of nowhere without a damn phone!"

Slick heard the click of Jewelz's gat as she jammed the barrel up against the back of ol' girl's head.

"What you mean you can't *let* him? Ain't nobody *asking* your ass!" Jewelz barked. "Give up the goddamn phone!"

The sky was lit up with stars overhead, but the only sound to be heard was the purring of the van's engine and the pounding of the chick's heart.

With trembling fingers, she dug around in her pocketbook then reluctantly held out her phone.

"Yo, hit this number for me real quick," Slick ordered. He started spitting out digits as she punched them in, and before he could finish Jewelz's mouth was hanging open and her eyes were shooting spiked daggers at him.

"*Really?*" she shrieked as Slick's cell phone flashed twice on his belt. Her and Honore both eyeballed his ass as the low purr of a vibration cut the air. "Nigga I *know* you ain't just give this bitch we shoulda deaded your goddamn number!"

Honore went in hard on him too.

"For real!" she said turning her lip up and smacking him with a disgusted look. "Don't nobody even want your number so don't be tryna get at me!"

Whitey laughed like a muthafucka and Wild Man started bitching again. "Ay, yo! What the fuck is you doing, my dude?"

Slick ignored all that noise as he opened his door and let the night air rush in. He jumped out and walked around to the back of the stretch van and lifted the hatch. With Noodles turned around and watching him silently from the rear seat, Slick grabbed the red leather briefcase and slid the two buttons over, releasing the lock. He raised the lid and saw a small white satin bag nestled inside some soft black foam, like an egg sitting in a protective crate.

Slick hesitated. His next moves could dictate the outcome of the hit and might just fuck him up forever. But that was a chance he was willing to take. Closing the briefcase, Slick slammed the rear hatch down and glanced around. Off in the distance came the sound of cars zooming up and down the Belt Parkway, but there wasn't a damn thing out there within shouting distance or walking distance either.

He made his decision and moved back around and opened the side door and glanced inside the van. He looked down towards the floor and chuckled to himself. Mami's shoes looked like they could break the fuck outta some ankles. She was gonna bitch and bark, but it was her choice. She could either stand out there in the darkness and hope somebody came along and rescued her ass, or she could hoof it to the highway and find a gas station when the sun came up.

"Yo, let her out," he instructed Jewelz.

Slick could see the rage bubbling under Jewelz's skin, but like a good soldier she obeyed his orders.

Narrowing her eyes, Jewelz jumped outta the van and whirled around lighter than a cat on her feet. Reaching back inside, she snatched the girl up in her chest and chucked her outta her seat so fast she didn't have time to react.

Honore tumbled outta the van and hit the ground face-first. Her phone flew outta her hand and landed a few feet away. She spit out a mouthful of dirt then rolled over and sat up staring up at Jewelz with rage burning in her pretty eyes.

This bitch had just crossed a fuckin line. In all the time she'd been hustling Honore had never once had a hammer pressed to her head. *Never!* And she'd never eaten a grain of fucking dirt neither!

She stared up at the beautiful brown-skinned chick with the long ponytail and she looked at that bitch real good. She would never forget her ass. *Never.*

Slick took a step forward and interrupted the killer stare-down that was going on between the two gorgeous women.

"Yo put your fuckin mask back on and get in the van!" he ordered Jewelz again. Slick knew his crew was gonna go bonkers and make all kinds of noise as soon as he got back in the van, but fuck it. They had accomplished their mission and now the only thing left to do was to make sure that Whitey dropped the briefcase off at the designated location, and have Wild Man ditch the guns and clean up their tracks.

"Ay, you better grab your cell phone, French Fry," Slick told the girl as she sat there breathing hard on the ground. Turning his back on her he climbed in the van and slammed his door shut, then he rolled his window down and looked around one last time as Whitey started pulling away. It was dark as fuck out there but if she started walking now she should make it back to civilization by the time the sun came up.

"Yeah," he said grinning underneath his mask. "Pick up ya cellular device and hold on to that shit real tight Miss Honor-*Ray* 'cause you damn sure gonna need it."

CHAPTER 11

Minor Setback, Major Comeback

As the tail-lights from the van disappeared into the darkness, Honore was left on her own to hump it out of the wild where the stick-up kids had dumped her ass.

She was mad as hell. They had abandoned her too far out in the bushes to pick up a phone signal, so she trudged along in the black night until all ten of her toes caught a corn on the top and blistered hot spots popped up on the back of both her heels.

Cursing under her breath with every step she took, Honore stumbled through the tumbleweeds and prickly bushes for about a good thirty minutes. Finally, she reached a dirt path that was dotted with piles of crusty horse shit. Her toes hurt so damn bad that she had kicked off her crazy-expensive Jimmy Choos about a mile back, and now the bottoms of her feet were hurting just as bad as the tops.

"Yes!" she shrieked out loud as she glanced down at her phone and saw what she had been praying to see. "Thank fuckin *God!*" She had been checking her phone every other minute and now she finally had a signal. The first person she dialed was a Belgium diamond connect she worked with named Avi.

Honore's hands were sweating and shaking as she punched in his digits. Avi was her link to the international black market jewelry trade and he was also one of the slickest diamond thieves in the world. He had helped her set her boss Joel up for the kill, and now he was waiting for her call.

The diamond she had been transporting in that red briefcase was valued at over five million dollars, and with Joel deaded and outta the way that was gonna be one less split that her and Avi had to make on the profit.

But thanks to those idiot-ass stick-up kids who had snatched her damn briefcase, everything was all fucked up now! With that diamond gone Honore stood to come outta this deal broke as hell and probably deceased too!

She bit down anxiously on her lip as she waited for Avi to pick up the phone. She had been in the business long enough to know the drill. The Jewish investors who had fronted Joel the sweet money were gonna think she had pulled a fast one and dipped with the diamond *and* their cash. They would never believe she had gotten picked and licked by a bunch of low-level petty thieves who were tryna rob a damn jewelry store!

Honore's heart pounded as the reality of that shit washed over her. Those stick-up kids had put her in a real fucked up predicament when they ran up in there looking for some cheap nameplates and grilles. They might as well have shot her between the eyes because she was about to have a target plastered on her forehead anyway. There was no way in hell them Jews were gonna let this shit slide, and if she was gonna stay her black ass alive then she had to find that briefcase and get that diamond back!

She shivered in the darkness as Avi's phone rang forever. Her mouth felt like it was full of dry sand as she tried to find the words to let him know that their five-million dollar diamond was lost out there somewhere on the streets of Crooklyn. The last thing she wanted to admit was that their multi-million dollar jewel was in the hands of a bunch of trap boys who didn't even know what the hell they had stolen!

"C'mon, c'mon, mothafucka! Pick up!" Honore muttered. She pressed her ear to the phone and listened to Avi's shit ring and ring, then she disconnected the call and dialed him back again.

He still didn't answer. Panic started creeping through her and the next call she made was to the only man she had been able to trust without fail for her whole damn life.

She called the Notorious Sly McFly.

$$$$$

Honore was ready to cry when she finally got through on the phone to Sly McFly. Sweating like a dog in the humid night air, she told him she was lost somewhere out in the dirt and weeds, and he told her to keep walking toward the lights and the sounds of the highway.

"Come and get me, goddammit!" she shrieked as she swatted a giant mosquito off the back of her neck. "It's scary out here and these goddamn bugs are eating me up!"

With her stylish pants suit ruined by sweat stains and dirt, Honore crammed her aching feet back inside her pinched Jimmy Choos. She stayed on the dusty path as long as she could; walking dead down the middle while cursing and dodging crusty horse turds like she was jumping hopscotch.

It was a long damn time before she made it to the bright lights of the highway, and by that time she was crying for real.

Sly McFly had pulled his whip over on the side of the road. He was sitting there flashing his headlights off and on as he guided her toward him. By the time

Honore stumbled outta the tall weeds and over to his car she was mad enough to spray some fuckin body.

She started shrieking as soon as Sly McFly leaned over and opened the passenger door.

"They got the goddamn diamond! They got that shit!"

"What! *Who* got it?"

"Some dumb-fuck stick-up kids robbed the damn jewelry store!" Honore gasped as she fell into the passenger seat dirty and exhausted. "They shot the security guard and took the briefcase and stole the fuckin diamond!"

"Why the hell you let them take you outta there, goddammit?" Sly McFly blasted on her like a scared parent who had just found his missing child. Rolling up on that jewelry store and finding a dead body on the floor and no Honore in sight had damn near given him a heart attack. His hands trembled as he stared at her like he wanted to knock her ass out.

"When you left outta that goddamn hotel I told you I was coming right behind you, didn't I?" he demanded. "You was supposed to make the drop and then wait your ass for me *right there* at that jewelry store!"

"I *couldn't!*" Honore cried out. "They made me go with them! Them niggas threw me in their van and not one of them bitches in my click was around to help me! Not one of them!"

"What the hell you mean?" Sly McFly spit. "We sent a whole damn team out there to watch your back! I set them up on the job and gave Cucci the reigns and told her to handle that shit!"

Honore shook her head. "Uh-uh. Hell no! *Fuck Cucci!* Wasn't nobody around but me and some old-ass security guard! And them stick-up kids banged on him right in the face!"

"Ahh, *shit!*" Sly McFly cursed. His jaw was set in a grim line and he had a death grip on the steering wheel as he cut into traffic and sped down the highway. "How in the hell did them lil gangbangers knock down your entire wall, baby? How the fuck did y'all let somebody snatch that five million dollar diamond???"

"I don't *know!*" Honore wailed in fear. The smell of stanking horse shit was rising off the bottoms of her aching feet but she was too terrified to care. "They came up at me outta nowhere—"

And then she remembered.

"Hold up! I got dude's number!"

"Dude *who?*"

"The cat who stuck up the jewelry shop!" she said, digging in her purse for her phone. "There was five of them and he was the boss."

Sly looked shocked as shit.

"And that muthafucka gave you his number?"

"Yep," Honore nodded, her eyes big. "He sure the fuck did. His boys wanted him to shoot me but he was feeling me. I could tell. He made me punch his number into my phone and call him. I could call him again right now!"

Sly McFly shook his head. "Uh-uh. Nah, you ain't gotta call him. He'll call *you*. I guarantee it. When a weak nigga pulls a bitch move like that you know for sure he ain't on his game."

Suddenly Honore's eyes got even wider and she turned her body around to face Sly McFly.

"Hey, you got that sweet money off Joel Samuelson, right? *Please* tell me you snatched that green duffle bag outta that hotel room and you sitting on half a million dollars right now!"

Sly McFly shook his head. "Nope. That slimeball greased us. Wasn't nothing in that duffle bag but a bunch of balled up old newspaper! I tore that fuckin room up from the wallpaper to the rug. Wasn't a dime in there."

"Oooh, *shit!!!*" Honore screeched in pure panic and buried her face in her hands. "What happened to all that *money???*" she wailed. "What the fuck is going *on*???"

Sly McFly's face was grim and a pulse twitched dangerously in his temple. "I don't know. But you know what time it is now, don't you?"

Honore nodded, unable to lift her head or speak.

"Yeah," Sly McFly grunted, both of them seeing the situation clearer than day. "Them rich Jewish bastards are gonna be all over your ass now, baby. Huh! Their half-a-mil is gone and the diamond is too? *Sheeit!* We gotta get that ice back, darling! We gotta get it back or get the fuck outta town! Nah," he corrected himself. "We gotta get it back or get the fuck outta the country! Nah, fuck that. Outta the muthafuckin *world!*"

$$$$$

Sly McFly's deadly predictions had Honore shook all down in her bones. She had sat there trembling in her seat as he drove her back to her posh apartment, and now she was soaking her aching body in her deep Jacuzzi tub with her devious mind calculating her dilemma from every possible angle.

The new day's sun was peeking into her bathroom window as Honore closed her eyes and thought about the stick-up kid who had pulled the jewelry store lick and then given her his digits. Dude had been tall and built real fine, and just like the rest of his click, he had worn a mask.

Dumb muthafucka!

That nigga musta been smelling her pussy right through her drawers because that was an amateur, sucker move if she had ever seen one! He musta been tripping when he threw her in the van with his crew! Honore turned her lip up and smirked. She *had* been looking real good in her cute lil suit though. The pants fit her so tight her pussy print stuck out in a nice fat V, so she could see why dude had lost his mind. He had been staring at her outta his one little eye and all he saw was what the head of his dick was able to see: tits and ass.

Don't let the big boobies fool you, she giggled as she cupped her juicy twin girls and blew into the huge mound of scented bubbles rising up outta her warm bath water. What kind of gun-boy goes to jam somebody up for their goods and then tries to holla at 'em instead?

A real stupid one, Honore smirked as her devious mind worked a hundred miles a minute to come up with a plan to recover the diamond so she could keep those cutthroat Jewish investors off her ass.

She closed her eyes again and replayed the entire scene over in her mind.

Ay! Jump on all that jewelry over there, yo! Bag that shit up! Make sure you pick that whole muthafuckin display case clean!

The leader of last night's stick up crew had had a sexy-ass voice on him and enough swagger on him to bang ten horny bitches. But as an armed robber he was just a stupid fuckin peon. Honore didn't know what dude looked like under that mask, but she had his cell phone number and she was gonna find his ass and get her diamond back! And as soon as she got her hands on that shit she was gonna go in hard on his entire thieving-ass crew and let 'em know exactly whose stolen property they had fucked with. Yeah, them niggas were gonna be taught a real valuable lesson because there was no way in hell she was gonna have a bunch of thieving mothafuckas thinking they could jam her for her jewels every time she made a drop!

Honore mighta looked like she was from Park Avenue but she was hood all the way down to her bone marrow. She had grown up motherless in the projects and she had scratched and fought for every damn thing she got. From an early age she had learned how to shake her shapely ass and bat her pretty eyes to manipulate niggas every which way in the game, and at this stage of her life she was tops at that shit.

Sure, a few blockers and enemies had popped up along her path to success, but those things came with the risky lifestyle that she chose to lead. She hustled enough stolen diamonds that she could afford to travel, shop, ball, and rub shoulders with New York's elite in the underworld and in the entertainment business too. She loved to be in the club popping bottles and flossing out in a room full of drug kingpins or rappers while none of them had a clue about how crucial she really was. She was a Queen in her own right, and as the leader of the Crushed Ice Clique she had the diamond embezzlement business on smiddash.

But even though she had fucked, sucked, and came up rough on her rise to the top, Honore was proud that she wasn't one of those food stamp tramps who had ten kids and was stuck in the projects. Fuck that. She was a risk-taker and she would rather die ducking bullets, living fast, and looking fly. She never wanted to be a bottom feeder, and that was the fire that fueled her passion to do whatever it took to remain sitting high on her throne.

Right now sitting in that top seat dictated that her first order of business was to deal with her clique for sleeping on the job and letting her get robbed in the first damn place! A storm was brewing in her as she stretched out in the warm bubbling water and wrapped her fingers around her full, sand-colored boobies with the stubby cinnamon nipples. She squeezed her girls and rubbed bubbles all over them as her calculating brain worked overtime. Never in a million years did she foresee last night's job going so wrong. All she knew is that she had to get that diamond back so Avi could sell it and she could pay off those investors.

Honore let her body go limp in the water and then she spread her legs open wide. She reached down to that slit between her triangle and rubbed her pussy as she forced herself to take a deep breath and tap into the power of her brain. With a finger inserted deeply in her hot tunnel, she reminded herself that she was smart and she was slick. Honore fucked herself and massaged her clit and told herself that she was ruthless and she was cunning. Squeezing her left titty and humping hard on her own finger, she swore up and down that she was gonna find that red goddamn briefcase. Ya goddamn right she would, she thought, just as she exploded and gasped in pleasure. They didn't call her the Queen of Diamonds for nothing!

CHAPTER 12

Niggas be Slippin

While Honore was busy worrying about how she was gonna get that sweet money back and save her ass from the Jewish investors, Slick was getting a nice-sized hole chewed in his ass by the members of the Zip 'em up Crew.

"Yo, man whassup with that? You coulda fucked this whole job up!" Wild Man blasted on him. "You getting soft, bruh. Last night proves it. 'Mister Perfect' is getting real fuckin soft!"

"He sure the hell is!" Jewelz's eyes flashed with anger as she got her shit off and went in on him too. "That hot mess you pulled last night was real unprofessional, Slick! I know your eyes stay glued to some bitch's ass, but last night took the damn cake. You put everybody's life on the line just because your dick got hard!"

Of course Noodles didn't say a word. He didn't have to. His disbelief and disappointment was written all over his face.

As usual Whitey was the cool head. "A'ight guys," he held up his hand. "That's enough. Shit happens. The only thing last night proves is that Mr. Perfect is just as human as the rest of us so I don't think we should take turns shitting on him right now. Slick's never made a bad move like this before and I still trust his leadership. What's done is done. We still have work to do so let's get over it and move on."

Slick had stayed silent throughout the entire tirade, facing his crew like a man and allowing each of them to talk they shit and get it off their chests. He didn't try to defend his actions because there was no excuse for them and he knew that shit. Whatever repercussions came behind the misstep he'd made last night he was gonna have to take it on the chin. That's all there was to it. But in the meantime Whitey was right. They were still a professional organization and there was still an after-action review of the job to accomplish.

"A'ight, I made a couple of dumb moves last night and I can admit that,"

Slick said. "I wanna apologize for putting y'all in a fucked up situation."

Slick stepped up to Whitey and offered a dap. "I'm sorry, man."

He went around to the entire crew offering a dap and an apology. Wild Man was the only one who was slow to give up the love.

"Yo, Wild Man. I fucked up and I'm sorry, my G," Slick said sincerely. "I was way outta order with my shit. But all in all, the hit was still a success."

Slick turned to Noodles. "You stashed the burners in the safe at the tucky spot and cleaned 'em all real good, bruh?"

Noodles nodded.

Slick turned to Wild Man. "Ayo, you torched that van, right?"

"Fuck yeah," Wild Man sneered and crossed his thick arms over his chest. "I always do what the fuck I'm supposed to do, homey."

Slick let that jab slide as he focused his attention on Whitey.

"Yo, Whitey, I know it was hot out there last night with those pig-ass cops all over the place. How'd it go when you went to drop that briefcase off in the city, man?"

Whitey shrugged. "Everything went cool, Slick. What you expect? I'm a tax-paying white man so I don't come up on the stop-and-frisk radar. I walked right past a whole crew of donut-eating pigs and none of them even looked at me twice. I stashed the briefcase in the locker you told me to. We good, man. The job is done."

"Yo, that was a bad-ass leather briefcase," Jewelz said outta the blue. "What the hell was in there anyway?"

Whitey glanced at her and shrugged again. "Beats me. I never opened it. Matter fact, it was locked."

$$$$$

The meeting had just ended and Wild Man and Whitey decided to take the stairs down from the rooftop. The stench of urine in the once-clean staircase was so sour it could make your nose twitch, and the graffiti-riddled walls were a sign that conditions in the old folks building had deteriorated and were getting worse.

But the two gunslingers were far from worried. They were hunters, not prey. If a slanga or a fiend was lurking on the staircase looking for something sweet, then they were the ones who needed to be worrying about Wild Man and his homeboy.

Whitey could feel the apprehension in his partner's vibe. Something was fucking with Wild Man and he was real bad at hiding his anger.

"Hey, what's going on with you, bro?" Whitey asked as they headed down the stairs. "Whatever it is, shake that shit off man."

"Nah," Wild Man said as he pulled his hoody up over his head and sulked. "Slick is acting like a savage out here on some sucka shit and I ain't feeling it."

"Fuck you mean?" Whitey asked.

They had reached the eighth floor and a short burley cat wearing a bunch of gold chains was wheezing his way up the steps counting his money. He didn't even look up as he slammed right into Whitey.

"Yo blood! Watch where you going, fam! You dead-ass almost stepped on my fresh KD's, nigga!" the short dude spit with much aggression.

He was sizing Whitey up like he could take him and not really paying any mind to Wild Man. "Kick rocks, white boy! What the fuck you doing in my building anyway?"

Whitey stood there with a smirk on his face, but he wasn't even thinking about moving out of dude's way. He was thinking about how fast he could snatch the guy's Adam's apple out of his pudgy-ass throat.

"Yo, chill, lil homey," Wild Man told the thug in a low tone. "The white boy is good money. He's with me."

"Who the fuck is you, nigga?" the short cat growled, straining to see Wild Man's face in the shadow of his hoody in the poorly lit stairwell. "Both of y'all better beat feet before I..."

"Before you do *what,* muthafucka?" Wild Man said as he snatched off his hoody and grilled the young slanga. In an instant Wild Man had a switchblade pressed to the young nigga's throat as he pinned him up against the wall.

"You hardbody right? So tell me what the fuck you gonna do if we don't beat feet? I will half-moon ya fat face right here, you lil bitch! This *my* muthafuckin hood!!"

"Damn Bruh! I ain't know that was you," the fat hustler stammered as he stared up at Wild Man. The sharp edge of the switchblade had slit his skin and drew blood, and dude was wide-eyed and scared to death.

"My fault, Wild Man!" he said with bulging eyes. "I don't want no problems with you, big bruh. You got it man. You got it!"

"You callin out my name? Where the fuck you know me from?"

"The streets talk man!" the fat nigga said with much fear and admiration in his tone. "Niggas know who to fuck with and who not to. Gimme a pass, bruh. I ain't mean no disrespect."

Wild Man let the little cat go and the fat boy clutched his bloody throat and hauled ass up the steps, grateful that his whole face wasn't sliced in half.

"Why'd you have to rough the little fucker up like that?" Whitey chuckled as they continued their descent toward the lobby. "I could have handled him on my own."

"Yo, I saw that look in your eyes, White Boy," Wild Man said as he shook his head. "I had to scare the kid off before you killed him. Who you think you fooling?"

"Well...maybe you're right," Whitey said as they shared a laugh and brushed the whole situation off.

"But like I was saying," Wild Man said as he picked his burden back up again. "Ya boy Slick was out there tryna play Captain Save-a-Hoe at that jewelry store the other night, man. Is he fuckin retarded?"

"I get what you're saying," Whitey agreed. "He was off his game but that could have been a good thing though. Slick is a fucking machine bro. He puts a lot of weight on his shoulders trying to keep us all alive and on the board. Maybe he needed that random piece of pussy to bring his ass back to human-mode."

"Fuck that!" Wild Man fired back. "He woulda never let that shit slide if one of us had pulled a move like that in the middle of a mission. He's quick to remind us when we fuck up, so I just thought it was time to call him out on his own shit."

"All right, you called him out, now let that shit go, man," Whitey said calmly. "It was impulsive and everything you're saying is legit. But Slick is a down cat and he keeps us all in the game. He deserves a little room to make his own mistakes. Plus you sounding like you real jelly right now, my guy. Lighten up."

"See, you got me fucked up, Whitey," Wild Man said, not letting up. "That nut-ass nigga mixed pleasure right in the middle of us conducting bizzness. Slick woulda never let me *or* you live that shit down. Fuck him!"

Whitey paused. "Damn bro," he said with concern in his eyes. "You going kinda hard right now. Sounds like you got some other issues with Slick that you might need to iron out. I hope you say all this fly shit to his face the next time something pops off."

"Oh trust me," Wild Man said with a bitter smirk. "He fuck around again and I'ma rain on that ass. You best be'lee that!"

CHAPTER 13

The Crushed Ice Clique

After masturbating and busting a quick nut in the bathtub, Honore had washed up then pittered around her apartment butt-naked for a few minutes as she fixed herself some toast and made a few phone calls. She picked some fly shit out to wear from the hundreds of designer outfits crammed into her two walk-in closets, and then she pulled her thick hair up on top of her head in a neat bun.

When she stepped outta her apartment building she was the straight-up definition of class and sass. She was draped from head to toe in jewels and finery, and her dreamy face and scrumptious body were making their own impact statement.

"How you doing today, goddess?" A well-dressed man walking outta a bodega clutching a cup of coffee greeted her. He swept his admiring eyes over her frame and Honore checked him out right back. He was the investment-baller type, over thirty-five, freshly groomed, and dressed in fashionable threads with all the right accessories.

"Fine and you," Honore replied as she put her nose in the air and swung her hips toward the corner where her whip was waiting. There was a time when a mature sugar-daddy like that woulda boggled her eyeballs and turned her head. But not no more. She didn't need no nigga to puff out her pockets. She had a hustle and she was making her own dollars now.

And what an exciting hustle it was! Honore had felt real lucky to land a gig at the New York Diamond and Jewelry Exchange. She was a lead diamond courier who transported low-level, gently-used stones around to other franchise stores and offered them for corporate resale at a discounted price.

She wasn't a high-level executive or nothing, but as a project-born chick whose primary education had been earned on the streets, she had risen up out of her hood shackles and gotten a toehold in the exclusive world of jewelry trading.

Of course, she had earned her stripes on her knees. Sucking and blowing the nuts of rich Jewish merchants like Joel Samuelson who ruled the industry with extra-tight reins. But it wasn't how you got your cheese that mattered in this game. It was how you kept that shit that counted, and Honore planned on keeping all of hers.

She had started out as a clerk behind the counter and she had been steady fucking her way up the ladder when Joel Samuelson tapped her for inclusion in the money-making side-hustle he had going on.

Not only was he a senior executive with the firm, Joel was also the leader of a ring of corrupt jewelers who grinded up stolen diamonds into chips and then sold them on the black market as untraceable "crushed ice."

Joel had a crew of thieves working for him who were tops in the trade, but Honore's cousin Cucci had begged him to hire her too, so he had relented and brought Honore on board.

Honore was all over it from the gate. As a representative who traveled to jewelry stores all over the five boroughs presenting display diamonds for sale, she had the right looks, the right personality, and the right amount of grime it took to get the job done. Since she was authorized to sign multiple diamonds out of the vault on a daily basis it was simple for her to delay their return for a day or two until a fake replica could be fabricated and stashed in their place.

Honore was making decent bread on this side gig, but she knew her shit was just a smalltime hustle in the big scheme of things. She was careful to pick diamonds that wouldn't raise any flags or sound off any alarms. She chose small stones that were only worth between ten and twenty g's each, and for every one that she stole, Joel hit her off with a cut of the profit and then he pocketed the rest of the change for himself

That little hustle had been all well and good in the beginning. However, a boss bitch like Honore wasn't the type to settle for no small chips for long. She made sure to keep her eyes and ears open while visiting jewelry stores in each of the five boroughs, and it wasn't long before she had lined up the type of low-wage workers, just like her, who were looking to earn some extra cash on the side.

In just a few short months Honore had a crew working for her in just about the same way she worked for Joel. But she had been real strict about only tapping females for her clique though. She knew a man would fuck her whole program up in a heartbeat because most of them had egos that were twice the size of their dicks. A lot of dudes had a real hard time bowing down and taking orders from a beautiful woman, and she couldn't afford to be second-guessing nobody's allegiance. If she was gonna get rich and stay outta jail, Honore knew she needed complete loyalty and obedience from the members of her clique. Utter and fucking complete!

She had started the Crushed Ice Clique using two chicks from the diamond business as her ponies, and her best friend and cousin Cucci as her manager. She had trained her girls on how to identify the kind of diamonds that nobody would miss, then they signed them out and passed them off to her so a dummy copy could be fabricated and returned to the vault, and the real thing could quickly be sold.

Business had been so good that there were now over two-dozen members working in her clique. Some chicks just straight up stole ice, while others were her personal stunt dummies, and a few more had been tasked to provide security for the team. Regardless of their assigned roles, the small diamonds they hustled and sold were putting some pretty nice dividends in everybody's pockets on the regular.

But today wasn't about padding nobody's pockets, Honore thought as she reached the corner where her whip was waiting. Today she was on a fact-finding mission and she was itching to let one fly from her gat.

Last night's drop had gone down the toilet bowl smelling real shitty. While Sly McFly had been busy murdering Joel Samuelson, somebody on Honore's look-out team had fucked up royally and now that somebody was about to pay.

"You ready to handle your bizzness?" Sly McFly asked her as she slid into the backseat of his whip. "You better take your goddamn pistol up there and put some fear in them bitches, baby girl!"

And that's exactly what Honore was about to do. They parked outside of a two-story building and minutes later she stepped into a brightly lit room and cocked her .38 special. With a look of pure death in her eyes, Honore stared into the startled faces of the slick and sexy diamond thieves known as the Crushed Ice Clique.

"Tell me something," she said quietly, glaring at her peeps as they sat huddled in a sacred circle in a bright room above Sly McFly's McBeauty Parlor. Her heat dangled loosely in her hand as she tried to decide who to aim that shit at first.

"Which one of y'all bitches fucked around and got caught sleeping last night?"

A chorus of "not me's" went up in the air and Honore felt her patience getting thin. Her feet still hurt and she was pissed off about the way the drop had fallen apart. She was a careful, meticulous planner, and she had covered all her bases. She depended on her girls to have her back, and it had fucked her up when the ski-masked crew busted in and snatched up Joel's briefcase and then planted a hot one in the old security guard's dome.

Fuck the dumb shit, that coulda been *her* laying on the floor with her brains shot out!

Honore lifted the muzzle of her gat. The charms on her silver wrist bracelet glittered under the bright lights as she held the burner out at chest-level and aimed it at her chief squad leader, Rayven "Cucci" Jones.

"What was your job supposed to be, Cucci Momma?"

"Excuse me?" the beautiful chocolate-skinned girl igged the loaded gun that was pointed at her as she twisted her sexy lips and smirked. "I did my fuckin job, Honore!"

Cucci was a stunna. She was almost as hot as Honore. Her waist was tight and her stacked hips looked luscious in her black and white sleeveless designer dress that barely covered her bubble ass and hit her high-thigh.

"*Sheeeit*," she leaned back and crossed one of her pretty legs over the other one as she wagged her foot in her shiny black stilettos. "You already know how I roll Honore so don't fuckin play with me! We go back way too far for that, heffa!"

Honore smirked. "You can miss me with that bullshit, Cucci! This wasn't no regular lil stick and lick shit. Y'all bitches knew we had an important job to do!"

Cucci waved at the crew of shame-faced chicks that were sitting in hot seats around the circle. "I had *all* these bitches lined up and on point like soldiers last night, baby! Everybody was supposed to be in they proper positions. They was locked and loaded, and all of them had their bang-up orders."

Cucci batted her fake eyelashes and started counting off on her three-inch manicured nails as she smirked at the dun dun chick who was sitting directly across from her.

"First of all, *Breezie* here was supposed to be her ass up on the roof!"

The barrel of Honore's gun swung around until it was aimed dead at Breezie's weaved head.

"I don't know if she was up there playing with her titties or what," Cucci spit, "but that bitch had her some binoculars, an iPad mini, a cell phone and the whole nine."

Cucci jerked her head sharply to her right and Honore's gat followed her gaze.

"India and Kellie was supposed to be holding down the back door. I told them to remind each other to be there thirty minutes in advance but for some fuckin reason dumb and dumber got there late!

"And *Man-Man*," Cucci got real swole as she swiveled her plump ass around in her chair. She faced to her left and glared at a cute light-skinned stud chick who had a shaved head and a ring in her nose.

Dressed in a plaid shirt and sagging jeans, Man-Man cringed as Honore's gat found a bulls-eye in the center of her forehead.

"I don't know what the fuck this bitch right here was thinking!" Cucci bucked her eyes open wide and barked, "Girl, you must didn't take me serious when I said to shut the whole fuckin street down, huh? I said nobody was supposed to get in or out, right? Nobody! So how the fuck did y'all let somebody get in there and snatch Honore like that?"

"That wasn't my fault!" Man-Man hollered, shrinking down in her seat like Honore's gat already had fire shooting outta the tip. "I had my ass on the scene exactly when you told me to be there! I had guards capped on both ends of the damn street too, but some kinda way we got caught out there!"

"You got peeped?" Honore cut in. "By who?"

"By *12!* We was chillin in the whips when 5-0 rolled up on us outta nowhere. They told us to clear the lane or get took downtown. There was mad other cars parked out there too, but we was the only ones they fucked with! I mean, I coulda bucked and whatnot, but with all them dirty guns we was packin we all woulda been spending the night on Rikers!"

Honore smirked. Some kinda way her look-outs had gotten caught out there. Her mind went into whirl mode as she listened to her crew describe how the po-po had rolled up and ran every last one of them off their spots.

"That's what happened to me too!" Breezy squealed as she flipped her silky hair outta her face. "I was up on that roof for a good minute when one-time bum-rushed me too! How the hell they spotted me way up there, I have no clue. But them blue boys told me I could either take the stairs or grow some wings, but they was gonna make sure my black ass came down off that rooftop."

Honore frowned. Something real flaky had gone down on Fulton Street last night. Somebody had cleared her team outta every single lane they was holding, and whoever it was had cost her a pot of sweet money and a very expensive diamond. Before it was all over that shit could end up costing her her life!

She thought hard about the crew of stick-up kids who had busted up in the shop and blasted on the security guard. There was no way in hell those weak ass herbs carried the kinda weight needed to clear a whole damn block and sic the blue boys on her squad! No way! Hell, their stiff-dick chief capo didn't even have enough smarts to lay all the witnesses down on the way out the door! Honore knew damn well his sucka ass didn't have the kinda connections it took to make no organized moves on a team of on-point females like hers.

There was no way the leak coulda came from anybody in her crew neither because Honore was operating on the sneak tip and none of her girls even knew what kinda heavyweight jewel she was actually transporting. But *somebody* musta known she was gonna be rolling up in that shop to get that stolen diamond fabricated! Somebody had set her black ass up to get jammed, and now a crew of petty thieves had *her* five-million-dollar jewel in *their* damn pockets!

Right on cue, the calculating and conniving Cucci spoke up like a mind-reader.

"So where exactly did them kick-door niggas take you last night, Honore? Did you get a good look at any of 'em?"

Honore hit her with the stank eye. "They took me someplace way out in the goddamn woods," she bitched. "And no I didn't see none of their faces. They had on masks!"

"But you said they got away with the diamond we was clocking for, right?" Cucci pressed with her eyes flashing greedily. "I mean, that shit musta been worth a grip for us to be posting up so strong on a run-down joint in Brooklyn like that. So how many dollars was you raking in and what kinda cut was the rest of us gonna get?"

"First of all, Honore snapped, cutting her eyes at Cucci. "It ain't about how much the diamond was worth! That shit was just slum money," she lied. "That lil piece of ice didn't mean shit. We was only gonna make around five g's each, but it's about the principle of the thing. It's about the *trust*. It's about my so-called *professional bitch*es acting like fuckin amateurs out there and not having my fucking back!"

With her lips real pinched tight, Honore turned her evil glare on India and Kellie, who were sitting side-by-side.

"So, India," she said to the cute little Pocahontas-looking chick who was wearing a white tank top and a dope beige cotton flair skirt. "What's your story, my sista? What happened when you went around to secure the back door? Did the cops roll up back there on y'all too?"

The soft baby edges of India's hair were slicked down on her face with Vaseline. She was mixed with Black and some other shit that she didn't even know what it was, but it was a stunning combination and it looked good on her. India shook her head full of curly hair and then hung it in shame.

"Nah, Honore, and I'm sorry. We didn't see any police in the back," she admitted. "We were on the way to the jewelry store when my period came down out of the blue so I asked Kellie to stop me at a store so I could get some tampons. Then some kinda way we took a wrong turn and got stuck in traffic. We got there late like Cucci said, but it wasn't our fault because like I said the traffic was so heavy—"

Boom! Boom!

Two shots rang out and India slumped over and pitched forward face-first out of her seat. Her body thudded to the floor and her skirt flew up in the back exposing her well-rounded cream-colored ass cheeks. She had on a rainbow-striped thong and there was a tampon string hanging outta her split. Her slender leg twitched twice, and then she lay still as a pool of blood leaked outta her blasted chest.

"Shit, *bitch!*" Kellie shrieked from the chair next to India. She leaned back in her seat and clutched her shoulder, then raised her knees to her chest and tried to ball her self up in a knot.

"You *shot* her! And you fuckin shot me too, Honore!" she screamed, looking like she was about to faint as a river of hot blood poured down her arm. "Why'd you sneak me like that, home girl? You just gonna pop on a bitch like that outta nowhere?"

"I apologize sweetie," Honore said quietly, still aiming her tool as Kellie moaned and groaned. "You're absolutely right. I was wrong to just pop off on you like that without no type of warning. I shoulda given you a chance to get ready. You ready now?"

Boom!

Kellie's body spun around backwards as the heat round entered her chest and flung her outta the chair. She landed on the floor just outside of their sacred circle, and as the blood pooled beneath her motionless frame Honore glanced coldly at the rest of her crew.

"Fuck around, lay around," she warned as she tucked her strap and switched her fine booty toward the door. She was halfway there when she stopped in her tracks. She turned around to gun-check Cucci, her bestie and blood-cousin who she had grown up with and had schemed and hung hard with her whole life.

All eyes were on Honore as she doubled back over to her best friend and planted the business end of her gat flush against her forehead. There were dollar signs beaming from Cucci's eyeballs and Honore knew her cousin was skeptical as fuck about the worth of that stolen diamond.

"Look, Cucci. I'm about to tell you something you better not never forget, homegirl," Honore spoke quietly. "Because of you, my ass got snatched up and I had to walk a hundred fuckin miles in horse shit last night! So when the game goes bad around here don't you never run me no lines about how you did your damn job! You must got it twisted because *your* job is to make sure that *my* job flows smoothly at all times. Twenty-four-seven. And when it don't flow like that—it's *all your fault.*"

Honore paused, breathing fire down at Cucci who sat there chewing her gum and still looking relaxed as fuck and cooler than a winter breeze.

"Now," Honore continued blasting on her girl, "I don't care which one of these bitches you told to do what! You can tell these chicks what to do, but you still gotta make sure that shit gets done! On the real, India and Kellie both ate a bullet for you today. The next one you're gonna have to eat yourself. I really need you to remember that shit *Hoochie Coochie Momma*, because the next time your ass comes up short you're gonna leave here dead. And that's my word!"

CHAPTER 14

Oh, She's Goode

The night after pulling the jewelry store jux Slick and Jewelz slid up to Club Goode Brothers. The joint was jammed-pack and jumping. Loud music blared from the doorway and people laughed and talked shit as they waited on the long line to get inside.

Jewelz had on a fitted off-the-shoulder white Versace dress with slits down both sides. She had long brown legs and two basketball-sized lumps in her glittering thong that stuck out for days. Crammed inside that sexy dress all her goodies were on full display.

Slick was dressed in a casual Michael Kors button-down with a pair of black Christian Louboutin shoes with the spikes on them. Nobody would have ever mistaken him for the scary bum called Sometimey. Not tonight. Niggas was sick to their stomachs when the couple stepped to the front of the line swaggin on 'em. Both of them was looking fresh to fuckin death, and all they was missing was a casket.

Slick and Jewelz weren't the only fly-looking people at the club, but the combination of seeing them together was pleasing to the eye. Even the bouncer gave them an approving nod as they approached.

"Are you two on the guest list tonight?" The big Spanish bouncer was asking Slick, but his eyes was all over Jewelz.

"Yup," Slick answered, swelling up like he was proud of his sexy bae. "First name 'Two' and last name 'Grand'." He pulled out two bands and handed them to the big man.

"Okay, you both have a great night Mr. and Mrs. Grand," the bouncer said, pocketing the money as he stepped back to let Slick and Jewelz pass through the door.

"Good looking out," Slick told him.

The whole club was lit. People of all different races were out on the dance floor gettin it. The money-hungry boppers were half-dressed and scheming, trying hard not to look like the thirsty hoes that they were. The broke niggas walked around with little ass overpriced glasses of Henny or whatever, while the ballers copped twenty bottles of Ciroc with the sparkles and made it light up in the spot.

Everybody seemed to be getting it in, but the two Zip 'em up Crew members were definitely not there to ball out. They were there to do surveillance on a certain drug kingpin who enjoyed stabbing little kids and recruiting hungry artists on Unsigned Hype night.

Dirty Mike, aka Handgun Goody, was well into his thirties now but he still looked young and fresh. A fly and flashy nigga, he had the hustle of a drug czar with the heart of a street enforcer. He knew if a nigga got money on the level that he did, he also had to protect it. Goody was a master at both. Getting it and keeping it was his specialty.

Like Slick had already discovered, Handgun Goody kept a tight-knit team of hood niggas around him that were extremely loyal. If he wasn't going somewhere for a specific event, then he was like a ghost on the street. Nobody knew his moves and he was seldom seen. What everybody did know was that his crew had shit on smash and he was the H.N.I.C.

"There's a whole lotta hood boogers in here tonight, Jewelz. You think you can get close to this nigga?" Slick asked her. They were sitting at the bar looking up at the balcony where Goody and his crew were spilling drinks on bitches and tossing money around like it was mere paper.

Jewelz gave him a look of contempt. "Ain't none of these hoes up in here got shit on me. I got this. Even though," she said, twisting her lips, "the nigga I really wanna get next to is busy acting like I don't even matter to him."

She took a sip of her drink and then glared at Slick with big, accusing eyes.

Jewelz was flipping the script and Slick knew better than to ask her what was wrong, but he didn't have to because she busted on him anyway.

"You know what? I'm feeling really shitted-on right now because you had the nerve to give that honey-mustard light-bright broad your damn number right in my face the other night, Slick! Not to mention that the bitch was a witness! She wasn't even supposed to leave the spot breathing. I mean, what the fuck is it, you think she looks better than me 'cause she's light-skinned or something? What's really good Slick? What the fuck is the deal?"

Slick stared deep into her eyes and saw right through her hostile front to her true turmoil inside. He knew what Jewelz was going through and he felt for her. Light-skinned, dark-skinned, none of that shit even mattered. The damn hit was the other fuckin night and she was still bitchin about it now.

Nah, she wasn't all that mad at him. She was just using her anger over his stupidity with Honore as a substitute for her rage over what had been done to her back in the day. They were out on a job and this wasn't the time to play psychoanalyst and get clinical, but if this was how Jewelz needed to play this shit out in order to get in her zone, then so be it. He'd play it out too.

"Come on, J-baby. Cut it out!" he said, flattering her. "You know hands down you badder than that girl eight days outta every week," Slick said, stroking her ego but meaning every word of it from his heart.

Jewelz nodded. "Damn right. I *am* badder than that bitch. But you won't even give me a chance to show you, Slick."

Slick sighed, then frowned. "Look. I care a lot about you Jewelz, you know I do. Just 'cause I don't want a relationship doesn't mean I don't have hella love for you baby."

For a very brief moment Slick allowed his eyes to gently kiss hers. "Now, c'mon. Forget about me. We came here to put in work, baby. That nigga upstairs got a debt he needs to repay us, remember? Let's get it in and get out."

For a long moment Jewelz just stared at him. She loved his eyes, his lips, everything about him. She would do anything for him. Anything. Yet, he wouldn't give her no kinda rhythm. No matter what she did she didn't feel good enough for him. He got mad pussy from other girls, but when it came down to her it was always about business with Slick. It was never about what they had shared and what she still needed from him.

Jewelz broke the glance then shook her head quickly. "Nah, you don't give a fuck about me, Slick. All you care about is how I murk these niggas and rock them to sleep. All you can see is the killer in me, never the woman in me."

Before Slick could deny it, she downed the last of her Effen vodka then slipped off the bar stool and wiggled her ass in her stunning white dress.

"You like big-booty bitches who kill it, right?" She smirked as Slick sat there grilling her frame with undeniable lust and appreciation in his eyes. "Cool," she said, turning to strut toward the staircase that led upstairs to the VIP area. "Keep your eyes on this bubble ass and watch how a killa in heels puts that work in."

$$$$$

While Slick monitored shit downstairs in the club, holding onto one drink and hanging in the shadows, Jewelz went upstairs to work her deadly magic on Handgun Goody. Right below the balcony, the stage area was poppin with male and female artists who were ready to spit their best shit for the Unsigned Hype showcase, which was right up her alley.

Just as the announcer was about to welcome in the acts, Jewelz made her way to the table where Handgun Goody and his gang were sitting. They were smoking fat blunts and had a lot of groupies hanging off their jocks, drinking, laughing, and shining like only the big boys can do. Jewelz stepped up to the table and looked directly at every nigga seated, giving each of them a playful and sexy grin until her gaze settled on Handgun Goody, the black-hearted sucka she hadn't laid eyes on since she was a helpless child.

"W'sup Gangsta?" Jewelz purred like a lioness.

All chatter at the large table stopped. Goody looked up into her eyes. He was caught off guard by her beauty and stunned even more by her bold forwardness.

A young Asian chick with bleached-blond hair sitting next to Goody threw Jewelz a cold look and said nastily, "Who this bitch?" as she mean-mugged the shit outta her.

Jewelz's eyes never left Goody's as everyone waited in silence for her response. She kept up the same seductive smirk, gazing at him in utter confidence as their eyes locked transfixed on each other.

"Hey, I said who the fuck is this bitch?" the chick riding Goody's jock busted on her again.

Jewelz broke the gaze she had locked on Goody and said to the chick very sweetly, "Okay, since you wanna know so bad, my name is Jewelz, and *your* name is, 'get the fuck up and trot away before I dog-walk you all around this club.' Now it was nice meeting you, goodnight," Jewelz dismissed her without even raising her voice.

The bleached blonde wasn't stupid. There was something about Jewelz that let her know she meant every word she'd said and the Asian girl just wasn't much of a fighter. She glanced up at Goody and his eyes told her the same thing. He wasn't offering her a drop of protection. She could either get up and leave, or risk getting a world-class ass-beating from this beautiful hood sista who was so clearly confident in her abilities.

Without another word the Asian groupie got up and made her exit. Goody's dick-boys laughed a little then went back to conversating with their female friends, and that's when Goody finally spoke for the first time.

"I can see you know who I am. So, w'sup with you, umm *Jewelz*, right?" he said sarcastically.

"That's right Mr. Goody," she said, sliding her plump ass into the vacated seat. "The name's Jewelz, and now that we've gotten the formalities out of the way I wanna talk a little business with you."

Goody couldn't help but laugh out loud, but in the back of his head he was a little leery. *Who the fuck did this fine bitch think she was?* he thought to himself. Yeah, she was bad as fuck, but she was coming at him just a little too hard. Yet not in the hungry hoodrat sorta way he was used to. This broad seemed to think she commanded the same level of respect that Goody did. Yeah, he was suspicious but he was also turned the fuck on. After all, power attracted power.

"Listen baby girl, as you can see my business is lit round here, ya heard! We good. That's why they call us the Goode Brothers. But since you chased away my lil jump-off for the night I think its only right that you take her place." He reached down and grabbed his dick under the table. "And that's all the business I can offer you," Goody said smoothly with a gangsta's charisma.

Jewelz laughed good-naturedly although there was a ton of hatred beating in her heart. She crossed her long legs and said smoothly, "Trust, you ain't ready for all this, Mr. Goode Brother. Number one, I'm not trying to have you chasing me just yet because you have to earn what I'm squeezing between these thighs.

Second, I'm here to holla at you about some bread that we can both get down on. I know you's a heavyweight and I'm trying to get my pockets closer to where yours are, you feel me?" Jewelz said sweetly.

Nah, Goody wasn't feeling her. He looked at her like she was some stray dog who had wandered in off the street and came sniffing her grimy nose around his gourmet table. Like she was trying to push her way into his business, trying to be down and shit and he ain't even know her.

His eyes suddenly turned cold and deadly. "Fuck is you? A wire-wearer, bitch? You come barging over here asking a lot of fuckin questions and right now you about to get me aggy."

His tone of voice caught the attention of his men who quickly got on their guard. One of his hoodlums who had a long nasty scar down his cheek stood up and growled at Jewelz, then looked at Goody and said, "Yo, you want me to make this hoe kick rocks, bro?"

But before Goody could answer Jewelz checked him real quick.

"First of all, cops in New York don't look this fucking good, Mr. Goody! Second of all, I was referring to me winning this Unsigned Hype shit you're sponsoring tonight. I know you got some side-money placed on the winner and you can bet your last Franklin I got this shit in the bag. I was just trying to put some extra bread in both our pockets but fuck it. You ain't 'bout that life. You talking some "wire-wearer" shit and got ya ugly-ass homey all extra-hyped for nothing!" She stood up abruptly. "Do it look like anything other than titties and ass can fit up underneath this dress? Forget it. I'm out, just watch me do me."

Goody sat there in mild shock as Jewelz turned her juicy ass toward his face like he could kiss it. He wasn't used to anybody talking to him in such a manner, let alone a female, which made him want Jewelz more than he wanted any other jawn in the building.

He watched her walk away from the table and down the steps, hungrily eyeing the way her sweet hips moved as her long ponytail swayed back and forth across her slender back. He looked up at his manz that she had just called ugly and grinned. Mami was right. He was an ugly muh'fucka.

"Yo, make sure that girl don't leave out the door without giving her my number, bruh," Goody pointed at Jewelz and barked. And then he took another sip of his drink and sat back and waited.

$$$$$

Jewelz made her way down to the stage where the second amateur performer was just finishing up his act. She whispered a few words into the DJ's ear and slipped him a few ends, assuring that she would be the next one to step to the microphone. A couple of niggas was looking salty because of the slick move but fuck it. Jewelz was about to shut shit down.

"Now," the announcer screamed, "ready to do her muthafuckin thing on the Unsigned Hype stage tonight is one gorgeously dangerous bitch! Give it up for *Jewelz!* Show her some Goode muthafuckin love y'all!"

The crowd cheered as Jewelz stepped up to the mic ready to put it down. Sitting at the far end of the bar, Slick glanced up at the balcony and saw the entire Goode Brothers Gang looking down over the railing and focused on Jewelz. He grinned with pride. Jewelz was stunning and carried just the right amount of class mixed with a confident hood chick's attitude. Not to mention she was a very well-trained assassin who could kill at will and slip away unnoticed. The tigress in Jewelz is what attracted most men, and it was what lulled them to sleep as well. The way Goody's eyes were sucking down her every move, Slick was confident that the kingpin would no doubt fall victim to the First Lady of the Zip 'em up Crew.

"Ayo drop, that beat, yea, now check me out....
Bum bitch never try to play me,
I don't chase these niggas they chase me,
I made him roll up the kush, put his face in my puss
Now his girlfriend wanna e-rase me,
He said god-damn Jewelz you *tasty,*
He kept saying that he had a big e-go,
So I got em for his bands/ tryna play superman,
But I ain't looking for no mothafucking he-ro."

Jewelz rhymed at a fast-paced pitch and the crowd went fuckin bananas. From the ladies to the niggas, they couldn't believe how this sexy, fly-ass chick could flex on the mic like that. She didn't come across too hard trying to be like a man, or too soft either, it was the perfect blend of aggression, style, and sexy feminine swag.

"Ciroc bottles they *been* popped,
And these other chicks know Jewelz *been* hot,
And ever since I got my bills up,
The hoez call me Mrs. *Big Shot!*
Step ya twat game up then get gwap,
Strap on my hip that *been* cocked,
You ugly bitches don't live this street shit,
So homegirl just keep it *hip hop*,
I said stop...hold up...wait a damn minute...
Bitch I'm always on my job,
I'm never late a *damn* minute!"

Jewelz proceeded to shut the whole club down. Goody leaned over and whispered into one of his goon's ears, "Yo, take five bands and give it to the announcer to add on to whatever the pot is. Make sure she knows who the bank is coming from. This bitch got some shit with her and I gotta see what it's hittin for."

"I spit them facts and get them stacks,
you violate and you get ate bitch straight like that,
I'm gone....."

Jewelz ended the ferocious show and dropped the mic on the stage as she walked off sashaying her fine body with her round ass on fleek in her white designer dress. The whole club was on tilt going nuts. The announcer met Jewelz at the bottom of the steps with a paper bag in his hands as he grinned from ear to ear.

"Yo that was dope ma, let's do a record!" and "ayo, you bodied that shit baby!" was all you heard as the other artists and club-goers scrambled to give Jewelz her props. Some even asked to get an autograph.

"This is yours Jewelz," the announcer said as he greeted her with a hug. "You smashed this shit by a landslide so don't worry about nobody catching feelings."

Jewelz smiled.

"Yo," he said, pushing the paper bag into her hands "Here go that bread, and a certain somebody upstairs added a little something extra," he told her as he pointed up to the balcony. They both watched as Handgun Goody raised a glass of champagne in a smooth lil toast and winked at Jewelz.

Jewelz took the bag of money and the card that came with it. A number was on the back along with a handwritten message that read, "Make good use of this, and I ain't talking bout the money. H.G. Goody."

Jewelz looked up at the balcony again and winked back at him. Then she told the announcer good looking out and made her way back toward the bar so she could go grab Slick.

$$$$$

Go Jewelz! Go Jewelz! Go Jewelz!

Slick couldn't believe it. Just like that the fuckin club was on tilt! Jewelz had that shit going way up! She had just slayed the whole competition on some effortless shit. Slick had known she could get down on the mic, but he ain't know she was gonna show out like that. As she headed in his direction he peeped how hard she was tryna fight back a smile from all the positive vibes and attention she was getting, but it wasn't working. She was loving every moment of it and Slick was hype as shit for her as well.

As Jewelz parted the sea of faces Slick saw niggas giving her high-fives and getting free rubs on her ass as she switched her hips past them. Jewelz took it all in stride and kept her head high as she made her way over to where he was waiting.

"Oh word?" Slick said with a grin. He damn near had to yell over the roar of the crowd. "You just gonna bomb shit, drop the mic, and then step off, huh? I see how you get down. Got these niggas in here going straight bananas!"

"I know you ain't expect anything less," Jewelz said as she waved off a hug by Slick. "Uh-uh, you. That nigga Goody got his eyes all on me right now. We don't need you on the radar. We need to make it look like you're my brother or something. Gimme some dap and a pat on the back or some shit."

Slick knew she was right. The way Jewelz was looking in that outfit Slick was sure the top Goode Brother had his sights on locked firmly on her ass. Which is just how he wanted it. Thanks to Jewelz, they had gotten exactly what they came there to get, and that was Goody's attention. Now it was time to dip out.

"Yeah, a'ight," Slick said as he gave her the Marlon Waynan's Brooklyn hug. She threw a fake punch at him and he laughed it off. "Since all of a sudden you famous and shit, the next time you getting me in this bitch for free, ya heard?"

As Slick turned around to head for the door, he collided dead into a nigga. The shorter, stocky cat's cup of Remy spilled all over Slick's shirt. Material shit never meant much to Slick and he was tryna be there on the low anyway, so he brushed his shirt off and was about to keep it moving, but the stocky nigga wasn't having it.

"Ayo, son," the nigga with the afro shouted. "Watch where the fuck ya tall ass is going, bruh. Fuck is wrong with you? You need glasses or some shit? I should slap the dog shit out'chu for making me spill my drink. As a matter of fact nigga, go buy me another one!"

"Nigga buy you what?" Slick barked as he clenched his fists so hard his own knuckles cracked. "Lil nigga move the fuck around 'fore I chin-check ya stupid ass up in here."

"Word up?" The cocky cat bucked and lifted up his shirt. The unmistakable handle of a Desert Eagle was poking outta his waistband. The two sexy females standing by his side looked excited by the drama.

"What the fuck is you saying, pussy? I'm Trill from the Ville, *Goode Gang* or *don't* bang nigga! Now make me wet yo goofy ass up!"

Slick saw the situation for what it was. Trill had two bitches on his hip and he was a shooter for one of the biggest gangstas in Crooklyn. The lil nigga's pride would make him clap Slick right there on the spot before he even thought about backing down.

But Slick was a gunslinger. He could kill this young punk with one blow from right where he stood. But that would fuck up everything him and Jewelz had planned and ruin what they wanted to accomplish long-term though.

"Let's go Lil Slick," Jewelz finally stepped in between the two Brooklyn hittas. "This ain't the time for this shit, yo. Fallback and let's ride out, it's just a misunderstanding. Come on, let's fucking go."

Slick let Jewelz guide him to the door by his arm while he grilled the wanna be tough guy on his way out.

"Yeah, you better listen to that bitch, *Lil Slick,*" Trill heckled. "'Fore it get ugly for yo bitch-ass in here. This *my* house nigga! Goody-Goody *always* hoody! You know how the fuck we get down."

CHAPTER 15

Hump Back, Hump Back, Cucci Momma

Stretched out on her mama's couch, Cucci was chewing some gum and thumbing down her Twitter timeline, silently laughing at the latest gossip in the social media world. She had just finished eating the Sunday dinner that her mother had lovingly prepared, and she was chilling in the living room while everybody else cleaned up the kitchen.

"If you don't get your ass off that phone and get in the damn kitchen," Honore complained as she walked in the living room carrying a broom and a dustpan.

"Everybody else is in there scrubbing pots and busting suds but I bet yo lazy ass is either on Twitter or the 'Gram. How about you get off your ass and act like you appreciate that meal Aunt Frita just stood up at the stove all day and cooked for you."

"How about you kiss my ass," Cucci responded softly. "I'm always on my job in more ways than one, homegirl. Nowadays if you got a bangin body all types of idiots try to holla at you on Instagram. I'm trying to cash out on these dumb asses."

"You crazy girl," Honore said as she laughed, but she knew Cucci was speaking the truth. "My inbox be lit too. It's full of thirsty niggas offering me all types of shit. Dudes and dyke bitches too. They don't even realize who they fucking with. If I run across the right one I'ma definitely line one of their asses up though."

"Speaking of niggas getting lined up," Cucci sat up quickly like she had just remembered something. "Bitch I just heard some breaking news that ya boy Samuelson got smoked in a hotel room the other night! What the fuck happened?"

"Your guess is as good as mine," Honore said keeping a straight face as she slid the broom under the couch and pulled out some dust bunnies. "Who knows what kinda drama he got caught up in. What did the news report say?"

"Basically it just said that Joel Samuelson got done dirty in a hotel room and some real gruesome shit went down. They think he got robbed for some jewelry. It's funny how he got slumped on the same day that you delivered that package and got stuck-up on Fulton Street. How convenient. A prime diamond gets stolen, Joel gets murked, and you get kidnapped. *Crazy*."

Honore shrugged. "Yeah. Real crazy."

"Uh, huh. But if you know like I know, that murder wasn't over no small-time charm bracelets or rings, if it went down like that. Joel was too smart to get caught out there and he kept his game tight. He prolly wasn't by himself in that hotel room neither. It sounds to me like some kinda back-door transaction that went all the way to the left."

"I guess his game just wasn't tight enough." Honore shrugged again. "That's fucked up though. He was good people. I wonder what's going to happen at the job now."

"Are you *sure* you don't know nothing about that shit?" Cucci probed.

"Bitch why you keep asking me that? I already told you I don't know nothing about that slimy dog getting slumped!"

"Well I'm just asking, damn! You sure seem real nonchalant about that shit, Honore!" Cucci said with an attitude. "You do realize his white ass was hitting us off with some real thick slices of bread, right? He was the one setting us up real nice with them licks! He was the *plug!* How the fuck are we supposed maintain what we got going on without him?"

"Why are you asking me all this shit like you don't know what's poppin?" Honore snapped. "Joel was in the same line of business that we're in. He took the same risks we do. Just cause he's a white dude with money don't mean he's exempt from getting touched. Plugs get wacked out here everyday. One monkey damn sure won't stop my flow! I'm more worried about the police or whoever smoked his ass finding out that we were working with him."

"Yeah, a'ight," Cucci said with a sly smirk. "Well I should be pretty safe then because you were working with him much closer than I was. Way closer. All my action with him got cancelled just as soon as I put your ass on to him. It's all good though. I still got your back."

"The fuck you tryna say?" Honore gave her cousin the death stare. "Bitch I was sucking his little stank dick for the both of us! You still got paid, didn't you? Did you miss any fucking meals? Are your bills overdue? Do you have money in the stash? A'ight then! Stop dry-hating and throwing shade. I didn't tell Joel to stop rocking with you. He just thought I was better suited for the job. I made sure me and you both ate regardless, so cut the shit, Cucci!"

"Damn you going all extra-hard for no reason," Cucci said trying to defuse the situation.

But something bothered her about the whole scene. For one thing, Honore had claimed she was transporting a lil weak under-priced diamond that night, but who the hell put mad security on a stone that wasn't even worth nothing? Plus, on the news they said Samuelson had gotten smoked for some high value pieces of jewelry. Could it have been a high-priced diamond? Including a high-priced *diamond!*

Honore was acting like Samuelson being rubbed out of the picture wasn't gonna affect their pockets at all. She was acting like she wasn't gonna miss those ends he helped them bring in. For all Cucci knew her cousin had made up that whole fantastical story about getting kidnapped by some stick-up kids. For all she knew Honore was walking around with a real grand diamond stuck up her ass, just'a sitting on that shit so it could hatch into a bunch of little Faberge eggs. Hell naw, Cucci wasn't buying it. She just couldn't shake the feeling that something was off.

"Relax, cuzzo," she said sweetly. "I was just stating the obvious and tryna see where ya mind was at now that the big boss is gone."

"My mind is on to the next hustle," Honore responded coldly. "Whatever happened to his old ass is his damn business. I'll tell you this much, I'm glad it was him who got slumped and not me. You don't know how deep that rich white man was in the game. He coulda owed somebody some bread or fucked over the wrong person. Shit happens."

Cucci let the conversation die down, but she kept asking herself why Honore was acting so cold-hearted and dismissive. Honore had been way up Joel Samuelson's ass and sucking his dick on a regular. The bitch was just like her dead damn mama when it came to men! Her sneaky ass had stolen Cucci's trick when Joel had been *her* sugar daddy from the gate!

Cucci's hood alarm was going off and ringing on a thousand. She was ready to put some money on the fact that Honore knew more about their boss's brutal murder than she was letting on. And if Honore knew something slick, then Cucci was damn sure gonna find out what it was.

CHAPTER 16

Ain't Nothin More Important Than the Moolah

It was a busy Monday morning at the New York Diamond and Jewelry Exchange. But instead of the usual friendly interactions with the rich clientele in the diamond industry, the back-office employees were walking around wide-eyed and talking amongst each other in hushed tones.

It had been on the news all weekend that one of their top supervisors had been gruesomely murdered in a hotel room, and all the white folks on staff were walking around looking pale in the face and stressed the hell out.

But not Cucci Momma. She was strutting her stuff and looking gorgeously cool and upbeat in her tan and red Kate Spade dress as she came out of a meeting room and strode across the large, elegantly decorated office in her red patent leather heels. With her eyes on rotate she squatted down discreetly near Honore's desk.

"The fuckin FBI is here!" Cucci spit from the side of her mouth. Reaching out to slide open a lower drawer, she pretended like she was searching for some documents.

"They're grilling everybody because that fucker Samuelson stole a major fuckin diamond! Them reporters lied and said it was just jewelry on the news, but it was a big *fat* diamond! When the investigators call you in don't say shit!" she hissed in warning. "Tell 'em you don't know a goddamn thing about that dead muthafucka!" Cucci stunted, knowing full well that she had already tickled their little pink ears off with all kinds of suspicious and incriminating shit about both Honore and Joel Samuelson.

"I can't be sure," Cucci had pressed her hand to her chest and dry snitched earlier when the alphabet men asked her if she'd ever noticed anything suspicious about Joel Samuelson and the way he handled the company's diamonds, "but I kinda got the feeling that he was living a double life, you know? I mean, I actually walked into a supply closet and saw him taking a diamond out of his pocket one day. He was on his cell phone whispering about finding a black-market trader, whatever in the world that means. Of course I couldn't hear everything that was being said, but he was definitely trying to hide something."

She had shrugged innocently while the investigators scribbled notes on their yellow pads and then added, "I never really knew Mr. Samuelson that well," she lied, "but he worked pretty closely with a girl here named Honore Morales. Please don't put my name in it, but my guess is, if anybody knows anything about him getting a little too close to the diamonds, it would be her."

And now, Cucci cut her eyes over at Honore.

"Bitch did you hear me?"

Nodding slightly to acknowledge Cucci's warning, Honore never looked up from the ledger she was writing in because she already knew the deal. Joel had signed out one of their largest diamonds on Friday morning and he got deaded before he got a chance to slip a fake one back in its place. With that big-ass empty spot in the vault it wasn't surprising that the federal authorities had closed in trying to connect the missing jewel to his murder.

The FBI agents on the scene today were both young white men and Honore had already peeped them way before Cucci's warning. She had seen their eyes crawl over her before they followed her boss into his office and firmly shut the door, and while her co-workers had crowded together in a huddle whispering and kicking up rumors, she had remained behind her desk working her ass off, just as she usually did.

Cucci had barely switched her apple ass back to her side of the office when Honore heard her boss's door open again and the agents stepped back out. She lowered her gaze and pretended to be focused real hard on reading something in her ledger, and then acted all surprised when she looked up and saw they were standing right in front of her desk.

"Oh!" she said sweetly in her pure-little-prissy-girl voice, her bright eyes going back and forth between her boss and the two agents. "Good morning Mister Goldberg! Is there something I can do for you?"

"Yes, there is, Honore," her boss answered quietly. "These gentlemen are from the FBI. They're here to investigate a possible connection between Mr. Samuelson's murder and the diamond he signed out on the day he was killed. I realize you were off work that day, but I'd appreciate it if you'd fully cooperate with them and assist them in any way you can."

"Of course," Honore said earnestly as she rose from her chair and followed the trio into the big boss's office. "I'd be happy to cooperate."

$$$$$

No sooner had the door to the boss's office slammed closed behind Honore did Cucci join the other clerks who were gathered around whispering amongst themselves. They went back and forth with the tongue-wagging, coming up with all sorts of cloak-and-dagger scenarios to fit their version of how shit had gone down.

"First the Pinkerton Detectives came by here earlier this morning," a young secretary squealed with excitement in her eyes, "and now the FBI! I overheard them say Mr. Samuelson might have been stealing diamonds for years! I mean, just think about it...he probably belonged to some intricate underground jewelry ring, because with a diamond that big he had to have help somewhere along the way."

"Really?" Cucci batted her eyelashes and butt-in. "You really think he's been stealing for years? I don't see how since our vault is always locked up tight. How could anyone be stealing diamonds for that long and get away with it?"

The secretary shrugged. "I guess that's what those agents are here to find out. Mr. Samuelson was kinda up there in senior management so he had a lot of access to the vault. I bet they're talking to Honore now because she's one of the people who worked steadily in his department. Maybe she noticed something fishy about him over the years."

"Wow," Cucci said, looking wide-eyed and impressed. "How much do you think that stolen diamond was worth?"

The secretary shook her head and shrugged again. "I'm not sure, but I know it's a lot. At least a few million dollars. It was one of our best pieces which is why only senior executives were allowed to sign it out."

The cackling group of hens suddenly scattered when the door to the boss's office opened and Honore and the agents walked out together. The staff pretended to be engrossed in the business of their day, when in reality all the ears and most of the eyes in the room were scoping shit as hard as they could.

Honore didn't even look at her co-workers as she walked calmly back to her desk and resumed her work. Whatever it was that those agents had said to her behind closed doors, she made sure that not one damn inch of her looked frazzled. Not a hair on her fuckin head was out of place, and there wasn't a drop of sweat anywhere on her body. Because them FBI agents didn't have shit on her. They didn't even have a clue. After submitting to their questions and agreeing to take a lie detector test, she was cool and collected and unfazed in every way.

Cucci watched from afar as one of the agents stapled a large flyer to the office bulletin board. Even from where she was standing she could see the picture of the stolen diamond and the words, "SEEKING INFORMATION" and "$100,000 REWARD" written in large bold letters.

Glancing around discreetly, she waited until the agent had walked away and then she grabbed some paperwork and swayed her hips closer to the bulletin board.

Opening the top drawer of a file cabinet, her eyes glinted deviously as they rushed over the words, "Seeking Information in the Recovery of a Valuable Diamond. A $100,000 REWARD is being offered for information leading to the identity and the arrest and conviction of any persons found to have committed burglary, robbery, or theft of the jewel on these premises."

Tossing her paperwork carelessly on top of the file cabinet, Cucci re-read the poster, then glanced over at Honore. Her eyes narrowed into slits as she looked at all them zeros on that poster and a zing of electricity shot through her whole body.

So them bitches wanna know about that diamond, huh? Well, somebody better hope I don't mess around and tell 'em about the diamond diva! The diamond fucking QUEEN!

Cucci's conniving mind was churning as she scooped up her paperwork and turned her back on her beloved cousin and best friend, barely able to hide her sneaky smile.

CHAPTER 17

Chasin Like Jason

It took about seventy-two hours for Honore to receive the phone call that she had been waiting for. She had been itching to hit those digits herself at least a thousand times in the last three days, but she had decided to take Sly McFly's good advice and hold off on making the first move.

Nah, don't call him. He'll call you. I guarantee it. When a weak nigga pulls a bitch-move like that you know for sure he ain't on his game.

"Hey whassup, French Fry. I'm just calling to check up on you like I said I would," he said, running her some old bullshit line.

Honore knew what time it was. He had worn a mask over his face but she'd seen the lust and intrigue in his eyes the night he snatched her, and she was surprised that he had held back from calling her for this long.

"Excuse me?" she said, faking like she was annoyed. "Who is this?"

His chuckle was low and sexy as it came through the phone line.

"Stop frontin girl. You know who this is."

"No, I don't," she said coldly. "I'm afraid I'm going to have to hang up. I have a class in fifteen minutes and besides, I don't talk to strangers."

"It's ya boy Slick," he said quickly, and she had to stop herself from laughing out loud.

Wide-open simp nigga!

"Slick?" she spit with disgust. "Sorry," she said. "I don't have any friends with that street name."

"I'm not a friend," came the response. "I'm that dude who saved your life the other night when my crew wanted to blast you into next week, remember?"

Honore held her breath and remained silent on the line, hoping he'd think she was shocked and didn't quite know what to say.

"Honore?" he said right on cue. "Honore are you there? Look, sweetheart. I'm sorry about the way things went down out there the other night, a'ight? I just wanted to holla so I could check on you. You know. Make sure you were straight."

"I-I'm here," she finally said, lowering her voice so she could yank the shit outta his stupid heart-strings. Her words quivered. "I was so damn scared that night . . . especially after seeing somebody get shot like that right in front of me. It was so scary because I've never been involved in anything violent like that before. But I'm doing a little better now. I'm trying to get my head back into my school work and I just wanna put everything about that night behind me."

"I hear you," Slick said. "You were just in the wrong place at the wrong time, mami. That's all. I'm sorry you even had to be exposed to that type of business. Check this out. Lemme make it up to you. Let me take you out tonight and show you a good time. You know, we can hang out and chill for awhile and you can relax, a'ight?"

"No," Honore sighed and lied. "I can't. I have class in a few. And then tutoring right after."

"What about tomorrow?" he persisted.

She sighed again. "I'm off tomorrow, but it's usually my day for homework and studying..."

"How about you work first and play later," Slick suggested. "Hit your books and do what you gotta do, and when you're finished let me take you out for a lil bit. It'll help you get all that drama off your mind."

"I don't know..." she said in a singsong voice.

"Say yes," he told her. "I wanna see you, Honore. I really wanna see you again."

Bingo! Honore hollered inside as she finally agreed to hook up with him the next night. She could barely keep the devious grin off her face as she mouthed evilly, *Yeah, you stupid muthafucka! I wanna see your black ass too!*

$$$$$

Noodles was known as the silent-but-deadly member of the Zip 'em up Crew. He was the straight-laced type who avoided trouble, stashed his money, and stayed taking care of his fam.

A year earlier he had met a chocolate-skinned sista named Ayesha and fallen head over heels for her. Ayesha was a single parent with three small kids who lived in a run-down tenement building on 149th Street. She wasn't no video vixen or no bad bitch with a big ass and fake everything and weave down to her ankles. Nah, she was just a struggling single mom and a college student who was hiding out from her fist-swinging baby-daddy named Massacre who stalked and terrorized her on the regular.

But when Noodles stepped into the picture he put the brakes on all that shit. Without a word he had convinced Ayesha to trust him with all her heart, and not only had he snuffed out that pussy-nigga Massacre, Noodles was taking damn good care of Ayesha and raising her three little children as if they were his own. Not a lot of men could do it for a ready-made family like he was doing it, but Noodles was far from the average man.

Today, Noodles had surprised Ayesha and the kids with a trip to a Ringling Brothers Circus show. The arena was jam-packed with families from all across the tri-state area. Ayesha's kids had missed out on so much in their young lives that Noodles spoiled them at every opportunity and let them have almost anything they wanted.

With pure happiness on their faces, all three kids grinned at him and started devouring their cotton candy and fruit snacks as soon as they jumped in the second row seats.

"I really appreciate you doing all this Noodles," Ayesha said she put her arm around her Superman. "I've never even been to a circus show before, and the kids are so excited and loving every moment. Shit I'm loving it my damn self."

Noodles grinned and started talking to her in sign language. He'd been teaching Ayesha how to sign for a few months now and she learned very quickly. At times when he would come home late at night she would be up taking an American Sign Language course online because she wanted to catch everything he said instead of him having to write stuff down. Noodles admired her dedication and her drive to grasp something that was foreign to her in order for them to communicate better with each other.

"This is what life is all about," Noodles said with his hand gestures. "Making the people that you love happy. The looks on the kids's faces are priceless. I'm just glad I get to experience these types of things with them. That's what I'm here to help provide, baby. Great adventures. I wanna let them be kids while they're young and have a happy and diverse upbringing in life."

Not only had Noodles stepped up to be a good father figure and male role-model, he had moved Ayesha and the children out of the clutches of the ghetto and into his own house to give them more stability and a better chance at happiness and success.

For the first time in their lives the kids had their own rooms and a green yard to play in every day. Noodles took them to the barbershop to get their hair cut every week, they played basketball together at the gym, and he paid for them to have music lessons too. The school district in his neighborhood was a big upgrade from the crumbling school they had been in, and the community was welcoming.

Ayesha was hesitant in her new surroundings at first because the hood was all she knew. Being intimidated and beaten up was just her fate in her mind, and she wouldn't have found an escape without Noodles coming along and protecting her and sheltering her children.

The love between them was genuine and strong. Ayesha knew she wasn't the prettiest chick running around and at times she could be highly insecure. She had sometimes felt as if that bitch-beater Massacre had been the only type of man she deserved.

But Noodles was changing her way of thinking through his kind-heartedness and his good loving. He was helping her fight those old insecurities by showing her that she was worth so much more. She was his one and only queen, natural hair and stretch marks and all, and before Noodles came into the picture Ayesha didn't have a damn clue about what that meant. It used to be all love and hip hop shit for her. But life was different now, and Noodles was absolutely the real damn deal.

"Thank you my love," she signed to him so she could show him how much she had learned. "I don't know what I've done to deserve a blessing like you. You've made me see things within myself that I didn't even know were there. My kids think the world of you, and so do I."

"You bring a peace to my life too, baby," Noodles signed back. "The kinda peace that keeps me human. What I do for a living is intense and I love coming home to you and the kids every day. Y'all help me relax and stay focused on what's really important, so I can clear all the foul shit from my mind."

"I feel you," Ayesha said. "Seems like something heavy has been on your mind for the past few days though, babe."

Noodles nodded. She was into him like that and he wasn't surprised that she had noticed. "I'm worried about Slick," he admitted with his fingers. "Some shit went down that got me saying, hmmmmm... But don't worry. It's all good, baby. They about to bring the elephants out now. Let's enjoy the show."

Ayesha started to push him for more, but instead she leaned over and kissed him as she ran her fingers through his long dreads. In an instant they heard a resounding, *"Ewwww!"* from the kids as they laughed and pointed fingers at them for kissing.

Noodles grinned and threw a handful of popcorn at the tykes. Then they sat back and enjoyed the show as a united family, happy and content in each other's presence.

CHAPTER 18

I Ain't Had a Crush in Years

Slick was having second thoughts as he pulled up in front of a pizza shop that was only a few blocks away from where him and his crew had hit the diamond jux.

"Fuck is you doing, son!" he shook his head and chastised himself in disbelief. "Bruh, you 'bout to play ya'self out!"

Tonight was gonna be a special occasion so he had pulled out the plum-red Aston Martin Vanquish with the peanut butter interior that he kept in a parking garage in Manhattan. It was an expensive car, and he only drove it when he felt like feeling sporty and stylish, which was very seldom.

The Vanquish was the type of machinery that would make a hater slap his chick for staring too hard at it or at the driver. Slick was much more comfortable playing the shell-shocked half-crippled "Sometimey" persona in Brownsville than he was ballin and flashing his wealth in the city. Stuntin didn't mean as much to him as it did to the other niggas around his way, although tonight he had on a fresh pair of blue and red Lebrons, with a black Polo t-shirt that complimented his blue and red Polo bubble vest. The Submariner Blue Rolex that hung on his wrist completed the deal, and The Low Life Crew—a played-out gang of Brooklyn knuckleheads who jammed department stores and boosted everything that had a Ralph Lauren label on it, woulda been proud of him.

All of that packaged with the Aston Martin had Slick's swag on a hundred thousand. He was looking more like he slung kilos than he pulled triggers. If niggas in his hood knew old bummy Sometimey was holding them kind of racks they woulda either jumped on his dick or robbed him blind.

But Slick was a highly trained professional killer. Maintaining a low profile and keeping his image in check was part of what made him such an expert on the trigger. He had very few vices and he cared for money and his pigeons way more than he did for beautiful women. He had always viewed females as an easy way to get killed.

Beautiful deceptions is what he liked to think of them as. But even with that in the forefront of his mind, he found himself about to go on a date with a woman who by all rights he shoulda smoked.

Instead, he had spared her life, and for the first time in a very long time he had acted on impulse instead of on intellect. Slick had broken some real crucial rules of survival and anonymity for this girl, and by hooking up with her tonight he was continuing to put himself and his whole crew at risk.

Lost in his own conflicted thoughts, Slick barely saw the shadow roll over his passenger-side door until somebody yanked the handle and tried to open it. He jumped and was just about to reach under the seat for his ratty, but then he saw it was her. Slick unlocked the door and Honore slowly slid into the type of car that street niggas called a spaceship. It damn sure mighta been one because the moment her ass touched the seat Slick felt like he was somewhere out in orbit.

He had a hard time looking into her hazel eyes as his gaze roamed from her Hermes high heels up her long legs and to her beautiful face. The perfume she had on smelled so sweet it was making him hungry.

"You looking type-nice right now, w'sup wit you?" Slick greeted her. If this was a normal date he woulda reached out to give her a hug, but this was some wild shit and he wasn't sure if she was open to physical contact or not.

Honore gazed back at him like she was partly in awe and partly in fear. He was more than attractive without his mask, she noted. In fact, he was fine as shit. He gave off an aura of power and authority. Although his swag was different than say, a gang banga or a drug kingpin, it was still powerful as hell. She sensed a disciplined intelligence and a sharp focus in him that you didn't find in stick-up kids too often.

"Thank you," Honore said as she gave him a smile that damn near brightened up the dark sky outside. She had lied and told him she lived in Brooklyn, so they had agreed to meet outside of a pizza shop near her crib. "I'm doing as well as can be expected. Oh yeah, and without that scary mask on you ain't looking too bad yourself."

"You ready to roll out?" Slick grinned as he sank back in his plush seat and checked her out. She was wearing glittery jewelry around her neck and a sleek, off-white sleeveless cat suit that showed off her toned shoulders and every one of her exploding curves.

"Why? You tryna let me drive?" Honore playfully asked.

Slick smirked. "Nah, baby. I don't know you like that. Plus, this thing might be a little too fast for you."

Honore rolled her eyes. "Um, being here with you right now is a little too fast for me, but guess what? I'm in the car and I'm still down to ride, right?" She laughed and then said cockily, "Don't get salty 'cause you scared I might whip ya wheels better than you do."

Slick had to crack a smile at her confidence. "I find that hard to believe. I'm the best at this shit, shorty."

He sped off in his Aston Martin into the Brooklyn streets. They rode in near silence at first, letting the sounds of J. Cole be the barrier between conversing with each other.

Honore broke the silence first. "So where are we heading? I'm not all that hungry or anything, what about you?"

Slick shrugged coolly. "I'ma swing by a little chill spot I hit every now and then. It's not a club or nothing, just a spot to grab a drink and relax. Is that cool with you?"

Honore shrugged right back. "Whatever. I'm a rider. I like cruising through the streets and taking in the atmosphere, but I'm down with grabbing a drink."

Smiling, she reached over and pushed the button to drop the convertible's top.

"Yo," Slick said in surprise. "What you know about these buttons? You been in one of these joints before?"

Honore smirked. "What? You think you the only one out here who been in some fly shit before? I'm far from a dumb-bum broad, so don't underestimate me baby."

Slick grinned and nodded. "Damn, my bad sexy. You right though. Matter fact, you didn't seem at all impressed by this shit from the gate," Slick said matter-of-factly.

Honore brushed it off. "No problem. Every chick I know likes a man who has fat pockets and a sense of style, but believe it, I get my own money and I drive my own car. It's them lil thirsty chickens out there who don't have much and get all worked up over material grub. Fortunately I'm not blinded by the fancy-life like most females are."

Slick nodded as he kept his foot on the pedal and cruised through the streets of the city that never slept. Already he was enjoying the space they were sharing, even though deep inside he knew it was stupid and crazy for him to even be there with her.

They rode in silence for a few, just listening to the music and taking in the urban sights and then, "Yo, lemme ask you something," Slick popped off outta the blue. "What made you decide to hook up with me tonight? I mean, I'm a thief, baby. You saw me and my team in action the other night. We stole a bunch of jewelry and left a witness to our crime behind. *You.* Why you ain't busted on us yet?"

Honore swung her head to the left and glared at him. "Hold up now, mister! I ain't no damn snitch! That little seven dollars and fifty cents an hour I get to intern in that jewelry store ain't enough to give me no diarrhea of the mouth! Besides, like you said, you saved my life when your friends wanted to erase me. I've got mad gratitude to you for that."

That plus the fact that you didn't know who I was or where to find me, Slick thought to himself.

He almost laughed when she shot him a dirty look then folded her arms over her breasts and scooted as close as she could get to her door, igging him.

"Hey now," Slick said playfully. "Don't be like that. I don't like it when chicks get too quiet. You pressing up on that door like you wanna jump out or something. You're safe, lil mama. Don't start acting all scary and shit."

She turned and looked at him strangely.

"What do I need to be scared of? If you was going to do something foul to me we wouldn't have made it this far, now would we? As a matter of fact," Honore blurted out, "Why did you let me go the other night anyway?"

"Forget about the other night," Slick said dismissing her question. "All that bizz is in the past. Me and you are chilling together *tonight.* Let's focus on that."

Honore shrugged and seemed to relax a bit. "You're the one who brought it up. I'm just tryna figure out where y'all offloaded all that stolen jewelry. I might wanna buy me a couple of pieces from you cut-rate. I damn sure couldn't buy none while it was in the store. So, just tell me where y'all gonna sell it—"

"Ah-ah-ah!" Slick raised his hand in the air, cutting her off as he shook his head. "We ain't doing that tonight. Now ain't the time for the extra questions and shit. Let's just kick back and enjoy our evening together, is that a'ight with you?" Slick said as he pulled up to the curb in a hood part of Brooklyn that Honore had never been to before.

Slick got out on his side and then came around and opened the door for her. Honore was a nice height for a female, but Slick was tall as hell. He towered over her as he led her over to the sidewalk and took her hand.

She hesitated and almost stumbled. *What the fuck*, she thought with her mind going into race mode. She didn't see no signs for a bar or an entrance to a nightclub. Her guard shot up and she felt a little nervous, but instead of asking questions she went with the flow.

Slick looked down at her like he was amused. "You a'ight, ma? You lookin a little petro."

"Yeah, I'm straight," Honore said as she glanced around with her eyes on rotate. "But where are we going? Are you sure you wanna leave your nice ride out here?"

Slick looked around like he was worried too. "Well, I don't know. I hope you strapped 'cause I'm not," he said with a dead serious face.

Honore didn't know what to think. Her instincts were riled. She was a Queens girl so Brooklyn wasn't her home territory. Niggas was real gutta in New York's largest borough. She was outta her element and she wondered if she was about to walk into a set up.

But then Slick bust out laughing as he gently squeezed her hand. "*Haaaaa!* Damn girl, you super-uptight! Come on, yo. Relax, baby. You with me. Ain't shit gonna happen to you. We 'bout to go kick it."

They walked into a corner bodega and Slick nodded at the huge Hispanic cat who was standing behind the counter. Honore was still looking shook as hell but she didn't bitch up, she just followed Slick's lead. They went straight to the back of the store and then pushed through two doors and walked down some steps. Slick knocked on another door and a huge, muscled-up bouncer dressed in a nice business suit opened it up.

"*Yooo,* w'sup Slick! How you been my dude?"

"I'm good, Mack," Slick responded coolly. "I just came out to relax with my lady friend for a minute."

"That's what's up," Mack said as he stood back to let Slick and Honore pass. "Enjoy ya'self my nigga."

They stepped into a huge room that was semi-packed with bodies. A bar was popping with customers. Some patrons were off to the side shooting pool, and even more people were sitting around at small tables playing cards.

Honore immediately recognized that this was an exclusive underground spot that not just anyone could get into. She was relieved to see that everyone was cool and dressed nice and the music was smooth. The patrons weren't the typical hood crowd that gave off a vibe of impending violence, and damn near everybody and their daddy was greeting Slick like he was an old homey that they were happy to see.

"If *I* ruled the world! I'd free *all my sons!"* Lauryn Hill's voice crooned throughout the joint as the crowd sang along and vibed to the classic Nas cut.

Honore bobbed her head to the sounds as her inhibitions began to fade. "This is a real cool lil place, Slick," she said, relaxing as they sat at the bar and settled in. "How did you find out about this joint?"

Slick laughed. "Damn...you crazy nosey ma, but if you must know I've been cool with the owner all my life. What you wanna drink?" he asked over the sounds of the music.

"I'll take some Ciroc and orange juice," Honore answered, her eyes scanning the room as she enjoyed the good vibes. "And after we wet our throats for a lil bit then I'll show you how to play some pool."

Slick gave Honore a *fuck outta here* look and then ordered their drinks. Just then his phone vibrated in his back pocket with a familiar rhythm. He could tell it was Jewelz calling him but he damn sure wasn't about to answer it right now.

They drank and cracked jokes on each other as they made their way over to the pool tables. Slick waxed her thoroughly in the first two games, but to his surprise Honore legitimately beat him in their final round.

"Yo, who taught you how to play pool?" he asked as their last game came to an end. "For real, shorty, you rack 'em better than a lot of niggas I know." He grinned. "Even though you got lucky on that last game."

Honore grinned back. Hard. Even though she was running game on this sherm her physical attraction to him was undeniable. "You know, I might go to college but I'm from the streets too, Slick," she said as she switched her sweet hips toward him. "I learned how to play pool just trying to keep some money in my pockets. But once I started winning big then niggas used to try and rob me because I'm a female so I had to chill."

The multiple shots of alcohol were starting to take effect and Honore found her caution and inhibitions flying right out the window.

"That's what's up," Slick said and nodded. "I gotta salute you for trying to get your hustle on."

"Okay, I give you your props on playing pool too," she said as she slipped her arms around Slick's waist and looked up at him seductively. "But can you dance?"

Slick smiled down into her beautiful, half-lit face. "Of course I can dance. Matter of fact, I can probably teach you a couple of moves. I got a mean-ass two step."

"Then let's do this!" Honore laughed and took his hand and led him over to the crowded dance floor.

You just gotta let my luv....let my luuuuuv...let Slick's luv adore you...

Slick put a lil twist on the Miguel track as it resonated through the club and him and Honore, along with multiple other couples, did their rhythmic two-step to the banga.

"You having a good time?" Slick whispered in her ear as he switched gears, pulling her into his arms as they danced real close to the classic jam.

"Yeah, I am," Honore said, slowly grinding her body into Slick's crotch as heat rose between them. "But honestly, though, I'm ready to leave."

"A'ight," Slick responded as he felt his phone vibrate again and his manhood rise. "I'm glad you enjoyed ya'self tonight, but cool. I'll get you back to your crib, baby."

"Uh-uh," Honore shook her head freely letting her body flow to the music. "I wanna go home with *you*, Slick. I'm not ready for this to end yet and I definitely don't want it to end here."

Slick was feeling it too, and he was instantly ready to get outta there and head to the crib and get up in her guts.

"Yo, you sure this is what you wanna do?" he asked quietly. *Don't let her in too close*, he cautioned himself. But he knew that shit was pointless because he was already a goner.

She nodded. "Hell yeah. Just don't be falling in love and shit when it's over 'cause I don't believe in being cuffed."

Slick hit her with that *fuck outta here* look again, and they laughed and made their way towards the exit.

$$$$$

The Manhattan skyline sparkled in the backdrop as Honore stared at the mega lights from the balcony of Slick's condo apartment. This nigga musta been a real good thief because she knew finery when she saw it. Slick's whole shit was laid and smooth. It was one of those ten to fifteen grand a month joints, and she figured he financed it by selling big time drugs and committing multiple armed robberies.

He had turned on some music and poured her a glass of champagne as soon as she stepped in the door, and she was feeling good as fuck as he came up behind her and pressed his nose into her neck.

"You like what you see?" he growled in a sexy voice.

His wood was on brick and poking the hell outta her from behind, and Honore laughed as she turned around and pulled her strapless cat suit all the way down until her naked crotch and titties were exposed.

"Naw, baby. Do you like what *you* see?"

Slick was mesmerized. Her skin looked like smooth buttercream. Her bulging breasts were a firm D-cup and her nipples stuck out like pencil erasers. Her triangle was spectacular. Her lady garden was curly and neatly trimmed, and her plump lil clitoris looked nice and suckable.

Enjoying his drool, Honore stepped completely out of her outfit and kicked it to the side. Her twenty-two-inch waist was toned and tight, and her hips flared out in two perfect curves. Wearing nothing but her sleek stiletto pumps and a big sexy smile, she turned around and walked back inside Slick's bedroom knowing his eyes were stuck like glue to her sculpted ass.

And Slick was damn sure watching too. That ass was flawless. It was smooth as baby cheeks and puffed out like pow! There was a deep dimple above each mound of her rump that perfected her rearview picture.

Honore stood by the bed and let him soak up her beauty. Slick swallowed it up and took it all in, then he stripped outta his gear and stood bold and naked in front of her too.

"What happened?" Honore asked, running her fingers over the scars on his chiseled stomach and buff chest.

Slick shrugged. "I was betrayed by somebody who was supposed to love me."

Honore nodded. Even with the scars she had to admit she was impressed. This nigga was fine and all cut up. Swole arms, chiseled six-pack, and enough thick black dick to satisfy five horny bitches. Honore knew for a fact that some good fuckin was about to be going on tonight!

And Slick damn sure didn't disappoint her. He walked up on her and took her in his strong arms. His chocolate skin felt like hot steel as he pulled her to his chest. His lips crushed hers and he thrust his tongue deep inside her mouth. Honore sighed and let herself go. He kissed her so thoroughly that she got dizzy and her pussy started leaking that good sticky stuff.

His hands roamed her body and ignited heat bombs everywhere he touched. Her breasts, her nipples, her ass, Slick had her about to explode like a firecracker. His tongue was expert as he licked all around her sand-colored aureoles before aiming for her erect nipples. Staring into her eyes, he got down on his knees on the carpet and kissed a path down her tight stomach and headed straight for that dugout.

Honore stood there gasping and trembling in anticipation. As the music played softly in the background, Slick massaged her outrageous ass with both hands like he had never seen a donk so gorgeous and round before. His breath was hot on her crotch as he gave her two quick taps on the hip so she could spread her legs wider. With sweetness already dripping down her leg, Honore was happy to comply.

Slick went to work on her like an expert and she almost lost her damn mind when he parted her pussy lips and his lips closed down firmly on her fat, sensitive clit. Honore shivered like crazy as sparks of pure pleasure spread throughout her whole damn body, and if Slick hadn't been bracing her with his strong arms she woulda fell the fuck over!

He took his time and licked her pussy out from one end to the other, sopping up all the juice she was squirting as he went. His tongue probed and flicked and teased and licked, and Honore was on cloud fuckin nine as she threw her head back and bucked against his face like a dopefiend getting a gigantic hit.

She felt a powerful orgasm rising inside her and she grabbed his head and whimpered as she humped and wiped her clit all over his stiffened tongue. When her explosion came it damn near knocked her out, and she sagged in Slick's arms and whimpered like a baby as he caressed every inch of her body.

And then it was time to really get loose.

The only reason Honore was with this dude in the first place was because he had something she wanted. And right now she wanted that *dick*. Yeah, she was gonna work this mothafucka over and get the info she was after. But not yet. Not tonight. Tonight, she told herself as they switched places and she kissed the rock-hard mounds of his chest and slid downward until the head of his magnificent dick throbbed heavily on her tongue, tonight she was gonna satisfy the part of her that not even money could touch.

After all, she was a killer and a cut-throat conniving trickster, but she was also a woman. She giggled inside as she gripped his thick long dick in her hands like a joystick and opened her mouth real wide. Nah, this wasn't written on her to-do list and it damn sure wasn't part of the game, but who woulda thought the Queen of Diamonds would be butt-naked in a mark's crib, crouched down on her hands and knees sucking dick like a chump and loving it?

CHAPTER 19

Some Dick and A Nut

While Honore was on her knees giving Slick some good brain, Cucci and her brand new bae named Ice Pick were in the back of Club Goode smoking hookah and sniffing coke. She had just wrapped her juicy lips around his dick and given him some mean-ass head, and right now his nuts were drained and satisfied.

"Ayo bitch, slow the fuck down," Ice Pick pushed hard against his new fuck-buddy as she leaned over a silver tray. "You sniffing that shit up like a vacuum cleaner! Save some for later. I don't need you getting too damn happy up in here."

"Relax, Papi," Cucci said in a daze of euphoria. She reached over and patted his crotch. "Just like this dick you got, I like the way this shit makes me feel. Besides you got that dynamite work. This shit got me on cloud nine, daddy."

"Yeah we do got that bomb pack," Ice Pick agreed as he exhaled a cloud of Hookah smoke. "Ay, don't you gotta work in the morning? When you gonna let me run up in that jewelry store and get some of that ice? We can act like you getting robbed and split the profits. Ya bosses won't know a damn thing."

"Nah baby," Cucci said coming to her senses. "I'm always down to hit a lick but I got other shit going on. I fucks with my job and they fucks with me. Plus we can scheme on some bigger shit than a little punk-ass jewelry spot."

Cucci wasn't about to have Ice Pick coming up to her damn job getting her arrested. She wasn't telling him shit about the business she had going on with Honore and the Crushed Ice Clique neither. *Sheeiit,* she was high but she wasn't stupid. A cardinal rule amongst the clique was to never expose plans, personal identities, or business relationships with anybody. Honore would kill her ass for disclosing information with an outside nigga like Ice Pick. Plus, even with Joel dead the money was still flowing in and her bank account was stacking lovely, so Cucci didn't wanna fuck nothing up. Ice Pick was good about giving up the dick and the dope, but he was shy about giving up the dollars. So for now she would keep her mouth closed and keep doing her thing.

But she had big plans for their future because this nigga Ice was a member of the biggest get-money gang in Brooklyn. He was a Goode Brother, and they were considered royalty in the Empire underworld. Cucci had been spending the weekend with her girlfriend in Brooklyn when she met him. Her girl had sucked a bouncer's dick to get them into the VIP section at Club Goode just so Cucci could get Ice Pick's attention. They had clicked together and hooked up, and since then they had gone out on a few dates where Ice Pick treated her to fancy food and some high-powered coke, and in return Cucci gave him the best fuck of his life every time she slid her thong off.

And her shit musta been super-good too because Ice Pick coulda had any bitch in the city he wanted, but so far he kept coming back to Cucci. But Ice was possessive and paranoid, so all the other niggas Cucci was entertaining had got cut the fuck off. Cucci got off on power, and she wasn't gonna mess up the chance to be with a boss-ass nigga like Ice Pick for some low-level fuck boy who couldn't even shine her bae's Gators. The power and notoriety Ice Pick had acquired in the streets was second only to his brother Handgun. Them dangerous but dapper Goode brothers had the streets in a headlock and everybody knew it. Bitches would line up and snake their own mommas for the opportunity to fuck with any one of the five brothers, and Cucci would do whatever it took to keep her gangsta on lock.

"You sure about that shit?" Ice asked skeptically, still thinking about hitting the diamond and jewelry exchange.

Cucci nodded. "Hell yeah. Plus they already up on shit like that at my job. As soon as somebody gets robbed the first person they look at is whoever she's fuckin with. Uh-uh. That ain't the move, daddy."

"I can dig it," Ice Pick said. "I might need you for some other shit anyway. There's a couple of deliveries I need you to drop for me sometime soon. I got some molly coming in that has to get distributed. Just because you got big lips and good pussy don't mean you ain't gonna work for this dick, you know Cucci. Everybody around me gotta be legit and produce. I don't put bitches on a pedestal."

"Nah, I'm with the shit, Ice Pick," Cucci said as she crossed her legs and looked at him seductively. "No doubt, I'm all in with that work daddy and I know how to earn my keep. I ain't no bum bitch asking for a handout. *Sheeiit,*" Cucci laughed. "Where they do that at?"

"You damn right," Ice Pick laughed with her as he sniffed a nostril full of coke. "But fuck all that, right now I need you to get back on ya knees. I'm ready for round two, ya heard."

Cucci grinned as she licked her lips and flexed her jaws. "One good dick-sucking, coming right up. I thought you would never ask."

Without hesitation she dropped to her knees and assumed the position. In a cocaine-filled daze Cucci went to work sucking and licking and pleasing her nigga. She knew her spot at Ice Pick's side wasn't guaranteed and the next bitch would love to take it, so she had to fuck and suck real good so he would realize that she was a thorough-ass rider who was worth keeping around. It was hard out there for a bitch. Keeping a good gangsta happy was no easy task, but Cucci was more than up for the challenge.

$$$$$

Honore had barely made it in her door before Sly McFly started blowing up her cell phone.

"What did you find out?" he barked as soon as she answered. "Where the hell did you go and how much info did that nigga give up?"

For the first time ever Honore found herself hiding something from the number one man in her life.

"Oh, we just chilled at some stupid lil club," she yawned real loud like she was exhausted. "I couldn't ask a whole bunch of questions all at once, but I got a lil something outta him. I mean, I'm gonna see him again so I'ma definitely probe for more, but at least I did get a lil something."

Sly McFly snorted loudly, the sound filled with disgust. "Yeah, your ass got something alright. I bet the fuck you did. Remember, them Jewish niggas want their money back and it's *your* ass that's on the line. So the next time you screw that thieving punk-ass nigga you better get more outta him than just some dick and a nut!"

CHAPTER 20

Going for the Kill

It wasn't easy to face your own death, and facing it all alone was even worse. Cancer was a killer, but payback was a mothafucka and Jewelz took comfort in the plan that was brewing in the back of her mind. There were certain things she had to do before she left this world, and she had been tracking down those two mangy dogs, Donnie Haskell and Chimp Charlie, in a quiet but determined way.

Part of the reason Jewelz had started working for Bajan Andy and his crew in the first place was to learn the necessary skills it would take to get some retribution on those who had done her wrong. For years she had fantasized about waging a suicide mission against Donnie and Charlie, with all three of them dying together in a blaze of glory that would finally satisfy her burning thirst for revenge.

It wasn't until Slick found her and put her on with his crew that Jewelz realized that her dreams could come true *and* she could body those who had wronged her without destroying herself in the process.

Bajan Andy had taught her how to strong-arm goons and bust a nigga's skull, but under Slick's training Jewelz had learned the art of stealth. She learned how to stalk her victims and execute them without them even knowing she was ever there. Jewelz was versatile and that made her excellent at role playing, infiltrating, and manipulating situations to get closer to the kill. In the assassin game she had become one of the most deadly women on the east coast.

And being part of a hit team that truly relied upon her and respected her had breathed new life into Jewelz. Although she was in the business of taking lives, she couldn't help but think that in many ways joining the Zip 'em up Crew is what had saved her own.

Being around Slick was her true peace. Slick had been there to witness her greatest moments of pain, and Jewelz wanted him to be the source of her greatest moments of joy. In all her fantasies Slick was her knight in shining armor and she was his fair lady. In her sweetest dreams Jewelz traveled the world with him and give birth to all of his beautiful seeds.

But those were just dreams. Life was a different story. Some days Jewelz felt like the most unstoppable bitch on the planet. On other days she felt vulnerable and she just wanted to be loved. But on this particular day it was the desire for revenge that weighed heavily on her soul.

I know a couple of hangouts that Donnie is known to slum around at, Jewelz thought as she stretched out in her plush bed. *Chimp Charlie seems to have slipped off the radar, but not even a New York City roach like him can hide forever. Them niggas thought they could pimp young pussies and ruin the lives of innocent girls without feeling some payback and retribution? Well they got another mothafucking think coming!*

Jewelz knew her rage could override her senses, so she picked up the phone to call Slick so she could run her plan past him real quick. She had already called him several times that night and left messages, but she figured she would try again.

She listened with a frown on her face as his phone just rang and rang. She waited and let a few minutes pass and then tried him again, but he still didn't pick up.

Fuck it, she thought, wondering what Slick was so busy doing that he couldn't pick up the phone for her. She tried not to let her imagination get the best of her, but that nigga knew she didn't just be calling him outta the blue just to chit-chat.

Yeah, fuck it, she said again. Maybe it was best to keep her plans on the low anyway. Never let your right hand know what your left hand was doing. Yeah, fuck all that. Every nigga who had ever done her wrong was gonna get something cruel back in return. Especially Donnie Hassell and Chimp Charlie. Them niggas were short-timers for this world. Jewelz was going to make sure of that. The monster that them bastards had created was gonna be the same monster who sent them both straight to hell.

CHAPTER 21

Size 'em Up

"Wow, bae, its kinda chilly out here. I should've bought a jacket," Honore said and tucked her arm underneath Slick's as they walked down a busy street in the city. Slick stood more than a full head taller than the average man, and he held her arm securely as they threaded through the thick crowd.

They were hanging out in Manhattan today, but Slick really wanted to be sniffing around in Crooklyn. He was getting more and more curious about the beautiful chick who was starting to work her way inside his heart. He wanted to know everything about her, and he especially wanted to know exactly where at in his borough Honore rested her head. Which is why he had offered to pick her up from her crib for their date today. But Honore had resisted.

"I already told you I live with my cousin not far from Fulton Street. She's real mean and nasty and she don't want no strange randoms coming by her apartment. Besides, you're a lil late to be picking me up anyway," Honore told him when he called and asked for her home address so he could jet by and snatch her up.

"I left my house a long time ago. It's a school day, remember? I'm already downtown, but you can meet me outside of that big deli by the school if you want to."

"Nah," Slick had said coldly. "The agreement was that I was gonna swing by your spot and pick you up. Do you remember that convo we had? Why you tell me I could come by if you knew you wasn't gonna be there?"

"Damn! Why you acting so hostile? I thought I *was* gonna be there. I'm in college, remember? I forgot I had to come in early and meet a few of my classmates so we could finish working on a group project. It's no biggie, Slick. Like I said, I live with my cousin and our place ain't that grand, so it's not like you missed out on nothing anyway."

But Slick felt like he *had* missed out and he was disappointed. This was some real shit they had going on. They were already past the cat and mouse stage where he pushed for the pussy and she held it out and then snatched it back. Their sheet thing was legit, and it was obvious that they had a real attraction to each other. Honore had been inside his castle twice now, yet he had never even laid eyes on hers. That shit just didn't feel right.

Swallowing his disappointment, he had agreed to meet her outside the deli by the college, and since Honore had a little free time before she needed to go study for her next class, Slick drove her across the Brooklyn Bridge and into Manhattan so they could do a little shopping.

"You seem like a real typical Brooklyn girl," Slick observed as Honore looked over her shoulder as they crossed the bridge and left New York's largest borough behind. "Don't worry. I'ma make sure you get back home."

Honore gave him the side eye. "I *am* a Brooklyn girl," she laughed as she lied. "I'm the sugar coating on the Big Apple, but there ain't nothing typical about me. You can believe that."

As they strode around the mighty borough of money-makin Manhattan, Honore snuggled up against Slick and they blended into a sea of their fellow New Yorkers.

"I gotta admit something, French Fry," Slick said as they walked through Midtown with bags full of Gucci, Louis V, and Prada from Saks Fifth Avenue. He put his arm around her waist and kissed her softly on her lips. "It feels real good hanging out with you. The way I stay on the grind and the way you stay in school, neither one of us has a whole lotta leisure time, but I'm always down to make time for you."

Honore let her lips linger on his and savored the heat that he sparked up inside her. It wasn't hard to play the lil girlfriend role with Slick at all, and she couldn't deny that she was sexually attracted to him. But putting all that lovey-dovey bullshit aside, she was determined to maintain her position and get what the hell she had come for.

She glanced up at him and reluctantly admitted to herself that if it wasn't for this dude she probably would have been shot dead the night his crew robbed that jewelry store. But even though she appreciated him, she had no room to be all mushy and emotional. At the end of the day *money* was her true motivation, and right now she didn't need no man or no fuckin love. She didn't need nothing but that damn diamond and her paper!

"I like kickin it with you too, baby," she said softly and gave him a sweet smile. She angled her body so she could rub her titty on his arm. "I wanna spend more time with you Slick, but I'm trying to keep my life as balanced as possible, know what I mean? Getting my schoolwork done and staying on top of my grades are my main priorities. I try not to deviate too much from that because I made a vow on my mother's grave that I would make something outta my life and not wind up like a lot of females that I grew up with in the projects."

"I feel you baby. I grew up in the 'jects too, so I can't be mad at that," Slick said as he grinned down at her. He admired this chick's fortitude and he was glad he had the cheese to take her shopping. He didn't mind blowing a few grand on whatever she wanted so she could rock all the latest fashions when she stepped up in that school.

"Tell the truth, Honore," he joked. "The only reason you going to college is 'cause you tryna join the NBA."

There was laughter in Slick's eyes, but he respected the fact that she was working hard for her future and he felt like he'd found something special in her. Sure, he knew the way they had met was fucked up, but he hoped in time that this girl would grow to trust him.

Honore looked confused. "The NBA? What in the world is that supposed to mean, baby?" She grinned and shook her head. "You know I'm not no athlete. I mean, I love to watch hoops and all, but I damn sure can't get into no NBA or no WNBA neither, for that matter. You seen my gigantic booty? I'm built for comfort homeboy, not for speed."

Slick smiled down at her again and admired her dimples. She was definitely a sexy muffucka, that was undeniable.

"Nah, I ain't even talking about sports, baby. I'm saying you're trying to join that other NBA. The Never Broke Again league. Nah'm sayin?"

Honore got the joke and busted out laughing. If he only knew how right he was! The Never Broke Again league! He was batting on a thousand with that one because she refused to go out like a sucka. It was money over *everything* with her, and she was just as hungry as a corner boy trying to work his way up to be a wholesaler!

The cold truth was, Honore would do whatever it took to get paid. She used the charms of her body when she had to, but most often she relied on the art of skullduggery. She was willing to lie in anybody's face, step on whoever's neck, or kill whatever the fuck got in the way of her achieving her goals.

And right now the goal was to get that goddamn diamond that Slick had stolen so Avi could sell it and she could pay back that sweet money that the Jews had fronted Joel Samuelson. But in order to do that, she had to stay on her game and out-slick the cat walking beside her who called himself Slick.

"Yeah," she said, playing coy so she could keep him talking. "Being broke is for the birds, but hey, look at you! Mad dollas, stank whip, hot crib. I can tell you ballin. Besides, you must have made off pretty good with that 'whatever' y'all stole in that red briefcase on Fulton Street that night, huh?"

Slick was almost caught off guard. His mind whirred like a computer. This girl worked right in the damn jewelry store that he had pulled a hit in. She probably knew what was in that red briefcase better than he did, and she must have thought his crew stole it and made some big bank off it.

And that's a good thing, Slick told himself, even though Whitey had disposed of the briefcase according to the BBU's instructions. *Yeah, let her think we just some regular old stick-up niggas who pulled a kick-door for some slum jewels.*

Even though she had him in his feelings and his nose was open on her guts, Slick had been real careful. He had never mentioned a word to Honore about his true profession. Everything in her little mind had come straight outta her imagination, so the conclusion she'd drawn made sense.

Slick chuckled to himself. This chick probably thought he was some kind of petty thief. Well, he was a thief all right, but he stole *lives*, not jewels.

"Well did y'all get something big outta that briefcase or nah?" she repeated.

Like a smooth-ass playa, Slick deflected her question.

"Nah," he said emotionlessly. "That wasn't no big payday for us, baby. Too much heat got aimed at that situation to mess around with it. But it's all good. I get my money by any means, so I'm not stuck scrambling in just one lane."

His words got Honore's interest because while he didn't say where her damn diamond might be, he implied that he hadn't gotten rid of it. That was a good start for now, and she believed that if she rubbed a little more titty on him and continued fucking his head up with her fluffy ass, she could squeeze the rest of the information out of him in due time.

Honore was devious and cunning. She was patient, too. She knew better than to show her hand by pushing the envelope too hard too early, so she threaded her fingers through his and let shit be.

For now…

$$$$$

The drive back to Brooklyn was one of the hottest of Honore's life. She knew Slick had felt some kinda way about not picking her up at her non-existent phony crib in Brooklyn, but she knew exactly how to get that nigga's head right back on track.

Not that it was gonna be difficult because Slick was so manned-up and self-assured with his shit that it came off sexy as fuck, and just being up under him had her moist in the crotch. She side-eyed him with a smirk as he pushed his whip down the Manhattan streets so he could take her back to school. He was comfortable in his role and his supreme confidence was enough to make any woman horny. His big old hands were capable and assured on the wheel, giving off the impression that he was in complete control of his large expensive car and of everything else in his life.

Honore's thoughts got her so worked up that she couldn't even help herself as Slick stopped for a traffic light and she reached over and placed her hand on his crotch and rubbed his soft dick.

Slick glanced at her and grinned. "Sup? You know what you doing girl? Don't fuck around and get ya'self in trouble a'ight. You might bite off more than ya lil mouth can handle."

Honore giggled and got real bold with it. In a flash she had his belt loose, his zipper down, and his dick in her hand.

"Wake up, black snake," she cooed as she squeezed and jacked his joint while he drove. "Lemme see you turn into a one-eye monster and start wrecking shit around here!"

Slick's monster didn't need no help coming to life. Before Honore could get outta her seatbelt and crawl up on her knees, his shit was on full-throttle brick and dripping at the tip.

"Yeah, that's what I'm talking about," Honore muttered as her mouth watered and her lips trembled with desire. Slick barely had time to push his seat back before she dove facedown into his lap and deep-throated his shit until it felt like his bone was gonna explode outta the top of her head.

"Goddamn, girl," Slick gasped as he drove with one hand and palmed her head with the other one. "You gonna fuck around and make me crash my shit up," he panted.

"Uh-uh," Honore disagreed from her throat as she licked and squeezed and slobbed all over his knob. She had no fear at all because she knew Slick was maintaining complete control over the situation as she gave him a blow-job that was outta this world.

Slick enjoyed that shit to the max as he drove back over the bridge. The excitement Honore generated had him feeling like a young bull as he navigated the whip and got his joint mouth-mauled at the same time.

When it was time for him to shoot his load, he grunted and moaned and his eyes damn near rolled back in his head, but he kept the car pointed steady and straight ahead.

"Yum," Honore said as she swallowed his hot seed and enjoyed the way his spurt felt sliding down her throat. "I think I just paid the tab for all the stuff you bought me today."

Slick chuckled as she tucked his dick back inside his pants. "The head was good but you don't owe me nothing, baby. My generosity ain't for sale. For the right woman it's free."

Honore stared. "Is that right?"

Slick looked over at her. Her lips were red and puffy and the thought of them sucking all over his joint was about to give him major wood again.

"That's right, baby. Ain't no dollar signs on this dick. You can get it anytime."

Honore smiled. "Well if that's the case I know of a nice hotel that's only a few blocks away. How about we swing by there and you can put some of that free love down on me in the proper way. Shit," she giggled, "I wanna cum too!"

"But what about school? Don't you have a class to go to?"

Honore waved that shit off. "I can get the notes from one of my friends. I already have an A average so missing one day won't set me back a bit."

Twenty minutes later Slick had Honore flat on her back in a swanky hotel room getting her shit smashed. With both of them naked, he lifted her in his arms and carried her over to the wall and pressed her up against it. Shifting his grip, he held her under her upper thighs as she reached between them and guided the head of his dick into that juicy spot between her legs.

Pausing at her entrance, Honore gripped his pulsating dick in her hand. She rubbed the swollen head all over her clit and shivered as electric sparks of pleasure spiraled through her entire body.

"Put it in," Slick whispered in a husky voice.

Using her tight pussy muscles, Honore slowly sucked him inside of her. His dick felt harder than solid cement and the sensation of him scraping up against her inner walls drove her wild.

Their sex thang was so strong they fucked like animals; grunting and heaving and panting and moaning. Honore had the body of his fantasies, and Slick got up in that pussy and filled her all the way up, stroking and pounding that ass like a hammer as she screamed out his name and nutted over and over again.

He carried her back to the bed so he could get his. Slick dicked her down slowly and properly, digging up in them guts and sloshing her pussy juice around with his long, strong tool. By the time they finished they had torn the sheets off the bed and both of their bodies were drenched in sweat.

Slick felt like the luckiest man in the universe as he lay back on the pillows and Honore crawled her beautiful self up in his arms. They snuggled close together, cuddling and feeling each other in their new-found attraction, and just before he closed his eyes and drifted off to sleep Slick thought to himself, *This shit feels dope as hell. A nigga might could one day fall for a girl like her.*

CHAPTER 22

Take 'em Out

It had been a long, banging ass night. One of the best in his whole fuckin life, and Slick was feeling like a sexed-out fiend as he walked his lil crooked-leg walk toward building 430.

On the outside he was back in Sometimey mode, but on the inside he was full on all the hot sex that sweet Honore had laid on him. She had dove down on him in the car while he was driving back to Brooklyn and sucked his dick like a champ until he blasted one off straight down her throat.

Honore had wanted to get her shit off too, so they had checked into a lavish hotel downtown and drank a bottle of wine and fucked like rabbits. Slick had waxed that ass for hours and he had her slobbering and grunting his name until she was hoarse and couldn't take no more. They'd fallen asleep for a couple of hours and then got up and ordered steak and shrimp from room service, and then Slick had picked her up in his strong arms and broke her off proper again.

They had spent hours in bed together and he hated making her miss her class like that, but he couldn't deny the feeling of deep satisfaction in his gut as he drove her to her classmate's crib later that night.

Never before had he put so much of his heart into making love to a chick. He almost felt like a sherm behind the way he had pulled out every trick in his book to turn her out. There wasn't no fuckin or no boning in it either. It had been pure loving making on his part, and for him to go all out like that over a girl he had practically just met and didn't even know was truly an uncommon thing.

But everything that had happened since the day he met her had been uncommon. Yeah, from the outside it prolly looked like he had slipped up on his game, but Honore was no common chick. She deserved everything that he had laid on her, and as Slick swung his pocket watch and walked stiff-legged toward his building, he couldn't wait to get with her again so he could shower her with everything she desired and then a little bit more.

Slick rounded the corner toward the building, and froze. There was a commotion going on near the porch. The cops were out there, the ambulance, the whole nine.

What the fuck? he thought, hoping like hell that none of the elderly residents had caught a heart attack and died. That was part of the pain of living in a building full of old people that you loved. They got sick, caught diseases, and sometimes they just upped and died for no reason at all.

Slick's mind ran through every apartment in the building, from the first floor all the way up to the fourteenth. There were a lot of tenants who had bad hearts, diabetes, and high blood pressure, but nobody he could think of seemed like they were knocking at death's door.

He frowned as the ambulance backed down the short walkway and then pulled off into the streets with its flashing lights turned off. The driver paused at the corner, taking his time like he wasn't in no hurry to get nowhere no time soon.

Oh shit, Slick thought, and then his worst fears were confirmed when he saw a coroner's van roll up and pull up in the walkway that the ambulance had just left.

Slick started booking it then. He moved as fast as he could while still maintaining Sometimey's distinctive half-crippled shuffle.

The yellow crime-scene tape that stretched across the front of the building brought shit home for him. And so did the crowd of old folks who were sitting on the benches and leaning on each other as they cried and shook their heads in disbelief.

"Hey, what happened?" he asked as he walked up on Pie Nichols, an older man who had lived in the building for as long as Slick could remember.

The well-lit porch was so packed with DTs and other officials from the 73rd precinct that Slick couldn't have gotten up in his apartment if he tried.

"What's wrong? Did Miss Walker have another seizure or something?"

Old man Pie shook his head.

"Naw, boy. Georgia Walker is fine. She's setting right over there on the bench." Pie put his hand on Slick's shoulder and stared at him from large, watery eyes.

"It was Maddie Taylor from the tenth floor, son. Your grandmother's best friend. They think somebody musta got a' hold of her when she was coming back from putting her trash in the incinerator. Louise Brown is the one who found her. She said Maddie was wedged in her doorway, stretched out on the floor with her feet sticking out in the hall. Whatever kinda animal attacked her, he spray-painted, "Payback" on her door.

The old man shrugged. "It was probably one of those little hoodlums who been hanging out pissing on the stairs and smoking dope all over the building. Whoever it was, he got poor Maddie and he got her real good."

Slick staggered on his feet. He felt gut-punched, and the harsh realization of the role he had played in Miss Taylor's murder almost smothered him with guilt.

"I just don't unnerstand this type of shit," Pie whispered as tears streamed from his eyes. "What kind of monster would do a poor old lady that way? Why? *Why?*"

Slick didn't answer. But he knew. Oh, muthafucka! He *knew!*

Miss Maddie's murder was payback from Handgun Goody for murking his two porch slangas, Dolla and Black Pearl. That old lady had died to pay for Slick's crimes, and the spray-painted message on her door had been meant for *him.*

$$$$$

The ambulance that had come for Miss Taylor left the neighborhood silently, but the sounds of sirens screaming in the air was nothing new. This was Brooklyn. To the longtime residents it was no different than hearing the ice cream truck coming down the block. Minutes after the ambulance left, the streets outside of the old folks building were quieting down. The crime scene was still active and the senseless act of viciousness that had been carried out by Miss Taylor's unknown attacker was being discussed behind nearly every closed door.

The crime had left the elderly residents feeling powerless and vulnerable. As the lobby and hallways emptied out and front doors slammed and were tightly locked, a handsome man crossed the street virtually unnoticed. He was dressed in a Sal's Pizza delivery uniform. His hat was low over his eyes and a sick smile was spread across his face. He had stood around on the edge of the crowd holding his pizza box and looking concerned just like everybody else, and nobody had bothered him at all. Nobody had bothered him earlier when he'd gone upstairs to make his fateful delivery on the 10th floor either.

And now, heading across the street to his beat up ride, he opened the box of pizza and looked down at the single slice that he had picked up for Miss Taylor. Since he knew for damn sure that her old ass would never be hungry again, he reached inside and took a nice big bite, then grinned coldly as he climbed in his whip and drove away.

$$$$$

It was sometime later that night, way after the coroner had carted Miss Maddie Taylor's body away and the crime scene tape had been torn down, that Slick exited his apartment and headed upstairs to the roof. He thought about Miss Taylor and swallowed a bolt of rage and shame as he remembered the message that had been spray-painted on her front door.

Payback!

Them Goode Brother bitches were the ones who were gonna pay, Slick promised the dead old lady from his heart. He remembered how she used to feed him and get him on and off the school bus when his grandmother first got sick. *I'm sorry I got you killed, Miss Taylor. But trust me, them muthafuckas is gonna PAY!*

Slick strode down the quiet hallway and hit the exit door hard. He jogged up the stairs and then stepped out onto the roof.

The stars up above looked so close and bright that he felt like he could jump up and grab one with his hand.

Moving over to the center of the roof, Slick took off his crusty boots and stripped down to his boxers. Taking his rage out on his muscles, he did a hundred quick jumping jacks, followed by a hundred deep push-ups and then two hundred solid crunches.

He rose to his feet with his buff brown body covered in a thin sheet of sweat that glistened brightly under the moonlight. With his mind focused like a laser, he went through ten complete series of mixed-martial arts routines, then shadow-boxed five imaginary enemies until he beat every last one of them bastards to death.

With his grief finally spent, Slick pulled on his pants and boots and walked bare-chested over to his pigeon coop. He checked out Dinkey, his prize messenger bird, and carefully removed the capsule that was attached to her tiny leg.

"Fuck is this?" Slick muttered under his breath as he opened it. "Another job?"

Business musta been booming in murderland because Body Bags Unlimited was handing down a new mission damn near every other day. Unfolding the square of paper Slick read the tiny words that were typed in black ink. It was only one line and it read:

Take out the Queen of Diamonds.

EMPIRE

STATE of MINE$!

(A Movie in a Book)

Episode 2

Queen of Diamonds

A NOIRE & REEM RAW JOINT

There are eight million stories in the naked city of New York.

These five are all the way live.

"Niggas out in Queens put you dead in a box,

Dishin off rocks and taking over y'all blocks!"

CHAPTER 1

Murder on the Menu

Pitch blackness reigned over the projects as Slick put his clothes back on and sat on the edge of the rooftop. It was hot and he was sweating bullets from the intense workout he had just performed. As he stretched his muscles and cooled down all he could think about was airing out the hoe-ass niggas who had beaten and strangled poor Miss Taylor to death.

Slick leaned over the rooftop railing and looked down on the chaos being perpetrated on the crime-ridden streets below. He felt like punishing somebody. Fucking somebody up. Brutal-style. And the next nigga on deck was gonna catch a mean one.

He glanced over at the wood-meshed pens that held his carrier pigeons. His favorite bird Dinky had come in a minute ago with a job slip attached to her leg. And now another bird, Dolemite, had just brought him home the specifics to accompany their latest assignment. Slick grunted in disappointment as he read that shit. The details on this job were the same as they had been on the last few jobs that had come in. Sketchy as fuck to say the least.

Slick twirled the small piece of paper he'd taken off his bird between his fingers. For once he was glad the rules of the Zip 'em up Crew dictated that every single member had to vote on every single hit. He was a decisive soldier and he had no problem calling the shots, but he was leery about sending his crew out into a killing field with only the weak amount of info that had come in with this latest assignment.

And that right there was the meat of his problem. As a boss Slick knew a successful hit depended on scoping out all reliable information before they confronted the target. The more scenarios they could anticipate in advance, the higher the chance they had of completing the job with the entire crew coming out alive and in one piece.

Yeah, there would always be X factors that arose in every situation, but as professional assassins they tried to minimize the unknowns as much as possible.

Slick's jaw tightened. He knew for a fact that them big-money cats over at Body Bags Unlimited didn't give two shits about the safety of his team. The only thing them billionaire muthafuckas gave a fuck about was handling the mission promptly and precisely. Dead hit-men were small-shit collateral damage in the criminal underworld. They were just a small cost of doing business in the world of the gunslingers.

Slick was definitely feeling some type of way. But on the real, this shit wasn't scientific. It was the murder bizz. Cut and dried. It was that ugly shit that they got paid very handsomely to do.

Slick watched the streets below and chilled as he waited for his crew to arrive. He had called for a meeting right after reading the message from the BBU. He'd forced himself to shake off the feeling of apprehension that gnawed at his stomach just from thinking about the assignment. Wasn't no need in worrying though, because his squad was tight and they were ready for whatever. The Zip 'em up Crew was the most feared group of headhunters in the whole fuckin bizz. They had earned a reputation of being cold and calculating, and most of all, of being precise. They were trained, they were certified, and they were surgical with their shit. But above all else they were gunslingers, and once they agreed to accept a contract on your life, your ass was as good as gone.

$$$$$

Jewelz was the first one to show up on the rooftop. She had on an off-white summer dress that hit her at the thigh, and it was a stark and sexy contrast to her smooth chocolate skin.

"Hey, what's going on?" she asked Slick softly. She was smelling good and looking perplexed in the face. "Damn, boy, we just had a meeting. Why you calling another one?"

"Yo," he said walking towards her. "You know that old lady Miss Taylor who be cooking me them good-ass Sunday dinners all the time, right?"

Jewelz nodded. "Yeah, her fried whities and potato salad plates be on fleek."

"Well some fuckin body got hold of her," Slick said fuming quietly. "She's dead."

"Aw, damn!" A huge wave of sympathy washed over Jewelz's face and Slick was comforted by the fact that there was somebody else in the world who could feel his pain. He would go down in a blaze of glory for any member of his set, but Jewelz was his heart and his soul. She was the only person in the entire world that he could lay his whole shit out there with, raw and raggedy. She was the only one who understood the tragedy of his history, and that's because she was the only one who had shared it.

"Damn," Jewelz muttered again and shook her head. "That poor old lady!

I'm so sorry, Slick. I know how much you loved her. What happened? Heart attack?"

"Nah, she got strangled. Choked the fuck out."

"What!?!" Jewelz shrieked. "Is you kidding me? Strangled? In this quiet-ass building?"

"The building ain't so quiet no more, baby. These days niggas be running around here pissing on the stairs and wildin out on the porch at all times of the night. I think it was that nigga Handgun Goody who did it, yo," Slick growled from deep in his chest. "I *know* it was that savage-ass bitch!"

Jewelz looked confused. "Goody? Why in the world would he wanna erase a sweet old lady?"

"It was retaliation," Slick said quietly. "I told you I had to dirt nap some of his lil homies. I cold snuffed them bitch-niggas out. And Miss Taylor was his payback."

"Hold up," Jewelz was still confused. "Does Goody know it was you who did his crew?"

Slick shook his head. "I doubt it. Them cats woulda set my grandmother's crib on fire by now if they thought I had something to do with it. Nah, that dope-slangin nigga don't know who it was. Everybody sleeps on Sometimey. Don't none of them niggas have the kind of eyes it takes to see me coming at 'em."

"So why do you think Miss Taylor's murder was specifically about *you* then?" Jewelz didn't sound convinced.

"It was about whoever slumped his lil mutts! Goody don't know *exactly* who to go gunning for, but he knows something popped off right here in this fuckin building!"

"Damn, baby," Jewelz said, stepping up close to him, "I'm sorry Miss Taylor is dead and I hope she didn't suffer too much."

Slick opened his arms and welcomed her warm, comforting touch. Her plump titties grazed his chest and her hands touched his thighs. Slick was seeking comfort but Jewelz was seeking something else. And what she wanted was giving him major wood.

Standing there under the glow of moonlight Jewelz pressed her cheek against Slick's hard chest and wrapped her arms around his waist. His body was still revved up from his workout and heat was coming off him in waves. And heat was coming off Jewelz's body too.

Slick struggled inside. He was turned the fuck on by this girl even though he didn't wanna be. He wanted her so fuckin *bad,* even though he didn't wanna want her! He lowered his head and pressed his lips to hers. Jewel opened up to him like a sweet blossoming rose. Her mouth was watering and her groin was pressing against his wood. Slick gripped her juicy ass-cheeks in his palms and grinded his hard dick up against her. He was reaching deeply between her mounds to get a swipe of that hot pussy when the door opened on the roof and Whitey stepped into view.

Slick broke the embrace. He reached down and grasped Jewelz's arms. Her skin felt hotter than an oven. He took a deep breath and stepped backward. Outta range of that desperate desire in her that he just couldn't bring himself to satisfy.

"Yo whattup, Whitey," Slick greeted his manz as he turned away for a second so he could adjust his bulging meat. He walked away without looking back because he knew exactly what he was gonna see in Jewelz's eyes. Feelings.

Minutes later the entire posse was fully assembled on the rooftop. They exchanged greetings and showed each other mad love. Then Slick pulled out his assignment scrap and laid the cards out on the table.

"We got another job," he said quietly. "Y'all already know the drill. We need to decide if we're gonna make a move on this shit or not."

He grilled his crew one by one.

"We got a mission to eliminate somebody called the Queen of Diamonds. We need to strike at three a.m. and the location will be a beauty parlor somewhere in Jamaica, Queens," Slick explained. "We don't have a visual description of her or nothing, but according to the BBU she'll be easy to spot because she'll be the only chick getting her hair done in the middle of the night."

Right on cue Wild Man bucked.

"Damn, here we go again! Yo, what's up with all this stupid shit? No pictures, no description, no real name, no details—if them BBU muthafuckas want us to erase somebody why don't they just tell us exactly who it is?"

Slick just shrugged. He didn't blame his homey for going hard, but there wasn't shit else he could tell him.

"So whattup, Slick?" Wild Man kept right on basing. "Them uppity clowns want us to go in ass-naked again and expose our throats like a bunch of blind mice, right?"

"Ay, I'm just delivering the message," Slick said calmly. "I'm giving you the same information the fuckin bird gave me."

Wild Man was still on one. "Nah, I'm itchin to make that paper just like the next muh'fucka but these BBU hits is starting to sound like suicide missions! Fuck that. Ain't none of us hurting that bad for cash that we gotta go for this one, dawg. By the way, what's the price tag on this Queen of Diamond's crown?"

"The same as it was on the last job," Slick answered. "Double the regular the pay."

Wild Man, Jewelz, and Noodles all shot each other a look. They were all about clockin that extra doe but they weren't completely sold on the job just yet.

"Nah, fuck that," Wild Man shook his head. "The hit is in Queens, right? So that's my territory and it makes *me* the lead man on the case. Them BBU niggas can *suck my dick!*"

He glanced at his hittas and grinned.

"Grab ya bird and send them bastards a message that ya crew wants *triple* the loot this time! Since they wanna send us in blind as bats we wanna be *compensated* for that shit. Y'all feel me on that?"

Whitey was dressed in a pizza delivery man's uniform and standing on Slick's right. He locked eyes with Slick real quick and then he chimed in with his usual level-headed common sense.

"I feel where you're coming from, Wild Man," he said calmly. "But double the pay for a one-target hit isn't too bad. I mean, we ain't the only team out here trying to get on with jobs, you know. If we fool around and get too greedy they'll just cross us off the roster and go with a cheaper crew. I'd be willing to do it for just the regular fee, so I'm good with double pay all day long."

Slick shook his head. "Nah, man. I'ma have to roll with Wild Man on this one, homey. These muthafuckas can't keep feeding us half-assed information and expect us to stay on our toes. If they wanna pass over us and hire somebody else, then let 'em. Fuck it. This ain't no video game we playing. If one of us drops we're maggot food," he continued. "There ain't no magical re-set button that'll bring us back to life so we can get up and try this shit again. I wanna take the job, but I say they gotta triple our payment this time too."

All eyes were now on Jewelz, who stood deep in thought with her arms folded over her chest and her foot tapping a hole in the ground.

Finally she shrugged. "Look, if they wanna give us these big boy hits then we need that big boy *paper!* Tell them rich bitches to cough that bread up! If they can offer us double then they can damn sure afford triple."

It was all on Noodles, who had turned his back on the group and was looking up at the sky in thought. He had a woman and three kids at home depending on him and they had shit they needed. Without turning around he pulled his tablet from his pocket then scribbled something on the screen with his finger. He passed it over his shoulder to Jewelz.

"I'm cool with whatever y'all wanna do," Jewelz read his words out loud. "If y'all wanna pop some Queen then that bitch is a done bun. Let's get it for triple."

Slick looked around at his posse one final time and then nodded.

"A'ight. Then that's it. I'll send the bird out with a message requesting our new price," he said firmly. "If our request comes back approved then we get to work. If it don't, then fuck it. Just keep in mind that if we end up doing this shit I'ma need everybody to be sharp and on point. We don't know what to expect so we got zero room for slip ups. We squeeze first and ask questions next year. Got it?"

The entire crew nodded in agreement and then they dispersed for the night to wait for further instructions.

CHAPTER 2

Only in New York

At exactly 8:12am the next morning the No. 4 train was barreling along the tracks as it headed uptown toward Grand Central Station in Manhattan.

Hundreds of passengers were crammed in shoulder-to-shoulder on the bench seats while even more riders were standing up holding onto the shiny silver poles and overhead bars.

The crowd was a mixed one. Young, old, and everything in between. The busy morning commute seemed the same as it did every other day. Passengers were either catching some quick zzz's, reading on electronic devices, or fiddling with their cell phones. It was a regular train ride, on a regular morning, with regular New York people.

Right up until the shit hit the fan and all hell broke loose.

The uptown express had just pulled out of the 36th Street station and entered the dark tunnel when a loud commotion broke out near the end of the subway car.

A heavyset white man was leaning against the conductor's door when suddenly he reached out and snatched a little boy right out of his mother's grasp.

The woman's shocked scream nearly got lost in the roar of the train, but the terror in her eyes as she lunged for her child was clear as day.

"Get your fuckin hands off my son!" the young sista screeched as she lunged forward and fought her way past the other passengers.

She had been holding onto a pole and minding her own business when the crazy-looking white man just upped and snatched her child. Terrified, she knocked a little old man outta her way and clawed toward her baby. But she stopped cold dead in her tracks when she saw what the deranged stranger was doing to her four-year-old little boy.

Dude had her baby yoked up in a chokehold. The kid's fragile neck was tightly compressed between the man's forearm and his jiggly body, and the tip of a glittering silver pistol was jammed down into the child's ear.

"Stay back!" the pyscho-looking white man yelled as he pressed back against the door that led to the next train car. He was short and flabby and he looked like he was in his late-twenties or early thirties. His hair was wild and greasy and he had on a pair of raggedy blue jeans and a grimy white t-shirt.

"Stay back or I'll blow his fuckin brains out!" he shrieked. "I'll *kill* this lil fucker! I swear I will!"

A nutcase brandishing a loaded gun was never a good thing on a crowded subway, and the good people of New York City started ducking and diving as they peeped what was going down.

"*A gun*! Run! *He's got a goddamn gun!*" Desperate screams of sheer panic rose in the air as the passengers stampeded together and sought to find cover and concealment. But trapped on the train in the middle of the underground subway system, there was no place to run.

Two teenage boys fought their way toward the opposite end of the train-car so they could escape into the next compartment, but the door was locked. Trapped, they banged their fists on the glass and tried to get the attention of the oblivious riders on the other side of the partition.

The rest of the passengers pressed backwards and fought to get out of bullet range. Two elderly Asian men sitting in the double-seater jumped up and tried to push their way into the middle of the panicked crowd, but the crowd spit their asses right back out again.

The young mother stood there in shock. In a jam-packed train-car she found herself facing a crazed gunman all alone. She was just a teenager and all she was trying to do was get to 42nd Street so she could go on a job-training interview. She had brought her little boy with her because her mother was sick and she couldn't find nobody else to watch him.

"Mister gimme my son back!" she screamed as she pleaded with the insanity in the gunman's eyes. Her mama would just *kill* her if she let something happen to her precious grandchild!

"Jamel, don't cry," the young mother called out helplessly to her son. "Mommy's right here, baby," she reached her arms out and tried to soothe him. "Everything is gonna be okay. Baby, don't cry. Somebody help me! Please, somebody *help!*"

But every last one of her fellow passengers was crouched into a frightened huddle and they had all abandoned her. Every last one of them except for a sucka-looking white guy in a Brooks Brothers suit. He sat there holding a bag and watching the action as he lounged calmly in the two-seater directly to her right.

Tearing her eyes off her son, the girl glanced into the crowd panting desperately. "Why is y'all just standing there?" she shrieked. "Please! He's got my baby, yo! Somebody please *do* something!"

Still, nobody moved.

"Does anyone have a signal down here?" a white woman hollered from her ducked-down position in the middle of the pack. "Dial 9-11! Someone should try to dial 9-11!"

"I'm gonna kill him!" the psychopath hollered as the train roared down the tracks. His beady eyes were wild and full of rage. "This little fucker's gonna *die!*"

"*Noooo!*" the young mother pleaded as she desperately reached for her son again. Her baby's eyes were bulging outta his head and a trail of saliva slid out the corner of his mouth. The look on his face sent a spear piercing into her heart, and she was just about to go for broke and bum rush his ass, but the sight of the gun's barrel pressed down in her baby's ear checked her feet right in place.

"Mister what do you *want?*" she shrieked as she held her hands up in surrender. "We don't even *know* your crazy ass! Why are you doing this to us? *Why?*"

"Because I'm *Jesus!!!*" the deluded man gave her a sickening smile. "I'm the holy fuckin spirit and I'm gonna nail this lil black bastard to a cross and drink his fuckin blood!"

"*Noooo!*" the terrified young girl stomped her feet and wailed. "Please gimme back my baby!"

"He's got twenty seconds," the psycho said quietly. The deranged smile fell from his face and he squeezed his arm tighter around the boy's neck, lifting the gasping kid off his feet.

"I'm counting to twenty," he said as the little boy kicked and wheezed in his arms. "And then I'm gonna blow this lil sinner's brains out!"

"*Noooo!*" the young mother shrieked again. She looked into the crowd one more time.

"Can y'all help me?" she begged desperately. "Can *anybody* help me?"

Her question was met with fear, horror, and even compassion in the eyes of her fellow passengers. But none of them, not even the buff-ass men, were willing to risk taking a bullet to help save a small child.

The crazy man began to count out loud.

"*One, two, three, four . . .*"

"C'mon, Mister!" The young girl snapped. "Stop fuckin playin! That's my *baby,* man . . . we didn't even *do* nothin to you . . ."

"*. . .five, six, seven . . .*"

The young mother turned her back on her child one last time as she searched the crowd for a savior. She begged God to bring forth just one brave soul who had the courage to rescue her little man. Just one!

"*. . .eight, nine, ten, eleven, twelve . . .*"

"Mister can you help us?" she took a step forward and pleaded with a tall brother who had neat dreadlocks hanging around his shoulders. Dude's chest swelled as he inhaled a deep breath and made a move like he was getting his courage up. But a quick glance down the barrel of the psycho's gun checked him where he stood and he dropped his eyes in shame and looked away.

"Can you?" The girl implored the biggest dude she saw. He was a muscled-up Hispanic guy dressed in sweatpants and a Brooklyn Nets t-shirt. "Please, Mister. Can you help me get this crazy maniac offa my son?"

Behind her, dude's voice was steady as he counted out clear and loud. "*...thirteen, fourteen . . .*"

The train was slowing down now as it pulled into the next stop.

"*Forty-Second Street,*" the conductor's voice crackled over the loudspeaker. "*Grand Central Station.*"

"*...fifteen, sixteen . . .*"

The young mother turned back around, completely defeated. "Jamel," she moaned about to pee on herself from fear. "Oooh, *baby!*"

She reached toward her son and braced herself for a real-life nightmare.

"Mommy loves you, baby. Mommy *loves* you!"

The train was grinding to a stop and frantic passengers started waving their arms and screaming out to the people who were waiting on the platform.

"Call the cops!" several people shouted and banged on the windows. "He snatched a kid! He's got a gun! Call the cops!"

Dude's voice grew even louder. "*...seventeen, eighteen. . .*"

The little boy's body went stiff and his eyes rolled back.

The train was at a complete stop now and the hydraulics hissed loudly as the doors got ready to open.

"*Nineteen—*"

Suddenly the white businessman sitting in the two-seater stood up and charged toward the exit doors. Carrying his bag, he reached in the pocket of his Brooks Brothers pants and withdrew a chrome object and—

Boom!

The gun blast sent glass flying and terrified passengers diving for cover as they dropped to the floor and held purses and briefcases over their heads like they were Teflon shields.

"*Jamel!*" the young mother screamed as she lunged for her child.

The body of the hostage-taker slid slowly to the glass-strewn floor. A single bullet had pierced his Adam's apple and torn out his larynx. He slumped down on his ass and made frantic whistling noises as he gasped for breath through the bright-red hole in his throat.

The train doors slid open and the waiting crowd spilled inside. Their eyes were on scan mode as they looked for vacant seats. But the moment they peeped the bloody carnage they immediately pressed backwards, shrieking in surprise as the frightened passengers on the train rushed the doors and tried to push their way out.

And in the midst of all the hysteria, while the young mother fell to her knees and clutched her precious little man-man in her grateful arms, not one person focused on the well-dressed gunslinger as he walked off the train.

Broken glass crunched beneath the soles of his two-thousand dollar shoes as he stepped lively through the station, moving like he was late for an important business meeting.

Moments later, without taking a single glance toward the life he had just taken, or the one he had just saved, the handsome gunslinger stashed his .38 Ruger in the pocket of his Brooks Brothers suit, then he blended into the crowded sea of other white businessmen and quickly disappeared.

CHAPTER 3

Cookies and Coke

Middle School 23 was located in the heart of Jamaica, in the quintessential town of Queens. It had a large minority population and quite a few of its students came from broken homes that fell well below the poverty line. A good number of their fathers were serving time in New York's penal system, and many young mothers were living for the city and just trying to get by.

Which is why when Fat Donnie Hassell, the warden of St. John's Home for Boys, was invited to D.A.R.E. Day to speak about the pitfalls of drugs and crime, he had jumped on the invitation.

Fat Donnie had stayed up late the night before writing his speech. He wrote all kinds of motivating shit and made sure to hit key points about how pursuing a life of crime could land you in a juvenile detention facility such as the one he ran for criminal-minded young boys.

Fat Donnie knew all about criminal-minded boys because he had been one himself. He'd been born and raised in the belly of Brooklyn, and he'd done a whole lotta wild, scandalous shit in his youth. He had an appetite for young, tender meat and it was only through sheer luck that he had been able to turn his life around, although truth be told, Fat Donnie was still a criminal at heart.

He arrived at the middle school bright and early and was escorted to the principal's office by a shriveled-up white woman in a pale pink dress.

He was ushered into a small reception room right outside the auditorium along with all the other program participants. There were at least six speakers scheduled to go onstage. Donnie was planning to dip out and take care of a little business before returning to work, so he needed folks to keep their bullshit speeches short and sweet.

Trays of freshly baked cookies and warm brownies had been set out by the D.A.R.E. organizers and a heavenly aroma was in the air. Never one to miss out on anything free and sweet, Fat Donnie headed straight for the cookies. He scooped up a napkin and palmed six giant chocolate-chip cookies in his paws, then he grabbed a paper cup of Coke and let his eyes scan the room.

There were several men and women standing around chatting in tight groups. Donnie recognized a few faces from local law enforcement and social service agencies but nobody acknowledged him or invited him to join them.

Donnie said fuck it as he stood on the edges of the crowd gobbling cookies and brownies and slurping down cup after cup of Coke. With his jaws steady moving, he let his mind wander to the real reason that he had agreed to come to Jamaica, Queens early this morning.

It was said that you could take the boy outta the hood, but you couldn't take the hood outta the boy, and Donnie knew that shit to be true. After years of living the grime-ball life he had moved on to bigger and better things, but he had never been fully rehabilitated or taken his fingers out of certain sweet, tight little pies. Matter fact, it was almost laughable that he had ended up in charge of a facility full of hardheaded young crooks and thieves when he was the biggest criminal of them all.

Donnie's plan for today was to get up on that microphone and spit some nonsense at these little convicts-in-the-making who would probably end up under the jail no matter what the hell he hollered at them.

And when he was done, Donnie planned to head over to a local family-owned pie shop where he would conduct a little give-and-take transaction in a parking stall behind the store. He would give the owner a couple of crisp greenbacks to get him to send his pretty teenaged niece outside, and then Donnie would take as many licks as he wanted from her sweet young pie.

Donnie grinned as he scooped up another handful of cookies and two more brownies. Peddling teenaged pussy from sleazy motel rooms was way in his past, but getting up in some tight young cat was still something he did as often as possible.

He was raising his cup of Coke to his lips when a stylish young black woman staggered away from a nearby group and started coughing violently.

She had on a tight black skirt and shiny red high heels, and Donnie stood frozen as she stumbled backward, pounding on her chest and making horrible choking noises like all the air was being squeezed from her body.

Concerned murmurs of, "Oh my God! Are you okay?" went up in the air, and the woman, who Donnie couldn't help noticing had the prettiest legs and the fattest ass he had seen in a good long while, bent over in her black skirt clutching her throat and coughing like crazy.

"Somebody do the Heimlich!" an old white lady screamed. Three men moved toward the coughing chick, but before they could reach her she lunged at Donnie and snatched his cup of Coke right outta his hand. Desperately, she slurped from it in several long swallows.

"S-s-sorry," she said, handing the cup back to him with tears streaming from her beautiful eyes. Donnie stood there with his mouth full of half-chewed brownies looking dumb as fuck as he eyed her shapely hips in that lil tight skirt.

The chick sniffled, then coughed real hard a few more times and stomped her foot.

"Whew!" she cleared her throat and finally said. Her pretty brown eyes glistened with tears as she flashed him a beautiful white smile. "You saved me! That cookie must have gone down the wrong pipe!"

Collective murmurs went up in the room as everyone smiled and breathed a sigh of relief.

"Thanks again," the sexy young thang said and then reached out and gave him a quick hug.

Fat Donnie was standing there thinking she smelled just like a fuckin honey bun when a secretary poked her head in the door and announced that it was time for the participants to take the stage.

Eyeballing the chick's wiggling round ass as it did amazing things to her skirt, Donnie tossed back the rest of his Coke and headed for the door.

$$$$$

The auditorium was packed full of noisy twelve and thirteen-year-olds and Donnie was slated to be the third speaker to address them. The first person to take the mic was the school's D.A.R.E. resource officer, and by the time dude was halfway through his speech Donnie knew he was in trouble.

He had to take a shit.

A really fuckin big one.

He shifted his weight in his chair, then gapped his legs open and laced his fingers over his gut to hold back the rumblings.

Too many muh'fuckin brownies, big boy, he chastised himself as he belched under his breath.

He frowned. That belch tasted nasty as fuck and it burned the hell outta his throat too.

By the time dude on the mic finished flapping his trap Donnie was in terrible pain. It felt like somebody had shoved both their fists up his asshole and grabbed his intestines and was wringing them back and forth.

"Hurry the fuck up," Donnie whispered as the other panel members on the stage clapped politely for the D.A.R.E. officer as he finished up his speech.

The next person up was a blond woman who was representing the department of social services. Donnie could see her mouth moving but he couldn't hear a damn thing she was saying.

His throat was burning even worse now, and all kinds of agonizing burps were rising up outta his boiling stomach. He was sweating too. Real bad. Even his ass felt hot. Like if he stood up he'd leave a stankin wet puddle of water in his chair.

By the time it was Fat Donnie's turn at bat he could barely talk and the kids were tired of listening anyway. The applause from the crowd sounded like a freight train rumbling through his brain. He tried to smile as he stumbled toward the podium and grabbed at the microphone.

"A'ight now, whaddup!" he said, trying to sound cool over the noisy pre-teens. He mopped his dripping forehead with his soggy cookie napkin, then held up his hand and got ready to use his jail warden's voice to grab the wildin kids's attention.

Y'all lil niggas shut the fuck up so I can speak real quick and then go find me a bathroom, is what Donnie wanted to say, but instead he swallowed the ball of fire in his throat and looked down at his speech.

To his horror the words were swimming all over the page. Not one of them shits would hold still so he could read it! Donnie looked out into the sea of juvenile faces and lowered his mouth to the mic so he could greet them again. But it wasn't the words of his speech that came out.

"I gotta *shit!!!*" he blurted into the mic then he clutched his stomach and belched real loud.

Adolescent laughter cut through the air and then a long stream of blood suddenly exploded from Donnie's mouth as he collapsed down hard on one knee.

Sweat poured down his jiggly cheeks in waves. He farted and filled his tighty-whitey drawers with a stream of soft warm poo-poo. Groaning in pain, he sank further down to the floor and wobbled there unsteadily.

A young girl in the front row of the audience screamed, and the lady from social services jumped out of her chair and rushed over to catch him before he collapsed.

But her lil ass was no match for Fat Donnie Hassell. His bulky, sweat-coated body slipped through her grasp like a pig greased with butter. And as his body thudded to the floor and the lights started to fade, Donnie's eyes flew open wide.

Pandemonium was kicking off in the auditorium full of screaming kids and the last thing Donnie saw was the gorgeous black chick with the sexy stiletto pumps and the wiggling ass.

That ass was still wiggling and jumping like Jordan as she got up from her chair and walked over to where he lay. Standing over him, she held up a white napkin with the word *Jewelz* written on it in bold black magic marker so he could see it very clearly.

"Now *you's* the young pussy getting fucked!" she snapped as she crumpled the napkin in her fist and spit dead down in his twisted face. Brimming with more than ten years worth of pent up rage, Jewelz threw her middle finger in the air and tooted up her lips again. She gathered all the spit that was left in her mouth and shot another thick wad down in that foul fucka's face.

And then she click-clacked her red high-heels quickly off the stage.

CHAPTER 4

The Great White Hope

Whitey Reynolds moved with a purpose as he emerged outta the belly of the screaming underground beast. He walked calmly up the stairs from Grand Central Station and began to move at the same pace as everyone else in the swaying New York City crowd.

Although he was a natural-born killer and one of the most dangerous men in the city, you couldn't tell it by his clean-cut appearance or by his youthful, handsome face.

Looking extra-sharp in his Brooks Brothers business suit, Whitey strode down the street with the confidence of a privileged white man in America.

He stayed in the thick of the moving crowd, blending in without even trying to because two out of every three people looked just like him: white, male, large, and in charge.

As he walked a cold shadow of ice crept into Whitey's piercing blue eyes. While he capitalized off false perceptions for a living, right now he gave less than a fuck about what people thought he looked like. For him, it was all about the red briefcase that the Zip 'em up Crew had been ordered to stash in a Manhattan locker after their Fulton Street hit.

Slick had sent his most trusted soldier to make that drop, and like a good little capo Whitey had done exactly what he was told to do. He had stashed that briefcase in a locker all right. But he stashed it in a joint that was ten spaces to the left of where he was *supposed* to stash it.

The feeling that had surged through him when he opened that shit up and saw what was inside had been indescribable. It was like tearing into a Cracker Jack box and discovering a million dollar jewel inside.

It was a gorgeous high-carat diamond and Whitey had pocketed the jawn knowing he'd have to lay low for a little while until shit cooled off. And while he was waiting he had done some homework and learned that the jewel in the briefcase was on the close-screen radar of both the Pinkerton Agency and the FBI.

The diamond had been stolen from a major New York City jewelry store, and news of the theft was being broadcasted twenty-four/seven on every television station in the tri-state area. The suspected thief was a dead guy named Joel Samuelson and he had worked as an executive at the New York Diamond and Jewelry Exchange.

Whitey had checked with a couple of his sources in law enforcement, and according to their reports Samuelson was supposed to be transporting the diamond to a trade show when he made a detour and ended up with his throat cut and his nuts chopped off in a downtown hotel room.

Security officials at the Diamond and Jewelry Exchange were speculating that Samuelson had either been killed and then robbed, or he'd sold the diamond and gotten himself killed for the cash. Either way he was gone and so was their five-million dollar gemstone.

After hearing that shit Whitey could only grin. How in the hell Joel Samuelson's stolen five-million dollar diamond had ended up in the hands of an elderly black man in a run-down jewelry shop in Brooklyn was anybody's guess. But Whitey didn't really give a fuck how it had gotten there. All he cared about was how he was going to offload that shit and rake in the cash it would bring on the underground market.

But in order to trade stolen goods on the black market you had to know a black market trader. And just as soon as he got that diamond out of the locker where he had stashed it, Whitey Reynolds was gonna find himself one.

Because something real big had been about to go down in that jewelry store on Fulton Street the night of the hit. Whitey was sure of it. That diamond was being dropped off there for a real good reason, and like the relentless bloodhound that he was, Whitey was gonna sniff out why.

He gave no fucks that he was disobeying BBU orders, and sliming around behind his team's back didn't fuck with him not even a little bit. Whitey was used to playing both sides of the fence. Pretending to be dependable, reliable, levelheaded, and responsible were skills that he'd practiced to a tee. But in reality they hid his truest nature. The gutter nature of a criminal-minded sneak-thief.

Plus, it didn't hurt that he had the right looks and the right attitude, and that he fronted like he didn't have a problem playing the number three or four man on the totem pole. Nah, Whitey Reynolds was a real actor, and getting people to sleep on him was his real talent. It was like he had the word "Trustworthy" stamped on his forehead and "Honest" stamped on his pale white ass.

Sure, his boy Slick was bound to pop off if he found out he was getting fucked sideways, but Whitey would worry about the Zip 'em up Crew later. Right now he needed to go retrieve that stolen diamond and make contact with whoever it was who had been waiting to receive it at that jewelry store.

Breaking out from the center of the moving crowd, Whitey walked past a bagel shop that smelled better than freshly powdered pussy. Moving closer so he could peer into the clear glass display window he cursed under his breath at the sight he saw reflected back at him.

Blood.

In a feathery spray pattern. All over the right side of his suit and the collar of his starched white shirt.

Damn! Even a harmless-looking white dude couldn't walk around New York City looking like he had just sparked off a bloody massacre.

Crazy son-of-a-bitch, Whitey thought as he pictured the fat slob that he had just slumped on the train in cold blood. What the hell was that maniac thinking, snatching up a lil kid and pressing the pistol to him like that? That psycho piece of shit had deserved two fuckin bullets. One to the dome and one to the nuts!

Whitey was in a fickle line of business and the rules changed every day. Most targets he whacked for money, but others he whacked for personal satisfaction. This morning's kill had come to him unplanned and unexpected, but it had definitely been satisfying. Satisfying on a deep and intimate level, because something about that young mother on the train, with her pretty chocolate skin and gorgeous hair, had reminded him of Jewelz.

Whitey jetted inside Macy's and purchased a fresh white business shirt and put it on in the bathroom. Then he made his way to the locker where he had stashed his take.

The red briefcase was right where he'd left it. After slipping his fingers inside the white cloth bag and pocketing the glittering jewel, he ditched the briefcase in a garbage can, then went outside and hailed the first passing taxicab he saw.

Feeling like five million big ones, Whitey grinned as he jumped in the backseat and barked out the address to the downtown Brooklyn jewelry store where the answers to all his questions waited.

CHAPTER 5

When Larceny Sets In

Cucci was standing at the reception desk of the New York Diamond and Jewelry Exchange wearing a classy peach designer dress and a fake smile. She talked shit in her head about every customer who came in the door, but no matter what she was thinking she kept a poised and professional look about her while she worked the front counter.

Cucci had mastered the art of hiding behind a mask, but she stayed scheming. She got so good at scoping people out that she could spot a customer who wasn't gonna buy shit and was just there to window shop as soon as they stepped through the door.

She also kept her eyes open for any unsavory characters who might be looking to score a lick. It was strictly against company rules, but she kept a baby Glock in her purse because she didn't put shit past nobody. Cucci wasn't willing to die to protect the store, but she was damn sure willing to spray somebody to save her own ass. She knew the consequences of not being prepared for the worst in this game because there was too much money out there to be made and lost. The murder of Joel Samuelson had confirmed that theory. Cucci knew there was always somebody out there plotting and planning to get the drop on an unsuspecting sucka because she stayed looking for a sucka her damn self.

And right now she was plotting and planning on her sucka-ass cousin, Honore. That heffa had called in sick first thing that morning and when Cucci had just hit her up to find out what was wrong, Honore had answered the phone sounding like she was getting turnt up.

"Ga'head with that, Slick!" Honore had squealed happily before she even said hello. "Boy you need to stop playing!"

"Slick?" Cucci had demanded, her ears on big alert. "Who the hell is *Slick?*"

"My new friend," Honore had giggled. "He's that dude I was telling you about. The one who snatched me up that night and tried to kidnap me. I'm just lining his ass up but this nigga is shook on this shit for real. He invited me out to a real nice restaurant for breakfast this morning and he just went up front to pay the bill."

"Bitch you out somewhere eating breakfast with a kidnapper? The secretary said you called in sick!"

Honore had sucked her teeth. "I'm sick of that fuckin job, that's what I'm sick of!"

"'Don't try to change the subject! You ditched work to go eat out with some fuckin stick-up kid?"

Honore sucked her teeth. "See I knew I shouldn'ta told you nothing. I'm still *working* bitch, I just ain't at the job right now."

Slick. Cucci was nobody's fool, and her gut instincts told her that her cousin was laying deep in the cut and hiding something real important. Because not too long ago when she had asked Honore straight up if she knew what them stick-up kids who snatched her looked like, the bitch had dead-ass lied.

"Whatever, I need a fill-in and I was thinking maybe we could go to the nail salon together. You wanna hook up when I get off work?" Cucci asked.

"Uh-uh," Honore said real quick. "I'll catch up with you tomorrow. Sly's taking me back to the Boatel tonight."

The Boatel? Cucci thought angrily as she hung up in Honore's face and stood at the reception desk tapping her finger loudly on the wood. *We supposed to be a money-making team but she be steady holing up with Sly at that fuckin Boatel plotting on the solo tip! Them two are cookin up something sweet. I can feel it. I know for damn sure they ain't out there relaxing on the water sipping Margaritas and getting no goddamn tans! Lately, Honore be keeping her some closed lips when I come around. And that means the bitch got something real heavy hanging off her bra strap. Well, two can play the shady game! I know she had something to do with Joel getting murked and with that diamond going missing too! Now the bitch tryna play a hustla like me for a sucka? I got something for her ass! Family or no goddamn family, if I find out she's holding out on me then I'm getting in that ass and all bets are off!*

CHAPTER 6

Diamonds are Forever

Walking up to the Brooklyn jewelry store in broad daylight was nowhere near as thrilling as rolling up brandishing a .44 under the dark of night.

Whitey was all charm and smiles as he pushed through the front door of the Fulton Street shop. The interior was cool and well-lit and displayed no signs of the bloody carnage that had gone down inside not too long ago. Whitey's gaze swept over the room as he strode over to the counter. He was happy to note that there were no other customers in the small showroom.

"Can I help you?" a mousy-looking white girl at the counter greeted him. She looked like an albino rabbit with her severe overbite and turned-down lips. She was young, less than twenty he guessed. The age where she should have been dating and dancing, but with her bucked teeth, pale skin, and crossed eyes, she was not attractive in the least.

"Can I help you?" she asked again.

"You'd better hope so," Whitey said, grinning as he faced her and leaned both elbows on the display glass.

Quicker than shit his hands snaked out and he jabbed into her flesh with his stiff thumb, damn near impaling her scrawny throat. She gasped and reached for her neck and he snapped his hands closed tight. He gripped the meat of her throat and dug in deeply with his fingers, threatening to tear her entire esophagus out with his bare hands.

Whitey waited for her to go limp, his smile never fading as the panicked girl kicked her feet and clawed at her neck and wheezed. Froth dripped from her lips as her eyes bulged and her back arched and her face turned bright crimson.

From the back room came the sound of rushing feet. An elderly man dressed in Jewish garb exploded in the room with a baseball bat held high over his head.

"You evil piece of shit!" the man screamed, swinging the bat so hard it almost slipped from his grasp. "Let her go!" he cried out. His aim was off and he totally missed Whitey as the bat cracked and shattered the clear glass of the jewelry counter. "Let her go!"

Whitey released the ugly chick and was on top of the Jewish man before her unconscious body hit the floor.

Their struggle was brief and uneventful. Whitey never even broke a sweat as he disarmed the older man and then dragged him into the back room and subdued him with a pair of flexi-cuffs. He pulled out his handkerchief and stuffed it deeply into the man's mouth, gagging the skinny old bastard until he choked.

Leaving the man writhing on the floor, Whitey made another trip into the front area to flip the OPEN sign to CLOSED. Then he locked the door and lifted the unconscious young clerk in his arms and carried her into the back room too.

Once there, he set the girl down then went about emptying his bag and organizing himself for the very important task he was about to perform. He tied the girl's hands behind her back and stuffed a wad of paper towels into her slack mouth. She started coming to when her obstructed airway made it difficult to breathe, and by that time Whitey felt like a surgeon: prepped and ready to operate.

"Okay, Mr. Lovitz," Whitey said, addressing the Jewish man by name as he lit the small blow-torch he'd brought with him and directed the burning tip at the now fully-awakened young girl's eyes.

"Noooo!" the old man cried past his gag in terror, confirming Whitey's suspicion that he was her father. "No-no-no-no-no-no!" he said, which came out sounding like, "Oh-oh-oh-oh-oh-oh!"

Whitey grinned and pulled back a bit. "Are you saying no? You don't want me to do that? You mean you don't wanna smell her eyeballs as they boil in their sockets and slide down her face like slimy gray gloop?"

The old man shook his head furiously and Whitey's grin widened. "Well, if you don't want me to do that then let's make a deal. I'm going to ask you a simple question and you're going to give me a simple answer, okay? The deal is, I'm only going to ask you once and you're going to tell me the truth. Because if you don't this ugly bitch'll be licking poached eyeball juice off her fuckin chin, you got it?"

$$$$$

Less than thirty minutes later the old man's hands were trembling as he untied his precious daughter and removed the soggy wad of paper towels from her gaping mouth.

"There, there," he said, as he cradled her pale face in his wrinkled old hands and rocked her back and forth. "It's okay dear," he told her as she cried softly in his arms. He felt terrible about the horrible thing that had almost happened to her, and he knew he was deeply responsible for the fright she had endured.

The old man cursed himself. He should have known something like this would happen sooner or later. He had been playing dirty in the jewelry business for many years. In fact, he'd been dabbling in the underground for so long that he didn't know what it meant to do business above the board.

His wife had been dead for many years, and his sweet, but unattractive daughter would never find a husband. It was just the two of them and they depended on each other. They were all each other had in the world, and he couldn't imagine life without her.

Which is why the old man didn't hesitate to give the maniac who had just left his shop exactly what he had coming looking for: Avi's contact information. Not only had he coughed up the Belgium jewelry trader's name, he'd spit out his address too.

Because Hymie Lovitz truly loved his ugly daughter. And it was his love for her that had prompted him to make a very important phone call just a few days earlier. A call that would finish the hit job that his partner-in-crime Joel Samuelson had started, yet failed to complete.

Hymie didn't understand where it had all gone wrong, because the two of them had planned their jewelry heist and murder-fire-hire scheme to perfection. During their last phone conversation all seemed to be going as arranged. Samuelson had warned him that the Queen of Diamonds was heading to his location. He said the Queen was bringing a briefcase to be placed in his safe, and Samuelson had urged him to get out of the shop as fast as he could.

Soon after that, the old man had been alerted by the police that there'd been a shooting at his shop. He had pretended to be shocked and frightened out of his mind.

But his shock had turned totally real when he walked into his store to find not a five million dollar diamond stashed in his safe and the dead body of a beautiful young black woman as he had expected, but rather the dead body of the old security guard who he had hired as an intern.

To make matters worse, the red briefcase containing the diamond was no place to be found, and Joel Samuelson had been discovered brutally murdered in his hotel room that very same night.

The old man had been scared shitless.

After all, it stood to reason that if the elderly intern and Joel Samuelson were both dead, then that meant the Queen of Diamonds was still alive. It also stood to reason that since she was still alive, that meant she had found out about their plan to rub her out and had beaten them to the draw.

And if that was the case, then there was no doubt in the old jeweler's mind that he was going to be the next target that she lined up in her sights.

So, old man Lovitz had quietly dipped into his healthy stash of cash and made himself a phone call of his own. He'd called a company called the BBU that was rumored to take care of business professionally and discreetly. And any day now his little problem, that beautiful black turd they called the Queen of Diamonds, would be eliminated for good.

The old man looked down at his precious daughter and shook with fear. He couldn't wait for that nigger bitch Honore Morales to be dead. He had been living on pins and needles waiting for the hit on her to go down, and he had assumed that Joel Samuelson's stolen diamond was still in the locker where it was supposed to be stashed. That diamond had actually been the last thing on his mind.

Until it had shown up just now in the hands of the maniac who threatened to cook the eyeballs of his precious daughter, that is! The old man gazed around his office and stared at a framed picture of his dearly departed wife.

It was definitely time to get out of the business. He had made quite a sum fabricating stolen diamonds for Samuelson and Avi over the years, but now it was time to cut his losses and get out while he still could. The New York City jewelry business had turned to scum. There was no way he could make a living selling gold chains to gangsters and fitting rappers for seedy grills. He had a brother in Florida who seemed to be doing well there. Maybe it was time to move south.

He thought about the look of pure evil he'd seen in the eyes of the young white man who had just walked out of his store. Yeah, it was definitely time to go. This last hustle with Joel Samuelson would have netted him a nice pot of gold, but what good was a fistful of money if you weren't alive to spend it?

He patted his daughter's face again and then got ready to shut his shop down for good. He had spent his entire life in the jewelry business, but after the craziness of the last couple of weeks he doubted if he'd miss it for a minute. Sure, it was true what they said about diamonds being forever. But then again, so was a cold deep grave.

CHAPTER 7

Dearly Departed

It was still pretty early in the morning and the large Queens mega-church was almost full when Chimp Charlie pulled up to the curb and let Honore, Cucci, and Sly McFly outta the whip. There was a bone-white hearse parked out front along with a slew of other cars that belonged to the many mourners who were attending the large funeral service inside.

They were late as hell getting there, and even from the outside they could hear the bootleg preacher in the pulpit shouting and putting on a show. An elderly usher dressed in all-white opened the doors and led the three of them over to the seats that had been reserved for them in the front row next to the family.

Honore was dressed in a sleek black and white polka-dot designer dress that stopped right above her knees. It was classy enough for a funeral but it didn't do a damn thing to hide her long legs and killer curves. Cucci was slaying a black-and-crème ankle-length pencil skirt with a matching top. With all that ass on her in that tight skirt she looked just like a sexy mermaid. Sly McFly was dressed in a black suit with a white shirt that was starched so crisp and sharp the edges coulda cut you. In fact, every stitch on him was made from the highest quality materials and tailored for his tall, lanky frame.

Sly draped his arm around Honore's shoulder as they sat in the front pew and pretended to pay attention to the preacher. Playing her role, Honore leaned her head on him as she gazed sorrowfully toward the open casket that was dead smack in front of her.

As usual, India looked real damn good. She had been a pretty chick when she was alive, and death hadn't changed that one bit. *Bitch was pretty but she was stupid too*, Honore thought as a fake tear slipped from her eye.

She could still feel the kick the powerful handgun had made after she shot India in the chest. By all rights she shoulda flew the bitch one to the dome, too.

Because it was India's own damn fault that she was laying up there with all these people snotting and crying over her. All she had to do was have her simple ass where she was supposed to be, and instead of being stretched out all cold and stiff she woulda still been flouncing her sexy ass around town stealing diamonds to be turned into crushed ice.

Honore's fake tears were really coming down now as she thought about that missing diamond. It was time to view the body and the mourners were marching slowly past the coffin. When it was her turn, Honore paused dramatically before India's cold corpse. She turned the waterworks up even higher and she was snotting and hiccupping and the whole nine as her knees sagged and she threw herself down on her old friend shrieking and crying.

"Indiaaaa! Girl why you had to gooooo...."

An old lady usher rushed over to fan Honore's face, but Sly McFly waved her off as him and Cucci lifted Honore to her feet and began slow-walking her down the aisle.

"Indiaaaaa!" Honore screeched as the organ music played louder and louder and the family screamed and wailed. She turned around and stretched her arms out toward her dead friend like she truly wanted to rush back and jump in the casket and join her. "Oh my gawddddd! *India!!!*"

"It's okay," Sly McFly pulled a starched white handkerchief outta his suit pocket and tried to sop up her overflowing tears. "She's resting in peace, baby," he comforted her loudly. Then he leaned in close and chuckled in Honore's ear, "The stupid little bitch is resting in peace."

$$$$$

There was a light breeze blowing outside when Cucci stomped outta the church and tipped down the front steps and made her exit. Funerals gave her a headache, and right now she was good and aggy. Sly had told her to excuse herself so him and Honore could go talk in the preacher's office and talk in private, and Cucci was fuming as she glided over to the whip in her mermaid skirt and plopped down in the passenger seat.

Slamming the door as hard as she could, Cucci had her lip poked out for days. Chimp Charlie watched her from the driver's seat, shaking his head as she fumbled in her bag and pulled out her weed grinder.

"What happened?" Charlie chuckled. "They done kicked you outta the damn funeral, huh? You so mad you can't even grind your weed up right. You dropping buds and residue all in the fucking car, girl!"

"Shut the fuck up," Cucci shot back. "How you talking shit when they made yo goofy ass stay out in the car the whole time? I swear to God, Sly and Honore act like I don't pull my weight, or I ain't supposed to be in on the shit they scheme up! I risk my freedom and put my life on the line just like they do!" she vented. "Something is gonna have to change big-time around here, and I mean that shit. Either I'm all in, or I'm all out. They got me all the way fucked up!"

"I feel you, baby. I ain't wanna go inside that fake-ass funeral anyway," Chimp said, trying to comfort her as he checked his mirrors and watched the street. "Sly pays me to drive and keep his secrets and you know I don't do no jaw-jackin. Just don't worry about it, sugar. Everybody's gonna come around and show their true colors in the end."

"Dead ass tho," Cucci said as she finally sparked up her trees. "I ain't nobody's flunky and I ain't stupid neither! I know you heard Honore got kidnapped with her dumb ass. What was the real deal going on with her in that jewelry store that night, Charlie? She ran me some wild story about some stick-up crew snatching her and dragging her out into the woods. You believe that shit?"

"I don't know for sure but I heard the same thang," Charlie said, nodding his head. "It might just be true too, because Sly took the car and went and picked her up that night. I know you and them girls was supposed to hold her down though, and y'all fucked that up." He chuckled and nodded toward the church. "You can go back inside and verify with poor India about that! But I wasn't driving that night so I don't know how Honore got into that situation or what the hell was really going on. Only her and Sly know the real scoop on it."

"And that's what pisses me off," Cucci snapped as she blew out a cloud of haze. "I should know every damn thing they know! Instead, I'm all in the dark and they keep giving me the run around like I don't know they hiding shit from me. I know when I'm being bullshitted, especially by my own cousin."

"Don't worry ya'self," Charlie said as he reached over and ran his rough hand up her leg. "Other than that, w'sup with you?"

The look on his face changed as his eyes dropped down to check out her hips and his big ol' hand squeezed her thigh. "You ain't been by to see me in a minute. You holding out on me? When I'ma get some more of that sweet shit you got up under your dress?"

"Get off me nigga," Cucci snapped as she slapped his hand away. "You can't be leaving ya paw prints on me and wrinkling up my shit. If Frita knew your old ass was fuckin me she'd cut ya damn dick off. You'll get some of this when I'm good and ready to give it to you. Until then keep paying them lil thots you be trickin on. You gots to peel off top dollars for this, and it's only when I say so."

"You know money ain't a issue, darling," Charlie said as he licked his fat crusty lips and damn near drooled on her. "And what Frita don't know won't hurt her neither. C'mon. Stop all that mean talk and slide through my place tonight, baby girl. Big Chimp Charlie always gonna treat you right. That dress is huggin them hips real nice you know."

"Calm down and quit breathing on me," Cucci said as she rolled her eyes. "And don't yeast ya'self up. The only thing big on you is that gut and them man boobs that you got sitting on top of it. I ain't thinking about yo ass Charlie! Ain't shit free over here! If you wanna get with me then what you need to be doing is keeping your eyes and ears open so I can get up on what's really good!

I'll give you what you want when you give me what I *need*. You copy?"

"Loud and clear baby," Charlie said with a perverted smile. "Loud and fuckin clear."

$$$$$

While Cucci was outside in the whip negotiating favors with Chimp Charlie, Sly McFly and Honore were sitting down the hall in the preacher's office, who happened to be one of Sly's old hustling partners from back in the day.

"You got black shit running down your face," Sly told Honore as he lit a blunt and kicked back in his manz's overstuffed chair.

Honore took her makeup compact from her purse and flipped it open. She peered in the mirror and used Sly's hankie to wipe away the mascara that her phony tears had washed from her eyelashes.

When she was done she looked around the small office that was just too damn junky to belong to a preacher. She could tell he was the bootleg-type because it looked like dude was having a garage sale up in that joint. There were funeral fans, bibles, crates filled with donated books, broken up televisions, triple beam scales, and stacks of old newspaper everywhere.

Honore sat back in her chair as Sly passed her the kush.

"I think I did pretty good shaking them FBI agents off at work you know," she said, inhaling the weed deeply into her lungs. "They asked me if I would take a lie detector test if they ever needed one and I said hell yeah, bring that shit on. They musta believed me though because they didn't come back asking no more questions."

Sly shrugged as his brows dropped low like he was thinking real hard. "That don't mean shit. They could be laying in the cut and waiting for the right time to strike. But fuck all that. Them gub'ment leeches ain't our biggest problem right now, Honore. Our biggest problem is them damn *investors!* You said Samuelson was gonna pay them off as soon as Avi sold that diamond, right?"

"Yeah," Honore nodded. "He told them he was gonna hand over all the money by the end of the month."

Sly frowned. "Well if the doe ain't in their hands by then they gonna send their goonies out looking for it. They're gonna want their sweet money back plus their cut off that diamond too. And trust me, with that Jew-boy Samuelson dead and gone, the first person they gonna come gunning for is *you*."

"But that shit ain't even right!" Honore bucked. "I did my fuckin job! I delivered the diamond where it was supposed to be! It ain't my fault that damn jewelry store got robbed! They gave *Joel Samuelson* that duffle bag full of sweet money, not me! They put it in *his* hands. I didn't get not nare penny of that doe."

Sly hit her with the crazy face. "Fuck does that matter? The deal was made in *both* of y'all names! Y'all was supposed to be working as a *team*, and with one half of the team gone they coming after the other half! We gotta find that diamond and sell it, baby girl," Sly muttered. "That's the only way we gonna get this heat up off your neck."

Honore was silent for a few seconds and then she asked quietly, "What if we blamed that shit on somebody else? What if we made them think it was somebody else who lost the diamond and not me?"

"Somebody like who?"

"Cucci," Honore said, tossing her cousin's name out there without missing a beat. "That bitch be asking too many stupid questions for her own good. What if we came up with a real good story and blamed it all on Cucci?"

Sly frowned and nodded. "Yeah, they'd probably kill her. If the story was good enough they'd smoke the shit outta her. But then they'd still kill you too. They want their sweet money *and* the profits they were supposed to make off that jewel. You were the one rollin with Samuelson. Not Cucci. Besides," Sly said, thinking of his main squeeze, Frita. "Cucci's family, baby. Blood family. She's supposed to be your best friend."

Honore snatched the bomb from him and took a long pull. There was real fear in her eyes and her hand shook as she inhaled again then passed the sticky back to Sly.

"You the one who told me that in this business you ain't got no friends!"

"Don't worry, baby girl," Sly told her in a soothing tone. "I got a few ears pressed to the ground out there and sooner or later something's gonna start rumbling."

"But what if it don't?" Honore wailed. "What if we don't never find that shit? What am I gonna do, run-duck-and-hide for the rest of my life? If they know the damn diamond got stolen then why should they still be expecting a cut? A cut of *what*? Nothing from nothing is *nothing!* Would them mothafuckas leave me alone if we just paid them back the sweet money?"

Sly shrugged. "Paying them back the sweet money might keep 'em off your ass for a second or two. Maybe long enough for us to find the diamond and get it to Avi so he can sell it. Why? You got a half mil in cheese stashed somewhere?"

"Nah," Honore shook her head. "I got some nice ends, but not that many. I got a little bit of crushed ice that I can sell though."

Sly McFly snipped the heat off the tip of the blunt with his calloused fingertips then stood up and brushed off his suit.

"You got something else, too, Honore. I don't know what the fuck you been out there doing witcha time but you sure as hell ain't been handling your business."

"What?" Honore asked, her head buzzing lightly and her mouth dry. "What are you talking about? What do I have?"

"You got that nigga's *address!* That sucka-for-luv nigga who snatched the diamond in the first fuckin place! If it was up to me we woulda been done ran up in there and folded that nigga up! He woulda been hung up on a rack by his nuts by now, begging to tell me what he did with that goddamn diamond!"

Slick!

The name exploded in her mind and Honore frowned, but just a little. She knew Sly McFly spoke truthfulness, but so far Slick had some real closed lips. Them shits seemed airtight and waterproof. No matter how deeply she probed him, or which direction she came at him from, that smoove nigga never leaked. He dipped and dodged, rolled and bounced. He stayed on his toes and guarded his game. He mighta been wide open on her delicious booty, but he wasn't giving up shit that had anything to do with a diamond!

"I feel you, Sly. I really do. And if we can't come up with nothing else then we might just have to roll on him like that. But it's gotta be our last resort. That nigga has a savage-ass killer crew too, and right now I don't need no extra hittas coming at my throat."

"A'ight." Sly shrugged. "But while you busy playing games you better get to work on his ass. Before I do. Now let's get the fuck outta here so Charlie can drop you and Cucci off at home. Funerals make me hungry and I got a taste for some Chinese food."

CHAPTER 8

Bullet Fried Rice

It was right before the lunch crowd and Wild Man was carrying big boxes of condiments through the back of Woo Shin's Chinese restaurant in Jamaica, Queens. He cradled as many boxes as he could in his strong arms and stacked them as neatly as possible in the back room.

As hard as he grinded for the Zip 'em up Crew, Wild Man still found time to run around to his father's chain of Chinese spots throughout the city. Whenever a little help was needed at a store he was glad to pitch in.

Shin, the long-time manager of the restaurant in Queens, was like an elderly uncle to Wild Man. He had a very sick wife and he had called on Wild Man to do a little manual labor for him.

Shin had been running the store since Wild Man was a young boy. He had taken a liking to Wild Man because they had similar personalities. He, too, had come from a street background and had lived his younger life in the trenches before he finally got his shit in order.

Wild Man had always respected Shin because he treated him as an equal without judging him too harshly. Shin knew what it was like to be Asian in an all-black neighborhood, and even though he was now a legitimate businessman he could relate to Wild Man's struggles.

"Is the truck empty yet, William?" Shin asked as he came in from the front of the store. "I have some cheesesteak eggrolls in the deep fryer for us."

"Almost. Just a couple of boxes left," Wild Man responded.

"Take your time young man, and don't strain your back," Shin said grinning. "If you are not strong enough to get the job done I'll give you hand, just say please."

Wild Man couldn't help but laugh at the short, small-boned man. Shin was a humorous old cat and being around him always lifted Wild Man's spirits.

"I think I can handle it old uncle," Wild Man said as he chuckled at Shin. "Just get those egg rolls ready while I finish up back here. I dropped a bottle of soy sauce but I'll clean it up after I eat."

"Fair enough. I'll save my strength for later," Shin said as he smiled at Wild Man. "How is your father doing by the way, William? I haven't spoken to him since last month."

"Yeah, well, you know pops stays busy. I go by and check on him at least once a week. He just buries himself in his work. You know how he does."

"I understand, William," Shin said. "Your father is a good man, and without his generosity I would have been dead a long time ago. He took a chance on me and showed me the meaning of hard work."

"I know, I know. You tell me this every time I see you," Wild Man muttered as he carried in the last of the boxes.

"Whatever it is in those streets that has you hooked, William, you'd better learn to let it go," Shin advised, loving Wild Man the way he would love his own son. "Before it catches up with you some day."

Wild Man wasn't dismissing what Shin was saying but he couldn't dwell on it either. Hell yeah he had a lot of pent up anger and frustration inside of him. What muthafucka walking the streets of New York City didn't?

"Look uncle, I ain't—" Wild Man opened his mouth to answer but was interrupted by a loud voice roaring from the front of the restaurant.

"Hey, where the fuck is everybody at? Hurry up and get out here! I'm hungry as hell, goddammit!"

"Yo, who is that?" Wild Man asked, reaching under his shirt for his gat as he peered through the doorway.

"That is a very bad man!" Shin leaned back and whispered with a frown. "You see my front window? Many years ago he beat a woman up in here and threw her right through the glass! It cost a lot of money to have that window replaced and he refused to pay me for it."

Shin shrugged and his face went blank. "But that was a long time ago. Time to get back to work," he said and disappeared through the doorway.

As Wild Man gripped his heat and set the last box down on the shelf, the sound of Shin out front raising his voice put his ears on high alert.

"Why must you always come into my store so disrespectfully and demand things? All these years I try to tell you that you don't own anything in here and I am not afraid of you!"

Wild Man almost chuckled as he walked up behind his uncle. Although Shin had a thick accent it was obvious he was from the streets. His words were very clear.

"Look at my window! This is my store and you still owe me money for the damage you caused so long ago!"

"Listen here, you chinky-eyed cat-killer," a tall, nicely dressed black man gripping a white cane blasted on Shin. "You want some money? Then shut the fuck up and take my order!"

"You are rude!" Shin yelled. "I am not afraid of you!"

"Is that right?" the old man said. "After all these years you wanna play with me, Shin? You wanna act like you don't know who the fuck I am? Fool, I can burn this store down to the ground and turn this whole shit into a vacant lot in less than an hour! Fuck with me and see."

Wild Man stood behind his uncle quietly. Shin was a small man but he was also a very proud man so he fought the urge to walk out from behind the glass and step to his defense.

"I know exactly who you are, Sly McFly!" Shin yelled, not backing down. "You are a *criminal!* A bad man who hurts helpless women! You are not tough when you kill a lady, you know. In my country that makes you a coward!"

"What did you just say, you soy sauce-slinging bastard?" Sly McFly growled, enraged as he slammed his palm on the bulletproof glass that separated him and Shin. "Mothafucka if I ever, *ever* hear you accuse me of some shit like that again I will cut your fuckin tongue outta your mouth and let my little homeys gang rape that flat-faced wife of your yours! You better watch what you say to me, you tiny yellow *bitch!*"

"Ayo, hold up!" Wild Man finally spoke up, then opened the glass door and rushed into the customer area where Sly McFly was standing. "Who the fuck is you talking to, old head? Fuck outta here with all them dry-ass threats, my man."

The older man turned and fixed him in a cold, killer glare.

"And *you* best stay your young ass in a child's place little nigga!" Sly said as he posted up eye-to-eye with Wild Man.

A sudden urge to kill rushed through Wild Man's blood. His instincts told him the old head was the real deal but he ain't give a shit. Wild Man was the real muthafuckin deal too.

"Yo, I ain't no little old man and I ain't ya fuckin girlfriend neither," Wild Man barked with venom as he stared Sly down. "If I just heard correctly you like to throw women around, right? Well ain't no pussy between my legs, old head! Get at me! I'll fuck your narrow ass up in here!"

Several customers had walked inside the restaurant but Sly ignored them as he glared at Shin and then back at Wild Man.

"You got a loud mouth my friend Shin, but trust me I'ma fix that shit for you," Sly said with a sick grin. "Right after I kill this Jet Li-looking shithead right here. Come on, muthafucka!"

Sly raised his cane ready to strike at Wild Man's head. Wild Man took a step back and put his fists up. His strong muscles flexed under his shirt.

"Go 'head. Swing that shit so I can shove it down your goddamn throat," Wild Man promised, ready to do battle with the older man that his uncle had called Sly.

"Stop it! Stop it! Not in my restaurant!"

Shin rushed out from behind the counter and wedged himself into the narrow gap between Wild Man and Sly.

"Mister McFly," he pleaded, pushing a bag of food into the black man's hand. "You are my old friend. We were once young men together, yes? I apologize for saying those bad things to you. It won't happen again," Shin said trying to defuse the volatile situation and keep his store from getting fucked up. "Please. Just leave. Enjoy your meal. It's free on me. I don't want any trouble here. I don't want my store burned. I don't want any trouble with my wife."

Wild Man looked at Shin angrily. He had never seen his proud uncle back down from anything before. Wild Man wanted tear off into the old head even more now. Sly had the look of a true killer about him and Wild Man could tell that if it popped off it would be a fight to the death. But for the sake of Shin and his livelihood, Wild Man stepped back and let it go. For the moment.

"That's what I thought," Sly said as he lowered his cane. "Yeah, we were boys together Shin, and you still a boy now. Next time you best remember your manners when a grown man steps up in this bitch!"

Sly turned to Wild Man and nailed him in a cold, vicious glare and spit, "Next time you see me you better watch ya mouth, young boy. Cause a nigga like me'll fuck around and serve you up a plate of bullet-fried rice, muthafucka!"

Then just as cool as he could be, Sly gave Shin and Wild Man both a bitter smile, then turned and walked out carrying his bag of free food.

"What the fuck was that about, uncle?" Wild Man said as Shin hurried to take care of his new customers.

"I told you he's a very bad man," Shin muttered as he snatched some money from the register and gave a young lady her change. "He scares a lot of people. I don't want any trouble. I must protect my wife. It's not worth it."

"Fuck him!" Wild Man spit. "That old crippled woman-beater bleeds just like everybody else out here! You just can't let people run over you like that man!"

"You might not understand the way this works, but I do, William," Shin snapped at him. "I said to let it go! I run a respectable business and I've been here for many years. Please don't bring any trouble around my wife. Thank you for your time. If the boxes are done then you can leave."

Shin took care of his remaining customers and then disappeared into the back room to check on his sick wife, leaving Wild Man by himself.

Wild Man cursed under his breath. He hadn't meant to upset Shin. He had only wanted to help. He went back and mopped up the soy sauce he had spilled in the storage room and straightened up as much as he could, and then shaking his head, he dipped outta the back door and breezed off.

CHAPTER 9

Rap Central

Jewelz stepped out of the taxicab holding a large designer umbrella. She paused for a moment as she stood in front of the Restoration Plaza located right on Fulton Street in the Stuy.

It had been sunny and warm earlier in the morning when she planted Fat Donnie with a poison pellet out in Queens. But here in Brooklyn the afternoon sky was gloomy and heavy drops of rain fell from the grey clouds that hung overhead.

The little brown capsule that Jewelz had spit into Fat Donnie's cup of Coke was one that she had used many times before. She had learned a lot about herbs and toxins when she first got sick and tried to heal her body holistically.

Today she had packed the tiny dissolvable capsule with a highly toxic chemical and then concealed it under her tongue. The inner contents of the capsule were safe from the mild acid in her saliva, but once the pellet hit that corrosive soda acid in the cup of Coke...well the outer shell had dissolved almost immediately allowing the poison that was packed inside to go straight to work.

One down and two to go, Jewelz thought happily as she walked down the street killin 'em softly in her tight black skirt, bright red patent-leather Giuseppe Zanotti pumps, and stylish black swing-shawl. She was about to enter the Royal Blue Recording Studios to meet Handgun Goody and she knew she was looking just right.

Ever since the night of the Unsigned Hype showcase when Jewelz had put her spit game on full display, Goody had been sweating her and waiting on her call. When she finally hit him up he was so anxious to get up with her that he offered her a lucrative recording contract right over the phone.

Jewelz had laughed inside. She could give two shits about a recording contract. Rapping was just a hobby that she was using as a tool to get the drop on the real target. And trust, that nigga was a target too. Jewelz understood the mindset of hood sharks like Goody. They used and abused the lil jump-off broads who fell at their feet and worshipped them like they were God's gift to the hood-rat universe. The powerful grip of that big-time money hypnotized these broke ghetto bitches to the point where they were just fine with being a nigga's toilet seat whenever he needed to take a shit.

But when a bad bitch like Jewelz came along the whole game changed. She had her own money and she stood on her own feet with dignity and intelligence, and with the pride of a lioness.

Chicks like her were rare in the hood, and it never failed that dopeboys were either gonna be intimidated by her stature or they would chase it. Jewelz planned on having Goody's ass running a fucking marathon to try and get a piece of what she was holding.

Pausing in the doorway of a pizza shop, she lowered her umbrella and hit Slick on the cellie real quick to put him down on her location. They had agreed to hook up together later on in the evening and compare notes, but Slick had insisted that she call him before she went in to meet with Goody, and he'd ordered her to keep in touch with him every step of the way. She had already called his ass once today but he hadn't picked up.

"Yo! Answer the phone!" she said, leaving him a voice message when he still didn't pick up. "I'm next door to Handgun Goody's recording studio about to line this snake up! You told me to call you before I went inside. Well I'm on my way in there and I'm about to finesse this nigga half to death!"

Jewelz hung up and stuck her phone back inside her purse and slid next door. As she stepped inside the building a security guard met her in the foyer, and after taking her name he politely escorted her upstairs to meet with the big boss.

"There you are sexy. So glad you could make it," Goody said as Jewelz strutted into a lounge area that was right outside the recording and engineer booth.

He was dressed in a black Sergio Armani tailor-fitted suit and posted up in his b-boy stance as he flashed a big grin at her.

She eyed him with her head held high. He was sharp. His teeth were bone white and stood in contrast to his deep chocolate skin. His shape-up was fresh, and an all-gold dope-boy Rolex was on his left wrist with the matching Jesus piece hanging around his neck.

Jewelz finally smiled a little, but she remained silent and queen-like as she analyzed her surroundings.

Handgun Goody kept his eyes locked on her as she inspected his shit like s she had on a white glove. He was hoping for her complete approval because he was intrigued by her style and her air of confidence. Goody recognized those qualities in her because he also had those same character traits and he prided himself on it.

Without a word, Jewelz strode across the floor and took a seat on a soft sofa in the lounge and crossed her long, shapely legs. The look in her eyes said his lil shit had passed her test and the plush leather sofa was good enough for her to sit her precious ass down on.

"This is a decent little establishment you have here, Mister Goode Brother." She waved her hand at his hard-earned finery like she was used to seeing much better everyday. "Thank you for inviting me."

"My pleasure, Mizz Jewelz," Goody nodded. "And thanks for coming. But before we take this any further lemme go 'head and apologize about how I spoke to you at the club the other night, a'ight? A nigga like me is naturally on point and suspicious of people who ask a lotta questions. Especially when those questions are coming from a beautiful woman, since that's every man's weakness to some degree," Goody said still giving her that million-dollar smile.

Jewelz smiled back and nodded like she knew she was all that. "I hear what you're saying, but my only motive was to put you up on game and not deceive you. It was pure strategy, you feel me? I already knew I was gonna win the contest, therefore I would get paid and you would be the first to get the credit for recognizing my superior talent."

She laughed and her eyes flashed at him sexily. "And see? I was right. You called me down here and you already offered me a contract, so I must have done something right."

Goody was stunned speechless as she uncrossed and re-crossed her long legs. He was leaning toward her with his mouth slightly gaped, in a daze, like he was getting high from the sweet fumes coming off her pussy.

"Oh, and by the way, apology accepted," Jewelz said in her sexy-savvy way. She glanced around again, thinking this wide-open nigga was lucky she didn't feel like snuffing his ass right then and there. She could almost kinda see herself in a corporate headquarters working for a big Fortune 500 company negotiating hostile takeovers. This nigga didn't even know how hostile she was! She would take his whole life over from right under his nose! The same way he had taken over hers!

Jewelz shrugged off the urge to kill him as she reminded herself to stay focused on the larger goals at hand. Revenge was sweet, but she was in the murder business and nothing gave her the type of thrill and exhilaration that annihilating a target did.

Her confident, sexy swag was throwing fuel on the fire that was burning inside of Goody. He knew he couldn't win her over with the flashy shit or the cash. He could tell she was sassy and wanted her own shit on her own terms. He had to admire it.

"I like the way you think, Mizz Jewelz, and if you agree to join my record label it would be my pleasure to start a flourishing business relationship with you. I know you're gonna have your own lawyer look over the contract, but I can assure you that if there are any changes you want made," Goody promised, "I'll put my lawyer on it immediately. Now, with that shit outta the way may we make a toast to our future together?"

Goody got up and walked over to a bar that was built right into the wall. He pulled out a gold bottle of Ace of Spades champagne and held it up for her approval.

Jewelz nodded, pretending not to catch the subliminal message in his words as she played along.

"I'm down with that," she answered sweetly as he poured.

Just as they tapped glasses in a celebratory toast, Goody's cell phone rang. He looked down at his screen and saw it was one of his partners from a main stash house.

"Please excuse me for a moment, Jewelz," Goody said as he walked over to the glass-enclosed engineering room. "I need to take this call real quick."

"Yo, w'sup lil homey? What's the problem?" Goody barked once he was behind the closed door. It was one of his young'uns named Tony, and since Tony was Goody's best ear out on the street, Goody had sent him on a little fact-finding mission.

"Everything's a'ight out here in the field," Tony said, "but I got a lil sumpin on that rapper chick you asked me to check out."

"Well, give it up, nigga," Goody said, eyeing Jewelz through the glass door. "Give it up!"

"Yo, man, that chick used to be an enforcer for Bajan Andy and his set. You know they had them loud packs on deck, and Jewelz used to make sure every shipment was on point for them. Andy told me she had the meanest gun game he'd ever seen. On a chick *or* a nigga. Then one day she upped and said she was done with all that shit and she disappeared. Word on the street is that she's retired. They say she'll still pop up in a club ere' now and then and tear the mic down, but when it's over she just takes the prize money and vanishes again. I couldn't find out where she rests her head or who she's eating with now. But Haitian Tisha said she was a penny-pincher. A squirrel stacking nuts. She lived at her crib for a minute, and Tisha said she's the type of chick who stashed all her cheese and stayed about her business."

Goody nodded. "Good work, my dude. That's more info than I had on her before she walked in my studio. Let Andy know I said good lookin out and make sure you tell him to let me know what the prices are on them kush clouds he got."

"I got you Big Bro," Tony said. "I'll hit ya later."

Goody walked back into the lounge where Jewelz was waiting. He knew Bajan Andy was a thorough nigga from the hood. The fact that Jewelz had worked for him gave strong validation to what his gut already told him. She was a stand-up bitch. It turned Goody on even more to know that she looked this good and could work a ratchet too. He loved the aura of mystery that surrounded Jewelz, and it beckoned him to her and made him want to learn more about this beautiful, and no doubt dangerous creature.

"Sorry I took so long," Goody said as he crossed the room and calmly sat down across from Jewelz. "One of my little homeys was handling some business for me that I had to attend to."

"That's quite alright," she said, sliding her cell phone back inside her purse. She had tried Slick's number again, and when he didn't answer she had clicked over and connected to an incoming call. "I had to take a call of my own," she said sweetly.

Jewelz picked up a pen and then leaned toward him and gave him a deep look. "So, Mr. Goody, tell me before I put my name on this contract, are you just some regular hoodlum with a couple of bucks and a studio who's trying to live out his 'CEO of a record label' fantasy? Because I refuse to put my name on some shit and six months later, God forbid, you get hit with some type of reck less charge and I'm stuck in a contract and hung out to dry."

Her tone was dead serious and the look on her face told Goody she was far from impressed with his set up.

"I mean," she continued, "I know nothing is promised in this game we're playing, but I need to know that you actually have a real *plan,* along with having the nuts and the smarts to carry out that plan."

Goody was totally impressed!

"Damn, Jewelz!" he said, laughing. "You keep a nigga on his toes don't you? I can appreciate that, and since we're on the topic of my nuts and my heart, let me clarify a few things for you."

He scooted his chair closer so he could run shit down to her properly. "First of all, I like to think of myself as a diamond in the rough. I used to be a skinny-ass, never-had-a-penny-ass nigga. Typical upbringing in the projects, all signs pointing to the graveyard or the bing. I got sent upstate and did some hard time and I'm not bitter about that shit. I'm not angry, and nor do I feel sorry for myself. All my hardships I use as pure motivation. I feel I was born and built to be even better than I am right now. I'm just using this druggin and thuggin shit as a platform to achieve my bigger goals. Success is my drug of choice and I can't get enough of it. That's my addiction!" Goody said with mad conviction in his eyes.

"I'm able to do what these other niggas out here can't do because I put it all on the line. I go hard in the trenches every single time, like I ain't got shit to lose. If I fail then fuck it, statistics show I was supposed to fail anyway right?"

"But what's real is, the hood dictates who and what's hot in this industry. The streets set the trends, the standards, and the lingo, so the streets say who's real and who's not."

He paused to flash her a quick grin. "Trust, baby girl, I *am* the streets, and I'm as real as it gets. I'm not one of them dumb niggas who jumps off a diving board without checking to make sure there's water in the pool! I'm the heart of the hood," Goody bragged. "These niggas out here love me *and* they fear me. I have the perfect combination of all attributes, and everything about me is strategic. I make it my mission to learn everything there is to know about my playing field, its strengths, its weaknesses, and its needs. I feel like with the right team behind me, and of course the right talent, I can crush this music shit!"

He stared at her deeply. "And that's where you come in, Mizz Jewelz. New York is ready for some new blood, a brand new wave. And somebody on my squad is gonna fill that gap."

Jewelz held his gaze sensing that he truly believed in himself and his dreams. Too bad he probably wouldn't live to see none of that shit come to fulfillment. She knew Goody hadn't gotten this far by being an idiot though, so she would have to be on her A-game at all times.

She nodded. "I can admire your ambition, and of course your reputation out here precedes you. I'm sure by now you did your homework on me and you can see I'm not exactly an angel or a fairy princess myself. I'm all about doing whatever it takes to make shit shake out here. It's a pit-eat-poodle world and can't nobody breathing tell me I can't eat."

She flashed him a fake grin. "So I hope you meant everything you said and you not selling me no dreams, because if this rap shit don't work I don't have any illusions of what I'm going back to."

Jewelz batted her eyes and giggled. "Shit, if this don't work I might need to go into some of your other businesses with you. What you think?" she asked as she smirked and slowly crossed her legs again so Goody could see the curve of her thighs against the fabric of her skirt. "Is there room for a Goode Sister in the Goode Brothers organization?"

Goody was mesmerized by her entire package and he found it hard to keep the lust from showing in his eyes. Jewelz had already known he would check up on her, and she was professional enough to expect and accept it. Letting her walk up in there unverified would've shown his hand as a weak-ass rookie.

"I would be souped up to have a woman of your stature aligned with my team," Handgun Goody said with a wide grin. "I can show you first-hand how I run these streets, get this paper, and how I've been able to take shit to the next level."

Jewelz didn't resist when Goody leaned over and pressed his lips to hers. She opened up to him as his tongue snaked inside her mouth and his rough hand slid up her thigh and over her curvy hip. She felt pure power in his hands and she could tell he was a rough-type lover just by the way he was gripping her. He took her hand and placed it over his bulging dick and urged her to squeeze it.

Jewelz knew his lil gunner boy was watching from the shadows of the doorway but she still went ahead and let him get his feel on. She was confident that she could get the drop and take both of them out, but that would defeat her and Slick's purpose. With Handgun dead, one of his brothers would just slide in his seat and take over the family hustle. Nah, she had to chill so they could pick off every last one of them rats. Her and Slick were gonna wipe the whole Goode Brother bloodline clean. They were gonna hit them niggas one at a time and save Handgun for last.

While Jewelz was mentally scheming, Handgun was enjoying the physical pleasures of her scrumptious body. His hands roamed over her freely and she felt so soft and good to the touch that his dick got even harder and he got even beastlier. He grabbed her plump titty and pinched her nipple painfully. He sucked her tongue like he wanted to tear it out from the root. And when he finally broke their kiss Jewelz's lips were bruised and swollen. She smiled and tipped back her glass of Spade and sipped from it daintily.

Goody let her get a couple of sips and then he took the glass from her and set it on the end table. He reached out and cupped her breast again and squeezed it hard as he thumbed her nipple back and forth. His hand slid up her shoulder to the back of her neck. He pulled her head forward, applying an insistent pressure.

Jewelz knew exactly what the fuck he wanted. It was a test. He wanted to see if she was running game, or if she was willing to submit to him the way the game demanded of her. He was gonna make her show and prove that her shit was legitimate, and that she knew her place.

Remember why you're doing this, she told herself as she leaned forward obediently and lowered her head deep down into his lap. *You're doing it for you and for Slick. You're doing it so y'all can get the revenge that you deserve.*

Goody unbuckled his pants and had his dick out quicker than shit. Jewelz eyed his shit. It was long and thick. Pretty as fuck. The kind she liked. But this nigga didn't even know who he was fucking with. Jewelz was a dick-sucking beast. Tops in the league. She was confident as hell as she prepared to lay her superior neck game down on him. She heard him moan above her and she smiled. She had this muthafucka. With her lick-a-dick skills she had him good. She was about to have him eating outta her hand, and she couldn't wait to report back to Slick and tell him how deep this fool was sniffing up her ass.

Jewelz put her face down closer in his crotch and visually examined his dick as she stroked it up and down. She cupped his balls and turned them over and around in her hand. Satisfied with what she saw, she opened her mouth and gave Handgun Goody what he was asking for.

Jewelz put on the performance of a lifetime as she tightened her lips around the base of his dick and gently sucked. She clamped the back of her throat down on the head of his shit and vibrated her neck pussy in a low hum.

Goody sucked his breath in and groaned. He didn't know how to act as he got his shit waxed by a pro. He didn't even expect this shit to be all that good. He had been testing her to see if she was really about that life, and this girl was proving to be an A+ head-of-the-class student.

Even though he was trying hard not to punk out, it wasn't long before Jewelz's skilled lips and killer tongue caused Goody to lose his head. He tried to hide the fact that he was turnt the fuck out, but he couldn't help shrieking like a lil bitch as she coaxed his seed up from his balls and sucked a hot walnut outta the tip of his dick.

"Damn girl..." Goody panted as he put his meat away and poured her some more champagne. "That shit was raw as fuck. I got a feeling me and you gonna be real tight, Miss Sexy."

"I'll drink to that," Jewelz smiled slyly as they locked glances and she fought to keep the chill outta her eyes. This nigga was really something. He would be fun to kill.

He was handsome and determined, but with that big dick he had on him he was also very prideful. And like they said, Jewelz thought as she licked her tender lips and completely drained her glass, pride goeth before a fall.

CHAPTER 10

All Play and No Fuckin Work!

Just hold on, we're going home…

Drake's banga floated from the speakers as Honore and Slick sat chilling on the living room floor of Slick's plush condo later that afternoon. His private piece of paradise was a totally tricked-out bachelor pad, nothing like his grandmother's humble project apartment in building 430.

Slick had bought the crib and had it completely renovated, and it had all the amenities he needed in his line of work. The neighborhood was quiet and upscale, and even though people minded their business for the most part, Slick still kept shit low key when he was there.

The young couple had just finished grubbing off delicious platters of steak and potatoes that Slick had masterfully chef'd up for their late lunch. He made good use of his decked-out kitchen and always cooked when he was there instead of ordering out.

He had put his special seasonings to work and grilled the hell outta the steaks. And now that lunch was over, him and Honore were engaged in an intense game of chess and they were both relishing in the ferocious battle.

Slick took his eyes off the chessboard and gazed at his date. It was still kinda early but he was drinking Henny straight outta the bottle and he asked Honore if she would like a glass of champagne.

"What?" she asked playfully. "You don't think I can fuck with the Hen rock? I ain't no light-weight," she said, dropping all her college-girl talk as she got loose and comfortable with him. "Pour it up, pour it up! I ain't drinking outta the damn bottle though, so can I have a glass please?"

Slick laughed. "Oh, you wanna play like you ain't never sucked it straight from the bottle?" he shot back as he got up to go get her a glass. "I guess you still have to keep it somewhat lady-like for me, huh?"

Honore waved him off like, please! "Um, can you change the music while you're up too, Mr. Slick? Are you Draking or nah? Are you having a moment? You thinking about ya lil ex or something?" she clowned him as they both burst into laughter.

Slick's phone vibrated in a special pattern as soon as he walked into the kitchen. He took it off his waist and glanced down as a sparkling diamond, Jewelz's avatar, flashed on his screen.

"Not right now," he muttered under his breath then quickly pressed the *call reject* button. He came back to the living room holding two glasses and still smiling from Honore's Drake joke.

"You heard what I said," Honore repeated. She pushed the chessboard aside. "Are you thinking about one of your ex's?"

"Naw," Slick laughed as he sat back down and poured them both a glass of Hen Dog. "I don't have any ex's worth thinking about. What about you? Do you find yourself getting caught up in old memories from the past?"

"The *past?*" Honore blurted out. "Fuck the past! If anything, I'm trying to run as far away from the past as I can get and bury the memories as deep in the ground as they can go."

She shook her head and smoothed back her hair then smiled a little. "Sorry, I didn't mean to blast on you. It's just that I'm the type who tries to only think about what's ahead of me. If I never do shit with my life from this point on, my future would still outshine my past by far."

Slick could hear the hint of pain and deep-seated anger in her voice. It was all too familiar and it made him want to know her story. He wanted to dig through and pick at some of the skeletons in her closet. Maybe they shared some of the same bones.

"It's cool baby. *We're all playing a mind game, were just stuck on different levels,*" Slick said as he swigged the cold Henny down without flinching. "*We facing the same type of hell, we just owe our souls to different devils.*"

Honore narrowed her eyes and looked at him real hard. "That was deep, did you come up with that yourself or did you get it out of some rap song you heard somewhere?"

Slick shrugged. "That's a bar from my boy, Jada Kiss that I put a lil twist on. I love that line 'cause it's real and it applies to my life."

"Ain't that the damn truth," Honore agreed as she got up and walked over to the window and gazed outside.

Slick stared at her with something hot in his eyes. Her tight jeans hugged the curves of her thick ass deliciously and it looked like he could fit his hands around her tiny waist and still have room to spare. He gave her a moment to chill, and then he walked up behind her and pulled her body close to his. He kissed the side of her warm neck and they fell into a comfortable silence as he waited patiently until she felt like talking again.

While he was waiting his phone vibrated on his waist in that special pattern again. He knew it was Jewelz, but he ignored it and said to Honore instead,

"What you thinking about, baby?"

Honore sniffled a little bit, drawing him in. "The past," she admitted softly. "I'm thinking about the bullshit, horrible past."

Those few words stirred something strong in Slick's stomach and he didn't like the feeling at all. He wasn't sure if he wanted to hear what might come outta her mouth next, but she kept going.

"Believe it or not, I used to be real dumb and innocent back in the day, Slick. But the little girl in me died the day I turned sixteen," Honore confessed. "No matter what happens to me now it could never hurt as much as I was hurt back then."

That there shit hit Slick right in the gut. He grunted under his breath and it came straight from his soul.

"A sixteenth birthday is supposed to be one of the happiest days in a young girl's life, you know?" Honore whispered as she turned away from the window and wrapped her arms around Slick's waist. He felt his phone vibrating with Jewelz's special tone again but he damn sure wasn't gonna answer it now.

"Shit wasn't supposed to go down so...so fucking horrible," she said. "It was my sweet-sixteen party for Christ's sake! And it ended up being the worst day of my whole fucking life."

Honore seemed to be fighting hard to push a lump in her throat down into the pit of her stomach. Slick heard the soft whimper behind her words and he hugged her tightly, like he was trying to keep her memories from harming her.

"What happened?" Slick managed to utter even though a part of him still didn't wanna know.

"My fuckin *father* happened," Honore said bitterly. Tears gathered in the corners of her eyes as she spoke.

"He was a true tweak-out type nigga, Slick. Real violent and way out there with his shit. He treated my mother like he hated her or something. She was so beautiful but he used to beat her until she was black and blue. He got mad one time and threw her straight through the front window of a Chinese restaurant. I was real little back then so I don't really remember it. But I do remember the horrible scars that were all over her back from where she got cut up and sliced by all that glass. It was totally bugged out."

"Damn," Slick said shaking his head. "Ain't no man supposed to be handling a female like that. It's fuckin madness."

"Yeah, well when I got older it got even worse than that. Like I said, I remember the night of my sixteenth birthday party. My father came home drunk after fucking some bitch he was running around with on the low. I could hear him and my mother in their room cussing each other out, not to mention the blows my father was throwing that had her crashing into the walls like crazy."

"My party had just started and all my friends were chilling in the living room," Honore said as she began to tremble. "We turned the music up and tried to ignore all the screaming and cussing. I was so embarrassed I told them we should just jet and go to another party a few buildings down that was going on at the same time."

Honore swallowed hard and trembled, and Slick ran his fingers through her hair trying to keep her calm.

"But before we could bounce my mother's screams changed. She started shrieking and calling my name.

"I...I rushed towards the back of the apartment to see what was going on," Honore said, "but the gunshots froze me right in my tracks."

The tears fell freely from her eyes and a world of hurt tumbled off her trembling lips.

"My father came staggering out the room looking wild and vicious. He had a gun in his hand." As she spoke her voice got softer and her eyes grew wider like she was reliving the moment.

"He looked *dead* at me, and he must have seen the terror on my face because all he could say was, "I'm sorry, Ray-Ray. He kept saying it over and over and over again. "I'm sorry, Ray-Ray. I'm sorry..."

Honore held onto Slick tightly and dug her nails into his back as she whimpered.

"And then right there in front of me he pressed the gun to his temple. I saw a quick flash and then his brains...his brains flew out the side of his head and he...he dropped to the floor."

Honore's body was shaking uncontrollably and Slick felt helpless as he listened to her reveal her deepest pain.

"That coward offed himself!" she cried out. "He murdered my mother on my sixteenth fuckin birthday and then he off'd himself right in front of me! Fuck that low-down bitch-nigga! Fuck him! He killed my mother! My *momma,* Slick! That animal murdered my mother and I hope hell is extra-hot for him!"

Slick had no way of knowing it, but Honore was lying her ass off. Her mother had been dead since she was three damn years old. It was true that she had been right there when her mother was killed, but she had slept through the whole thing and she didn't remember none of it.

Honore had grown up totally unaware of the details of that day, but she got curious when she turned thirteen so her aunt Frita and Sly McFly had sat her down and told her the whole story.

Frita and Sly told her the thing between her mother and father was one of those, "If I can't have you, can't no fuckin body have you," type of thangs. They said her parents had a fuck-a-lot, fight-a-lot relationship, and one night shit got way outta pocket.

Sly was Honore's godfather, and he said her mother had called him to come over and help her when they got to fighting that night. But by the time he got there it was too late. Sly actually cried when he told Honore that when he walked in the door her mother was already dead and her father was long gone. Sly said Honore had slept through the whole thing peacefully in her bed, and consumed by grief he had snatched her up and taken her to her Aunt Frita's house and placed her in her auntie's arms, where he knew she'd always be safe and well-taken care of.

Honore pressed her face deeper into Slick's neck hoping he'd think she was consumed with grief and anger. But on the real, she couldn't care less. Her father was never caught, so she had never met the clown and she had no idea who he was or what he looked like, and she didn't give a fuck neither.

Holding her tightly in his arms and surrounded by her silence, there was nothing for Slick to say. He felt sick to his stomach and all he could do was be there for her. He couldn't believe that they had been through almost the same fuckin thing. He knew exactly how it felt to watch your mother get murdered right in front of you. Slick also knew what it was like to have everything you held dear to your heart ripped away from you by a fuckin lunatic who was supposed to love you.

They stood there rocking in a close embrace, enduring the painful moment together as Slick whispered soothing words and let Honore cry her grief outta her system. All this shit was his fault for even mentioning the past, and the last thing he wanted was for their evening together to go down the drain. He was just about to say something to switch up the mood real quick when he felt his phone vibrating on his waist again.

"Come on," he said, taking Honore's hand as he looked down at his phone. Jewelz needed to fuckin chill. This was like the fourth time she had called. They were supposed to meet up tonight and talk bizzness, but with Honore feeling like this it wasn't happening. He pressed the call reject button and then gave Honore a long kiss as he wiped the tears from her face.

"Grab ya stuff, shorty. Let's go out and get some fresh air. Lemme take you for a spin in the whip so we can relax for a little bit."

"Okay," Honore said softly, rubbing her teary eyes. "Thanks."

She turned away from Slick holding her head down and fighting back a wicked smile. Yeah, she had this nigga. She was all up in his lil pea-brained head! She had also busted his lil amateur move with his cell phone too, which made her giggle her ass off under her breath. Whoever the bitch was who kept calling him, her pussy must not be that lethal because he was fronting her calls right off!

"I'm sorry, Slick," Honore said softly as she picked up her purse. "I didn't mean to fuck our groove up like that. You shouldn'ta let me have that Henny. That yak be having me in my feelings sometimes though."

"It's all good baby girl," Slick said making sure she knew it was cool. "I'm glad you felt close enough to me to share that kinda pain. It means you trust me. Now let's get outta here and go have some fun."

Slick scraped their plates and tossed their steak bones in the garbage, and then he sat their plates in the sink and their liquor glasses on the counter. His phone vibrated again, and he snuck another quick peek at the caller ID, confirming what he already knew. Whatever Jewelz wanted it was gonna have to wait. Determined to wipe that look of pain outta Honore's eyes, Slick turned the phone off then scooped up his car keys as him and Honore broke out and got ready to go swing from some vines in the concrete jungle.

$$$$$

Coney Island was warm and packed to capacity as Slick and Honore walked together holding hands on the crowded boardwalk. People of all races and ages had come out to enjoy the rides and the games. The smell of popcorn, cotton candy, and buttery corn on the cob, along with the loud cheers of happy kids, filled the Brooklyn air.

"Damn," Slick said as he looked over at the huge Cyclone ride spinning around like crazy. "I ain't been out here in years. My grandmother used to bring me here to get on the rides whenever she had a little extra money and I used to love it. Especially the Hell Hole."

"Yeah, it's been a real long time for me too," Honore lied as she leaned in closer to Slick. On the real, she didn't know shit about Coney Island or about nothing else in Brooklyn neither, for that matter. She was a Queens girl and she was only claiming dirty Crooklyn to throw Slick off. "I used to come out here when I was a teenager," she perpetrated. "This joint used to be popping back in the day."

"Yeah, you hungry?" Slick asked her, eyeing the sign for Nathan's restaurant. "You like frog legs?"

Honore frowned and shook her head. "Yuck. Hell no. Besides, we just ate steak. What I want with some nasty frog?"

"Ay," Slick said patting his stomach and fronting. "I still got room to grub. Wait right here for a minute. I'ma run in Nathan's and get me a frank."

Slick jetted inside the restaurant and placed an order, then he turned on his phone and checked his messages real quick. Jewelz had been blowing his shit up. There were voicemails out the ass from her but he only had time to listen to the last one where he heard her say, "I can't believe I actually did that shit, Slick. But I did! I did it for *us*."

"Ay, let's go down to the beach," Slick said to Honore as he walked out of Nathan's carrying a frank drenched in ketchup and relish and some thick-cut fries.

"I'ono about that," Honore said doubtfully as she stopped and looked down at her shoes. "That sand is kinda wet and I ain't trying to mess these Steve Madden Proto's up."

Slick bit off half of his frank and gave her a look like he hoped she wasn't that vain. "Chill, I can buy you a million pairs of those shits, French Fry."

Honore rolled her eyes. "Don't be looking at me like that. I'm just playing. I might even stick my feet in that dirty ass water."

Slick grinned, happy to see that the dark cloud that had been hanging over her was completely gone. "A'ight cool. And I might just dunk yo *ass* in that dirty water too!"

"Yeah, a'ight," Honore laughed as she punched Slick in his arm playfully.

"I'ma drown ya punk ass, don't play with me."

She grinned devilishly. "Let's go, Papi. And get rid of that nasty frank, too," she said, frowning toward the last little bit of Slick's food. "If you still hungry when we get back to the crib then I got something nice and sweet for you to eat."

Honore stepped outta her designer shoes and picked them up, then she took off running toward the water kicking sand up behind her.

Watching her hips shake, Slick didn't hesitate a lick. Forgetting all about Jewelz's message he tossed the rest of the delicious frank over his shoulder and took off running after his sexy new bae.

$$$$$

Jewelz was puzzled as fuck. It was getting late and she had left Handgun Goody's studio hours ago. She had been trying to get in touch with Slick all damn day long and she just couldn't understand why he wasn't answering his phone. He was the one who had been barking about staying in touch and getting together to talk bizzness that night, and if there was one thing that boy was about it was his bizzness.

She replayed their last conversation over and over in her mind.

Yo, stay on your toes around that sucka and keep in close contact with me at all times, ya heard? Slick had warned her. *If that nigga so much as looks at you the wrong way I want you to bail the fuck outta there and hit me up real quick so I can come kill him.*

Jewelz frowned. She had hit his ass up, all right. She had hit him up, down, left and right, over and over again, and he hadn't picked up the phone not one damn time. She was a little concerned about that but she was still amped as fuck and riding a high from today's events. She couldn't wait to get with Slick so she could update him on all the things she had learned about the Goode Brothers Gang.

Jewelz thought about the brief call she had taken when Handgun Goody had stepped outta the studio to answer his phone. Her doctor had been on the line warning her that the cancer cells in her blood were multiplying and that she needed to come in to receive treatment at once.

Jewelz didn't like to be rude, but she had told that doctor the same damn thing that she had already told his frantic nurse: She wasn't coming in for her next appointment, or for the one after that, or for the one after that neither.

She was fed up with all that chemo bullshit, and radiation treatment was definitely out too. At least for now. Maybe she'd try to get everything started up again after she had completed her mission and gotten her revenge, but there was no way in hell she could commit to continuing that type of thing right now.

Chemo could make life horrible. It was impossible to focus on a mission and function as a killer with all that pharmaceutical poison coursing through her body. All the vomiting and sweating and shitting and the feeling of being too weak to even stand up on her own two feet...nah, Jewelz just couldn't do it.

And even after listening to the frantic warnings from her doctor, Jewelz was proud of the way that she had handled that dirty-ass nigga Mike aka Handgun Goody today. She was even prouder that she hadn't sank her teeth into his chunky dick-meat and ripped his throbbing bone off at the root when he stuck it down her throat.

All of this was on Jewelz's mind as she walked through Van Dyke projects listening to Slick's phone ring in her ear. It was still rolling over to voicemail when she entered the old folks building and rode the elevator up to the fourteenth floor.

She called him again while she stood outside of his grandmother's apartment and banged on the door. He didn't answer the door neither, and when she hit the stairs and went up another flight, he wasn't up on the roof fooling around with his birds.

It was dark outside by the time Jewelz hopped in a bootleg taxi and gave the driver Slick's other address. She figured he was probably taking a lil break from his Sometimey role and chilling in the sweet two-bedroom condo that he used as a retreat when he needed to get away.

Jewelz remembered how grateful she had felt when she first got on with the Zip 'em up Crew. Slick had been real generous and he had let her crash at his condo until she could get a place of her own.

He had stayed there at the condo with her off and on sometimes, but it was like that dude had an invisible force field around him and no matter how hard she tried to get up on him, Slick had refused to give up a single beat of his banging-ass rhythm.

Jewelz still had the key to his crib. Not because she was trying to check for him, but because he had never asked for it back. She paid the cab driver and then unlocked the outside door and rode up to the twelfth floor where he rested.

"Slick?" she called out softly after ringing the bell like a million times. "Slick, are you in there?"

Wondering if he was knocked out sleeping, she stuck the key in the lock and turned it, then walked inside. It was stark quiet in the condo and it only took her a couple of seconds to take a peek in the two stylish bedrooms and realize that the apartment was empty.

It only took her a few more seconds to realize something else too. Jewelz's nose itched like a mutha as she walked into the kitchen. She saw two glasses on the counter, two eaten-off plates in the sink, and two big-ass steak bones in the trash.

And then she sneezed. A strong cloud of perfume lingered over the entire eat-in area. It was a sweet, cloistering brand that she would never forget. Poison by Dior.

Ha-chuu! Ha-chuu!

That sneaky-ass sucka! Jewelz hissed under her breath as she frowned at the gnawed down steak bones sitting at the top of the open trash.

That dirty ass dick-swinger!

Jewelz knew *exactly* who had been up in Slick's crib sucking on a fuckin cow bone and getting treated to a little candlelight dinner for two! She bet that wasn't the only bone that bitch had been sucking on too!

She sneezed again violently as the perfume particles tickled her sinuses. Jewelz couldn't see straight and she damn sure couldn't think. The only thing on her mind was the incredible fact that Slick had actually been with that bitch and brought her to his crib!

Pain flooded her heart as Jewelz sniffed the air deeply, hoping like hell she was wrong. Hoping that there was some other explanation for what her heart already knew.

But then she sneezed again.

Haaa-chuuu!

Jewelz shook her head as her sinuses burned and tears sprung to her eyes. She was like a bloodhound and her nose never lied. That bitch had been up in there. The truth was right there in the air to be smelled.

Jewelz's heart crumpled and ached. That nigga Slick had meat bone for every chick except her! While she'd been laid up letting Handgun Goody pinch all over her titties and jam his big black dick all down her throat, Slick had really, really, *really* been with that bitch!

CHAPTER 11

We Lit!

They'd had a blast chillin on the rides at Coney Island, and Slick just wasn't ready for the night to end yet. He had called ahead to a sweet hotel and told the concierge that he would pay him triple if he could get his best suite ready to his specifications in less than an hour.

Slick drove to the spot with Honore complaining that she didn't bring no extra gear with her the whole time.

"You shoulda told me we was going somewhere else. I didn't bring shit with me, Slick!"

"You with me, baby," Slick reassured her smoothly. "Any damn thing you need I can provide."

Honore had a lot more objections to spit, but when she walked into that deluxe penthouse suite and saw the glow of one hundred flickering candles and the soft petals from seventy-five pink and red roses stretched out in front of her like a long fragrant carpet, all of her complaints went right out the window.

"Oooh, Slick!" she turned to him and squealed. Throwing her arms around his neck, she stood up on her toes and planted soft kisses all over his face. "This is so damn sweet of you baby. You sure know how to make a girl feel good."

They kicked back on the real bear-skin rug drinking Moet and eating the grapes and cheese that Slick had ordered up as a light snack. The sounds of smooth R&B music played in the background as they grooved together and got turnt up.

After a few minutes Slick left Honore stretched out on her back and wiggling all over the soft rug and he went inside the expansive bathroom and ran them a bath. The concierge had been on his j.o.b. and there were mad shimmering candles and flower petals arranged around the honeymoon bathtub that was shaped like a great big heart and had Jacuzzi jets inside.

The whole scene was like some shit outta a fairytale as Slick took Honore by the hand and led her into the bathroom. She gasped in delight as she saw the spread, knowing she was about to be treated like a queen.

And Slick didn't disappoint her neither. As the candles flickered and threw tantalizing shadows against the walls, Slick slowly undressed her, taking his sweet time and staring into her beautiful eyes as he removed every stitch of her clothing.

When she was naked Honore stood there proudly in front of him, letting him see all that magnificence she was holding and knowing damn well how good her body looked from head to toe.

Slick came up outta his gear quickly. His dick was long and thick as he let Honore check his shit out, confidant that he looked like a prime stallion who could win any kinda race. He helped her into the warm sudsy water, and then he climbed in after her. Slick sat with his back against the tub and Honore nestled herself between his thighs and leaned back against his chest.

With his wood poking a hole in her back, Slick kissed her neck as he cupped warm water in his hands and then let it trickle down over her shoulders and cascade back into the tub. His fingers explored her body and glided over her beautiful skin with slippery goodness.

His hands snaked up her side and found her breasts. He rubbed bubbles all over her pert nipples and sucked up a hickey on the back of her neck while Honore moaned and played in her pussy under the water.

Turnt on beyond his wildest dreams, Slick urged Honore to lean forward and he stood up suddenly. Without a word, he reached down and picked her up in his strong arms, and dripping water, he carried her back inside the room and laid her down on the bed.

The next hour was a blur of licking and sucking and groaning and fucking. Honore ended up on top, riding his dick like it was a golden pony. She bounced on that shit and bucked her ass back and forth, growling deep in her throat as she had the orgasm of her life. Shrieking, she squirted cum and coated his dick in her slippery sugar as she fell forward, totally fucked out.

And when Slick couldn't hold back no longer, he let loose too. He gripped her by her tight waist and banged his dick up inside of her until his whole damn back locked up. He massaged her ass with both hands as he shot his load and grunted out loud, loving every bit of Honore and her delicious body.

Two hours later Slick was feeling good about the sight of Honore leaning back and catching some zzz's in the passenger seat of his whip as he drove her to her friend's crib. That warm bath, that hot fucking, and the cool air that she had soaked up earlier near the salty ocean water of Coney Island was like the ultimate sleeping pill for her. Her head was bobbing with the car's movements, and every now and then a soft snore escaped her parted lips.

Slick drove down the Brooklyn streets feeling gooder than shit. Every now and then he would glance over at Honore and wonder how he had gotten lucky enough to land such a beautiful chick who had all the attributes he wanted in a woman: a sharp wit, high intelligence, a good sense of humor, and a fire burning in her heart.

"I need a soda." Honore sat up abruptly and opened her eyes. They were a couple of blocks away from her friend's spot in Bed-Stuy where he was dropping her off. "Can we stop at the corner store?"

Slick nodded. They coulda stopped on the fuckin moon if she wanted to. Matter fact, any damn thing this girl wanted to do was all the way cool with him.

He pulled his whip up in front of a local bodega and killed the engine. There were nigs standing around outside manning the corner and regulating the streets with a vengeance, but Slick wasn't worried in the least as he got out and went around to the passenger side to open Honore's door.

Mami was a lady, and she definitely knew how she was supposed to be treated. Slick laughed to himself as she sat there perched in her seat, just waiting for him to open her door and offer her his hand. Some old regular nigga from the hood mighta jumped outta his ride and hit the store without even looking back for her, but Slick's grandma had raised him better than that.

Slick led her straight through the crowd of thug niggas who were standing around outside. He knew better than to walk a path around them wolves and give them that kind of respect. Nah, predatory niggas caught the scent of other predatory niggas. With his grip firmly on Honore's hand Slick parted the crowd like Black Jesus and walked inside strong as fuck, without the slightest bit of fear in his heart.

Honore got a Nehi grape soda and a bag of Lays potato chips. Slick picked up a cold one, and after paying the old Arab dude at the counter they headed toward the door.

Once again Slick pushed right through the lil slangas crowded around the doorway. He stood tall like a boss, and although he saw the cold heat lurking in a few eyes, he saw respect there too.

He had just put Honore back in the car and was walking around the front to get in the driver's seat when somebody called his name.

"Yo, Slick! Sup?" Wild Man hollered, as he ran across the street dodging traffic.

"Sup wit'chu?" Slick grinned, dapping his boy out. "Fuck is you doing way over here, man?"

Wild Man nodded at the blinking lights of Wong Fu Chinese restaurant across the street. "I just swung by to close up the restaurant for my uncle Ming."

He peered through the front window of the whip and hit Slick with a shocked look. "But what the fuck is *you* doin over here, ak?"

Slick shrugged and cracked the cap on his cold brew.

"I'm just giving a honey a lil ride home. I'm about to drop her off and head back across town."

"Yo, slime," Wild Man said, leaning forward so he could see into the car better. "Please tell me that ain't the chick from that jewelry joint on Fulton Street. *Please* tell me it ain't her."

Before Slick could answer Wild Man snatched the passenger door open and eyeballed the delicious-looking chick who was perched in the front seat.

"How you doing, Miss Lady?" Wild Man said grinning as the fine chick gave him a real curious look.

"You probably don't remember me," he said as his hot Asian eyes swept over her from her bulging breasts down to her slim ankles. "But I damn sure remember you."

"Nope," Honore said. "I don't remember you."

"That's probably because I had on a mas—"

"Yo shut the fuck up!" Slick barked as he elbowed his boy in the chest and quickly slammed Honore's door closed. "Don't be fuckin around like that stupid ass," he growled, his voice low and hard.

Wild Man kept right on grinning but the burning question in his eyes was definitely gonna be asked.

"Yo, my man. How long you been shittin where you eat at, bruh?"

Slick shook his head. "It ain't even like that, homey. You got it twisted, nigga."

"Oh yeah?" Wild Man looked skeptical, but he eased off that shit and backed up anyway. "That's good to know, muh'fucka. 'Cause if one of us gotta have his shit twisted then I damn sure hope it's me."

CHAPTER 12

Love Jones

The next day Jewelz played it cucumber-cool when she got the call she'd been waiting for. It was Slick. He wanted to take her out to eat so they could go over the details of her meeting with Handgun Goody.

"Oh, so now you wanna talk to me?" Jewelz had spit, then she backed off. "Never mind," she said. They wasn't doing this shit over the phone. Nah, she wanted to be looking dead in Slick's eyes when she started firing shots. She wanted to blast on his monkey ass face-to-face! "What time you wanna meet up?" she asked him. "And where?"

The childhood friends met at a table for two at Mitchell's Soul Food Kitchen on Vanderbilt Avenue in Brooklyn. The joint was packed out with hungry patrons who came to get some of that sweet southern soul food in their bellies. The waiters were good-natured and outgoing, which was almost as pleasing as the delicious platters of chicken, ribs, fish, and turkey wings that they served.

Slick was going ham on his plate of fried chicken, collard greens, potato salad, and rice with gravy, but Jewelz was barely picking at her food.

"Damn!" she eyed him as he dug into his plate. "Slow down before you choke ya damn self out. I'm good at a lotta shit but the Heimlich maneuver ain't my thang."

Slick laughed and kept right on devouring his grub. "I'm hungry, yo. A nigga gotta eat."

He raised his eyes from his plate for a moment and eyed her picking over her baked mac and cheese, meat loaf, cabbage, and candy yams.

"Yo, baby, you look like you getting kinda skinny over there. Eat all that shit up and then let me buy you some banana pudding for dessert."

Jewelz smirked. "Skinny? It's called discipline, Slick, and don't get it fucked up. Have you peeked back there at my ass lately? It's far from bony, baby. I'm fit and firm. I stick to a healthy diet and I keep my junk food intake to a minimum because I gotta stay on point. That's how I stay ahead of these haters, you dig me?"

She stared into his eyes and put out so much emotion that it made Slick uneasy and he put his head back down in his plate. It was a look of lust mixed with deep love, sadness, and pain.

"Look, we came out here to eat and talk bizzness, a'ight?" he mumbled. "Just fuckin eat girl. And then we can talk."

"*Tuh!*" Jewelz flicked her hand at him. "See, that's your problem, Slick. You always so damn serious! I know the shit we do requires us to play a kissing game with death, but you ain't dead yet! Every King needs to have him a Queen by his side. You know exactly how I feel about you," she pleaded, "I just don't understand why you gotta look for what you want someplace else when I'm offering you everything you need right here!"

Slick put his fork down and sighed. He didn't wanna go there with this girl. Their shit was way too complicated to fuck with and he wasn't sure if he totally understood it himself.

"It ain't that simple, Jewelz," Slick tried to explain. "I got a lotta shit I need to overcome as a man. My heart just ain't ready to love a woman like you just yet 'cause it's still cold, you feel me? Why you think I got into this bizz in the first place, huh? Because I didn't have nobody to give a fuck about! That's what allows me to do what I do! I just can't turn that shit on and off, baby. To keep it a hunnid, if I let you get too close I'ma start worrying about you while we out there on the job. And that's the type of stupid shit that can get both of us killed. I don't know why you can't seem to understand that, tho. You need to stop living in what it used to be and start living in what it is right now. That don't mean I don't care about you, Jewelz. I do care. I care a whole lot. I just think you'd be better off with a different type of hitta, that's all."

Slick knew his little speech was all for nothing when he saw the anger on her face and the tears that began to well up in her eyes.

"Boy, *bye!*" she snapped. "Excuses, excuses, *excuses!* You can just cut the fucking crap, okay? You over there slaughtering that damn greasy chicken like you starving when you and some random bitch just chowed down on some big old steaks last night! You think I don't know about that shit? If you mashing it up with that stupid bitch then why don't you just say so?"

"Girl what the hell you talking about?" Slick spit through his teeth, motioning for her to keep her voice down low.

But Jewelz didn't give a damn that people had noticed them and were starting to whisper and stare.

"For real, Slick. Why you do me like that, huh? I would do *any* fucking thing for you! I've pushed niggas for you, I've gotten close to niggas for you, and if you hadn't turned your phone off last night when I was tryna call you then you woulda known that I've even s— "

Jewelz shook her head and bit back her words and swallowed them painfully. "Forget it. You let some bitch make you igg my calls when you knew damn well I was out there working on a mission for *us*. That shit was foul, nigga. Real flagrant."

Slick was caught out there wearing the stupid face. There was no way to deny that she was speaking the truth. So he did what most dudes in a situation like that did. He played dumb and lied.

"Yo, ain't no bitch make me turn off my phone! I'on't know what the fuck you talking about—"

"You've got somebody, don't you?" Jewelz cut in and demanded the truth. A look of such intense pain was in her eyes that Slick found it hard to look in her face. "You have a girlfriend, don't you?"

Slick threw up his hands. "I'm a *man,* Jewelz. Hell yeah I like to fuck and I get with females sometimes, a'ight?"

"It's that *bitch*, ain't it? You fucking with that bitch named Honore that we snatched off'a Fulton Street that night, right?"

Guilt fell over Slick's head like a thick winter blanket. He had no room to move other than backwards.

"Yo, how you know who I been with? You been following me or something? And how you know what the fuck I been eating in my crib? You got me under surveillance or something?"

"I swung by your place last night," Jewelz admitted calmly. "I couldn't wait to tell you all about my meeting with Goody. I had called you like a thousand times but you didn't answer, and since I wasn't that far away I popped up on your ass."

"You popped up and did what? Went looking through my damn trash?"

Jewelz's bottom lip quivered.

"You really like her type, don't you, Slick? I mean, you like her type better than you like my type, right?"

"What *type?*" he blasted on her.

"Why is that, Slick?" Jewelz asked like she really, really just wanted to know. "I mean, I know I'm beautiful from head to toe, and that's undeniable. So is it because she's in college? Is it because she talks proper and acts all high-class and educated and I didn't even make it outta high school?"

"*Jewelz!*"

"No, dead-ass. I wanna know for real. What is it? Is it because she's a redbone and I'm milk chocolate? Is it her long hair?" She reached up and touched the baseball cap covering her head. "Because you know I got some long hair too! Or," Jewelz said, her voice starting to really quiver, "is it because she can have a baby for you and I can't? Or maybe its all them men I used to fuck when Fat Donnie and Chimp Charlie snatched me and had me out there working them motel rooms—"

"Jewelz! Baby *please—*"

"Just *tell* me," she insisted quietly, her pain turning to rage. "You can tell me, Lil Slick! I swear to *God* I can take it! I mean, after all the crazy shit I been through in this life I can take *anything*, so just tell me," she jumped to her feet and swung her fist at him viciously.

"What exactly does that bitch have on me???"

Slick caught her wrist and held it firmly in his grip. Everybody in the joint was staring in hushed silence as tears streamed down her cheeks and her body shook with sobs.

Slick stood up slowly. He looked into the windows of her soul for a few seconds. Then he gently brought her fist forward and pressed his lips tenderly to the back of her hand and kissed her warm skin.

"I'm sorry baby girl," he said quietly. "I'm sorry."

A young cat with braids who had been sitting at the next table with two older women got up outta his chair and stepped over to them.

"Yo, sweetheart," he said, placing his hand gently on Jewelz's shoulder. "You a'ight, lovely? You too fine to be crying over some chump."

He sneered at Slick and smirked. "Any other time I would snuff this bitch-nigga out for you right on the spot, but my moms and my auntie are sitting in that booth right there and they both worried about you. You want me to slide your chair over so you can eat with us?"

Jewelz shook her head. "No. Thank you, but I'm not hungry no more. I'm just gonna leave."

"A'ight, that's cool. Then maybe me and my mother can give you a ride someplace?"

Jewelz looked like she wanted to say something more, but then she snatched her hand from Slick's grip and bit down on her lip. She rambled through her Birkin bag and pulled out some money and dropped it on the table.

Then without even looking in Slick's direction she slid on her Ray-Ban shades and lifted her chin and strutted out the restaurant refusing to say another word.

"*Pussy-ass nigga!*" the dude with the cornrows barked at Slick with a look of cold contempt in his eyes.

Slick igged the young nigga as he sat back down and watched Jewelz leave the restaurant. People nearby were staring at him and throwing him shade like he had just beat her down with his fists or something.

He picked up a chicken wing but his appetite flew out the window as he pondered on his fucked up situation. Jewelz's words had been bitter cold, and to Slick's surprise they had cut him deeper than a knife.

CHAPTER 13

Beautiful Deceptions

The sky was darkening with an approaching late afternoon rainstorm. Shoppers were scurrying up and down Jamaica Avenue in Queens trying to make it home before the clouds split open and dumped a ton of rain down on the urban streets.

Totally stressed out over the looming deadline that was approaching with those killer investors, Honore had decided to take a quick walk to try to clear her head. She left her apartment and ended up wandering into a brand new high-end spa. She had a deep-tissue massage that lasted over an hour, and she was surprised by how much it relieved her anxiety and mellowed her mood.

Feeling a whole lot better, Honore swung by her favorite nail salon to get a mani and a pedi. The splatter of hard rain was pelting the shop's glass windows as she quickly paid for her services and left a generous tip.

She pushed out the door and was rushing across the wet sidewalk with her head down against the rain when she literally bumped right into him.

"Yo, my bad," he said, grabbing her wrist to steady her as she stumbled and fought to stay on her feet. "Damn," he said, ignoring the falling rain as he stared deeply into her eyes. "Excuse me, pretty lady. For failing to notice the sexiest woman in New York when she was crossing right in front of me."

Honore ignored the rain too as she gave him a cold, scornful look. What were the odds of running into him way out here? He was a different type of dude than she was used to, but with his buff body, saggy jeans, and fresh Jordans, it was obvious that he came from the streets. But not from *these* streets.

"What are you doing around here?" she asked, shaking his hand off of hers. "Are you following me or something?"

He grinned and nodded towards a Chinese hole-in-the-wall nearby. "Nah, I'm not following you, sweetheart. I just came outta that joint right there. I do a few solids for the owner sometimes."

Honore stared into his slanted eyes to see if he was lying. She found no deception in him and he did smell a little bit like Egg-Fu-Young.

He grinned even wider as she grilled him, and his handsome face seemed to light up the gray sky.

"Don't look at me like that. I'm being for real," he said laughing. "You studying me like you got a lie detector in your eyes or some shit, shorty. What you doing way out here in Queens? I thought you lived in Brooklyn?"

"I *do* live in Brooklyn," Honore lied with an attitude. "I had to hook up with one of my classmates on a project today. She lives in Queens so I came out here to handle it."

He nodded, and even through the raindrops Honore couldn't help but notice how fine he was in a different sorta way.

"Ay," he ducked his head as fat drops of rain slid down the back of his neck. "It's starting to really come down, you know? If you need a ride back to Brooklyn I can take you," he offered.

She shook her head quickly. "Nah, no thank you," she declined. "I don't fuck with strangers."

"That's good," he said, not pressed in the least. "'Cause I ain't a stranger."

"You are to me. I don't know you like that."

He nodded, hunching his shoulders against the rain. The wind had suddenly kicked up a few notches too.

"A'ight, cool. It's about to be a storm out here sweetheart, but there's a nice little lounge right up the block. How about you let me buy you a drink so we can get dry and get to know each other a little better?"

Honore opened her mouth to say hell fuckin no, but then she hesitated as her devious nature kicked into gear.

"What's your name again?" she asked him.

"William Choo," he said. "But they call me Wild Man."

Raindrops brushed her cheeks as she hit him with a sly, but sexy smirk.

"Oh really? What's so *wild* about you?"

He laughed, then grabbed her hand and pulled her toward his parked ride.

"Hop in the whip with me and you'll find out."

$$$$$

It was now or never. Jewelz paused outside the thick wooden door and made sure her shit was thoroughly smooth before she rang the bell.

It had been a long and painful day for her and she needed to relax and unwind. She especially needed to take her mind off that nigga Slick and all the heartache and confusion that he had caused her in the soul food restaurant earlier that day.

Jewelz loved that dude with all her heart, but it looked like love just wasn't in her cards, and it damn sure wasn't what she needed right now.

Nah, what she needed right now was a stress reliever. A muscle relaxer. Something quick and hard and hot to take her mind off her turmoil and bring her some inner-peace.

She'd had to overcome a lot of guilt and shame for her to come here tonight, and a big part of her hated what she was about to do. But the stress she was under had her emotions running all over the damn place. Her heart was hungry and her body was too. No matter how she looked at it, it all came down to the same thing.

She was lonely as hell and she wanted to lay down with a man.

And what was wrong with that? Why couldn't she have the same thing that other grown women had? Why couldn't some of her dreams ever come true?

Jewelz was sick and tired of playing the stand-on-your-own-two-feet role. Forget all that shit. Them type of chicks who couldn't admit they needed a man were just a bunch of unfulfilled bitter bitches.

Right now Jewelz was standing all in her need and owning that shit. She wanted her a man. But she wasn't tryna hot-sheet it with just any old random piece of dick. She was way classier than that, and after what she had endured as a teenager, she'd had enough off-brand sex to last her a lifetime.

Nah, what she needed tonight was a soul connection. Somebody who was gonna hold her in his arms and love her like a natural woman. Jewelz knew her time on this earth was short and she couldn't afford to wait around for Slick to get his shit together. And that's why she was here right now.

Staring at the thick wooden door, she tried to talk herself out of it one last time. She had already told ol' boy she wasn't coming over, and even when he begged her to change her mind, she had still refused.

Because the truth was, as much as this dude satisfied her physical thang and treated her like she was the only woman in the world, there was some deep shame up in Jewelz's game.

No, she wasn't cuffed to nobody and she wasn't the cheating type neither, but Jewelz couldn't help feeling some kinda way about being with him. She knew plenty of bitches who woulda loved to be in her place because not only was he fine as hell with a tight body, he was a perfect gentlemen and he treated her with the utmost respect. This dude had a special way of looking into the deepest parts of her and seeing all her insecurities, and then making them seem like they were all her greatest assets. And oh yeah, the package he was holding was long and strong and he could fuck his ass off too.

Jewelz stood there staring at the door. She knew she should resist, but instead of turning around and heading back to her car, her need got the best of her. Taking a deep breath she poked out her finger and rang that bell, knowing damn well what she was gonna get from the man standing on the other side of the door.

"Hey, brown sugar," the handsome dude said as he opened the door. He was naked from the waist up and wearing just a pair of black boxer shorts on the bottom. "I'm glad you changed your mind."

Jewelz stood back and eyed him for a moment. He was just a little over average height but his body was solid and muscular. His chest and arms were cut-up like a sculpture and she knew from experience that he was stronger than the average man. On top of all that, dude had a dangerous swagger about him that was hot and sexually exciting, and Jewelz already knew he was thorough as hell in the streets and in the sheets.

He reached out and tugged Jewelz by her waist and pulled her close. His deep sigh told her he loved the way her curvy body felt against his, and he inhaled her scent as he pressed his nose and warm lips into the crease of her neck.

Tears gathered in Jewelz's eyes as she gave in and allowed her greedy hands to roam all over his muscular back. A gigantic spark of fire ignited between her legs that she couldn't wait for him to put out. She knew she was wrong but she couldn't help herself. Her pussy was leaking and she needed the comfort of a man. She leaned against him, loving the feeling of his hard body pressed up against hers. He was all over her too. Lips, hands, tongue. Like he had been feening his whole damn life, just for her.

Why can't Slick need me this way?

Jewelz's knees grew weak as she stepped deeper inside his spacious house in a high-end Staten Island neighborhood. The man picked her up in his strong arms and carried her across his threshold. Her tears fell on his bare shoulder and he looked down at her in surprise.

"Hey," he said softly. "It's okay, beautiful." He dried her eyes with his tender kisses. Then he nudged the front door shut with his foot and it automatically locked behind him.

"Ssssh…don't cry," he whispered between his kisses. "Please don't cry."

Jewelz's tears flowed even harder as the reality of what she was about to do sank in and all kinds of guilt washed over her heart.

"Come on now, what you got to cry about?" her secret lover asked softly as his hungry lips grazed her ear.

"Whitey's here, baby. I got you, Jewelz, and I ain't never gonna let you go."

CHAPTER 14

Art and Murder

Way on the other side of New York, Wild Man and Honore were sitting at a table at the Nuyorican Poets Café. The lights were dimmed low and the large animated crowd was starting to settle in for the festivities.

The Lower East Side café hosted some of the dopest up-and-coming spoken-word poets, hip-hop, and performing artists from all around the city. People of all colors and backgrounds came here to be entertained and inspired.

"Check it out, *Wild Man*," Honore said with a snide grin on her face. She was sipping on the Henny he had ordered for her and feeling real relaxed. "I realize we don't know each other like that, but can I keep it real with you for a minute?"

"Aww man, here we go," Wild Man said as he smirked playfully. "When a chick starts out with a statement like that then you know something crazy is coming up next. But a'ight, whassup? What's on your mind, sweetheart?"

"*Wellll*," Honore said as she looked around the spot. "What made you bring me here? I mean, it's definitely not 'right up the block' like you said, but regardless this just don't seem like your kind of scene. You look like the street type who takes chicks to gangsta rap concerts instead of bringing them to diverse cultural places like this."

"Oh, it's like that?" Wild Man fronted like he was offended as he took down a double shot of Henny with one swallow. "A'ight, ga'head. Keep underestimating me. A sharp cookie like you should know better than to judge a book by the cover. I'm all about culture and diversity, sweetie, and the raw talent that comes through these doors is legendary. These cats up in here are lyrical geniuses. They express themselves in a way that I can't."

"Well, I like to think of myself as poetry in motion," Honore clowned as she grinned and batted her eyelashes. "I shop and get my hair done with such style and grace it's unbelievable. I'm also that bad bitch Beyoncé when I sing in the shower too."

They both laughed at Honore's vain statement as they continued to soak up the eclectic ambiance of the crowd.

"So," Honore said a few moments later. "If you're not a poet and you're not one to spit on the mic, how do you express your inner feelings?" she asked innocently.

"Oh, I don't spit, but I consider myself an artist nevertheless," Wild Man said, as he stared dead into her gorgeous hazel eyes. "Except my paint brush is usually a gun and my canvas is the New York City streets."

"So in other words, you're just a thug, huh?" Honore said deciding to push his buttons a little bit. "A petty thief. Are you also the type to get your rocks off by oppressing and destroying your own neighborhood? Are you one of them dudes who's motivated strictly by the money?"

"Please don't insult me," Wild Man said as he leaned back in his chair and grilled her. "I've been all the way around the world, sweetheart. Trust me, can't no lil dumb thug-nigga do what I do. I'm the type who takes pride in his work. The satisfaction lies in the quality of how I line shit up and execute my plans. The thrill of the hunt is what fuels me. Money is just the bonus I get for doing what I do best."

Honore's eyes narrowed as she prepared to match wits with him. She could spot a wolf a mile a fuckin way. Although she had to admit the sheep's clothing this wolf was wearing looked damn good on him.

She studied him even closer. She had never fucked with an Asian who sounded and acted like a brotha before. Wild Man had a sharp tongue and everything he said seemed to have a double meaning. Honore sensed a darkness in him and she had to admit that it intrigued her. She could tell he was definitely cunning and on his game, yet she also detected a weakness in his armor. A tiny chink in his coat of steel. He seemed to enjoy bragging about his street skills, and that's where Honore saw her opening.

"So, since you're such a sharp hunter how did your plans work out the night you busted up in that jewelry store and stormed into my life?" she asked quietly as she stared at him intently.

He shrugged. "What makes you ask that?"

"I ask because I'm not convinced your little band of thieves came shooting shit up at my job just for the love of the sport. There must have been something real valuable in that briefcase y'all stole, huh?"

Wild Man opened his mouth to answer but he was interrupted by a couple of artists who recognized him as a regular and came over to greet him. They dapped each other out and showed some love before moving on.

"You're right, Honore," Wild Man said coldly after the dudes were gone. "Monetary needs gotta get met in order to stay up on bigger goals, but what I'm saying is that cash isn't my main motivation. Everything ain't always as it seems, ya dig? Yeah, I ain't gonna lie. We snatched that briefcase, and what was in there will be put to good use when need be. Trust me, its in safe hands. But that's just one piece of the puzzle."

Honore shrugged, faking outward indifference to what he was rapping, but on the inside the wheels of wrath were rapidly turning in her head. Because the way she was reading between the lines, Wild Man was basically saying that his crew still had the briefcase and they hadn't done anything yet with the contents. And that's exactly what she had wanted to hear.

Honore knew this was just a vague little clue, but it was enough to boost her hopes that she might just recover that diamond and save her ass. And judging by the way this cat was staring at the deep slit between her plump titties she was pretty sure that if she pushed and probed the right way she could get him to say even more. She could definitely tell how badly Wild Man wanted to smash her. Now it was her job to figure out how to use his wants to take care of her needs.

But before Honore could ask another question the Café's host came to the stage and grabbed the mic.

Whattup, yo! I hope y'all are ready for some of the illest underground poets that this city we call home has to offer! Tonight we 'bout to be doing it big y'all. So give your undivided attention to these artists as they rock the muthafuckin house! It's time to get shit started!

One by one, talented young poets and lyricists, both male and female, got up on stage and started doing their thing. They conveyed emotions and deep thoughts through rising and falling rhythms complimented by intriguing word patterns. Some styles were aggressive in delivery and others were subtle cries from the heart. The content touched on subjects of race, love, pain, failure and success with such creativity that it captivated the spirit of the audience. The joint erupted in applause each time a performance was finished, and Honore immediately understood why this was considered one of the dopest forums for spoken word in the whole city.

At the end of the set the host announced that there was going to be a brief intermission, so Wild Man took the opportunity to order them some more drinks.

"Yo this shit is sweet. I'm really glad you brought me here Wild Man," Honore said, amped up from the liquor and the good energy that filled the room. "They're going hard in here tonight. This is way different from the usual hip-hop spots and strip clubs. You know, the typical type of low-level joints that some guys wanna take a girl to."

Wild Man laughed. "What? You mean my man Slick ain't never brought you out to nothing classy like this before?" he asked as he grinned at her. "Yo, Slick comes through here on the regular, and since y'all been spending so much time together lately I woulda thought he'd have exposed you to this form of art by now."

Honore shrugged. "Yeah, me and Slick hang out a little bit sometimes," she said, downplaying their relationship. "But it ain't nothing serious. So don't get it twisted. I do my own thing. Although I occasionally like to be tied up, I'm *never* tied down. If you catch my drift."

Wild Man laughed at the remark and responded, "Yeah, I get what you're saying. You move them sexy hips to the beat of your own drum."

"Exactly," Honore said as she crossed her legs and eyed him seductively.

The announcer made his way back to the stage to introduce the next poet of the evening.

"I hope y'all are enjoying these dope young men and women who've been killing the scene tonight. Coming up next is the two-time Poet Of the Month who hails from Castle Hill Projects in the Bronx. Lets give it up y'all for Albie Anthony!"

Dude stepped up to the mic and started heating that shit up.

"I'm America's problem!...young black angry and from the bottom! I ain't asking to be saved...I could never fit in with nine to fives...or suits and ties...me and minez move them pies...so it's either you do or die or muthafucka, move aside! Pops who? Moms where? I'm statistically a victim...born with an itch I could never scratch...just a product of somebody's nasty addiction!

The scruffy-looking kid with the nappy Afro kept spilling his dark tale that had the audience hanging off every word. The crazy shit about it was he didn't look a day older than the age of twelve. Yet his delivery reached out and grabbed you while his graphic depictions were high definition vivid images to the mind's eye. You could just tell his pain was genuine. The old folks would say, *that lil nigga been here before!*

I'ma go hard nigga...I make something out of nothing...got the heart to go and get it...ain't no faking or no frontin...I'm the coldest nigga out...broken hearted...discarded and forgotten about...I'm the one they always locked out the house...but love never lived here...no fucks to give here...my life is too real you fake niggas can't pretend here...I'm America's problem! It started and it ends...here.

The crowd erupted with a loud roar of cheers, hands clapping, and snapping fingers.

"Talk that shit, Al!" A hyped-up fan yelled from the corner of the club.

Albie stood there visibly shaking as raw emotion raced through him. He had given the mic everything he had and he was breathing heavily. When he regained his composure Albie waved to the crowd in appreciation. He had just put in *work*.

Honore smiled over at Wild Man as the crowd stood up and continued to go crazy. "Hey, you got some pull around here, right? Can you introduce me to that kid, Albie?" she asked with her eyes wide.

Wild Man thought about it for a second.

"I got you." He got up from the table and disappeared into the sea of people. Honore sipped on some more of her drink and a few moments later the cheers in the lounge started to erupt again. She looked up and saw Wild Man cutting through the crowd and making his way back to the table with Albie right behind him as the crowd showed their love.

"Albie," Wild Man said as he made a hand gesture towards Honore. "This is my lady friend, Honore. She was feeling your flow and wanted to meet you."

Honore peeped the nonchalant demeanor the young kid displayed. He was from the streets and he looked like everything he had portrayed in his poetry piece. Albie's eyes were dark and unforgiving. He didn't look too happy to be there at all.

"W'sup, Albie," Honore said as she smiled at him. "I don't wanna take up too much of your time, I just wanted you to know that you were astounding tonight. I know that look in your eyes because I've had it in minez before, too. But I ain't here to preach to you. I'm here to be a blessing."

Honore reached in her purse and pulled out a knot of bills totaling a thousand dollars and handed it to the kid.

"You have the gift of words, young man," Honore said as she looked him dead in his eyes and matched his cold stare. "Find a way to make it work for you. Channel those inner demons. Weak men sell their souls to these streets. Strong men use their brains and try to find ways outta the streets. Which one are you?"

The young boy nodded as if he understood, but he hesitated with the money in his hand. He couldn't believe that somebody he didn't even know was being that generous and he didn't trust it. Wild Man looked at Honore then reached into his own pocket and pulled out a knot of hundreds. He counted off ten bills and handed them to Albie too.

"That's yours, little homey," Wild Man said as put his hand on Albie's shoulder. "This ain't no handout bro, it's an investment. Both of us see the potential in you and we want you to rise above this madness, a'ight? Take heed to what this pretty lady right here just said and keep fighting, you dig?"

This time Albie cracked a smile as he accepted the cash and then he nodded in appreciation. "Thanks to both of y'all," he said as he turned around to walk away.

He took a few steps and then spun back around and spoke from his soul.

"By the way," he said as he stared at Honore like she was the most beautiful thing he had ever seen in his life. "You asked me what kind of man am I? I'm one of the strong ones."

"I know you are, baby," Honore said softly as she nodded at the young boy. Something in his eyes told her that he was taking what she'd said to heart. She'd actually found some joy in helping Albie, and looking at Wild Man she could tell he'd found joy in it also.

"Ay, let's get out of here," Wild Man suggested in a low voice when the boy walked away. Honore agreed. She stood up and grabbed her purse, admitting to herself that she had really had a good time. And when outta nowhere Wild Man stepped to her and started tonguing her down with mad heat right there at the table, she knew her night was about to get even better.

$$$$$

What had started out as a completely shitty day was turning out to be a real hot night. The drinks that Honore had guzzled down with Wild Man at the spoken word club had her head in the clouds. She had rode with him to a nearby hotel and both of them had talked shit the whole way. Honore liked Wild Man's easy back and forth banter. There was a little verbal competition thang going on between them, and their playful sparring with words was something they both greatly enjoyed.

"I hope you ready to put your money where your mouth is and take this L," Wild Man joked as they got inside the hotel room and prepared to go at it.

Honore just laughed. If there was one thing she was at all times, it was confident about her shit. She was practically flawless. Not only was she straight beautiful in the face, she had the type of body that drove men wild.

They stripped outta their clothes and Honore checked Wild Man out. She had never fucked an Asian before but she was game for it. Wild Man was overly buff in the body, with massive arms and shoulders that looked like Superman. With all them fuckin outrageous muscles she had expected him to have one of them lil undersized dicks, but instead Mister Chinaman had a nice hunk of tube-steak swinging down against his thigh.

In an instant their lips were locked and their hands were roaming and exploring new territory. Honore soon realized that Wild Man was a titty man, and he handled her tits and nipples with expert care. Wasn't none of that harsh squeezing and excruciating nipple-pulling that some amateur niggas did. Nah, Wild Man stroked and massaged her breasts with just the right amount of care and pressure. He paid sweet attention to her nipples as he guided one to his mouth and sucked it between his lips like it was a sweet golden raisin.

Honore moaned and squirmed as he flicked his tongue back and forth over her sensitive bud, all the white rubbing and cupping her other breast with his free hand.

Keeping up his tongue game, Wild Man slid his hand over Honore's shoulder and down to her hip. He pressed her down flat on the bed and his fingers trailed lower as he grasped her thigh.

Spreading her legs wide, he took his lips off her big titty and let it bound free. As she gasped in pleasure he lowered his head down to that spot in the middle of her triangle, and took a long, deep sniff.

"Peach pie," he said, staring at her pretty pussy as his mouth watered for a taste. Honore's dugout was just as beautiful as the rest of her. Neatly trimmed, her slit leaked creamy sweetness as she anticipated what she was about to get.

Wild Man dove in face first and went to town. He pushed Honore's legs back until they formed an "M" shape, then stuck his nose up in her slit and wiped her juices all over his face.

Honore squirmed around on the bed as Wild Man showed her what he was working with. He put his pussy-eating skills on full display as he sucked her clit between his lips and ran his tongue back and forth over the tip of it until Honore couldn't take no more and bucked her hips and tried to get away.

But Wild Man wasn't having that shit. He grabbed her hips and attacked that pussy again with his tongue, extending it out as far as he could and stiffening it like it was a dagger. With expert precision he slid his mouth-meat in and outta her cave, pausing every now and then to give her clit a swirl and then lick her sweet asshole.

Flipping her over, Wild Man snatched his pants off the floor and put on a glove, then he jerked her up by her hips until she was on all fours in the doggie position. He guided the head of his dick into her spot and eased himself in. Honore pointed her ass in the air and moaned as his thickness filled her up to the brim.

Wild Man thrust his dick in and out of her juicy pussy as his meat swelled up and got even harder. Going up on his knees, he helped Honore raise up too, without dislodging him from her hot sucking tunnel. Leaning back on his heels, Wild Man cupped both of her breasts in his hands and nibbled on her ear. He fucked her from behind, enjoying the way her fleshy ass slapped up against his balls.

Letting a titty go he gripped her hip and held her in place, and banged himself up in her until she yelped in painful pleasure.

He dug her out so good that before long Honore was ready to throw up a white flag and surrender. She reached down and felt his joint sliding in and outta her pussy, then fingered her own clit deliciously, pressing and squeezing her lady meat until her pussy squirted hot liquid and she came with a yell.

Honore collapsed forward on her stomach and Wild Man dove down on top of her with his dick still lodged inside her snatch. Gripping her ass-cheeks, he spread her butt open wide and gave three mighty thrusts and pounded that pussy until his balls erupted and warm cum filled up his glove.

All Honore could do was lay there, all fucked out and slobbering on the sheet. She took great pride in her fuck game, but Wild Man was clearly an expert and going for round two with him was definitely gonna be a hellacious challenge!

CHAPTER 15

Homey Hoppin Hoes

It had been a great night of freaky sex with a bad and beautiful bitch, and now it was time to make the donuts and greet a new day. Honore had told him not to worry about her 'cause she was taking a cab back to Brooklyn, so Wild Man left her sleeping in the hotel bed and jumped into his Lexus coup. He lit up a blunt and sat back in his seat and relaxed. He exhaled the Sour Diesel smoke and replayed the little turn up he'd had with Honore in his head.

The girl had some sweet pussy on her and wasn't no denying that. Wild Man knew the main reason he had fucked with her was to prove a point to Slick, but shit was sure to get crucial if the lines between them fucked around and got blurred. Besides, if Honore was turning up with him then she couldn't be feeling Slick as much as Slick thought she was. Either way, bitches were disposable and Wild Man didn't give a fuck. He was doing him and having fun in the process.

His phone started vibrating in his pocket and he pulled it out and glanced at the number then clicked it on.

"Thinking of the devil," Wild Man said with a snide laugh. "W'sup, boss man?"

"Cut it out nigga," Slick responded. "Where the fuck is you? I texted you last night and told you to call me."

Wild Man cursed. "Damn! My bad. I was boning this cute lil chickenhead and the time got away from me. What did I miss?"

"Put your scrambler on," Slick instructed him.

"A'ight," Wild Man said, fitting the high-tech device over his phone. "It's on."

"Cool. The bird came back on that job and it's a green light on the triple pay," Slick informed him.

"*Sayyy daaatt*," Wild Man drawled as he got excited. "See what did I tell you? We the best like D.J. Khalid my nigga! We deserve every penny! Fuck all that low-ball shit. They know who to get with when they want some shit cleaned up nice and proper-like."

"I feel you on that," Slick said. "But dig the move. Queens is your main bitch, right? Make sure she dresses real nice and her performance is flawless. A good chick should be the reflection of her good man, you feel me?"

Despite the scrambling device Slick was still talking in code. He was saying the borough of Queens was Wild Man's responsibility. Wild Man was gonna be the lead gunman on the Queen of Diamonds mission, and it was his job to make sure everything was planned and executed correctly.

"Did we get any more info? A day, a time, a place?"

"Nah. Not yet. We still waiting on that part."

"This shit is crazy," Wild Man shook his head and said.

"Relax, son. It's all good. If you need some help get with Noodles," Slick said. "He's gonna hold you down, a'ight. See what you can find out and then let me know w'sup."

"Come on, slime," Wild Man said in a cocky tone. "I got this shit covered, Slick. I'ma line shit up properly and then fill you in the next time we link up."

"Say no more," Slick said. "So what you doing, nigga? You still laid up witcha lil slide-off joint?"

"Naw," Wildman chuckled. "I left that ratchet bitch knocked out and snoring in a hotel room. She's stupid bangin in the body and she got a mean head game, but I don't trust no bitches in my crib, yo. You know how these thotties is nowadays bruh. You turn ya head for one fuckin minute and they'll be lickin and humpin your best friend."

"Whatever nigga," Slick joked him. "She's probably just your imaginary friend anyway!"

"Oh, I made her imagine something," Wild Man joked right back.

"What?" Slick laughed. "You some type of pimp or something now nigga? Don't no real bitch want you! Niggas like you be walking around here smelling like gunpowder and pork-fried-fried!"

"Fuck outta here," Wild Man said as he laughed right along with his manz. "You'd be surprised at the chicks who wanna rock with a big boy like me."

"That's cause you's the trick-daddy type, my nigga!" Slick kept going strong. "Don't lemme find out you blowing all your money on these *thots*, bruh!"

"I'm from the Ville, muthafucka!" Wild Man laughed. "We don't pay to play! I'll fuck around and rob one of these bitches blind before I give any of 'em a dollar. You know how I get down."

"You burnt the fuck out, yo," Slick said as he cracked up. "A'ight I'ma holla at you, G."

"One hunnid."

Still grinning, Wild Man started up his Lex and peeled off from the curb. Slick was a solid nigga since day one. But these homey hoppin hoes wasn't loyal. Especially chicks like Honore. Wild Man didn't give a fuck who felt some type of way about him tapping that ass. He was a *wild* muthafuckin *man*, and when it came to slangin dick he didn't live by nobody's rules but his own.

CHAPTER 16

Stick 'Em

It was a sunny mid-morning and Honore was in Midtown Manhattan shopping her ass off. All fucked out from her crazy night with Wild Man, and surrounded by designer clothes and expensive jewels, she shoulda been feeling herself. But unfortunately she was dragging a hood-rat extraordinaire around with her who was shopping her ass off too.

Walking next to her cousin Cucci, Honore's hips were looking heavenly in the fifteen hundred dollar imported Balmain biker jeans Slick had bought her when he took her shopping at Barneys. The cute little emerald earrings that he'd picked out for her dangled sexily from her lobes.

"Ooooh, Honor-Ray!" the hood rat walking on the other side of her exclaimed.

Honore was chaperoning the sixteen-year-old thotty as they walked down the aisles of one of the most expensive department stores in New York City. The girl's grubby little hands were roaming all over shit and Honore had to stop herself from reaching out and popping the mess outta her.

"This store is fuckin beast!" the girl exclaimed loudly. "They got Versace and Herpes up in here too?"

It's Hermes not Herpes, stupid ass now quit touching shit!

That's what Honore wanted to say, but instead she glanced over at Cucci then gave the young chick a fake smile and said gently, "Yes, Indigo. This is a very classy, high-end retailer so they carry all the top designer brands."

Honore's voice dripped with honey as she disentangled the four-hundred dollar Hermes scarf from the girl's hands. She smoothed it down before passing it to Cucci to return to the shelf.

Distracted by all the sweet scents in the air, the excited young chick rushed over to the perfume section. She started squirting fragrances from a million different tester bottles in all directions.

"Damn!" Cucci muttered and covered her nose. "You can't take a project bitch no damn where!"

Honore nodded in agreement as hot disgust bubbled around in her stomach.

If there was one thing Honore and Cucci were a true team at it was shopping. And right now this greedy little hood chick was throwing off their flow.

But it served them right, Honore admitted to herself reluctantly. Little Indigo had been so broken down after her sister India's funeral that Honore had consoled her by offering to take her shopping one day.

Well, that day had come, and so far Honore had dished out over five grand on shoes, clothing, and jewelry for the ghetto-fabulous lil youngster.

My girl India had way more going for her than this hoochie scripper right here, Honore thought, looking down her nose as the teenager snatched a five hundred dollar knit sweater off a shelf and pulled it over her head and tried it on right there in the aisle.

Cucci glared at the young scrub too and rolled her eyes in silent agreement with her cousin. Indigo wasn't nowhere near as smooth and sophisticated as her sister India had been. Although she was blessed with the same pretty face and banging body, she was definitely much lighter on the cap.

As they shopped up and down the aisles Honore helped the young girl pick out all the fly, classy shit that she would have bought for herself. She had already noted that her and Indigo were roughly the same size and weight, and that they had the same small waist and blossoming booty. She had even picked out and purchased several pairs of designer shoes for the girl, making sure to try them on herself too, even though they wore the same size.

The three of them got their shop on as they jetted from store, to store, to store, picking out all the finest shit on the racks. Cucci had a sharp eye for fashion so she had the best tastes in both clothes and shoes, but for a broke chick from the projects Indigo had some real expensive tastes too. Everything her little ghetto hands reached for was on the top shelf and had a heavy price tag hanging from it.

Those are the kind of bird moves you make when somebody else is paying for your shit at the cash register, Honore thought with a smirk as she took care of the girl's purchases with countless crisp one hundred dollar bills.

The trio dropped their bags off with the concierge at the five-star hotel next door, and then rode upstairs on the elegant, gold-carved elevator to have lunch in the exclusive dining room.

Honore ordered soup and salad, and Cucci ordered some hot herbal tea and a crab cake, but Indigo's greedy eyes were scurrying over the menu like lice running around in some real thick coochie hairs.

"Umm, lemme get two of them lobster tails and a jumbo skrimp salad—but keep the damn salad. Just bring me some of them big-ass skrimps, okay? I think I want me a couple of them crab cakes that Cucci's getting too. Plus...I'll take some crab and spinach dip with tortilla chips, and do y'all have any cheesy biscuits? *What?* No cheesy biscuits? Well they sure got 'em at Red Lobster! Okay, then can you just bring me a biscuit and slice it in half and stick a piece of cheese up in there? Yep, cool. That'll work."

Of course the chick's eyes were way bigger than her stomach and she wasn't shy about hollering for a doggie bag so she could take her leftover shit back to the projects with her.

When they were done eating they all went back downstairs and the concierge loaded their bags and boxes onto a cart and pushed it outside to the curb where Sly McFly stood waiting near a limo driven by Chimp Charlie.

Impeccably dressed from the bottom to the top as usual, Sly McFly looked like a real grand gentleman as he helped all three chicks get settled in the back of the whip. Honore turned her lip up as the little project chicken immediately made a grab for the miniature bottles of Henny, Smirnoff's, Remy, and Cuervo that were stacked in the traveling bar.

"Um, how old is you?" Cucci blurted, checking the young girl with her eyes.

"I'm sixteen, about to be seventeen and that's grown," the girl answered as she bit into the silver seal on the skinny neck of a bottle of Seagram's and ripped it off with her front teeth.

Honore opened her mouth to say something slick, but then she closed it again. Fuck it. Let the little slut get juiced up. What this skank did with a bottle of knotty-head was not her concern.

They drove through the city streets until they crossed the bridge back into Queens. The sight of the dilapidated projects outlined against the New York skyline brought a sour feeling to Honore's stomach. She hated the slums. She had been born and raised in the hood but she worked hard everyday trying to claw her way up outta that bitch.

She was glad when the limo finally pulled up outside the girl's building. Her little ass had drained bottles and gotten toasted all the way home, and the glint in her eyes and her rapid fire speech were evidence that she was about to step into the gutter and get loose.

"Thanks, Honor-Ray," Indigo waved as she sucked air outta the last bottle and slid her bubble-ass across the soft leather seat. "Girl, I see why India was your friend. I really appreciate all the bank you dropped on me today and if you ever need another shopping partner just holla at ya girl, 'kay?"

She reached over to give Honore a hug and Honore twisted up her lips. Not only was the chick musty as hell, she smelled like a nasty combo of weak deodorant, top shelf liquor, and a million different brands of perfume.

"Thanks again, Ray-Ray."

"You're welcome, baby girl. You know you good with me. Your sister was my girl. I truly loved her ass. Matter fact, I loved her to *death*. Anytime I can do anything for you, you know I will."

Cucci was steady giggling under her breath as Chimp Charlie unloaded the girl's stuff from the car and Honore punched a number into her cell phone. Indigo had so much shit to carry that she had to balance her bags left and right, in both of her hands.

"T-Bone! Listen up, mothafucka!" Honore barked when Sly's favorite young hustla answered the phone. T-Bone was Sly's lil stunt dummy, and after following them around all day he was parked directly behind them in a beat-up blue Toyota.

"Get your ass in that building and stick that lil bitch up before she gets on the elevator," Honore ordered as she watched Indigo stagger up the walkway carrying her hard-earned money in a million designer bags.

"*Rob* that ass and bring me all my shit back!" Honore demanded. "I'm serious! Ain't nobody got no money to be tricking off on her stank ass! Go stick that drunk hoe up, T-Bone, and bring me back *all* of minez!"

By now Cucci was laughing so hard she had keeled over in her seat.

"You's a cold bitch, Honore!" she cackled loudly with mad love and admiration shining in her eyes. "A cold *dirty* bitch!"

CHAPTER 17

No Church in the Wild

It was early afternoon in the notorious neighborhood of Brownsville as Slick watched his enemies pace back and forth in front of the old folk's building. Goody had sent in an extra squad of shooters to kick up some dust and find out who had slumped his workers Dolla and Black Pearl, but so far the streets ain't have no answers for him.

Slick stood across the street at a distance that was safe enough not to be noticed. Leaning up against a fence in his birdman hat, wrinkled clothes, and shitted-on boots, his blood boiled hotly as he watched Goody's goons harass and intimidate the elderly people who were hurrying to get off the streets and into the safety of their apartments before the sun went down.

To the casual passerby Slick looked like the slow, crazy bum Sometimey. His lips curled up in a dumb half-smile, and his eyes were glazed over like his inner light switch had been flipped all the way off.

But Slick's fake mask of ignorance hid the fact that deep inside he was seeing red as visions of a massacre surged through his very core. He wanted to rip apart and destroy every last one of the hunters that Handgun Goody had sent to disturb the tranquility of the place he held most dear.

Yeah, he said to himself. *You just keep on sending ya mutts out Goody, and I'll keep on zippin 'em up. I'ma send all them bitch-ass niggas back to you headless in a box.*

With his mind stuck in murder-mode, Slick turned away. He walked around the corner stiff-legged style, plotting like a muthafucka as he waited for the sun to go down so he could do what he did best.

$$$$$

QUEEN OF DIAMONDS

Darkness had fallen over the ballistic borough of Brooklyn, but the air was still hot and muggy around the projects. It was 3:30 in the morning and Goody's goon squad was still lurking in front of the old folks building. They had been loud as fuck earlier in the night, but after guzzling a few pints of Henny and wolfing down turkey and cheese heroes and bags of chips, they were getting lazy and tired.

"Yo, son," a tall, brolick nigga called Ricky Rollack said. Rollack was a hired gun whose name rung bells throughout the five boroughs. He was a certified enforcer and one of Goody's most efficient shooters, and due to his rep he always got paid nicely for his services.

"Where the fuck could this dumb-ass nigga be laying low at man?" Rollack bitched. "I mean how hard can it be to catch one muh'fucka lackin?"

"Word up, son," said his lil homey, Cajiid. He was Ricky's young gunner who held shit down and would pop off at the first sign of static. "I'm ready to fly this nigga's head off and get the fuck up outta here, but don't nobody know what he look like."

Cajiid took a swig of Corona and smirked. "I heard some old lady just got choked out in this building last week so I know niggas get it poppin in here." He shook his head. "Fuck all that. A nigga like me puts in real work, nahm'sayin? I don't fuck with old people."

The sharp sound of gunfire popped off in rapid succession a few blocks to their right, but that was no surprise nor did it rouse any suspicion. These were stick-up kid hours, the time where the goons and the goblins took over the streets. Smokers drifted around like zombies, scheming or begging for their next hit, and gangbangers robbed, looted, and exacted revenge on each other under the cover of darkness.

"Yo, it's almost time for the police patrol to roll through," Ricky told his young'un as he stood up from the crate he was sitting on in front of the building. "Let's duck in the lobby till they bounce. We don't wanna get spotted before we rock this nigga to sleep."

"A'ight," Cajiid said as his big homey pushed opened the front door. "I'ma take a piss right quick and then I'll double back and scope out the back door one more time. I'll meet you inside in a minute."

Standing in roughly the same spot he had stood in earlier that night, Slick watched as the big goon walked into the building and the younger one strode off in the opposite direction towards the side of the building.

Slick had on an all-black polo hoody with a dark ski-mask pulled down slightly on his forehead. He was deep in predator mode, salivating for a meal, and these two niggas was looking just like steak.

Moving outta his spot, Slick stalked the young slanga as he kept his head down and walked at a pace that was steady, but didn't draw attention. Cajiid strolled toward the side of the building with the confident bop of a young killer. He stayed strapped and was usually on point. But he was no match for the man that had him in his crosshairs. Cajiid didn't yet posses the sixth sense that you needed when you played with the big boys. He could only see what was in front of him, and that would be the cause of his demise.

The young slanga stopped near a small shrub, unzipped his fly, and pulled his dick out to take a piss. He barely heard the two soft footsteps behind him, and by the time he turned his head a sharp object he didn't even see coming was jammed up into the soft spot right under his chin.

The long blade penetrated deep up into the roof of Cajiid's mouth and immediately he let go of his dick as his hands flew up to clutch at the wound. With his tongue pierced and choking on his own blood, Cajiid staggered away from his killer, piss spraying all over his pants and sneakers as he lost control of himself.

He hit the ground coughing as blood rapidly soaked his shirt and the life began to fade from his eyes. Cajiid's 45-caliber handgun fell harmlessly from his waistband, without even the slightest chance of being used.

Slick stood over him and watched the be-boy try to shake off the clutches of death.

Slick shook his head and grinned. "So you too light in the ass to fuck with me young nigga, but your little bitch-ass is good with killing old folks huh?"

Slick lifted his ski mask up, then he gathered some saliva in his mouth and spit dead into Cajiid's face.

Moving quickly, Slick raised his right knee as high as he could in the air and sent the heel of his scuffed boot crashing down on the bridge of Cajiid's nose with such force that both of Cajiid's legs lifted straight off the ground at the impact.

Slick delivered the fatal death-blow without an ounce of remorse for the slaying of such a tender youngster. There was no church in the wild. Even the young got eaten in the jungle. There was no doubt in Slick's mind that if he was the one who'd gotten caught out there with his dick hanging out, the young boy wouldn'ta shown him a shred of mercy neither.

The dark part of Slick's nature had enjoyed this kill because this wasn't a contract murder that stemmed from a business obligation. Nah, this shit was personal. He was righting a wrong and protecting those who couldn't protect themselves.

Slick's senses tingled and he whirled around to see a bum staring at him from the street. The wino was clutching a bottle and standing under a light pole swaying back and forth. He looked at Slick then glanced down at the body at Slick's feet. Without a word, he simply shook his head and staggered off drunkenly. After all, this was Brownsville, a wolf-eat-dog jungle where the weak and faint-hearted became food for the brave.

Slick got back to work. He grabbed the young'un by his ankles and dragged his body down the walkway that led to a ramp and tucked him out of sight. But his job was far from over. Slick was in a killing zone and he was anxious to take out the big guy on the scene.

And right at that moment Ricky Rollack was in the lobby of the building wondering where the fuck his lil manz Cajiid was at.

"Lemme go check on this little nigga," Ricky muttered under his breath as he finished smoking his Newport 100 and headed for the door. "His young ass can dumb-out sometimes and I don't need him fucking this money up."

Ricky reached for the door handle but Slick made it there from the other side first. Slick yanked that shit open and stood staring at the six-foot-seven, two-hundred-and-sixty pound man who was posted up in front of him.

"Where you headed, you big muthafucka, you?" Slick said through the ski-mask as he stared into the eyes of the gigantic goon. "Lemme holla at you for a quick minute, yo. I just tried to have a chat with ya little homey out there, but he ain't got too much to say right now."

Slick watched as Ricky's eyes dropped and stared at the dark blood that was dripping from his knife and splattering over the toes of his boots. He saw realization start to spread across Ricky's face and he anticipated correctly that the big bear was just about to go for his burner.

"You's a dead man, you fuckin coward!" Ricky yelled as he yanked the gun from his waistband.

And that's when Slick crouched low and lunged at him. He drove the knife deep into Ricky's gut, forcing the big man to yelp and drop his weapon, which skidded across the floor to the other side of the lobby.

"*Ahhhhh! You bitch-nigga!*" Ricky screamed. Then he grabbed Slick by his throat and the crotch of his jeans at the same time. He lifted Slick clear off his feet and tossed him high into the air.

Slick's long body crashed down hard against the elevator door. Sharp pain radiated throughout his spine as he slid to the floor and landed in a jumbled heap.

This wasn't how shit was supposed to go down, and Slick knew he had to recover quickly. He could see the big guy wasn't gonna go down as easily as his boy Cajiid did.

Ricky stood there bleeding from the gut like a stuck pig, but the fire and desire to either plant a bullet in Slick's heart or snap his fuckin neck in two kept him steady on his feet.

Slick ripped off his ski mask then jumped to his feet with the knife clenched in his hand, waiting for the big guy's next move.

"You chose the wrong fuckin building tonight," Slick muttered as he kept one eye on Ricky's fallen gat. "I know y'all niggas slumped that old lady on the 10th floor, bitch! Now you gotta pay the price and the receipt is gonna come from *me,* pussy!"

Slick lunged at him again but with a little too much fury and not enough precision.

Ricky dodged the strike and grabbed Slick by the back of his hoody. He pulled Slick close into his chest then wrapped his powerful arm around Slick's neck and latched his right hand onto his left forearm, clutching him up in the dope-fiend position.

This coulda been the end of the game and Slick knew it. Ricky flexed and tightened his strong muscles trying to squeeze Slick's neck hard enough to pop his eyeballs out of their sockets.

"*Yeah,* mothafucka," the big man growled as he gripped and squeezed. "Talk that shit *now*, bitch! Me and my dawgs don't *fuck* with old ladies! I'm a *wolf*, nigga, and I'm about to chew right through yo bitch ass! This is for me *and* my little nigga, Cajiid!"

Slick was flailing his arms back and forth and feeling the effects of the oxygen being cut off to his brain. He didn't mind dying in the building that he had grown up in and had sworn to protect. But now wasn't his time, and he damn sure wasn't going out at the hands of this big nigga.

Before the last bit of coherent thought faded from his brain Slick rotated the knife in his hand and jammed it down into Ricky's upper thigh. The second he felt Rollacks's grip slacken he twisted the blade in even deeper and then he yanked it out again.

Both men fell to the lobby's floor gasping in pain. It took a moment for them to gather their senses as they got ready to go in for the kill again.

Ricky was fucked up. Blood was flowing from his stomach and his right thigh was spurting a stream and painting the lobby red with every beat of his heart.

Slick was on his knees gasping for air as he tried to shake off the effects of near unconsciousness.

Ricky started to crawl towards the 9 millimeter that was still on the floor. Slick hurled himself over and kicked the gun further across the lobby. Still breathing heavily, he pulled himself up and stood over Ricky's bleeding body.

"Goody is gonna get yo ass for this, boy," Ricky looked up at Slick and vowed as he bled out through his gut and an artery in his thigh. "Yeah, mutha-fucka…Handgun is gonna eat yo food when he catches you!" Ricky gagged as he started choking on the blood that bubbled up from his stomach and filled his mouth. "Nigga he's gonna eat yo fuckin food! That's my word!"

Slick nodded. "That's cool, big man. I hope he's keeping my plate nice and hot 'cause I'ma take a bite outta Goody's ass soon enough too. But right now I got a table reserved for you in hell and I would hate for you to be late for the entertainment."

With that, Slick dropped to one knee, and in a single deadly motion he slit Ricky's carotid artery.

Hot blood spurted in the air and landed everywhere, including all over Slick. He made no attempt to avoid it. He didn't mind the up-close-and-dirty action. His murks weren't usually this messy, but right now he was good with the gore. The whole damn lobby looked like a butcher shop, but it made Slick feel real good to know that at least for now, on this dark and dangerous night, every-one he cared about was safe.

CHAPTER 18

Day Dreams and Nightmares

Snuggled up next to her sleeping man, Ayesha was caught up in a dream that was more like a nightmare. A thunderous scream split the air, and she took off running as fast as she could toward the sound. She knew that voice. Even though she had never heard it in her real life, gripped in the throes of her dream she knew that voice very well.

It was Noodles. And he was screaming her name.

He sounded like he was in great pain, and Ayesha could barely stand the sound of his blood-curdling cries for help. As she sprinted as fast as she could towards his screams in the darkness, her greatest fear was that she wouldn't make it to him in time.

Noodles was more than the love of her life. He was the love of her *everything*. He was her savior and her knight in shining armor who had rescued her from a life that had almost killed her. Noodles was the man who had stepped up to the plate to be a father to her kids. He was her light at the end of the tunnel, and right now she was running and crashing through the woods like a crazed bear, all for him.

But when she finally stumbled into a clearing and came upon her king, Ayesha saw that it was much too late. His head had been detached from his body and the life had faded from his eyes. The grass around him was soaked with blood. Ayesha dove on top his body and snapped. She screamed at the top of her lungs, pounding her fists and wailing out her agony. And that's when Noodles reached up and grabbed her.

Making small smacking sounds with his lips, he held her by the shoulders and shook her gently. His eyes were a bright question mark in the darkness as he pulled her into his arms.

Ayesha gasped, her eyes darting around the room in fear. Noodles was holding her by her shoulders with a look of utter confusion on his face, and suddenly she realized that it had all been just a nightmare.

Noodles kissed her forehead and held her closely. He wiped the sweat from her face as she trembled in the safety of his huge arms.

"Oh baby I was so fucking scared," Ayesha said as her voice cracked. "I was dreaming and it seemed so real...I ran as fast as I could but I couldn't get to you in time. I tried to get there. I swear to God, I tried Noodles."

Calm down sweetheart, Noodles signed to her. *It was just a bad dream my love. I'm right here, and I'm fine. Chill, baby. I promise you it was just a dream.*

"No, you don't understand Noodles," Ayesha insisted as she grabbed his hands. "I come from a family of dreamers and I take shit like this real serious! For real, Noodles. Not once since you brought me here have I asked you *anything* about what you do out there in the street! Your work is your work, and I'm not tryna probe for nothing you don't wanna tell me. But I swear, Noodles. Whatever you do I need you to get away from it. Just fuckin stop it and walk away! You can do something else. Please find another hustle baby, because me and the kids need you. We won't make it out here without you!"

Baby, what's up? Noodles signed to her and sat straight up in the bed. *All this just because of a lil bad dream? Everything is chill, Ayesha. Trust me, I have a plan and it's all gonna work out. Don't worry, I been stackin my money and one day soon you're gonna get everything you been dreaming of. It won't be too much longer now. I'm gonna make sure my moms is straight and then me and you are gonna take the kids and get the hell outta this city. We'll go someplace real nice,* he gathered her closer in his arms and started dream-building with her for the future. *Someplace warm, okay? We're gonna have us a real big house, a fancy car, and take plenty of vacations. There's a lotta love and life waiting for us, Ayesha. Just hold on, baby. I'm almost at the finish line and then they'll be no more need for me to work. Just trust me. I got us, baby. It's gonna be us and the kids forever.*

"How much longer before you're out?" Ayesha pleaded. "Six months? A year?"

Noodles shook his head and signed, *Less than that. Two months, tops. Okay?*

Ayesha nodded, finally satisfied. Noodles helped her lay back down and get comfortable. She cuddled in his arms with her face pressed against his chest, listening to his heart beat. After a while Ayesha dozed off and her breathing became heavy, but Noodles stayed wide awake. He wasn't worried about her dream not one damn bit. Ayesha didn't know it, but he had already picked out her wedding ring and stashed it with Slick. He was gonna ask her to marry him, and he had a plot of land waiting in Guatemala and she was gonna be able to build her any kind of house she wanted.

He had already been planning to get outta the game, and he knew it would happen in due time. Nobody stayed on top forever. He was gonna get on this unfinished business he needed to handle, and then he would get out for good. Noodles started to wake Ayesha up and tell her the whole shit right then and there. He started to tell her about the trip to Guatemala, the engagement ring, the new house, everything. But hey, he thought as she snored and snuggled deeper in his arms, why ruin the surprise?

CHAPTER 19

Underhanded Situations

Text Message From Akeem: *Flight delay, change of plans. Will arrive at the Boatel an hour late. Business associate is willing to pay same price as last time.*

Akeem? Cucci stared down at the message on her cell phone with a look of bewilderment on her face. She was at the gym working out on the elliptical and sweating like a pig, and for a second she thought some idiot hater was tryna play head games with her. *Akeem.* As her leg movements slowed, Cucci's mind raced up and down the block and all around the corner.

Akeem was a big African dude who used to be one of Joel Samuelson's top clients. Akeem purchased stolen diamonds in the states so he could trade them dirt-cheap on the black-market all over England. When Honore first got on deck at the New York Diamond and Jewelry Exchange, Joel had handed Akeem to Cucci and Honore as a tester. He became their solo client, sorta as a get your feet wet and pop-ya-cherry type of thang.

Akeem specialized in buying small diamonds for crushed ice, and him and Cucci and Honore had hooked up back and forth on a couple of deals here and there. But they hadn't done business together in a good minute now, since way before Joel got bodied. So why in the hell his big black ass was texting her outta the blue about some mysterious meeting at the Boatel was anybody's guess. And who was his business associate? What damn prices was he talking about from last time? Last time *when?*

What you want, Akeem? Cucci texted. *What meeting?*

In just a moment he texted her back. *Is this Honore?*

Cucci frowned. This cat thought he was texting Honore!

Her fingers flew across the phone. *Yeah. This is her. What you got for me?*

50K. Same as last time.

Cucci narrowed her eyes. Last time? So them sneaky bitches had done some transacting together for fifty grand and didn't tell her nothing about it? And they were planning on doing some more under-the-covers fucking again today?

As she climbed down off the elliptical and grabbed her towel the truth of the matter washed over Cucci like a cold wave and she started catching killer vapors. Honore must think she was real stupid. Yeah, that trick thought she was a punk. That thief-ass bitch was tryna play her like a fucking sucka! Flinging her towel over her shoulder, Cucci's fingers flew again.

What time at the Boatel?

Six.

She typed, *Bet.*

Cucci nodded and started heading toward the locker room as a plan of action began to form in her brain. She thought about the bag of stolen diamonds that her and Honore had in their lil secret sista stockpile. They had agreed not to tell nobody else about their emergency shit-hit-the-fan stash, but if Honore was planning on selling off some crushed ice to Akeem, then that meant she was planning on stealing that shit from Cucci because that ice belonged to her too!

Cucci grabbed her gym bag outta the locker and rushed outside to her car. She plopped down behind the steering wheel and lit a tree. She inhaled that shit deeply as she drove home with her thinking cap on, trying to come up with a way to catch Honore in the act and catch her ass out there at the same damn time.

Cucci got home and stretched out on her sofa in her sweaty gym clothes. It took her two more trees and a shot of Henny, but finally she had it. Cucci was gonna cold bust Honore and *yap* that greedy bitch! Just like that greedy bitch was trying to yap her!

$$$$$

Honore had a whole lotta shit to fit into her day, and messing around with Cucci wasn't hardly on her agenda.

"Sorry," she told her cousin when Cucci popped up at her crib asking if she wanted to go get a Brazilian wax and a facial at five o'clock that evening. Waxing was something they always did together, but Honore was tryna find a way to get her money up so she was going to the Boatel at five to hook up with an African client that her and Cucci used to sell diamonds to.

"I got a date with an old friend," Honore told her, "and then after that I'm gonna chill with Sly at the Boatel for the night, you know, just so I can relax."

"Um, old friend, *who?*" Cucci demanded, ignoring the Boatel remark. "I thought *I* was ya damn friend! You know what, heffa? Never mind. Lately I been feeling like I don't even know you no more. Every time I ask you to do something with me you always got something better to do. So now you curving me for some nigga, huh? Well who is he? That petty-ass thief again? What's his name, Slick?"

"Hell no," Honore laughed. "I ain't going out with him. Besides, he's a new friend, not an old one. And don't even start talking no crazy shit either! You know I don't be tryna brush you off or nothing, Cucci. You know you my day-one cuzzo and I love you girl. It's just that I already made plans and it's too late to change them. Next weekend, okay? Next weekend it's gonna be all about me and you. I promise."

Cucci gave Honore a puppy-dog look that was designed to make her feel guilty, and then her face brightened up slightly. "Okay," she relented. "But what about tomorrow night? You still going to the Sunday Nite Oldies, right?"

"Hell yeah!" Honore said with a smile. "I wouldn't miss it. Blondie's House of Hair is hosting it this weekend. She's gonna put a perm in my hair so I'll definitely be there."

"Good," Cucci said, her face glowing as her heart hardened. "You go ahead and enjoy your Saturday night without me," she said as she flounced outta Honore's apartment. It's all good. I'll catch up with you on Sunday, cuzzo. Deuces bitch!"

CHAPTER 20

The Hand Off

It was close to six-thirty and Honore was sitting at the bar on a small Boatel that floated at Marina 59 near Far Rockaway, Queens. Music could be heard playing outside and several people were laughing and splashing as they swam and kayaked in the mild inlet waters off Jamaica Bay.

The Boatel belonged to Sly McFly, and it was really just a tiny two-room cabin in a very small boat, but it was also a sanctuary where they could kick back and scheme and strategize.

Way back in the day Sly McFly had gotten down with the owners and invested some cash in the marina to make it a more diverse environment that catered to the local people of different backgrounds. He had introduced Honore to the scene a while back, and she had immediately fallen in love with the place.

As usual, the marina was crowded with a mixture of hipsters and musicians who came around just to hang out and express their artistic talents. But the private space that Sly McFly owned was on the side of the harbor that was off-limits to the general public. It was where the serene waters blended best into the open bay.

Sly, being the crafty nigga that he was, understood the importance of having a low-key get-away spot at all times. Right now he was sippin and pimpin as Honore and her two foreign business associates sat at the bar conducting a cash transaction for some crushed ice that she was selling.

The African men expertly analyzed the merchandise they were being offered as Sly took care of collecting their cool crisp doe. He had two straps in the closet and he felt safe and secure while Honore and the Africans poured glasses of rose and toasted each other to deal successfully completed.

Although Sly and Honore were playing it off and looked blasé and indifferent on the outside, they were desperate to make this sale. They needed to get their pockets up to pay back that sweet money Honore owed, and every dollar helped.

There wasn't a whole lotta cash involved with this transaction but Honore was selling off some low-grade diamonds that her and Cucci had stashed away for a rainy day. The diamonds were too flawed to flip on the international market, but they could be dished off here in the states for a quick twenty-five grand a piece and Cucci wouldn't be getting a dime of it.

Honore sighed as she flashed a phony smile at one of the Africans. She loved reigning as the Queen of Diamonds, aka boss-bitch of the jewelry underworld, but right now all she wanted to do was get paid and get those investor muthafuckas off her back.

Between her piggy bank and Sly McFly's, they now had about half of what they needed in the stash. But that meant they were still half of what they needed in the hole, and with the end of the month coming it was getting real hard not to start panicking and shitting bricks.

"I wanna thank you both for coming," Sly McFly said to their African guests as they were wrapping up the transaction. "And even though y'all fuckers kept us waiting for over an hour, it was a pleasure doing business with you gentlemen and the Queen looks forward to cashing out again with you in the future."

Sly flashed that killer smile of his and added, "The Queen also highly appreciates your discretion and your professionalism, which of course means—*y'all niggas better keep ya goddamn mouths closed!*

"Now, good day, my Nigerian brothers," he laughed. "It's time for you to go. Head back outside and climb up on your camels."

Honore rose from her stool and shook hands with the traders, and Sly McFly did the same before watching the two men leave the Boatel.

"Okay, now," Sly said, locking the door as soon as they were gone. "We ain't make out too bad, now did we sugar?" he asked as he ran stacks of hundred dollar bills through the money counting machine and then quickly banded them and tossed them into a leather carrying bag.

"True," Honore answered. "Now all we gotta do is get the rest of the money up and maybe my ass can stay alive."

"We still have a little more time to come up with something," Sly soothed her. "Don't worry. I don't trust those Jewish kikes as far as I can throw their asses, but I ain't gonna never let nothing happen to you. We gonna come up with the rest of the sweet money and get that fuckin diamond back and sell it too."

Sly McFly said that shit with such assuredness and conviction that Honore truly believed him. Matter fact, she had believed every word that had come outta his mouth for the past twenty-something years of her life. Sly had always been there for her. He had always protected her from anything that could harm her. It was Sly who had made Honore believe that with the right amount of intelligence, muscle, and power they could live large and do just about anything they wanted to do. He had made Honore envision a life beyond the project buildings that had condemned so many of the people she'd grown up with.

Fuck that, Honore said as she went over to the table to help him count the stacks. There would be no sucking dick for pennies or flipping burgers, or letting poverty chain her to the brick project tomb that she was raised in. She was gonna get her money up and find that diamond because she was determined to live like a Queen for the rest of her life. Anything less would be the death of her.

She had just inserted a stack of hundred dollar bills into the machine when the unmistakable thunder of gunfire erupted outside. She heard somebody yelling frantically as male voices squealed and shrieked like they had been hit with something hot.

Sly and Honore stared at each other as immediate thoughts of a double-cross flew through both of their minds.

Sly was the first to move.

"Those camel-walkin bastards!" he said, rushing over to the window to peek out. He saw madness erupting out there. People were running and screaming up and down the dock as blasts went off in the air. Sly watched a fat white woman and both of the Africans get hit and all three fall to the ground. A moment later a swarm of thug niggas rushed over to them and started going through their pockets, ignoring the bullets and obviously looking for something sweet.

"Time to go!" Sly said, rushing back to the money. His hands were a blur as he scooped the bills up off the table and threw them into the leather bag. Those cats had probably come from one of the projects right across the street, and if them niggas were hip to the Africans then that meant they were coming after him and Honore next. "We gotta haul ass outta here *right now!*"

Sly tossed Honore a key and started zipping up the bag of money as he yelled, "Get the Mac outta the closet!"

Honore darted across the room and reached for the pantry door. She flung that shit open and extracted two pieces of heat.

"Yeah, this baby right here'll keep them niggas off our backs!" Sly muttered as Honore handed him the automatic weapon and kept the handgun for herself.

They were moving toward the door when Sly checked her with a firm hand. "Hold up." He ran back over to the window and looked outside again. A barrage of shots chased them hood nigs off the Africans, and frantic white people were shrieking and grabbing their kids as shots popped off in the air.

"Check it," he told Honore. "Let's chill for just a second, but when we get out there I want you to head straight for one of the speed boats at the end of the dock," he ordered. "Don't bother looking back 'cause I'll be holding us down," he said as he passed her the bag of cash. "You just hold tight to the fuckin money and run!"

Screams from the passengers on the other boats could now be heard in between the volley of shots being fired. It sounded like people were being slaughtered on their own boats. Sly counted to twenty and waited. As soon as there was a pause in the noise he stepped outside and glanced around, ready to bang the entire marina with the thirty-two shot Mac 10 that he gripped tightly in his fists.

"Oh, *shit!*" he yelled and jumped back inside, damn near knocking Honore off her feet as a round whizzed by his face.

"It's those double-crossing fucking Africans, ain't it?" Honore shrieked, mad as hell at the thought of being fucked over once again.

"Nah," Sly said panting. "Them two camel-riding niggas are out there taking a concrete nap. Them niggas got hit!"

Sly knew him and Honore were sitting ducks. He counted to twenty again and waited, and then the two of them hit the door and made their way outside. It sounded like the bullets had stopped flying but crazy pandemonium was still ensuing on the dock. Blood was splattered and bodies were down everywhere. Mad people were now rushing toward their cars, others were trying to set sail away from the dock, and some had even jumped into the cold water trying to escape the stray bullets.

Honore and Sly took advantage of all the running and screaming as they raced toward the end of the marina. Sly was back-pedaling with his weapon locked, cocked, and ready to rock all the way.

But lots of other people fleeing had beaten them to the edge of the dock. An older white couple had just jumped into the last speedboat and were trying to make a quick escape.

"*Hey muthafuckas!*" Sly shouted down at them as he pointed his weapon and aimed heat at the frightened pair. "Put your fuckin hands up!"

The passengers on the speedboat froze in horror as they stared down the barrel of Sly's big gun. Him and Honore moved quickly as they ran down the dock and jumped into the boat and started barking demands.

"In the water!" Sly waved his heat and ordered the man and his terrified wife. "Gun it up, baby!" he shouted to Honore, then he turned back to the white couple and barked as the boat lurched away from the dock, "*Out* the fuckin boat and *in* the fuckin water!"

The white man nodded and grabbed his wife's hand, then both of them dove over the side of the boat and swam back toward the dock like minnows.

Honore was speechless as Sly took over and guided the boat out into the open waters of the bay. Why them two Africans were dead as a doorknob and her and Sly were still alive was a fuckin mystery to her.

"What the hell just happened back there?" she shouted over the noise of the speedboat. "What the hell are we gonna *do*, Sly?"

Sly shrugged as he powered the boat forward. "Relax. We'll find out what happened from Twitter in about five seconds. Every time a bullet pops off it ain't gotta be about us," he said.

Honore was shook. She wanted to believe him. She needed to believe him. But her whole life had just flashed before her eyes and she was scared as fuck.

"You don't think it was those investors coming at me, do you? You don't think they got tired of waiting for their sweet money and just came after my ass?"

Sly McFly shook his head and smoothed back his wavy hair as they got ghost and circled around the waterway under the cover of night.

"Uh-uh. Hell nah. Them *hebe* niggas don't miss nothing they aim at. If it was them they woulda laid the whole dock down to get at you. They ain't leaving no money on the table. Trust me, not a dime. If it was them, then that lil bit of cash we got from them Africans and your beautiful black ass woulda *both* been gone, baby. Long gone."

$$$$$

Floating out there on the cool waters Pier 59, Honore and Sly were thankful to be alive. But back on dry land there were four armed thugs whose hearts were filled with disappointment.

"Yo, it was a massacre out there!" Tragedy barked into his cell phone as him and his cousins sped away from the Boatel in a souped-up Chevy hatchback. "There was some wild shit poppin off right on the dock, yo! We found Honore's Boatel and was about to blitz, but we didn't even get to run down on that bitch because some maniac fuckin white boy was out there shootin shit up!"

"Shooting shit up?" the woman on the other end echoed.

"Yeah! Somebody said the white dude used to work out there but he got fired. That nigga came back packin a choppa and started clearing his boss and a whole bunch of other muthafuckas clean out!"

"So y'all ain't get the fifty grand?" the female voice on the other end of the phone asked coldly. "You telling me y'all niggas left up outta there empty-handed? I gave you all the info you needed, stupid ass! How did y'all fuck it up?"

"Yo, I'ono," he muttered. "It was bullets flying and mad white people out there runnin and shit--"

"I don't care what color them assholes was out there! That bitch Honore shitted all over your sister, nigga! You was supposed to do it for *India!* I told you Honore and Sly was going out there to conduct a cash transaction with some Africans! Man, both of them be wearing jewels and carrying around boo-coo cash! Especially that old yellow nigga Sly! You was supposed to rob both of them bitches and get *paid!*"

"Yo! I did what the fuck I could do!" Tragedy spit viciously. "But I'm telling you it was some Wild Wild West shit going on out there! Before we could even pop shit off the place was going bananas. We caught up with the two African cats coming outta her joint though. We banged on both of them bitches and took some real pretty diamonds off they asses. But then the psycho white boy rolled up airing shit out and we had to breeze like asap."

"So she really sold the diamonds, huh?" the female on the other end spoke with quiet disappointment. "That dirty bitch really, really, *really* sold my damn diamonds!"

"I guess so. All I know is one of them Africans we deaded had 'em in his pocket."

That was it for Cucci Momma! That was the last fuckin straw!

"Yo," Tragedy said, "we 'bout to run them diamonds to the pawn shop right
quick and see what kinda yardage we can get."

"No!" Cucci snapped sharply. "No pawn shops, stupid! I hustled my ass off for those bad boys! You bring those diamonds back to me and I'll dish 'em off my damn self. And the next time I give you a big-money lead you better not fuck it up!"

Perched on her sofa, Cucci Momma clicked off the phone then snatched up her glass of Bacardi and took a big swallow. That sneaky bitch! Honore had sold the diamonds to them Africans clients without telling her! That dirty crab! Cucci was the best damn thief in the whole damn Crushed Ice Clique and them diamonds belonged to both of them! That oily roach didn't have no intentions on giving up Cucci's share of the cut either! Nah, she had done her dirt on the low and now she was gonna keep the whole pot to herself.

Cucci fumed. The only reason that skank-ass heffa was still in the game in the first place was because Cucci had loved and trusted her. She coulda *been* done turned that snake in and bagged that reward money from the FBI! She had been holding off outta her sense of family loyalty, but now all of that was about to change! Ya damn right! Shit was about to get poppin for real!

Cucci took a deep breath and tried to relax and think rationally as the liquor hit her stomach with a slow burn. It was her fault that Tragedy had lined Honore up in his crosshairs and then couldn't deliver. That's what she got for fucking with amateurs. Tragedy and his niggas were a bunch of low-budget lightweights. It was gonna take some professional action to put Honore in check and get Cucci's pockets right.

Cucci was mad, but she wasn't sad. What goes around, comes around, she told herself. She had failed to get what she wanted this time, but life was all about making the right moves at the right time, and right now she knew exactly what she needed to do to make sure her opportunity came rolling back around again.

CHAPTER 21

Droppin Dimes

At exactly 8:04am on Sunday a call came through on the FBI hotline. The middle-aged agent who took the call had been a bureau employee for two decades and he knew the intricacies of his job inside and out.

"Hello?" a female voice whispered through the line. "Is this the number where you call in tips so you can collect a reward?"

"Yes it is," the agent said in a bored but professional voice as he kicked back in his chair and crossed his feet at the ankles.

To his trained ear this sounded like another useless dud call. He could tell right away that the voice on the line was young and black, and if he had a dollar for every dumb-ass tip he received from a lying nigger who was bucking for reward money he would have been a very rich man. "How can I help you, ma'am?"

"Well, I seen a wanted poster saying y'all was looking for the person who stole a real expensive diamond from the New York Diamond and Jewelry Exchange not too long ago."

Immediately the agent uncrossed his feet and sat up straight.

"Yes," he reached into his pocket and retrieved a small magnet and pressed it against the phone, scrambling the line. "What information can you provide about that crime?"

"Uh-uh," the girl said and sucked her teeth. "Ain't nobody stupid. If I just up and tell you everything I know how am I supposed to get the reward money then?"

"If your tip pans out then you can apply for the reward money by filling out a form," the agent replied sincerely. "Don't worry, before we hang up I'll take your name and address, and if you like you can come in and speak to an agent and he can help you fill out the form right here in the office."

"Well," the girl whispered, "I just wanna tell you that the person you're looking for is called the Queen of Diamonds, and I know where y'all can catch her at tonight," she said. "But y'all gotta show up exactly when I tell you to, you got it?"

"Got it," the agent said as he listened to the story the young woman was running down on him. He scribbled some notes on a pad with the location and times the girl specified, and before he hung up he took down the name she gave him, which he knew was fake, and assured her that someone from the Bureau would follow up on her information in less than twenty-four hours.

After disconnecting the call the agent signaled to his co-worker in the next booth that he needed to take a quick trip to the men's room. Breaking strict company policy, he failed to log the call that had just come in. Instead, he walked out on the balcony and discreetly placed a call of his own. Because unlike the ten other seasoned agents who manned the nation's telephone hotlines, this agent didn't just work for the FBI.

He also worked for the BBU.

CHAPTER 22

Life's on the Line

Care for me, care for me. I thought Slick cared for me. There for me, there for me...Slick should be there for me...

Jewelz was lounging in her posh Manhattan crib and singing along with Lauryn Hill as she dried herself off with a big soft towel. She was fresh outta her morning shower and had just begun smoothing some Estee Lauder *Nutritious* lotion onto her long athletic legs.

The smell of coconut incense floated through the air as the in-ceiling speakers blasted the angelic vocals of Lauryn on her *Ex-Factor* album.

Today Jewelz was feeling better than she had in a good minute. She was looking forward to dressing up and feeling sexy, which is something she rarely felt like doing these days. There was a lot she wanted to accomplish in the little bit of time she had left in the world, and the icing on the cake was gonna be slumping the beloved family members of the infamous Handgun Goody.

Despite the fact that she was sick, thinking about this mission had Jewelz feeling invigorated and energized. The monster from her past had scarred her in more ways than he probably even remembered. She felt a gratifying sense of elation at the thought of stalking him like prey and making him feel the same type of pain that her and Slick had felt as kids.

But killing Goody and his family wasn't going to be like any of her other missions where she'd killed with coldblooded indifference and zero emotion. Uh-uh. Just thinking about this one had Jewelz salivating like a lioness over what would be the most thrilling meal of her life.

The plan was to erase every fuckin body that Goody loved before devouring him at the end. She was fantasizing about killing his favorite brother Ice Pick when she heard a loud knock at her door.

Jewelz grabbed the semi automatic propped against the wall by her bed.

She never had unexpected company come over so there was no need for anybody to be at her door. Especially banging on that shit like they were gonna tear it down. She put on her wig, then threw on a sports bra, a t-shirt, and some loose basketball shorts and approached the door with caution.

"Who the fuck is it!" Jewelz yelled as she gripped her heat and kept her distance. She knew better than to approach the door to look through the peep-hole because plenty of idiots had gotten their domes split doing stupid shit like that.

"Get away from my door before I clap your ass!"

"I'm looking for Miss Diamond Jordan!" a woman called out loudly. "My name is Beverly Gaines and I was sent from Memorial Sloan Kettering Cancer Center to check on you."

Jewelz paused for a few moments, and then responded.

"What do you want?" Jewelz asked, walking towards the door with the shocked face on. Hiding the gun behind her back, she unlocked it and then opened it just as far as the chain would allow and peered at the small black woman. "Why in the world are you banging on my door like you crazy? You could have just called me and saved yourself some time."

"We've been calling you over and over but you never answer," Beverly said quietly. "Our staff is worried about you, Diamond. Do you remember Nancy? The head nurse? Well, she's really fond of you and she wants to know why you haven't shown up for the treatments she scheduled for you."

Jewelz's gaze fell to the floor. She had been running off pure rage and adrenaline ever since Slick put her on Goody's trail, and nothing other than killing him had mattered to her.

"Um, tell Nurse Nancy that I appreciate her concern," Jewelz said slowly, "but I can't come in right now. I have a few things to take care of that absolutely can't wait. I'm sorry."

"I really wish you would reconsider, baby," Beverly pleaded like a caring grandmother. "Without a strict drug regiment and consistent treatment you know what will happen to you, don't you? Over time your body will get weak and your organs will start to fail and shut down. This is something you can't fight alone. Let us help you, Diamond."

"Now is not the time," Jewelz said firmly. "I know the risks and I'm fully prepared to accept whatever consequences that come with my decision. Tell Nurse Nancy that I'll come in as soon as I can."

The old lady looked sad. "It might be too late by then."

Jewelz nodded. "That's a chance I'll just have to take."

Jewelz slammed the door closed and pressed her back to it. She knew the words that Miss Beverly had spoken were true. Yet she couldn't allow her mind to dwell on none of that. Right now she felt halfway strong, and as long as she had strength left in her body she was gonna get her revenge on Handgun Goody.

Or die trying.

$$$$$

Fifteen minutes after Jewelz had closed the door on the lady from the hospital, somebody was out there knocking on her door again.

Damn, I got random folks bangin on my door twice in one day?

But when Jewelz answered the door this time the person standing there dressed in a dark imported suit was far from random.

"What are you doing here?" she stared into his eyes and asked quietly.

He stared at her right back. His blue eyes were gentle, but they never wavered.

"Where are your manners, girl? Are you gonna leave me standing out here in the hallway or are you gonna let me in?"

Reluctantly, Jewelz opened the door a little wider and stepped back, allowing him to come inside.

"So, what brings you over this way?" she asked him as she looked down at the floor. The last time they'd been alone together she had sucked his dick and given up the pussy like a shameless freak and she felt some kinda way about that. She felt guilty for being so damned needy. "I know you didn't just happen to be wandering around in my neighborhood."

He held out a brown paper bag that was rolled tightly at the top. "You were on my mind. I figured you were holed up in here by yourself and probably not eating, so I came all the way to Manhattan to bring you some grub. You ran out of my house in a hurry the last time, and I wanted to make sure everything was cool with you, Jewelz. That's all."

Jewelz led him into her spacious and trendy living room, and when she sat down on the sofa Whitey sat down right beside her.

"My phone works you know," Jewelz said, eyeing the cell phone that sat on her end table. "You coulda just called and saved yourself a trip."

"Yeah, I know," Whitey said with a serious look in his eyes. "But I wanted to bring you something to eat and I also have a few questions I wanted to ask you. Because I brought you something else besides the food too."

Jewelz watched as Whitey stood up and took off his suit jacket. He reached into his pants pocket and came out with something gripped tightly in his fist. Her face was a big question mark as he got down on his knees in front of her and pressed it into her hands.

"Jewelz," he whispered as a look of mad worry entered his eyes. "I don't know what the fuck is going on, but I found this on the floor after you spent the night at my crib. I been noticing other little things about you too, but this right here scared the hell outta me, girl. Seriously. I'm worried about you. I'm more than worried. I'm terrified."

Jewelz stared down at the long clump of hair that Whitey had pushed into her hand, then reached up and touched her wig. She sighed deeply. There was no doubt that it was hers. She had been shedding mad hair for a minute now, and right now underneath her wig she was almost completely bald.

Jewelz pursed her lips and turned away from all the questions in Whitey's eyes. Chemo was a bitch and you never knew where you were gonna be when your shit fell out.

"Umm, yeah," she said, leaning over to place the loose hair in an ashtray so she could burn it later. "Sorry about that. My doctors have me on some medication right now that has some real weird side effects."

"What *kind* of medicine?" Whitey asked, drilling her with his ocean-blue eyes. "The only kind of medication I can think of that makes your hair just fall out like that is chemotherapy. But only people who have cancer usually take that kind of drug. So what's going on with you, Jewelz? What's really real?"

The amount of pain and distress in Whitey's voice and eyes hit Jewelz like a sledgehammer. He was truly, truly worried about her. He was on his knees clutching her hands and massaging her flesh with his thumbs, and Jewelz couldn't help but collapse under the weight of his genuine concern.

"W-Whitey," she licked her lips nervously and began. "I-I just don't know how to tell you this…I mean I just don't want nobody all up in my business like that…feeling sorry for me and all…"

"C'mon, Jewelz," he urged her. "I'm not just any old body. Look at me. I'm the guy who's always there for you, right? I'm your Whitey-on-the-spot. Hell, I'm down here killing my knees like a sucker for you right now. Whatever's going on you don't have to hide it from me, Jewelz. I promise you can trust me, baby. You know you can."

Strong emotions rushed through Jewelz's entire body. She had been carrying the weight and bearing the burden of her disease all alone for so damn long. She had convinced herself that there was nobody in this world who truly gave a fuck about her. That there was nobody to share her pain and her fears with. That there was nobody who would really be affected if she lived or died.

But maybe there was Whitey.

Jewelz gazed into his eyes and what she saw shining there suddenly satisfied a burning, desperate need in her that stretched out like a gaping black hole.

You are not alone. I am here with you.

Jewelz mentally collapsed. She was only fuckin human, and she broke down and cried hot, pain-filled tears as all that 'strong backbone' and 'stiff upper lip' shit went right out the window.

"Whitey I've got cancer," she blurted out as the tears ran down her cheeks. "For the second damn time in my life, I've got cancer."

It was Whitey's turn to collapse. He slumped forward and buried his face in Jewelz's lap as he cried out in sympathy for her.

"Jewelz, Jewelz," he moaned as she ran her fingers through his hair and cried with him. "I'm so sorry you're going through this. Oh my God, it must be terrible for you, baby. Just terrible…"

"It's been horrible," Jewelz admitted. "It's been a *nightmare*…but please, Whitey. Please don't tell nobody. You gotta promise me that you won't tell nobody!"

"Sshh..." he pressed his finger to her lips. "Don't worry. I won't tell a soul. I swear I won't."

In the stillness of the apartment Jewelz and Whitey clung together. Jewelz's body shook with soft sobs as Whitey crouched on his knees and held her around the waist. He let her cry it out, then he wiped her tears and murmured words of love and comfort that felt like a soothing balm washing straight over her heart.

Jewelz wasn't sure when the dynamics of their situation actually changed, but at some point she realized that Whitey's touch and his loving caresses had become different. His hands became more intimate and insistent. From his knees, he gripped her by the thighs and ran his palms up and down over the flesh of her hips. His face pressed deeply into her groin as he reached inward and slid his fingers up the leg of her basketball shorts and caressed her smooth skin.

"Whitey..." Jewelz pulled away and reached for his wrist. "Yo, Whitey hold up..."

But he had already dipped his head low and his lips were on her inner-thigh now. His tongue too. Ignoring her protests, he was nibbling and licking his way up her shorts toward that moist place that he knew so well.

Jewelz shivered all the way down to her bones. It felt so good to be touched and tempted, and as guilty as she felt, she just didn't have the strength to stop him.

Whitey went deeper up the leg of her shorts and pulled the crotch aside. He stroked her kitty-kat until Jewelz gave up the fight and lay back on the sofa and moaned in pleasurable surrender. She pulled up her t-shirt and freed her titties, then lay there playing with her nipples as he stirred up a pulsating beat between her legs.

Whitey took advantage of her excitement to unbutton his starched shirt and strip it off. He inched Jewelz's basketball shorts down past her hips and dragged them down her legs.

With nothing stopping him from getting what he wanted, Whitey parted her lower lips and sighed at the marvelous sight of her milk chocolate candy with the sweet pink center. He planted small wet kisses on the smooth area of Jewelz's groin before moving closer and getting to the good part.

Lifting her slim legs over his shoulders Whitey ate that pussy like he was at a soul food buffet. Everything about Jewelz was delicious to him. He loved the way her body was shaped, the tastiness of her cream, the scent her pussy gave off when it was hot, and the way she hissed and moaned when his tongue flicked over the exact right spot.

Making Jewelz feel good was Whitey's main priority, and even though he was dying to make love to her, he didn't even think about taking his hard dick outta his pants because today it was all about Jewelz.

Laying flat on the couch and gripped in the throes of her passion, Jewelz was all the way cool with that shit. She stretched out and allowed Whitey to give her the oral workout that she felt she deserved. There was such little joy in her life these days, so little love, that she couldn't help but take advantage of the opportunity for any kind of gratification when it presented itself.

Whitey sensed all this in Jewelz, and because he was truly connected to her with his heart, he doubled his efforts to bring her to the heights of arousal. Although after her first nut she shrieked and moaned and tried to buck him off, he held her tight and wouldn't let her up until she had exploded with two more orgasms and her legs were trembling with exhaustion.

When it was over Whitey helped her sit up and handed her her shorts.

"You wanna take a quick shower while I step in the kitchen and pop your soup in the microwave? I can run you a hot bath if you want," Whitey offered as Jewelz pulled her sports bra back down over her titties and put on her shorts. "I'll even wash your back for you."

She shook her head.

"Uh-uh. That's okay. I'm good."

Letting Whitey in the shower with her was outta the question. Not only didn't Jewelz want him or anybody else to see her without her wig on, suddenly she didn't want him up in her crib like that neither.

"Um, you know what? Thanks for everything, Whitey, but I'm really tired," she told him as she passed him his shirt, then stood up and led him towards the door. "I really appreciate you coming over here and checking for me, but I was up late last night and I think I already overdid it today. I need to lay down and relax for a little while."

Whitey got it. He felt like he had a real connection going on with Jewelz and in her fragile condition he could dig her need to get some extra rest.

"Cool." He slid back into his shirt and then picked up his suit jacket and made sure his gear was straight. Like an obedient puppy he followed Jewelz over to the door and stepped outside. But instead of leaving, he leaned against the doorframe with his body halfway across the threshold.

"You know, if you ever need anything I'm only a phone call away. Just hit my digits and I'll come running, a'ight?"

Jewelz nodded. "Yeah. Thanks. And remember, don't tell anybody about what's going on with me okay?"

"I won't," Whitey promised her. "You have my word, baby."

Jewelz stared at him for a brief second then said, "Especially Slick. Don't tell Slick."

"Slick!" Whitey spit out the corner of his mouth as his whole face changed. Just the sound of that nigga's name sent his jealousy raging from zero to a hundred in about two seconds flat.

"*Fuck Slick!* Why are you so worried about that idiot finding out? He shouldn't even be a part of this damn equation, Jewelz! I don't see him over here bringing you no food, or rubbing your back, or eating your fucking pussy!"

"Boy calm down and stop making all that noise!" Jewelz hissed as she glanced at her neighbor's door and hoped nobody had overheard him. "Fuck's wrong with you? This ain't even about Slick!"

"Then why'd you have to mention his fuckin name? Why does he even have to be on your mind?" Whitey demanded. "What's it gonna take for you to realize that Slick doesn't give a shit about you, Jewelz? You're not even a woman to him, you know. You're nothing more than an expendable *gunslinger* to that slimeball!"

Suddenly he stood up tall and sneered down at her. "And why would you even wanna *fuck with* a man who can send you out there on the streets to die everyday? What kind of *woman* wants a dude who can do her like that? Is that all you're worth, Jewelz? A gun and no roses? Just what kind of sadistic bitch are you anyway?"

Jewelz shook her head, which was suddenly pounding. "Gone, Whitey. You all in your feelings and you about to get real outta pocket right now, baby. Gone."

"Oh, so the man who cares about you has to leave, but if Slick rolled up in here right now you'd welcome him with open legs, wouldn't you?"

"What? Are you crazy?" Jewelz spit back with mad attitude. She was fronting with the crazy look on her face, but deep down inside both of them knew Whitey was absolutely right.

It had always been about Slick with her. Slick, Slick, *Slick*. And yes, if he walked his fine black ass off that elevator right now then yes, Jewelz would make a liar outta herself and come clean outta her panties because he could damn sure get it. All of it.

"Look, it's no secret how I feel about you, Jewelz," Whitey pleaded. "All I wanna do is be with you and *make you mine*. If you were my woman you would never have to grip another ratchet or go out on another job again. *Never*. I swear I would put you up on a pedestal for *life*. I would take you outta this stinking Empire State and surround you with more finery and luxury than you could ever imagine. *Fuck* Slick, baby! Choose *me!*"

Jewelz shook her head tiredly as she closed the door in Whitey's face. He was a cool dude and he had really been there for her when she needed him. But she wasn't trying to belong to him. Her heart already belonged to somebody else. And the heart was stubborn like that. It wanted what it wanted. No matter how many other men she was with, Jewelz's heart belonged to Slick, and there wasn't a damn thing she could do about it.

CHAPTER 23

Beauty Parlors and Blood

"A'ight people it's about that time," Wild Man informed his squad as they assembled at a refurnished warehouse in Queens. He was the lead gunslinger on the job and he had sounded the alarm at one a.m. and demanded that every member of the Zip 'em Up Crew report locked and cocked to their warehouse location no later than two o'clock.

"This shit don't make no fuckin sense," Jewelz bitched under her breath as they suited up and packed the weapons, silencers, and ammo that Wild Man had provided for them.

"We supposed to hit some Queen of Diamonds in the middle of the night at a *beauty parlor*? Don't no real bitch get her hair did on no Sunday night at three o'clock in the morning!"

"A gunslinger is on call twenty-four-seven," Whitey said, sticking two magazines of ammo down in his jacket pocket. "This is the job you signed up for, remember?"

"Was anybody talking to you? Jewelz snapped. She was still mad that he had caught her in a weak moment earlier that morning. She had let that bastard eat up her whole pussy after blabbing to him about all her business, and then he got out in her hallway and showed his ass. "How about you speak when spoken to, stupid ass!"

Slick side-eyed her curiously. "Just chill and strap up," he said to both of them. His voice was low and cold, but on the real, the shit didn't make much sense to him neither.

But the message he'd received from Body Bags Unlimited had been straight and to the point: Eliminate the target at three a.m. at a beauty shop in Queens. Everything about this hit was perplexing to Slick, but those were their orders and they were obligated to carry them out. Besides, the fact that the BBU had agreed to tear off triple dollars to his team told him how crucial this hit was to the person who had ordered it.

"Yo, bruh, do we at least know who owns the beauty shop?" Wild Man asked. Queens was his territory, so the responsibility for the job fell on his shoulders. Like everybody else he was feeling some kinda way about rolling in half-blind, but he took his leadership role very seriously and he was ready to get it in.

Slick shook his head. "Nah. We don't know shit but the address. I sent Noodles ahead to try to scope it out a little bit before we get there, but we got a real narrow timeframe to work with. According to the BBU, the best time to catch the Queen of Diamonds out there lightly guarded will be at three a.m. After that the bitch'll probably sky-up and who knows when we'll be able to roll on her again."

"But what about her click?" Wild Man asked. "Them bitches said "lightly guarded?" What kinda security team do she usually be holding?"

Slick shrugged. "That we don't know. We just need to be ready for any and *every* fuckin thing, nah'm sayin? It don't really matter how many muthafuckas she got watching that ass. We going in for a piece of it, and we ain't leaving until we get it."

$$$$$

There were five beautician chairs in Blondie's House of Hair located off Jamaica Avenue, but on this particular night in the quantum town of Queens, only one chair was open for business.

It was close to three a.m. and as usual they were celebrating Sunday Nite Oldies. It was a lil late-night social mixer and get-together that the old school beauty and barbershop owners in Queens had been participating in every week for years. Since most of them worked on the weekends and their shops were closed on Mondays, each Sunday night after closing up, the old-head owners came together at a selected shop where they drank, smoked weed, played Bid Whist and Spades, laid down some Domino bones, and ate pig feet and collard greens with potato salad.

This week they were chilling at Blondie's joint. Everybody else was partying in the side room and getting tipsy, but Blondie was standing up on her tired feet working like a dog.

Sly McFly's goddaughter Honore was sitting in Blondie's chair with her long hair hanging around her shoulders. Her tender scalp was burning like hell from the salon perm that Blondie had slathered all over her roots and new growth. The shit was sizzling so hot that Honore was squirming around in her seat like she had crabs in her drawers and she couldn't wait for the first blast of cool water to hit her head.

"Damn! How much longer?" Honore bitched. Her eyes watered as she shook her leg and tapped her foot against the pain.

"Calm down," Blondie said, shifting her weight on her bare, aching feet. "I know it's tingling a little bit," she told her, "but that's to be expected when your scalp gets real dry and you scratch up all your flakes like that."

"But I didn't even scratch it all that much," Honore protested. She fanned her hands uselessly around her head tryna stir up a breeze. "You sure this stuff is mild because it's cookin the shit outta my scalp and my hair ain't even that nappy."

"Yep, it's mild. That's the only strength that your type of hair can take."

"Well the shit don't feel mild," Honore muttered under her breath as her eyes watered from the intense pain.

"Well all that scratching and digging you did got your scalp inflamed and outta control. Try to relax for just a few more minutes. The tingling shouldn't get any worse than it is right now."

Honore sucked her teeth and closed her eyes. Tingling hell. Her damn scalp was *burning*. Especially around the edges and near her forehead. That shit was burning hotter than hell!

A door opened and Sly McFly came out of the noisy side room. He was dressed in a sharp white suit and holding a bottle of beer and puffing on an expensive cigar. A "No Smoking" sign was prominently displayed on the wall next to him but he paid that shit no mind as the smoke trailed up toward the ceiling.

"You win anything?" Blondie asked.

Sly grinned happily as he leaned on his cane, then slid his hand across her plump ass and copped him a feel. "Hell yeah I won. I took Flip and Sammy to Boston on a six no-trump. Cleaned them nigga's pockets right the fuck out."

The door to the side room opened again and Cucci Momma staggered out looking lit. She had been in there drinking and dancing and getting her freak nasty on with all the drunk old men and a big smile was on her face.

"It's hot as hell up in this bitch," she said loudly. Her hair was sweated out and her curls had dropped. Her mini-skirt had slid around till the zipper was crooked on her ass from the hungry hands of all the old men who had felt her up while they danced.

"I'm going outside to get me some fresh air," she announced. "I'll be right back."

Blondie nodded. Almost ready to rinse, she adjusted the smock around Honore's neck and pulled on some fresh plastic gloves. Ordinarily she woulda been making all kinds of small talk with a client but she knew better than to start flapping her gums with this one here.

Sly had slid her some nice ends and asked her to hook the girl up while he got his bid whist on, and Blondie had grumbled inside because it was Sunday night and she wanted to drank and play some whist her damn self!

Plus, he had his own damn shop so Sly coulda done Honore's hair on his own damn dime. But as bad as her feet hurt and as tired as she was, she knew better than to say no. In fact, fuck the money. Blondie woulda permed Honore's shit up for free if she had to because despite the grin on his face Sly McFly was a brutal old gangsta who could have her *and* her shop burnt down to the ground for crossing him.

So she rubbed her aching toes together and kept her mouth shut as she gave the perm one last go through Honore's thick strands. Not that this chick really needed a perm because she had some real nice shit to work with. But some people hated the curly look, so Blondie's hands worked expertly as she smoothed Honore's roots and made sure every single one of them strands was bone-ass straight.

"Okay, let's get ready to rinse," Blondie said as she lowered Honore's chair back and let her long hair fall into the sink.

"It's about fuckin time..." Honore sucked her teeth and muttered under her breath.

Above her, Blondie smirked. *You salty young bitch! I didn't wanna do your damn hair no way!*

She had just cut on the faucet and was waiting for the hot water to kick in good when—

BOOM!!!

Blondie looked up just as her front door caved in. Shattered pellets of glass flew into the room and washed over them like a blizzard of tiny needles.

The sound of whizzing bullets cut through the air and Blondie screamed and instinctively turned her face away from the blast.

And that's when the lights flickered out. The whole joint was bathed in utter blackness. The music blaring from the side room died abruptly and the people dancing hollered in surprise and then...

Phewttt! Phewttt! Phewttt!

Blondie was a veteran diva from the streets and her urban warfare senses kicked in hard. With her bare feet coming down on the sharp glass, she took off running toward the back of the shop where a rear door opened onto an escape alley.

Honore jumped up outta her chair and took off right behind her. The whole joint was being sprayed with rounds, and blackness and gunpowder filled the air. The perm in Honore's hair was burning fuckin hot, but not as hot as the bullets that were whizzing past her in the darkness.

Blondie made it to the back of the shop. Her bare feet were cut open and bloody, but she didn't feel a goddamn thing except the desire to survive. She was about three steps away from the exit door when she felt a hand clamp down hard on her shoulder.

"Move it, bitch! Get yo fuckin ass out the way!" Sly McFly hollered as he yanked her backwards and flung her down to the floor. Her tailbone fractured as she hit the ground hard. She rolled over in agony and her knee cracked hard against a door jam. Her lower leg first surged with a bolt of bright pain, then it went numb from her hip all the way down to her toes.

Blondie screamed in pain. She clawed out with her hands in the darkness, but all she saw was a white blur as Sly McFly's long legs jetted past her and he hit the back door at a sprint.

"Wait for me!" Blondie sobbed from the floor. She rolled over and scooted toward the door on her stomach. Her shattered leg trailed uselessly behind her.

"*Please*….wait for me!"

Hot lead was flying everywhere and all poor Blondie could do was pray none of the bullets were aimed down low. She had just heaved the top part of her body outta the back door when a female voice screamed out behind her in pain and surprise.

"Ouch! *Shit!!!*"

Then something heavy landed hard on Blondie's pillowtop ass. She grunted and collapsed forward in agony.

"*Aggh!*" she groaned as Honore leapfrogged through a hail of bullets and stomped dead on her spine.

The pain shifted as Honore ran straight up Blondie's back and stepped on her neck, then took a flying leap out the back door.

The bullets were coming even faster in the darkness now. There were pounding footsteps getting closer too. Blondie rose up painfully on her knees. She tried to crawl across the threshold but the moment she felt something hot pierce her back she knew she was a dead woman.

The last thing Blondie saw as she collapsed in the doorway leading to the alley was that cane-leaning mothafucka Sly McFly. He was hauling ass down the alley on two good legs, and that uppity hoe Honore was beating feet right behind him.

With goo-gobs of perm dripping from her hair.

CHAPTER 24

Bullets But No Body

"Did we get her?"

Wild Man's voice was high-pitched from adrenaline as his words rang out in the cool night air. The partying patrons in the shop had scattered, and the gun smoke was starting to clear as he walked up behind Jewelz. She stood gazing down the alley behind the beauty shop, gripping her hot gat in both hands.

Wild Man aimed his tool at the female body that was sprawled on the concrete and laying right at Jewelz's feet.

"Is this the bitch?" he demanded. "Is this the goddamn Queen of Diamonds?"

"Hell nah," Slick answered as he exited the beauty parlor and walked up from behind them. He stuck his foot out and flipped the slim woman's body over with the toe of his boot and stared down into her slack face. "This ain't her."

"Yo, how you know it ain't her, man?"

"Cause I got eyes, nigga! This is the chick who owns the shop. Her picture was all over the poster on the front door."

"Fuck!" Wild Man snatched off his mask and cursed as Jewel took a few steps down the deserted alley. "We missed the fuckin hit!" he barked. "We missed her!"

"Nah, we didn't miss her," Jewelz said quietly. "We got that bitch. *I* got her."

"No," Whitey corrected her with a smug attitude as he walked up on the scene and joined them. "I think you missed her, Jewelz. If you had hit her then she'd be laying out here dead, don'tcha think?"

"*No*," Jewelz rolled her eyes at him and corrected him right back as she pointed down at a small splatter of bloody droplets that stained the concrete red.

"I got that heffa. I *tagged* that ass! I ain't saying the Queen of Diamonds is dead, but the bitch is sho'nuff bleeding!

EMPIRE

STATE of MINE$!

(A Movie in a Book)

Episode 3

Money Makin Manhattan

A NOIRE & REEM RAW JOINT

There are eight million stories in the naked city of New York.

These five are all the way live.

"Harlem niggas don't fade away,

Money Makin Manhattan get it every day!

CHAPTER 1

Shot in the Ass!

"Ouch, goddammit! *Ouch!*" Honore shrieked as she clenched her booty cheeks together and arched her back in sheer agony. She had caught an ass-shot and the pain was outta this world!

"They hit me, Sly! They hit me! Shit! Shit! *Shit!* Them mothafuckas *hit* me!"

The Queen of Diamonds trembled in pain as her right ass cheek throbbed and burned. She was stretched out on her stomach on a dusty table in Sly's emergency tucky spot with both her scalp *and* her behind on fire!

They had fled the ambush at Blondie's House of Hair and ended up in the back room of an old bar where Sly McFly used to stash heroin, coke, and illegal weapons back in the day. He had paid cash money for the place back when he was still pushing packs on the street, and through the years it sat abandoned unless he needed someplace safe to lay low on this side of town.

It wasn't his grandest tucky spot but it had been the closest one to Blondie's joint. Sly kept a generator on hand for a power source and some emergency weapons and ammo and shit, but otherwise the place was dirty and empty and it smelled like damp wood and wet rat shit.

"What the fuck is going *on?*" Honore hollered as she reached back to touch her bloody ass. "Why them fuckin Jews coming at us like that already? The sweet money ain't even due yet! Sly please tell me what the hell just happened?"

Sly McFly just shook his head because he didn't fuckin know. The attack had been vicious and it had come outta nowhere. One second they were listening to old jams and getting fucked up on some Smirnoff's and weed, and the next second hot bullets with no name on them were whizzing through the air looking to rip some fuckin body up.

Leaving Blondie laid out and stretched, Honore and Sly McFly had made a mad dash out the back door. Hauling ass, they had dove face-first into the waiting whip driven by Chimp Charlie.

"Where's Cucci?" Charlie had hollered as Sly and Honore hit the floor mats and hugged them shits tight.

"Fuck that bitch!" Sly screamed with his face damn near under the seat. "Just drive, nigga! Drive!"

Charlie had punched the gas pedal and pushed the whip at warp speed until they came to a dark, industrial area that had once been home to large commercial warehouses and a few small shops and pubs.

They pulled up in an alley and Honore flung her door open and jumped outta the car like it had a bomb in it. Sly could barely get the key in the lock before she busted through the door and rushed over to a sink full of trash and threw her head down in that bitch.

"Water! *Water!*" Honore stomped her feet and fumbled frantically with the faucet as she spun the dials around in circles. "I need some fuckin *water!*"

She dipped her head lower in the sink and damn near shit when spiders and water-bugs and even a mouse scurried up outta that bad boy. The old pipes strained and belched and farted, and then finally produced a thin trickle of rust-tinged water.

Trembling, she thrust her head up under it as fast as she could. "Ooooh," she moaned and shuddered as she turned her head from side to side and panted through the pain. "Oooooh, *shit!*"

"Damn," Chimp Charlie yelped behind her. "Girl you bleeding like a bitch!"

Honore igged him. The warm blood that was soaking the back of her pants and running down her leg was some bad shit, but right now the only thing she gave a fuck about was the fire that was burning on her scalp.

With nothing but a tiny stream of cold water coming outta the faucet it took forever to rinse that creamy crack outta her hair. It had been sitting on there caking and baking and melting her scalp for so long that hunks of hair and patches of skin slid down the clogged drain right along with it.

"Oh, my *goddddd*!" Honore shivered and moaned as she cried. Her whole head was on blaze as she swirled it around trying to hit all the spots that burned the worst. "Ooooh, shit, shit, *shit!*"

"Keep rinsing," Sly told her. "Keep ya fuckin head under that water, girl!"

"Why is this happening?" Honore sobbed into the sink as the thin stream of water trickled through her hair. "Why is all this shit happening to *meeee*?"

"Here," Sly told her when she finally got most of the perm rinsed out. He handed her some balled up paper towels to dry her head and neck. Her shit was patchy as fuck and it looked shot totally out.

"Forget ya damn hair," Sly spit as Honore whimpered and felt around her flaming head with her fingertips. "Just put some Vaseline around the front and that shit'll grow back. Now get your ass up on that table and let me see how bad that bullet bit you."

Sly helped her limp over to the table and stretch out on her stomach, and now she lay there sniffling and cursing and looking fucked up from all directions.

"*Owww!* This fuckin shit *hurts!*" she wailed as her tears dripped onto the dusty old table. "I need a doctor, Sly. I need something for this pain! I need some weed, some whiskey, some *something!* I need you to get somebody over here to help me!"

Sly was already on it. He was barking into his phone and he took it from his ear as he turned to look at her.

"Hold on, baby girl. Just hold on. I got Doc on the line right now. He's gonna come take a look at you and then I'm gonna find out who shot you and drop a *bag* on that fucka's head!"

Sly began to yell back into the phone. "Just get the fuck over here, muthafucka! I don't give a damn *what* time it is on a Sunday night, bitch! You get paid in advance for situations like this, so be here in fifteen fuckin minutes or you gonna be needing a doctor ya goddamn self!"

Sly glanced around the filthy room as he deaded the call to the street doctor. While this was one of his oldest safe houses, it didn't feel all that safe to him right now. He turned to Honore and gently helped her take off her pants, and then he patted her wound dry with his handkerchief and Chimp Charlie's t-shirt. Sly was making moves while remaining vigilant and on full alert because for all he knew this spot coulda been compromised too.

Them bitches tried to catch us out there at a beauty shop, he thought, shaking his head in rage. *At a fuckin beauty shop. Ain't that a bitch!*

This right here felt way different than that disgruntled white guy's shoot-out down at the Boatel. He didn't wanna scare Honore, but the guns tonight were definitely aimed at them and there was no denying it. Somebody had lined them up and almost murdered Honore!

Sly went ice cold. If something ever happened to that girl he didn't know what he would do. Honore was the apple of his eye, and whoever did it was gonna get smashed. Oh hell yeah. He owed some fuckin body a slice of hood retribution that he was gonna serve up in the worst sort of way. He was Sly "King-of-Queens" *McFly* and you didn't just roll up in his presence any old kinda way and not get tagged with some dirty payback.

It took exactly fifteen minutes for the street doctor to arrive to stitch up the bullet wound that had skimmed across Honore's right ass-cheek. The whole time the doctor was working on her Honore was crying and Sly was pacing back and forth with his gat in his hand and his mind moving a million miles a minute.

"*Sly they shot meeee!*" Honore howled as the doctor scrubbed out her wound with soap and a rough brush. "I can't believe it! I got fuckin *shot!*"

"Yeah you did," Sly said bitterly. "You got shot right in your ass, baby! But whoever them cowards is they didn't do what they *came* to do!" he muttered as he continued to pace with his blood on high boil.

"They shot you but they ain't *kill* you. Nah, they ain't come *correct* and that was a fatal mistake when you fuckin with a nigga like me!"

A deadly look darkened Sly's stone-cold face. His bloody reign of running the dangerous blocks of Jamaica, Queens had fine-tuned all of his instincts, and not even his advancing old age could detract from that.

"Them cats must think they fuckin with some young sucka who ain't 'bout that life," Sly fumed. "I got something for they ass! Somebody's gonna get *buried* behind this shit!"

Then he turned to Honore. "I want you to remember one thing about tonight baby girl, if you don't remember shit else."

He grilled his young protégé closely. "It ain't about who strikes first in this game, sugar. It's about who strikes *the hardest!* Whoever them niggas was they fucked up tonight, and when I catch 'em they gonna know it. Yeah, they tagged you a lil bit, but the way those bullets were flying we wasn't even supposed to make it outta there alive. But we did! And now the ball is in *our* court!"

Honore answered him through clenched teeth. "It was them fucking *Jews!* I know it was! They think I ripped them for that diamond! That sweet money from Samuelson ain't even due until the end of the month and these assholes coming at me all early!"

Sly McFly didn't respond but he was thinking the same thing about the Jews being the culprits. He didn't put nothing past those greedy fucks but he wasn't completely sold on the idea that it could *only* be them. It pissed him off that somebody had gotten the drop on him and nipped Honore in the process, but this was the Empire State and there were haters of all sizes, shapes, and colors crawling around in the woodwork out there.

Sly had long ago disciplined himself to look at situations from multiple angles and to avoid ruling out any possibilities. He himself had done a lot of dirt in the hood, and when living that type of lifestyle you never knew how many undercover enemies you might have racked up.

But the streets kept a careful score and they didn't forget shit. Naw, he wasn't absolutely sure it was the Jews who had blasted on them, but he knew whoever it was they were professionals and they would most likely try to finish the job.

The street doctor took advantage of their short silence to say his piece.

"Well, thankfully the wound isn't as bad as it looks. It will take a few weeks for it to heal and you'll need to get on some antibiotics to make sure you don't get an infection. It's gonna be sore as hell, but other than the pain you should be fine," he told Honore.

"Yeah," Sly McFly said, cracking a joke as he eased up and lit a cigar. "And after you heal up I'll buy you some ass implants if you want. That's the new shit all the chicks are into these days, ain't it?"

Honore rolled her teary eyes and smirked, but she chuckled a little bit too. "No thank you, I got enough tail back there for two chicks. You can send them implants to Aunt Frita since she likes to shake her tail-feather, okay?"

"Don't worry about Frita," Sly answered. "Just worry about getting that shiny diamond back, baby girl. We lost some good people back there at Blondie's and for all we know we mighta lost Cucci too. Them fools want their money and they ain't going away, darling. But count ya'self lucky. The way them heat rounds was flying your forehead coulda got twisted back instead of your ass."

CHAPTER 2

Shutting Shit Down

The sun was coming up and the warehouse in Queens where the Zip 'em up Crew had gathered was buzzing off the chart. It was the first time the gunslingers had ever failed to complete a mission and their raw anger was about to tear the roof straight off the joint.

The entire set was hyped as tempers flared and fingers pointed every which way. The normally tight and cohesive crew was all over the board as they shot out accusations, threw low blows, and sprayed blame for blowing the hit and sending the mission totally off fuckin track.

"Yo, we gotta figure out what the fuck went wrong back there!" Slick barked, tasting the failure all down in his gut.

"*You* went wrong, muthafucka!" Wild Man raged. "I knew we shouldn'ta took that job from the gate, slime! Not even for triple the money! You sent us in there with our hands tied behind our backs! You shoulda known this type a shit was liable to go down!"

"Get the fuck outta here with that ol' *bull*shit!" Slick barked. "We *voted*, you lil *bitch!* You knew the risks straight outta the gate and you was the main one hollering for triple pay, remember? So now that the job got fucked up you wanna belly up on that shit, huh?"

All eyes were on Wild Man but none were colder and filled with more scorn and contempt than Noodles's.

You steady blaming Slick, but that was some low-level, amateur-ass, rookie-style shit you planned for us, son, Noodles wrote on his tablet as he sat on an overturned crate. *That whole shit was doomed from the beginning. You lucky none of us ain't get stretched out tonight.*

Noodles finished writing then tossed the tablet to Wild Man to read.

As soon as he finished reading Wild Man flew up outta his seat and lunged. He barreled his whole body into Noodles and knocked him backwards off the crate. Noodles's trach tube went flying outta his throat and the metal appliance clinked loudly as it hit the floor. In a flash Wild Man had his hands around Noodles's neck so fast that none of them had time to register what was going down.

"Nah, *pussy!*" Wild Man roared. There was murder in his eyes as he squeezed his hands together and tried to choke the shit outta Noodles. "It was ya weak-ass surveillance that almost got us fuckin whacked! It was *your* fault, you bitch-ass punk!"

As Noodles fought to retrieve his trach tube and catch his breath, Whitey and Jewelz rushed to pull Wild Man off of him. With his finger pressed over the hole in his throat, Noodles made his move. Slick lunged at his gun hand, catching it just in time to keep Noodles from snatching his .44 off his waist and squeezing it off.

"Back the fuck up, stupid ass!" Whitey yelled, gripping Wild Man by his massive arms. He rushed over to help Noodles slide his tube back in his throat and then he helped Slick clench the dreadlocked killer up tight so he couldn't get his furious bone-breaking hands on Wild Man.

"Your shit is way out there, Wild Man!" the white boy of the bunch spit. "You need to check yourself, homey, because you damn sure wasn't on your A-game tonight, mothafucka!"

"Fuck wrong wit'chu?" Slick whirled on Wild Man and sneered as the reality of what had just gone down began to sink in. "That shit was foul, nigga! It was low and it was foul."

"All y'all little boys need to calm the fuck down," Jewelz chimed in sounding weak and weary. "This ain't no big dick pissing contest. Everybody knew the risks involved with this job from the jump, and we also knew there was a chance this shit wouldn't go our way. Now ain't the time for y'all to be fighting and trying to kill each other. Instead of blaming Slick or Wild Man or anybody else, we need to put our heads together and figure out what we're gonna do to fix this shit."

Cloaked in a cloud of fury, Noodles was mutely rocking back and forth and struggling to control himself. The look of pure rage on his face was indescribable as he lost the battle and reached down in his Timbs for his back-up piece.

"Chill the fuck out, man." Slick moved quickly to put himself in the line of fire. He placed his palm over the .32 gripped in Noodles's hand and tried to calm his boy down. "Fall back bruh, damn. Be cool."

Noodle's eyes were straight on kill-mode as he gestured wildly at his throat with rage and disbelief that Wild Man would dare put his fuckin hands on him in that manner. In that area.

"I know, I know," Slick said, eyeing Wild Man with a look of burning disgust. "He was wrong for that shit, my nigga. But he's still your brother and you can't shoot him man."

"So how the fuck did this happen?" Slick asked quietly when the men had finally gotten themselves under control. He spoke so softly it made the entire room go silent and all attention was focused on him. He sat down on a crate then leaned forward and tapped the muzzle of Noodles's .32 on the table. He knew how fucked up his crew felt. Eating defeat was a foreign taste for them and without the proper leadership they would turn on each other like a pack of snarling wolves.

"We've executed plenty of hits off sketchy intelligence before," Slick continued. "The difficulty level of this job wasn't something so great that we couldn't handle it. Our crew has wiped niggas off the map and disappeared before their bodies hit the ground. We're the best at what we do, and we're the best squad in this whole fuckin game!"

Slick continued to tap the gun on the table with his eyes seeming to stare somewhere way beyond the warehouse.

"But for some reason we slipped up tonight. We slipped up and dropped the damn ball. I don't know," he shrugged. "Our shit just feels off. Way off. I been thinking...maybe there wasn't nothing wrong about the hit, y'all. Maybe there's something wrong about *us*."

Those words hung in the air thicker than gun smoke. Everybody kept the poker face in place but it was clear that they all understood. This thing was bigger than just a simple fuckup. It was an internal cancer, and if they kept it up sooner or later somebody was gonna get deaded.

Slick stood up and tossed Noodles his gat. "Yo, fam. I think we need to take a break," he said, turning his back on his team as he walked toward the warehouse exit.

"Yeah, fuck the bullshit," he said without looking back. "We need a break."

CHAPTER 3

Everything Ain't 100

Noodles was flying on one thousand. Deep rage was an enemy he already struggled with on a daily basis, and right now puffs of hot smoke were seeping through the cracks of his self-control. He was doing his best to slam the bitter blackness deep into his gut, because experience told him if he lost this battle he had no chance of ever winning the war.

He strode back and forth along the narrow ledge behind his house like a mountain lion pacing at the top of a ridge. Visions of the bloody carnage he could have caused tonight flew through his mind like gory scenes out of a horror movie.

Wild Man had put his fuckin mitts on him. That muthafucka had lunged at him and gone straight for his throat. The last cat who had pawed him up like that had triggered a bloodbath so gruesome it had landed Noodles in the womb of a tomb called the Asshole.

He had been two seconds off of blowing Wild Man's thoughts clean outta his head in that warehouse tonight, and it was only his respect and obedience to Slick that had kept him from aiming his gat and squeezing one off.

But he had just barely managed it. He knew he owed it to Slick to keep a leash on the beast that lived inside him. His manz had put his life on the line over Noodles's rage once before and almost got buried because of it. He couldn't throw his dude's sacrifice away just because some chink nigga stepped outta pocket and wanted to act ill.

"Noodles," Ayesha stuck her head out the window and called out to him softly. "Come on inside, baby. The kids just woke up and they're asking for you. They want some pancakes for breakfast like you promised them."

Noodles didn't look at her but he detected the tremble of concern in her voice. The sun had gotten high in the sky and he had been out there for hours trying to keep his rage away from her. What he carried inside of him was too big for her. Too violent. And after all the shit her and the kids had been through he refused to bring that type of destructive energy into their home.

Nodding once, he continued to pace back and forth until he felt the glow of his personal demon shrinking and getting smaller and smaller. When it was finally tiny enough for him to handle it, he stuffed it back inside his mental box and psychologically threw away the key.

Yeah, this was much better, Noodles told himself as he went inside the house. When he calmed the fuck down he was able to think clearer. He was able to strategize and rationalize. Yeah, the hit had been fucked up from the gate, and since it was Wild Man's gig the nigga had cause to be on one.

But even with the shitty surveillance and without the proper background info, something felt real grimy about the entire Zip 'em up program. It seemed like there was some type of hidden conspiracy floating around that Noodles couldn't quite put his finger on.

But he had his suspicions, though. He didn't wanna ring no alarms to Slick just yet without having something concrete to show and prove, but some fuckin body in the click was smelling shady as fuck. And even though all the details hadn't revealed themselves to him yet, Noodles couldn't shake the feeling that certain niggas in his set was living foul.

Noodles knew this was the wrong time for him to be having these hunches but he just couldn't shake them. His mother was sick in Guatemala and he had made arrangements to go see her. He had bought tickets for Ayesha and the kids to go with him, and not only was he gonna surprise her with the trip, while he was there he was gonna get down on his knees and ask her to be his wife.

Noodles gazed at her standing near the kitchen table setting out plates and he smiled inside. Everything in his life had turned to sugar ever since his woman and her kids had come into his world. For the first time since he got outta prison Noodles's life had a purpose. He had peace of mind and peace of heart, and he slept damn good every single night.

He forced himself to smile as Ayesha came over and stood on her tip-toes in front of him. She reached up for a kiss and touched the side of his face lovingly.

"You don't have to tell me what's bothering you," she said softly. "But whatever it is, I just want you to remember that life's too short to hold grudges."

Noodles nodded. He loved Ayesha way more than he had thought it was possible to ever love a woman. No other chick in the world, no matter how fine she was or what she was throwing at him, could ever claim a piece of his heart. Ayesha had it all. She had the whole fuckin thing. And he was gonna show and prove that shit to her when they got to Guatemala and he asked her to be his wife. And to top it all off, he was also gonna ask the children to take his last name and to give him the honor of adopting them and becoming their legal father.

Noodles couldn't wait for all that to happen, but right now his gut was talking to him and his gut didn't lie. As he lifted their youngest son up high and placed him on his broad shoulders, he knew for a fact that something wasn't right in his set. Matter fact, something was far from right. Noodles didn't know what the fuck was what yet, but given some time he was sure as hell gonna find out.

CHAPTER 4

Bury Me a G

The afternoon rain fell in heavy sheets over Cypress Hills cemetery as the Goode Brothers Gang gathered to bury two of their very best young gunners.

Dressed in all-black and standing under large umbrellas, they listened to the preacher utter the last prayers over the closed caskets of Ricky Rollack and his sidekick, Cajiid.

Close family members and street niggas from several different boroughs were in attendance. Ricky had been a certified goon who was well-respected among his peers. He had looked out for his hittas in the street and was extremely loyal to his crew.

Cajiid was like Ricky's little brother, a young soldier on the come-up who was being mentored by the best. In his short lifetime he had been battle-tested many times and had come out on top. The fact that such a young cannon with a lot of heart and potential had been put in the dirt was hard for his homeys to accept.

Handgun Goody had a lot of love for both of the men who were laid out cold in their caskets. He was taking their deaths personally. With his crew gathered around him getting soaked in the rain, Goody began to talk and thunder fell outta his mouth.

"Yo, they got my young bulls man! They were Goode Brothers and nobody touches a hair on a Goode Brother's head!" Goody's whole body trembled with rage as he spoke.

"These niggas out here think we soft? A'ight," he nodded and a dark look of utter brutality crept into his eyes. "When we find them rats I want all their grandmothers tossed off a fuckin project roof!"

He clenched his jaw and nodded again. "I want their baby mama's guts mauled out by pit bulls right in the lobby of their buildings! I want their fuckin kid's heads cracked open with Louisville Sluggers and their bodies stuffed down the fucking incinerators, do y'all bitches OVERSTAND ME?"

Goody glared around at his crew and they all nodded their heads in silence. A shooter named Bolly who was standing next to him spoke up.

"That's all well and understood, big homey. You want they fam tortured until they suffer the most unspeakable pain and horror imaginable. We got you. But what about when we find the coward who actually did this shit? Their leader. How do you want us to take *him* out?"

Goody stood in silence for a moment as he watched the caskets being lowered into the ground. He thought about it for a second then answered Bolly in a voice that was colder than a wet grave.

"Bring that muthafucka to me. I'll dish out his punishment. That clown owes me some blood and I'm gonna collect every drop of it. This thing ain't coming from the pockets no more," Goody growled like a bear about to tear into a warm carcass. "This shit is coming from the heart."

His men nodded in acknowledgement of their marching orders and Goody stepped over to the gaping hole that the luxurious caskets had just been lowered into.

Standing there with his expensive shoes sinking down in the mud, he looked down and spoke out loud to his fallen comrades.

"I got mad love for y'all niggas and y'all have my word that revenge will come sweet and swift. It don't matter who put y'all in this hole—I'ma slay them niggas faithfully in the memory of your sacrifice. If y'all niggas made it to Heaven then sneak me in the back door when I get to them pearly gates. If y'all tearing shit up in hell, then do me a favor. Tell the Devil to keep it hot until ya nigga Handgun Goody gets there!"

Handgun paused and held two white carnations up in the air.

"Goody-Goody, *always* hoody!" he recited the Goode Brothers motto out loud and then leaned forward and threw one flower down into each freshly dug hole. Moments later he was heading off, back to the hood, fully intending to keep the promise that he had made to his dead soldiers.

CHAPTER 5

The Origin of a Kingpin

Dawn was breaking over the naked city of New York, and Handgun Goody was laying in his king-sized bed brooding with his eyes wide open.

Burying his lil porch slangas Dolla and Black Pearl a while back had been cause for concern, but putting Ricky and Cajiid in the ground had taken shit to a whole different level.

Somebody was testing his gangsta. They were probing his power range and slaughtering his niggas at an alarming rate. And so far none of his soldiers had been able to bring him the muthafucka he was hunting for.

Goody was older and wiser than the average kingpin on the streets. He had gone to prison at a young age and come into his manhood amongst some of the most brutal criminals in the country. The joint had been good to him in a number of ways. He had been taught to think like a war general. To analyze conditions from every direction and to anticipate his enemy's attack from every possible scenario. He had also been taught how to launch a vicious and effective counter-attack too.

Goody knew he had an unseen but skilled enemy out there who was coming for his throat. The dead soldiers stacking up on his side of the line made that very clear. It was only a matter of time before he was next on deck, so right now Goody was using all of his mental energy to figure out what moves he needed to make in order to get the drop on the muthafucka who was waging war on his click. Goody had been targeted for death many times before so he knew what it took to survive.

As the moon faded from the sky and the sun came out to announce the new day, Goody looked out the window and thought about the time he almost got smoked while pulling his first bid on Rikers Island.

There was a pecking order established in jail where the strong ruled and preyed upon the weak. Goody was a sharp nigga and he was quick to realize that the guards weren't there to protect him. Some of them even encouraged the cruelty and violence to keep the inmates off their backs.

A certain group of Jamaicans ran the cellblock where Handgun Goody was located and they were young and ruthless. Goody had been nervous just like any other first timer when he stepped on deck, but he was far from a punk and he refused to be oppressed.

Coming to Rikers Island was a rite of passage for young men in the hood. It was the place where the most dangerous dudes from all five boroughs met up for the clash-up.

There were three main things that provoked most of the violence on the Rock: the phone, the food, and the television. Dudes were regularly getting shook down for their commissary and forced to pay a tax on the food they received. They called that shit "paying rent," like the cellblocks were a bunch of high-rise condos.

Goody was green, but he knew he'd have to get his hands dirty in order to gain the respect of the wolves. He was ready for it.

For the first couple of months he stayed outta trouble and flew under the radar. He worked out every night intensely in his cell, building muscle and anticipating the day he would have to fuck somebody up. He realized it was a matter of when and not if, because fighting was a fact of life behind those walls if you refused to be treated like a bitch.

Goody needed some money on his books and he had to use the phone to call his peoples. After breakfast one morning he approached a Jamaican who was standing next to a phone.

"Ayo son, I know how shit goes around here and I need to use the phone so w'sup?" he stepped to the Jamaican and asked with full confidence.

The Jamaican was at least six inches taller than Goody and black as midnight. He wasn't crazy muscular, but he was lean and athletic.

"Dat's gwon cost you ten soup and a box a Newpawts on commissary."

Goody let the cost of the call sink in and kept his poker face on and then responded.

"A'ight, let me get this straight. I'm supposed to pay you ten soups and a whole carton of Newports just to use the phone, right?" Goody said it in a way that reflected his disgust for the terms of using the phone.

"Ju a funny nigga, huh? Did I fucking studda? Don make me kill you idiot bwoy!!! Pay me mine on Friday or me cut your bloodclot troat," the Jamaican said with evil intent as he walked away.

"Oh yeah. I'ma pay you dread. On Neveraury thirty-second muthafucka," Goody muttered under his breath as he made his phone call then went back to his cell.

It wasn't like Goody didn't know niggas in jail, but most of the Brownsville cats was on another cellblock. The few he recognized on his block were already getting extorted or he had beef with them from the street.

"Ayo, Q, who the fuck is the tall Jamaican nigga who think he running shit around here?" Goody asked his celly Quan from Corona, Queens. Quan was a laid-back Five Percenter who was waiting to go up north for attempted murder.

"Oh that's Mittens and he does run shit around here. He put together a mean team, and as you can see they got shit on smash. Yeah, I heard about the conversation you and him had earlier," Quan said as he hung his sheet from one side of the bunk and connected it to a hook on the wall so he could take a shit in private.

"Mittens is over-charging you for the phone tho, my nigga. I don't know why, but the usual price is five soups and five packs of smokes. When you the boss you can make up your own prices though," Quan said casually as he relieved himself behind the sheet.

"Yo how the fuck you hear about that shit? It was just me and Mittens standing over there talking," Goody said.

"Nigga this is *jail*," Quan farted and responded with a chuckle. "Walls have ears in here and they spill the word, ya dig?"

Goody dug it but he had no intentions on paying anybody. He was from Brownsville. "Never ran, never will," was the motto, and that was Goody's whole fuckin attitude. There was no way he was going out like a sucka to a nigga who breathed the same air that he did. Goody would rather die on his feet than live on his knees.

So Friday morning came around and Goody was well prepared. He stepped outta his cell with a shank made out of a piece of metal from a dustpan wrapped in thick wet toilet paper until it had hardened. He stashed it in the elastic band of the boxer briefs he had on.

Goody had already decided not to wait until he was approached by Mittens and his crew. He was a man, and he was gonna take matters into his own hands. After breakfast the inmates were being called to receive their commissary. Goody got his bag of food, clothes, and toiletries, and took it all back into his cell. He then went into the day space and confronted Mittens who was watching TV with his homies.

"Ayo Mittens, let me holla at you my G. Let's talk about what I owe you," Goody said as he kept his right hand in his jumpsuit, gripping the shank.

Mittens and his gang got up quickly and began to surround Goody. Showing no fear, Goody looked in the eyes of the menacing Jamaican and was about to jab the shank deep into his face. He didn't give a fuck about the repercussions. Goody was ready to go all out. If nothing else his name would ring bells wherever he went from this point on.

But then Mittens spoke.

"Me received a kite earlier not to let no harm befall you, mon. It seems you are in good graces with da monsta dey call Haz. He sent me a picture of me mother and sista. Said if anyting happens to you they will be dealt wit accordingly. My apologies for any miscommunication between us," Mittens said, and signaled his crew to back off and go back to watching television.

Handgun Goody's jaw almost hit the damn floor as he tried to stop his heart from jumping outta his chest. He couldn't fuckin believe it. Goody didn't realize Haz's rep was so strong, but he was thankful. He was under the protection of a crazy muthafucka, and he knew why.

Goody was well aware that if things had gone down differently in Big Slick's apartment that long ago night that he wouldn't even be breathing air. If he hadn't done what the fuck Haz had told him to do, he woulda got planted.

As it was, he coulda been murked in here off of Haz's word too. That psycho nigga didn't love him. He was sending him a reminder to keep his fuckin mouth shut. Haz was letting Goody know that he controlled his life and his death, and that his black ass wasn't even safe from his reach in jail.

That was the day that Goody decided he wanted the ultimate power. With the right mix of street smarts and brutal dominance he could be a heavyweight in the underworld. Like Haz, he would be able to rule over his own kingdom and decide the fate of others. The strength of his word would either condemn a man, or set a man free.

CHAPTER 6

Sticky Situations

The VIP pool party that was going down on the rooftop at a Central Park West condo was way beyond jumping. Jewelz had just taken the elevator upstairs after being cleared by tight security and using the passcode that Handgun Goody had provided her.

His invitation to hang out with him had come outta nowhere and at the last minute, but Jewelz didn't complain. It was her job to be on the ready no matter when that nigga called. After all, her goal was to get closer to him and to probe deeply into all his weak spots, and that's exactly what she was gonna do.

The rooftop was packed out and it didn't take long for Jewelz to realize that she was in a high-powered sexually charged atmosphere. There were security-types out the ass, posted up discreetly to keep the patrons safe.

Drunk ballers draped in expensive gear were partying hard and chasing ass-naked model-worthy chicks all around the damn place. Jewelz hadn't seen Goody yet as she walked through the crowd, but she was curiously surprised by the reckless environment.

She peeped a few executive heads sitting at a table having a great time sniffing what looked like a half a key of cocaine piled up in an ivory mound. A young white guy was kicked back stuffing his bong full of weed, while a Spanish chick with long dark hair was pouring shots of Effen Vodka like it was water.

A pretty white girl sitting with them made eye contact with Jewelz and shouted, "Hello there, sexy!" She beckoned Jewelz over and asked with a smile, "Would you like to join us? There's plenty of room over here on my lap. I got what you need. This is the best blow in the city, baby. We can make something work together."

"No thanks," Jewelz said politely. Getting hit on by chicks was understandable and nothing new to her. She was looking sexy as fuck in her hot-pink romper shorts that stopped just under her curvy ass cheeks and highlighted her milk-chocolate skin tone. The top of the outfit was puffed out nicely around her breasts, hiding the burner that was strapped to her chest.

"You sure?" the red-headed chick asked, licking her lips.

"Yeah, I think I'm gonna pass for right now," Jewelz gave her a small smile. "Would you happen to know where Handgun Goody is though?"

"Sure," the woman said and then sniffed a blood vessel worth of coke up her swollen nose. "I think he's over by the pool."

Jewelz walked in the direction the chick pointed in and noticed a gorgeous bare-breasted woman who was straddling a black guy's lap with her back up against his chest. She looked exotic, like a bronzed Brazilian, and she was stacked like a brick building in all the right places.

The beautiful seductress had a blonde-haired white chick crouched down on her knees in front of her. The chick was licking and sucking all over her chocolate chip nipples while the black guy humped on the Brazilian's ass and reached around and massaged her lush titties.

The white girl busted Jewelz watching and let a nipple go and smiled. She stared at Jewelz with a slight smirk, then stuck her pink tongue out and licked the air, as if she was inviting Jewelz to come join them without saying a word.

Dayum, Jewelz thought as she sashayed on by. There was enough pussy up on that rooftop for Handgun to fuck a different bitch every night for six months. *What type of porno freak-fests do this nigga Goody be running over here?*

"You like what you see?"

Jewelz looked up and saw Goody coming toward her with a grin on his face. He looked absolutely handsome with his navy blue dress shirt on and his chest muscles bulging underneath it. He got up closer and hit her with that big radiant smile that showed all of his pearly white teeth, and Jewelz found that shit totally irresistible.

"*Do* you?" he asked again.

"Well, it depends on what you're talking about," Jewelz said with a seductive look in her eye. "Shorty over there looks real nice and all that, but I'm not interested in pussy. I have my own pussy and it's pretty damn good. Wouldn't you like to know?"

"Damn," Goody said still grinning. "You always got a fly-ass comeback. Just how I like it." He gazed down at her with an approving grin. "You killin that pink shit, ma. Come on, let's walk."

Goody grabbed Jewelz by the hand and led her over to the pool. He introduced her to a few shot-callers and they all complimented Jewelz on her grace and beauty.

By the time Jewelz and Goody sat down and stuck their feet in the pool she was feeling a little more comfortable in the midst of the wildly poppin turn up. Goody signaled for a waitress to bring him some weed, and after offering some to Jewelz, which she declined, he rolled himself a nice fat blunt and puffed away.

"So who the hell are all these people?" Jewelz asked as she dragged her slender pedicured feet through the cool water and watched tray after silver tray of cocaine go passing by. "They up here on this roof getting fucked *down!* This ain't no hole-in-the-wall type action. This is some high class upper-echelon shit."

"Exactly," Goody said as he sipped a glass of Krug champagne. "This is a private event that I finance for my power circle every now and then. Lawyers, judges, councilmen, and drug connects. Shit you might fuck around and catch Mayor D.B. up in this bitch sometimes. This shit right here is for the movers and shakers of New York City. I don't care what your occupation is, or what side of the law you standing on. Good pussy and free blow will keep 'em loyal every time."

"So that's what you looking for? Loyalty?"

"Damn right. That's the whole pact right there. I keep these fuckers entertained, and they keep me insulated from all the legal bullshit. This is how you step your game up."

"Big boy shit, huh?" Jewelz said like she was impressed. "I can dig that. So it's all work and no play for you? Where's the balance at? I'm sure something in your life has to be motivating you besides all this money."

"Yeah, my kids motivate me," Goody said. "I got five shawtys and shit. All girls. I don't see them that much 'cause I can't stand they fuckin mothers. I rather just write the child support checks and keep it pushing. I mean, they mines but I'm not the daddy-type of nigga. I'm their human ATM and I don't mind. I make sure they don't need shit and they look good, and that's about it."

Hearing that shit had Jewelz hurt and furious on the inside. Sitting there next to that bastard it took everything she had in her to hide it. She couldn't birth any seeds right now today because of how this fuck-boy had damaged her womb and scarred her body for life, and here he had five daughters and he didn't want shit to do with none of them?

Man, if God ever saw fit to bless her with just *one* daughter, let alone five, Jewelz knew she would be the best mother in the whole wide world. She would move heaven and earth for her little girl, and nothing would stop her from showering her daughter with every drop of love and affection she had inside her.

But with her womb totally destroyed, the possibility of ever becoming a mother had been stolen from her. It had been snatched from her when she was just a mere child. By the mothafucka who was sitting right next to her!

It took everything in Jewelz not to reach over and poke Goody's eyeball out and then push his ass in the pool!

And let his niggas bark.

She would pull out her strap and spray every last one of these mothafuckas on the way out if she had to. She closed her eyes and held back the hot tears brewing up inside her. She forced herself to push the pain out of her mind and to keep her game-face straight so this fool didn't get suspicious.

"So what about you?" Goody asked. "You got any kids? Any crazy baby-daddies I should be worried about?"

"Nah," Jewelz said coolly as she turned her head and fanned away his cloud of weed. She wiped her eyes like they were burning from the smoke. "No kids for me. I'm on the paper chase, baby. I got unfinished business I need to take care of. I don't have time to be chasing after no lil brats."

They hung out together kicking it for awhile as they got to know each other better. Jewelz made up all kinds of lies about the family she didn't have, and Goody told her that his father was dead and his mother was a sanctified Evangelist who was deep in the church.

Soon the party started to wind down and Goody's VIP guests started to file out. Jewelz was glad for the invite but what she really needed was to find out where Goody lived and to see how he had his shit set up on the inside. But all of that in due time.

"Well, I think I should be heading home my damn self," Jewelz said as she gathered her purse and slung it over her shoulder. "It's getting late but I had a good time. Thank you, Mr. Goody. This was a fly-ass get together."

"So when can we get with each other again?" Goody asked as he reached out and stroked her jaw. "You be tryna have me chasing and shit."

Jewelz smiled. She knew he was remembering that lip-lock game she had put down on him in his studio that day.

"Can you cook?" she asked. "If you wanna get together with me then you need to know that I like home-cooked meals and Netflix. I'm not one of them motel room bitches that you probably used to dealing with. I'm no hot dogs and French fries floozy. So get ya'self a cookbook and invite me to your crib when you learn how to follow some recipes."

"Oh you got jokes," Goody grinned. "But we ain't gotta stand over no hot stove and dirty up no dishes, bae. You see the spread I just financed up here? Shit, I got the lettuce to hire you a gourmet chef, sweetheart. I can take you to some of the fanciest restaurants in this whole damn city," he said, sliding right outta her trap. "What type of food you wanna eat? When can I take you out?"

"I'll call you," Jewelz said mischievously. This nigga was smoove. She had been trying every which way to get up in his crib, and so far he had blocked and resisted her every effort. She leaned up on her toes and kissed him on his cheek, and he reached out and grabbed her by her ass-cheek. She felt his hunger as he massaged her ass and sucked her bottom lip greedily between his. Right off the bat his shit got bricked up in a major way and as soon as Jewelz felt it poking her she pushed him off and laughed.

"Look at you," she teased him. "You wouldn't even want this pussy if I didn't make you chase it, now would you?"

Goody could only gaze at her and grin.

"You right, baby," he admitted. "You right."

$$$$$

Despite the carefree role she had played with Handgun Goody, Jewelz's face was carved from stone the next night as she unlocked the door to her apartment and let Slick inside. They had scheduled a meeting to go over the next phase of their plan to spread grief and misery over every member of Handgun Goody's clan, and she had some real good intel for him.

"I got that info you wanted," she said quietly as Slick sat down on her designer leather sofa. Her crib was spotless and stylish as fuck. It was a sanctuary with good vibes flowing all around. The only thing disturbing the peace right now was all that pent-up madness that Jewelz had going on over Slick.

"So whuddup?" Slick asked. Dressed in fine attire, he was all bizz.

"Believe it or not, Dirty Mike is somebody's dirty daddy. He threw a sex party up on a rooftop yesterday and he invited me over. That trifling nigga has the nerve to have five daughters. He buys their clothes and pays child support, but that's about it. He ain't no real father."

Slick nodded. "That shit don't surprise me."

"Well, you also said you wanted to plant Goody's daddy."

Slick nodded.

"Sorry, boo. I hate to disappoint you but that old dirty bastard died a long time ago," Jewelz said as she plopped down on a plush ivory ottoman directly across from him.

"Handgun and his brothers were raised by their mother," she continued. "She's a sanctified old church lady. She tried to bring them up right, but all six of them suckas was already crooks and criminals by the time they were ten years old."

Slick shrugged. He still wasn't surprised. That whole fuckin bloodline was foul. Them Goode Brothers wasn't shit and had never been shit from the gate.

Jewelz smirked. "Like I said, they momma is a sanctified church mother and she still lives in the projects. Goody and them bought her a plush house but she won't even step foot inside that devil's playground. She won't take none of their money neither because it ain't holy. She's one of those heavenly bound saints who ain't no more earthly good."

Slick nodded again. He knew the type. "Cool. We gonna put Momma right outta her misery and send her to her heavenly reward. I been tracking that nigga Razorblade. I'ma hit his ass first."

Jewelz shrugged. "Why him?"

"'Cause he's the baby," Slick said simply. "Ere'body loves the baby. Matter fact, I think we should smash them muthafuckas with a double-header. Let's send Razorblade *and* his momma both to hell at the same time."

"Fine," Jewelz said as she stood up and looked at the door like he needed to get up and step. "Let me know when you get the details worked out."

Slick sat there and looked her up and down. He stared at her peach miniskirt and teal high heels like he was just noticing how finely she was dressed and how different she was wearing her hair.

"You look real nice, Jewelz. *Real* nice."

"Thanks." She touched the wig on her head self-consciously, then eyeballed the door again and stared at him.

"You tryna tell me to bounce?" Slick asked with a half-smile.

"Yeah, something like that."

"What? You having company?" he joked her. "You about to grill some bum-nigga a steak?"

Jewelz smirked. "Nigga, please. I don't drag trashy shit home with me outta the gutter! And don't get me confused with that low-budget bitch you be feeding neither. If I want a steak I can go buy me one or I can get me a real man to take me out to eat one."

Slick nodded. "So you *are* having company tonight then, huh?"

Jewelz put her hand on her hip and strutted over to the door with her needle-thin high-heels stabbing the floor.

"For your information I'm on my way to the studio to hook up with Handgun," she said coldly. "He's laying down some tracks and he asked me to come by."

"Damn!" Slick bucked hard. "You was just with him last night and you steppin out with that nigga *again*?"

"I'm on a *job*, remember? Some of us *professionals* know how to keep our business separate from our pleasure and still put in *work*."

"Yo, I put in work too, Jewelz. Ere' fuckin day."

"Whatever." She shrugged. "You wanted to know when I was gonna make another move on Goody. Okay, so I'm letting you know. I'm making a move."

"A'ight, no doubt," Slick said standing up. He walked over to the door and looked down at her quietly. "You be careful fuckin with that dirty nigga Mike though, Jewelz. Stay focused and keep ya head in the game. I know you still mad at me, but Goody ain't no light-weight nigga. You go up in that studio smelling good and looking all fine like that and he'll try to lull ya ass to sleep. And as soon as you close your eyes he'll bite the shit outta you. Trust me, baby, you gone hafta be up on your toes at all times with that nigga. You gonna hafta—"

"Nigga chill I'm straight!" Jewelz snapped. "Goody is a monster but I ain't no slouch neither! If we wasn't tryna sweep up his whole damn family I would smoke his ass right there in that studio and take his whole click out with him *tonight*."

"Jewelz—"

"Don't worry." She whirled around and snatched open the front door. Slick caught a nice whiff of her scent as her pretty skirt twirled in a cloud of perfume. His heart banged in his chest and his dick jumped on wood.

"I'ma stick to the script," she said with a grin. "I'll let you know what it's hitting for when I get back. I'm about to mind-fuck this nigga to death and get him all strung out."

"A'ight, do ya thing." Slick threw his hands up reluctantly as he walked out with her. He couldn't help feeling some kinda way about sending her off into the lion's den all alone and he paused to give her a few more words of advice.

"Look, Jewelz. Just be careful and make sure you stay in contact with me.

If he tries some foul shit on you I'll come kill that pussy with my bare fuckin hands."

"I'm good. Relax, nigga. I'm in my zone."

"But Jewelz…yo maybe I oughtta go down there with you..." Slick opened and closed his mouth as he tried to find the words. The words to tell her how worried he was about her. The words to say that he would lay down and die if something ever happened to her.

Jewelz smirked. "Nigga you jelly or something? Just keep ya jack on," she said, strutting her sexy ass down the hallway like she didn't have a care in the world. "I'm out."

CHAPTER 7

Remember the First Time

Slick left Jewelz's crib feeling jealous all down in his gut. She wasn't supposed to be looking so damn good or having so much damn fun slumming around with that slimy nigga Handgun Goody.

Deep in his feelings, Slick had gotten on the train and headed back to Brooklyn and now, an hour later, he was standing on the rooftop of building 430 reading and re-reading the message he'd just taken off his bird and trying to get that shit to make some sense.

As a penalty for failing to complete two consecutive assignments your organization has been formally suspended from all business activities until further notice.

What the fuck? The BBU was putting his crew up on a shelf. They were fuckin suspended!

Slick read that shit again. *As a penalty for failing to complete two consecutive assignments your organization has been formally suspended from all business activities until further notice.*

"Yo, hold up. *Two* assignments?" Slick muttered under his breath as he racked his brain tryna figure that shit out. "What the fuck y'all bitches talking about we failed to complete *two hits*?"

Slick was so surprised that his voice had risen way up high.

"Hell, nah!" he paced back and forth on the grainy rooftop. "Y'all goofy niggas got it wrong! My gunslingers only fucked up *once!*"

Suspended. Slick knew what type of crucial shit this meant for his crew. It wasn't just that the BBU was punishing his set for fucking up that last mission. And it wasn't like them billionaire muthafuckas was gonna ask for their client's money back neither.

Nah, what them bastards *could* do though, was cut the Zip 'em up Crew off at the knees and cripple them. They could put the word out on the underground wire that Slick's crew was unreliable and couldn't be trusted to complete a job no more. And if that happened it would fuck up any chance they had of getting on with another organization and picking up future assignments. Yeah, the BBU could use their power to fuck with their pockets in a major way, and if that shit happened then where would his click be?

Slick was furious as he paced around on the rooftop. Even though he had told his hittas to take a break he wasn't talking about forever. The negative ratings from a suspension would kill their credibility quicker than shit and dry up their contract jobs damn near overnight.

Slick had worked too long and too fuckin hard picking the right crew and molding them into a solid team just to get pushed outta business like this. His plan was to stay in the hit game until he could amass and stash at least ten million duckets and he wasn't ready to retire just yet.

The only solution at hand was for the Zip 'em up Crew to redeem themselves. They had to get back out there and fix what they had fucked up. They had to restore the BBU's trust and confidence in their organization.

But that shit was easier said than done. Nerves were already raggedy in the group and everybody was quick to get in their feelings these days. Slick had a major morale problem amongst his posse and he wasn't feeling that shit one bit.

Because theirs was the type of business where one bad apple would fill a whole fuckin basket up with worms. Slick was gonna have to do an assessment of where the bad blood was coming from and determine which member of his family had become the problem child.

Deep in his heart he had his finger pointed in one specific direction, but Slick wasn't the type to jump to conclusions or make decisions based on emotions. It was no secret that him and Wild Man went toe-to-toe at times, or that they had some past animosity that they had to iron out every now and then.

Wild Man was naturally off the cuff with his game, and him and Slick had butted heads ever since they were tykes. It was only natural. Two alpha muthafuckas was always gonna bump heads and clench up. It had happened to Slick over and over again when he was in the military because he was the type of nigga that cats envied.

Slick shrugged that haterade off. He knew he was the shit. And the shit attracted flies. That was part of the game.

Besides, when you cut through all the bullshit, Wild Man was always gonna be his dude, regardless. He had been there for Slick through some rough and hungry years, and Slick had been there for him too. There was no way he was gonna curb his partner. No fuckin way.

Slick's head was heavy and he needed a distraction. He needed to be deep up in some sweet warm pussy. He needed to be held in some soft, female arms. He needed that beautiful chick that he just couldn't get off his mind. The one that he couldn't keep from getting in his heart. He needed him some Honore.

Sitting on the ledge of the roof, Slick placed a call and waited while her phone rang on the other end. He was tired as fuck with his nuts dragging down on the ground, and he couldn't wait to hear his baby's voice.

"Honore," her name practically fell outta his mouth when she finally answered the phone. "Wus good, sweetheart? How you feeling tonight baby?"

"Who's this?"

His stomach got tight.

"C'mon, French Fry. It's ya dude Slick. You don't know my voice by now? How you doing sweetie? Tell me something good."

"I'm fine," she answered, and those two words were so cold and sharp they smacked Slick across the grill like a corner bitch being pimp-slapped to the other side of the street.

"Yo, 'sup with that? What's going on? Why you sound like that?"

"Why I sound like *what*?"

Slick slid down off the ledge. He forced a mental wall to rise up around him and he made damn sure Honore was standing on the other side of it.

"Why you sound like you got a *problem*, Miss Lady? Check it out," he said in a voice that was just as cold as hers. He didn't know what she was crackin for but two could play this bullshit game. "Something's hittin on my other line. I'll holla."

Slick didn't wait around to hear her response. He cut off the call and slid his phone down in his pocket. A moment later he pulled it back out and dialed another number.

"*Jewelz*," he said, grateful to hear her voice when she answered on the other end.

"*What?*" she hissed, sounding all aggravated and annoyed. "What you calling me for, Slick? I told you I was getting with Goody at the studio tonight! That nigga went in the engineer's booth but he's coming back out now. I gotta go!" *Click.*

Slick stared down at his phone and then pushed that shit back down in his front pocket again.

Fuckin females, man.

He sat down on the roof and leaned his back against the ledge. Then he shoved his hand down in his drawers and gripped his meaty dick. He stared up at the moonlight and the stars for a minute, and then he closed his eyes and thought about how a nigga like him had gotten in the murder game in the first damn place.

$$$$$

As the childhood survivor of an extremely bloody massacre, Slick had developed an appetite for slaughter and his first kill had been his tastiest.

The heat had been real hot that summer in Brownsville. It was the time of year when everybody in the hood was outside enjoying the city flow. Ladies walked around half-naked and hustlers flashed their jewelry and rode around in shiny new cars trying to bag the pretty young thots.

On this particular day the block parties and cookouts were jumping while the kids played in the open spray of fire hydrants and everyone enjoyed the good food and good drank.

Slick was not too long out of high school and he had just passed the test to get into the military. He had completed all the necessary paperwork and physicals and he was ready to go.

His outlook on the future was hopeful because he was young, strong, and in the best shape of his life. Yeah, it was gonna be hard for him to leave the wonders of New York City behind, but too many bad memories had stained his soul and he was ready to venture away from the projects in search of some new experiences.

But he still had some unfinished business to settle before he left.

Hassan "Haz" Williams, the man who had murdered Slick's family and left him to die in pool of his own blood, had recently been released from prison. After all the anguish he had caused, that big pyscho nigga was still out there walking the streets of New York City alive and free. Over the years Slick had figured that somebody had already planted that bogus bastard, but fortunately that wasn't the case.

It was a little after eleven p.m. on a hot-ass night and the local drug crews were going about their usual games of cee-low in Nehemiah Park on Livonia and Watkins. The games were held every Friday night, and five or six games would be going on at one time.

It was a regularly held event and the cops stayed away. Rival gangstas from Brownsville and East New York came together to flex on each other and to try to win as much money as they could just for bragging rights. Most of these gatherings usually ended in gunfire, so each crew had their goons waiting on the sidelines just in case some static popped off.

Slick had recently heard through the nigga-network that his uncle was outta the joint, and he had studied and tracked Haz's moves so he could line his ass up properly. Occasionally he had spotted Haz from a distance on the streets and struggled with the urge to kill him on sight, but Haz was a dangerous felon and Slick was trying to survive the encounter.

Slick was young and he had never slumped anybody before, but at the same time he had never wanted somebody dead so badly. Haz represented the destruction of Slick's childhood. He was responsible for the nightmares and the cold sweats that Slick had woken up to almost every night for over ten long years.

Haz Williams was the reason that Slick would never see his mother's beautiful smile or hear her sweet voice again. He was the reason Big Slick hadn't been around to teach his son how to navigate the world and be a man. His uncle Haz represented the boogeyman under Slick's bed, and he was the monster in all his dreams. The next couple of days would find Slick in a military uniform with his whole future stretched out in front of him, and he'd vowed that this was the night he would slay that fuckin boogeyman or die trying.

After a few minutes of careful watching, a chance to catch Haz slipping presented itself and Slick jumped on it.

"Nigga I ain't paying you shit, son!" a fat dude named Oink blasted on Haz, who had just rolled a triple fever.

Haz growled. "You already know what time it is, bitch. Pay me minez or I'ma moon-walk your wig back! I don't give a fuck if it rolled in ya baby momma's *mouth*, nigga! It's trip five's so pay me!"

Everybody out there tossing dice knew Oink was a pussy and he was gonna pay Haz, even though Haz was supposed to shoot it back.

"Man, whatever! Here, take this shit! I'ma get it back anyway nigga! That was a lucky-ass roll," Oink stated trying to save face after getting bitched for his money.

"Yeah, yeah, yeah! Whatever, stop bitching nigga! You mad aggy. If you rolled trips in a crack *I* woulda paid *you*," Haz said with a smirk. He was lying through his damn teeth and everybody knew it.

Over the years Haz had let his physique go, and after getting locked up he was even flabbier than he used to be. If these niggas out here called themselves goons, then one would have to call Haz a goblin. He was considered a bonafied psychopath both in the penitentiary *and* on the city streets. And even though he was fat and sloppy he continued to command a high level of respect and fear. He was still a boss, but most of the time he moved like he was doing now. Like a reckless stick-up kid who had something to prove. Bottom line, the nigga was wild and unpredictable.

"Yeah right, it sounds good mothafucka," Oink said under his breath as he handed over the bread to Haz.

"Yo," Haz said as he snatched all the money from the pot and started walking off, "winning this cheese from y'all bum-ass niggas got my stomach hurting. I'll be right back."

The other dice games were still jumping. Niggas were laughing and joking and talking shit as money was getting made and lost. But even though it looked all good, the tension and excitement was always high. All it took was for somebody to lose too much doe or hear one joke too fuckin many, and that's when the bullets would start flying.

"Yo Haz, you want me to walk with you bro?" one of Haz's young soldiers called out to him.

Haz glared over his shoulder like that nigga was crazy. "Fuck you mean walk with me? Nigga you ain't my bitch! This *my* house! I wish a mothafucka would! Matter fact, com'mere right quick." Haz waved the young'un over to him.

"Here," he said, retrieving his burner from the small of his back and handing it to the pup. "I'm going up to Gina's house on the fifth floor to take a shit. Take this gat and these couple of stacks and keep these niggas playing until I get back. Anybody try some funny shit then you man-down one of these niggas, you heard?" Haz said to his little homey.

Dude nodded. "I got you big bruh. These fools know how I get down out here. I ain't playing with these clown-ass niggas. I'ma keep shit cracking until you get back."

"A'ight, say no more son. I'm out," Haz said and sped off.

Slick was standing nearby and overheard the whole conversation. The night was hot and sticky and several bystanders had towels draped over their heads to keep the sweat off their faces, and Slick blended right in with his.

Slick proceeded to follow Haz into the Tilden Houses that were located across the street from the park. This was the moment he'd been waiting for. His heart was pounding in his chest and sweat broke out across his forehead. He had expected to feel fear when the time finally arrived, but it was actually excitement and adrenaline that was shooting through his blood right now.

Slick hung back as he watched Haz stop and holla at a few niggas who were chilling in front of building 315.

"Y'all porch-monkey niggas *stay* in front of this fuckin building man!" Haz spit at the young bucks who were posted up trying to get they money up.

"What? Y'all too shook to go across the street and get at a couple dollas?"

Haz knew these young niggas didn't have enough money to participate in the games. He also knew that deep down they wanted to stick the whole park up, just like he used to do when he was their age. But even if these niggas had the heart they weren't dumb enough to attempt it. With his towel over his head, Slick walked right past Haz and into the building as his uncle continued to antagonize the young boys.

"Don't look all stupid in the face. You lil niggas will get your turn. You gotta start from the bottom like everybody else. Pay ya dues and then maybe one day you can get it like I get it," Haz joked as he eyeballed the young niggas with an evil grin.

The youngsters didn't even look back at him. They knew Haz was a deranged nigga and they were just trying to get they money up while the big boys were off at the dice game.

"Y'all a bunch of soft lil niggas, man. Holla at me when y'all tryin to make some real doe. Punk ass niggas!" Haz growled as he walked into the building with his stomach bubbling.

Slick had jetted up the stairs and he was already on the fifth floor waiting. He assumed Haz's fat ass was going to take the elevator so Slick waited around the corner and out of view just in case.

Slick was gripping the old .38 snub in his hand that he'd bought off the street for a hundred dollars, and he could hardly wait to put a body on it, if didn't already have one. He heard the elevator open and it seemed like everything started to move in slow motion. He peeked from around the corner and saw Haz walking with his head down counting some bread.

"Ayo, big boy. How you been?" Slick's voice cracked a little as he held the pistol aimed directly at his uncle's head. His adrenaline was running high and beads of sweat formed in his armpits.

Haz looked up at the young man standing before him with a burner gripped in his hand and didn't even flinch. He didn't recognize Slick, nor did he seem to be concerned about the sight of the gun.

"What you want nigga? This lil bit of change right here?" Haz said referring to the ten thousand he had in his hands.

"You can have this shit, just get the fuck out my way nigga," Haz said casually showing not a hint of nervousness. "I'm tryna go take a shit and you holding me up. But I'm glad somebody in this lame-ass building got the heart to do what they gotta do. Makes me proud. Even though you won't live to spend it."

Slick looked at him with a sideways grin and shook his head. Something in that grin looked all too familiar to Haz and a look of confusion slowly crept into his eyes.

"Yeah, big nigga Haz. That's the look I been waiting to see. That priceless look in your eyes that you have right fuckin now," Slick spit in a low, menacing tone as his anger steadily rose. "I been feenin my entire life for this moment, my nigga. Can you smell that shit I'm smelling, Haz? It's the smell of sweet vengeance, you fat fuck."

Slick grinned as he glared at his uncle and gun-checked him with his heat. "You can keep your lil money though 'cause I came to take your soul with me tonight. If you can even call what you have a soul. Tonight you pay for what you did to my fuckin family," Slick said as a blind rage started to overtake him. "Tonight you *die*, muthafucka!"

"Yo, hold up," Haz said calmly, waving the money in the air and trying to stall for time. "Cool the fuck out young nigga. I'm sure we can come to some type of agreement. I'm a Brooklyn bandit. I did a lot of shit to a lot of muthafuckas back in the day. But it was never personal, it was all business. I know one thing, though. Money can smooth a whole lotta shit over. So relax, I know something can be worked out."

"SHUT THE FUCK UP YOU BITCH ASS NIGGA!" Slick roared. His voice echoed loudly in the project hallway as he tried to keep his gun hand steady. The overwhelming flood of emotions surging through his eighteen-year-old body surprised him as he stood face to face with his uncle.

"You killed my mother and my father and my lil brothers and sisters too, you grimy piece of shit!" Slick spit as a single tear fell from his right eye. "You took everything I had! You took the people who loved me *and* you the most!"

When the light bulb in his head finally went off Haz's asshole got weak and he almost shitted on himself right then and there.

It was his nephew. His firstborn nephew. The nephew he used to toss a football to and walk around the projects with riding on his shoulders. The nephew he had taught to dribble a basketball and to shoot cee-low. The nephew he thought he had killed more than a decade earlier, but who was somehow standing right there in front of him, all grown up.

Haz was like a deer caught in headlights and the money he was holding slipped from his grasp and rained down all over the piss-stained floor of the hallway.

"Lil Slick is that *you*?" Haz whispered incredulously as sweat broke out all over his forehead and nose. His stomach bubbled like boiling water on a stove;

it's liquid contents threatening to explode straight outta his ass at any moment.

"That can't be you, man. It...it fuckin *can't* be you."

Slick grinned sickly. "Naw, Unc. You murdered Lil Slick a long time ago. I'm *Big Karma* tonight, mothafucka! I'm the ghost of that boy you left to die on the floor with the rest of his family that night! You can pick up all ya fuckin money and put it in ya pocket cause you gots to pay me in *blood* tonight, you goddamn coward!"

Haz stood there in total fuckin disbelief. He'd thought he had buried those demons a long time ago, yet the spitting image of his older brother was standing before him alive and well.

"Lil Slick, listen to me, Neph," he mumbled. "I was fucked up in the head back then, a'ight? You was too young to understand man, but Big Slick was trying to play me out and...."

Haz stopped in mid-sentence as Slick cocked the hammer back on his weapon.

"Fuck you and your explanations, nigga," Slick said in a venomous tone. "You can explain that shit to God if you ever get to meet him. He forgives. I don't."

The last two surviving Williams men locked eyes and they were both filled with fire. Slick thought for a second that he peeped a bolt of fear flash through Haz, but he quickly realized that wasn't the case. That nigga wasn't scared. He was laughing.

"You think I want your forgiveness, lil nigga?" Haz chuckled with a smirk on his face. "You must be fuckin stupid! Nah, what I was saying before I was interrupted was that your punk-ass daddy was tryna play me. That big brother shit was dead way before I killed him," Haz said, his face straight and colder than ice. "You don't know? I'm the original *Monster* nigga! *I'm* the one who got these niggas out here scared to death! I'm *God* out on these muthafuckin streets, boy!" Haz spat through clinched teeth fully believing every word he said. "And a true God has no mother, no father, no brother, and no muthafuckin *nephew!*"

Haz made his move and it was the final mistake of his life. He reached for the gun he usually carried in the small of his back and—

POP!

The sound of the Slick's bullet slamming into his uncle's shoulder was deafening inside the project hallway. Haz stumbled backwards but he didn't go down. He clamped his finger over the bleeding bullet wound like he was trying to plug up the hole.

"Relax, you fat stankin nigga," Slick said with a grin. All the nervousness was gone from his heart. His mind was sharp and he was ready to do what he had waited his whole fuckin life to do.

"You must be in a hurry to get slaughtered tonight Unc, but I ain't gonna let you go out that easy."

Haz was breathing heavy and holding his bleeding shoulder meat. He realized that Lil Slick had missed the kill shot on purpose. His eyes darted back and forth as he cursed himself for handing off his heat and getting caught out there unarmed. Secretly, he wished some nosey fuck in one of these apartments would poke their head out the door and call the pigs. But that shit was just a pipe dream though. People in the projects minded their own damn business when they heard bullets poppin and the cops never made it in time to save anybody anyway.

"Yo," Haz tried to switch shit up. "Hold the fuck up now. We family, youngblood. Family."

Slick chuckled. "Chill, nigga. Don't start bitching up now cause that was just a lil scratch."

Slick gripped his strap and placed it in the small of his back. He saw the gangstafied aura of Haz starting to melt away and give in to something that looked like real fear.

"You a'ight Monster?" Slick asked with a grin. "I see you sweating kinda heavy over there, Unc. What happened to all that murder-murder kill-kill shit you was just talking?"

"Suck my fuckin dick nigga!" Haz exploded with his face contorted with rage. His blood pressure was skyrocketing and he was getting dizzy. He wanted to lunge at Slick and twist him up and snatch his gun away from him, but he knew he didn't have the foot speed to make it without getting popped again.

But he still had a whole lotta shit to talk outta his mouth.

"I see you got more heart than ya punk-ass daddy did," he taunted Slick as he took a step forward. "You better finish me off right now, lil nigga, cause if I get my hands on you again I won't make the same mistake twice."

"Oh is that right, beloved?" Slick taunted him right back as he pulled a switchblade from his hoody pocket. "Don't worry. I been studying hard for this test and I'ma get this shit right the first go round nigga."

Slick crouched low and lunged at Haz with speed and athleticism. He thrust out his switchblade and stuck Haz in the same spot where his hot bullet had just struck him.

Haz yelped in pain and tried to throw a punch and bear hug him, but he moved far too slow and Slick ducked smoothly out of the way.

"This shit is too easy," Slick said as he roundhouse-kicked Haz in his head then bounced on his toes like Bruce Lee.

Haz's head snapped to the side, and sweating like a fat pig, he staggered under the brutal blow.

Slick laughed. "Man, I wish you was still in your prime so it could be a fairer fight, Unc. But then again, I wasn't in my prime when you stuck me and my baby brothers and sisters with your knife, right? You remember that shit don't you?"

Before Haz could respond Slick rushed him again. He threw a swift, crushing kick to Haz's kneecap that, along with his overweight frame, caused it to buck backward and shatter.

Slick watched coldly as his only living relative hit the floor screaming in excruciating pain. The echo was deafening in the hallway and sure to alert the residents that were huddled behind the closed doors, but Slick didn't care.

He raised his foot and heel-smacked Haz on the side of his meaty head again, and then he pushed him over onto his back and plunged the knife deep into his beefy guts.

Stretched out as helpless as a beached whale, Haz grunted and swung his good arm trying to fend him off.

"Yeah, muthafucka," Slick breathed fire down on him. "This is for my *family,* you grimy-ass bitch!"

"Go to...hell, nigga!" Crazy Haz gasped as blood flecked on his lips. "Go to fuckin hell!"

Slick grinned. "How about I meet you there. And when I see ya ass you better fuckin run 'cause not even the Devil is gonna keep me offa you!"

"You can suck my big black dick!" Haz wheezed, "Just like Kea, your tramp-ass *mama* did!"

"What?" Slick amped out at the mention of his mother's name. He was made of pure murder as he drove the knife blade straight into Haz's forehead.

"W'sup now, huh nigga?" Slick screamed like a maniac as he stuck the knife any and everywhere on Haz's body that he could stick it. "Say her name again!" he dared him and jabbed the knife into Haz's bloated, flabby meat. "Say her fuckin name!"

His uncle did his best to shield off the attack but Slick was zoned out. He ripped, sliced, tore, and plunged his blade into Haz with a sickening degree of rage. "TALK THAT HOT SHIT NOW YOU BITCH ASS NIGGA!"

By the time Slick came back to reality the hallway looked like the type of shit you see in mass killing documentary. He didn't know how much time had passed but he looked down at his uncle and dude's face was damn near unrecognizable.

The hallway smelled like blood, piss and shit. Haz was still twitching and coughing from the fluids that were seeping into his lungs. Slick was out of breath and the muscles in his arms ached from the violent carnage that he had inflicted. His hoodie and pants were soaked in his uncle's life liquid but he paid it no mind. He could hear people in their apartments sliding their peephole covers over. He realized they were looking out into the hallway and that he had to dip out fast, but Haz was still moving. Slick pulled his gun from the small of his back and let it spark.

"POP!! POP!! POP!!

Slick's eardrums ached from the loud blasts as he emptied the rounds into Haz's face and head.

"That's for my *family,* you pussy-ass nigga! We can meet up in hell and go for round two one day, and maybe you can get you a second chance, but for now yo ass is zipped the fuck up!"

As Slick raced down the stairs and ran outta the back door of the building the satisfaction he felt was immediate and soul cleansing. He had just slumped the boogeyman. He had avenged his mother's honor and made his father proud.

All Slick wanted to do now was get the fuck outta Crooklyn so that his demons, and his peoples, could finally rest in peace.

CHAPTER 8

Regrouping

It was Saturday and a big jewelry conference was in town. The New York Diamond and Jewelry Exchange was sponsoring it, so Honore and everyone else in her office had to attend, with time-and-a-half pay of course.

Wearing a colorful scarf tied over her hair to hide the lye burns and bald patches on her scalp, Honore stood up in the back of the conference room shifting her weight from one foot to the other. She had gotten a few curious stares and a couple of patted seats from co-workers inviting her to sit down beside them, but there was no way in hell she could put all her weight down on her wounded ass. Even if she did lean mostly on one booty cheek.

After getting shot she had taken a few days off from work and laid in bed on her stomach, doped up on painkillers and feeling sorry for herself the whole time. Her bestie Cucci had taken off from work too. She spent her time running around Honore's apartment like she was her little housemaid; cooking and cleaning and waiting on her favorite cousin hand and foot.

"I don't know how you didn't see them muthafuckas coming when they rolled on the shop," Honore had bitched the morning after Blondie's beauty joint had got hit.

She was laying on her stomach feeling like pure shit. Cucci had just finished rubbing some Neosporin around the blistered edges of her hair and now she was sliding a plate of grits, sausage, and cheesy scrambled eggs under Honore's nose.

Hungry as hell, Honore had propped herself up on her elbows and winced with pain as she took the fork Cucci was holding out and got busy digging into the grub.

"Them bastards busted right in through the front door and chased us out the back," Honore said, sounding disappointed that Cucci didn't get caught up in the crossfire too. "I just don't see how you coulda missed seeing them because I remember you went outside to get some air right before they kicked the shit in."

"Yeah, I went outside but I didn't just stand out there on the corner like a hoe, stupid!" Cucci said hotly. "Girl it was damn near three o'clock in the morning. I took my ass down the block to the 24-hour rib joint and ordered me a plate. I jetted in the bathroom to pee real quick while they was fixing that shit, and the next thing I knew Big Red was running around hollering and screaming about somebody was shooting shit up in the beauty parlor."

"Unh," Honore had grunted, picking at her food with her lips poked out. Getting shot in the ass was gonna throw some salt in her game. Not only would the healing process slow her down, she'd had to act like a damn clown and front Slick off when he called trying to get with her too. There was no way in hell she could be around that boy and him not wanna get up in her pussy. And there was also no way in hell she could pull off her panties in front of him and explain how she got a bullet hole in her ass neither!

"Here," Cucci had said, passing her a tall glass of orange juice filled with ice cubes. "You thirsty, boo?"

Honore had nodded, letting her cousin fuss over her and make her comfortable.

"It's time to take your antibiotics," Cucci told her, twisting the cap off the bottle and passing Honore two pills. "How's that booty feeling? You think the bandage needs to be changed?"

"Yeah," Honore said weakly as she tossed the pills back and chased them with the juice. "It feels kinda wet back there. I think it's bleeding again."

Cucci's hands had been so gentle as she changed the bandage on her cousin's ass that she shoulda been a nurse. Honore was grateful to have her bestie by her side, and when she needed to go pee Cucci had been right there holding on to her while she screamed in pain from the mere act of squatting her ass down to sit on the toilet.

"It's gonna feel better soon," Cucci stood in front of her cousin and promised as Honore clung to her waist and cried as she peed. When she was done Cucci had balled up some toilet tissue and passed it to her girl, then flushed the toilet for her and helped her shuffle over to the sink to wash her hands.

"Don't cry, Honore," Cucci had pet her bestie and supported her weight as she crawled back into the bed on her stomach. "It's gonna all feel better soon, and until it does, I'll be right here to take care of you."

And now, with both of them back at work in time for the big jewelry conference, Honore wished she had stayed home to rest for a few more days. All that standing and sitting was taking its toll, and her patience and her temper were both growing short.

She slipped outta the conference room the moment they dimmed the lights and a PowerPoint slide appeared on the screen. She headed straight to the bathroom where she popped two Motrin and two Tylenol and then locked herself in a stall and squatted down painfully to pee.

Honore had just flushed the toilet when her cell phone vibrated in her jacket pocket. She glanced at the caller ID and saw that it was her new friend. Wild Man.

His call was right on time! Immediately the pain in her ass was gone and Honore morphed into scheme mode as she leaned against the stall wall and chatted with him.

She giggled inside as she listened to him flap his gums a hundred miles an hour. This fine Asian freak wasn't nothing but an info pigeon. He was somebody she could definitely manipulate and put the squeeze on for some information. She knew she had the skills to get some data outta him because his type was usually hard in the bed but soft on the cap. The fact that he was willing to fuck behind his man Slick told her that this dude was probably the weakest link on their entire team.

Honore had a feeling she could lay her best weapon down on Wild Man and get him to cough up some of that critical info that Slick had refused to disclose.

Yeah, she thought, listening to the Asian cat yap as they arranged to hook up later that day for another date. His ass was steady running his mouth as Honore walked outta the stall and lifted her skirt up and pulled her panties down again. Standing in front of a full-length mirror, she turned around and carefully peeled back her bandage and gazed at the angry red flesh wound on the crown of her juicy ass. It didn't look as wet and nasty as it had yesterday. In fact, it seemed to be changing for the better, and maybe her luck was too.

Instead of going back inside the conference room Honore hung out in the bathroom and kept right on chatting the Asian dude up, stringing him along like a simple-minded sherm as he flapped his loose lips. Running into him in Queens that day had been some real good fuckin luck because right now she needed her a serious pigeon. And from where she was standing this gullible yellow nigga looked like he had bird feathers coming straight outta his ass!

CHAPTER 9

Playin With Fire

It was gusty as hell that Saturday morning but the sun was shining brightly over Van Dyke Houses when the young man stepped out of his car. Residents walking through the project breezeways fought against the howling wind as they hurried from the liquor store, the pizza shop, the bus stop, and the train station.

At any other time a man like this one woulda stuck out like a target in the projects of Brownsville, Brooklyn. But this particular man knew how to blend in. Today he was dressed in black slacks and a crisp white chef's jacket with the stupid matching hat. Balanced in his hands he carried a thermal bag that looked like it was full of delicious food, and he walked with an air of urgency like he needed to deliver it while it was hot.

Nearby, the number 3 train roared past on the Livonia Avenue El and the shrieking sound of metal-on-metal followed the young man into the lobby of building 430.

There were several stooped over and tired-looking senior citizens standing around waiting for the elevator to arrive, but the young man in the white jacket moved swiftly past them and disappeared through the stairwell door.

The strong and athletic type, he took the steps up two at a time and he didn't slow down until he got to the fourteenth floor. Then he went up one more flight and stood in front of the exit door that led out to the roof.

Pausing for just a second, he unzipped the thermal bag and reached inside. He felt around and extracted an 8-inch serrated-edge hunting knife. Skimming his index finger lightly over the blade, he pushed through the door and got ready to do what he had come there to do.

Put in some muthafuckin work.

$$$$$

Gamma and Turk got off the elevator on the fourteenth floor in building 430 and held the door open as they waited for their slime Trill to get off too.

"Yo, nigga, you comin or what?" Turk spit, grilling his manz who stood planted in the elevator like he was scared to get off.

Trill didn't move.

"Man, come the fuck on!" Turk said as he slammed his hand against the rubber panel that forced the elevator doors to stay open. "Ain't nobody got all morning to be fuckin around up here. I got some pussy sleepin in my bed back at the crib."

Trill took a deep breath before stepping outta the elevator car. He was feeling some kinda way about getting assigned to ride out with these two young fuck-ups and the expression on his mug showed it.

Six months ago he'd been taken off the streets and brought up to the big house. His favorite uncle, Handgun Goody, had promoted him from worker-ant to security guard, and up until now Trill had spent most of his time hanging out at Club Goody making sure shit ran smoothly for the Goode Brothers Gang.

Getting sent out on a Saturday morning project mission with frick-ass Turk and his frack-friend Gamma felt like a big fuckin demotion to him. Trill was Hammerhead Goody's firstborn son, and even though his father was the fuck-up of the family, he still had Goode Brother blood running through his veins. Trill shoulda been way past the little petty hustler grind that these two basic niggas was on, and he felt fuckin embarrassed and insulted to be slumming around anywhere near these dumb-ass cats.

But Handgun had ordered all three of them to sniff around the project building. They were supposed to find out if anybody new had recently moved into the building and scare the old residents into coughing up some info about the murders of Handgun's fallen hittas, so that's exactly what they had to do.

"I want y'all niggas to wipe that whole fuckin building down!" Goody had commanded. "Smoke that fuckin rat outta his hole, straight the fuck up! Start on the top floor and work your way all the way down to the lobby. Bang on doors and get up in some faces, too, my niggas! I want them old dusty folks shittin in their Depends, you hear me? Some fuckin body in that building either saw something fishy or they heard something funky! Don't bring y'all asses back here until you find out who the *fuck* that somebody is!!!"

Trill was feeling some kinda way, but he had no choice but to follow the two clowns over to the projects and start knocking on doors.

"Yo, let's split up," he demanded as he walked off the elevator. He sent them to the left and he headed to the right by himself. It was bad enough that the old folks were looking outta their peepholes scary as fuck. They damn sure wasn't gonna be opening their doors if they saw three killer-looking hard-bodies standing out there in the hall.

Trill walked down his side of the hall shaking his goddamn head. He had to obey Goody's shake down orders but he wasn't feeling this shit. He wasn't feeling it at all.

$$$$$

By the time Goody's three thugs stepped off the elevator on the building's top floor, the dude in the white chef's hat had already finished handling his handle up on the roof.

He paused at the top of the stairwell for a split second as he heard them on the fourteenth floor, knocking on doors up and down the hallway and talking in loud voices. Quickly, he jetted down the steps to the twelfth floor, pushed through the exit door, and then jabbed at the call button and waited for the elevator to arrive.

Right on time, he grinned to himself as the elevator car coasted to a smooth stop. When the doors opened he stepped inside, whistling softly as he swung the thermal bag carelessly by the handle like he had just made a delivery.

The elevator descended toward the lobby, stopping quite a few times on its way down. Several tenants got on at various floors. Some nodded and said hello, and others got on and immediately turned their backs on him as they stared straight ahead.

None of them noticed the fact that his crisp white jacket had *Fook U Tu* embroidered on the nametag. They didn't know that the bag dangling from his hand was full of balled up old newspapers. And they definitely didn't notice the wet streaks of blood that covered the bottom of his black pants, or the faint red prints on the floor that were left by his shoes.

$$$$$

Goody's three hoods had already banged on doors and harassed everybody on the fourteenth and the thirteenth floors, and they were jogging down the staircase to the twelfth floor when they saw him.

"Yo, *Sometimey!*" Turk hollered as the tall bum with the grimy hat ran up the stairs three at a time toward them. "Where the fuck is you runnin to so fast, my nigga?"

The peasy-headed bum tried to push his way past them but Gamma hooked his hand under dude's arm and flung him back around hard.

"You heard him, nigga!" Gamma growled. "Where the fuck is you going so goddamn fast?"

Sometimey trembled in fear and his knees knocked together under his stained jeans. He ducked his peasy head down and mumbled some type of gibberish under his breath.

"Open season!" Turk suddenly hollered and then,

Smack!

He swung his open palm down hard and slapped the back of Sometimey's neck like he was trying to kill a giant mosquito. The cracking sound echoed throughout the stairwell as Sometimey yelped in pain and covered the stinging skin on the back of his neck with both hands.

"Chill, Turk!" Trill barked as the two low-level mutts laughed like stupid hyenas. "Y'all dumb fucks need to stop playing so much!"

Trill turned to the dingy-looking bum who stood there with his head hanging down even lower. Dude's face was damn near touching his chest, and in a way Trill could understand why Gamma had taken the opportunity to serve him up. The "open season" game had been around forever and even the stupidest bum shoulda known to protect his neck.

"Ga'head, nigga," Trill urged the raggedy tard-head, waving him off toward the top of the stairs. "Be about your bizz, my man. But stay up on ya fuckin neck, bruh. You heard what that nigga said, didn't you? It's always open fuckin season in the hood, slime. It's always open season."

$$$$$

Sometimey was known as a scaredy-cat muthafucka, and after getting slapped like that it took everything Slick had in him not to blow his cover and start breaking those young niggas into pieces.

He had forced himself to take the vicious slap to the back of his neck without retaliating, and while he had stood there trembling in what looked like pain and fear, it was really rage and a heroic attempt at self-control that had him shaking in his bird shit-covered boots.

It was Saturday and the Zip 'em up Crew members were each off doing their own thing. Slick was helping out the elderly folks around the building, and he had just made a run to check on old man Pie when the trio of slangas surprised him as he was on his way back upstairs to his grandmother's crib.

Slick hardly ever encountered anyone on the staircase this high up in the building because all of his neighbors were too old and sick to walk up that far, so they took the elevators up and down instead.

Fuck is these clowns doing up here? Slick had silently asked himself as the corner boys put their hands on Sometimey and clowned him. He had breathed a sigh of relief when one of the dudes nodded and told him to get going. Slick knew he coulda taken all three of them out right then and there if he needed to, but he was much more interested in knowing why they were lurking around on his fuckin staircase than he was in getting his hands bloody.

That nigga Goody must not'a got my message, Slick thought coldly as he pictured the brutality he had inflicted on them soft soldiers Ricky Rollack and Cajiid.

Them lil bitches better let me be and stay the fuck outta my building! he thought as he ran up the stairs with the sound of their harsh laughter filling his ears.

Slick paused at the exit door on the 14th floor and put his hand on the doorknob. His body tensed up like he was gonna push the door open and walk on through, but his hood senses tingled as he glanced toward the dark flight of stairs leading up to the roof, so he changed his mind and jetted up there instead.

$$$$$

Standing on the rooftop Slick was so dizzy he was almost blind. His heart lurched as he stumbled toward his bird pens with his eyes bulging wide.

Nah, he whispered to himself as he stared down at the pebbly tarpaper that covered the rooftop. He stepped on something soft and recoiled in disgust as he lifted his foot up and saw what it was.

Nah, nah, hell fuckin NAH!

His birds.

Them niggas had gotten to his birds. Sliced them up. Damn near all of them. The locks had been shot off the pens and the doors stood wide open. Most of his flock had been slaughtered, even Dinky. Only a few of the messenger types hovered around flapping their wings. No doubt, they had flown outta the coop before they could be cut the fuck up.

The sound of his blood boiling in his veins rushed to Slick's ears. The rooftop was stained with red liquid and the tiny feet that had been cut off his birds were scattered everywhere. Countless hobbled bodies still lurched and twitched on the ground, wings flapping uselessly as they bled out and died.

Slick stood there enraged for what seemed like a whole fuckin hour, but in reality was less than sixty seconds. The scent of fresh fowl blood slid up his nose and soured his stomach, and it was the nausea that rose to the back of his throat that freed him from his paralysis.

Goody!

The name shot through his mind like a cannon as Slick tore off his Sometimey cap, wheeled around, and dashed back through the door. He bounded down the steps silently, three and four at a time as his hand burrowed deep inside his front pocket and he came out with what he wanted.

It was open fuckin season all right, and Slick was about to get him some neck too.

He rushed them niggas from behind, taking the trio of slangas by surprise as he rolled up slashing and swinging.

"*Argghh!*" the one they'd called Turk squeaked like a bitch as Slick clasped his forehead back with one hand and slit his throat with the other. Dude stumbled down two steps clutching at his neck as he gurgled frothy red bubbles from his brand new smiley face.

Slick didn't pick and choose which one of the other cats he was gonna do first. He just pounced on the first nigga he could get his hands on.

Gamma half-turned and threw his arm up to protect himself. Slick blocked it with his left, and reached under and stuck him in the throat at the same time. The blade went in deep, like it was driving through a ripe peach, and when it hit the nerve between the bones of dude's spine, his knees buckled and he collapsed like his feet had been cut off, just like those birds.

The third cat was the smartest and the fastest. He had taken off running the moment he spotted Slick. He was on the move before the first "*Argghh!*" even came outta Turk's mouth.

Dude bolted down the steps like he was running on air, and by the time

Slick pulled his blade outta Gamma's throat that other muthafucka was already three floors down.

Slick chased that nigga with a vengeance. He was rounding the corner on the 4th floor when he heard dude hit the exit door leading to the lobby at a dead run. Several moments later Slick hit that bitch too, but by the time he pushed into the lobby dude had busted outta the building and was sprinting down the walkway like an Olympic track star.

Slick took off after him. His feet moved like lightening as his chest heaved with every breath. Dude was running wild. He leaped over a fence without even touching that shit, and cut across the grass as he dashed toward his home territory.

But long-legged Slick was closing in. Closing in fast. He fell back on his days in the Army and sprinted at full speed, eager to catch that bitch-nigga and stick his knife right through his heart.

The corner boy must have felt the heat approaching on his back. He hopped over a chain-link fence and headed toward a building across the street where his boys were chilling on the porch and he knew he would be safe. He glanced back over his shoulder with wild, wide eyes, and when he peeped Slick bearing down on him he threw his head back and his legs started moving even faster.

Them shits were moving so damn fast that there was no time to put on the brakes when he saw the garbage truck coming through the intersection. He darted out in front of it, tucking his ass in and praying he wouldn't get clipped and smashed.

Slick was right up on the truck when it slammed into the dude with a sickening crunch. It caught him on the hip, and Slick watched that nigga twirl around and fly high in the air and sail halfway down the street. Then he slammed into the concrete ground with a loud, hollow thud.

Tires screeched in the air and people up and down the street started yelling and screaming. Slick took a step forward to finish the job, intending to rush over and stab that nigga while he was down, but the way the cat's body was twisted up and the angle of his neck, not to mention the spreading puddle of blood that was fanning out all around him, all that told Slick that the job was already done.

CHAPTER 10

Showing Luv

Damn it feels good out here this morning! Time to get the festivities started. The kids are gonna love this shit.

Jewelz was enjoying the warm breezy Saturday in Bucktown, New York, but something about the vibe today was just a little bit different than usual. Today was Old Timer's Day, where nearly the whole hood came out on the blocks to have a good time. People who had moved away years ago flocked back to Brownsville to hang out with old friends. It was a time-honored tradition that had been going on for over seventy-five years.

The energy around the projects was upbeat, positive, and cheerful, and that was rare for one of the worst neighborhoods in the entire Empire State. The local gangs and drug crews had called an unspoken truce for the day, and people knew it was safe to come out for block parties and to and enjoy them some loud music, a drank or two, and some good-ass soul food.

The neighborhood playgrounds and parks were filled with kids and parents who were jamming out the Brownsville way. Pitkin Avenue was live as hell, and all the cute chickenheads rocked their get 'em girl outfits and clucked for the attention of all the real right niggas in the hood.

This was a time of year that Jewelz really liked. She loved watching all the project kids run around and play. It reminded her of how she used to run around the playgrounds with Slick and his brothers and sisters when they were little.

This year Jewelz was continuing her own personal tradition of giving back to her community with a little twist. She called it her Dollar Day, where she lined up all the children in the building she used to live in and gave them each a few dollars so they could rush to the corner store and get as much junk as they wanted.

Jewelz made sure the kids didn't fight each other over the money and she looked out for the weaker ones. She walked to the store with them to make sure they didn't get jacked by no winos, and she always had encouraging words for them all.

So much of her own childhood had been filled with scars and misery that it really brought her joy to put smiles on these babies's faces. Jewelz felt real good about giving these kids the money to get chips and cookies and stuff. She liked easing the tension in the town that she called home.

There had been very few smiles for Jewelz when she was a kid. Growing up in Brownsville was like going to gladiator school. Nobody had two nickels to rub together and a lot of people were out for self. It was a stressful placc that would test the hardest of hearts, and you could bet your ass that only the strong survived in the concrete jungle.

This year Jewelz had some help so she'd decided to do things a little differently. Noodles had offered to participate in her Dollar Day and help her make the event even bigger.

Forget the penny candies and quarter waters from the corner store. Noodles had gone to the outlet mall and shut down the Nike store a few days ago and blew a good five grand as he filled his truck up with boxes and boxes of nice kicks to give away. Jewelz blew a few racks on book bags, school supplies, and coats for when the weather got cold and the kids had to walk back and forth to school.

Together they had set up a bunch of big folding tables in Betsy Head Park and stacked them up high with the latest Jordan sneakers and other gifts for little boys and girls of all sizes.

"Thanks again, Noodles," Jewelz said. She was out of breath and sweating from making trips back and forth to the truck as they got ready for their giveaway. "The kids are gonna love all this shit you bought them. Now that everybody can have something nice to put on their feet maybe they'll stop trying to kill each other over a simple pair of sneakers."

Noodles nodded in agreement. After all the death they dealt with in their profession it felt good to give something to the youngsters who represented the future life-force of The Ville.

"But we gotta put some rules down on this shit," Jewelz said as she stacked a bunch of colorful book bags up on a table. "Nobody gets a damn thing this year until they tell us their future goals and give us the names of two foreign countries that they wanna visit one day. We need to help stimulate these young minds, and I figure we can start by letting them know that there's a world out there beyond these projects."

As Jewelz explained her plans, Wild Man walked up eating a chocolate-and-vanilla Mister Softee swirl ice cream cone. A bunch of little kids were surrounding him and eating cones of their own, and they were thanking him for his treat as he smiled and gave them all high fives.

"Wild Man, w'sup! What are you doing out here?" Jewelz asked, surprised to see him.

"Rolling through," Wild Man responded. "I was sitting in my whip talking on the phone when I peeped y'all standing over here."

"Well since you put on the brakes why don't you chill for awhile and help us give out some of these goodies to the kids today."

Wild Man shrugged. "A'ight. I can hang out for a few. I usually don't fuck with Old Timer's Day, but this is my hood so I'm always down to show love. I can't stay all day though," he warned. "I gotta bounce out to Queens to pick up this lil honey I got a date with later."

"I'm not staying out here too long either," Jewelz said. "I'm going to a basketball jam in Money Makin Manhattan this afternoon. It's at Rucker Park."

Wild Man looked over at Noodles who was hitting him with the killer glare. They hadn't seen each other since the night they got into that lil scuffle after the failed Queen of Diamonds hit. Wild Man had straight violated the rules of brotherhood and Noodles still wanted to drill him behind that shit.

"Noodles. W'sup bro," Wild Man said as he walked over and offered Noodles some dap. "I ain't seen you in a minute, my slime. What's poppin with you?"

Noodles looked down at his hand coldly. He was itching to pull out his gat, and not one move was made to reciprocate the love.

Instead of trying to flip and wild out, Wild Man kept it cool.

"Look man, I apologize for what went down that other night," he said sincerely. "You know me, dawg. Sometimes I bug the fuck out but deep inside I don't mean no harm. I was wrong for what I did, though. My bad for disrespecting you and getting outta pocket like that. You my brotha, Noodles. Whether you like it or not, ain't nothing gonna ever change that, and even if you stop fuckin with me I'll still ride out and take a bullet for your silent ass any day of the week."

Jewelz gave Wild Man the side-eye as she watched him humble himself, which was a very rare sight. Noodles still wasn't feeling it at first, but after a few more moments he gave Wild Man some dap and just like that shit was all good again.

"I'm sorry, man. For real, I love you like a brother," Wild Man said and hugged Noodles real quick. "We all in this game together."

Jewelz laughed and clapped her hands. "See that's what I like to see! Family over everything. Now let's get a group hug going," she said as she pulled both men toward her by their massive arms.

"Gimme a kiss Noodles," she said and laughed as he kissed her cheek. "Now give Wild Man a kiss."

Both men gave her the *fuck outta here* look as she giggled her ass off.

"Yo, I ain't kissin you either muthafucka," Wild Man joked, "but like I said, Noodles you my ace, my day-one nigga, and I got mad love for you, G."

Noodles stared at Wild Man for a second and then he nodded as he heard Ayesha's sweet voice echoing in his ear. He wrote something on his tablet and passed it to Wild Man.

That's Snapple Facts. I got love for you too. Life is too short to hold grudges.

CHAPTER 11

Plottin and Plannin

The jewelry conference had dragged on like a mothafucka that morning but Honore found herself in a much better mood after talking to Wild Man. She had ducked outta the conference early and gone home and changed into some fly sexy shit in preparation for the Saturday afternoon date they had lined up. Hot 97 was killing the radio with classic 90's hip hop and R&B, and her and Wild Man were riding down the street with the windows open battling each other to see who knew the words to every song.

People driving next to them gave them crazy looks as they sang at the top of their lungs and goofed off. Honore was sitting on one ass-cheek working her grind, but she was actually having fun too. She felt like she could be more playful with Wild Man than she could with Slick because this cat was less guarded with his info and he was definitely a whole lot lighter in the forehead.

In spite of her playfulness Honore's mind was firmly on the task at hand, but she couldn't front like she wasn't feeling dude a lil bit. However, it was bizz over bullshit, so if she could squeeze some info outta him while they hung out it would be a win-win situation.

"So, where are we going? You taking me to another poetry club?" Honore asked as they cruised through a neighborhood called Chelsea all the way on the west side of Money Makin Manhattan.

"Nah, not exactly," Wild Man said with a mischievous grin. "This place is a little more intense than the poetry spot."

"Oh really? What do you mean by intense?" Honore said as she looked at him suspiciously with a half-grin. "Why you gotta make shit so secretive. I don't even like surprises."

Wild Man didn't answer, but a few moments later he pulled over and parked the car. He nodded his head in the direction of a building.

"Well, surprise!" Wild Man said grinning even harder than before.

Honore looked up and saw a sign that read Westside Rifle and Pistol Range.

"What the hell?" she blurted out. "You taking me to a goddamn shooting range?" *Was this mothafucka serious?* As sore as her ass was the last thing she wanted to see was a fuckin bullet!

"I know you ain't nervous around guns, Little Miss Tough Ass," Wild Man teased her as he came around and opened the passenger door so she could get out.

"No, I'm actually glad you brought me here," Honore said as she got outta the car being careful not to slide too hard and scuff up her tender ass.

"Hanging out with you I'ma need to learn how to handle myself cuz ain't no telling what's gonna happen! I never knew a stick-up kid who actually practiced at a gun range before."

"Ay, I'm a professional...stick-up kid." Wild Man said reluctantly. He hated associating himself with petty thieves but he wasn't about to expose her to what he really did for a living. "I believe if you're gonna do something you might as well try to be the best at it."

"Well, it's a little disturbing but I know what you mean," Honore said and winked her eye at him as she smiled.

As they walked inside the range they were directed to go to an area where they were required to attend a mandatory gun safety class. The instructors were polite but urged people to listen carefully and to take their precautions seriously.

"Have you ever fired on a gun range before?" Wild Man whispered to her.

Naw, but I've practiced on some human beings before, Honore thought to herself with a smile.

"No," she whispered back. "This is my first time. I don't think I'll be very good at it."

"You'll be fine," Wild Man said, patting her arm. "I got you, baby."

The gun safety class only lasted about twenty minutes and then they were given the option to choose the type of guns they wanted to shoot.

"I wanna try the rifles," Honore said before Wild Man could make a suggestion. "I mean, if that's cool with you."

Wild Man looked surprised that she would choose the rifles over the smaller pistols that she could handle a lot better, but he didn't object.

"Yo, I'm good with whatever," he shrugged. "Let's do it."

Honore put her ear protectors and protective glasses on, and then she elected to shoot first. She picked out a .22 rifle that she thought she'd feel comfortable with. She tried out the grip and peered down the sights as Wild Man loaded the magazines with their rounds of ammunition.

"Now take aim and if the bulls-eye looks blurry you should change your rifle because your shot will never be true," an instructor informed Honore.

"It looks fine," Honore said as she took aim at the Zombie targets that Wild Man had purchased and placed twenty-five yards away. "I'm ready."

"Fire at will," said the instructor.

Honore concentrated on the target, then she took a deep breath and began firing.

POP! POP! POP! POP! POP!

She looked focused and totally comfortable as she got in a zone. She hit the bulls-eye on the zombie's forehead on her first try and the rest of her shots were center mass and headshots. Wild Man and the instructor were both impressed at her seemingly natural ability to handle the rifle.

"*Woo-hooo!* I fucked that zombie up, didn't I?" Honore shrieked in total jubilation as she gave Wild Man a high five.

"Damn girl, you put in work on that nigga!" Wild Man said truly surprised. "You did way better than I expected you to."

The instructor smiled and walked away.

"Tank you, tank you!" Honore clowned, still excited. "I do my best. Now that you see how I put it down with the blicky maybe I can join you and your team on your next kick door mission, huh?"

"Haaa-haaa, now you pushing it," Wild Man said as he laughed and got into position to shoot his rifle.

Wild Man had the target moved back to about fifty feet and got bizzy. He picked specific areas to attack on the zombie and hit them with effortless accuracy.

"Yeah!!! Now that's how you get it in *right there!*" Wild Man yelled then turned and grinned at Honore.

The smell of the gunpowder and the act of yanking the trigger had Honore real excited. She didn't know why she hadn't thought of going to a gun range before. Popping off rounds sure relieved a whole lotta stress and she was starting to really feel herself.

"See there," she grinned at Wild Man, impressed with his shooting, "you just tryna show off. You lucky I'm a college girl because if I really wanted to I could get on some stick 'em up shit with you too."

Wild Man shook his head. "Don't get me wrong, you're a New Yorker so I'm sure you've seen ill shit all ya life. But you don't strike me as the type of person who has the stomach for getting your hands dirty like that. Those college books you be studying don't have the answers to the type of shit I'm into, you best believe that."

Honore shrugged and shook her head as she reloaded her magazine like the instructor had taught them during the safety class.

"What's so hard about running up in jewelry stores and blasting on mothafuckas? What? You want a cookie for that? That's just regular hood-nigga shit. Y'all didn't do anything spectacular that night you know," Honore said dropping into ghetto zone and setting the bait for him to bite.

"Y'all robbed a jewelry store and probably got some gold ropes just so you could wear some shines. Whoopty-fuckin-doo."

"Ay! I don't give a *fuck* about no jewelry," Wild Man barked. "I'm not attracted to the bullshit bling-bling them idiots be out there killing each other over."

He was insulted now and Honore knew she had him.

"So do y'all have any pieces left or did y'all sell it all?" she pressed. "I mean, I used to sit up in there and look at all those nice necklaces and rings and wish I could afford one. I'll buy a couple of pieces from you if you got any left." She grinned. "Cut rate of course."

Wild Man shrugged. "Whatever we got from that jewelry store is put up. Stashed. Wasn't nothing but small-time jewels in that display case anyway. Slum shit. You should know that."

"Uh-huh, I do. But what about what was in that *briefcase* y'all took?" Honore probed even deeper. "That there alone musta been a real big-time take, wasn't it?"

Wild Man stared at her through slitted eyes. "*What* fuckin briefcase? What do you think was in it?"

Honore shrugged innocently even though his anger had her excited. "Beats me. I just figured it had to be something kinda special because the police keep asking me about it."

"Oh yeah?"

"Yup. Since I worked in the jewelry store they made me go down to the station and look at mad mug shots the day after the robbery. And guess what? You really are a thief because I saw yours!"

Wild Man cracked a crooked smile. "Liar. It takes a thief to spot one, now don't it?"

"Yeah, whatever." Honore shrugged him off with a laugh. "I'm not into boosting trinkets, but like I said, I'd buy a few pieces from you real quick if they were still available."

"I already told you I don't have nothing to sell."

She smirked. "That's some bullshit! Why you holding out on me? What kinda kick-door thieves don't wanna offload their stolen shit?"

Wild Man threw his hands up like he was caught out there.

"A'ight, you got me baby. You right. I prolly shouldn't even be telling you this, but Slick is the one sitting on all that jewelry. He said that shit is too hot to dish off right now so won't nobody wanna buy it. So we just waiting for the streets to cool down. That's all."

Honore smiled brightly. *Blabbermouth!*

"Well wait no more! *I* wanna buy it! You looking at a cash customer right here! Do you know how long I been waiting for that jewelry to go on sale? My boss was so damn cheap he wouldn't even give me an employee discount! I know y'all made off with more than just some old earrings and bracelets too, so don't try to hold out on me. Just let me see everything that was in that red briefcase and I'll buy as much of it as I can, bet?"

Wild Man nodded. "Yeah, bet, baby. Lemme get with my crew and see what we got. I'll let you know."

"You gonna gimme the homegirl hook-up, right?" Honore pressed. "I want the biggest and the best shit y'all took, ya heard? But what I really want is a nice big diamond."

"A'ight. I'll see what I can do. I can tell you don't know shit about jewelry though. Just because something is the biggest don't mean it's the best."

"I know enough about jewelry to know what I like," she said playing it off. "Besides, I'm a smart chick and a quick learner. Look at my target, yo! With a little bit more practice I could probably out-shoot you all day long." She laughed. "And then I can start my own stick-up click and get it poppin."

Ignoring the look that crossed his face, Honore stepped up on deck and picked up her piece. She kept the target at the same distance that Wild Man had just shot from. Her first few shots were slightly off the bulls-eye, but the next ones started to hit vital marks. By the time her clip was empty she'd done almost as well as she did on her first set of rounds.

Wild Man stood back as she fired, looking real impressed. With some more practice she could definitely be a good shooter. Most people didn't have the patience for it. He could tell that Honore did.

"You like what you see, now don't you?" she grinned when she was done banging at the target. "Go head. Admit it. My gun-game is nice."

"Why you tryna be so damn tough?" Wild Man asked with a grin of his own. "Stay in school, little college girl. You don't go hard enough. I do what the big boys do. Them little niggas in ya hood couldn't tie my Lebrons."

Honore was covered in a light sweat from handling the kick of the rifle but she felt energized as she got ready to chomp down on this fool and eat him alive.

"School ain't got a damn thing to do with this. You can save that "little girl" shit too, 'cause with all this booty I'm packing it's obvious that I'm grown as hell," she said putting her hands on her sweet hips and taking the conversation where she wanted it to go.

Honore grinned deviously inside as his hungry eyes shot down to her hips. She was gonna get with this fine Asian nigga again. Yeah, her ass-cheek was still sore and fucked up, but she played a mean head game from her knees.

"Besides," she continued and smirked at him sexily, "I'm tough because life is tough. Now how about we hook up someplace private for the rest of the night so I can show you just how tough and grown I am. Since it's my gangsta that you're questioning."

With the sound of guns popping off all around them Wild Man and Honore stared at each other with crazy lust in their eyes. Both of them were remembering the wild night they had spent together and how good the sex had been. It was silently understood between them exactly what was gonna go down next.

"Say no more," Wild Man said as he stared at Slick's fine-ass side piece and rubbed his hands together in anticipation of getting up to his balls in summa that.

Say no more...

EMPIRE STATE OF MINE$!

$$$$$

It was late Saturday afternoon and Jewelz and Whitey stood in the middle of a crowd watching Jay-Z's team beat the shit out of P-Diddy's team in some hoops at the Rucker Park. The annual basketball tournament was packed to capacity and had the city on fire. The park was hittin with all kinds of celebrities and some of the flyest gangsters and thirsty trap bitches from across the city were in attendance.

Back in the day, when Jewelz was still working for Bajan Andy, she used to deliver packages out here to some of the biggest dealers in the entire Empire State. They all still respected Jewelz as a thorough bitch, and they had invited her to come out to chill with them on Diddy's side, even though her roots were in Brooklyn.

Jewelz was feeling pretty good today and she was having a real good time. Yeah, she was peeping how some niggas were giving Whitey funny looks as he stood posted up next to her, but her posture made it clear that the white boy was with her and everything was one hunnid.

"I'm surprised you wanted to hang out with me today," Jewelz leaned toward Whitey and said as they stood in the hot sun watching the intense game go down. "I didn't even know you were into basketball."

Whitey chuckled. "What you tryna say?" he said as he looked down at her. "White boys can't jump or some shit? Tell Jay to let me lace up for his team and watch me Larry Bird this whole situation out here."

Jewelz burst into laughter and shook her head.

"Shut thee hell up," she told him playfully. "I know you got muscles and you a lil athletic and all that, but you ain't got no jumper, boy."

"Why don't you put your heart where your mouth is," Whitey shot back. He slid behind Jewelz and wrapped his arms around her waist and nuzzled her sweet neck. He felt the softness of her ample ass-cheeks rubbing up against him and he whispered smoothly in her ear.

"Let's play some one on one. The stakes can be your future happiness. For real, on some Love and Basketball shit. If I win, you give me your everything. You let me take care of you. You let me protect you and provide for you. You let me be everything that Slick can never be for you."

"Okay, here we fucking go," Jewelz bitched as she shrugged his arms off and moved away from him. "You sure know how to fuck up a moment don't you? I was gonna play along with ya lil shit until you bought Slick's name up. This isn't even the time to be discussing all that, so cool out with all the Slick stuff, okay? I keep telling you that what's between me and Slick is complicated. Remember, me and you are *friends* Whitey, okay? Just friends."

"You always do that," Whitey said as he stepped in front of her. He stared down at her with his intense ocean blue eyes. "Excuse me for telling you how I feel about you, Jewelz. But I can see all the stress and strain he's putting you through."

"You need to stop. Slick's not putting me through anything. I'm a grown woman. I do what I wanna do."

"Yeah, but he's making you chase him and you deserve better than that, Jewelz. All I'm saying is if you want a real man who's gonna be there standing solid for you every single day and can give you everything you need, then that's me. I know you, baby. You need love and affection. You need a man who's willing to show up for you and show you how much he cares. I mean damn, you got me standing right here willing to go all out for you and do all that every day, but somehow that just ain't enough."

OHHHHHHHHHH!!!!

The spectators in the park erupted in a loud cheer as one of the shooting guards for Team Diddy did a 360 windmill slam and drove everybody insane. The action broke the tension that was brewing between Whitey and Jewelz for the moment and they both stood there quietly for a few moments.

"Listen to me," Jewelz finally said, wanting to make shit real clear. "I don't wanna come across like I'm not diggin the love that you have for me. You're a good dude, Whitey. It ain't just that the sex is great, but you make me feel special and you give me a lot of comfort whenever I need it. I really appreciate all the love you offer me, but like I told you before, you can't force it on me. The issues that me and Slick have are strictly between us, so please don't talk about things you know nothing about."

"And please don't let him know that I'm fuckin you when you wanna be fuckin him, huh?" Whitey shot back. "What type of woman doesn't wanna have something real, huh? Whatever you think Slick had for you back in the day, it's dead. He's already proven that. So how long are you gonna keep chasing that ghost? Goddammit, Jewelz! I'm the one who's there for you through thick and thin and everything in between. I'm not asking you to commit to shit, I'm just asking you to open your eyes and not be stupid all your damn life."

Shots had been fired and Jewelz was just about to open her mouth and start firing back, but suddenly she felt all the eyes that were on her and Whitey. Niggas out here were hostile. They already weren't feeling her getting pawed up by no white boy, but to have him screaming on her with base in his voice was way too much. She peeped a couple of hittas looking like that wanted to rush up and steal on Whitey's ass, but Jewelz knew that would be the mistake of their lives, and if they flexed on Whitey their people would be reading about their murder in the next day's Daily News.

She put her hand on Whitey's arm and squeezed it gently. She didn't feel like arguing and deep down inside she knew he was talking some for true, for true, shit anyway.

"A'ight Whitey damn," Jewelz conceded. "Can we talk about this shit later? It's a beautiful day and all I wanna do is watch this game and forget about all the extra emotional shit. Can we do that please?"

Whitey's anger subsided as fast as it had come on. He had a real jones going for Jewelz and he just couldn't let it go. He wanted this girl and he wanted her bad. Her chocolate smooth skin and her thick ass hips, those brown eyes and that smile...she had him head over fuckin heels.

"You got it," Whitey said and smiled. "You know I get crazy when it comes to you, Jewelz. I can't help it."

"Okay but remember, we're just friends, right?" Jewelz clarified as she stared into his eyes. "Just *friends*."

He flashed her that killer grin and shrugged. "Cool. You can call it whatever you wanna call it. Sure, I'm your friend. Any man who wants to be with you should be your friend. Ain't that right?"

"Yeah, you right," Jewelz said as she smiled and reached out to hug him. "Your ass still can't play no ball. Larry Nerd."

Jewelz let him kiss her on the lips and then they settled in to enjoy the rest of the game at the Rucker. Jewelz had smoothed things over with Whitey for now, but the white boy was wide open on her and she knew without a doubt that sooner or later something was gonna have to give.

CHAPTER 12

My Brother's Keeper

As Handgun Goody and his goon squad pushed through the doors of Brookdale Hospital's emergency room his usual ice-cold-under-pressure demeanor was nonexistent.

His lil nephew Trill was in critical condition after being smashed by a big-ass garbage truck. He had sent Trill and two pop-off dummies named Gamma and Turk into the old folks building to see what they could find out about his hittas Rickey Rollack and Cajiid getting pushed, and this was what the fuck had happened.

A couple of dope boys who had witnessed Trill's accident said it looked like Trill was running for his life right before he got hit. Goody figured it to be true because the two flunkies he was with, Turk and Gamma, had both been found bodied in the building's staircase.

As a kingpin who was trying to expand his stranglehold on the streets of Brooklyn, Goody had of course expected to meet with some opposition. He knew a fair share of niggas would respect his gangsta and go along with the program, and he knew he could make deals and form alliances with other sets to keep shit moving like clockwork.

Goody also understood that there would be other niggas that he'd have to straight up take to war, and there would be cold dead bodies that he would have to drop in order to get his point across.

But that was the nature of the business. The nature of the entire drug game. It was a constant fight for positioning amongst the combatants, and the ultimate take was highly lucrative. There were spots in his territory that could produce up to fifteen thousand dollars of straight profit on a good day. And sometimes even more.

In a hood like Brownsville, with one of the highest concentrations of projects in the Empire State, the more buildings you had under your control the more power you possessed and the more money you could rake in.

Goody himself would go at *anybody's* neck if the ends justified the means in terms of dollar bills. So it was no surprise to him that niggas were willing to die in order to keep those spots and that dope bread for themselves.

But with two of his best hittas murdered ruthlessly in the streets, and now this latest mayhem in the old folks building where somebody had slumped a couple of his most thoroughbred young'uns and left his nephew in critical condition?

Goody could only shake his head at that one.

This here shit seemed to be way outside of the game because as far as Goody knew didn't nobody have that spot on lock. Wasn't nobody even competing for it. Nah, something real fuckin funny was going down in that building and he needed to know what it was because the body count from his side just wasn't adding up. In fact, he was starting to think this shit was personal, which of course could make things difficult and get way bloodier than just an ordinary power move.

"W'sup, Ma," Goody walked up and addressed the big-boned West Indian lady at the emergency room's reception desk. "My lil fam just got hit by a truck and they bought him in here. I need to get back there and see him."

"Uh-uh. Nope," the receptionist twisted her lips and shook her head like Goody had just asked her to suck his dick. "Sorry, I can't let you back there unless I see some identification and you fill out these forms."

Goody looked down at the stack of papers on the clipboard she was trying to hand him.

"Listen, Miss Lady," he growled, leaning over the counter until his nose was damn near poking her in her eyeball. "Please don't waste my time with no frivolous shit like *paperwork,*" he said in a calm but cold tone as he looked straight into her eyes. "Now, I'ma need you to find out where they got my neph at and point me in that direction."

He reached over the counter and put his paw down on the lady's left shoulder. "And if I have to ask you again these murderous wolves standing behind me will be waiting for you outside when your shift is over," Goody motioned toward his goons, "and you can discuss all that *paperwork* shit with them."

The receptionist nodded quick-fast. She had no fucking doubt in her mind that this scary bastard meant business. Brookdale wasn't paying her nearly enough to get fucked up over some paperwork. She had a life to live and grandbabies to make it home to. So without any further hesitation she typed something into her computer and then gave Goody the room number he wanted and got the fuck out the way.

"This shit don't feel right," Goody muttered as him and his brothers walked down the hallway to check on one of their own. They had fuckin flipped when they found out that Trill had almost gotten killed tryna put in work.

But Goody had never once considered giving up and leaving the old folks building alone. He had lost some good men over there but he still wanted that shit. He would whack the fuck outta whoever was behind their murders and still get the building jumping, just like he had planned.

"Yo, Trill," Goody said as he stood over his nephew's bed. Trill was laid out stiff as hell with tubes coming and going everywhere. He was bruised and bandaged and all bent the fuck up.

"I know you can't hear me, son, but I need you to pull through my nigga. I need you to wake up so you can tell me who did this shit to you. I need you to tell me who the fuck I need to kill."

Goody had said his piece but on the real he wasn't sure if his fam was gonna ever wake up. Death was stankin up the air all around Trill's bed, and if he was blessed enough to pull through with the ability to think and speak clearly again, it would be a miracle.

Goody was no stranger to death and he had no fear of it. He was still searching for leads to the bitch-made dirt bag who had dared to spill his soldier's blood, and standing there looking at Trill's broken body the coldness of unsatisfied revenge consumed his heart.

He was gonna *smash* the muthafucka who had done this to his little neph. To his mother's firstborn grandson. He was gonna knock out his teeth and crack his fuckin collarbone. Yeah, he was gonna torture that nigga. Stick a match to him and burn him up like a dried-out twig.

All he need to do was find out who the shithead was. He just needed to catch one whiff of the bastard who was smoking his crew, and he was gonna plant that muthafucka a country-mile below the ground.

"Rest up my nigga," Goody said to his unconscious soldier. "Rest up good, too. 'Cause when you wake up I want you to tell me who the fuck did this to you. And don't worry. I got something real special planned for them niggas," Goody promised.

The machine that was breathing for Trill moved his chest up and down, but otherwise the young man lay deathly still. He was the only one who could supply his uncle with the names, faces, times, and places, but unfortunately for Handgun Goody, it would be a minute before he'd be able to tell him.

CHAPTER 13

A Monster Unleashed

When there was a sharp economic downturn the poor and the weak always suffered, which is why Monday morning found Whitey Reynolds doing just fuckin fine.

Although the Zip 'em up Crew's last hit had gone sour and the solidarity of his crew had damn near dissolved, the white boy of the group wasn't worried in the least.

Whitey was definitely what you would call an opportunist, but above all else he was a predator. There wasn't a weak bone in his body and being poor was for the dumb suckers of the world. It was for those ignorant idiots who lacked the guts and brutality to take whatever they wanted out of life.

Today Whitey's guts were telling him that he was very close to getting what he wanted. A while back he had gone to Fulton Street and squeezed a name out of the old Jewish kike who owned the store, and after taking his time to do some research, he had formulated a plan.

This morning he was laying in the cut outside of a ritzy twelve-story apartment building in one of Money-Making Manhattan's most expensive neighborhoods. Whitey wasn't looking to close out a high-priced real estate transaction as one might assume, but he *was* looking to trade his stolen diamond for a suitcase full of cash.

A born and bred blue-blooded native New Yorker, Whitey was as American as baseball and apple pie. He knew very little about the ways of the French and he had never in life been to Paris or Belgium, but right now he had his eye on a sho'nuff tasty-looking French pastry.

Her hair was flaming red and she was dressed in a short black dress and the white bib apron of a professional maid. Whitey pretended to tie his shoe as she walked past him and hurried toward the building, and when she unlocked the gated door and stepped into the foyer he pushed in right behind her.

"*Parlez vous France?*" he whispered in her ear as he cupped his hand over her mouth so hard she was momentarily paralyzed. He hooked his other arm around her chest and lifted her in the air.

"Wanna see my French tickler?" he asked, carrying her toward the stairwell entrance.

The maid bucked. She twisted and squirmed and tried to hold on to the doorframe as Whitey barged through the stairwell entrance with her in his arms.

He flung her against the wall the moment they were inside. Then before she could draw a breath he thrust thc flat of his palm against the ridge of her nose and snapped it.

"Aggh!" she cried out weakly. All the fight was gone out of her as she gripped her gushing nose and slid down to the floor.

Whitey stood back and lit a French cigar as she gasped and writhed on her knees in pain.

"Avi," he said after taking his first toke. "The Belgium dude who does the diamonds. Which apartment?"

Stark terror was in the maid's eyes as she cupped her broken nose and cried. "I-I-I don't know!" she babbled with a stream bright red blood flowing into her palm. "I don't know!"

Whitey was disappointed. This bitch wasn't French. Her accent placed her from somewhere in South Jersey.

He toked his cigar again and the ember at the tip glowed orange-red.

"Avi. What's his last name?"

The frightened young woman shuddered as she sat back on her ass and shook her head from side to side. "Please!" she whimpered, blood spraying from her nose. "I don't know his name! I don't have that information!"

Whitey sighed heavily. He squatted down close beside her and smoothed her bangs away from her sweaty forehead. He gripped its warm roundness firmly in his palm. He took another puff from his cigar and then maneuvered himself until his knee was pressing against her feeble chest. Extending his arm, he leaned his full weight down on her forehead and then took the cigar from his mouth and aimed the glowing ember toward her right eyelid.

Immediately she squeezed her eyes closed and tried to jerk her head away.

"Avi?" he asked simply, then pressed the ember to her eyelid and listened to it sizzle.

Her scream was immediate and intense. It was a bloody-fuckin-murder scream, but Whitey didn't even hear it.

"Avi?" he repeated.

"I don't know!" his captive whimpered as she tried to wag her head from side to side. But that simply wasn't true. She *did* know. Whitey knew she knew. And after one more deep eyelid burn that made her shit her drawers as the orange embers nearly melted straight through to her eyeball, she told.

Finishing her off only took a minute or so. By the time her tongue was protruding from her mouth and her eyes had rolled back in her head, Whitey had already formulated his next steps.

He wrinkled his nose as the smell of loose shit and sizzling flesh rose in the air. After taking one last toke before clipping off his cigar, he brushed off his suit and exited the stairwell with his stomach growling.

Whitey walked out into the sunshine hungry as fuck. He had skipped breakfast, and now he had a taste for a nice Belgium waffle, or maybe even a slice or two of delicious French toast!

CHAPTER 14

No Rest for the Weary

There were smiles greeting her from every direction as Jewelz walked down the hall of the hospital's oncology ward. Most of the staff was familiar to her as she had been down this road before. And as she made her way to the nurse's station she got warm greetings and "welcome backs" out the ass.

It had taken two more home visits and quite a few more harassing phone calls, but she had finally agreed to come into the clinic to sign some paperwork stating that she was voluntarily withdrawing herself from the cancer treatment program.

Jewelz had no problem signing the documents because aside from her hair loss and fatigue she'd been feeling pretty good during the day. She figured it was just all the partying and hanging out she'd been doing with Handgun Goody that had her feeling tired and run down at night. She had been doubling up on her vitamins and supplements but she still wasn't going back on no damn chemo.

Besides, with the BBU acting funny Slick had told everybody to take a short break, so she was gonna start catching up on her rest and get more sleep now that they had stopped going out on missions every other night.

Jewelz was placed in a small office, and a few minutes later she looked up as the door opened and her smiling doctor walked in.

"It's good to see you, Diamond," he said, extending his hand. "How've you been feeling?"

"I'm good Dr. Ford," she answered. "I've been feeling pretty good."

"Well, I'm glad to hear you're feeling okay, but you're still a very sick person, you know. Despite how you may feel, your body can't fight this disease on it's own and you could take a downhill slide at any time," the doctor told her with serious concern in his eyes.

"You really need to take the rest of the chemotherapy that we have scheduled for you. The doses you already took are still working in your body, but they're not enough. Every day you forego additional treatment is a day you allow your cancer cells to multiply and a day of potential healing that you give up."

Jewelz nodded her head as she looked around the office that had mad medical degrees and certificates mounted on the walls.

"I understand all that, but I can't finish the chemo right now. I'm not saying I'll *never* finish it. I'm just saying I can't finish it right now."

The doctor leaned forward and frowned at her like he just didn't understand.

"I've never had a patient stop chemotherapy treatment before they even get halfway through it, Diamond. What could you be doing that's more important than saving your own life? Whatever it is, can't it wait?"

Jewelz shook her head.

"No, it can't," she said thinking about the date that she had planned with Handgun Goody's fam later that night. "I'm doing a lot of stuff right now. Important stuff that I can't do if I'm sick and can't function. I'll get back on my treatments soon. I promise."

The doctor shook his head sadly. "I hate to say it, but this thing could kill you, you know. By the time you come back in to resume your treatment it might be too late."

Jewelz nodded. She was an informed patient and she knew what kind of death she was facing.

"I know," she said signing the paperwork as she stood up to leave. "But that's a chance I'll just have to take."

CHAPTER 15

Brother for Brother, Mother for Mother

Slick sat inside a beat-up hoopty with his seat reclined low and a chrome ratchet gripped in his hand. It had taken him a few days to track down the youngest Goode brother, Razorblade Goody, and tonight Slick had followed him to a party being held at an apartment on Chester Street in Marcus Garvey Houses.

Just like Haz had done with Big Slick, Razorblade took advantage of the popularity and status that came with having an older brother who was a kingpin. He kept a few yes-men type niggas by his side and a flock of young hoes ready to jump on his dick. Razorblade had a nice ride parked outside and a pocket full of money. That's all you needed in order to be somebody in the hood.

But what the youngblood didn't have was the slightest idea that a wolf like Slick had been on his heels for half a week. It was only a matter of time before the baby hoodlum made a mistake. And it would be a mistake that Slick would capitalize on to turn his little ass into fertilizer.

As Slick sat watching a crew of niggas smoking blunts and drinking on the porch of the small building, the light on his phone vibrated. It was a text message from Jewelz.

About to meet momma for dinner. I'll save you a plate baby. Call me on your way home.

Slick smirked then put the phone in his pocket. Jewelz was about to carry out her end of the coordinated attack that they had planned together. She had found out where Handgun's mother lived and she was about to turn her old ass into a distant memory.

Slick was about to hold up his end of the plan too. Suddenly his mother Kea's face flashed in his mind. Her eyes were hard and her lips were frowned up as she looked down at him. Slick blinked real hard and shook his head.

Stay focused nigga. Now ain't the fuckin time to start catching no guilty conscience. Kea's gone and she ain't coming back. Fuck that! Goody had a hand in taking my mother away and now his fuckin momma gotta go too. But Miss Goode won't be traveling alone. Her baby boy Razorblade is going to hell in a casket right behind her.

Seeing Kea's image flash before his eyes angered Slick. He wasn't no natural born killer, but life-altering situations had made him this way. If them niggas Haz and Dirty Mike hadn't massacred his entire family then maybe he woulda turned out to be somebody completely different. But his trauma and loss had him hell bent on revenge, and tonight he was gonna get him some.

Sorry, Momma. I'm about to hit these bitch-niggas where it hurts the most. Right in their fuckin hearts!

Slick got hyped when the door opened and he saw Razorblade Goody stumbling out of the apartment with his arm around the shoulders of a nice thick chocolate girl. The two were slipping off alone, without any of his yes-men following them. The chick laughed out loud when baby boy slid his hand across her waist and gripped her meaty ass cheek, and then bent to nuzzle her neck.

Slick grinned. Razorblade was dipping off to get him some pussy, and this was the type of error that Slick had been waiting patiently for him to make.

Slick coulda picked him off right there without even getting out of the ride, but he wanted to do something a little more dramatic. He was gonna send a message to the Goode Brothers Gang, and a stray bullet wouldn't make his statement clear enough.

Slick started his car and slowly pulled outta the parking space. Razorblade patted the young girl on her jiggly ass again and then walked over to the driver's side of his car.

Slick slid his toolie under the front seat and rolled his window all the way down. He reached for the Molotov cocktail on the passenger seat and lit that shit as he pulled right up on Razorblade's ass.

"W'sup young blood," Slick said quietly. "That Goode Brother shit is dead out here, B."

With his dick hard and his head in a haze of drugs and alcohol, Razorblade wasn't quick enough to react. He barely jumped as the glass bottle splashed down at his feet, and in the next moment he was engulfed in flames.

Slick pulled away from the curb looking back through his rearview mirror with a wicked grin. A big ball of human flames was rolling around in the street and the sound of a horrified female screaming her head off filled the air.

Slick drove through the intersection smirking to himself. One of them porch niggas might run up and take a long-distance piss on Razorblade, but wasn't nobody gonna get burned up tryna put that nigga out. He'd be a crispy muthafuckin steak bone by the time the ambulance arrived. Oh yeah, the Goode Brothers Gang was about to hear his message loud, and they were gonna hear it clear too.

Slick drove with one hand and leaned back in his seat as he replied to Jewelz's text.*You ain't gotta save me no plate, baby. I just ate a nice big juicy Outback steak.*

It was kinda burnt, but that shit was great. I'll holla.

$$$$$

Jewelz was wearing a dark blue Housing Authority maintenance uniform that she had picked up just for this special occasion. She was also rocking a brand new wig and had caked her face up with a bunch of make up. She was so done up that she couldn't even recognize herself when she looked in the mirror.

Standing outside the apartment door of her target, she took a deep breath. *Gone in there and get your shit off, girl,* she urged herself. *She's just a mean old lady and this is probably gonna be the easiest hit you've ever done.*

But an unfamiliar sinking feeling entered her stomach and Jewelz hesitated. She had never zipped up an older black woman before. Matter fact, she had never in life fucked with an elder or hurt somebody's harmless grandmomma.

Uh-uh. She mentally kicked herself in the ass. *Fuck the dumb shit. That harmless old lady spawned a half-dozen fuckin demons! It's her fault that every last one of her sons turned out to be all fucked up!*

Jewelz was there to handle her handle and there was no turning back. Her and Slick had spent a lot of time planning this shit. She got ready to shake that shit off and do what she had come to do.

Fuck all this sentimental shit. That old bitch ain't special! How many innocent mothers have her sons caused to grieve over their children? Them monsters of hers have caused so much suffering that it's only right that their mama should catch some of that hell too! She's probably a ratchet old bitch anyway!

Jewelz was armed with a clipboard, a metal wrench, a small caliber pistol that wouldn't make too much noise, a small bottle of poisonous herbs, and a piano wire that she could use if the situation called for it. She knocked on the project door and waited.

"May I help you?" called a shaky voice from the other side. Jewelz heard a slight click and knew the old lady was looking through the peephole. She could have put her gun up to the lens and popped her right then and there, but that wasn't part of the plan.

"It's Housing," Jewelz called out loudly.

"Housing? At this hour? Is there something wrong?" the old lady asked sounding worried.

"Sorry to bother you, ma'am. I'm Miranda from the Housing maintenance department," Jewelz explained through the door. She jumped right into character and started talking her game.

"The water pipes just busted in an apartment upstairs. A few of your neighbors called in to complain about a leak. I just need to check your bathroom to make sure we don't need to send a plumbing team in for you." Jewelz heard the door being unlocked and a second later a little old lady opened it.

"Hey sweetie," the elderly woman said. She wore a raggedy old blue nightgown and had about ten gigantic pink foam rollers clamped in her thin hair.

"Come on in and check it out. Lord knows I don't need any problems with any floods."

"Thank you," Jewelz said as she stepped inside and closed the door behind her.

The apartment was small and typically modest, project-style. Old-school furniture covered in tight clear plastic was in the living room, and there were pictures of Jesus nailed to the cross hanging from the dingy walls.

Jewelz could tell right away that Handgun had told the truth when he said his momma didn't accept none of her son's drug money. With the thin linoleum and faded curtains it didn't look like The Goode Brothers Gang was looking out for their mother at all.

Jewelz glanced down at her clipboard. "Are you Judith Goode? The leaseholder on the apartment?"

"Yes, I am," the old lady said. "I've been living in this apartment for the past forty years and I ain't never had a lick of trouble with no pipes! I suppose everything is getting old around here though, including me."

"Well, I'm sorry for knocking so late," Jewelz said with a smile. "I'll check things out and be right on my way. This shouldn't take long at all."

Ms. Goode pointed down a short hall toward the bathroom. "Go on back there. It's the first door on the left, sweetie. I was just finishing up my dishes so I could make myself some tea to help me relax. Would you like a cup?" Ms. Goode asked. "I make the best hot tea in Brownsville, young lady."

"Sure why not," Jewelz accepted the offer with a smile. "I couldn't possibly turn that down. Thank you, ma'am."

Jewelz walked down the hall and fiddled around under the cluttered sink in the small bathroom. There was all types of old lady shit up under there. Poly-Grip. Rubbing alcohol. BenGay. Robitussin. Mothballs. Peroxide. A small red tin of Dixie Peach hair grease, and of course some good old-fashioned Vaseline.

Jewelz's mind raced as she stuck her head under the sink and clinked her wrench back and forth against the pipes. Ms. Goode was nothing like she had imagined. Jewelz had thought Goody's mama was gonna be some old Newport-smoking self-righteous church hag with a hairy chin and a big-time attitude. But so far Ms. Goode seemed as sweet as pie and was making her feel real comfortable. She had the aura of a wise elder about her. Jewelz had never had a grandmother before, but Ms. Goode seemed to be exactly what she imagined a good grandmother would be.

After a few more minutes of tinkering under the sink, Jewelz put everything back in place and joined Dirty Mike's mother in the kitchen.

"Everything looks alright in there," Jewelz said as she scribbled some nonsense on her clipboard. "If you find any problems later on feel free to give us a call, but right now it all seems straight."

"Thank the Lord for that," Ms. Goode said, relieved. "Now sit down and drink this tea, young lady. I don't get much company so I'm glad you're here. Even if it is kinda late. I don't sleep much anyway."

"Do you live alone Ms. Goode?" Jewelz asked pleasantly as she picked up the steaming cup and sipped from it. "Your apartment is very nice. It reminds me of my grandmother's house," she lied.

"Yes, I live alone," the old woman responded. "I have six sons," she said, pointing up at a row of elementary school pictures of cute lil boys that were taped to the wall. "Michael is the oldest, and there's Melvin, and Malcolm, and Malik, and Marlon and Maurice. They're all grown now, but none of them come by here anymore. Their father died a long time ago so I've just been hanging strong with the Lord. I don't mind too much though."

"Wow, that's sad," Jewelz said as she continued to sip her tea. "Why don't your sons come by and check on you? I mean, if you don't mind me asking."

"They don't come by because I won't allow them to," Ms. Goode said with very little emotion. "My sons have all fallen victim to the streets. I'm a woman of God, and although I recognize the allure of that life and how it attracts so many young men, I will never condone it. I worked my fingers to the bone so my boys could grow up and be something. They turned out the exact opposite. So," she sighed and gave a sad smile, "as long as they're out on the streets selling that dope and doing the devil's work they are not allowed through my door."

"I understand what you mean," Jewelz said quietly. "That's such a complicated position to be in."

"Not really," the old lady shook her head. "Not when you have your faith and your principles. I wanted my sons to do exactly what it looks like you did."

She pointed at Jewelz's uniform. "You found a way to get yourself a real job. A respectable job where you work hard and pay taxes without hurting anyone. I wanted them to do that too."

Jewelz nodded. She was finding it hard as hell to look Ms. Goode in the eye and that tea had her sweating hot. But she knew what she had to do. As soon as the old woman turned her back Jewelz was gonna get shit poppin. She was either gonna hit her in the head with the wrench and crack her skull, or she was gonna pull out her piano wire and wrap it around the old lady's bony neck.

Yeah, that was it. Jewelz was gonna choke the life outta Dirty Mike's mama. She was gonna leave that mothafucka an orphan, just like him and Big Haz had left her and Lil Slick.

"I'm sorry," Jewelz muttered under her breath.

"No need to be sorry, darling. I came to peace with it a long time ago," Ms. Goode said. "Those boys are my flesh and blood and I love them. I pray for them everyday, but I had to let them go. I can only hope that God answers my prayers one day and that he removes the seal of evil from their hearts and minds. Are you done with your tea?"

"Y-y-yes I am," Jewelz stuttered. Her heart had risen straight up to her throat and she knew the wheels of revenge were about to be set in motion. "And you're right, Ms. Goode. Your tea is the best in town. It was very, very good. Thank you again."

"Glad you enjoyed it," Ms. Goode said. Her eyes twinkled as she smiled.

"Now let me get up and wash out these cups and finish up my dishes."

Ms. Goode stood up and picked up both cups. Humming an old church tune, she turned around to walk slowly toward the sink.

And that's when Jewelz made her move.

CHAPTER 16

She Don't Put it Down Like You

Hanging out with Wild Man at the gun range had been a real cool and exciting date. And after sucking his dick and humping his face later that night in a Manhattan hotel, Honore's good gushy had that nigga's nose wide open.

But unfortunately that pup had been blowing up her cell phone left and right ever since. Every time she turned around he was begging to swing by her crib so he could get him another bite of her cinnamon cookie.

"Yo, so can I get with you tonight?" he had just called and asked her for the umpteenth time.

And of course Honore had refused once again. She had loved the Asian dude's head game, but he was gonna have to bring a lot more than a dope tongue to the table if he was gonna start camping out between her legs.

Honore was used to having niggas hanging off her bra straps by their teeth. From the drug lord roughnecks to the Wall Street-type investment ballers, Honore was the kind of chick who could get with the dude of her choice at the drop of a hat.

But the clock was ticking down on her thirty day grace period, and if she couldn't find that diamond and pay the Kosher Nostra back their sweet money it didn't matter how fine she was because her life wasn't gonna be worth shit.

So, hell nah. She had to get more than just a nut outta Wild Man. And if he wasn't willing to give up no more info then she wasn't willing to waste no more time on him.

"Nah, I don't think so," she told him when he tried to press her. He was really, really tryna get up in her crib. *Mothafucka is you crazy?* she wanted to ask him. But instead she said, "I just don't feel like having company right now."

"Really?" he countered like his lil feelings were hurt. "You sure you don't feel like having no company? Or is it that you just don't wanna spend no more time with *me?*"

Honore giggled inside. *Nigga if you know then why you asking?* She shoulda known from the jump that letting this lil Asian boy get a lick and a smell was gonna be risky. After all, what had she expected? It was only right that Wild Man was wide open on her beautiful body and her unique bedroom skills. Her neck tendencies alone had damn near turned him into a stalker.

"Actually," she said sexily with just a hint of cruelty, "you're right. I just don't wanna be with *you*. The truth is, I'm planning on getting with Slick tonight. Remember, I was fucking with him first so you shouldn't be surprised."

To her amazement Wild Man laughed loud as hell on the other end.

"Nah, baby. I ain't surprised about you getting with Slick. But what I *am* surprised about," he said, with just a little cruelty of his own, "is that you still chasin a cat who clearly ain't banging you the right way."

"How you know what me and Slick do when we're together, boo? That nigga got a two-way mirror or you been chillin like a fly on his wall?"

Wild Man laughed again.

"It ain't gotta be about none of that. It's obvious he ain't handling you superbly or you never woulda opened up them pretty butterscotch legs for me."

Honore cracked up right back. "Look at you! Some kinda homeboy you are! Damn, you don't even know me like that but you throwing shade on Slick's dick so you can slide up in my sheets tonight. With friends like you Slick damn sure don't need no enemies!"

Wild Man tried to front her off. "Nah, sexy. Slick is squad. My ace muthafucka. But you and him ain't even on the same page, baby. You way up on the balcony and that cat is in the basement."

"Damn, that's hard. Why you say that?"

"I ain't tryna throw no shade, doll. But Slick just ain't in your league. That nigga can't do nothing for you. Why you wanna hang with him?"

She tested him. "Well, that jewelry store y'all hit done closed down and went out of business so now I'm looking for me another job. If I hang out with you tonight will you help me find one?"

"Yo, I'll help you do any fuckin thing you wanna do," Wild Man assured her. "You wanna shoot up a liquor store? I'm ya hitta. You wanna rob some corner boyz? I got the heat and I'm rolling witcha."

Honore giggled. "What if I wanna buy me some stolen jewelry? Would you be down to help me do that?"

She heard him chuckle under his breath.

"Don't underestimate me, baby girl. They call me *Wild Man*. I'm down for whatever."

"So, what time did you wanna get together tonight?" Honore asked, thoroughly feeling his sexy little rap.

"Umm," he stammered like he was caught off guard by her switch-up. "Eleven. Gimme your address. I can prolly be at your crib by eleven."

"No," Honore said firmly. That shit was out. She hadn't even let Slick peep where she rested at and she damn sure wasn't gonna let blabbermouth Wild Man fly his bird-ass up in her nest!

"I'll come over to *your* crib," she told him. "I want you to sit back and relax tonight. Since you're so willing to help me out I'll deliver the pussy to you in a gift box. I'll even put a big pink bow on it for you."

CHAPTER 17

Blood on the Leaves

"Burnt up?" Surrounded by his entourage, Goody paused with a glass of Ace of Spades halfway to his lips. "Fuck you mean Raze got burnt up?"

Handgun had been ballin out in Club Goode and getting turnt up when one of his young bulls named Tookie walked into the VIP area and dropped some bad news in his ear.

"Yeah, I just heard about it from this chick I be smashin," Tookie spoke casually with a blunt hanging outta the side of his mouth. "She said her sister is in the hospital with burns all over her hands and shit. She said she got fucked up tryna save Raze because somebody caught him in Marcus Garvey and set him on fire."

Handgun's heart banged hard in his chest and his entire body pulsed with sudden fury. He glanced over at his brother Ice Pick who was sitting on the other side of the booth squeezing and licking all over his bitch Cucci's fat luscious titties.

"Yo Ice!" Handgun tried to bark but that shit came out sounding like a high-octave shriek. "Nigga get the fuck over here right fuckin now, son!"

Ice Pick left Cucci with her lush titties hanging out and jetted over to his brother, who pointed, "This pussy-ass punk just came over here spittin some stupid shit about Raze!" Handgun swelled up on the lanky dude who was squinting through the trail of smoke that was coming off the tip of his blunt.

"Bitch say that fuckin shit again!" Handgun demanded of Tookie as him and Ice Pick pinned the young pup in their killer glares. "Say it a' fuckin 'gin!"

Peeping game, young Tookie sensed danger and swallowed hard. "Ay, I'on't really know what exactly went down, man. I just heard my man Razorblade got burnt to a crisp, that's all."

He shrugged and took a step backwards. "He's ya lil bruh and shit so I thought y'all would wanna kn—"

Smash!

The Ace of Spades bottle damn near tore the side of that nigga's face off as Handgun gripped it by the neck and smacked it against his cheekbone. The glass cut into Tookie's dark flesh and lifted a flap of pink meat right off the bone.

"Ahhh!!!" Tookie screamed, clutching his cheek as he stumbled backward and fell down on his ass. His blunt smoldered on the floor as he tried like hell to hold his face together through the dripping blood.

"Ahhhh!!! Tookie shrieked again as loud as he could while rolling and flopping on the floor like a fish outta water.

"Go get the rest of my brothers!" Handgun ordered his chief security guard who was standing by with his finger on the trigger. "Tell 'em to get in my fuckin office *right now!"*

Goody glanced down at the wounded pup Tookie, who was still screaming and howling and rolling all over the floor and barked, "You go get my brothers, then toss this stupid nigga in the Dumpster out back and shut his bitch ass up!"

$$$$$

Led by their oldest brother Handgun, the Goode Brothers were having a deep discussion regarding the untimely and horrific death of their youngest brother, Razorblade.

Some of them believed Raze had been set up for a robbery by the bitch he had been about to go fuck, and others, including Handgun, believed the origin of his murder was far more sinister and deadlier than that.

"I'm telling you, this shit smells like a direct hit," Cannonball Goody said with tears in his eyes. Raze had been their baby bro. Just knowing somebody had the fuckin guts to reach out and touch him was an infuriating thing. The entire Goode Brothers Gang had gone up to the hospital to try to see Raze, but unfortunately young Tookie had been right. Raze had been burnt to a crisp and there wasn't enough left of him to see, let alone identify, except through his dental records.

"Mama's gonna have a fit," Ice Pick predicted as he paced back and forth. "She already mad about Trill, and Raze was her favorite. This shit is gonna kill her."

Handgun could only nod as he listened to his brothers and brooded inside. Ice was right. Razorblade had been their mother's baby boy and her favorite son. She had cursed Handgun up and down for allowing his lifestyle to attract and lure her youngest child away from the church and into the gutter with him. Razorblade's death was gonna hit her hard, and Handgun knew without a doubt that somehow it was gonna be all his fault.

"Yo, who the fuck is gonna tell Mama?" Hammerhead asked fearfully.

As usual, the weight of the brotherhood fell squarely on Handgun's shoulders.

"Me," he said quietly. "I'll tell her."

CHAPTER 18

Sent Messages

If there was one thing Wild Man couldn't get enough of it was hot butterscotch pudding. Yeah, he knew there was a type of thang going on between his manz Slick and the sexy Honore, but ask him if he gave a fuck! The way he saw it, it was a free-for-all on Honore's golden sweet ass. That pillow-top shit was up for grabs and tonight he was damn sure gonna get him another piece!

She was an hour late showing up, but her actions let him know from the gate that she was gonna be well worth the wait.

"Uh-uh," she said, stiff-arming him in the chest when he tried to get up on her right at the door. "Don't be attacking me with ya tongue hanging all out like a dog chasin a bone, Wild Man!" she said as she walked in shaking her hips. "Act like you got some chill witcha shit, damn!"

But Wild Man couldn't help himself because from head to toe she was looking sexy as fuck! Her thick nipples were poking a hole in her shirt, her pretty hair was out and flowing down her back in waves, and she smelled like something he wanted to throw down on the floor and fuck the shit out of!

Honore stepped deeper inside and looked around his crib with her nose turned up. Her eyes skimmed over the Shoji screen and the hand-painted nesting tables, and the Chinoiserie armoire, and then a smile lit up her face. "Your rest don't look that smoove from the outside but it's really kinda laid in here."

She pointed toward a wall shelf. "Is that a backgammon set over there?"

"Yeah," Wild Man said. "But that's for grown folks and I don't think you wanna mess with that."

Honore smirked and cut her eyes at him like he just didn't know. Kicking off her designer flats and slipping outta her long sweater, she switched her lush ass over to the shelf and took the rectangular box down. She walked over to the low Qing-style glass coffee table and sat down cross-legged, then plopped the backgammon box down and looked at him with the ultimate challenge in her eyes.

"Set it up."

Wild Man grinned. He poured two glasses of wine right quick and passed her a blunt, then he set up the backgammon board and sat down across from her.

They spent the next hour mentally sparring over their game and engaging in playful shit-talking back and forth between them. By the time Honore had waxed his ass off the board for the second time, they had smoked some trees and polished off a bottle of wine and Wild Man was ready to move on to bigger and better things.

And so was Honore.

"Do you have a deck of cards?" she asked him.

Wild Man went and got some Tally Ho's from his kitchen drawer, and when he came back Honore had a big smile on her face.

"What's so funny? What we playing?"

"Strip poker," she said. "Now let's shuffle and cut."

By the time Wild Man figured out that Honore was a straight-up card shark with the gift of the poker-face, he was ass naked and she was still fully clothed.

"You cheated," he accused her as he stood up with his dick long and hard and hanging down along his thigh.

Honore laughed and stood up too. She could barely take her eyes off his pretty wood and she started coming outta her clothes with a quickness. She didn't have on much, just a skimpy bra and a thong under her denim skirt and light-blue tank top.

With her eyes fixed on his, Honore did a sexy lil strip-tease, peeling her shit off piece by piece using the utmost in tantalizing and sensuous moves, and then tossing her discarded clothing high up in the air for effect.

Enjoying the show, Wild Man waited until she was naked and then he stepped up on her and tongued her down. Her lips were sweet as hell and his hands snaked around and cupped her monster ass-cheeks.

They stood there kissing and grinding up against each other and Wild Man rubbed and massaged Honore's ass until her pussy started leaking. Running his hands up her sides, he cupped her fat titties as she scraped her stiff nipples back and forth against his chest.

Wild Man wanted to fuck her so bad his dick was throbbing and his balls were aching. With his tongue still swirling hotly around hers, he lifted Honore up by her hips and then braced his forearm under her ass as she wrapped her legs around his waist and held on tight.

He carried her into his room and stopped in front of an oversized Feng Shui chair that sat in the corner. Easing her feet down to the floor, he turned her around and grasped her under her right thigh, bending her over and lifting her foot up to the seat of the chair.

Wild Man ran his big hand all over the softness of her naked back as he wrapped his shit up tight, and then he reached around and cupped her firm breasts. Her nipples felt like pencil erasers and she moaned as he rubbed and fingered them as he humped her from behind.

Damn near outta control, Wild Man grabbed his dick and guided it down the crack of her ass and down towards her pussy. He spread her cheeks wide and impaled her with a deep long stroke, enjoying the startled gasp that escaped from her parted lips.

He dug her out from a wide-legged stance, holding on tight to her broad ass and banging all the way up in them guts until his balls slapped against her soft pussy hairs.

Honore was bent over that damn chair wheezing and whining. All that shit-talking she was known for was out the damn window now as she bucked her ass back at him and hollered, "*Yesss!* Oooh, goddamn! That shit feels soooo fuckin *goood!!!*"

Wild Man held her in his arms as she leaned back and nutted. She squeezed her pussy muscles tight and fingered her own clit, trembling the whole time like she was having a seizure.

When she was done Wild Man moved them both over to the bed where he told her to lay on her stomach, then he got back in that pussy again and proceeded to bang her lights out.

Wild Man was on cloud nine. The explosion that was about to burst outta his nuts felt too good to be true. Just as he was about to nut he pumped twice and then snatched his joint outta her wet pussy and aimed it at her gorgeous ass. Wild Man's dick jerked and spasmed as hot cum shot outta the tip in waves and coated her butterscotch-colored skin.

"Aggghhh!" he yelled as his knees wobbled and he collapsed down on top of her. He gasped as he tried to catch his breath, and when he finally did he rolled Honore over and pulled her into his arms. Their bodies were hot and sticky as they held on to each other and drifted off into a deep, fuck-out type of sleep.

She was snoring softly in the crook of his arm when he heard it.

Downstairs, under his bedroom window. It wasn't more than a scratch. Not even enough to wake up a mouse.

But Wild Man had heard it.

His ears had been trained to detect the slightest abnormality in his environment, and two seconds after the sound reached him he was wide-awake and on high alert.

His leaned over and got his gat outta his nightstand drawer as he inched his other arm out from under Honore's sleeping head and lowered her gently to the pillow. Without disturbing her, he sprang to his feet like a cat. Reaching under the bed, he swept his pants up with one hand and pulled them on. Moments later he was jetting outta his front door, his pockets heavy with the tools of his trade.

The air outside was damp and misty as Wild Man exited his building bare-footed and bare-chested. Silently he crept around the corner and crouched down behind a row of parked cars. He was cloaked in the shadows as he stared up at his guest room window and assessed the situation in just a quick second.

Darting toward the building, his powerful legs were like springboards. Wild Man leaped in the air and grasped the last rung of the fire escape in his strong grip. Pulling himself up by his massive arms, he scrambled up on the metal platform and scared the living shit outta the dude who was crouched down by his window trying his best to bust the lock.

"Agghh!" dude cried out sharply as Wild Man jabbed an icepick deep into the back of his neck. He yelped again as Wild Man snatched him up by his jacket and sent him flying over the fire escape's railing.

The cat burglar hit the damp ground with a sickening crunch. Moments later Wild Man lowered himself down the fire escape and landed right beside him, and dude immediately started begging.

"Yo, I'm hurt, fam," the thugsta moaned in pain. "You ain't hafta toss a nigga down to the ground like that! Fuck man, I think I'm bleeding on the inside. I'm sorry, son. I'm sorry. I'm all busted up inside. Call me an ambulance. *Pleeeease.* I think my leg is broke. Call a fuckin ambulance!"

"I got your fuckin ambulance," Wild Man muttered as he grabbed him by the ankle and started dragging him down a short ramp that led to the basement door.

"What the fuck you doin, god!" The cat screamed in pain and bucked his hips up and down as he struggled to get free. "Hold the fuck up, goddamn it!" he screeched, kicking out with his good foot. "I think my fuckin leg is broke!"

"Probably is," Wild Man said coldly as he kept right on dragging his ass down the ramp.

Dude started really begging now. "A'ight. You got me, a'ight? *You got me!!!* Lemme 'fess up, god. I was gonna rob ya ass! I was gonna clean your crib the fuck out! But c'mon, now! I didn't even get inside, yo. No harm, no foul cause I didn't even take shit from you. Lemme go, man! *Lemme go!*"

Wild Man cracked a smile at that one. If dude wanted to perpetrate like he was some type of ordinary cat burglar, then let him. But game recognized game and Wild Man had peeped this fucka right from the gate. This lil bitch wasn't tryna get in his window cause he wanted to steal. Hell nah. This amateur idiot had been up on his fire escape because he wanted to *kill.*

Wild Man chuckled deep inside. He didn't know who the fuck had sent this lame muthafucka to sleep walk him, but he was damn sure about to find out.

$$$$$

Almost fifteen minutes had passed. The bloody body sprawled at Wild Man's feet looked like a flat tire that had sprung a thousand leaks.

The basement under his apartment building was cool and damp, and Wild Man had turned that bitch into a slaughterhouse. It was pure-dee torture. He had started out poking deep holes in the young coward with his trusted icepick, and for the last few minutes he'd been carving tick-tack-toes everywhere this mutha-fucka had a smooth spot.

"I'ma ask you again. Who sent you?" Wild Man inquired calmly. He had fucked around and hit an artery in ol' boy's thigh, and dude was laying in a widening pool of warm dark blood.

Wild Man dropped his meat cleaver and picked up his ice pick again. He jabbed it deep into the cat's thick shoulder muscle.

The would-be killer winced and moaned, but he was all out of screams.

Wild Man went for broke. Rising to his feet, he snatched dude's pants and drawers down to his ankles and stood over him sweating. Dude wasn't lying. His fuckin leg *was* broke. And judging from the angle of his kneecap and the white bone that protruded from his shin that shit was broken in at least two places.

"I'ma ask you one more time," Wild Man warned him. "And then the next hole I poke is gonna be in ya nuts. Who the fuck sent you?"

Dude bit down on his lip and squeezed his eyes shut tightly. He was in agony and desperate to live, but there was no way in fuck he could answer that question. At least not truthfully.

Because T-Bone knew that if he gave up that info it wouldn't just be *his* balls on the line. It would be his mama, his grandmama, his bae, and both of his precious kids who got smoked too. Nah, no matter what the fuck this psycho-ass Asian did to him, there were two words that wasn't *never* gonna come outta his mouth: *Sly* and *McFly*.

So when Wild Man gripped his shriveled nut sack in his fist and roared in dude's face, "*Who the fuck sent you, muthafucka!*?!?"

T-Bone swallowed a mouthful of blood and lied through his sliced up lips. "The Queen sent me, yo! It was *Honore!*"

CHAPTER 19

Outta Sight, Outta Mind

"That shiesty slant-eyed bastard!" Honore bitched as she sat up naked and alone in the empty bed. She kicked off the sexed-up sheets and scrambled to her feet, fuming mad.

She looked around Wild Man's empty bedroom and sneered. "Oh, so your grimy ass waited until I fell asleep so you could go creep with some other bitch, huh?"

Storming into the living room she reaching for her tank top and pulled it over her bouncing titties, then she bent over and snatched up her short denim skirt. She wanted to kick her own self up the ass. Just like a true sucka, she had given up the booty before she got the info she had come there for!

Ignoring the thong that she had tossed across the room, Honore pulled the skirt up over her hips then slid her bare feet into her flats and grabbed her purse and sweater up off the glass table.

"If that pie-faced fucker was feening for some random pussy he coulda just woke me up and sent my black ass home!"

Honore stomped outta the small crib punching in a number on her cell phone. She slammed the apartment door hard on her way out, and her footsteps echoed in the empty hallway as she stormed down the steps madder than fuck.

"Charlie!" she spit into the phone as soon as it was picked up on the other line. "I need you to come and get me. *Yeah,* mothafucka! *Right now!* I don't give a fuck what time it is, come and get me!"

She listened to him for a moment as she pushed the heavy front door open and stepped outta the building and into the dampness of the cool night air. "Alright, bet. Yeah, that'll work. Meet me at the all-night joint on the corner. I'm heading towards the avenue right now."

Click.

Honore had stormed halfway up the block when she turned around and glared at Wild Man's apartment building over her shoulder. She twisted her lips as she looked up at his window and spit, "I hope you busting a real nice nut up in ya lil skank-ass bitch because there'll be no more of this good pussy for you, Mr. William fuckin *Wild Man* Choo! You hear me, minute-man? On everything I love!"

$$$$$

The sky was colored in the greyness of pre-dawn when Wild Man re-entered his apartment. Gripping his bloody icepick in his hand he stormed straight to his bedroom and walked over to his bed.

The sheets were rumpled and the smell of hot sex and expensive perfume still lingered in the air, but the chick he had just smashed the shit out of was nowhere to be found.

He stood there fuming mad with a whole bunch of questions to ask, but no one to ask them of.

Because Honore was gone.

$$$$$

Goody's insides felt like they were boiling in acid as he stepped inside the project elevator. He knew better than anyone the casualties you faced when playing the type of game he played. No matter how arrogant and ambitious he was out there on the streets, Handgun knew full well that no one was untouchable. No one was off limits. The only thing a gangsta could do was try to make the penalty for violating so severe that it sent a deadly message to his enemies. Fear was much stronger than love, and it was an emotion that was universally respected whether you were a common crook or a Wall Street banker.

And at that particular moment Handgun had to admit that he was feeling a little fearful himself. He was riding the pissy graffiti-streaked elevator up to the apartment of the woman who had given birth to him. It was his responsibility to tell her that her baby boy had been murdered under his watch, and the ruthless drug lord who sat at the head of one of the most powerful gangs in New York City had the jitters as he knocked on his mother's door and prepared to give her the bad news.

"Who is it?" Ms. Goode called out in a surprised voice from the other side of the door.

"It's Hand—" Goody started to say and then checked himself. "It's Michael, Momma. It's Mike."

Ms. Goode unlocked multiple locks and chains and cracked the door open slightly.

"Hello Michael," Ms. Goode said as she stared at him up and down. She was dressed in all white and disappointment filled her eyes as she gazed at her oldest boy. "You know you aren't allowed in my house, is there something I can do for you?"

"I just came by to tell you what's going on," Handgun said quietly. He didn't care if she didn't invite him in because he didn't wanna step foot up in her house no way. There were too many bad memories and shitty regrets in there for him to handle. "I gotta talk to you for a minute. Can you at least step out in the hallway? Please, Ma?"

"What is it Michael?" Ms. Goode said as she stepped across her threshold. "You're wearing expensive clothes and shiny shoes so I know you haven't stopped selling dope and gone broke. What do you want of me?"

"This is not about me, Ma," Handgun said quietly as he stared down at the grimy project floor. "It's about Maurice. Mama I'm sorry, but Mo was murdered last night. I wanted to tell you before you heard it someplace else. I'll be handling the cost of the funeral and everything so you don't have to worry about none of that. They said he was at some party and—"

"It doesn't matter how it happened or where he was at!" Ms. Goode snapped. "What's dead is done," she said firmly. "I tried to raise all my boys—you, Malik, Marcus, Melvin, Marlon and especially Maurice, to be stand-up men like your Daddy was. Poor Mo was just out there trying to follow your path of destruction, boy. I worked my fingers to the bone trying to keep my baby outta those streets but you still managed to pull him right down in the gutter with you! It don't matter who killed him. You're responsible for this, Michael. *You're* the one who started this unholy domino effect with your little brothers, and now my baby's blood is on your hands. You deal with it!"

Before Goody could say anything his mother stepped back inside her apartment and slammed the door in his face. He stood there speechless and alone. The expression of straight disgust on his mother's face had looked real familiar to him. He'd been seeing that recriminating look in her eyes ever since his Dirty Mike days.

But she was absolutely right, though. His baby brother's blood was on his hands. Goody gritted his teeth and clenched his fists as he walked away from his childhood home. The tongue-lashing his mother had put on him was inspirational and it burned motivation deep in his soul. He knew what had to be done, and he was on his way to put vengeance into motion.

Thirty minutes later he was issuing his bang-up orders.

"Y'all better beat these fucking blocks up, son!" Goody roared at his hittas. The Boss of Bosses had called a meeting with his remaining brothers, his soldiers, his corner boys, and even all the young chickenheads that he paid to keep an ear out on the blocks.

"Somebody set my fuckin baby brother on fire in the middle of the street and I want y'all to flush 'em the fuck out! I got an eighty-thousand dollar bonus for the mothafucka who finds out who did this shit and brings me back a body!"

Goody's gang sat in the room stone-faced and dead serious, brandishing burners and ready to get bizzy. That amount of bread on a nigga's head made all the wolves thirsty. They could all use a piece of that change, and they would put their best foot forward to try and get at it.

"I don't give a fuck who it is!" Goody screamed. "I don't care what click they rollin with or who they big homey is! It's a green light on anybody who even knew about this shit! Y'all got my full support and backing. Do I make myself dead-ass clear?"

All it took was a head nod from his crew. The mission was set and now it was time for the goons to earn their keep. Blood would flow in the streets of Crooklyn and everybody knew it. Goody's wrath would be felt in more ways than one.

CHAPTER 20

Sex, Money, Murder

Razorblade Goody was dead and buried, and Slick and Jewelz were ready to scratch another name off the Goode Brother's kill list.

Tonight the sky was dark as they sat in a dilapidated Chevy with out-of-state license plates on the back. They had driven way outta Brooklyn and followed a tricked-out burgundy Cadillac to a McDonald's located on the Lower East Side of the magnificent town of Manhattan.

"He's going through the drive-thru," Jewelz said, pointing towards Hammerhead Goody's whip as it pulled up at the end of a long line of waiting cars. Hammerhead was the second oldest Goode brother and he was also the softest and the least disciplined of the bunch. He was sloppy-fat in appearance and prone to doing stupid shit.

Jewelz sucked her teeth as she eyed the crazy line snaking around the golden arches. "He's gonna be all damn night in that line," she complained as they watched several cars slide up behind him and box him in. "They must be selling crack on that damn dollar menu."

"That's a good thing," Slick said as he trained a pair of binoculars on the Caddy and scoped shit out.

Suddenly he froze.

"Goddamn," he muttered under his breath. "That stupid *fuck!*"

"What?" Jewelz demanded. They had been following the fat boy all around town and she was tired as hell. She couldn't wait to get this job over and done with so she could go home and hit her pillow and crash out.

"Check this shit out," Slick said, passing her the binoculars. "That wanksta got a lil kid with him."

Jewelz peered through the lenses for a few seconds and then nodded her head when she saw a little arm waving around in the air.

"He sure do! Why he got that little one hanging out so late at night? He ain't even in a car seat! That child's mama oughtta kick his ass for riding her baby around in the front like that. I guess we gotta fall back and call it off. I can't believe we wasted all this time following Hammerhead's fat ass around for nothing!"

Slick cut his eyes and gave her a cold look.

"Fuck outta here. Take this wheel girl." He grabbed his gat from under the front seat then opened his door and started getting out the car.

"Where you going?" Jewelz demanded.

"Yo, as soon as you see that muthafucka pull up to the first window I want you to drive around to the other side of the restaurant. Pick me up right at the front door. You dig?"

"But he's got a lil kid with him!"

"*Fuck that shit!*" Slick barked, his eyes shooting cold fury down at her. "My mama had lil kids with her too! Now drive your ass around to the muthafuckin front and meet me over there!"

Moments later Slick was crouching down low and hauling ass across the street. He ran across the grass toward the line of cars that were waiting in the drive-thru lane, and Jewelz lost sight of him as he slipped between some hedges.

"Shit!" she cursed out loud as she climbed over the center console and plopped her ass down in the driver's seat. She rolled down both front windows, then pulled the seat forward and adjusted her mirrors. Satisfied, Jewelz put the car in drive and eased it outta the parking lot. She kept her eyes steady trained on Hammerhead Goody's ride as he advanced in the fast food line and approached the first window.

Jewelz had nosed the car across the narrow street and was just pulling into the McDonald's lot when she saw the back door of Hammerhead's car open and a figure jump in. Before the door slammed shut Jewelz heard the faint but unmistakable sound of two gunshots.

Pop! Pop!

She hit the gas and cut the wheel as she pulled forward and stopped right outside the fast food doors, just like she was instructed. Moments later Slick pushed through the front door and strolled out looking unfazed and winter cool.

Jewelz's eyes were all over him as he hopped in the passenger seat, and as soon as his door slammed shut she pulled outta the lot and merged into the light traffic.

"Did you clip both of them?" she swallowed hard and asked him, her heart sinking deep down into her stomach. "Don't tell me you popped that lil baby too?"

The look Slick gave her was evil and icy. It was filled with rage and bitter contempt.

"Fuck you think?" he spit and grilled her like the stone-cold killer that he was. "Da *fuck* do you think?"

$$$$$

Judith Goode jumped out of the Uber cab and made her way to the front of the jammed-packed nightclub. It was nippy outside, and she was dressed in all white like she was going to church. The line for the club was packed all the way down the block and around the corner, and Judith knew if she went to the end she would probably never make it inside. But she had no intention on waiting because she was the only woman on line who wasn't there to party. Judith walked straight up to the bouncer who was standing at the entryway taking money and patting down patrons.

"'C'mon now, grandma, you can't just skip the line," the bouncer said as Judith tried to get in. "We don't have no old lady discount specials 'round here so take yo ass to the back of the line just like everybody else."

"I'm here to see my son Michael," Judith said respectfully. "Can you either let me inside or go get him for me, please."

"Listen, lady," the bouncer said, clutching a fistful of dollas and getting agitated. "I don't know no damn *Michael* and I'ma need you to step off from 'round the doorway so I can do my damn job."

Judith was holding up the line, and all the young, half-dressed chicks waiting to get inside started to talk shit and suck their teeth in frustration.

"Look, young man! My last name is on the front of this godforsaken club!" Ms. Goode said as she glared at the bouncer with anger and impatience. "Now I suggest you let me in right now to see my boy, Michael! You and I both know he won't take kindly to you making his mother stand out here freezing while you talk this nonsense to me."

The bouncer looked wide-eyed at the woman as he considered what she was insinuating. If this was really Ms. Goode, Handgun's mother, he damn sure didn't wanna take the chance of disrespecting her. He had already played her out in front of a crowd, and that alone could mean a death sentence.

"I'm sorry, ma'am," the bouncer said. He motioned for his partner to take over collecting cash for him at the door. "Right this way please. I'll take you right to him."

Judith Goode was led upstairs through the loud ass smoked-filled club and through a set of doors that led to the VIP section, and then onward to an area where Handgun had his office in the back. The bouncer gave a special knock on the door and was greeted by another huge security guard.

"I need you to wait right here for just one second please, miss," the bouncer told her. "I promise I'll be right back with you."

The bouncer went through another set of doors and saw Handgun sitting at his big cherrywood desk counting stacks of crisp money.

"Goode brother," the bouncer said. "There's an old woman out here demanding to see you. She said she was looking for Michael. I don't know who the hell she really is, boss. You want me to pat her down?"

Handgun looked up from the table wide-eyed and angry. There was only one person on this earth who called him by his government name, and he knew it had to be his moms. Handgun also knew that his mother was crazy enough to show up at his place of business at this time of night too. He came from behind the desk in silence and walked up on the bouncer real strong. Without hesitation he hit his employee with a powerful uppercut that busted his lip and dropped him right on his ass.

"Don't you even *talk* about putting your dirty-ass hands on my mother!" Handgun stood over him glaring in a sudden rage. "Now get the fuck up and go let her in here."

A few moments later Judith was escorted into her son's office by the bloody-mouthed bouncer who had given her a hard time.

"Momma what are you doing here?" Goody asked in concern. "You feeling alright? Sit down and let me get you some hot tea or something. What's the matter?"

"You tell me what the hell the matter is!" Judith said turning down his offer to have a seat and standing right next to him instead. "Why do I have to hear on the news that another one of my sons has been killed? Malik is dead, and they're calling it some sort of gang war. Is this what you got your brothers out here doing? Fighting in the devil's war?"

"W-w-what?" Goody damn near dropped to the floor. "What you talking about, Momma? Malik ain't dead!"

"Oh yes he is!" Judith Goode snapped. "I just saw the report on TV. He was at a McDonald's somewhere down on the Lower East Side of Manhattan. He had Boo-Boo in the car with him and the police said somebody ambushed him. Your brother is dead, Michael! My *son* is dead!

Hammerhead!

Handgun was shaking like a leaf as he dropped his eyes to the floor. Hammerhead, the brother who was just ten months younger than him, the cat that he had shared a baby crib and a milk bottle with, was gone. He couldn't even look in his mother's face. The pain and sorrow in her eyes were enough to stop his heart. For a moment Goody considered getting outta the game while he still had three brothers left. Not for his own sake, but for the sake of their mother. No matter what he did out there in the streets, he never wanted his mother to suffer the bitter repercussions of his decisions.

"I'm sorry, Momma," Handgun whispered, hanging his head. "I don't know what happened to Malik, but I swear I'ma find out. I didn't have him fighting no war over there in Manhattan, though. I swear I didn't."

Judith reached over and slapped the shit out of her oldest son.

"Don't you sit here in my face and play me for no fool Michael! Malik is dead because I failed to keep him away from you, and you failed him by introducing him to this life!" She shook her head in disgust. "I don't know how I gave birth to such a monster. You have a lot to atone for, and I hope the Lord has mercy on your devil-filled soul, boy! If I have to come looking for you again because one of my children, I will throw gasoline all over this building and strike a match! I swear I will, and then I'll ask the Lord to have mercy on *my* soul!"

Handgun took the slap and the harsh words into his heart as his emotions boiled inside him like hot lava. Hammerhead was dead, and the guilt and shame that his mother had just dropped on his shoulders only fueled his thirst for blood. As Goody walked his mother out of the office he barked a set of orders to the bouncer who was waiting outside the door.

"Get the keys to the limo and take my mother home. Make sure you ride her upstairs to her apartment and wait until she gets inside."

Handgun Goody turned to his mother and said, "I'm sorry, Ma. I'm sorry."

But Judith Goode paid him no mind. With her head in the air, she followed the bouncer out without so much as a backwards glance at her son.

Goody took her rejection in stride. He understood how she was feeling. Because murder was hanging like a thick fog inside his mind, and he was ready to lash out and kill in his brother's name. *Yeah,* Goody thought as he watched his mother walk away in her starched white skirt with her spine straight and tall. Heads were gonna fuckin roll all over the Empire State. And if he rolled enough heads he would eventually get to the one who was responsible for spilling his family's blood.

CHAPTER 21

Set For Life

Life for Honore was anything but grand these days. She had totally failed in her efforts to dig up some information about the stolen five-million dollar diamond, and with a thirty-day time bomb ticking over her head, her nerves were a hot mess.

It was a work day, and she had been sitting at her desk and staring at the same piece of paper for over an hour. She was feeling nervous as fuck, and she was totally unable to get her brain working and come up with another solid plan of action.

She sighed and smoothed her hair back from her face. As the other employees of the New York Diamond and Jewelry Exchange went about their day without a care in the world, Honore's forehead was banging like a drum and her mind was moving on a million. She was scheduled to go around the city selling minimally-priced diamonds to other stores today, but with a half-million dollar bounty on her ass, the last thing she wanted to be dealing with right now was some low-budget ice that could only bring in shitty ends.

She was tidying up her desk and gathering all her documents in a stack when she noticed a copy of the latest employee bulletin that had just come in from human resources.

Immediately the brilliant picture on the front cover caught her attention and she sat up straight in her chair as she read the headline:

Brand New Sotheby's Location Auctioning 'Pink Lady' Diamond After Original Buyer Defaults.

Honore's greedy eyes feasted on a full color photo of the most breathtaking diamond she had ever seen. It was a dazzling coral-pink in color, and the caption said the thirty-carat gem had originally sold for forty-seven million dollars in Brazil. But somehow after out-bidding three other investors, the buyer was unable to come up with enough cash to complete the transaction.

"What the *fuck...*" Honore whispered under her breath as she continued reading. That little five million-dollar diamond that Joel Samuelson had jacked was nothing compared to this one. Fuck thirty days, this was the type of mega-money that those big willies in La Kosher Nostra would have killed a mothafucka for on sight.

Honore read and re-read the article several times.

"How the hell do you default on an *auction*?" she wanted to know. That was like ordering up a gourmet meal at a fancy steakhouse knowing damn well you only had enough doe in your pockets to buy a White Castle hamburger!

She smirked. It was all good for Sotheby's, though. They still had their diamond, and they were gonna make a shitload of money when they brought it to their new location on Staten Island and sold that baby all over again. But this time she bet they would make damn sure they had the cold hard cash in their hands before that auctioneer banged his fuckin gavel and hollered *sold!*

Honore pursed her lips tightly as a crazy thought tried to sneak into her head. Setting the bulletin aside, she picked up her cell phone and did a Google search on a few key words.

Her eyes rotated in their sockets like marbles as she read article after article on a subject she knew well. By the time she was done her headache was completely gone and her lips were turned up real sly-style.

Suddenly the idea was shining so bright in her head that it damn near blinded her. She didn't know why she hadn't thought of this shit before! Yeah, it was risky, but when you had a bunch of matzo-ball mafia muthafuckas gunning for your head, what the hell did you have to lose?

Honore had to stop herself from giggling as she looked around the office as the unsuspecting employees of the New York Diamond and Jewelry Exchange went on about their business.

She was smirking like a mutha as she dialed her old friend Avi's phone number. She was so excited it felt like she was on that stupid game show *Jeopardy* as a burning question formed on her lips.

Category: Diamonds for forty-seven million, Alex.

Question: *If you lost a five million dollar diamond what was the best way to get yourself another one?*

The answer was simple as shit.

You steal it, goddammit! *You steal that fuckin shit!*

$$$$$

A couple of days later Honore sat posted up in the Food Court at Queens Center Mall. It was that time of month and she was on some emotional shit as she read an article from the Daily News website on her iPad.

Five young boys had just been murdered in a gangland killing in her old neighborhood. The young'uns had been snatched off the street and tortured to death. Honore recognized three of the names, especially a kid named Malice who used to work for Sly, and she knew the rest of them as little wannabe hustlas from around the way too.

She was surprised by her sudden rush of sympathy because she was born and raised to be hard-hearted. Niggas got rocked to sleep everyday where she was from. But something about the slaughter of these young'uns had her in her feelings.

Their early demise made Honore think about all the rotten shit that she had seen in her short life. It reminded her of all the shady, cut-throat niggas and bitches that she had involved herself with over the years.

Life was a mothafucka. Everybody was out there on their own trying to win. Trying to step on the back of the next hustla and get an edge on his or her fellow crab in the barrel.

It was a vicious cycle of savagery that Honore and her get-money peers had damn sure contributed to. She swallowed hard as she thought about the kinda violence that her own mother had lived with. One of the few memories Honore had about her mother was of sitting on the bed and running her tiny hands all over the scars on her mother's back. Back when she was little she didn't know what those scars meant. But as a grown woman she realized that the scars her mother bore were a testament to the years of violence and abuse she took from the man she loved. Why in the hell did she stay around and let some nigga put her through all that? Honore wondered. What in the world coulda been going through her mind when she went flying through the glass window of that Chinese restaurant all those years ago?

Honore was thinking on that shit real hard when she was interrupted.

"Good afternoon," Avi said. He had walked up outta nowhere looking sophisticated and suave as usual. His clothes were top-shelf and his Versace shades went perfectly with his jacket.

"What's wrong?" the foreign-born man asked as he eyed Honore's distressed face. Pull yourself together. You look like you just lost your best friend."

"I'm fine," Honore said quickly as she snapped out of her funk. "Thanks for coming. This was too big to talk about over the phone."

"No problem," Avi responded. "Tell me what's on your mind."

"Money," Honore said as her face brightened right up. "Mega money is on my mind. Listen, boo. This shit I'm scheming on right now is gonna change the whole game! I'm talking *retirement* money. I'm talking *new identity* money. I'm talking *never coming back to this hellhole they call America,* money! You feel me?"

"I'm listening," Avi said calmly. In his line of work you had to have nerves of steel and right now his were on full display. "Give me the details."

"I'll give you three fucking words," Honore said in almost a whisper. "The. Pink. Lady. Look her up. She's one of the baddest hoes on the planet. I'm talking Beyoncé, Janet, and Rhianna bad! I think we can get next to that bitch. We can get right up under the covers with her. I know when she's coming to town, who she's fucking with, and how she rolls. Me and my crew can snatch her up and deposit her right in your hands. The rest is up to you."

"Hmmm," Avi said like he was unimpressed. "Do you know what kind of backing and support it would take to get next to a superstar on the level of Ms. Carter and Ms. Jackson and Ms. Fenty? Why do you think no one has ever gotten close to her before?"

"Put it this way," Honore said as she took off her shades and looked dead in Avi's eyes. "If I can get that hoe to hop in the bed with you and make her take off her panties, then you can finger-fuck her until she cums. I know your type, Av. You like your bitches big and pretty. Well this pink skank is move-outta-America fine, and travel-to-the-ends-of-the-earth thick."

"Okay," Avi finally grinned. "I'll have to get with a few of my associates and check things out. A superstar of this nature will require a lot of financial backing from people overseas who have a lot of clout. They'll want their share of the pie too, of course, but that's the cost of doing business. It'll take me some time to network and make my connections though."

"Bet. Just Google that lady and see what you find out," Honore said firmly. "They should be announcing everything about her arrival on the news. Make sure you're watching. When you see for yourself what this bitch is working with, then get with your people and see what they think. I'll wait a few days for you to get back to me. Just don't take too long because if we jump on this the right way it's game over baby. Game over and I'm gone."

Honore expected the underground jewelry trader to ask a lot more questions, but to her surprise Avi stood up and smiled, and then without another word he turned toward the door and headed out of the mall.

She started to call after him, but instead Honore sat in her chair feeling like the planet was just about to start rotating in the right direction for her. This shit just had to work out. It had too. Because her time was just about up. That sweet money payment would be coming due with those Jewish investors way before she had a chance to get her hands on the Pink Lady diamond. She was about to be in default and that meant she was gonna have to watch her ass and stay outta sight.

Honore thought about all those millions she could get if this thing went the right way and she forced herself to brighten up. All she had to do was stay alive long enough to pull this shit off. Once Avi did his homework she had no doubts that him and his investor friends would find that the Pink Lady hoe was everything she'd said she would be, and they'd jump all over that bitch.

Even though she'd have to hand Avi and his investors a substantial cut of the cash, a diamond of that status and beauty would bring in enough for everybody to retire from the game if they wanted to. Honore's mind was in fiend-mode as she tried to calm her growing excitement.

Could this job be the big one? Could this be the jewelry heist of her lifetime? Honore didn't know for sure, but she was damn sure game to steal that diamond and find out!

CHAPTER 22

No New Friends

Avi had just picked up his six-year-old sons from the private elementary school they attended. They were both in the backseat asking him a million questions at the same time. His twin boys, Andre and Antoine, were his pride and joy. Avi's wife had died a few years back from breast cancer and he was still adjusting to being a single father. It was a role that he'd wholeheartedly stepped into and therefore he tried to give his kids everything that they asked for. The three of them had taken his wife's death very hard, but his boys had kept the love in Avi's heart. They were his world.

As a jewelry expert, Avi was a middleman and consultant for several legal and illegal diamond buyers and distributors, both here and abroad. He got paid handsomely for doing his type of business, and he could afford to give his little boys the type of childhood he'd never had.

"So, are you little monsters hungry?" Avi asked as he looked through his rearview mirror and gazed at his sons sitting in the backseat.

"Noooo, Daddy," the boys called out in unison.

"Do you boys want to go to the library today?" Avi asked.

"Noooo, Daddy," the boys called out again. The slightly taller Antoine spoke for them both. "We want to go to the park."

"Is that right?" Avi asked. His sons were two little bundles of energy. They weren't heavily into video game systems, although they had plenty of them. No, Avi's boys preferred to read books and play outside, which was a blessing in the technological age that they lived in. "Would you like to go to the park too, Andre?"

"Yes, daddy," Andre responded with a smile. "I love going to the park. We have so much fun there."

"Well, okay. If that's what you boys want to do then let's do it," Avi said as he rolled the windows up in his Benz and turned on the air conditioner and made his way toward the Imagination Kingdom Park.

Minutes later Avi pulled up at the park and let his boys out of the car. He kept a football in the trunk that he usually tossed around with them, but today they preferred to check out the attractions on the playground.

"Look at me, Daddy! Look at me!" Antoine yelled as he slid down the sliding board on his stomach with his brother Andre right behind him.

"Good job, boys," Avi yelled as he sat on the benches where a few other parents were relaxing and watching their children play.

As thc kids found playmatcs and took off running and scrcaming their heads off in a lively game of tag, Avi pulled out a copy of the Wall Street Journal and began to read. Moments later, a well-dressed man with a friendly smile came over and sat down beside him.

"Hello, how are you? Nice day out today," Avi said in his foreign, courteous way.

"Yes," the man said evenly, keeping his cold blue eyes trained forward. "Yes, it's a very nice day today, Avi. It's a very nice day to die."

Avi gripped his newspaper in his fist and sat up straight. His inner alarm bells were ringing off the chart. "Excuse me sir? What did you say? How do you know my name?"

"That's not important," the man said quietly as he watched Avi's sons play. His eyes followed the little boys like an eagle on a rodent. Like he was a predator itching to pounce.

"How's your housekeeper?" the man asked with a smile.

Avi's whole body shook. "W-w-what?" he stammered. His housekeeper had recently been tortured and brutally murdered. He had sent a huge bouquet of flowers to her funeral service. "What do you mean?"

"You're a smart guy, Avi," the man continued, "so I'm going to cut right to the chase. I have in my possession a very special diamond. Your friend Hymie Lovitz told me that you were the person I needed to see in order to turn my glistening stone into cold hard cash."

"I-I-I don't know what you mean," Avi stammered.

The man nodded. "That's the same bullshit line that old Hymie gave me. Until I promised to murder his daughter, that is."

Suddenly complete fear seized Avi. It gripped him right by his heart and all the color drained from his face. He knew what time it was and he couldn't believe it was actually happening. He'd always known the old Jew Hymie was a coward, and now he'd put Avi and his family in danger.

The strange man reached over and took the newspaper from Avi's trembling hands and pretended to read it while he slipped the diamond from his overcoat and showed it to Avi discreetly.

"I need to get rid of this and it has to be fast," the man said. "And I want a good price for it too."

"I-I-I swear I don't know what you're talking about, my friend," Avi tried again to play stupid, hoping and praying he wouldn't pay for his act with his life.

The man sighed as he slipped the diamond back inside his coat pocket. "Why must you dumb mothafuckers always do things the hard way?" he bitched quietly as he slid a pistol with a red beam and a silencer from his waist. He kept it concealed behind the newspaper.

"Now Avi," he said coldly but calmly. "Which one of your handsome little boys should I bury first? Or must I kill both of them to prove that I'm not fucking around? And after I blow their brains out, should I go to your parent's fancy townhouse in Manhattan and scatter your mother's thoughts all over her fucking breakfast table? Tell me, have you found a replacement for your cute redheaded housekeeper yet?"

"Daddy!" Little Andre suddenly yelled out. "Can you come push us on the swings, Daddy?"

Avi stiffened. "I'll be there in a minute, son!" he cried out weakly. "Just stay over there and play with your brother!"

"Avi," the man said, aiming steadily as he lifted the newspaper slightly and placed the red beam on the back of little Andre's head. "Fuck with me and I will slaughter every kid in this park and make you watch. Believe me, I'm seven steps ahead of whatever dumb-ass idea is running through your brain right now. You wanna see how fast I can take out little Andre and then tag little Antoine before anybody even notices his brother's body has dropped?"

"Okay, okay!" Avi whispered. "Just relax! Okay, I-I-I can sell the diamond for you!" Avi promised, panicking and sweating profusely. "But not right now. No matter what you threaten me with it's just too hot of an item right now. The authorities have their radars all over that thing. You're just going to have to sit on it and wait until the heat dies down. Trust me, if I try to smuggle it out of the country any time soon I'll go to jail for a million years and you will never see a penny of the money."

The mysterious man sat in silence for a few moments while he contemplated what Avi had just told him.

"Why do I get the feeling you're trying to play me, Avi?" he asked quietly. Little Andre turned around laughing and the red dot appeared in the center of his pale forehead. "Must I fuck around and show you just how real shit can get?"

"Noooo!" Avi yelled out, attracting the attention and curious stares of the other parents. "I mean, no sir!" he lowered his voice to a whisper. I swear to God I'm not lying! I can't sell that diamond for you right now, but...I can get you involved with another diamond that's worth much more than that one. If you promise to stay away from my sons I could cut you in on something I have brewing that could leave both of us well-off for the rest of our lives...

"Something like what?" the stranger demanded, his gun-grip steady.

With his eyes bucked open wide, Avi swallowed hard and asked in a whisper, "Have you ever heard of the Pink Lady?"

CHAPTER 23

Putting the Pieces Together

Jewelz was tired as hell but she was also very excited as she stood in the mirror applying glue to her new wig so she could fasten it to her bald scalp.

She'd gotten a real strange call earlier in the day from Handgun Goody saying that he wanted to see her. It had rained cats and dogs all day and she had been knocked out cold and slobbering on her pillow when her phone rang.

Goody sounded tired. He told her he'd just gotten home from a meeting, and instead of attending a school play for his blind second-grader cousin like he was supposed to do that night, he wanted to take her out to dinner instead.

"You mean you'd rather take me out for some shrimp and lobster than sit in an elementary school and watch your lil cousin pretend to be a stalk of celery?" Jewelz had joked as she stretched her body and rolled over in her designer sheets. "Now that's real sweet, but I'm not sure I'm worth you missing out on something like that."

"Trust me, it's all good," Handgun Goody had told her. "Jasmine is my cuzzo Winky's little girl, and she's my goddaughter too. Winky is a longtime Goode Brother himself, so he knows how I make shit happen. I'll send Jazzy a nice big gift and catch them at the next event cause tonight a nigga just wanna be with you."

Jewelz's mind raced as she came up with a quick plan. She hung up the phone knowing she only had a couple of hours to get her shit off and make it to the restaurant on time without him suspecting anything.

The first thing she did was look up all the elementary schools in the district, and then she started calling around to see which one was holding a school play that evening.

"Oh, it starts at five o'clock?" she asked, hitting the jackpot on her fourth call. "And it's free to the public? Thanks for the info. Bye!"

Jewel went to her medicine closet and took a good look around. She had researched a lot of toxins and poisons and had perfected delivering them shits in the most covert ways possible. She usually tried to drop something deadly in a target's food or drink, but when that wasn't possible she resorted to other measures. Like she planned on doing with Handgun Goody's cousin Winky tonight.

At five-thirty p.m. Jewel was sitting in her parked car near the entrance of P.S. 133 and scoping shit out with a small pair of binoculars.

Her eyes scanned over every parent and every child who approached the doors to enter the school, hoping to pick out her target. She knew there was a possibility of zeroing in on the wrong kid but shit, how many blind second-grade actors could one damn school have?

Her phone buzzed and Jewelz let it go to voicemail. A few seconds later she listened to the message. She frowned as she heard her doctor's voice. *Diamond, this is Dr. Ford. I just wanted to remind you that your condition is very grave, and if you continue to refuse your chemotherapy your life will be in danger.*

Jewelz disconnected the message and deleted that shit, then went back to scanning for her target.

Before long, she spotted them. A man and his young daughter. Winky's name rang bells around the club scene, and Jewelz knew he ran a territory and pushed packs for the Goode Brothers Gang.

Even without the binoculars she could tell he had some Goode Brothers blood in him. He was tall and built real broad in the shoulders, and he had the same rugged mug, smooth chocolate skin, and wavy hair as his cousins.

"That's them," Jewelz muttered under her breath as the man gripped the shoulder of a little girl who carried a telltale guide-stick for the blind in her hand. It was long and silver-gray and it had strips of reflective red tape wrapped around the bottom.

Jewelz trained her binoculars on dude's handsome face. She noted his every feature, and when she felt like she had gotten a perfect look and memorized his mug, she lowered her binoculars and watched as the pair walked slowly toward the entrance of the school. "Yeah, I'm sure as shit that's *them,*" she said again. And then she smiled.

$$$$$

On the other side of the bridge, Honore sat in the back of the rented black stretch Navigator sipping Belaire Rose and waiting for her partner-in-crime to arrive. The limo was parked near Battery Park on the tip of Manhattan, and a torrent of rain was coming down heavily. She had instructed her hired driver to go wait across the street in a small bodega while she conducted a very important meeting.

Honore had wanted to stay home and be nice and cozy this evening, but when Avi called and said it was urgent she knew better than to drag her feet. Avi was gonna be a major key to her success, and she had to jump to it when he called.

As she whipped out her makeup kit from her beige and black Celine bag she couldn't help but think about how far she had come in the game. She was young and beautiful, getting money, and basically doing whatever the fuck she wanted to do.

But because of that missing diamond and those killer Jews, the fear of an early death stayed on her mind. With an entire organization of cut-throat criminals gunning for her ass, would it have just been better to stay poor and broke? She took a look in the little mirror and quickly dismissed that bullshit.

I do the shit these average bitches only dream about doing. I live the life that most of these hoez would kill for. I'm a bad bitch in every sense of the word. I'm a boss in a world full of peasants who don't have the guts to go out and take what the hell they want outta life. Fuck that. I'm doing exactly what I was born to do. I'm a Queen!

Honore's little mental pep talk was interrupted when a dark car pulled up along side her Navi. She unlocked the doors and Avi got in quickly.

"Thanks for meeting me on such short notice," Avi said as he wiped the rainwater off his face. "Although I think we could have picked someplace a little drier and a lot more pleasant."

Honore looked out the window. Even through the midst the Statue of Liberty rose up outta the waters of the upper bay like a woman on a mission. "The Lady" as she was called, stood watch over her Empire like the queen bitch of the city, which is exactly how Honore had been feeling ever since she'd decided to yank that precious pink diamond.

"Manhattan is all the way live," she said as she took another sip of her Rose. "It's the money-making capitol of the world, so it's only right that we should meet up right here. Now what was so important that you got me out here in this nasty-ass weather?"

"Well, there are a few changes in our plans that I think you need to be updated on," Avi said as he declined a glass of wine she offered from the minibar.

"Oh yeah? What kind of changes?"

"For one thing, I had to bring in a new partner. He's someone I just met and he'll need to be included in on our plans and get a cut of the pot too."

"*What?*" Honore stared at Avi like he was off his fucking meds. "What the hell do you mean you have a new partner?" she barked with much New York attitude.

"Hell no." Honore shook her head. "Nopety-fuckin *no*. We not bringing in nobody else! I shouldn't have to explain the fucking magnitude of this operation to you, Avi! The less mothafuckas involved is the less mothafuckin chance we got of getting ratted on. What the hell was you thinking, stupid? Haven't you ever heard the phrase, 'no new friends'?"

"Stupid? Do you really think *I'm* the one in this car who's fucking stupid?" Avi glared at Honore with a dangerous look in his eyes. "This was an agreement that was not up for my debate! I was given an ultimatum, and since I love my children and I also love breathing, I didn't have a choice in the matter. The Pink Lady is a forty-seven million dollar rock. There's no need to be so damn greedy with the profit split anyway."

"Yo, hold up," Honore barked back as she quickly put two and two together. "You mean to tell me you let some stray nigga muscle you down to get a piece of *our* goddamn deal? And now we gotta split the money with him and the investors too? Are you fuckin crazy???"

"I'm far from crazy," Avi said calmly. "I'm sane and I'm smart. Sometimes you have to take a step backward in order to take two steps forward. That's something you might hope to learn one day."

Honore smirked and waved her hand. She wasn't stupid enough to say it out loud, but she had just made up her mind. Avi wasn't getting shit. Not one fuckin penny. He had helped her scheme on whacking Joel Samuelson, and now she was about to scheme on his ass too! And it was all his own fault because he was stupid and he was weak. He didn't deserve shit! She was gonna find somebody else to do the black-market trading overseas, and then she'd cut Avi's bitch-ass right outta the picture the same way her and Sly had done Joel!

"Okay, whatever," she said with a shrug. "Fuck you and your new friend. His cut is coming out of *your* pocket, I want you to know that. And he better not turn out to be no fucking federal agent or some shit, Avi! I don't wanna meet this guy or even know his name. I'm keeping my shit on the low. The less people who know me, the better off I am. This is *your* problem and you gotta deal with it. I'm still trying to figure out the best way to go about getting up in the Sotheby and pulling this whole shit off."

Avi sparked up a Cuban cigar and closed his eyes as he thought about his twin sons and the white devil who had threatened to kill them. He had always been good at making decisions under pressure, but this type of up-close danger that threatened all he held dear had made his decision to cooperate that much easier. As a matter of fact, it had been a no-brainer.

"I think you're looking at this thing the wrong way, Honore," Avi said after he exhaled some smoke. "Every eye in the world is going to be on the Sotheby. Security is going to be tighter than a prick in a virgin butt-hole. We need to get our hands on the Pink Lady before it even arrives at the museum. *That's* what you should be focusing on. Forget hitting the auction at the Sotheby. Let those bastards sell the diamond. Me and you will just wait outside and rob whoever buys it."

CHAPTER 24

Blood in the Wine

It was a beautiful night, and Jewelz was looking truly lovely in her shimmery gold Chanel dress as Handgun Goody's security chief escorted her out of the limo. Ruth's Chris restaurant, located in Money Making Manhattan, was packed with patrons and the air was filled with the aroma of hot delicious steak.

Goody had reserved a private window booth for them and he sat there waiting patiently for her arrival. He had been trying to get Jewelz out on a formal date for a minute now, but she knew his typical birds went bananas over lobster and steak so she had steadily declined him.

A cock-sure man like Goody had to be handled a certain way, and Jewelz had that shit perfected to a tee. Unlike the bitches he was used to nipping and biting all on his jock, Jewelz constantly let it be known that she didn't need his money, his food, or his dope, so the chase was always gonna be in a one-directional lane: him chasing her.

Although the restaurant was very nice Jewelz wasn't interested in a meal. She was exhilarated about the kill she'd made earlier in the evening, and what she wanted right now was to get closer to Goody so she could discover even more of his weaknesses.

"My...my...don't you look handsome this evening Mr. Goode Brother," Jewelz beamed, complimenting him on his smoke-grey Tom Ford designer suit.

"Thank you, Mizz Jewelz. You know I gotta keep myself on point when I'm in the presence of greatness," Goody fired back while flashing his perfect white teeth that accentuated his smooth dark skin. He had just left the hospital after visiting his nephew Trill again, and although his mind was still churning with bitter thoughts of the streets, his outward demeanor was suave and charming.

"I was watching you as you walked in," Goody admitted. "Those Derrick Lambs look perfect on your feet by the way."

Jewelz gave him a slight smile with a smirk hidden underneath. It wasn't every day that a notorious monster like him poured on the charm. She had to admit that he was rather sharp with his shit though.

"Thank you! I can tell you're highly knowledgeable when it comes to fashion. You seem to know your designers very well," Jewelz remarked with genuine surprise.

Goody nodded. "I try to keep up on what's trendy. I'm a man who makes a living by paying attention to details and I can appreciate a good shoe when I see one," he said as he picked up the menu.

For the millionth time Jewelz had to remind herself of what a monster Goody really was. He had a good sense of humor and an aura of power that would have the average chick ready to strip outta her panties and throw them babies dead at him. He was also a smooth operator who seemed to love playing the cat and mouse game that Jewelz challenged him with so readily. If she hadn't actually been a victim to his cruelty she would've found it hard to believe that he possessed so much evil way down in his soul.

The waiter came over and offered them drinks as they looked over the menu.

"Good evening, my name is Felix and I will be your waiter for tonight. What would you like for a beverage, sir?" he asked Goody with a respectful smile and a positive attitude.

"Give me whatever the stunning woman sitting across from me is having Felix," Goody said as he turned the attention to Jewelz.

Jewelz grinned, ready to play her role. "Good evening, Felix. We'll start off with a bottle of your finest Chablis and two glasses of carbonated water with fresh lemon wedges please," she said politely.

"No problem, madam. I'll get that right out to you and we can discuss the main course whenever you are ready," Felix said and then turned and left the table.

"Their finest wine?" Goody said with a look of mock shock on his face. "A'ight now. Don't let me find out you tryna get me drunk and take me back to your crib and do nasty shit to me. I'm onto your little scheme Mizz Jewelz, and I'm not the type to give my shit up that easy."

Jewelz couldn't help but laugh at his clowning. He was sharp with the mouth and Jewelz liked that in a man because she was definitely the same way.

"Boy please!" she countered shooting him a seductive look. "You *wish* knockin your boots was on my agenda. If I wanted to do some nasty stuff to you I doubt if I'd have to get you drunk first to do it."

They laughed together again and then Jewelz turned her head to gaze out the window that overlooked the city. They sat in silence for a moment listening to the light chatter that filled the air in the restaurant.

While Jewelz knew he would strip her naked and dig her out if she gave him permission, Goody couldn't tell what kind of progress he was making with Jewelz. She had sucked his dick one good delicious time, and now he was like a crackhead, feening for another hit.

But Jewelz was very good at stringing him along and masking her emotions, and she was a very strong-willed woman too. He loved the class she personified, but after seeing her in the club and listening to her lyrics, he also believed she could cock a nigga cold just as quick as any man he knew.

"Yo, Mizz Jewelz," Goody said as he leaned back in his seat and grinned at the mysterious and sexy creature in front of him. "I'm glad you decided to come rock with me tonight. You're human so I know you gotta eat, but you're a very hard lady to convince to have dinner. Are you scared to let me see how you get down with your grub or something?"

Jewelz busted out laughing and shook her head as she pulled her sweater over her shoulders to ward off the chill in the air-conditioned restaurant.

"Scared of you?" She laughed again, twisting his words. "You're just full of jokes tonight, huh Mr. Goode Brother. But I can dig it. You have quite a fearsome reputation on the streets so I can see how you might scare off a lot of ordinary chicks. But I'm cut from a different cloth," Jewelz said as the waiter finally came with a bottle of vintage wine. "I fear no man."

"Yeah, I know...I know..." Goody joked her. "I forgot you're big bad Jewelz the gangstress on the mic. I'm just messing with you, baby. I know you gotta keep your defenses up. It's a cold world out there and you gotta be just as cold when you playing on them corners," Goody said as he took a sip of his wine and tried to keep the mood light.

Jewelz and Goody both ordered broiled steak and shrimp and a grilled lobster tail, and the waiter filled and refilled their wine glasses as they waited for their meals to arrive.

"Check it out," Goody leaned close to her and said. "It's no secret that I'm very interested in you. You intrigue me. There ain't many chicks like you where I roam. You can't be bought or wined and dined. I know I need to step to you correct if I wanna get in deep with you, so that's what I'm trying to do. A woman with your mix of intelligence, instincts, and discipline is truly a rare thing to find these days, and I like it," Goody admitted as he spoke from the heart keeping it all the way one hundred with her.

Jewelz crossed her legs daintily and put her hands in her lap as she gave him a look of real interest for the first time since walking through the door.

"You're right, Mr. Goody. I'm very disciplined and I'm far from the typical bitch out here who's just trying to trap any baller who's holding a couple of racks. You intrigue me too, and I *do* find you attractive. Maybe if we keep it real with each other we can get to know each other a little deeper," Jewelz said as she looked into Goody's murderous eyes and saw them light up.

"But as you can see, nothing comes easy with me. You're gonna have to show and prove your genuineness to me because I'm worth it. I have zero tolerance for stupid shit. I'm too smart for that. And as you can probably tell, I ain't chasing no niggas because I'm fine by myself. So how do you suggest we go about this?" Jewelz asked sweetly.

Just as Goody started to answer the waiter came back with steaming platters of shrimp and steak, and huge lobster tails that instantly had their taste buds on high alert. Goody thanked the waiter as they said a prayer over the food, and then both of them began to dig in.

After knocking down a few shrimp Goody continued their conversation.

"You asked me how I suggest we go about getting to know each other deeper, and I'm about to tell you. I'm a get-right nigga, baby. I work hard and I play hard too. I seldom hold back and do shit on a small scale the way other niggas do, because in my line of work tomorrow might not come. What I'm saying is, I'd like you to take an all-expenses paid trip to Jamaica with me," he said, fully expecting her to buck and put up some resistance.

"On the real, I recently put a couple of my young G's and two of my beloved brothers in the ground, and I need to take a step back so I can see the big picture from multiple angles. An all-expenses paid trip to the islands on my dime might give us a chance to talk and get to know each other in a more relaxed environment."

Jewelz swallowed hard and went in on some breadsticks and a couple of strips of steak before she answered.

"An island vacation might be nice, Mister Goody. Ain't nothing wrong with getting away from the city grind every once in a while. But we haven't really spent any quality time together here at all. You ain't never invited me to your crib, and I've never even been alone with you without one of your security guards looking up your ass. See how your boy standing right over there has his eyeballs all down my throat right now? I bet you he can tell you how many times I chewed my steak. How about we spend a little more time together right here in this country first before we go jetting off half-way around the world," Jewelz said calmly.

Goody nodded. "A'ight then. But just like you got your lil defenses in place, I got mine too. I'm a gangsta, baby. I put niggas down for long naps in the dirt. I can't afford to get caught slipping so I'm careful about who I let in my circle," he grinned. "Shit, I wanna be alone and up in a lil something with you too, but females are far more dangerous and unpredictable than men are. I gotta stay on my toes with you more than I do with any nigga in this game. If you from the streets like you say you are, then I'm sure you can understand that."

Jewelz signaled the waiter to pour her another glass of wine as she picked over her meal. Suddenly she was tired as fuck. Her head was spinning and her stomach was acting ill.

"I hear you," she said with a small smile. "I might just need a little vacation too. I'll think about what you said and get back to you, okay?"

Goody was nodding when his phone chirped in a weird pattern on his waist. He held one finger up and snatched it up and answered it.

"I'm out wit'a female, muh'fucka!" the charm was all gone and the brute was back in him as he growled in a low, dangerous voice. "Fuck is you calling me for son?"

Jewelz took a sip of carbonated water and watched his face change right before her eyes.

"*What???*" he exploded, his eyes narrowing in rage and disbelief. "Is you fuckin kidding me?"

All the blood seemed to rush to Jewelz's head as she watched him listening intently to the person on the other end of the phone.

"How the *fuck* did that happen?" Goody demanded sharply. "And he's gone just like that? Y'all sure he's *gone*?"

Jewelz woulda been happy as hell if she wasn't feeling so damn shitty. It was obvious that Handgun Goody was getting word about that hurting she'd put on his cousin Winky. The toxic powder she'd wiped on his arm when she "accidentally" bumped into him in the auditorium after the play must have done its job.

Suddenly her head started spinning and dark spots appeared in her vision. Jewelz braced her elbows on the table and fought to remain upright in her chair. Doctor Ford was right. She was sliding downhill real fast. She felt flush in the face and her stomach churned with sweet wine and acid, and she was just about to signal the waiter and ask for some water when Goody slammed his phone down hard on the table.

"Yo, my fuckin cousin Winky is dead!" he spit grimly. "Tell me how the fuck does a young strong-ass muthafucka drop dead of a heart attack just like that outta nowhere? I don't believe this shit! Another Goode Brother gone in just a matter of weeks? I'm out here burying mad good soldiers and my brothers is getting smoked left and right! My lil nephew not too long ago fucked around and got run over by a truck! I just can't believe—"

Jewelz jumped up from the table with her stomach lurching. She grabbed her cloth napkin and pressed it to her mouth and it was all she could do to whirl around and jet toward the bathroom as a forceful gush of liquid rose out of her stomach and filled her mouth.

She hit the bathroom door at a sprint. She heard Goody's voice calling out behind her in panic and concern, but there was no way she could answer as she busted into a stall and expelled the heaving rush of hot liquid that sprayed from her mouth.

When the gushing finally ceased Jewelz nearly passed out at the sight of the mess she'd made. It looked like a crime scene up in that stall. The toilet, the floor, and the starched white napkin she still gripped in her hand were all covered in the same thing.

Blood.

CHAPTER 25

Saved by the Enemy

The sight of her splattered blood had sent Jewelz tumbling down to her knees in the toilet stall. Moaning in fear, she had blacked completely out on the bathroom floor, and when she regained consciousness Handgun Goody was cradling her in his arms and calling out her name.

"Jewelz!" he tapped her face and yelled loudly. "Jewelz! Wake up, baby! C'mon, girl. Please *wake up!*"

The first thing Jewelz saw when she was finally able to focus her gaze were the tears of concern in Goody's eyes. For such a hardcore gangsta who liked shooting, stabbing, and torturing his enemies, he sure was displaying a whole lotta fuckin emotion!

"What the hell happened to you, baby?" he pleaded with her. "Was it something you ate? What's wrong???" But then he shook his head. "Nah, fuck that. Don't even try to talk. We gonna get you to the hospital right now," he said, getting ready to lift her up in his strong arms. "Don't worry, baby. I'ma take you to the emergency room and get you some help."

"No!" Jewelz tried to push him away. "No hospitals!"

Goody turned around and barked at his dun-duns over his beefy shoulder, "Yo what the fuck y'all muthafuckas standing around staring for? Go get me some fuckin paper towels, stupid! Wet 'em up and make sure they're nice and warm!"

Snug in his arms, Jewelz could only lay there in submission as his boys scrambled to get him some wet paper towels and Goody wiped away at the blood that was all over her face and clothes. All the while he was whispering soothing words to her and cleaning her up tenderly, like she was his baby.

Moments later a bunch of concerned waiters and the restaurant manager had crowded into the bathroom too.

"She's sick," Goody told them with his voice tight. "She just threw up a whole lotta fuckin blood. I gotta get her to the emergency room."

Jewelz struggled in his arms again as he picked her up and she protested profusely.

"No!" she arched her back and tried to squirm out of his grasp. "I said no hospitals! I'm fine. Please, put me down! I'm a'ight. I'm *fine!*"

But Goody had her firmly in his grip and he refused to let her go. Jewelz fussed and fought so much that he carried her straight outta the bathroom and through the restaurant just like she was a cranky toddler having a fit. And when they got outside he climbed in the back of his waiting limo with her still bitching and protesting.

"Call me a cab!" Jewelz wailed struggling against him as he held her close. "I don't wanna go to no hospital! Take me home!"

"A'ight, *a'ight!*" he said getting her settled down on the plush seat. "You don't have to go to the hospital, sugar. But you ain't going home, neither. And I mean that shit, Jewelz. You *sick*, baby. Did you see all that damn blood? Something is *wrong* with you! If I take you home I'll just be up worrying about you all damn night long."

"But I wanna go home," Jewelz whimpered weakly. "I'm tired and I just wanna go home."

Goody put his rough palm on her cheek, then leaned over and kissed her on her forehead.

"You going home all right, sweetie," he said gently, and then he nodded at his driver giving him the okay to take off. "You going home with *me*."

$$$$$

Jewelz must have passed out again because the next thing she remembered was coming awake in a cool room that must have been big as shit because the sound in it echoed. A deep male voice was talking in a low tone, and for some reason it scared the shit outta her.

"Yo, Ice Pick. I'm at the crib, slime. I heard about Winkey and that shit is wild as hell, son.... Nah, I can't leave yet cause I got a lil situation with a female right now, but I'll be over that way later...Hell no I ain't smashing it, she's knocked out sleep, nigga and I ain't into the rape game.

But check it out...I need you to handle some light work, man. Tell Chainsaw I want him to drop them packs off in the Pink Houses first thing Monday morning, and then have him slide over to meet Frankie in Seth Low and pick up that stash, a'ight?

And oh yeah, let him know I'm putting a green light on Bajan Andy and his whole fuckin set. The streets is whispering, my nigga. Word is that them cats is the ones behind all this hit-and-run shit goin down. That's right. I'm kinda skeptical that they went after Raze or Hammer, or I woulda burnt that Bajan nigga to a crisp right in his own bed. But I do think they did Rollack and Cajiid, and Dolla and his manz Black too.

Proof? Fuck you mean proof? Nigga I know what my gut is tellin me and I want that

Bajan cat's head and I want it now!

So check it out, have Cannonball—nah fuck that make it Chainsaw. Yeah, tell Chain to round up a few hittas and swing through Andy's gym Tuesday around midnight and wipe that bitch clean. From here on out Andy is food, *and I'm gonna eat every Bajan in the entire fuckin borough until I make my message clear. You copy?*

Jewelz shivered. She was locked in on every word Handgun Goody said, and as she lay there with her eyes closed in the darkness she forced herself to memorize his chilling conversation.

Because that nigga was about to make a power move on her old boss, Andy. Goody thought it was the Bajan gang who had been rocking his click to sleep and fucking up his business! Jewelz knew she had to get a hold of Slick and tell him what was about to go down, but right now she was too weak to swallow the spit in her mouth, let alone to find the strength to get up and figure out where her purse and her cell phone were at.

A huge wave of nausea washed over her and a low moan escaped her lips. Dazed, Jewelz remembered her predicament and reached for her wig. She felt around her hairline and made sure it was still glued firmly in place, and when she spread her arms out and explored around further with her fingers, she realized she was in a big fluffy bed and surrounded by a whole bunch of pillows.

Jewelz was struggling to sit up when she locked gazes with him. Goody was sitting in a big leather recliner near the foot of the bed and his eyes were fixed firmly on hers. He had taken off his shirt and a huge tattoo that said HEARTLESS in big bold letters stood out on his muscular chest.

"Where are we?" Jewelz licked her lips and asked softly.

"*Shhhh...*" he said, pocketing his cell phone as he stood up from his chair. "Don't worry, you're safe, baby. We're at my crib. You're in my bed. You're safe."

Jewelz was hella dizzy and weak, but the irony of how she had finally ended up in the monster's lair after all her failed efforts to get up close on him almost made her smile.

Because Handgun Goody was most definitely a monster. But he was a monster who was all about *her.* If Jewelz hadn't known that he was the same man who had hurt her all those years ago she coulda seen herself falling real hard for him. In just a few weeks Handgun Goody had treated her with more tender loving care and respect than any man had ever shown her in her whole damn life. She was starting to think that she might just need to go on that all-expenses paid vacation to Jamaica with him after all. While she still had a little bit of life left in her.

"How you feeling?" Goody asked in a worried tone as he came over and sat down next to her. He looked mad relieved as he reached out and rubbed the back of his hand tenderly over her forehead.

"You want some juice or some water? Is your stomach good now? Do you want something to eat? Tell me what you want, baby. Just tell me, Jewelz, and you got it."

As sick as she was Jewelz just couldn't believe how worried this hardbody street killer was about her health.

"I'm okay," she said softly. "I don't think I can put anything in my stomach just yet though."

Goody let out a big sigh.

"Look here, Jewelz. I don't know whattup witchu baby doll, but that was a whole lotta fuckin blood that came outta ya mouth, yo! Let me take you to the hospital, a'ight? I promise, no matter what they say is wrong with you I'll get you the best doctors that money can buy. I don't wanna see you suffering and I damn sure don't wanna lose you. I got a lotta people dropping around me like flies these days and I just don't want nothing to happen to you, a'ight?"

Jewelz could only shake her head. She was finally in a room alone with Handgun Goody and she didn't have the strength or the will to kill him.

"No hospitals, Mister Goody. Please. I promise you I'm straight now. I got an appointment with my doctor next week anyhow," she lied. "I probably got one of them bleeding ulcers or something in my stomach. It's probably nothing more than that."

"I hope you right about that, girl," Goody muttered. He touched Jewelz's cheek gently again then pulled a blunt from behind his ear and sparked it up.

Here," he said holding the weed out to her. "See if this kush makes you feel a little better."

Despite herself, Jewelz took a few tokes of haze and then fell back onto the soft pillows and closed her eyes. She heard the sounds of Handgun's zipper going down as he took off his pants. Then she felt him lay his muscular frame down next to her on the bed. She didn't have the desire to resist when Goody pulled her into his arms and rubbed his hands gently all over her back. He massaged her arms, her stomach, her ass and her thighs. His hands were everywhere on her, touching her all the way down to her soul, but there was nothing sexual about it.

Swept up in another wave of pain, Jewelz couldn't remember the last time she had been held so close or touched with such tenderness. Despite the fact that these were the same two hands that had brutally plunged a knife into her womb, she couldn't help but enjoy the feelings of adoration and safety that Handgun Goody was stroking up in her now.

The last thing Jewelz remembered thinking before the potent weed and Goody's strong, soothing hands eased her back into a sweet dark slumber was, *Why, dammit? Why couldn't Slick love her like this?*

CHAPTER 26

Back-Alley Bullets

Wild Man was speeding up the New York Thruway in a Con Edison truck and blasting some Notorious B.I.G. as he rushed his scoob Noodles to an event that was taking place just south of Westchester County.

You're nobody...till somebody...kills you... Biggie rapped through the speakers as both men nodded their heads to the classic Puffy beat.

Noodles was rolling out on a solo mission today and he had asked Wild Man to give him a ride. That lil falling out they'd had over the failed beauty parlor hit was way behind them now, and once Wild Man had apologized for his actions they'd gone back to hanging out together again like true blood brothers do.

They had met up at Slick's crib in the projects early in the day and the three of them had played some poker and put back some brewskis. Around lunchtime Slick said he had to break out to take care of some issues for one of the old ladies in the building, so Noodles had asked Wild Man to do him a solid.

I need a favor, yo, Noodles wrote on his text-to-speech device. *I need you to gimme a ride up to Westchester. I got a lil job to handle so I need you to drop me off and then come back and pick me up later.*

Wild Man had shrugged. "Cool. I got a lil something to handle today my-self, but I can make time for you, my G. As long as you ain't got a problem riding around in the raggedy Con Ed truck I'm pushing."

"Yo," Slick asked, tossing back the last corner of his brew, "Y'all niggas got some bizzness that I don't know about? What kinda job you got happening up in Westchester, Noodles?"

Instead of answering, Noodles had dapped his boss manz out and grinned as him and Wild Man got ready to break out. He knew Slick was curious, but Noodles was from the school of closed lips and he didn't give up nothing until he was good and ready.

Chilling in the Con Ed truck, Wild Man and Noodles shot the shit back and forth as they rolled outta Brooklyn and headed into Manhattan.

"Ayo," Wild Man said, bouncing in his seat as the truck flew over potholes that were as deep as graves. Noodles was his muthafuckin bro, and it felt good to be back chilling with him again.

"Lemme run something by you. I ain't pulled Slick's coat to this shit yet, but you know that fine chick he picked up after that hit at the jewelry store on Fulton Street that night?"

Noodles nodded.

"That bitch is shady," Wild Man said. "Check this out. I had to poke a coupla holes in some young nigga the other night, man. He was outside my window tryna violate. That lil sucka sang like a bird before I off'd him, and while he was singing he spit some wild shit in my ear that sounded suspicious as fuck."

Noodles didn't need to type his response into his text-to-talk device this time. The curious look on his face said it all.

"Ay," Wild Man took his eyes off the road and turned to him for a second so Noodles could see just how serious he was. "I don't think Slick's new honey is no innocent lil college chick like she tried to make us believe. I think she's fraudin, man. I'm about to go check something out so I can get the real scoop on that bitch."

Noodles's fingers moved furiously as he typed on his device. *Yeah, she might be a minor problem but she ain't our MAJOR problem. We might have us a snake sliding up even closer to home than that, my nigga.*

Wild Man shot him a look. "What you saying, man?"

Noodles shrugged and typed. *I ain't saying shit right now. But I'll know something for sure by the time you pick me up.*

"Yo, fuck is going on up in Westchester?" Wild Man asked, repeating Slick's earlier question.

But Noodles's lips were still closed. He was tracking hard and sniffing up on something big, and the only thing he would say right now was, *Hurry up, man. I'm running late.*

Thirty minutes later they pulled up in an alley about a block away from their destination.

Pick me up right here in exactly an hour and a half, Noodles typed on his device.

"Bet dat," Wild Man nodded setting the timer on his Apple watch. "Ninety minutes. I'm on it. I got you, bruh."

Noodles nodded back then grabbed his duffel bag off the floor. He gave Wild Man a pound and then jumped outta the truck and prepared to get shit started.

$$$$$

EMPIRE STATE OF MINE$!

Noodles had been putting his counterintelligence training to good use ever since he got kicked outta the Marine Corps. Recently, he had tapped into a certain phone line and found out about a back-room meeting that was gonna take place at the Jewish Center while a bar mitzvah was going on.

Noodles was like a bloodhound sniffing out this funny-style shit. He'd been watching this one particular cat on the sly for a minute now, and as good as dude was at operating under the radar and covering his tracks, he wasn't better at the game than Noodles was.

But dude was definitely up to something, and lately the slimy snake seemed to show up everywhere he wasn't supposed to be. But Noodles took pride in the fact that he beat that bastard to the spot every single time. By the time son arrived on the scene Noodles had usually already been waiting and watching in the shadows for hours.

All of Noodles's surveillance was about to pay off though. Not being able to talk had made him a damn good listener, and after hearing all the coded chatter going back and forth about a major diamond getting snatched, his suspicions had only deepened.

"We gotta go see Benny," Noodles had dipped in on an intercepted conversation between his target and a cat he'd peeped as an international diamond dealer named Avi.

"Me?" Avi had continued, "I'm just a small-fry peon. Guys like Benny are the real movers and shakers. They have all the money and all the power. Without Benny's help nothing moves and we can't make anything happen. I'll introduce you as my business partner during his son's bar mitzvah."

Just hearing that shit over the wire had told Noodles what kind of amateur his target was dealing with. Benny was one of the biggest Jewish mobsters in New York, and even the Italian gangsters were leery of him. The middle-aged shyster had his hands in all kinds of rackets and extortion schemes, and anybody who opposed him was getting knocked off with ruthless brutality and professional efficiency. If Benny ever found out that his peon was spitting his name and discussing business over the phone, he would lay dude's whole family down.

The cat Noodles was stalking today was somebody he loved from the heart. Somebody he had fought side-by-side with and stood back-to-back with and woulda given his life for, no questions asked. For Noodles, suspecting somebody you had love for of doing the ultimate foul shit went against the laws of nature.

But the minute he had busted his boy lying and disobeying orders and tryna pull a fast one on Slick, a nagging feeling had jumped on Noodles and it just wouldn't let him go. That one transgression had led to another one, and then to another one, until a building block of doubt and distrust found Noodles trailing Whitey's grimy ass all over the city of New York.

See, not too long ago he had followed Whitey to a locker in Manhattan where he was supposed to drop off a briefcase from that jewelry store hit in Brooklyn. To Noodles's surprise, Whitey had fucked around and stashed the red briefcase in a completely different locker than the one he was told to. That right there had convinced Noodles that his man was a snake, and he'd been on that muthafucka's ass like a thong on a stripper from that point on.

Today's job was crucial because Noodles was gonna get the video proof he needed to rally the rest of the posse together and bring a major charge of treason up on that bastard Whitey Reynolds. And the penalty for that type of betrayal was cold death.

Noodles had done some research and found out which restaurant had been hired to cater the food for today's bar mitzvah, and then he dropped a rack of doe to convince the manager in charge of food services to switch places with him.

Fernando, the manager, had called his crew and told them that a man named Michael Wallace would be filling in for him at the event. Noodles had gotten himself an ID badge made in the name of Michael Wallace, and got his waiter gear together and he was set to go.

Fernando had assured Noodles that his serving crew could handle the job and all he had to do was look like he was making everything run smoothly. He'd also informed Noodles that there would be no weapons and no cameras allowed at the bar mitzvah. The Feds had Benny paranoid as fuck and he had a very strict rule about that sort of thing.

"They're gonna pat you down and make sure you ain't hiding nothing under your nuts," Felix had warned him. "So be prepared for that shit, homey."

The bar mitzvah was being held at the Jewish Recreational Center owned by Benny and located in a nice area up past Yonkers and just below Westchester. Noodles headed deep into the shadows of the alley and switched into the proper threads for the event. Five minutes later he was neatly dressed in black pants and a matching black vest, a starched white dress shirt and a black bow tie. His shoes were nice and shiny and he was properly groomed.

When he stepped outta the shadows the cat called Noodles was gone and Michael Wallace, the event supervisor for Wine and Dine catering, was ready for action.

He made his way to the back door of the recreation center where he saw a long line of employees waiting to enter. When Noodles finally got inside the large kitchen the cooks and waiters were hustling and bustling trying to get everything in order.

"Oh hello, Michael," an older white guy said as he read Noodles's nametag. "I'm Tommy, the co-manager. Felix told me you'd be filling in for him today so let me know if you need anything. Nice to meet you, but excuse me while I run next door and check on the auditorium crew. You gotta make sure you look busy around here, you know. The big boss is a fanatic. He doesn't like wasting his time or his money."

$$$$$

Wild Man had a reputation for being a spark-it-up hothead, but in reality he was real crafty with his shit. He had to be. It was an Asian thing, which was about to be demonstrated as his cell phone rang and he glanced down and saw it was his homey Detective Wayne "Flaco" Choo.

Detective Choo was in no way related to him even though their parents had come from the same region in China. But that was a small thing. The Asian community was all about the "hook up" and they lived and breathed that shit every single day.

So when Wild Man had hit his manz up and told him he needed to check out some video from a recent crime scene, he knew it wasn't gonna take no whole lotta convincing to get his dude to cooperate. It was gonna take a whole lotta cash, but not a whole lotta convincing.

"Yo, whattup Flaco," he spoke into the phone. "What's good, what you got for me?"

Flaco was a young cop who was on Wild Man's family payroll. He used to run the streets with Wild Man when they were coming up, but he'd managed to stay out of trouble long enough to become a police officer. Flaco did small favors for most of the Chinese business owners in Brooklyn, to include Wild Man's father. He wasn't a gangsta but he wasn't a church-boy neither. He had grown up despising the cops just like everybody else in the hood did, but Flaco was smart enough to know that being on the right side of the law could have some real sweet future benefits. Even though him and Wild Man ran on opposite sides of the tracks they still considered themselves old friends, and Wild Man always hit him up with a few dollars and paid him nicely for his services.

"Yo, what's good, fam?" Flaco said, sounding like he was in a rush. "Check it, I got that tape you asked for. Getting hold of that shit wasn't easy and I'ma need to dish it off as fast as possible. Where you at?"

"I'm around," Wild Man said. "I'ma swing by there but you gotta give me a little time though. I had to make a lil run up past the Bronx, man."

Flaco scoffed. "Fuck that! You wanna see that goddamn footage, right? Check it, I got about forty-five minutes until I'm due at a briefing with my chief. You gotta come peep it real quick 'cause I don't trust nobody in here to sit on it. I took that shit outta the evidence locker and I gotta make sure I cover my ass and put it right back."

Wild Man glanced down at his watch. He had less than an hour and a half left before he had to scoop Noodles up. At this time of day he could probably push it to Flaco's station in forty minutes or less and hopefully be back up in Westchester in forty minutes too.

"A'ight, yeah I got you, son," Wild Man said, already putting his truck in gear. "I'm on my way, nigga, just don't leave. Yo, what's the damage gonna be on this one?"

"We can square up on my fee later," Flaco said. "Just hurry up so I can get this shit back in the locker and outta my hands."

"Say no more, I'll be there in few, my G," Wild Man promised as he ended the call.

Wild Man pulled into traffic and got ready to haul ass to Brooklyn. He knew he was gonna have to push it hard in the big raggedy truck, but he was confident that he could make it there and back to Westchester in time to pick Noodles up.

He drove away from the Lincoln Park Jewish Center and jetted south down eighty-seven and into the Major Deegan Expressway. He kept south until he hit the FDR Drive, then following the curve of Harlem River, he zipped toward Lower Manhattan and crossed the Brooklyn Bridge and headed toward the precinct.

Less than forty-five minutes later Wild Man was pulling into an expensive pay-for-parking garage near the police station where Flaco worked. He pulled a ticket and drove to a secluded spot way in the back. It was their designated meeting spot, and as soon as he parked the truck Wild Man texted Flaco and waited for him to arrive.

Five minutes later Flaco arrived and tapped on the window, then climbed into the passenger seat of the truck.

"Wuddup, Flaco," Wild Man grinned as he gave up some dap and greeted his homey.

"Same shit different day, you know how it goes. Trying to maintain some honor around these wack-ass cops," Flaco joked as they laughed at the irony.

"Yo, what the fuck are you doing with this Con Edison truck? You got a legitimate gig now?" Flaco shook his head and grinned. "Nah, fuck it. Don't even answer that man, cause I don't even wanna know. You're a wild bastard, though. I'll give you that!"

Wild Man chuckled in amusement. "C'mon, now. You know I never limit my game to just one hustle, baby. I'm a jack-of-all-trades, my G. A man who wears many hats. Now lemme see what you got for me, homey."

Flaco reached into his jacket pocket and passed Wild Man a small object. "It's on this flash drive, bro. It took a lot of pull to get this shit out of the evidence locker, but you know I always come through."

Wild Man pulled his tablet out from under his seat and connected the flash drive to the port. He punched a few keys and waited for the data to load, then he stared at the screen as the color images from the security camera at the Fulton Street jewelry store came into focus.

Wild Man hawk-eyed the footage as he prepared to soak up every detail. The cameras had been set to record a single still frame every three seconds, and Wild Man stared at the screen as he saw the back door of the jewelry shop swing open.

Moments later, a young woman wearing a light blue pants suit and a big red hat that concealed her face appeared in the doorway, and she was carrying something in her hand.

The next frame showed her raising her free hand up at a balding old man who was sitting in a chair dressed in a plaid shirt and dark slacks.

Wild Man blinked for a quick second and suddenly the old man was crouched down on the floor like he was picking something up. And in the next frame he was up on his feet again.

The following frame showed the old man and the younger woman exchanging the items each of them held in their hands.

And in the very next frame Wild Man saw himself and the rest of his masked crew entering the camera's frame.

They were dressed in all-black from head to toe and they were totally unidentifiable.

The flash of multiple popping muzzles lit up the next frame, but Wild Man wasn't interested in none of that.

"Oh shit—gotta go back!" he muttered out loud. "Gotta go the fuck back!"

He swiped the feed-flow button backwards a couple of times and there it was. Right in front of his eyes.

The muthafuckin hand-off!

Wild Man stared at the still photo of the young chick who seemed to be snatching a big book away from the older cat. The book looked thick and white, and Wild Man woulda bet his left nut that it said, *Basic Biology* on the front cover.

He kept his eyes on the footage and in the very next frame it happened. The young chick slid the object she had carried into the shop into the hands of the older black man, and then she pointed somewhere off-camera.

"Well would you look at that pretty-ass *monkey!*" Wild Man spit under his breath as he stared at the image of the elderly man that his crew had straight-up murdered. In his last picture alive, the old dude was reaching out to accept the very item that had gotten him murked. A red briefcase.

That bitch! Wild Man fumed inside as he stared at the beautiful female who was half-pictured on the screen. *That shiesty fuckin bitch!*

Suddenly the footage went black as Jewelz aimed her pistol and shot out the security camera. Cursing under his breath, Wild Man snatched the zip drive from his device and handed it back to his manz.

"Yo, whassup?" Flaco asked eyeing him intently. "You know that chick? Can you make a positive ID on her?"

"Nah," Wild Man lied, fronting his homey off. "I ain't never laid eyes on that bitch before in my life," he muttered.

But of course he knew who that jawn was. He knew how that trick tasted between her legs and how she smelled all up in her guts. She smelled like a monkey. A monkey with a red briefcase!

Ain't this some high-level bullshit? Wild Man thought as his mind raced on a hunnid. He could still hear that pussy-nigga he'd poked full of holes in his basement crying clearly in his ears.

"The Queen sent me, yo! It was Honore!"

Now Wild Man knew dude had been spittin truth. So that bitch Honore had made a drop at the jewelry store on Fulton Street and she was all about diamonds too? She had asked him over and over again what was in that red damn briefcase, and now Wild Man knew why. Yeah, two and two had finally added up to four because homeboy outside his window had definitely been telling the muthafuckin truth! That bitch Honore was wearing a dual fuckin crown! She was the Queen of fuckin Diamonds, and she was the monkey with the red briefcase too! *Wait till I tell Slick!*

CHAPTER 27

Get In Where You Fit In

It's ShowTime! Noodles thought as he made his way into the main area of the Jewish Recreational Center. For the past hour or so he'd been lurking on the low, blending into the shadows and making himself invisible as he scoped shit out and got a nose for who was in the building.

Right now Benny's friends and family were taking their seats inside the huge auditorium. Everyone was having a good time and engaged in lively conversation. Little kids were running around playing underfoot, totally oblivious to the cluster of hardcore murderers, extortionists, gangsters, and thugs in suits that were sitting just a few feet away from them.

Noodles spotted a young boy who had been getting a lot of hugs and kisses from old ladies all day long. He figured him to be Benny's son, the celebrated bar mitzvah boy.

Noodles moved discreetly from table to table, shadowing the waiter staff as he pretended to oversee their work. On his face was a professional expression, and in his hand was a miniature palm-held video camera that was connected to a thin wire that slid in and out of his shirtsleeve.

None of the guests even noticed him and they paid little to no attention to the catering team as they were consumed by their conversations while awaiting the ceremony. Noodles made his way around the room with his recorder busy gathering evidence and doing its job.

"Good evening, can I have everyone's attention?" Benny's wife tapped on the mic as she spoke from the stage.

"I'd like to thank all of our family and friends for your attendance at the bar mitzvah for our only son. We hope you enjoy the good food and the good company and we'll be beginning the program momentarily."

Noodles played the cut while the program got underway. Young Benny Jr.

was happily showered with money and gifts as male members of the family got up on stage and spoke to the audience and welcomed him into the fold of manhood. Everything was flowing smoothly for the mobster and his family, but as the afternoon wore on Noodles's hopes were slowly fading because it was looking like his suspicions were off the mark and probably wouldn't pan out.

But then he peeped a tall guy dressed in a dark suit walk over and whisper something in Benny's ear. Their eyes traveled to the right, and Noodles's eyes did too.

Suddenly the auditorium doors swung open. Noodles's gaze grew hard as fuck as in walked none other than his fake-ass homey.

Whitey Reynolds.

The palest member of the Zip 'em up Crew slid up in the joint looking smooth as peanut butter. He was accompanied by a nervous-looking fellow that Noodles knew from his surveillance to be the underground diamond trader they called Avi.

Backstabbing mutt! Noodles fumed at his manz from afar. *Shittin on his whole fuckin click!*

Avi looked hesitant as he made his way over to pay his respects to Benny, and then he gestured toward Whitey like he was introducing the two men.

Noodles stepped back further into the shadows to make sure he wasn't spotted. He knew Whitey's ass like a fuckin book, and no matter how innocent that snake looked he had eyes in the back of his head and he was always on the hunt for prey.

Frowning, Noodles glanced down to make sure his camera was recording that grimy turncoat live and in color, and when he looked back up again his eyes bucked open wide and he did a quick double-take.

The auditorium door had swung open again and the person walking in this time caught Noodles by surprise and damn near blew his mind.

What in the entire FUCK? he thought as he watched the fine-ass chick slide in looking like a million big ones sitting on a diamond-crusted platter.

Beauty on top of beauty, she rolled in fuckin 'em up from head to toe. Led by a tall gangsta-looking cat who was spiffed up in an imported suit and what looked like real snake-skinned shoes, the chick that Wild Man had just been tryna put him up on, the same chick that they had snatched outta that jewelry shop and tossed into their van that night, Slick's brand new piece of ass, walked up to Big Benny and held out her hand so he could kiss her ring.

Noodles stared at the two of them, steadily recording and focused like fuck. *Now if this ain't some dirty underhanded bullshit that's about to go down!*

Benny stood up and the entire entourage, including his shady-looking boys, started walking towards a backroom where Noodles knew a meeting of the minds and a plan of the pockets was about to take place.

He also knew that there was no way in fuck he was getting inside that meeting room with them. But that was cool because he already had enough evidence on camera to bring a charge on that traitorous snake Whitey. And on that shady bitch Honore too.

Yeah, muffuckas! Noodles thought as his icy eyes followed them from deep in the darkness of the shadows. *I got dat ass! Y'all bitches is cold fuckin busted! Wait till I tell Slick!*

$$$$$

Eager to dip out and get back to Brooklyn, Noodles fell in step with a group of waiters who were carrying trays of dirty dishes back to the kitchen. They had just exited the auditorium door when one of Benny's beefy-ass security guards backed into Noodles on accident.

Noodles stumbled forward and bumped into a serving girl. Her tray full of dirty dishes and his palm-held video camera both went flying in the air, and when the camera hit the floor it landed right at the security guard's feet.

"Ay!" the thick-necked cat barked as he bent down and snatched up Noodles's miniature recorder. "What the hell is this?"

Noodles shrugged and calmly went to reach for it but the guard snatched it back.

"Uh-uh," dude said, shaking the recorder just out of Noodles's reach. "What the fuck is this, wise guy? We specifically told your company no cameras or recording devices were allowed, Sambo!"

The guard peered closely at the device then started pressing its buttons. "What the fuck do you got on here?" he demanded, trying to access the video feed.

Noodles just couldn't allow that shit.

In a flash he smashed the guard in his nose with a quick right fist that dropped the fat man to one knee. Noodles grabbed dude's wrist and began wrestling for his tiny camera, but big boy jammed his hand in close to his body and belly-flopped down on that bitch, trapping both the camera and Noodles's hand beneath his massive weight.

"*Bennyyyy!*" the man roared from his gut as frightened children and guests started screaming and scattering at the sight of the commotion. "Get a guard!" The man yelled, grappling for his gun. "Security! Security! *Security!*"

Noodles grabbed dude's gun hand and clenched his thumb. He squeezed tight and bent it all the way back, breaking it. Dude howled and snatched his hand away and Noodles went to work. Digging under the man's fat lard stomach, Noodles grabbed his camera and squeezed it in a death grip. Pushing through the crowd of startled waiters he beat feet through the kitchen, hauling ass like Usain Bolt.

Outta nowhere two security guards came at him from opposite sides and lunged at him. Noodles staggered and his knees buckled, but on the way down he gripped both men in headlocks and took them down to the mat with him.

His shoulder muscles bulged and his forearm strength was on a hunnid as he squeezed their necks against his massive chest until their eyes bugged out.

Both men were throwing weak glancing punches at him but Noodles had them bitches caught in a steel vice-grip and he wasn't letting go.

Dude clenched up under his left armpit was gasping and strangling and he slumped over first. Noodles released his death-grip and shook the cat's body loose, then he slammed his left fist into the mug of the man he was clenching with his right arm. The man's face was reddish-purple as he gasped in pain, but when Noodles eased up a bit and placed the flat of his palm against the cat's head and pushed it sharply until his neck popped, the man collapsed without making another sound.

But there were all kinds of sounds and screams splitting the air behind him as Noodles scrambled to his feet and hauled ass again. Benny's goons were breathing heat on his neck as he busted through the back door like a bat outta hell and exploded outta the Jewish Recreational Center and into the bright daylight.

"Shoot that son-of-a-bitch!" Noodles heard a white voice yell as rushing feet slapped against the pavement behind him.

Kicking it up a gear, Noodles jetted toward the corner and ran down the busy street like a track star, feet furiously flying as he headed for the rally point where his boy Wild Man would be waiting in the cut with the blicky on the ready.

Just like the rest of his crew, Noodles was in top physical shape and unless those fluffy pancake-eatin fatties chasing him were willing to start banging right out in the open, they wasn't about to catch him.

It's on now, bitches! Noodles's mind raced right along with his feet. *Wait the fuck till I tell Slick!*

He couldn't wait to expose that rat-ass turncoat Whitey, and to warn Slick about that grimy *thot* he was fuckin with too!

The corner loomed in front of him and Noodles took that bitch at a full-out sprint, putting even more distance between him and his pursuers as he headed toward the meet-up spot at the other end of the block.

But the moment he turned into the alley Noodles's whole shit fell off.

The sight that greeted him made his heart drop straight down into his nut-sack.

The alley was empty.

He could see all the way down to the other end and there wasn't no Con Ed truck, no Wild Man, no blickys, no *nothing.*

The fuck? Noodles thought in wild disbelief. *Where the fuck is he?*

Footsteps were thundering behind him and Noodles almost panicked.

Fuck!!! He started running again, hauling ass toward the far end of the alley, praying like a muthafucka for Wild Man to come speeding around that corner in his Con Ed truck with his burner spittin heat.

POP! POP! POP!

The sound of hot bullets whizzing through the air put Noodles's ass in a whole 'nother gear. Benny's shooters were gunning hard for him and without a gat he was assed all the way out.

Desperately Noodles yanked his cell phone outta his front pocket. He fumbled to hit the text key but his vision was blurry and hot rounds were flying left and right.

POP! POP! POP!

Noodles's sweaty finger was slipping and sliding all over his fuckin phone. Wasn't no way in hell he could send a text, so he ran as hard as he could and hit the first number he came to on speed dial.

"Whattup my nigga?" Slick said casually as he picked up on the first ring.

"*Hhhhhhh!*" Noodles screamed out in a long whisper. His feet were flying as his useless vocal cords strained to produce something that resembled language while hot bullets skipped off bricks right behind his head. "*Hhhhhhh!*"

POP! POP! POP!

Noodles zigzagged like a running back as he tried to outrun the zinging lead that was flying his way.

"Hhhhhhh!" he hissed into the phone again as he tried his damnest to communicate with his manz Slick. *"Hhhhhhh!"*

"Ayo *Noodles!*" Slick panicked as he recognized the unmistakable cracks of bullets popping off and the horrible sounds of desperate fear coming outta his main manz's mouth. "What's wrong? What the fuck is happenin man!?!"

With Slick's voice ringing out in his ear, Noodle pounded his feet all the way to the very end of the alley. And then suddenly he stopped.

He glanced quickly to his right, praying like hell to see Wild Man rolling up in the cut, but the street was empty. Wasn't shit out there. Wild Man wasn't there and his Con Edison truck wasn't neither.

Fuck, Noodles thought, giving up in defeat as the sound of Slick screaming at him through the phone cut into the air.

That nigga played me, Noodles thought grimly as he accepted his fate and prepared to die. His only thoughts were of Ayesha and the kids, and the beautiful life of love and security that he would never be able to give them.

But then the bullets started flying again and the will to survive kicked into overdrive.

Noodles took off running again. Faster this time.

"*Hhhhhhh!*" he pressed the phone to his face and hissed out to Slick as he hauled ass toward the street beyond the alley.

"*Hhhhhhhh!!! Hhhhhhhh!!!*"

EMPIRE

STATE of MINE$!

(A Movie in a Book)

Episode 4

Boogie Down Bronx

A NOIRE & REEM RAW JOINT

There are eight million stories in the naked city of New York.

These five are all the way live.

"If it wasn't for the Bronx there'd be no boogie goin down,

So let's give it up for all the hittas in this town!"

CHAPTER 1

Best Friends Become Strangers

Wild Man was running about five minutes late as he burnt rubber down the mean streets of the Boogie-Down Bronx.

"I *knew* that bitch was dirty!" he cursed under his breath as he punched the gas pedal and zipped his truck in and out of traffic. "I fuckin *knew* it!"

The images of Honore that he had seen on the jewelry store's security camera were burned into his mind as he raced back up the Major Deegan. He was headed back to the Jewish Community Center so he could scoop up his bro, Noodles and he was gonna be about five minutes late.

"*Yeah!* I shoulda plugged that bitch in the dome the first night I saw her!" Wild Man muttered, gunning the engine and dodging potholes as his mind replayed the sight of Honore with a stylish red briefcase swinging from her hand.

Bitter rage coursed through his blood, and not just because the bad-ass trick had played him and his entire posse for a bunch of weak pussies. Nah, Wild Man was mad as fuck because now he knew for a fact that when that sucka-ass sneak thief who tried to break into his window said it was Honore who had sent him, he had been telling the truth. That bitch had tried to wax him!

He couldn't wait to bust her ass out!

"Wait till I tell Slick!" he spit as he weaved in and out of traffic before jumping off the highway at his exit. Minutes later he rounded the corner and entered the cut where Noodles had said he'd be waiting. "I can't *believe* this shit!" Wild Man fumed out loud. "Just wait till I fuckin tell Sli—"

The words froze in his throat as he rolled into the alley and spotted a figure laying sprawled out in the middle of the road.

It was a body. A body dressed in black and white waiter clothes. It was stretched out on the hot concrete directly in front of him. It was—

"Oh, *shit!*" Wild Man shrieked as he slammed the gear into park and jumped outta the truck like he'd been auto-ejected from that bitch. "Nooo, nooo, *nooo* muthafucka, *nooooooooo!*"

Wild Man ran around the truck's front bumper. He dropped down to his knees and snatched his bro up in his arms as he hollered his name out with his head thrown back to the sky.

"*Noodles!!!!*" he screamed, gripping his friend's shoulders and shaking the shit outta him. "Noodles!!! Son, get the fuck up! C'mon. Please. Get the fuck up!!!"

Noodles's glazed-over eyes were open but his body was completely limp. There were no signs of him breathing and the white shirt of his waiter uniform was soaked in blood. Wild Man pressed his hand to his manz's heart and felt for a beat. Nothing. He grabbed at his wrist to check his pulse and something small and metallic fell outta Noodles's lifeless palm.

Wild Man scooped it up and moaned deep in his throat. His homey was fucked up. Bullet holes dotted his entire upper body. Somebody had swiss-cheesed the fuck outta his slime and he was leaking life liquid everywhere.

"Noodles don't die! Just hold on!" Wild Man begged uselessly. "Please just fuckin hold on!"

The light had already faded from Noodles's eyes and his skin was growing cool, but none of that registered with Wild Man because he refused to accept or acknowledge it.

"I gotta get you to the hospital, bruh," he said, denying the reality of what was in front of him as he gathered his friend closer in his arms and started carrying him toward the truck.

He had only gone a few steps when a faint sound cut the air and Wild Man glanced down. A cell phone lay on the ground nearby. It was Noodles's joint, and hearing a barely audible voice coming from it Wild Man lowered Noodles to the ground and snatched the phone up and pressed it to his ear.

"Yo, Noodles!" somebody screamed, and right away Wild Man knew exactly who it was. "What the fuck is going on?" the voice demanded. "You a'ight, baby? Talk to me, nigga! *Talk to me!*"

"*Slick!*" Wild Man hollered back as an indescribable wave of guilt ripped through his chest. "It's *me!* Noodles got hit up, son! Somebody fuckin *rocked* him!"

"Yo call the fuckin ambulance!" Slick yelled. "Where they hit him at? Is he breathing? Is the muthafucka breathing? Yo call a fuckin ambulance, nigga!"

Wild Man's whole body shook as he sank back down to his knees beside the body of his friend.

"It's too late," he moaned into the phone, suddenly conscious of the fact that his hands and his conscience were both covered in his brother's blood.

"Slick..." Wild Man moaned and cried. "It's too fuckin late, fam. They deaded him," he sobbed into the phone. "Noodles is fuckin *dead!*"

$$$$$

The Zip 'em up Crew was up on the rooftop of building 430 going at it hard.

Fuck the brotherhood. That shit was over and done with and Slick and Wild Man were bare-knuckle boxing like bitter enemies who had crossed each other up in the streets.

It was some of the worst shit Jewelz had ever seen in her life. If her heart wasn't hurting so bad for Noodles she woulda been up on her feet swinging on that fuck-up artist Wild Man too.

Slick had sounded the emergency alarm to alert the entire crew to the loss of their treasured brother and friend. Jewelz had been stunned with grief as she rushed to the rooftop to be with Slick as they waited for Wild Man and Whitey to show up. It took both of them a long time to finally get there, and she had held Slick in her arms the whole time as they waited together and cried.

Whitey had arrived first, and a couple of minutes later Wild Man had burst through the rooftop door covered in blood and looking a total fuckin wreck.

Losing Noodles was bad enough, but he was even more tore down because the cops had rolled up and he'd been forced to abandon Noodles's body in the alley and skate off. Slick and Jewelz were both mad as fuck when, through his tears, Wild Man 'fessed up and admitted that he had been late getting to the meeting spot to pick Noodles up.

"What meeting spot? Where the hell was y'all at?" Whitey demanded. "Where did all this shit go down?"

"We was up by Westchester! Noodles had to go check something out and he told me to drop him off! I was late picking him up but I swear it was only like four minutes," Wild Man insisted as he sat slumped on a crate with his face buried in his hands. "*Four fuckin minutes!* Not even five! I had dipped down to Brooklyn real quick to take a look at those—"

He never got to finish because Slick lunged at him and started swinging like a young Mike Tyson.

"Four minutes?" he rushed the shit outta Wild Man and knocked him backwards off the crate.

"You was *late,* bitch! You shoulda stayed right there wit' him! You got him *stretched* you stupid fuck!" Slick charged again as he snuffed out Wild Man with a flurry of killer punches.

"Yo! He told me to drop him off!" Wild Man yelled from the ground as he raised his arm over his head to protect himself. "I let him out where he told me to let him out, and then I went to look at the fuckin tapes from that—"

"Stupid ass!!!" Slick threw a quick jab that snapped Wild Man's whole head back. Stunned, Wild Man lunged forward and caught Slick with a pounding jab of his own.

"Back the fuck off me, bitch! I went to look at the—"

"I don't give a fuck *where* you went!" Slick raged as he swung on his boy and smashed him again. "Late means *dead* in this game, muthafucka! Late means *DEAD!!!*"

"It wasn't my fault!" Wild Man jumped to his feet and charged forward. He lowered his massive shoulders and grunted as he tried to clench Slick up in a chokehold.

But Slick was quick and nimble. He ducked and sidestepped then caught Wild Man with another brick-breaker on his temple that sent him stumbling. Wild Man crumpled to one knee and both his hands hit the ground to brace his fall. He was pushing off to stand up when he felt the rigid barrel of steel heat jammed up against the back of his head.

"You jealous-ass pussy!" Slick said coldly as he cocked his pistol with a cool, steady finger. "Noodles is dead and it *is* your fault! You left him out there by himself so it ain't nobody's fuckin fault but *yours!*"

Wild Man was frozen on one knee with his sweat-drenched face twisted in a mask of grief and disbelief.

"Slick?" he whispered hoarsely. "Oh word? Is you posting up on me, my nigga?" His eyes bulged in shock and a tear ran down his face. "Is you really pressing ya strap on *me?*"

"You fuckin right! I oughtta blast your slimy brains out, you lil *bitch!* You left him out there on purpose, you weak-hearted clown!" Slick spit through clenched teeth. "You was still aggy at him from that other shit and you got him rocked on *purpose*, you grimy pussy! You got him *bodied!*"

"Noodles *told* me to leave!" Wild Man bucked. "You was standing right there! He didn't want nobody to know what he was doing! He told me to drop him the fuck off!"

"Yeah, and he told you to show the fuck back up too! He told ya ass to show up *on time* like professionals do! Like *brothers* do!"

"But I went to look at the—"

"Just pop him!" Jewelz shrieked. She couldn't take this shit no more. She watched through a haze of tears as Slick held the muzzle of his blicky jammed hard behind Wild Man's ear. "*Clap* his bogus-ass, Slick!"

"Jewelz!" Wild Man whirled on her with a look of unbelievable anguish in his eyes. "You turning on me too? You *too?*"

Still on his knees, he turned back to Slick. "Yeah, ga' head, B," Wild Man sneered. A sick grin spread across his face as he dared Slick to blast him without a smidgen of fear. "You think my shit is sideways like that?" He rose to his feet and turned to face his former dude. "Zip me up then, Slick! Let one fly and zip me the fuck up!"

"Hold up!" Whitey barked storming over. He was dressed in a real expensive suit like he'd just come from a business meeting. He slammed his palm into Slick's chest and wedged his body between the two men. "Put the fuckin heat down!" he raged at Slick. "Put that shit DOWN!"

"Nah, Whitey, man...he shoulda been there," Slick moaned with his face contorted in grief as a single tear gathered in his left eye. "Noodles is dead, yo...this bitch-made show off shoulda *been there*, man!"

"Yeah," Whitey nodded. He snatched the tool outta Slick's hand but kept it aimed in Wild Man's direction. "He fucking shoulda been there," he said glaring at Wild Man with heat in his eyes. "He's a shifty-ass hothead, but he's still your brother. So you can't fucking kill him."

"Fuck all of y'all!" Wild Man sneered then took a step forward and pimp-smacked the gat straight outta Whitey's hand. "All of y'all blind bitches can suck my dick! Get the fuck outta here with that dumb shit!"

"Nah *you* get the fuck outta here!" Slick barked on his former manz as Whitey struggled to hold him back. "You's a fuckin problem child, you wild-ass muthafucka! A wanna-be fuckin renegade! You off the team, pussy! You ain't dependable and can't nobody count on you! Now step the fuck off before I fly you over that railing and send you downstairs the short way, *nigga!*"

"*Fuck* you, Slick!" Wild Man barked again. His rage was subsiding but there was deep pain in his eyes. "You playing that "Mr. Perfect" role but ere'body on this team got skeletons in they fuckin closet, man! Everybody! Noodles knew something was up! He was tryna get up on that shit when he got rocked! But you so blinded you can't even tell when you getting fucked over backwards, homey!"

"Get gone! You don't mean shit to me no more, nigga!" Slick hollered as Wild Man whirled around and stormed toward the roof's door. "You better get the fuck *gone* and don't bring ya ass up on this roof no more neither! Stay the fuck away from my click! If you show ya mug around here again I'ma man-down ya ass, bruh! Just like Noodles, you gonna be a *dead* man!"

"Suck my dick!" Wild Man yelled as he busted through the door like he was greener than the Hulk. "That's why I ain't putting you down, and I ain't telling your blind ass *shit*, muthafucka! Figure it out by ya goddamn self! I ain't telling you *shit!*"

As he stormed down the stairs the last three members of the Zip 'em up Crew stood on the rooftop either consumed with grief or shocked into silence. But the cold hard fact was not lost on any of them that they had just lost Noodles and Wild Man at the same damn time.

$$$$$

Wild Man's rage was damn near as big as the pain that was gripping his heart. He wasn't no punk in these fuckin streets, and when bitten by a pit bull his natural instincts were to bite back even harder.

I ain't telling him *shit!*" he vowed as he took the stairs down from the rooftop where his former homey had just kicked him off the team and barred him from all activities with the Zip 'em up Crew.

Stay the fuck away from my set! If you show ya mug around here again you's a dead man, muthafucka!

Slick had spit those words at him right before he left, and that statement alone was enough to blow Wild Man's fuckin mind.

This shit was insane! He had been out there tryna do a solid for the whole fuckin team! The very thing that had made him late getting back to Noodles coulda been the very thing that saved Slick's life, but nah, *fuck* that idiot! Calling him jealous and accusing him of setting Noodles up to get murked?

"Fuck I look like?" Wild Man fumed as he rounded the stairwell on the fourth floor. "Slick's punk ass better hope he can stay ten toes down! As long as I been riding for him he oughtta know me better than that!"

He was racing high on anger but the pain in his heart was the true source of his fuel.

"Let his funny-actin ass find out the hard way!" Wild Man slammed his fist into the concrete wall, sending a welcome explosion of pain radiating through his entire arm.

"Let that smut-ass bird Honore plant some truth right in his fuckin forehead! Mister Perfect is about to take a fuckin fall 'cause I ain't putting him down on *shit!*"

CHAPTER 2

Switch Siders

Slick adjusted his tie and buttoned the jacket of his midnight-black Armani suit. It was windy outside and the clouds cast a sullen look on an already gloomy occasion.

They were at Woodlawn cemetery in the Bronx, and Slick stared down at the shiny blue casket containing the body of his homey Noodles as they lowered it into the ground.

Ayesha and the kids were totally broken up with grief. All four of them were standing nearby and crying with looks of shock and disbelief on their faces. Noodles had never gotten a chance to propose to Ayesha and ask for her hand in matrimony. In fact, she didn't even know he had bought her a ring. He had asked Slick to come to Guatemala and be his best man, and it broke Slick's heart to have to tell Ayesha about the wedding she was never gonna have.

Noodles's mother in Guatemala was technically still his next of kin, but she was on the waiting list for a heart transplant so she was way too sick to fly in. She had cried pitifully over the phone when Slick called her to notify her that her cherished son was dead. She gave Slick permission to make all the arrangements for the funeral and burial, and Slick had shared those responsibilities with Ayesha.

The whole click knew that Noodles had not only taken care of Ayesha and the three kids that weren't biologically his, but he had also been his mother's financial lifesaver too. Every month he sent her the money she needed for the barrage of drugs that kept her weak heart beating. Slick had vowed to continue those payments for as long as Noodles's mother lived, and he also vowed to make sure Ayesha and her children were set for life and never wanted for a damn thing.

It was hard to come to grips with Noodles taking a bullet, but Slick knew it could have been any one of them. He fully accepted the risks that came with his lifestyle, but losing his friend made him think real hard about the moves he was making.

The type of work the Zip 'em up Crew did caused other people to have funerals every day. It was different when it struck close to home though. It cut deeper when it was you who had to say goodbye to somebody that you loved.

But the good thing was, there wasn't a damn thing left unsaid between him and Noodles. No final words or feelings that Slick wished he woulda had a chance to express. Him and Noodles had loved each other like brothers. And the two of them had shared the only fuckin thing that mattered in the street-life they lived.

Loyalty.

That shit was solid and true. Slick had went all-out without a second thought for Noodles and vice versa. Fuck what death said. They were gonna be homeys forever.

Slick stood there with the wind whipping around him and he thought back to the day his brotherhood with Noodles was forged. Everything in life happened for a reason, and if it wasn't for that charge he had taken for Noodles, they never woulda got put on with the BBU in the first place...

They called it the Devil's Asshole.

Slick was entombed at the bottom of a hole so dark and black it felt like the earth had cracked open and swallowed him whole. It was so fuckin black that he couldn't see his hand right in front of his face or tell if his eyes were open or closed.

But it wasn't a jail cell that they had thrown him into. Nah, that woulda been too merciful. The hole they'd buried Slick in was built to shatter a man's psyche. It was a cold, damp place with no light, no sound, a thin lumpy mattress for a bed, and a reeking hole in the ground for him to piss and shit.

Slick huddled there as naked and helpless as the day he had come into the world. He had no perception of space or time. Once a day, at random times, a tiny slot in the door opened and a sandwich made of stale bread and mystery meat was thrown in. A cup of warm water followed.

Over time, even the strongest of men were reduced to crazed lunacy by this type of sensory and food deprivation. It was a technique meant to torture, degrade, and drive a man insane. And it worked.

Surrounded by men who wanted him dead, Slick knew full well that his own mind was his worst enemy. In the silence of the darkness he was alone with his personal demons and he was forced to battle them to the death. But Slick also knew that if he fought wildly, like so many others before him, he was sure to lose. Just as they had lost.

So Slick embraced that shit. He embraced the darkness, the bitterness, and the hopelessness of it too.

He immersed himself in every ounce of pain, suffering, and rage that he had ever endured, and he let himself be swept up in its current and thrust into an ocean of nothingness. He replayed his entire life from as far back as he could remember, like a movie rolling in slow motion. Even the most painful parts. He forced himself into a state of suspended animation and floated between the scenes of his own existence. Slick welcomed the hallucina-

tions and met his fears head-on as he reminded himself:

I am Samir Williams, Junior. Son of Samir and Kea Williams. I'm strong. I'm a muthafuckin man! I will survive!

Slick was serving hard time for the murder of a fellow soldier. His boy Noodles had committed the crime, but Slick was taking the charge. For years he had been searching to find meaning in the cold desolation that his life had become, He had gone into the military to satisfy a recklessness that was left inside him, but even danger and top-level training wasn't enough to plug up the holes that the murders of his family had left in his heart.

Ever since basic training Slick had displayed a superior level of ability in everything from sharpshooting, to land navigation, to physical training. Slick was not only the best soldier in his entire military company, he was fearless and better at everything than most of the men who held rank over him and who were considered the nation's top-level elites.

This had created a lot of envy and hostility in the ranks, which was further fueled by the fact that Slick was vocal and unapologetic about his superior skills. The good old boys couldn't stand Slick's cocky attitude and they hated the fact that they couldn't break his uppity black ass down.

Any and every test that was put in front of Slick he passed with flying colors, and then he dared his superiors to do that shit better than him. He was undermining and openly challenging his higher-ranking officers to the point where the other soldiers had a lot of respect for him and they held his words in the highest regard.

So when Slick suddenly confessed to a heinous and highly publicized murder in an attempt to save his right-hand-manz Noodles's life, the senior officers started salivating at the mouth because they finally had him by the balls.

Normally, Slick would have been placed in a regular military holding cell. But because of the enemies that he'd amassed from almost day one, the powers-that-be decided to punish him harshly. They decided to send him to a place where if he refused to bend then he was guaranteed to break. With the utmost glee and delight, they shoved him into the deepest recesses of a place they called The Devil's Asshole.

It was solitary confinement to the tenth power. Trapped in complete darkness with no outside interaction and a bucket of water for a shower every other week, it was the harshest punishment available and it was every inmate's nightmare.

But one day the door slid open and Slick was snatched out of the Asshole with no warning. A black bag was pulled over his head and he was led into a room and forced to sit at a metal table.

The bag was yanked off his head and Slick threw his hands over his eyes and recoiled in pain. He had spent so much time in darkness that the light was excruciating. He struggled to sit upright. His body was weak and malnourished and his bones ached when he moved.

A door opened and a well-dressed white man with a cold look in his eyes walked in and sat across the table from him.

"My name is Walter Reynolds. I'm an attorney with the Department of Defense and I'm here to offer you representation at a new trial."

Slick peered at the man in front of him through squinting eyes before he responded.

"You, Mr. White Boy, are a goddamn liar. I know DOD when I see it and you're not

it. So how about you run that bullshit by me again."

"You're pretty sharp," the white man responded. "And that's why I'm here. You've been inside the Devil's Asshole for nine months. I've been monitoring you the entire time. Most men scream, mutilate, or even try to cannibalize themselves under those extreme conditions but not you, Mr. Williams. You've displayed a will and a patience that I haven't seen before. I'll be done with my stint of working for the government in just a few months and then I'm going into business for myself. I need a solid team and I can use a man like you to lead it."

"What do I have to do?" Slick asked warily.

"Let me file an appeal and a request for a retrial on your behalf. And then let me defend you. I've studied your case and I guarantee that I can get you off on a technicality and have your sentence overturned. And once you're free, I'll advance you a hundred thousand dollars and pay you more in one weekend than you were making in six months of Army pay. I'll even let you recruit the rest of the team."

Slick rubbed his long, dried-up beard as he thought it over. His mind calculated as crusty flakes of dead skin and sour dandruff fell onto the table between them. "Damn, nigga!" he finally said to the white man. "Fuck I gotta do to earn all that?"

"You're a killer, right?" the man who Slick would come to know as Whitey Reynolds said with a grin as he opened his briefcase and slid Slick a stack of papers to sign. "All you have to do is that killing thing that you do best."

Slick stood looking down into the six-foot hole containing Noodles's casket. It seemed like so long ago that he been granted an unconditional release after his retrial. Whitey was a brilliant fuckin lawyer and strategist, but Slick knew the fight had been fixed from the gate. The BBU had been in control of the judge and of the appeal panel too, and once he'd accepted Whitey's proposition it had been a done deal.

Slick had been revitalized by the overturned verdict, and he had walked outta the Devil's Asshole and recruited Noodles, Wild Man, and later Jewelz, for his team.

He'd always known there was a possibility that one of them could catch a bullet on the job and get taken down, but he never thought it would go south like this for Noodles. His manz had survived so much, only to get hit up for something that none of them even understood.

And that was the hardest part. Why? *Why?* Why was Noodles dead? Who killed him and what the fuck was it all about? Slick stood over his friend's open grave and said a silent prayer:

I'ma miss you, Noodles. You was always barking about that lil bid I did for you, but I can't count how many times you saved my ass out there on the job. Your momz and your fam are gonna be straight. I promise you they'll never go without for as long as I'm drawing breath. When you see my family up there... tell them how much I miss them. Let my mother and father know that I think about them everyday. Let my lil brothers and sisters know that I'm sorry I wasn't big enough and strong enough to protect them. Tell my father I squared shit up with Haz for him, and that Dirty Mike is gonna get his next. Hold it down in Heaven for me, bruh. I'll see you when I get there, my nigga. Till we meet again.

Slick finished up his short prayer for his homey and then he stepped back and gave Jewelz some room to step up and say a prayer of her own. He could see how bad she was hurting and it was hard to even look at her in such intense pain.

Funerals were tough on both of them. After his family was murdered, him and Jewelz had sat through the combined funeral service clinging to each other and crying pitifully the whole time.

There had been a long row of white caskets stretched out before them containing the bodies of his mother and father and the mutilated bodies of his young siblings too.

Terrified, Slick and Jewelz had snuck a million looks over their shoulders expecting Crazy Haz to bust into the church and finish what he'd started.

But even as scared as they were, they were project kids and they knew better than to open their mouths and tell the cops who had stabbed them. Him and Jewelz had just sat there shell-shocked in the front pew together, holding hands and moaning and grieving. When it came time to close the caskets Slick had broken down like a motherless child and Jewelz had fallen to the floor and cried even harder than him.

And now, Slick gazed into her eyes knowing that she was sharing his memories. He was shocked by how weak and fragile she looked. Like she was tired as hell.

Slick was tired too. He had been speed racing through life. Gunning his motor and flying fast. His gut instinct was telling him that him and his crew could easily collide and crash into the concrete walls of destiny. He just hoped it didn't end up with every last one of them stretched out cold in a box. He shook his head. He didn't have his ten million in cream stashed away yet, but maybe it was time to think about an exit strategy for getting outta the game.

"This is fucked up, bro," Whitey said as he came up behind Slick. "Noodles was the heartbeat of the crew and we all loved him. The only thing we can do now is try to hold it all together. We both know that's what Noodles would've wanted."

"Yeah," Slick said quietly. "But payback is a bitch and Noodles woulda wanted us to get summa that shit too!"

"Damn right," Whitey agreed. "When the time is right we'll raise some hell."

Slick shook his head. "Why we gotta wait? We can't just sit back and take this shit in slow-motion, my friend. We gotta roll up to Westchester and lay a bunch of muthafuckas down, homey. We need a name and a face. We gotta make somebody *pay* for this shit!"

"In due time," Whitey said again.

"Yo, time ain't on our side. We gotta figure out what the hell Noodles went up there scoping for in the first place! What the fuck made him go out on his own? Who was he going after? What the fuck was he trying to find out?"

Whitey shrugged and shook his head. "I don't know, but now isn't the time to worry about that bro," he said gently. "Noodles took the answers to those questions with him to his grave. But you just leave everything to me. I promise you I'm on this shit. I'll do some looking around and find out what Noodles was going after and exactly who he ran across. Whoever did this, we'll give those motherfuckas what they deserve, but right now we gotta concentrate on getting Noodles buried and putting our squad back together."

"What squad?" Slick was about to say, but just then a figure in a grove of trees just beyond some small tombstones caught his eye.

"That coward-ass *bitch!*" Slick tensed up and cursed as Whitey followed his gaze. "Fuck is he doing showing up here?"

"C'mon," Whitey said. "He's grieving too man—"

"I'ma drill 'im," Slick spit bitterly as he turned back to the limo to go get his piece. "I told him not to come around me! I'ma dirt-nap his ass right fuckin here!"

Whitey grabbed Slick's arm and Slick glared at him and pulled away. "Fuck offa me!" he exploded. But when he looked toward the trees again, Wild Man was gone.

"Fuckin *herb!*" Slick spit, eyeing the empty spot as he clenched his jaw. "I swear to God the next time I see that lil pussy I'ma rip his ass! Son better stay clean the fuck from around me because if I see him again I'm take him right off this planet."

$$$$$

Whitey knew he had just dodged a major fuckin bullet. It was obvious that there had been some hidden eyes on him when he attended that business meeting with Avi up in Westchester. Eyes that had peeped his game and were trying to smoke him out. But even before that his former partner must have been pulling recon on his moves and tracking him like a bloodhound.

Whitey drove out of the cemetery and away from Noodles's burial with the full realization that if Noodles had made it back to Brooklyn to sound the alarm, then *his* white ass would have been the one stretched out in that cemetery taking a long nap in the dirt right now.

Whitey had strong-armed Avi into taking him to that meeting so he could size up Don Benny and the rest of the jewelry-ring crew. They had gotten together to discuss the logistics of the heist, and everyone involved had the poker face on, to include the Jewish mobster who was financing the entire operation.

The conversation had gone back and forth for a few, but then tempers started getting heated and all eyes had suddenly aimed full metal jackets straight toward Whitey.

"I'd like to introduce everyone to my new partner," Avi had explained. "His name is Mr. Blanco and he'll be helping me line up a few foreign appraisers in the underground market overseas."

"Wait a hot fuckin minute!" an older black man dressed in a fine suit had stood up and bitched. Avi had introduced him as Sly McFly, and right off the bat Whitey sensed the old dude was gonna be a problem.

"First of all," Sly spit, "who is this Blanco muthafucka and where did he come from? And who said you could bring this new nigga into the goddamn picture? We ain't cutting the cheese in no more slices, asshole. What type of rookie shit is you on right now?"

"Relax, Mr. McFly," Avi had said, keeping his cool. He didn't care what any of them said. Whitey was staying. His sons' lives were on the line and there was no way he was backing off.

"Mr. Blanco is with me and there's no need to worry. Such a valuable stone will require a joint appraisal effort. Besides, there's enough money to go around and I'll be compensating him from my cut. Just relax. Everything's going to be fine."

"Let me put it to you like this so you don't get it confused," Sly McFly stood up and drawled sounding evil as hell. "I don't trust nan'one of y'all muthafuckas up in this bitch! Not you, not you, and," he pointed at Big Benny, "definitely not fuckin *you!* The more dirty fingers you stick in the pot the greater the chance for somebody to fuck it up! It ain't just about the money split either, simple-ass. It's about the fuckin Feds!"

Don Benny held up his hand.

"Alright, that's enough! You came to me asking for financial support and all I care about is getting a return on my investment. I don't give a shit who shares their cut with who. As long as I get my full portion Avi can bring in whoever he thinks might help us. I don't give a fuck who it is."

Sly McFly bucked again. "You don't give a fuck because you ain't got no ass in the game! You ain't putting nothing on the line but money! You gonna be sitting up nice and safe in the big house while us field hands are out there pounding dick on the streets! If we get caught and the po-po starts clicking them metal bracelets down on us you won't be nowhere around!"

Whitey had been amused as fuck as he listened to the back-and-forth banter because there was no way in hell Avi was gonna agree to cut him out. He had him bent too far over the barrel with his dick too deep up his ass for that.

"Here's the deal," the Don said to Avi as he leaned back in his chair and put his feet up on the table. "I'm going to provide the trucks, the explosives, and the firepower for the mission. I'll also finance the airline tickets overseas and the cost for security until the diamond is sold. *That's* our agreement. Now I want to hear what your plan is on obtaining the goods."

"We're going to hit whoever buys the diamond at the auction," Avi said with extreme confidence. "We'll wait until the auction has been completed and then we'll ambush the buyer. We'll strike as soon as they leave the building, and then we'll head straight to the airport with the diamond."

"Um, hold up," Honore stood up and interrupted. "That plan is wack as hell, Avi. I think we need to switch it up because I don't see how that shit can work. What we need to do is hit the damn delivery truck *before* the diamond even gets to the Sotheby. Nobody's gonna be checking for it while it's rolling down the street. *Everybody's* gonna be checking for it once it's inside that damn museum, you feel me? Nah, let's dead that old plan. We gotta steal them suckas when they're on the road and not paying attention. That's how I envision this thang going down."

Whitey could barely stop himself from laughing. The beautiful black chick was acting like a shot-caller today, but the night of that jewelry store hit she had been all hiccups and tears. She had no idea that he had been there that night because he'd worn a mask and she'd never seen his face. But he had damn sure seen hers. He'd seen her face and that beautiful ass she had on her too.

Avi frowned as she spoke, then he nodded in agreement. "Okay. So let's say we intercept the delivery truck before it gets to the museum. We can set up a couple of explosions or heavy-duty concrete trucks to create a roadblock and a diversion to soften the level of security. Yes, that would work perfectly."

He turned to the Jewish boss. "We appreciate your financial contributions and I can assure you that no matter what strategy we employ this endeavor will be a great success. Just leave the details to us, Don Benny. You provide the money and we'll provide the brains."

Sly McFly snorted. "Brains? Sounds like you got a pile of *shit* for brains to me," he muttered while side-eyeing and throwing shade at Whitey.

Whitey stayed cool with a slight smile playing on his lips, but before Avi could respond two security guards busted up in the room shouting that they'd caught somebody taking pictures at the event and they'd just bodied him outside in an alley. Everybody stood up looking surprised as the guards took Benny aside to provide him with more details.

Almost immediately after Don Benny walked off with his security team, Whitey's phone vibrated in his pocket. He retrieved it and turned toward the wall to answer it, and he was surprised as hell to hear Slick on the line hollering something about Noodles getting shot up in Westchester.

"Get over here right now!" Slick barked. "Noodles got *bodied*, man! Somebody popped him somewhere in an alley. He's fuckin *dead!*"

Whitey's stomach sank. Ignoring the other people in the room, he pressed his forehead against the wall and banged that shit one good time. Slick sounded pitiful as fuck on the phone and it didn't take a genius to put two and two together.

"Hurry up," Slick had insisted. "We're on the roof, man. Wherever the fuck you are, get your ass up here ASAP!"

Of course Whitey had broken out from the joint right away. Noodles was his manz and he loved him. But during the drive back to Brooklyn he kicked himself up the ass the whole damn way. How the hell had this happened? Either he was falling asleep on the game, or Noodles had come at him extra hard with his surveillance skills because he had never even felt the gunslinger stalking him. And there was no doubt in Whitey's mind that Noodles had been tracking *him*. Yet Whitey's fuckin Spidey senses had never once tingled. Why?

Whitey had no answer to that question, but he was damn sure grateful. Because if those security guards hadn't popped Noodles then he definitely would have run back and exposed Whitey to the crew. And that kind of betrayal would have earned Whitey an immediate death sentence.

A sentence of death that would have been most especially cruel and unusual, and handed down by the grieving man he'd just stood next to at the cemetery, the chief gunslinger himself. Slick.

Stay on your toes, goddammit, Whitey chastised himself as he peeled outta the cemetery and headed toward his crib. *Stay on your goddamn toes!*

$$$$$

Wild Man was driving through the Bronx with his head spinning with crazy thoughts. As he pushed his black-on-black Benz down the troubled blocks of the bombastical Boogie-Down, all he could think about was his boy Noodles and his untimely demise.

It was hard to wrap his mind around everything that had happened over the past few days. He had just peeped Slick at the cemetery where Noodles was being buried and it hurt him to his heart that his closest road dawgs had turned their backs on him.

As fucked up as they were treating him, nobody was harder on him than he was on himself. Wild Man felt responsible for Noodles's death, and he understood that he had made an unpardonable error at a crucial time.

For the past couple of nights he'd been having some crazy nightmares about his manz. In his dreams, every time he turned into that alley and tried to save Noodles he would get there too late. Wild Man would wake up sweating and panting like a dopefiend. He'd be re-living the grief and horror of seeing his friend's bullet-ridden body stretched out in a back alley in Westchester all over again.

Wild Man wasn't the type of clown to keep feeling sorry for himself. That's because he was usually at peace with whatever decisions he made and he gave a fuck about the consequences. However, this situation was different.

Noodles's death had him in a fucked up state of mind. The only thing he could do was try to find out what his boy was doing up in that fuckin town that was so important when he died.

Wild Man looked down at the small metal device that had fallen out of Noodles's hand when he searched for his pulse on the street. Wild Man had never seen anything like it before, but he had a cousin who worked for Intel and he was the tech king of the entire family.

His cousin would know what he was sitting on, Wild Man was pretty sure of that. Yeah, his cousin was outta town right now, but as soon as he came back Wild Man was gonna have to pay his fam a lil visit so he could find out exactly what Noodles had been creepin on when he went up to Westchester and got himself slumped.

CHAPTER 3

Playin Catch Up

It was late-night in the brazen town of the Bronx. Movement on the dark streets was furtive and sparse. All the straight-laced squares and working folks were locked safely behind closed doors, and the criminal element of the city was coming alive.

Still grieving over Noodles, Slick was lurking in the shadows of a front porch at a house across the street from Bajan Andy's boxing gym. He had gotten word from Jewelz that the Goode Brothers Gang was planning to embark on a killing spree to wipe out certain members of Andy's Bajan crew.

"I heard him talking to one of his brothers and giving him the order to rock Andy out," Jewelz had come back and reported to him. "I was in his bed and he thought I was sleep—"

"Fuck you mean you was in his bed?" Slick had damn near roared.

"Calm down, stupid!" Jewelz snapped. "I got sick and I rode home with him from a restaurant! I left as soon as I was feeling better. I didn't give up no pussy so it was no big deal."

Slick had got jelly as fuck just hearing about Jewelz getting that close to Handgun Goody, but the info she had gathered was vital and now he was overjoyed. This was his big opportunity to tag another Goode Brother, and he was standing by ready to take potshots and pick them niggas off like sitting ducks.

According to the info that Jewelz had given him, Chainsaw Goody and his shooters would be arriving in just a minute. Waiting in the darkness, Slick's tongue started tingling in his mouth like it usually did at times like these. It was a weird sensation that seemed to get his adrenaline flowing and sharpen his focus. It only happened when he went into beast-mode and was about to put a body on his hammer, and Slick loved it.

The last time he was at Bajan Andy's gym was the night that he had laid eyes on Jewelz again for the first time in years. Slick didn't have to split nobody's shit that night but tonight would be much different.

Slick was dressed in all-black and he was standing on somebody's shadow-filled porch just like he lived there. He had a clear line of sight directly to the back door of the gym, which would be the only place that Goody's men could attack from and make a clean getaway.

Slick stood in the shadows watching quietly as Bajan Andy himself stepped outside. He was followed by a tall skinny chick who had her hair at the top of her head in a bun.

Slick could tell the girl was a chickenhead, even before he heard the tinkling sounds of her giggles as she said, "What you want, Mr. Andy, huh?"

As Slick watched, Andy went in his pocket and pulled out his wallet. He tore the girl off some bills and she laughed again, then dropped down to her knees. Slick couldn't hear Andy's zipper going down, but he had a pretty good hunch that it did.

Unaware that he was being scoped out, Andy leaned back against the wall of his gym and put his head back. Moans and groans escaped his lips as the jump-off's head bobbed up and down against his groin. Before long Andy's moans got louder and he cursed and praised the girl's skills as he got his nut.

Suck it baby, suck it. Yeah...suck it just like that...

Gripping his ratchet tight, Slick chuckled under his breath.

How ironic is it that you could be coming and going at the same damn time, Andy? Hur'rup and get ya nut, my nigga. If it's up to Handgun Goody and his hittas it'll be the last one you ever blast off.

As the gym rocked inside with occupants, Slick looked down the quiet block and saw a dark brown Cadillac cut its lights and pull up and park on the corner. Slick knew what time it was. Handgun Goody's dogs had arrived and they were ready to eat.

Finished with her job and standing near the doorway, the young dick-sucker laughed out loud then turned around and went back inside the gym. Andy remained out back. With his balls nice and empty he had lit himself a cigarette and was now looking down at his cell phone and steady puffing.

Slick was hyped and on the ready. He knew that once those niggas rounded the corner the Bajan kingpin would have zero reaction time. His ass would get shot full of holes, and then the gunmen would go inside and light up the rest of the gym.

That was the type of cut-throat message that Goody was trying to send to the Bajans. He wanted them bitches to know that he would roll up and shit in their mouths right in their own fuckin territory.

Slick watched as the five shooters emerged from the old Caddie and popped the trunk. Led by Chainsaw, they were carrying AK 47's and probably some handguns too.

Although Slick had the drop on them from his vantage point, his margin of error was slim. With the kind of weaponry them cats were carrying they could lay down mega bodies without even stepping foot inside Andy's gym. All they had to do was aim and shoot at the building. Those full metal choppa rounds were just that deadly.

Bajan Andy flicked his lit cigarette into the grass and walked back inside his gym just as the shooters closed the Caddy's doors.

It's ShowTime baby.

The shooters moved fast, and as soon as they were past him Slick came down off the porch and fell in behind them. He moved silently and light on his feet with twin Glock 9's in his hands as he trailed them toward the boxing gym. Slick paused and ducked behind a parked car until they got to the back door of Andy's joint, and that's when he started cutting them down.

Handgun sent y'all cocksuckers here to die tonight! He's got one foot in the grave right along with y'all niggas though!

Before the first shooter could reach for the doorknob Slick was already firing at a fast and precise clip.

He let off on Chainsaw first.

Blat! Blat! Blat!

Slick dodged and squeezed. He was close enough not to miss, but he didn't wanna risk them raising the choppas and letting off at him if he was stationary. With fleet feet he moved from side to side ripping at the other four young gunners.

And as the gunshots cracked and echoed in the night air, Slick began counting down a mental clock in his head. By now he was sure Andy could hear what sounded like World War Three going down behind his gym. The cops were about to get called and the block would be getting hot in just a few minutes.

Slick didn't stop shooting until he was sure Goody's gunners were good and dead. Then, as he always did, he made a silent escape and slipped right outta the danger zone.

Slick's actions were sure to spark off some major shit between the two strong street coalitions. He knew the type of backlash that was gonna come down and he welcomed it. Andy would find these stiff flunkies laid out behind his joint and figure the Goode Brothers Gang had gotten bent up on their way in to kill him. The how and the why of it all wouldn't even matter. Only the bloody payback would be relevant.

And that's when shit would really start to get interesting.

CHAPTER 4

Black Hands of Death

All muthafuckin hell was about to break loose in the penthouse apartment above Club Goode Brothers. Blue Willie had just rushed in to deliver the bad news and right off the bat he knew shit wasn't gonna end good for him.

"What the fuck did you say, pussy?" Handgun stepped up on him peering through bulging eyes. He was so mad his breath was coming out in short puffs as a raging pulse jumped up on the side of his head and pounded like a drum.

"What the *fuck* did you just say to me?" Handgun barked on repeat, gripping his heat. "Say it again, goddammit! I *dare* you, nigga! Say it a' fuckin 'gin!"

Blue Willie stood there breathing hard and shaking in his drawers. He had run all the way up the stairs to tell his boss what he had just heard, and now he was wishing he had called his deranged ass up and told him over the phone.

He glanced over at Ice Pick, Cannonball, and their cousin Pistol Preem. They stared back at him with shocked expressions on their faces, but none of them niggas could rescue him from the heat that was coming outta Handgun Goody's eyes.

"I'ma ask you one more goddamn time. What the *fuck* did you just say?" Goody growled low in his chest.

Blue Willie licked his lips and mumbled, "I-I-I said some crazy shit popped off up in the Bronx, boss."

He hunched his shoulders and took a small step backward.

"I don't know if it's legit or not...but some nigga downstairs said Chainsaw and 'nem just got bodied at Bajan Andy's gym."

A blast rang out and Blue Willie dropped to the ground. A bullet hole dotted his chest and his dead eyes rolled up toward the ceiling.

Handgun stared down at the gun in his trembling hand.

"Nooooo," a low, anguished wail came from behind him. Handgun turned

and saw his brother, Ice Pick. He was bent over clutching his stomach like his guts had just gotten ripped out.

"Not *Chain*, what the fuck! *Noooo!*" Ice Pick's face was twisted in pain. "How the fuck could some shit like this happen?" He gripped his gat like he was ready to pop off and shoot somebody too. "Yo, I'm the one that sent him out there," he moaned. "I sent Chain and them boyz out there to *die!*"

"No," Handgun said quietly. "I sent him out there. It was *me*. I green-lit the situation and both of y'all followed my orders."

Ice Pick snatched his phone from his pocket then pressed in some digits and stormcd into thc bathroom. Thc door slammcd loudly behind him and suddenly Goody's knees felt weak and his legs could no longer support him.

He stumbled forward and+ collapsed in a nearby chair as his entire body trembled like an electric current was running through him.

Razorblade, Hammerhead, Chainsaw!

What had started out as a brotherhood of six had been brutally cut down to three. Half of the Goode brother's bloodline had been wiped out in street violence, and as the leader of the family Handgun had no answers. He had no who, why, or how.

"*FUCK!*" Cannonball slammed his fist into the wall and screamed in rage. His huge muscles bulged as he paced the floor with tears falling from his eyes. Him and Chainsaw were close in age and they had been tight. Tighter than tight.

"We sent five of them muthafuckas out there!" Cannonball spit with grief. "*Five!* You mean to tell me Andy's niggas got the drop on all *five* of them? So how many bodies did our set stretch out? How many of them Bajan bitches did Chainsaw bend up before he got hit?"

Handgun shook his head. None of this was making sense to him and he didn't know shit. He just didn't know shit.

"Son!" Ice Pick came outta the bathroom a few moments later and sounded off again. "I just talked to my nigga in the Boogie Down. He said the crime scene looked like a fuckin massacre, yo! None of Andy's bangas got clipped because Chain and the click never even got a chance to run up in the gym! They got caught right at the back door and all five of them got stretched out cold right there."

"Ain't no fuckin way!" Cannonball barked. "Ain't no fuckin way all of our niggas got took without squeezing some shit off too! Somebody picked them off, man. Somebody musta knew they were coming and picked 'em clean the fuck off!"

Preem nodded. "You prolly right! How much you wanna bet them niggas got shot in the back, coward-style? They prolly got sniped from a rooftop up there in the dirty-ass Bronx! Yeah, our cats was dead in the water 'cause somebody set em up!"

"Who coulda knew, nigga?" Ice Pick demanded. "We didn't tell no fuckin body and every last one of them niggas who went knew the code we live by! Nobody coulda fuckin known what we was planning. I just don't see it, man..."

"Either way," Preem prophesized, "Andy knows we came at him now. And he knows somebody came at us, too."

"Nah, fuck that! It was *Andy* from the gate, yo!" Cannonball declared firmly. "That nigga got wind of the party and he set our fam up. I think he's the one that got Raze and Hammer too! I swear to God that Bajan nigga better vest up 'cause when I see him I'ma peel the skin off his fuckin scalp! On the grave of my *three dead brothers*, before the week is over that nigga's gonna see the inside of a morgue!"

Still seated, Handgun Goody closed his eyes and buried his face in his hands. He fought to reject the image of his younger brother's body laid out in the street, bloody and shot full of holes.

As his cousin and brothers argued back and forth and came up with a hundred different scenarios of how Chainsaw coulda met his fate, Handgun sat there and quietly pondered his own fate. He couldn't put his finger on it yet, but something didn't feel right. One minute he had been sitting at the top of the world, and the next minute he had all kinds of low niggas coming after his set.

"Yeah, that's what the fuck I'm talking about," Ice Pick said loudly as he dapped Cannonball out. "Ay, after we pay our respects and bury our soldiers that nigga Andy is a dub. We doing that shit our damn selves too. No flunkies, no soldiers, no nothing. Only ones who gon' know about this shit is us right here in this fuckin room! Niggas must think shit is sweet. It's time to get our hands nice and dirty again."

Handgun sat there listening quietly. His mind raced in a thousand different directions as he tried to wrap his head around shit. He was feeling what his brothers and cousin said, but his gut wasn't screaming out Andy's name. He just wasn't convinced the Bajan drug man was responsible this time.

One thing was clear though. It was time to go to war. It was time to throw all his weight behind digging out his enemy and making that fuck-boy pay. Big Haz had once told him it was better to be feared than respected. *Goody-Goody, always hoody*. Well, it was time to put the fear of Goody back in the streets.

"Yo," Cannonball suddenly stopped ranting about slaughtering the entire borough of the Bronx and barked, "Who's gonna tell Mama?"

The room fell silent. Handgun let out a deep sigh and then pulled himself to his feet and stood up like a man.

"Me," he said, his whole body filled with guilt and dread. "I'll tell her."

CHAPTER 5

Painful Lessons

Slick was crouched down on the rooftop of a drug store that was located right next to Carter's Funeral Home. He had a bird's eye view of the massive procession of dope-boys, street thugs, and common killers as they filed out the doors and gathered around the hearse.

Shiny black stretch limos lined the street as the mourners stood around talking quietly after paying their respects to young Chainsaw Goody, who had been shot dead behind a boxing gym in the Bronx.

Slick was pretty sure the Feds were posted up somewhere nearby watching the whole scene too. With so many criminals gathered together from all across the five boroughs it was a prime opportunity for law enforcement to check shit out and see who was associating with who.

Tension was high down on the street and the energy was wild. Wannabe gangsters and willing side-bitches lined the sidewalks and observed with sullen looks. Suddenly the doors opened and six pallbearers came out carrying a shiny white casket. The mourning family followed, boo-hooing and walking slow behind their deceased loved one.

Slick's eyes narrowed as he saw a familiar face mixed in with the family. He knew her like the back of his hand and he could spot her fineness anywhere. She had on some large shades that covered part of her face and her hair looked real different, but it was her.

Jewelz.

As usual she was on the job and playing her role to perfection. She was shuffling along with the rest of the mourners who were slow-walking Chainsaw Goody to his final car ride. Slick noted how the people in the crowd were paying extremely close attention to the family, but it wasn't because of Chainsaw or Jewelz.

All eyes were on the head nigga in charge. Handgun Goody. He was holding tightly to Jewelz's hand and the poker face that thugs like him spent their whole life perfecting and mastering was long gone. Consumed with grief, that tough outer-shell of his was cracked like an egg and his gangsta was nowhere to be found as the tears ran down his face and he wept like a little boy who had just lost his momma.

Slick knew that look all too well. But that nigga got not one drop of sympathy from him because he had *been* that lost little boy with no momma to be found. If anything, Goody needed to buck the fuck up because it was a shame to see a kingpin so broken down and shattered and displaying emotional weakness in the hood like that.

Yeah, Slick thought, nodding his head in satisfaction. The chickens were definitely coming home to roost for the Goode Brothers Gang. Especially for Handgun. His soldiers getting knocked off had hurt him pretty bad, but his flesh and blood brothers getting touched was about to destroy him.

Slick grunted in satisfaction. He liked seeing that nigga drowning in a sea of pain and misery. His plan to crush Goody's heart by destroying his family before he dusted him off, was working to perfection.

Slick watched as a couple of Handgun's tight-knit soldiers rushed over to his side and tried to calm him down. But Goody was racked with sorrow and beyond their help. Shrugging Jewelz off, he balled his fists up tightly as sweat dripped from his face. That nigga looked wild and beastly as he started pacing back and forth in his expensive suit, raging and cursing and crying for the entire hood to see.

Pushing his way toward the curb, he jumped up on the hood of a parked limousine and barked loud enough for the whole neighborhood to hear him.

"Yo, I'm telling y'all niggas right muthafuckin *now!*" Goody roared to the crowd of onlookers. "One of y'all bitch-made cornballs standing out here knows who murked my little brother! One of y'all niggas prolly *did it!* And when I find out who the fuck it is, there won't be no cop, no district fuckin attorney, no mayor, or no muthafuckin *President* who can stop me from murdering everybody you ever loved in your life, nigga! That's my word, nigga!" he screamed hysterically. "You hear me? Whoever you is, I'm taking everybody you ever loved in *ya bitch-ass life!*"

Up on the rooftop Slick chuckled as a hush fell over the large crowd. You could hear a pin drop as Goody glared at the crowd with rage and venom rushing outta his pores. The streets now had the word. Straight from the horse's mouth. Handgun Goody was going on a killing spree.

Suddenly a strong female voice cut through the crowd. It was filled with quiet authority.

"Boy, get your tail down from that car and quit all that yelling," commanded an elderly woman who was dressed in all white from head to toe.

She pushed her way out of the funeral parlor like she was gonna whip Goody's ass with an extension cord.

"And hush up with all them nasty words coming outta your mouth and have some respect for the dead!"

The sound of her voice instantly killed Goody's rage. His head whipped around toward her and he jumped down off of the limo and rushed to her side.

"*Mama,*" Goody blurted out as Ice Pick and Cannonball jetted over too and tried to help him lead the woman over to a sleek stretch limo that was parked right behind the hearse.

But the old lady wasn't having it. She shook her head and pushed them all away, and the thick crowd parted like the Red Sea as she took off storming down the block all by herself.

Mama? Slick thought.

Chilling up on the rooftop he followed the old woman with his eyes. She walked to the corner and sat down on a bench at a bus stop. Her shoulders shook a little bit like she mighta been crying, and when she dabbed at her eyes with a tissue Slick knew that she definitely was.

And that's when it hit Slick.

Somebody had fuckin lied. He had asked Jewelz how the hit on Ms. Goode had gone down and he could still hear her voice echoing in his ear:

It went great. I took care of business. I gave that old lady exactly what she deserved.

He peered at the old woman sitting on the bench under the plastic enclosure and then looked back at the Goode Brothers as they stood around on the sidewalk looking helplessly toward the bus stop.

Slick stared over at Jewelz again, then looked back at the old lady.

Yeah, *Ms. Goode.* Handgun's momma. If her ass was sitting at that bus stop alive and breathing, then that meant Jewelz had lied. She damn sure didn't do what the fuck she said she did the night she went to that old lady's apartment to smoke her.

I gave her exactly what she deserved, is what Jewelz had told him, but the evidence of that lie was sitting right there at that damn bus stop.

Fuck was up with that? *Da fuck was going on?*

CHAPTER 6

Time to Eat

The New York Diamond and Jewelry Exchange was a hopping joint and customers stayed coming and going all day long.

Wild Man was dressed to impress and wearing his best "Innocent Asian" face as he approached a fly black chick standing at the front counter. He gazed at her hungrily because he was on a bitch-hunt and he was eager to bite some prey.

"I'm looking for Honore Morales," he said and flashed the girl a handsome smile.

"Ummmm," the chick said slowly. Her curious gaze crawled all over the bouquet of bright, colorful flowers that Wild Man was holding in his hands. "You looking for Honore? Ummmm, she ain't here right now but can I help you with something?"

Wild Man glanced at the gold nametag pinned to the girl's bright yellow shirt. It said Rayven Jones and he couldn't help but notice that she had some big old chocolate titties under that shirt and the outline of her nipples were poking out real nice.

"No," he declined politely. "That's okay I'll come back later.

"Wait, hold up," the girl said, her eyeballs sliding all over him like she was a buzzard about to jump on a fresh piece of meat.

This bitch is thirsty, Wild Man thought with a chuckle. *Real thirsty.*

"Umm, I think Honore might be taking her lunch break right now. Yeah, that's where she is. Them flowers are real pretty but is this visit business-related? Can I take a message or something? What's your name? Who should I tell her came by?"

The muthafuckin boogeyman, Wild Man thought coldly.

"Just tell her an old friend is trying to catch up with her. She'll know who

I am."

But Ratchet Raven wasn't about to give up that easy.

"Okay, cool, I'll tell her." She nodded at the flowers. "You wanna leave those with me and I'll make sure to give them to her for you?"

"Nah. Do you know what time she'll be back? I wanna give them to her myself."

"*Welllll,*" the glamorous hood chick drawled, and then suddenly something changed about her eyes and her voice grew a whole lot louder.

"Ummm...see, I don't usually be telling people's business but I don't think *Honore* is coming back today! Matter fact, I think *Honore* got sick right before lunch and she probably won't be nowhere near here for the rest of the day!"

Wild Man heard the warning in her voice and knew what time it was. He turned around and followed the path of the chick's eyes and saw the Queen of Diamonds herself as she paused to say something to an older white lady and then continued switching her sexy hips across the large room.

He gave Raven a killer smirk and turned away.

"Hold up, Mister!" she yelled at his back. "Yo Mister! Hold up!"

Wild Man igged that ass as he walked right up on that bitch Honore and shoved the bouquet of flowers in her face and gripped her by the neck at the same time.

"Whattup, Queen?" he said, enjoying the look of shock and fear that jumped into her pretty eyes. "Why you dip out on me the other night? All that creaming you did on my sheets and I still wasn't smashing it good enough for you?"

Honore opened her mouth to scream and Wild Man checked her with his cruel laugh.

"Ah-ah-*ahhh*," he whispered as her eyes bulged toward the elderly security guard. "I wouldn't do that shit if I was you. Trust me, I'll have your neck snapped in three pieces before that old bastard can fart and get up off his ass."

"Get the fuck off me!" she gasped. Her eyes darted left and right seeking help. "What the fuck is wrong with you!"

Wild Man chuckled. "Nah, what the fuck is wrong with *you,* Miss Queen of Diamonds? What was in that red briefcase you dropped off at the jewelry joint that night?"

"*What?* I didn't drop off no red briefcase!"

He gripped her throat tighter.

"You lying bitch!"

"Get the fuck off! How the hell did you find me?" she squeaked.

Wild Man shrugged. "I followed my nose and sniffed your stank ass out."

"What do you want? Why you choking me?"

"You sent that weak nigga to my crib the other night to fade me, didn't you!"

Honore squinched her face up. "*What?*" she whispered shaking her head wildly. "What the hell are you talking about? No I didn't! I ain't send nobody nowhere!"

"Bitch stop lying! Your shit is wide open! You sent that lil punk-ass nigga to my crib and I poked a bunch of holes in his ass!"

"Boy what the hell is you talking about! I swear to God I didn't send nobody to your house!"

"So why you run off then, huh?"

"You ran off *first,* fuck you mean!" Honore hissed. "You snuck off to go bone some other *bitch* as soon as I started snoring! I woke up and your doggish ass was gone! You left me in there by myself!"

"That's because a coward with a banga was coming in my window!"

"Yeah, right! Save that old bullshit for somebody else! You was out there swinging that *dick!* Get the fuck offa me!"

Wild Man's eyes hardened and narrowed into little slits as he gripped her up and clenched her neck even harder. "Don't fuck with me," he warned. "I'll push your shit back right up against this wall. Fuck around and find out."

"W-why you gotta bring this shit to my damn job?" Tears came to her eyes as Honore realized he was up on her game. "What the hell do you *want?*"

Wild Man's grin grew even wider.

"I want what was in that red briefcase, sexy mama. Matter fact, I want a piece of every muthafuckin criminal thing you got going on, pretty lady. I want *in.*"

$$$$$

Cucci Momma was all eyeballs, corneas, irises, and pupils as the fine Asian guy in the business suit stood yoking Honore up against the wall in the midst of the busy showroom.

His left arm was wrapped completely around Honore's shoulders and the huge bouquet of flowers he gripped hid the fact that his other hand was choking the shit outta her cousin's neck.

The Asian was grinning his ass off. He had run up on Honore so smooth and breezy it looked like he was her loving bae and about to tongue her down.

"*What the fugg is that nigga doing pawing Honore up like that?*" Cucci muttered under her breath as she peered at the pair. Her family loyalty had her about to rush up on that bastard and dig the edge of a stapler into the back of his head. But her conniving instincts checked her and told her to chill right where she was so she could watch and learn.

The two of them exchanged a bunch of words and Honore looked real red in the face when ol' boy finally let her loose and stepped away. Cucci knew something was up for real when he didn't even give her the flowers he had brought with him. Instead, he waited until Honore nodded her head and took off walking real fast down the hall, then he headed toward the exit and dumped the flowers in the garbage can on his way out the door.

"Uh-uh," Cucci shook her head. If she wasn't by herself at the reception desk she woulda sprinted her nosey ass behind Honore like a track star. "I know I ain't the only one who peeped that shit."

But as she glanced around the busy showroom where every member of the staff was working with a customer and doing their own thing, she knew she was.

She smirked and drummed her long, gel-baked nails on the marble counter in mad irritation. You couldn't trust no damn body these days. Not only was Honore still holding out on her, Cucci had called that FBI hotline again and screamed on them muthafuckas for shooting up the whole damn beauty parlor the night they came gunning for her cousin's head.

"Y'all bitches is some slow-ass *amateurs!*" she had blasted hard on the bastard who answered the phone. Cucci wanted that moolah but she felt guilty as fuck behind getting her cousin shot. "All I wanted was the reward money, stupid! Y'all was supposed to lock her up, not shoot her in the ass!"

The agent on the line had the nerve to act bored and front her off like he didn't know what she was talking about. He denied knowing anything about the tip she called in *or* the $100,000 reward money she was due, and he told her she could come into the office in person if she wanted to file a complaint.

Cucci wasn't stupid enough to walk up in no government building telling no crazy stories. This was the Corrupted States of America and wasn't no telling what them snakes woulda done to her if they got her behind closed doors. Prolly woulda made her disappear into the solitary guts of some secret underground torture chamber or some shit.

But not trusting the FBI was one thing, and not trusting her own cousin was something else. Yeah, something fishy was up with that Asian dude and Honore, and as soon as somebody came to take over at the reception desk Cucci Momma was gonna find out what it was!

$$$$$

Jewelz couldn't even front. It was the fourth time she'd been up in Handgun Goody's crib and she was feeling comfortable as fuck. Her body was relaxed, and for once her mind was completely mellow. Laid out across Handgun Goody's bed, she was listening to The Weekend's new jam as she puffed on the best purp in New York City.

Jewelz toked and exhaled again. She enjoyed the way the stress left her body as the cloud of smoke drifted up to the ceiling. Since she wasn't going to the hospital to undergo her chemo treatments, this was the best form of therapy for her weakened body. The combination of smooth music and good weed put her at ease, and she was totally relaxed and at peace as she lay in the center of Goody's bed like prey in the middle of a spider's web.

The sensation of her warm skin up against the cool designer sheets of the very nigga she planned on eradicating felt exhilarating to Jewelz. It gave her such a rush.

Some people used love to ignite their inner fire, some used hate and anger.

But for Jewelz it was vengeance that got her going. It burned hot way down in the pit of her soul. It's what compelled her to stick to the script instead of simply decapitating Goody's fucking head right off his shoulders as he lay sleeping beside her at night.

But even though she kept it real with herself regarding her intentions, Jewelz just couldn't deny the way Handgun Goody made her feel inside. There were parts of her heart that were conflicted as fuck as she fought to separate the sins of Dirty Mike from the virtues of Handgun Goody. Yeah, the charming drug kingpin mighta been a G'd up beast of a nigga in the streets, but here, behind closed doors, Goody was a loving bae and he treated her like nothing less than a queen.

They had spent a long night of hot sex together the night before, and Jewelz was so exhausted by the time the sun came up and Goody got ready to head out that he had told her to just stay in bed and hold his crib down until he came back later that night. He had some important bizz to handle with his brothers he said, and Jewelz instinctively knew that whatever his business was, it was related to his brother Chainsaw's murder.

Jewelz had been standing right by Goody's side when they buried Chainsaw, and the way that nigga had sniveled and carried on like a lil bitch was a sight to behold. Matter fact, the devastation that she'd seen on Goody's face was exactly what her and Slick had been hoping for. It had been confirmation that they had hit that nigga dead in his heart, which made the job Jewelz was doing truly worthwhile.

Goody had cried all over her titties when they got home after the funeral as she held him in her arms and stroked his face with soothing words. And when he reached down and rubbed her ass, then closed his warm lips down on her nipple and started flicking it with his tongue, Jewelz had given up the ass and rode his dick like she was an innocent little angel.

Today she had spent the whole day sleeping and lounging around in Goody's bedroom. A few of his dick boys were out there in the living room keeping lookout, so Jewelz couldn't just roam around and search the joint like she wanted to.

By nightfall she had decided to get lifted again, and she was lost in the haze of her thoughts when the bedroom door swung open so fast she almost dropped her lit blunt down on the bed.

It was Handgun, dressed in all-black and bulked up with what Jewelz recognized as a bulletproof vest under his hoodie. He looked at her with a cold stare as he stood there with a strong grip on his .40 cal.

"Hey, what's going on," Jewelz asked as she sat up and set the blunt in an ashtray. Goody's face looked like cold death and a rush of fear suddenly surged through her. Dressed in a wife-beater and a thong, she was strapless and she didn't know what kinda insane shit was on this nigga's brain. He looked like he was in a zone, the same way her Zip 'em up Crew members looked after they had just dropped a couple of bodies.

"What's wrong," Jewelz asked again, licking her lips nervously. "You 'bout to clap at me or something?"

Goody's demeanor changed and his whole body relaxed as he strode over to the bed and sat down beside her.

"Nah, baby. Never. I could never do you no harm. I'm just feeling real good right now, that's all," Goody said. His eyes looked wild and his chest heaved up and down. He tossed his gun down on the bed next to Jewelz. Then he took off his gloves and his hoodie and said, "Shit got real out there tonight. I ain't been on this kind of high in a long, long time."

Jewelz knew that look in his eye and the feeling he was describing very well. Not only could she smell it on him, she could damn near taste it. She knew without a doubt what Goody had been doing out there in them streets. The only thing she didn't know was exactly who he had smoked. A part of her didn't even wanna know.

"I guess them niggas thought I had a pussy between my legs," Handgun said as he turned to look at Jewelz.

She forced a puzzled look onto her face and he nodded like he understood her confusion.

"Don't worry. It should be on the news in a minute and you'll see what I'm talking about. We just put in work and made a movie outta every last one of them bitch-ass niggas. Grab that remote baby. I want you see how me and my hittas get down."

Jewelz tossed him the remote and Goody clicked on the huge flat screen television. He turned to the local news where they were busy reporting on a recent carnage.

"...Ten people were murdered in a bloodbath tonight that spanned at least two boroughs. Six men and four women were found shot to death in what looks to be two closely-related gangland killings. The dead were all alleged members of a drug and prostitution ring led by Anderson Archer, better known in the underworld circles as Bajan Andy. Police are canvassing the area in an attempt to locate any witnesses who can provide information related to the crime. No arrests have been made yet in connection with the murders..."

"C'mere, girl," Goody said as he leaned over and pushed Jewelz down on her back. He was so excited from his kill that his dick was hard as hell and his rough hands roamed all over her curves.

Goody got undressed and knelt on the bed with his dick pointing straight at her. He lifted the edge of her wife-beater and then pulled that shit completely over her head.

Jewelz's bouncing brown beauties leaped free and jiggled up and down as the cool air hardened her nipples. Hooking his hands through the side of her thong, Goody ripped the fabric and tore that shit straight off.

Jewelz understood his frenzied desire. She had no choice but to play along with the program, and when he placed his strong thigh between her legs and spread them wide apart she didn't resist.

Goody shoved his dick up in her guts dry.

Jewelz winced, and bit her lip to keep from hollering. Handgun plunged his joint in and out of her, stroking her down with a beastly fury. Jewelz was yelping and scooting up toward the headboard trying to get away from his violent thrusts, and when he realized that her cries were coming from pain, he immediately stopped and pulled out.

"Damn, I'm sorry, Jewelz. I ain't mean to hurt you, baby. You know I would never do nothing to hurt you girl..."

Goody kissed her lips and trailed over to her neck. His fingers found her clit and he massaged it slowly as he licked her collarbone and tongued her earlobe.

Jewelz's nipples were pointing straight at the ceiling and Goody lowered his head and pulled one between his lips and gently sucked it. That shit felt good and Jewelz moaned a little bit. Taking this as a positive sign, Goody's hands got to roaming again. He slid down her brown body and kissed a trail down her stomach. He paused at all the old scars that she told him had come from female troubles, then he kissed them tenderly and lowered his head and licked out her pussy until she was nice and wet.

Licking her juice from his lips, he guided his hard dick to her wet slit and entered her properly this time. Slowly, he inched his hard dick forward until it was jammed up in her and packing her tunnel, and then he rotated his hips and got to fucking her again.

"Is that better, baby?" he whispered as he grinded up in her.

Jewelz nodded and wrapped her long legs tightly around his waist. "Yeah. Much better."

"You know I luh you right?" Goody muttered as his swinging balls slapped her ass and he pounded his rock hard meat deep up inside her. "This some real good pussy, bae. You know I luh you girl..."

Jewelz had been dying to hear those words coming out of a man's mouth for the longest time, and even though she knew it was just Goody's balls talking, it still felt good to hear it. Warning herself to ignore his lil pillow talk, Jewelz arched her back and squeezed him between her thighs as she submitted to his frantic humps and thrusts.

Goody was consumed with the need to get him a nut, but staring over his shoulder at the television screen, Jewelz wasn't really thinking about sex at all. She was replaying that news broadcast over and over in her mind, and it caused her to push back a big lump that had suddenly risen in her throat.

Andy wasn't the best or the worst crook that Jewelz had ever known, but he had been real cool with her. Him and Haitian Tisha had treated her decently when she started working for them, and they made sure that she was straight at all times.

And now, because of her, Andy and his whole squad had been laid out over some shit they didn't even do. It could all be charged to the cut-throat game they all played, but deep inside it still made Jewelz feel some kinda way.

CHAPTER 7

Never Trust A Grimy Ass New Yorker

It was early Saturday afternoon on Fordham Road, and Wild Man was parked on a busy street across from a popular dress shop. Young and old, male and female, people of all sorts walked up and down the streets in both directions.

Fordham Road was the Bronx's version of Brooklyn's Pitkin Avenue. There was an array of bustling stores that offered cheap items such as clothes, shoes, electronics, and of course lots of pizza parlors, hero shops, Chinese restaurants, and other random storefront places to eat.

Wild Man had been waiting on a special phone call ever since he had yoked Honore up at her job, and he was on a big one right now. That slick bitch had ducked out on him, and no matter how many times he hit her digits he came up dry.

So he had switched up his tactics. Instead of hunting for Honore, he had put a tracker on somebody that he was sure would lead him straight to her. And right now Wild Man had his eye trained on a sleek white Bentley that was being driven by a fat black man who looked like King Kong.

Wild Man cruised behind the stylish whip as it slid into a parking spot across from the Korean-owned dress shop. An older gentlemen with light skin and a long wavy ponytail sat on the passenger side of the front seat, and a beautiful woman rode in the back.

The chick was Honore, and Wild Man was itchin to snatch her up by her scheming neck again. He had finally managed to get with his tech-head cousin Phu who worked for Intel. His cuzzo had informed Wild Man that the device Noodles had been carrying was actually a high-tech video camera, and after downloading the film Wild Man saw some shit that took him completely by surprise.

As he watched the footage play out on his cousin's monitor he saw a large group of people participating in some sort of celebration. As Wild Man checked out who was clicked up with who, it wasn't long before the answers to all his questions fell right in place.

No wonder Noodles had gone up to Westchester on a find-and-destroy recon mission! No wonder his scoob had been so fuckin careful with his suspicions that he wanted to go in alone and get the evidence first, before telling anybody else about it.

Noodles had been so smart and so fuckin loyal that he had gotten enough proof on tape to send the Zip 'em up Crew's whole house of cards tumbling down.

All Wild Man could do was shake his fuckin head as he watched what was going down on the screen. Because the video that Noodles had shot on the day he died was proof that Honore's scandalous ass was into some shit that was even deeper than what he had suspected.

Noodles's video had shed light on the fact that scandalous Honore and the vicious old head Sly McFly were clicked up tight together, but it also proved that their boy Whitey was dirty as fuck too. And somehow Honore was deep in the bed with him. Grinding her ass under the covers with that rat just like a bitch in heat.

Wild Man knew there would be plenty of time to chop off Whitey's head, so right now he killed his engine and just sat and watched the car that was parked in front of him. Minutes later the older cat hopped outta the front passenger seat of the Bentley and pimp-walked around to the back passenger door.

He paused for a few, surveying the scene, and when he was satisfied that everything was legit he opened the door and Honore got outta the back seat looking immaculate as fuck.

Wild Man took a moment to admire her sexiness as she walked into the dress shop. She was a dime piece for real. The first thing that came to his mind was "project princess." But Honore was business savvy too, and you could tell she was about her bread. He already knew she wasn't just a pretty face who fucked niggas for an outfit and some sneaker money. And she wasn't the type of chick to wait around for a nigga to make no moves for her neither. Honore was a get-money bitch who had a deadly game on her. She was street and sweet all in one grimy, dangerous package.

Sliding on his Ray Bans, Wild Man got out and sat on the hood of his car. He recognized the older guy she was with right off the bat. He could tell dude was a street nigga by the way he had looked in all directions before he let Honore get out the car. It was a different type of wariness than a bodyguard. The old head moved like a hood veteran. As if he was used to walking the front line.

"Yeah, OG," Wild Man muttered under his breath. "Look like you ain't new to this, you true to this. What role do you play in Honore's life, homey? She swinging you around by your old nuts too?"

While Honore went inside the dress store to shop, the older cat waited outside the car with his arms crossed and alert. Just like the last time they had crossed paths, the old head was immaculately dressed in an expensive suit and he gave off a vibe that had a lotta swag and a killer's confidence.

But the last time they'd met it was under much different circumstances, and Wild Man felt this was a prime opportunity to re-introduce himself.

Wild Man moved his gun from his hip to the small of his back to conceal it better. If he had to bang on somebody it wouldn't be difficult for him to get to it. As usual he had a hawk on him too. Just in case he would rather cut a nigga to the bone first. Ready to go dumb, he proceeded to walk over to the tall cat they called Sly McFly doing a lil New York diddy-bop pimp-walk of his own.

"Ayo, w'sup, Slim! Yo bruh, I couldn't help but notice the sexy chocolate queen that just hopped outta ya ride. Is that your daughter, yo?" Wild Man said with as much animation and excitement that he could muster.

Sly McFly stayed cool as a fan. He acted like he had never seen Wild Man before. Like he had never disrespected his fam Shin in that Chinese restaurant or threatened his fuckin life. Matter fact, the slim-built light-skinned Snoop Dog-looking nigga wasn't really tryna acknowledge Wild Man's existence at all.

That didn't discourage him though. Wild Man kept right on playing the role of a clown-ass corn-ball thirsty nigga, because he was sure the old man wouldn't put up with it for long.

"No disrespect home-slice, but I wanna slide on that! Can you put in a good word for me?"

Ignoring dude's silence, Wild Man kept right on trolling him. "Ay, did you see that donk-donk fat-back she got on her? She bad as a muthafucka, OG! Damn, nigga! I gots to have me summa that!" Wild Man laughed hard as shit until the old head finally had enough.

"Listen here you fried-rice-face lil shrimp," the old head spoke in an icy tone just above a whisper as he removed his Gucci shades and peered coldly into Wild Man's eyes. "I highly suggest you get the fuck outta my way and keep it moving. Step the fuck off before I decide to break your fucking neck out here, you sucka-ass nigga."

Game recognized game and Sly had the unmistakable look of a seasoned killer in his eyes. Madness mixed with cunning radiated off him in waves, and his jaw twitched like he was two steps away from committing a murder.

"Yeah, my nigga," Wild Man grinned, dropping his jive act and loving the animal reaction he had provoked in the old man. "Ga'head. Show your true shit. A killer like you can only hold back for so long. Trust me, I know how hard it is."

They glared at each other for a moment having a silent conversation. Both men, young and old, probed for a sign of fear or weakness that could be exploited. It wasn't a mean mug competition by any means, because a wolf knew when he was in the presence of another wolf.

Their unspoken communication was a vital trait that all true goons possessed, and it was how they assessed the pending threat level. And right now Sly

McFly was telling Wild Man to get ready for the grave.

Wild Man was good with that. Wasn't no family-owned Chinese restaurant out here on these streets. Wasn't no Uncle Shin and his sick wife standing between them now. Wasn't no bullet-proof glass, neither. His silent gaze said if the old head wanted any problems then they could bang to the death right there on the spot.

"Nigga you must not know who the fuck I be," Sly finally growled under his breath.

"You must not know 'bout me neither so allow me to remind you, playa. My name is Wild Man, and I'm about to take yo bitch, Honore."

"*Wild Man*," Sly spit with mad amusement. "You wanna step to a chick like Honore with a bitch-ass name like that? I ain't never heard of you little nigga. Y'all young cats be having the toughest names nowadays and be the pussiest niggas in the hood. Who gave you that bullshit name? Ya fortune cookie-eating mama?"

Wild Man grinned. "Naw, you not gonna hear my name ringing in the streets, old man. That's not good for the type of business I'm involved in, nah'mean? But I promise if you make another reference about my mother I'll show you just how accurate my name is and how well I hold it down out here in these streets," Wild Man stunted as he postured himself to pop off if Sly tested his word.

"What the hell are y'all two doing out here acting all extra and shit?" a familiar voice spoke from behind Wild Man.

Honore had just come out of the dress shop and she could tell right off the bat that some stupid shit was about to pop off.

"Wild Man?" her pretty face looked annoyed. "What you doing up here in the Bronx?"

Wild Man chuckled. "What? You thought you was outta range and safe up here? I'm well-connected in the Boogie Down too, baby. Ain't nowhere in the whole Empire State for you to hide from me. C'mere. Let's take a lil walk so I can holla at you right quick."

"Honore don't you move one fuckin muscle," Sly spit, hefting his killer cane in his grip. "I was just about to put the paws on his ugly yellow ass."

Honore shrugged it off. "Relax, Sly. It's cool."

She turned to Wild Man with a smirk on her face and her hand perched on her hip. "First you roll up at my job showing your ass, and now you lurking like a stalker while I'm out shopping. The fuck is you doing, following me?"

Wild Man grinned. "Hell yeah I'm following you! We made a deal, lil mama. Remember? You promised to put me on but you ain't answering your phone or holding up your end of the bargain, sweetheart. I mean, you got a real good head game going but your wet-neck ain't *that* poppin for me to just roll over and let you play me, nah'm saying?"

Wild Man chuckled loudly as he ignored the heat waves coming off Sly McFly.

"Shut the fuck up, chatty patty!" Honore snapped, snatching him by his arm before he could let any more skeleton bones fall outta his mouth. This nigga was half-crazy. He didn't have to blow her spot up like that! Sly didn't need to know she had fucked with this meatball and sucked his damn dick! She was so embarrassed she couldn't even look her godfather in the eye. "Come on," she yanked Wild Man's sleeve. "Let's walk up the block."

"You ain't going nowhere by ya'self with this clown," Sly objected as he leaned forward and thrust his cane in between Wild Man and Honore.

"He's good, Sly," Honore held up her hand and smiled. "I promise he is. Don't worry. We just gonna take a little walk up the street and come right back. He's stupid as hell, but he's good."

$$$$$

"Yo, is that antique-looking nigga your pops, your uncle, or your sugar daddy?" Wild Man joked as him and Honore walked slowly up the block.

"Don't worry about who he is!" Honore said hotly. "That's my peoples so cut it the fuck out and say what you gotta say because I got shit to do."

Wild Man had shit to do too so he didn't beat around the bush.

"Like I told you that day at your job, I want in," Wild Man said, displaying no emotion as they walked down crowded Fordham. "Don't try to front me off this time neither because I'm dead fuckin serious. Whatever kind of down-low and underhanded filthy shit you got going on, I want in on it."

"You don't know shit about me or what I got going on."

"I know you ain't no fucking college student, my Queen," Wild Man said with every bit of certainty.

Honore kept her cool and didn't so much as break her stride. She didn't deviate from her game face at all because she didn't know exactly what kind of evidence Wild Man had on her.

"I don't know what the hell you're talking about. I *am* a student. I'm a student of the game and I hustle for minez just like everybody else. But what about you? You ain't shit but a stick-up kid. Niggas like you audition everyday to be morgue-meat and they come a dime a dozen," Honore shot back.

"Baby be for real. You know I'm way more ambitious than a stick-up kid, and I know you gives a fuck about reading, writing, and basic biology. I peeped that security tape, pretty lady. You know, the one from the jewelry store that night where you tossed the red briefcase to the old man right before we banged on him?"

Wild Man chuckled inside. Yeah, the Zip 'em up Crew had hit the wrong target that night, but this Queen of Diamonds bitch didn't even know somebody had put a hit out on her stupid ass! Nah, not one fuckin hit. *Two!*

Honore didn't even bat an eyelash. If Sly McFly was the one who had taught her about this street shit then he did a hell of a good job. She kept her composure very well. That was a vital skill the most men couldn't even master.

"A'ight," she twisted her lips and said. "I'll put you down. I had a diamond stashed in that red briefcase. A real big one. Help me find it and I'll split the profits with you fifty-fifty."

"How much was that shit worth?"

"Five million."

Wild Man whistled. "Is that right? So what about that other deal? How much is that jawn worth?"

"*What* other deal?"

"That scheme y'all was cooking up at that community center in Westchester."

Honore stumbled. "Westchester? I ain't been up in no Westchester!"

"Fraud bitch! My dude filmed you, sweetie. Once again I peeped ya ass right on camera! How long you been getting down with that dirty white dude?"

"White dude? I don't even know that cracker!"

"Yeah, a'ight," Wild Man said, backing off and chilling. "Ay, I ain't here to drop no dimes or fuck up your plans or nothin," he assured her. "And I ain't knockin your hustle neither. A nigga just wanna get down with you and get his foot in the door, nah'm sayin?"

"No," Honore snapped as she regained her composure and shimmied beside him looking like a sweet lemon Italian icee. "I don't know what the hell you're saying."

"I'm saying, unless I get a slice of that cheesy pizza the Feds are gonna get a copy of that security tape with your name on it. And just in case you thinking about doing shit funny-style, if anything happens to me then my fam is gonna make sure that tape is streamed to the Feds within an hour."

Honore poked out her lip and cut her pretty eyes at him. "How much you trying to get?"

"Same amount you getting."

"Nigga you just greedy. Straight greedy."

"I ain't greedy, baby. I'm willing to work for minez. Look at it like this. I'm Asian, so that means I'm good with numbers. I wanna be your business partner. I think me and you can make some power moves together."

Honore rolled her eyes. "I already got a partner. I got a few of them. And Asians ain't special. Niggas and white folks know how to count past ten too. We moving powerful shit just fine without you."

"You ever been to Rikers?" Wild Man asked quietly. "I hear Rosie gets real crowded this time of year."

"Ain't nobody scared of Rosie!"

"You ever did time in a Fed joint? Eighty-five percent of twenty years is a real long time, baby."

Honore shut up on that one and Wild Man knew he had her by the pussy hairs. This chick was wrapped up in some big-time shit, and if she was in as deep as he thought she was, then the last thing she wanted to do was get hauled off to the Rock.

Wild Man had her squeezed so tight he almost felt sorry for her. It was hard not to be blinded by her beautiful exterior, and he could see how she could have a man breaking his own rules. He saw how weak she had gotten his homeboy Slick, but Wild Man wasn't going out like that. Just because he had slept with her didn't mean he was stupid enough to sleep *on* her. Hell, naw. He was an assassin and he had some very deadly tools in his arsenal. But he knew the deadliest weapon of them all was pussy. Better men than him had fallen victim to that sweet, delicious fruit. It could bring an entire dynasty trembling to its knees.

Naw, he was nothing like that weak bitch Slick. Some cats were born to be slaves to the drawers, and some cats were born to pimp them drawers out. In the words of Jada Kiss, Wild Man thought, *I'd rather die from a bullet than a nasty bitch!*

"You gonna 'fess up or what, Queen?"

Honore was steady grilling him. "Okay! So you seen me on a tape!"

Wild Man laughed. "No, I seen you on *two* tapes. *Two* tapes, shorty!"

"So what!" she flicked him off. "You already knew I was at the jewelry store that night anyway."

"But I didn't know you was a jewelry *thief*, baby. You was up in Westchester plotting with that boss Don Benny too. Do you know how much time the Feds would give you if they knew you were conspiring with a mega criminal like him? What's the take on that deal?"

"About forty-something million," Honore reluctantly admitted. "Close to fifty. But why you gotta push up on my hustle? I thought you had your own thing going on with you and Slick? Don't y'all niggas have your own crew?"

Wild Man smirked because he had expected that question. "Fuck that crew and fuck Slick too. This shit right here is about *me*. I'm riding solo now, baby. I'm repping for *self*."

"Oh really?" Honore stopped walking and whirled around to face him. "So what happened between you and Slick? What's that shit about?"

"It ain't about nothing. Me and Slick just have different visions and outlooks on how to handle our business, that's all. Sometimes people just grow apart and wanna explore new options." He chuckled. "It's time for me to take my talents elsewhere like Bron-Bron did."

"Uh-huh. Is that the case?" Honore asked with sarcasm suddenly dripping from her voice. "It seems to me like business was going quite well for you and your band of thieves not too long ago. Something tells me that it's *you* who mighta been the issue."

"*Me*? Fuck is you talkin about?"

"Yeah, *you*. What happened between y'all, Wild Man? Did you do some "wild man" shit that didn't go over too well with your homeys? Yeah. I can see that happening. You the type of cat who don't know when to chill. Niggas like you are foolish. You do stupid, rebel-without-a-cause shit at the risk of other soldiers, and you probably cost your crew something valuable."

She smirked at him sideways as she stepped off and continued rolling her hips down the street, knowing full well that she was reading him like a book and pushing his buttons like he was an elevator.

"See, a chick like me? I do what I do to perfection. You coming at me like a walking liability, my dude. That's probably why your crew cut you off. You ain't got no friends no more 'cause niggas like you sink ships," Honore cut him up harshly with her tongue. "You sink 'em down to the bottom of the deep blue mothafuckin sea."

Wild Man reacted in a flash. He reached out and gripped her up by the arms and tossed her against the glass window of a grocery store. He got up in her face like he was gonna wring her fuckin neck right out there on the busy street.

"Bitch you need to watch your fucking mouth!" he said hotly, guilt swelling all up in his chest. "You don't know shit about me or my crew! Don't nobody gotta be my friend! I'ma get minez by any means, and right now bitch I want in on *yours!* Now make that shit happen pretty lady or we can see how fast I sink ya ship and drown every rat in your set right along with you!"

Click-Clack!

Wild Man heard a gun cocking and felt a cold piece of steel pressed to the side of his temple.

"Get your pork-fried-rice oven mitts off her before I blow your last thoughts all up and down Fordham Road, you chink-ass clown," Sly McFly growled as he aimed his loaded Glock at Wild Man's dome with deadly intentions.

Wild Man didn't let her go right away. Instead he stared deeper into Honore's hazel eyes and he was shocked to see them dancing with excitement.

Suddenly Wild Man was pissed the hell off. This bitch had punked him. She had straight up lured him in like a fish on a baited hook. And he had fallen right into her trap and lost his head, just the way she had wanted him to.

People on the street peeped the Glock and started scattering out of bullet range as quickly as possible. Sly's finger was tightening on the trigger and it looked like he was about to make good on his threat right there in broad daylight.

"Don't shoot him, Sly," Honore said calmly as she shrugged Wild Man's hand off her arm.

"That was just a little love tap he gave me just now, that's all. He's not hurting me. He's just a little sensitive these days. He'll be a'ight."

Wild Man turned his head slowly toward the gun and met the familiar look of murder in Sly McFly's eyes. Honore was right. He wasn't trying to hurt her. Slowly, he let go of her and nodded.

"A'ight, sweetheart. I'ma holla at you later and this time you better answer ya jack," Wild Man told her as he grilled Sly fearlessly. With a look of mockery in his eyes, he turned his back on the old man and headed calmly back down the street.

"I'ma kill that muthafucka," Sly said as he watched the brolick Asian dude walk off. "Young boys like him think they too tough for they own damn good.

What the fuck was he spitting to you about anyway?"

"Money," Honore said quietly as they made their way back to the whip where Chimp Charlie was waiting. "We gotta put that bitch-nigga on."

Sly eyed her. "Put him on with what?"

"With the Pink Lady! We gotta give him a cut from the sale."

Sly scoffed and chuckled. "You must be outta your fuckin mind, darling. We ain't putting him on with shit!"

"We *have* to, Mr. Mack," Honore said firmly. "He's blackmailing me. Some kinda way he got his hands on the security tape from Hymie's jewelry store the night I lost the diamond. He seen me tossing the briefcase to the guard and he knows I don't go to no damn college. He seen us with Benny at that meeting up in Westchester too."

"Fuck him!" Sly said again. "When I kill that coward whatever he seen won't fuckin matter."

"Yeah, but if we smoke him then somebody else will just step up with another copy of the tape. I'm not going to jail for nobody! If the Feds find out I'm the one on that video in the jewelry store, I'm fucked. If they find out I'm scheming with Benny I might as well be dead. Nah, we gotta make Wild Man think we're putting him on for some cash. He's a little reckless, but he runs his mouth and he's stupid as fuck. I can use that to my advantage. Trust me, he has a weak spot when it comes to me," Honore said as they got in the car and Chimp Charlie pulled off down the street.

"Oh there's some weak spots in this chink's armor all right!" Sly agreed bitterly. "You got niggas thinking they can just walk up on you in the streets and manhandle you any old kinda way? I know good and goddamn well I raised you better than that!"

"It was nothing," Honore shrugged and turned her head toward the window. "Just let me handle Wild Man. I know I can get something outta him."

Sly bit back the cutting words that were about to fly outta his mouth, but as far as he was concerned Wild Man's fate was sealed. That bitch wasn't getting shit. He had peeped the groove between Honore and the Asian cat. She had been damn near creaming in her drawers even as that nigga's hands was wrapped around her throat.

Yeah, Sly thought, shaking his head. Honore was young and dick-whipped. She was slipping and sliding off her game just like a cat in heat.

But Wild Man wasn't getting a cut of *shit.* The only thing that chink muthafucka was gonna get a cut of was the dirt falling down into his open grave!

CHAPTER 8

Squad Shit Only

Cucci had just finished putting a mean dick-riding game down on dog-ugly Chimp Charlie and she was laying in his bed with her left eye jumping like crazy. Charlie was stretched out naked beside her with his breathing still erratic and sweating like a pig with his saggy balls on empty.

Chimp Charlie's dick game was weak as hell, but he broke Cucci off with stacks of them crispy hundreds whenever she asked for it. He also kept her up on what was going on with Sly and Honore, which was highly beneficial these days.

Cucci was using him to the max and she didn't mind throwing him some pussy from time to time because it wasn't like he was putting a hurting on her anyway. The nigga's name shoulda been Limp Charlie 'cause he could barely keep it up long enough to put it in, and the nigga nutted and came faster than a speeding bullet.

But right now Cucci's left eye was jumping like some dirty bitch was talking about her and she knew it was Honore. Her cousin had been even more secretive and hush-hush lately, and whatever her scandalous ass was cooking up to dish out was anybody's guess.

Cucci's mind wandered as she sprawled across the California king-sized bed and thought about her favorite nigga Ice Pick Goody, and how good he broke her back in when they fucked.

"Did you get your nut off, baby?" Chimp Charlie interrupted her thoughts as he reached for the sheet and wiped off his sweaty balls. "I know you did, 'cause Old Charlie knows how to put it down."

"Nigga *puh-leez*," Cucci rolled over and looked at Charlie with the, you-can't-be-serious face. "This ain't even about yo dick Charlie, so let's not even get this shit confused, homey. I got what you need and you got what I want.

That's it."

"Yeah-yeah-yeah," Charlie said as he chuckled. "You can lie to me all you want to but this Cucci-juice dripping all over my joint says different. I be having you gushing girl. Now reach over there and hand me one of them Newports off the nightstand."

"Yeah, I get super wet, don't I?" Cucci giggled as she threw the pack of cigs right on top of his fat stomach. "That's cause I be thinking about the nigga who *really* be knockin the bottom outta this pussy, stupid! That's the only way I can even get moist fucking with you."

Chimp Charlie didn't really give a fuck what got her aroused and what didn't. He was an old school playa and giving up a little cash to get some young fresh trim didn't mean shit to him. As long as he blew a good load he could care less if she was pleased or not. Cucci wasn't the only young chick he tricked on, she just happened to have the best box around and there was something about her that always got him going strong.

"Whateva," Charlie said as he sparked up his cancer stick and started to harmonize. "I got *mineee*, so I'm *goooood*. Just wait. When I help Sly and Honore make this big-money move I'ma be surrounded by the finest bitches on Planet Earth. I'ma be laid up under a palm tree on an island with a glass of wine in one hand and a big hunk of ass in the other one!"

This little revelation got Cucci's attention but she didn't wanna come off as extra pressed about it. But her jumping eye was trying to tell her something, and the only time it jumped like this was when some skank-ass hoe was plotting to do her wrong.

"What you mean you gonna be on some Island, Charlie? Damn, you gonna have sex on the beach without me and shit?" she said, adding a little sweetness to her voice as she slid her thick thigh over his.

"Look, you might have a weak dick, Charlie but it's *my* weak dick, goddammit! You ain't going to no island without me." She kissed him on the cheek and whispered softly, "So, what kind of moves do Honore got going on with Sly?"

"Ain't you Honore's best friend?" Charlie chuckled. "If you don't know what's going down then it's not my place to say nothing. Shit, I ain't even supposed to know what I know, but them mothafuckas talk like I ain't even there sometimes. Which is cool wit'me cause old Chimp Charlie knows ere'thang."

Now Cucci *really* needed to know what the fuck was going down. She had been trying to get a step ahead of Honore for a minute now and something always seemed to go wrong. Honore had her lips zipped real tight and it seemed like the universe was protecting that bitch.

Cucci knew her cousin was up to something that was related to money, but as hard as she tried she couldn't find a way to get the info she needed. Charlie seemed to have the scoop on what was being plotted on the jux, and she wasn't letting this nigga outta the bed until she knew everything his pot-bellied ass was withholding. No matter how she had to get that info she was determined to get it. So she reached under the sheets and grabbed his limp dick and began to bring the sticky little pecker back to life again.

"I know you ain't holding out on me Big Poppa, are you?" Cucci cooed as she gripped him firmly and stroked him slow and steady. "I need to know these things, Daddy. Honore is more than my cousin, you know. She's my best friend and I have her best interests at heart. You know she's just gonna to tell me the whole plan anyway. I just wanna have a heads up, ya know baby?"

Charlie closed his eyes as he enjoyed the pleasure of Cucci's skilled hand job. She always knew how to work him over and a few strokes later his shit was on full brick. He didn't really wanna tell her anything because he knew how Sly was about his business. This was some life-changing shit they were planning and he wanted to keep what he knew to himself.

But his dick wasn't agreeing with what his mind was telling him. Besides, Cucci was family. Like she said, Honore was gonna tell her the whole shit anyway. He reached over and started playing with Cucci's dark nipples as he got turned on even more.

"Nigga start talking," Cucci said as she stopped stroking for a second and squeezed the head of his joint real tight in her hot fist. "I know you want me to put my mouth on it. So tell me what's going on and I'ma take real good care of you. Don't I do it better than all them other hoes?"

Charlie nodded. He was desperate for her to keep jacking his joint and he couldn't wait to feel Cucci's juicy lips stroking and slobbing his meat.

"Well, uhh," Charlie started as he tried to find the right words to pluck from his lust-filled thoughts. "Sly and Honore plan on jacking this crazy high-priced diamond."

"For how much?" Cucci demanded as she pumped and squeezed.

"Tens of millions. Enough for all of us to live off for the rest of our lives. The shit is called the Pink Lady and it's gonna take all the tricks they got in the book to pull this one off. It's gonna be the scam of a fuckin lifetime."

"Oh really?" Cucci said as she tossed the sheet to the side and looked down at Charlie's erect little wanker. In the blink of an eye she put her head down and deep throated his stiff little woody. She let Charlie hump into her mouth a few times before coming back up for air. A glistening string of saliva hung from her bottom lip and connected to the tip of Charlie's dick like it was linking them together.

"Be a good boy and tell me all the details," Cucci pressed. "I need to know it *all,* from the beginning to the end. If you do that for me I will suck your bone *dry*, Big Daddy. You know how much you love this tight neck pussy, right?"

Moments later Cucci got to sucking like the professional she was. The nasty old man in bed with her humped and cried out and shivered and moaned under her jutting neck, frantic tongue, and expert fist grip. And when she was finished and he had blown his bitter load into her mouth and it was sliding hotly down her throat, just like he had promised her, Chimp Charlie got to talking.

CHAPTER 9

Everything is All Real

Cucci's mind was steady clicking like a calculator the next afternoon as she exited her whip and swayed down the avenue toward the project building where her mother lived.

Clean as a bean in her stylish peach and crème dress, she looked like a million-dollar beach condo as she walked toward the trash-strewn dilapidated high-rise tower where she had grown up.

Today was her mother's birthday and they were gonna celebrate it with a project barbeque. They were sparking up the grill and her mother's friends had cooked up all kinds of side dishes, and the entire fam, to include Honore, was gonna be there.

Cucci sucked her teeth. She had some words coming for Honore's trick ass. After listening to Chimp Charlie spill his guts in the sheets last night, Cucci had tried her best to corner Honore at work and find out what the hell was going on that morning. But every time she rolled up Honore either ducked into the boss's office or pretended like she was on the phone with a client.

"That's all right," Cucci had told herself. "I'ma pounce on that bitch and hem her up after work," but she was real disappointed at five o'clock when she looked around and realized that Honore had already clocked out for the day.

That's cool too, Cucci thought as she headed toward the porch where niggas outta the ass stood smoking trees and listening to music. She knew Honore couldn't avoid her forever. Her sneaky tail was gonna have to face her sooner or later, and if Cucci had her way it would be sooner. Like right damn now.

Her heels clicked on the pavement as she switched her ass seductively up the walkway, catching every male eye within a ten-block radius. Her thigh-high dress was made of a soft, slinky material that accentuated her abundant curves. She had worn a matching scarf tied around her neck at work, but she'd taken it off in the car and now her titties were bouncing up outta the plunge-neck top and trying to jump free.

"Hoochie Cucci!" A skinny dude with long dreads yelled out to her from the porch. "Long time no see! You lookin good as shit, ma!"

Cucci grinned to herself, glowing under the compliment as she kept right on moving. She wasn't tryna turn nobody on because couldn't none of these two-bit boogers do nothing for her that her man Ice Pick Goody couldn't do better. Every last one of these low-level slangas had been tryna get in her panties since she was twelve-years-old, but it wasn't happening back then when she was broke, and it damn sure wasn't happening now that she had herself a baller with heavy pockets. These chump-niggas in Queens could kiss her ass. Ice-Pick Goody was her main squeeze and she was rolling Brooklyn-style now!

Because if there was one thing Cucci understood it was the value of her pussy, and every last one of these nasty porch niggas could keep right on dreaming.

The block party was jumping in true Queens fashion when she walked around to the street side of the building. An old head had just broke open the fire hydrant for the little kids and they ran through the cool water without a care in the world. Older children were jumping double Dutch and playing skelly, jacks, and bat n' ball.

You could smell the odor of sweet kush being blown from Dutch Master blunts and the sounds of Hot 97 rap cuts being bumped at high volumes. The bucket-head broads were looking thirsty for attention as they strutted up and down the block in their favorite rompers and booty shorts.

Cucci walked into the large fenced-off area where multiple card tables and chairs were set out and the barbeque grill was smoking hot. The smell of ribs, franks, and spicy chicken wings was in the air.

Frita and her home-girls were laughing loudly as a bunch of them did a Chicago-style line dance in the grass, while the men were pouring beer and bbq sauce on the meat, drinking Heineken and rum, playing bones, and talking major shit.

Cucci walked through the bald patches of grass and pushed her way into the loud crowd of aunts, uncles, cousins, and friends. Everybody for miles around knew the smart-mouth, kind-hearted, but quick-to-cut you Frita. She came from a large family and she was loved and respected in the projects. Frita saw her daughter coming and made her way over to a long table to pour herself another deep cup of Bacardi 151 and Coke.

"Happy birthday, Mama." Cucci dropped her bags then kissed and hugged her mom warmly. Cucci was Frita's mini-me. She was a younger replica of her mother, and when you looked at Frita you could see exactly where Cucci got her good looks and banging hourglass shape from. "How you feeling today, old lady?"

"Ain't shit old about me baby," Frita said taking a sip of her liq. "I'm still a spring chicken and I ain't too old to kick yo ass."

"You funny as hell, ma," Cucci said with a smile. Her mother always had a smart remark no matter what was going on. That shit would never change. "You always tryna turn up on somebody. And that's why I love you."

"Thank you, baby girl," Frita said, plopping down in a plastic chair. "I love you too. Now go get me one of them ribs off the grill. I'm about to tear this food up and play me some pitty pat. I'm gonna get wasted off this rum too because it's my birthday!"

Cucci was turning around to head to the grill when she bumped dead into her cousin.

"Happy birthday, Auntie," Honore said as she moved past Cucci and reached down to hug Frita. "Sorry I'm late but I had to stop at the street vendor and get you some of those smell-good oils you love so much."

Honore greeted the other friends and family members out there with smiles and hugs. She was so busy cheesing she didn't even peep Cucci standing there giving her the side eye.

Cucci couldn't believe this bitch. She had been mad as hell when Chimp Charlie confessed that Honore and Sly McFly were going after some Pink Lady diamond on the low. Cucci knew Honore was shiesty but she couldn't believe her dear cousin and supposed-to-be bestie was fixin to cut her out of the payday of a lifetime.

That type of betrayal had hurt her real deep, and as far as Cucci was concerned it was go-to-war time now. Honore was just as good as dead in the heart of Cucci, and she might as well have been any other bitch on the street.

Anger rushed all up in Cucci's chest and even though it was her mama's birthday celebration she just couldn't hold it back.

"You funny-style as hell, bitch," Cucci spit nastily to her cousin. "Why don't you get ya fake ass gone and keep it moving up outta my mama's party."

"What the hell is your problem?" Honore said looking confused. "Why you coming at me all crazy like that? Don't be jealous. I got you some oils too. They're in my bag."

"Fuck your oil!" Cucci said gaining more steam. "How about you get me some of that Pink Lady shit you got going on?"

"What the hell are you talking about?" Honore hissed, looking around with the guilty face. "Bitch your lips are looser than ya damn pussy!"

"You know exactly what I'm talking about, Honore! You's a shady hoe! Always running around preaching this family loyalty shit but your snake-ass is fake as fuck!"

"Girl why you tripping? Ain't nobody fake but you—"

"Well lemme give it to you real-style, then! I ain't got no more love for your bum-ass! Best believe I'm done being your invisible sidekick, bitch! We supposed to be hustling together and going hard fifty-fifty on everything we do, but your sneaky ass is all about hiding out and holding out! You don't mean shit to me no more, Honore! Now raise the fuck up outta this yard before I rock yo ass!"

Honore looked puzzled. "What in the world are you talking about, Cucci? Ain't nobody been holding out on nothing!"

"You fuckin *liar!* Sneaking around tryna stack all the chips for yourself! I know all about that lil transaction that went down at the Boatel. And I know about all the other shit you scheming on too! We supposed to be a team, but you keeping secrets and going behind my back and making ya own little side deals without me!"

Knowing she was caught dead out there, Honore went for broke.

"Yeah? Well the reason I gotta keep shit a secret is because you too damn thirsty and your mouth is too fuckin big! A gutter bitch like you can't hold *water* and I'm supposed to let you fuck my shit up?"

By now everybody in the entire backyard had stopped and turned their attention to the argument that was going down. Before Frita could intervene Cucci did the worst thing you could do to anybody, let alone to a member of your own family.

She opened her mouth and let a big fat glob of saliva fly right in Honore's face.

In a blur Honore began digging into her cousin's ass with a combination of punches that would have impressed Mike Tyson. In mere seconds Honore had Cucci's big-mouth self down on the ground pounding her into the dirt.

"Bitch you *spit* on me? I'ma beat the shit outta you out here!" Honore shrieked. She was scratching and mauling Cucci like a wild animal in the woods.

"Let her go, Honore!" Frita and a bunch of her girlfriends jumped in and were trying to pull Honore up off of Cucci but it wasn't working. "Turn her loose, goddammit!"

The two cousins were scratching and thumping. Cucci was wind-milling her arms from the ground and throwing haymakers. Honore was fist-gripping Cucci's weave and slanging her head violently from side to side.

"You jealous fuckin hoe!" She pounded Cucci in the face. "You could never fuck with me! You just a can't-get-right type a' smut! I bet I'll be the last bitch you spit on in ya whole miserable fuckin life!

Finally Frita and her girls unbent Honore's clenching fingers and pried her off of Cucci, but not before Honore landed a solid kick square in Cucci's mouth. The force busted her lip instantly and blood squirted in the air then dribbled down her chin and splattered her dress.

Cucci shrieked in pain and rage. She tore off after Honore and grabbed her by the hair and started swinging killer blows, popping her hard in the nose. The backyard was in total chaos as the partygoers grabbed Honore and broke shit up again.

"Y'all dirty hoes was holding me back!" Honore accused, glaring around at her cousins and aunts. "Why the fuck was y'all holding me back but y'all let this bitch keep on swinging?"

"Y'all two *stop it!*" Frita pleaded ready to whip both of their asses. "Cut this shit out! Showing your tails out here in the street like this! Both of y'all was raised better than that! You was raised up together like *sisters!*"

"She ain't my fuckin sister!" Cucci screamed.

"You ain't my damn sister neither!" Honore hollered back, and then she turned her lips down at her aunt and said, "And you wasn't no kinda sister to my mother neither!"

"Stop it," Frita panted, pressing her hand to her heart. "Y'all just stop it. We family, y'all. We are *family!*"

Cucci sucked her teeth. "That shady fuckin hater ain't shit to me!"

Honore clutched her nose as a stream of blood dripped from her left nostril. "You ain't shit to me neither, bitch!" she snapped as she bent over and snatched up her bag. She came up staring at her aunt Frita and spit real nasty outta her mouth, "Like I said, don't neither one of y'all tricks know how to be a *sister!*"

That was it for Frita.

"Look at you!" the older woman sneered as she glared at her niece with blazing Bacardi eyes. "You just like your ungrateful ass *mama!* That fuckin dick-rider always did think she was cute! All the time violating some damn body! And you take right after her too!"

"Well she musta been riding it way better than you," Honore snapped. "'Cause she took your fuckin man, now didn't she?"

"*What?*" It was Frita's turn to break as her elderly homegirls rushed to hold her back. "That hoe ain't take *shit* from me!" she screamed, wind-milling her arms as she tried to break free of the hands holding her back.

"You got it backwards, baby!" Frita screamed. "I'm the one who took his ass from *her!* And now her cute ass is dead and gone, and me and my man are still right here together! That means while she's riding a tombstone I'm riding that nigga's *dick* anytime I want it! I tell you what though, you lil ungrateful *bitch!* After everything I done for you, you got the nerve to talk that kinda way to me? I ain't Cucci Momma, baby! I'll knock you into next week and slap the mothafuckin taste right outta—"

"Happy birthday, Auntie!" Honore barked as she stomped past her aunts and cousins. She turned around and gave Frita the stank face. "You and Cucci might not be two peas in the pod, but y'all are damn sure two crackheads on the corner!"

"*Bitch!*" Frita and Cucci screamed at the same time.

"Bitch, hell. Fuck all y'all fake-ass family members!" Honore spit bitterly as she sashayed out the gate waving her middle finger high in the air and poking her bouncy ass way out like they could all kiss it. "Don't try to come for me unless I send for you! I'm gone!"

CHAPTER 10

Unforgiving

It was getting dark outside when Slick got off the number 4 train. He walked through the concrete jungle with his hands buried deep in his pockets and his mind spinning in thought.

He had called Jewelz a little while earlier and lied about being in her neighborhood and asked her if he could swing by and chill for a little while.

Seeing her all up under Handgun Goody at Chainsaw's funeral, holding that nigga's hand and wiping away his fuckin tears, had messed his head up. Especially since he had peeped Goody's moms there too, alive and kicking.

Jewelz lived in a real nice apartment building in an upscale hood, but there were two low-budget Section 8 tenements just a few blocks away.

Slick approached the six-story buildings with his eyes on scan and his hoody covering his head. An intense argument was going on between two cats who were standing outside the lobby of the first building. A short Puerto Rican cat seemed to be getting hostile and aggressive with a taller darker-skinned black dude.

"W'sup, *puta!* I told you if I ever saw yo bitch ass over here again I was gonna *off* you didn't I?" the short stocky 'Rican roared.

"*Mchhh*," the skinny brother let out a sound of disrespect. "Nigga this *my* hood! I stomp where the fuck I wanna stomp. Fuck is you talking about?"

Slick slowed his pace and studied the body language and movements of both men as they argued back and forth about who the hood belonged to.

The black kid is shitting bricks although he's putting up a good front. The 'Rican dude is posturing. He's putting on a show because he likes the attention. The 'Rican looks like he can take the Black guy, but he's talking too fuckin much. He shoulda popped smooth the fuck off right after he said what he had to say. That's gonna be his downfall.

Between his knowledge of the streets and the training he had received in the military, Slick could calculate a certain outcome of a situation in just a matter of seconds. This type of battle intuition is what had saved his life plenty of times on the job, and it made him a highly efficient killing machine.

Shoot and move, my nigga, Slick urged the Hispanic cat. *Shoot and fuckin move!*

Suddenly in the mix of the argument the dark-skinned cat turned slightly to his right then made a slick move. In the blink of an eye he spit a razor blade into his palm then swung hard and slashed the 'Rican's neck while he was in mid-sentence.

They started fighting like bulls and Slick peeped the 'Rican trying to reach for the gat that was stuffed down in his waistband. The Black kid was all over him though, slicing viciously and carving him up so fast that bloody gashes seem to magically open up all over his face and neck and even the backs of his hands.

Screams and curses of alarm were coming from the spectators but no one dared to interfere. The Puerto Rican kid was losing a lot of blood and could no longer withstand the razor-sharp flurries as he dropped to his knees.

A deep cut from his forehead to his chin opened up in a gruesome display of white meat and blood. He was trying desperately to hold his collapsing face together while he continued to take a massive beating.

The black guy stood over him swinging his blade with a complete look of insanity in his eyes as he ripped up the cat's face and neck until dude fell over and was no longer moving.

Women in the crowd screamed from horror and disgust. A fat nigga shouted loudly for somebody to call 911. Slick gazed at the bloody mess and proceeded to move on. His prediction had been right on the money. The Puerto Rican kid was laid out on the concrete shredded up like spaghetti and mozzarella cheese and inches away from death. And his gun was still on his fuckin hip.

You was doing too much talkin and not enough movin, B, Slick thought coldly. *A scared man is a dangerous one. His only mistake was leaving you alive.*

The black guy whirled around and ran off down the block while the group of bystanders inched up closer and gawked over the wounded man who was barely breathing.

Slick walked past dude's shredded mug without even looking down at him. This was New York. The Empire State. Careless niggas got ripped out here every single day.

$$$$$

Jewelz's upscale apartment building was several blocks away. She buzzed him in, and the moment he walked through her door Slick was bombarded by the strong odor of some good-ass trees.

"Sup?" He reached out to give her a hug and took a good look at the tell-tale redness in her eyes.

Jewelz half-hugged him and she patted him a couple of times on his back, but she kept the eye contact real brief as she quickly turned away and walked down the hall.

Slick followed her with his eyes. She was dressed in a wife-beater with no bra on underneath, and a pair of red and white candy-striped boy shorts that were hugging a lot looser on her curves than he remembered. She had a bright red scarf tied around her head too, and when it flapped up and down in the back Slick saw straight through to her naked skull.

Da fuck?

Slick frowned deeply as Jewelz switched her diminished ass towards the kitchen.

This crazy-ass girl done gone and cut-off all her fuckin hair or nah?

He was burning with the need to ask her what was up, but lately she had been on some other shit. He didn't want no repeat of that crazy scene she had caused in the soul food restaurant, but he just had to know.

"Ay, what the hell happened to all your hair?"

Jewelz kept her back to him as she shrugged and replied, "Charity. I shaved it off. I donated it to sick kids who need hair, and as soon as mine grows back in a little more I'm getting me a sew-on weave. No biggie."

Slick kept his thoughts to himself as he joined her in the kitchen.

"Yo, I wanna let you know we got suspended," Slick said quietly. "The crew ain't just on a break, Jewelz. The BBU said we missed two hits in a row and they suspended us."

Jewelz shrugged. "Well, them bitches must can't count because we know that's a lie."

"Right," Slick agreed. "We missed the Queen of Diamonds, but we got the monkey with the red briefcase. The old man we left rocked on the floor was proof of that."

Jewelz shrugged again. "Whatever. I'm cool with it. I ain't got the energy to be out there blasting on niggas no way. You hungry?" she asked over her shoulder as she picked up a tightly rolled spliff from an ashtray and sparked it up. She took a few pulls and held them in for a few, then she slowly exhaled and let the smoke out. "I cooked a pot of ox tails and potatoes this morning. You want some?"

Slick nodded as he watched her closely. "Yeah, you can fix me a plate. Thanks. I ain't ate much of nothing all day."

"Me neither," she said as she picked up a big spoon and started digging into the pot. "I gotta get nice and buzzed just to work up a little bit of an appetite these days."

"Why? What's up with that?" Slick asked with a look of concern in his eyes. "For real, you don't look too good, J. You been smoking that sticky all day?"

Jewelz set his plate down hard on the counter.

"*Fuck* you! Don't walk up in here tryna come for me! You don't look too hot your damn self, nigga! Are *you* doing okay?" she shot back angrily. "I been out here making mad power plays for you. The last thing you need to be worrying about is how much weed I smoke!"

Slick held his hands up in surrender. "My bad, lovely. I didn't mean no harm and I didn't come over here to argue with you neither," he said calmly.

He got a fork from the silverware drawer and moved over to the table with his steaming hot plate of stew.

"So gimme a quick update," he said, changing the subject as he dug into the grub. "I peeped you at Chainsaw's funeral the other day. What's the buzz on Goody and his crew? That nigga still walking around town crying like a lil bitch?"

Jewelz stared him down as she stood leaning on the counter puffing her sticky and tapping her foot like she was pissed the hell off.

"Goody is doing just fine," she snapped. "He's probably just a little stressed out, that's all. Matter fact, he asked me to go on a trip to Jamaica with him just to get away from all this bullshit for a while. On the real, I'm thinking about packing my shit and hopping on that flight."

Slick raised his eyebrow and paused with the fork halfway to his mouth.

"What the hell you talking about, Jewelz?" he spit, looking at her real crazy. "You talking about traveling somewhere alone with that nigga? For real? You sound like you feelin him or something!"

"What the hell do you care about who I'm feeling?" Jewelz snapped again. "Goody ain't the monster you think he is anyway. That dude stays splurging on me, showing me crazy love. Don't worry about me, okay? Worry about that little fake-ass jump-off you be running around with."

"Yo, goddammit!" Slick pushed his plate back so hard it skidded to the other side of the table. "The fuck is wrong with you girl? Did you forget this is a fuckin *job*? You done let that nigga get up in ya head like that? Do you remember what the fuck he did to us? How he stole my entire fucking family?"

"*Our* family! He stole *our* family! Big Slick and Miss Kea were all I had in this whole world too!"

"A'ight, then! *Our* family! So how the fuck could you be thinking about going across the water somewhere with that grime ball then?"

"People *change!*" Jewelz shrieked. "All that shit happened twenty fuckin years ago! Goody ain't the same dude who did those terrible things. He was just young and dumb back then, Slick! A fuckin teenager! He was just doing what Haz *made* him do! Haz woulda killed him too if Goody didn't get down with him and you know that!"

Slick stood up trembling with rage. "Yo," he said slowly shaking his head. "You wild delusional with ya shit, girl. You straight up fuckin buggin, ma."

"Why I gotta be buggin?" Jewelz demanded, shifting her hips and crossing her arms over her breasts. "You the one who keeps telling me to forget the past! You said to stop living in what it used to be and start living in what it is right now! Well, *this* is what it is right now *for me!* Right now is *all* I got! So you can just come down off ya high-horse, homeboy. You got you somebody, and now I got me somebody too! I ain't saying I'm not gonna kill Goody. I can still rock him just like we planned it. But...not now," she lowered her eyes and stared down at the floor. "Not yet…"

Slick whirled around furiously and put his fist straight through the front of her china cabinet. Shattered slivers flew everywhere and when he drew his hand back a long shard of glass was stuck down between his first two knuckles.

"*Stupid ass!*" he hissed on her, ignoring the blood that dripped down his fingers and splattered to the floor.

"What the *fuck* do you think that nigga's gonna do when he finds out who you really are? Huh? You think he's just gonna say 'my bad' and let you walk ya ass up outta there? I told you that nigga was gonna lull you to sleep then bite you! He's gonna *kill* you, Jewelz! He'll cut you the fuck up for real this time!"

"Nah." Jewelz shook her head. "Goody wouldn't do nothing to hurt me. He ain't that scared young fiend no more. He's a grown man now and he loves me, Slick. He wants to protect me. He wants to make sure I'm straight."

Goddammit, I love you! I wanna protect you! I wanna make sure you stay straight! were the words that blasted through Slick's mind.

But instead of saying them he just shook his head, furious at her blindness. "You must be fuckin *tweakin*, Jewelz! If I'da known you was this fuckin stupid I woulda never put you on this job!"

Slick grabbed a dishcloth and pulled the shard of glass from his flesh. His wound was deep, but the only pain he felt was from the realization that once again he had failed to protect Jewelz. From the realization that he had fucked around and let her walk straight into a danger zone. He couldn't believe he was hearing this blasphemous shit coming outta her mouth. He had just lost Noodles and he wasn't about to lose her too. Not when he was just starting to realize how much he really lo—

"I'm pulling you off this jawn," Slick spit as he wrapped the dishtowel around his throbbing fist. "You can just clock out and cut off the lights right now baby girl, because it's over. This job is officially fuckin *cancelled!* I want you to fall your ass back from Goody and his gang and forget that nigga ever existed, you hear me?"

Jewelz broke. "I'm a grown-ass woman, Slick! I play my own fuckin cards! You don't come up in here telling me when to pluck and when to fold! I takes care of *myself*, muthafucka! Don't you or no other nigga get to tell me how to make my moves!"

"How long you been fuckin that nigga?" Slick asked quietly, his murderous brown eyes boring a hole in hers. "*How long*?"

Jewelz threw her hands in the air and turned her back on him.

"So that's what this is all about?" she demanded, cutting her eyes over her shoulder. "Nigga you just *jealous!* You don't want me, but you don't want no other man to have me neither! Don't worry about who been smashin this pussy!" she said, whirling around with her hands on her hips. "How long have you been fuckin *Honore?*"

For the longest time Slick just stood there looking at her. His eyes cut like razors as he pinned her in his glare. When he finally spoke his voice was lowered to a bone-chilling whisper.

"I want you to listen to me carefully, Diamond," he said quietly. "Handgun Goody is a *dead man walking*. You hear me? That nigga is a dead man walking! And so is every muthafuckin body left in his shitty-ass family! *Everybody!*"

Slick had the look of a serial killer about him as he stepped up on Jewelz and let the blood-soaked towel fall from his hand. He stared at her with such murderous intentions that it sent chills running down her spine.

"I swear on my mother's grave, Jewelz…word is bond on my muthafuckin momma's *grave!* I'ma kill Handgun Goody. I'm gonna *cook* his ass! And if you get in my way tryna live out some bullshit fairytale fantasy I will fuckin cook you too!"

$$$$$

Honore was sitting in her car looking up at the tall project building. Even though some time had passed, that fist-fight between her and Cucci had been weighing heavily on her conscience.

Honore had violated the family rules when she ran off at the mouth and aired dirty laundry in front of everybody at her aunt's birthday barbeque. But not only did she show out and beat the brakes off her cousin, she had also disrespected her beloved Aunt Frita in a real foul type of way. Honore was an orphan. She only had a few good people in this world that she could count on, and her Aunt Frita had always been one of them. It was time for her to be a woman about the situation and apologize for all the nasty things she had said.

On the real, she had no problem being humble when it came to her auntie, but she could give a fuck less about Cucci's conniving ass. Honore felt like Cucci had been acting real shitty towards her lately anyway. She had deserved to get checked. But Frita was an elder, and she damn sure didn't deserve the tongue-lashing that Honore had put down on her.

Fuck it. For once I'ma just go ahead and do the right damn thing!

Honore hopped outta her car and entered the project building, then she made her way upstairs to her aunt's apartment and rang the bell.

"The fuck you want?" Frita demanded with a raised eyebrow as she opened the door and grilled her niece with the stank face. She was holding an icy can of Olde English in her hand with a napkin wrapped around it to soak up the cold sweat. "Is there something this old crackhead on the corner can help you with?"

"Auntie just let me come inside so we can talk," Honore pleaded. She could tell Frita had been drinking for a minute so she wasn't surprised by the attitude she was getting from her. "I know you mad, but I'm still your niece and we need to put all of this petty mess behind us."

"Oh, it's behind me!" the older lady snapped. She ran her hand down her hourglass figure. "Do I look like I got any worries? It's *way* behind me!"

"Well it's not behind me because I owe you an apology," Honore said humbly. "You raised me for practically as long as I can remember and I didn't have no right to open my mouth and say all that nasty stuff to you, Aunt Frita. And I'm sorry for that. I didn't mean none of it, and I don't even know nothing about all that crap that went on between you and my mother anyway. I was just repeating some of the stupid rumors I heard over the years because Cucci started some shit with me and my feelings got hurt so I wanted to hurt y'all back. But I didn't mean none of it, Auntie. I swear I didn't. I appreciate everything you ever did for me, and I love you just like you my real mother. Because in my heart you are, and that's the truth." Honore leaned forward and planted a big kiss on her auntie's cheek. "Do you forgive me?"

"Mmm-hmm," Frita rolled her eyes and then stepped back reluctantly and let her inside.

The apartment was filled with the delicious smells of sweet potato pie, and Honore could tell her aunt was burning it down in the kitchen. The sweet aroma of cinnamon and nutmeg brought back good memories of Honore's childhood growing up with Frita and Cucci, and she couldn't help but smile.

"Bring yo ass in here and sit down," Frita said as she opened up the oven and took a peek inside. "You looking mighty peaked girl, but you right on time for this good shit I just baked up."

"Yeah, I been real stressed out lately, Auntie," Honore admitted as she plopped down in a kitchen chair. She watched her aunt spread a dishrag out on the counter then set the pies on it so they could cool. "There's been so much stuff going on all at once. From my boss breathing down my neck at work, to people on my back saying I owe them this and owe them that..." she shook her head and frowned. "I'm just out here trying to keep my head up, that's all."

"I hear that," Frita said sweetly. "I know it's rough out there but don't stress yourself out too much over them sons-of-bitches at yo job, baby. Fuck 'em! When you clock outta there you gotta learn to leave that shit where it's at and live your life.

"And as for whatever people you owe," Frita laughed. "You ain't gotta pay 'em shit! As long as you owe 'em they'll never go broke!" Frita laughed again, then said seriously, "Listen, baby. I know Sly be looking out for you and all, but you always need to be maneuvering the best way you know how out there. Ain't nobody got you like you got you."

Honore knew exactly what her aunt was saying. Self had to look out for self. Right now she was in a bind, but deep down inside she was confident that she could finesse her way out of it. It was all about timing and attitude. She loved talking to Frita because she could always come up with some good advice without even knowing all the details of a situation. Frita had been a Queen bitch back in her day, and Honore loved and respected her mind and her gangsta.

"Yeah, well I can't stay too long, Auntie," Honore said with her mouth watering. Them damn sweet potato pies were invading her nostrils. "Me and Cucci still have us some issues we need to take care of, but you were never the problem. I was trippin out and being extra, and again, I apologize."

"Baby, don't even worry about it," Frita said gently. "We all have our moments. I was in my liquor that day and I said some things I shouldn't have said either. I didn't mean to hurt your feelings, and if I did I'm sorry too. You know how my mouth gets sometimes, and I guess Cucci got it honest from me. This is what families go through every now and then, but at the end of the day we still family and I'm always gonna love you."

"Thank you, Auntie," Honore said with a smile. "I'm always gonna love you more."

"Huh—take this," Frita said as she cut a big slice of pie for Honore. She set it on a piece of foil then pinched off the corner piece and stuck it in Honore's mouth. "Eat that and then tell me how it tastes." She peered at Honore as she chewed and frowned. "Hot damn! You look like you need some dick in ya life girl! You better go get you summa that get-right!"

Honore almost spit out her damn pie she was laughing so hard. Her aunt Frita was crazy as hell, and just like that things were back to normal between the two of them again.

CHAPTER 11

Break Ups to Make Ups

Slick had just got finished watering the plants in his grandmother's apartment and he stood looking out the tiny kitchen window at the city streets below.

Taking care of the houseplants was something he used to do for his grandmother every day growing up, and even though she was long gone it was still like second nature to him.

Being raised by his father's mother was one of the few childhood memories that brought a smile to Slick's face. For all the bad shit that had gone on in his life, home was sweet because she had made it that way. The spirit of his grandmother was still alive and well inside the apartment and Slick kept paying the rent every month because the place was like a sanctuary for him.

As he thought about the past and looked out over the projects, his mind slipped back to Jewelz. The last time he had seen her shit had gotten real rocky between them. Slick felt like she was falling in too deep with Goody. She was talking crazy shit about going away on some kinda tropical vacation with that nigga, and just the thought of it had made Slick lose all his cool.

He had popped off at the mouth and said some pretty foul shit to her, but the more he thought about it the more he realized how wrong he was. How could he blame Jewelz for falling for some knucklehead nigga who treated her right? How could he blame her for wanting the same thing out of a man that every other woman wanted? True love and affection, and the knowledge that everything about you was wanted and desired?

Slick was well aware of how hard Jewelz was feeling him. He knew exactly what it was that she needed and wanted outta him, and deep down inside he had always wanted that same thing from her too, from the time he was a kid.

But it was the small voice of that seven-year-old kid in him that said he wasn't good enough for her. It was that nagging voice that told him that Jewelz deserved better than him. It was that helpless, stabbed-up little boy in him that continued to fuck with his head and his heart.

That little boy just kept reminding Slick that he'd been too young, too weak, and too incomplete to protect his fam from the Crazy Haz's and the Dirty Mikes of this world. It reminded him that he had lain right there next to Jewelz while she was being violated and hurt, and there hadn't been a damn thing he could do to help her.

But even still, there was no doubt in his mind that Jewelz was a rider for him. Through thick and thin, she was down for Slick no matter what. When the Zip 'em up Crew had voted against the hit on the Goode Brothers Gang, it was Jewelz who had stood by his side with her ratchet in her hand. Just like Slick woulda laid down his life for her, Jewelz was ready to die for him too.

And that's why he had to make things right between them. Slick knew he had to make amends and show Jewelz how stupid he felt over the way he had acted. The only reason he had amped out like that in the first place is because he cared about her so much and he didn't want nothing to happen to her.

The type of fear and protectiveness that Slick felt for Jewelz held mad power over him. It dictated all his moves and clouded his decisions. That shit actually scared him. And the closer she tried to get to him, the scareder he got. It was a fucked up feeling because after the type of childhood terror Slick had lived through he wasn't tryna be scared of nothing else ever again.

Which is why he knew for sure that it was time to stop living in the past like he had accused Jewelz of doing. Slick knew he needed to take the chains off his heart and make a clean start. He needed to forgive himself for failing Jewelz in their childhood, and then reclaim that love and the soul-deep connection that they had once shared. The truth was, he was in love with her. He always had been, and he always would be. He had just been too damn traumatized and scared to admit it, especially to himself. Yeah. It was time for him to stop fighting his reality and embrace that shit. Life was too short. It was time for both of them to start *really* living.

So he picked up his celly and called her.

"Hello?" Jewelz answered on the second ring.

"Hey sweet chocolate," Slick said smoothly. "What you up to?"

"None of ya damn business," Jewelz snapped with a big-time attitude. "Why are you calling me?"

"A'ight, listen," Slick started off calmly, "I know you probably still mad and everything, but I just wanna apologize for the way I came up in ya crib acting the other day, nah'm sayin? You know I got mad love for you, girl. My brain just be everywhere sometimes. You the last person I would ever wanna flip out on, Jewelz. I'm sorry. I was way outta bounds. My fault yo."

"You daggone right it was your fault," Jewelz spit. "How you gonna come up in my house and insult me, break my damn furniture up, and then threaten me too? That shit is a no-go! You must be crazy!"

"Yeah," Slick said quietly. "I do be crazy sometimes. When you said you was thinking about going off to some fuckin island with Dirty Mike I felt real crazy."

"Why?" Jewelz exploded. "Why can't I go with him? Are you the only one who can floss and fuck and have all the fun? I'm a grown woman, son! I have grown woman needs!"

"I got scared for you," Slick admitted in a whisper. "Yo, on the real, I got mad regrets about sending you after Goody in the first place. I shoulda never even told you about that nigga, Jewelz. I put you in danger and I'm pissed off at myself for that. Not at you. So can we just rewind and x-out all the extra shit that I said? Please? Can we be tight again? You all the family I got in the world and I would never hurt you. I'd fuck myself up before I ever let anything happen to you, Jewelz. You feel me?"

On the other end of the line, Jewelz took a deep drag off her blunt and was silent for a long, long moment.

"Jewelz," Slick finally said. "Talk to me. Please."

"I hate yo ass, Samir," Jewelz whispered as she exhaled the smoke. She set her blunt down in the ashtray and closed her eyes. "Your smoove ass knows exactly how to make me give in to you. But you ain't getting off that easy. Food on you, muh'fucka."

Slick let out a big sigh and then he laughed. "A'ight that's cool. Food's on me. But do me a favor. Cut that Samir shit out, a'ight? Ain't nobody called me that name since never. And forget about slappin me up in another restaurant. How about you swing by my grandmother's crib tomorrow for lunch and I'll cook us up something real nice. We'll eat some old school shit like fried baloney and cheese sandwiches or maybe some Spam and scrambled eggs or corn-beef hash with Ritz crackers. Just like we used to do back in the day."

"That'll be dope," Jewelz said, getting excited despite herself. "I got this new Biggie mix I just copped from the bootleg spot. We can get our grub on and rock out with some sounds like we did at your mother's crib when we were little."

"I'm down with that," Slick smiled as he thought about those good old-jam sessions his parents used to throw when they were alive.

"Okay, cool!" Jewelz's bad attitude was gone and she was sounding real lighthearted now. "I'll be over there tomorrow around noon," she said sweetly.

"Bye, baby," Slick said softly.

"Bye," Jewelz giggled, and then she hung up.

CHAPTER 12

The Real Make the Fake Niggas Kneel

"A'ight, so let me run this shit by you one more time just so I know I got it right," Wild Man said to Honore as he shot Sly McFly a look of distrust. The pair of crooks sitting in front of him had agreed to put him on with their diamond-snatching scheme but neither one of them looked happy about that shit.

To his surprise, Honore had answered the phone when he called and they had agreed to hook up and discuss his share of the cut. Wild Man had met them at a table way in the back of a rundown KFC and he was anxious to hear all the details. That wrinkled-dick bitch Sly McFly was sitting there eyeing him like a snake on a mouse, but Wild Man was still hyped as shit.

"So, you saying the Pink Lady diamond is being flown into a commuter airport on Staten Island and it's getting picked up by an armed courier service, right?" he said, running Honore's words back to her.

Honore nodded, twisting her lips like she was bored.

"But instead of jumping on the diamond right there at the airport," Wild Man said, "we're gonna let the couriers bring that shit to the Sotheby museum and drop it off there?"

Honore nodded again. "Yeah. How many times I gotta say the same dog-gone thing? We gonna be chilling in the basement of the museum waiting for 'em. Laying low in the cut. All you gotta do is meet us there," she said, then thought to herself, *so Sly can roll up behind you and stick the blade of his cane right through your sucka-ass heart!*

Wild Man shook his head like he still wasn't getting it.

"So when the diamond gets sold at the auction then we move in on whoever buys it and we snatch it? Is that the big plan? Y'all sure about that shit?"

"That's right," Honore lied, rolling her eyes like she was tired of explaining the same damn thing over and over again. "I already told you it's safer to wait and hit the buyer when they're leaving the museum than it is to pull a heist on the airfield. Planes is expensive! You know how many cops and cameras they got out there on them bitches? Not to mention all them electrified wire fences and shit. So for the last freakin time get it through your head, asshole! As soon as the couriers roll up at the museum and they transfer custody of the diamond to them rich cats at the Sotheby, then we make our move. We're gonna wait till the jewel gets sold, and then come up outta the basement and hit it, and hit it *hard*. Now, you jumped your greedy ass all up in the picture and said you wanted to be down with the program, right?"

The hungry look in Wild Man's eyes was answer enough and Honore turned her top lip up and smirked.

"Yeah, well, *that's* the fuckin program, nigga," she spit coldly as she stood up from the table and grabbed her purse. "Be down with it or be gone."

CHAPTER 13

We Goode Brothas in the Hood Brothas!

While Sly McFly was scheming on some murderous thoughts about Wild Man, and Slick was busy contemplating murderous methods of planting Handgun Goody, Mister Handgun Goody was contemplating a few murderous moves of his own.

Goody had been mourning his dead brothers and sending mega members of his squad out into the streets to scope shit out. But something still kept telling him that the old folks building held the answers to his questions. Some of his best men had been smoked in that building, and he just couldn't shake the feeling that his soldiers were out there sleeping on something real important. Their instructions were to find out who the fuck was dropping his men like they were flies, but no matter who he sent out, every one of them had come back empty-handed or dead as fuck.

"Mama always said if you want something done right you gotta do that shit yourself," he muttered under his breath as he stepped outta his whip flanked by a small entourage of triggermen who were strapped to the max and ready to bang.

They strode toward the porch of building 430 with purpose and intent, and Goody had his eyes on scan the whole time. He didn't know exactly what he was looking for, but he knew if something looked outta place he would spot that shit.

And that's exactly what happened as they pushed through the door of the building's lobby. It was right around noon and the senior citizen free-lunch truck had just pulled off. In the lobby there were mad old people lined up holding their trays as they waited to take the elevator upstairs to eat and then catch an afternoon nap.

Goody probably wouldn'ta seen her if she hadn't darted outta the crowd and took off running toward the stairwell, but he did see her. In fact, he *busted* that ass!

$$$$$

Jewelz had been smoking a lot of weed lately to keep her pain in check, but it musta been some kinda paranoid sixth sense that sent those chills running down the back of her neck.

Slick had been trying real hard to get back on her good side. He had called her talking about how sorry he was for going off on her, and he apologized for barking on her over the vacation she had planned with Goody.

Jewelz had listened with her lips tooted up as he begged her to let him do something special to make it up to her. She had finally agreed to hook up with him at his grandmother's crib so they could share an old-timey lunch, and she was hoping they could reminisce about the brief innocence of the childhood they had spent together.

Jewelz had dressed to impress in a peach tank top and a tangerine-colored flared hula skirt. Her .22 burner was strapped up high on the outside of her thigh. She had put on a long curly wig and tied a bright orange scarf down over it, and put on some big hoop earrings too.

She had also smoked a nice-sized joint before leaving the house, just to make sure she'd have some type of appetite and she'd be able to eat whatever Slick had fixed for her. Jewelz made a quick stop at the corner store and picked up some orange juice. As she traveled to his crib she was hoping that Slick had hooked up some fried baloney and cheese sammiches on Wonder bread, or maybe some fish sticks and buttery grits, just like his mother used to feed them on Saturday mornings while they watched Thunder Cats cartoons when they were little.

But one minute Jewelz was standing in the lobby of building 430 clutching a carton of Tropicana and waiting for the elevator to come, and the next minute something told her to look over her shoulder. And what she saw made her bowels lurch low in her gut.

Goody!

Her mind screamed loud as shit as she peeped him walking up on the porch and about to push through the front door of the old folk's building.

Jewelz panicked. She ducked down low and tried to hide in the pack of elderly people who had just come in from the lunch truck and were waiting for the elevator. By the grace of God she saw a clear path between all the walkers and canes that led straight to the stairwell door, and she headed that way.

Playing it cool, she stared straight in front of her as she jetted toward the staircase and hoped like hell she could get outta sight before Goody peeped her.

After pushing through the doorway she hauled ass up the steps two at a time with her skirt flapping and sailing around her thighs like a kite. She had made it halfway up to the third floor before she heard the door open down below, and then suddenly the sound of stomping footsteps rushed up behind her.

The familiar smell of his powerful cologne chased her up the stairs and Jewelz put her ass in high gear as she beat feet up to the fourth floor. She didn't have the strength to run up any further, so she hit the exit door hard, busting straight through that shit as she jetted down the long hall and headed toward the row of apartments with red-painted doors.

She could hear his footsteps slapping the concrete as he chased her up. Her mind raced like crazy as she fled down the hall. Jewelz knew there was only one way outta this mess, and she knew what she had to do.

By the time the stairwell door burst open behind her and Handgun Goody emerged and hollered, "*Jewelz!*" she had already lifted the metal door knocker and was banging as hard as she could on apartment 4B.

"*Aunt Lou!*" Jewelz shrieked as she bam-bam-bammed on the door like a cop on a drug raid. "Open the door Aunt Lou! Open the door!"

"*Jewelz!*"

She whirled around with her eyes wide like she was caught by surprise.

Handgun Goody stood there looking like a thug-monster-killer. He was swole and breathing hard, and his muscled-up shoulders looked like they were about as wide as the whole damn hallway.

Jewelz's hand went to her thigh. She was gun-strapped under her hula skirt, and if she had to she would shoot the shit outta that big bitch and all his goonies too.

"Hey!" she said, smiling all bright like she was glad to see him. Then she pressed her knees together in the classic, *I gotta piss bad as hell* pose and banged on the door again. "What you doing here, bae?"

"Nah," Goody growled as him and three psycho niggas from his squad advanced down the hall like they was about to twist her grill. "What the fuck is *you* doing here?"

Jewelz squeezed her legs together and hopped from foot to foot as she gripped that door-knocker and slammed it up and down as fast as she could.

"My auntie lives here!" she lied over her shoulder as she damn near banged down the door. "She's old and half-deaf and I gotta pee." She grinned at him again. "You know I don't be pissing on the staircase like some of these project birds be doing so I wish she would hurry up and open up this goddamn—"

The sound of the door being unlocked was like sweet music to Jewelz's ears. A confused-looking elderly woman wearing a starched apron tied over a pale pink duster opened the door just a crack.

That was all Jewelz needed. She bum-rushed that bad boy open and jumped right into the old lady's arms.

"Aunt Lou!" she hollered, pressing herself into the old woman's fluffy bosom. "You didn't hear me out here knockin? Why you ain't got on your hearing-aid, Auntie? I been standing out here forever! What took you so long to answer the door?"

Jewelz grabbed the woman's cheeks and planted a bunch of loud wet smack-smacks all over her face.

"W-w-well…" the old lady stuttered, looking confused as fuck. She turned up her lip and wrinkled her nose but submitted to Jewelz's kisses as her eyes went suspiciously from Jewelz to the four hulking dudes who were now standing almost inside her doorway. "I was just back there using the restroom and…"

"Whew!" Jewelz yelled. "I hope you're finished 'cause I gotta pay my water bill!"

Standing back, Jewelz pushed the carton of orange juice into the old lady's hands and asked, "You feeling any better today, Auntie? I bought the orange juice you wanted. I got Tropicana 'cause I know it's your favorite kind."

She turned to Goody and mouthed, "I'll call you later," then hugged the old lady again and said real loud as she pushed them niggas up outta the front door, "Whew! I'm about to tinkle on myself, Auntie! I really gotta *go!*"

The moment the door slammed Jewelz hurried up and locked that shit. And then she turned around to face the baffled old woman.

"Baby," the elderly lady said staring at Jewelz with puzzlement shining in her droopy eyes. "I appreciate the hugs and kisses and the juice and all, but my name is Reenie, not Lou. And if you don't mind me asking, who in the world is *you?*"

CHAPTER 14

It's Gon Be What It's Gon Be

Slick was running late. He had told Jewelz to meet him at his grandmother's crib for lunch so he could calm shit down between them and apologize for acting ill and breaking shit up in her crib.

But he had jacked his dick to a skin flick a little earlier, then he fell asleep and burnt up the fish sticks he was trying to cook for her, so he had ran up on the avenue to grab something else for their lunch real quick.

He was coming outta the corner bodega holding two tall cans of Arizona ice tea and two turkey and cheese heroes when his phone started buzzing on his hip. Slick glanced down at it real quick.

What the fuck do she want?

The last time he called her she ain't have shit for him. She had fronted him off like she didn't even recognize his voice.

"Ayo," Slick said as he connected his earpiece into his phone and answered the call.

"Hey Slick," Honore said sounding sweet and happy. "Ain't nothing much happening, just checking on you. I just wanted to see how you was holding up."

"Haaa-haaa," Slick laughed like she was full of shit. "What's wrong? You thought I was gonna break the fuck down and start bleeding outta my ears because you stopped talking to me or something? Nah, you ain't gotta check for me, French Fry. I'm always gonna be good. Remember that."

"Damn you ain't gotta go in like that." Honore sucked her teeth. She started to get aggy and say something smart, but then she thought about how she had played him to the left because of that bullet wound in her ass and she calmed down and tried again.

She didn't want no fight with Slick. Besides, she had actually missed him and she had been hoping he would call her back. Slick was a real one. The type that she could actually see herself getting cuffed up with. True, she had shit on him with his boy Wild Man, but that was business. This was turning into pleasure. Chicks was probably lined up on both sides of the street waiting to be Slick's wifey, and there was no way in fuck Honore was gonna let him get away. Especially now that she was scheming on a bigger and better diamond.

"Look, I'm just calling because we haven't spoke in a minute and I wanted to make sure you was good. It's crazy out there in them streets and I care about you, boo."

Slick didn't say shit. He stopped to give an old wino he knew a couple of dollars for a cold one, then he walked over to his car and hopped in.

"Oh, so now you concerned about my well-being, huh?" he finally replied in a slick-ass tone. He heard Honore suck her teeth again but he didn't give a fuck. "Never mind. Anyway, thanks for the call though. But like I said, I'm a'ight. I got shit to handle so I'll holla at you whenever the next blue moon rolls around."

"Slick, wait," Honore blurted out. "I know the last time you tried to get with me I was on some other shit. I don't know what I was thinking. I just felt like we were moving too fast and I didn't wanna get hurt. Just give me a chance to try and explain myself face-to-face, okay?"

Slick thought about it for a minute. She had something to say to him? Yeah, well he had some shit to say to her too. He couldn't front like he didn't dig her, but it was *adios* time and he had to let her go. His heart was in a crazy place right now and he refused to be that sucka nigga that Honore could just string along.

"For real, Slick," Honore pleaded. "I just wanna look you in the eye and tell you how I really feel about you. I'm dead serious."

Slick paused for a long moment. "A'ight, you know where Melody Lanes is at?" he finally asked.

"You talking about that bowling alley up in Sunset Park?" Honore responded. "You know how to bowl or something?"

"Meet me up there in thirty minutes if you wanna rap with me, but leave all ya bullshit at home," Slick said ignoring her question. "And don't be late neither 'cause I got shit to do."

"Okay, fine, but you can leave your attitude at home too, a'ight," Honore said, excited that she would get to see him and hoping they could hit a hotel and get naked real quick. "I'ma be there Slick, but you know thirty minutes ain't enough time for me to get ready. Make it an hour, baby. You can't rush perfection."

"Thirty minutes."

"Forty-five!"

Before Slick could protest she hung up the phone.

Slick stared down at that shit with a slight grin on his mug. Then he quickly hit a number on speed dial and listened as the phone rang on the other end.

"Yo Jewelz—"

"Boy where the hell are you!" Jewelz screeched. "I'm standing outside your grandmother's apartment! You in there on the damn toilet or something? Open up the door and let me in!"

"Um, I ain't even in there," Slick tried to explain. "I had to run to the store to get some grub real quick and now I gotta—"

"Hurry up and get up here!" Jewelz said. "I gotta tell you what happened! You ain't gonna *believe* who I just ran into right here in this building!"

"Ay, look," Slick said quickly. "Something important just came up. I need to make a lil run so gimme a couple of hours, a'ight? Matter fact, I'ma prolly be gone for a good minute, so let's get together tomorrow, cool?"

"Mutha*fucka!*" Jewelz spit from way down in her gut. "I *knew* I shouldn'ta brought my ass over here fuckin with you! *Hell no* that shit ain't cool! Got me running up in old ladies apartments bustin in the door like I'm crazy! Somebody coulda got blasted up in this bitch today! Shit coulda been blazin up in this building!"

"Damn, baby! It's only lunch—"

"Nigga you *begged* me to hook up with you! You said you wanted to do something special for me! You said we was gonna eat some back-in-the-day grub like we used to do when we was little! Well, *fuck you*, Slick! You can eat my ass like it's *groceries*, nigga! *Fuck you!*"

Click!

Slick stared down at the dead phone and then at the lunch he clutched in his hand. He couldn't believe it. All that fuckin noise over a turkey and cheese hero? That shit just didn't make no sense to him. He started to call her back and ask her what she meant about shit getting blazing, but instead he shook his head. He'd get with Jewelz later. He thought about that day at the soul food restaurant when she had actually swung on him, and he shook his head. Jewelz was too emotional. He was definitely gonna make lunch up to her, but she was way too turnt up to be reasoned with right now.

With his mind steady on the future, Slick started his car and headed toward the bowling alley so he could dump Honore.

CHAPTER 15

Deep Love or Cheap Lust

The bowling alley wasn't all that crowded when Slick arrived so he paid for a lane and picked out a couple of bowling balls. Honore was only ten minutes late and that was making very good time for a self-absorbed chick like her.

Slick spotted her as soon as she walked in the door. Her hair was loose and hanging free. She was wearing a skintight pink sweatshirt and black leggings that highlighted her bulging titties and all the curves on her shapely booty.

"W'sup baby," Honore smiled as she walked up to Slick smelling good. He stood there stiff as a board as she gave him a real big hug. It's good to see you. You ready to get yo ass handed to you? I'ono bout you but I do this bowling shit for real and I ain't taking no losses."

"I ain't never scared," Slick said as he checked her out. She looked even better than he had remembered. "I already put our names in the computer. All you gotta do is go pick out a ball."

Honore went over to the rack and sorted through a couple of bowling balls until she found one that fit her fingers. The sounds of old-school hip-hop jams blared through the overhead speakers while they started going head to head on the lanes.

Honore was sticking out her titties and flirting her ass off. Slick played right along with her. He knew what he had come there to do, and he was gonna do it. But he felt some kinda way because Honore looked so happy that he couldn't just cut her off like that. He had to wait for the right time. He decided to save his lil goodbye speech until the end of the game. He'd let her win, then toss her off gently and go back home and make shit right with Jewelz.

With his decision made, Slick relaxed and they started getting in a groove. Honore was a decent bowler so when it was her turn to get on the line Slick would yell or go up behind her and smack her on the ass to distract her from hitting a strike.

After awhile they were both starting to feel like they had never even been apart. They were having fun and falling back into the comfortable groove that they'd had going between them from the gate.

"Hey, listen Slick," Honore said turning serious while they took a break to share an order of cheese fries. "I wanna apologize for the way I acted when you called me that night, yo. I started thinking too hard and I guess I just went into panic mode," she said and flashed him a soft dimpled smile. "I mean, I gave up the ass to you way faster than I normally would and it made me insecure. Plus, I had my aunt and my cousin in my ear telling me you probably had a ton of other bitches too. They said sooner or later you were gonna toss me to the side and I fell for that shit. On top of that I started slipping in school and I felt like you were becoming a big distraction to my education."

Slick stayed quiet and took everything that she was telling him in. None of it sat right with him, but he knew how emotional some females could be.

"I hear what you saying," Slick looked deep into her hazel eyes and admitted, "but I'm not the type to let no woman run in and out of my life. I rarely let females get close to me at all, so when I show genuine care I expect to get it back. I ain't no sucka, Honore. And I won't be played like one. If you was wishy-washy with your shit then you shoulda let me know from the gate whether you was fuckin with me, or just fuckin around."

"I know you ain't no sucka, and yes, I *am* fucking with you," Honore smiled like she knew she was about to get back in good with him. "I'm fucking with you all the way to the end! I apologize, bae. I swear it won't happen again. I just be skitzzin sometimes."

Slick shrugged her off. "That's cool, ma. It was good while it lasted. Maybe ya next dude will have more tolerance for that type of shit than I do."

Honore laughed and traced squiggly lines on the back of his hand with her finger. "Stop playing. There ain't gonna be no next dude. You can kill all them jokes because your sexy ass ain't going nowhere."

"I'm dead-ass serious though," Slick said, even though his resolve was weakening with every whiff of her perfume. "My life is too real to be wasting time. I ain't saying we was supposed to plan a future together, but that hot and cold shit got in the way."

"You right, Daddy," Honore said as she got up from her seat and straddled his lap and wrapped her legs around his waist. She slipped her tongue deeply inside his mouth as Slick's dick bricked up and he held her in his arms.

"Let's start all over, okay?" she asked softly. "As of today, no more on-and-off shit between us, no more hot and cold. Let's be for real. I ain't never felt for no other man the way I feel for you, Slick. I swear to God. Never. I love you, boo. I really do."

"A'ight," Slick said as he stood up and gripped her hips until she was firmly back on her feet. "You said ya piece, now I'ma turn up on you in this bowling shit."

Honore laughed, even though she had expected to hear 'I love you too' roll outta his mouth. She didn't sweat it though. She had wronged him and she had to let him show his pride.

"You can't handle me, boo," she said with a big smile. "I was taking it easy on you. Now you gotta go."

Honore wound up winning the first game and Slick won the next three. Slick bought her a grape soda to make her feel better about the losses, and also because he loved their little playful competition.

He had to admit that Honore was beautiful and it was real cool being with her and all, but still. He wasn't impressed no more. Yeah, that ass was lumped up and them titties were sweet, but whatever. There was no doubt in Slick's mind that their lil sex thang was dead. Because the whole time he was busy checking for Honore, he couldn't stop thinking about Jewelz.

$$$$$

Two whole days had passed since Slick had ditched out on their lunch date, and as Jewelz left the pharmacy and walked back to her apartment she was looking and feeling more tired than ever before in her life.

She had cried her eyes out over him for a whole day and an entire night, and the stress of it all had caused her health to take a serious nosedive.

Slick had been blowing her phone up non-stop, and he had even popped up banging on her door twice the night before. Jewelz had ignored him as she wrapped herself up in a thick blanket and lay there shivering with a bone-chilling fever.

She had woken up this morning dry-heaving her guts out. She'd laid in bed and smoked a joint hoping it would mellow her out and make her feel better, but an hour later she was shaking so bad she'd broken down and called the hospital. The nurse had been sympathetic and the doctor had prescribed her a painkiller and some medication to help calm her stomach.

Right now Jewelz looked a wrung-out mess as she headed back to her crib after picking up the medicine from the pharmacy a few blocks away. She was dragging herself home slowly, clutching her bottle of pills tightly in her hand and trying her best to put one foot in front of the other when somebody called her name.

"Jewelz!"

She turned around slowly with her tired eyes searching.

"Uh-uh, bitch!" a heavyset light-skinned chick with a ratchet mint-green weave and a ton of makeup threw her hand in the air and twisted her lips. "Oh, so you just gonna walk past and act like you don't know me, huh?"

It took a moment for recognition to set in, but when it hit her, it hit her hard. As bad as Jewelz was feeling a huge smile spread over her face.

"Trina..." she grinned, holding her arms out to embrace her old friend as a million painful memories flooded her heart. The chick grabbed Jewelz in a bear hug and held her tight.

"*Trina, Trina, Trina...*" Jewelz whispered as she pressed her face into the girl's bosom and her eyes filled with tears.

"Jewelz...it's so good to see you. I thought you was lost forever..." Trina's lip quivered as a flood of tears ran down her jiggly cheeks. "Girl, I didn't know what them muthafuckas had did with you."

Trina sniffed and wiped her eyes on her sleeve. "I mean, one day you was chained up right there next to me, and the next day you was gone. I thought them niggas dead-ass killed you," she whispered. "I thought you was in a Dumpster somewhere and wouldn't nobody never see you again."

A long-buried ache filled Jewelz's chest. Her and Trina went way back. They had been held captive as teenaged sex slaves together and they'd suffered horrible years of sexual exploitation as victims of Chimp Charlie's pimp reign.

"I ran away when Chimp Charlie took me to dance at a strip joint," Jewelz said slowly, taking her old friend's hand and leading her over to lean against a parked car.

"The cops ran down and raided the joint and I broke the hell out. I didn't stop running until I was damn near on the other side of the city."

Trina sniffled and wiped at her eyes again. "I felt so lost and alone when you left. I mean, I'm glad you got out and all, but I hated not having nobody to talk to and to watch my back. They moved us to a new location that same night. Fat Donnie said since you was gone I had to work overtime. They ran tricks through our room day and night to make up for all the bank you used to bring in."

"I'm sorry I left you," Jewelz said, patting Trina's hand and leaning her head on her shoulder. "I just couldn't take that shit no more, Trina. If I hadn't got out then I woulda died up in that bitch. I swear to God, I woulda died."

Trina nodded. "I feel you girl. I wasn't mad at you. I just missed you, that's all." She frowned. "All them years those niggas had us locked up and selling pussy for them. We wasn't nothing but babies. Them fuckin predators did us so damn filthy!"

Jewelz nodded as old feelings of rage and helplessness sparked up in her too. "I know. I hated them old nasty fuckers. Both of them."

"They probably still got some young girls out there tricking for them right now," Trina said sadly. "They probably never even stopped."

"Uh-uh," Jewelz shook her head quickly. "Fat Donnie ain't trickin *nobody!* His greasy ass is dead so the only thing he's trickin on is a pitchfork down in hell!"

"But what about Chimp Charlie, that ape-looking muthafucka?"

Jewelz frowned then shrugged. "He's still around. For now."

Trina nodded, then smiled and looked Jewelz up and down. "So what you doing now a' days? You dressed real decent so I know you ain't in the life no more."

Jewelz shook her head. "Nah, I been left that kinda thing alone. I'm doing okay, though. I got me a little freelance job that I work here and there, part-time. I live right here in Manhattan now, though. You still in Brooklyn?"

Trina shook her head quickly. "Hell, nah. I got the fuck outta there. I moved up to the Bronx a while back with this dude who got me strung out. I had three kids back to back before my nigga got locked up. But my family stayed in Brooklyn, though. My pops kept the house there and he had custody of all my kids until he got shot in a jewelry store robbery down on Fulton Street a little bit ago."

Jewelz's pulse jumped and she froze.

"Your father got shot?" she yelped. "Are you serious?"

Trina nodded. "Yep, girl. In a fuckin jewelry store. Some wanna be crook-ass niggas busted up at his job and shot him in the face. It was terrible, honey. My mother almost lost her mind. Matter fact, I'm about to move back to Brooklyn so I can help her take care of my kids."

"Trina....Oh my God," Jewelz moaned, covering her mouth with her hand.

"I know," Trina nodded. "My father had just went back to school tryna graduate and shit, and the college had set him up with a job at the jewelry store. The owners made him work late one night and they ended up getting robbed. Poppa Duke got killed, and since my mother's still so tore up I'm tryna get my custody back so the state don't put my kids in foster care."

Jewelz slumped against the car in a daze. If she thought she had felt sick earlier she was really, really sick now. She had spent countless hours locked up in motel rooms with Trina and she had heard a million tales about the humor and goodness of her father, Papa Duke. Jewelz's hands shook and she felt faint as she gave Trina her number and told her she had to run. The good-bye hug she gave her friend was extra-long because it was filled with so much guilt and unspeakable pain.

"If you or your kids ever need anything," Jewelz said, sniffing back her shame-faced tears," call me, okay? If there's *anything* I can ever do for you or your family, I swear I will."

Jewelz walked home with her head in a spin cycle. She kept hearing Trina's words in her ears, and replaying the night of that Fulton Street hit over and over in her mind. And each time she came up with a scenario that was so slick and grimy it was damn near incomprehensible.

"It just can't be," she muttered to herself as she rushed into her apartment and headed straight for her iPad. Her fingers felt like ice as she typed a few search words into the Google bar and stared at what came up.

According to the online news reports Trina's father had been a seventy-two year old college intern at the time of his murder. He had been studying to complete an associate's degree in liberal arts so he could get a promotion at his job.

Jewelz's eyes grew big as shit as she read. Her heart pounded heavily in her chest. It was all right there. Right there in black and white.

The Zip 'em up Crew had fucked up big time. They had gotten the whole thing wrong. The old man they had gunned down hadn't done a damn thing except step into their line of fire holding the wrong damn thing in his hand. He had been minding his business and trying to make a better life for his family when the crew walked in the door and cut him all the way down.

Jewelz felt terrible. She had helped kill the father of one of her closest friends and she would never ever forgive herself for that!

For the very first time she regretted ever jumping on with the Zip 'em up Crew. They were supposed to be a professional hit team, but professionals didn't take out the wrong fucking targets!

Jewelz's first instinct had been to grab her phone so she could call and tell Slick, but then she chilled as she remembered how he had left her hanging out to dry in his grandmother's building. Fuck him! That nigga could get whatever was coming to him because she wasn't telling him shit!

But still, Jewelz just didn't understand it. There were only two people in the jewelry joint when they busted in the door that night. Their assignment had been to hit the monkey carrying a red briefcase, and the old black man was the one who had it in his hand!

But, Jewelz asked herself, if Poppa Duke was the college intern who was studying for a biology test, *then who the fuck was Honore?*

CHAPTER 16

Show Up and Show Out

Wearing the shit outta a money-green designer romper and a pair of stylish pencil-heeled gold stilettos, Cucci Momma looked like a million fat ones. She was chillin out in Crooklyn, and she sat sipping champagne in her man Ice Pick Goody's living room as she waited for him to come home from putting in work on the streets.

She crossed her sleek, perfumed legs and brushed her silky bangs back from her face as she lounged on a butter-soft sofa and gave herself a great big pat on the back.

This was the first time that Ice Pick had left her in his crib alone, and she had gotten down on her hands and knees and gone over the joint with a pair of white gloves, snooping and stealing and scheming her ass off as she ran her greedy eyeballs twelve inches deep inside every nook and cranny up in the bitch.

And now, after pocketing five G's she'd found in a shoebox and about ten grams of coke that she'd discovered taped to the back of Ice Pick's headboard, she was busy flipping through the pages of a trendy magazine while scheming up a plan that would knock her grimy cousin Honore right off her high horse.

As the leader of the Crushed Ice Clique, Honore had been the shot-caller for everything that went down with the all-female crew. But now it was time for Cucci to step up and take what she felt like was owed to her.

Her best shot at grabbing the top spot had been that sweet tip-off that she had given to the Feds so they could lock Honore up, but them bumbling-ass numbskulls had fucked around and blown the whole damn plan up.

Cucci had actually been tasting the sweetness of that hundred grand reward money all on her tongue. She had given them assholes very specific details and lined the whole scene up lovely as hell, and it wasn't her goddamn fault that those idiots couldn't close the damn deal!

Every time she thought about the way those federal suits had fucked up the mission she got pissed off all over again. She just couldn't understand how Honore had escaped that hail of bullets with nothing more than a hunk of meat gouged outta the fat of her ass!

Everything in Cucci had wanted to see her favorite cousin get handcuffed and picked up off the street like a mangy dog. But since the first plan got busted she had been forced to come up with a back-up strategy. And that's where her nigga Ice Pick Goody and his gully brother Handgun were gonna come in.

She was sipping pretty on her second glass of bubbly when she heard keys turning in the door lock. Seconds later, in walked Ice Pick and his fine-ass older brother.

Cucci sighed. Handgun Goody was fly as shit from head to toe, and he looked way longer and stronger than her man Ice Pick did. She was getting moist just looking at that beefy-necked nigga, but she only glanced at him for a few quick seconds because she didn't wanna get caught out there staring at his crotch with her tongue hanging out.

"Yo, w'sup witchu, bae," Ice Pick said as he walked over to the couch and gave her a stank and sloppy kiss that tasted like Newports and 'Ronas. "What the fuck you been doing while I was gone?"

"Nothing much," Cucci batted her fake eyelashes and cooed in the sexy kitten voice that he loved. "I took a bath and cleaned up around here a little bit, then I just been waiting on you to get home, Daddy."

"Well I'm home now. We need to holla at Handgun and put him up on that lil bizzness me and you was kicking back and forth before."

"Hi, Handgun," Cucci cooed shyly, batting her fake eyelashes. "Its good to see you again witcha fine lookin self."

"Yo, bruh," Ice Pick said glancing at her coldly, "my bitch here got some info on a lil mission I think you might be interested in."

"A'ight, then," Handgun said as he took off his Tom Ford jacket and his muscles bulged underneath. He pulled a .45 pistol outta his waistband and set it on the table across from the sofa that Cucci was sitting on.

"Have ya bitch go pour us a drink," he directed Ice Pick, and then let's get down to business."

Cucci got up and hopped right to it, and when she came back with the liquor she sat down on the couch next to Ice Pick and crossed her legs sexily at the knee.

"Now tell my brother what you told me," Ice Pick said, passing Goody a tall glass of peach Ciroc.

"Which part?" Cucci asked.

"The part about the diamond and that nigga they call Slick."

Cucci shrugged. "Oh, Slick? He's just some thieving nigga who came up outta the woodwork. My cousin Honore fucks with him. She said he's a stick-up kid. She met him one night when we was clockin this jewelry store on Fulton Street. He kidnapped Honore and jacked her for a diamond. That shady bitch tried to play me like that shit was only worth pennies but I found out later that it was really worth five mill."

Handgun glanced at his brother and then stared across the table at Cucci closely. "This dude Slick. I used to know a dopeman with that name from back in the day. Is he from Brooklyn?"

She nodded. "Yeah. He's from right here. At least that's what Honore told me. She said Slick is a project nigga but he got another crib somewhere in the city too."

"You know where?"

"Nah, but I just found out that Honore is tryna rip for this other diamond that's worth a lot of fucking Benjamins. Way more than five million this time."

Forgetting his interest in Slick, Goody's eyebrow shot up. "More than five million? Is that right?"

Cucci nodded. She had studied the Pink Lady diamond like she was taking a test and she knew everything there was to know about that bitch.

"The diamond is called the Pink Lady and it'll bring in enough cash for all of us to get a cut and get the fuck outta the hustle game for life."

Handgun frowned. "I don't know too much about diamonds except the ones in my watch and my chain," he said. "How much money are we talking about?"

"Somewhere in the forty to fifty million range," Cucci said with dollar signs dancing in her eyes. "But first we gotta jack it."

Handgun looked at his brother Ice Pick with raised interest, shocked at the price value.

"See, muh'fucka?" Ice Pick grinned at Handgun as he picked up his glass and took a swallow of his drank. "I told you this shit would be worth listening to, bro."

"For forty to fitty mill I'll sit here and listen to this bitch move her lips all night," Handgun said enthusiastically as he turned back to Cucci. "But if we jack the diamond then how the fuck do we sell it once we get a hold of it? Rolling up on that kinda doe sounds real good, but at the same time that shit could get us locked down for forever and day."

"So can all this other extra shit we doing right now!" Ice Pick barked. "But in this case the reward is even higher than the risk, yo."

"Very true, little bruh," Handgun nodded agreeing wholeheartedly.

"And that's where I come in," Cucci spoke up with authority so she could let these niggas know she had already formulated the master plan.

"I was in the diamond bizz way before Honore came along. Our old boss introduced me to a lotta peeps who work underground. I got the connections and the clientele who can handle a transaction for us overseas. All I need y'all to do is get the diamond for me and knock Honore off her square in the process."

"Yo," Ice Pick said suspiciously. "I thought that chick was ya fam? Why you and her ain't huddle up and hit the diamond together?"

"I'm done with that bitch," Cucci said with authority. "Her conniving ass ain't breakin bread the right way and besides, she's moving too sloppy runnin behind that nigga Slick all the time. It ain't personal between us, it's business. This is my big chance to get where I need to be and I'm going for it."

Handgun could clearly see the cutthroat and conniving side of Cucci coming to the surface. He knew damn well that a big part of her issue was straight up personal. Yet he understood. He knew the mechanics of the game. He understood the plotting, scheming, and double-crossing that was required to get on top at all costs. Everybody had their own reasons for shitting on the next nigga. People who craved power and control had been doing that shit since the beginning of time.

"You seem pretty ambitious, Cucci," said Handgun. "I kinda like your style. I can tell you're all about your business. So the reason you haven't rocked Honore yourself is because you need to get the diamond first, am I right?"

"Yes, that's part of it," Cucci told Handgun as she took a sip of her drink. "With me it's always business before pleasure. Plus she got this nigga named Sly McFly who watches over her like a hawk. He's an old school gangsta who holds her down. He would chop me up and stuff me down a fucking incinerator if I was caught betraying them."

"I see, I see," Handgun said as he sat back on the sofa and internalized everything Cucci was saying to him.

"Yo, what we need to do is come up with a plan," Ice Pick said.

"A'ight," Goody agreed, "but before we go for the gusto I wanna know more about that nigga Slick your cousin is fuckin with. Ain't no way he can be the same dude I used to know, but the name is real familiar."

Cucci picked up her drink and slurped. "Well, that lil petty thief ain't nobody special so y'all can deal with him on your own time. But do you think you can bag Honore and get to that diamond before she can get it? And what about Sly McFly?" she asked impatiently. "Which one of y'all niggas got a pair of balls big enough to handle his old ass?"

"*Bitch!*" Handgun barked suddenly. He reached across the low table and pimp smacked Cucci hard upside her head. "Don't you see two muthafuckin men talking? Just shut the fuck up and stay in your lane and be ready to roll when Ice Pick says it's time to make a move!"

"Yo!" Ice Pick grabbed Cucci by the neck and yanked her over to him. "Since you got that mouth open so wide bring them big-ass lips over here and get on ya fuckin knees!" Ice Pick told her as he forced her down in front of him. He unbuckled his belt and took out his soft shit and gripped it in his fist.

"Get my shit up!" he demanded.

Everything about the situation had changed and even the air in the room felt hostile. Cucci had been around plenty of killas before and her mama didn't raise no fools.

"Okay, Daddy..." she said meekly.

She scrambled down in front of Ice Pick's crotch with a quickness. Grabbing his limp man-meat she swooped down on it and started jacking it in her hands and licking underneath his hairy balls like they were two apple-flavored Blow-Pops.

Ice Pick reached down inside the front of her romper and yanked her titties outta the top. Then he unsnapped the crotch and pulled it up in the back so he could rub on her ass and play in her pussy while she worked.

Cucci slobbed on his knob until that shit was wet and shiny and standing straight up in the air. Sucking dick was a skill that Cucci was tops at and she could give brain in her sleep. She was well aware that she was being chastised and Ice Pick was checking her in front of his brother for a reason. The fact that Handgun was watching her closely didn't escape her either. In fact, it excited her and turned her on, and she wanted his fine, paid ass to see exactly what his lil brother was getting and he was missing out on.

Cucci dug in deep and gave Ice Pick a blow-job that was worthy of the big screen. She stuck out her tongue and licked that chocolate shit from the mushroom-capped head all the way down to his coffee-colored balls, taking care to make sure her visual performance was just as good as her physical one.

With Handgun watching, she got up on Ice like a porn star and rubbed the wet head of his dick all over her nipples, giving herself a thorough titty fuck. Next, she sandwiched his throbbing meat in the hollow between her breasts like a hot dog in a bun. She slid her titties up and down while squeezing them together and licking the sugar off the head of his dick at the same time.

As Ice Pick moaned and gasped, Cucci went to work with her teeth. Gently, she nibbled up and down the length of his dick, then she poked her tongue way out and swirled it around and around the crown of his shaft like it was an ice cream cone. Faster and faster she milked his balls in both hands, then swooped down and deep-throated his wood while vibrating her throat and jutting her head back and forth like a chicken.

It wasn't long before she felt Ice Pick's nut building up in his balls, and when she felt his spurt shooting up the chute of his dick like a miniature volcano, she pulled back a little and jacked that shit, smearing his pearl-colored cum all over her lips and letting it drip down the side of his dick.

Cucci was damn proud of herself. She knew she had done a top-notch job and put on a premiere performance, and Ice Pick confirmed that shit for her when he fell back on the sofa and pushed her away and said, "Goddamn! That shit was tops, baby! You rocked my whole muthafuckin world! Now take them pretty lips on over there. My brother want his dick sucked too."

With shock shining in her eyes, Cucci turned toward Handgun as that nigga unbuckled his pants and yanked out his big dick and said, "Sho do!"

CHAPTER 17

Personal Demons

Being so sick made it rough going for Jewelz, and she tossed and turned all night. When she wasn't crawling into the bathroom to heave the contents of her stomach into the toilet, she was huddled under her blanket shivering and shaking like a leaf.

By the time the sun came up her pain was getting crucial and she was ready to give up on life. Despite the medication the doctor had prescribed she was feeling much, much worse. She wasn't surprised because she knew what time it was. Her body just couldn't take it no more and she was losing her fight against the deadly disease that had invaded her blood cells.

"Okay," she relented and told Nurse Shelly when the phone rang a few hours later. The nurse's weekly call had found Jewelz huddled under her blankets sipping from a warm can of Ensure. Her will was still strong, but the bone-tiring weakness was too much for her to bear, so she had finally agreed to restart her chemotherapy treatments.

"Okay, I'll come back to the clinic," Jewelz told the nurse, "but it'll have to be tomorrow because I can't come in today."

"Now, Diamond," the nurse said gently. "A person with your prognosis should know that every single day counts. C'mon, baby. You're already so far behind in your treatment plan that even hours matter at this point. Minutes too. What's so important that you're willing to d—that you can't come in today? Why can't you just come in right now?"

Nurse Shelly had caught herself before she said the d-word, but Jewelz had heard her anyway. The cancer nurse had started to ask Jewelz what was so important that she was willing to die for it, and the answer was something that Jewelz really didn't expect anyone to understand.

Because she had already made up her mind that today was going to be the day. Today was the day that she was going to kill Chimp Charlie. It was now or never and she was gonna kill that ugly-ass predator dead.

She didn't care if it took her to her last dying breath, she was gonna murder that old nasty bastard. All the filthy shit he had forced her to do with her young mouth and pussy was unspeakable and unpardonable, and with the last drop of strength in her body she was gonna make him pay.

Today.

"Nope," Jewelz told Nurse Shelly firmly as she got up slowly and headed toward the bathroom to pull herself together. "I can't come in right now. Not today."

Jewelz knew she had a long hard day ahead of her. She could only pray that God would bless her so that her strength would hold up long enough to satisfy her thirst for revenge.

"Tomorrow," she promised the disappointed nurse. "Like I said, I've got something real important I gotta do today, but I swear to God I'll check myself into the hospital the first thing tomorrow."

CHAPTER 18

Pure Slick

Handgun Goody and his surviving brothers were crammed into a room at Brookdale Hospital right off Linden Boulevard. They had gotten a call that their nephew Trill was finally out of his coma, and they rushed over there to see about him. All three of the Goode brothers felt fucked up about Trill's situation, and they felt they owed it to their dead brother Hammerhead to make sure his seed was straight.

When they got there the youngblood was not only up, he was also eating and talking, and Handgun, Ice Pick, and Cannonball huddled around his bed blasting him with questions and catching every word that came outta his mouth. Although Trill's body was still all broke the fuck up, his mind and his memory were clear as hell.

"I'm telling you it was that bum-nigga Sometimey, man!" Trill insisted. "We ran into him on the staircase and Turk played open season on his neck. I told that psycho nigga to step off and go on about his business, then me and Turk and Gamma headed down the stairs to bang on some more doors and make a lotta noise just like you told us to."

"So what happened?" Ice Pick asked.

"So we had just finished banging on doors on the twelfth floor and we was heading down to eleven, and the next thing I know here comes this wild-ass nigga rushing up behind us outta nowhere!

"That nigga had on the same raggedy clothes that Sometimey had on, but some kinda way he was missing all that nappy hair. Before I could blink he cold-slashed Turk and Gamma, and then he came straight at me!"

"*Sometimey?*" Ice Pick shook his head and patted his lil nephew on the shoulder. "That tall bummy cat who be limping around swinging that watch? Nigga you still sleep. That pissy-ass nigga Sometimey is harmless, yo. Ain't no way he went after all three of y'all like no psycho."

"Fuck that!" Trill bitched. "I swear to God it was him! But like I said, his hair was way short when he came at us, and he didn't have on that shitted-up lil hat no more. His eyes even looked totally different, man. But yo, I'm telling you, my nigga. I seen that mutt nigga somewhere without his lil hat way before that. For real, I know I seen him before."

"Where, nigga?" Handgun demanded. "Where?"

"I seen him twice. The first time was at the club on Unsigned Hype night. Then I seen him again when me and my moms took Aunt La-La out to eat for her birthday."

"*What?*" Handgun Goody shook his head. "What you talking about, man?"

Trill stared hard at Handgun. "Listen, Unc. When that nigga came running down the steps he wasn't Sometimey no more! He was that same clown I seen arguing with your girl in a soul food restaurant one day."

Goody bucked. "Arguing with *my* girl? My fuckin girl *who?*"

"You know who I'm talking about! The broad with the real big ass you was hollerin at in the club. The one who shit on the mic real nice and you gave her a contract. I think her name is Jewelz."

Handgun Goody stumbled backward in the small room. He bumped up against Cannonball's rock hard chest as his brain tried to process the crazy shit he was hearing.

"That nigga was in my club?"

"Hell yeah. I spilled my drink on his punk ass and he didn't even flex."

"And you telling me that bum nigga Sometimey is down with *Jewelz?*"

Trill nodded. "Yeah. That's what the fuck I'm telling you. They was arguing real loud in Mitchell's Soul Food Kitchen while we was eating one day. My moms sent me over there to make sure ya girl was straight and he wasn't putting his hands on her. And that's when I heard her call him Lil Slick."

"*Lil Slick?*" Handgun demanded, his mind flying all the way back to his Dirty Mike days. "She called Sometimey *Lil Slick?*"

"Yeah. I remember laughing to myself when she said it 'cause that long-tall nigga didn't look all that little or all that slick to me. Matter fact, ya mutt Jewelz was runnin off at the mouth and chumpin that nigga like he was a fuckin simp. She even swung on him and ere'thang."

Goody's heart banged in his throat as he plopped down in a hospital chair. He pictured the scars that he had kissed on Jewelz's belly and it felt like somebody had just smashed him over the head with a sledgehammer. He couldn't fuckin believe it. He didn't wanna believe it. Lil Slick was still alive. Alive and well. Alive and in alliance with the beautiful woman that Goody had fallen hard for. With the woman that he loved.

Jewelz.

Reality crashed down all around him.

So that's what Jewelz was doing in the building when I ran down on her ass that day! Goody pictured her banging on the door and holding that container of orange juice and kissing all over that old lady, and he knew what time it was for sure.

Them trench-bitches had played him. Lined him right up for the kill! Guilt surged through Goody as he thought about the first night he had brought Jewelz home to his bed. He knew exactly where his leak had come from now, and he knew why too.

That bitch had tried to sleepwalk him. She had laid right in his bed acting like she was sick. And his pussy-drunk ass had issued killing orders to his brother in the presence of a turncoat infiltrator! Goody had been played like a sucka-ass simp, and his little brother Chainsaw had paid the price for it.

As his brothers continued to question Trill, Handgun sat there stunned and consumed in a state of quiet rage. The blinders had fallen off his eyes. One and one was finally adding up to two.

It wasn't Bajan Andy who had come at his set and picked all his boys off like ducks, he now realized. It was Lil Slick. Crazy Haz's nephew. And Goody was pretty sure he knew exactly who the fuck Jewelz was too.

The memory of her small, bloody body swam into his vision and Handgun felt sick to his stomach about what Haz had made him do that day. His criminal actions had brought death down on his entire family. On his whole fuckin empire! Goody was physically sick with this knowledge, but he was too ashamed to admit it to his brothers. They didn't know nothing about his fiendish past, or about the unforgivable acts he had committed on a bunch of helpless kids that day.

He glanced across the room where Cannonball was steady grilling Trill.

"So you seriously saying this Slick nigga was strong enough to fuck all three of y'all up without pulling out no gat?" Cannonball questioned.

Trill nodded his head slowly. "Yo, that muthafucka *ran down* on Turk and Gamma! You shoulda seen how swift and smoove he dropped they asses. He moved so fast with his blade that I didn't even have time to think about fighting back, Unc. The only thing I could do was tuck my ass in and rise and fly."

Ice Pick pressed. "So you *really* think that Sometimey nigga is some kinda undercover savage named Slick?"

"I don't think, my nigga! I *know!* I just told you I seen him with my own two eyes! I walked up and looked dead at him when we was in that restaurant. I even tried to give that chick Jewelz a ride home but she said nah and bounced."

"Damn. So that retarded bum-shit Sometimey be walking around playing is all a fuckin act then, huh," Cannonball said quietly.

Trill's laugh was short and bitter. "Just look at me laying here all fucked up. That wasn't no Sometimey-shit that put me in this bed and our niggas in the ground, homey. That shit was pure Slick!"

$$$$$

So many fallen soldiers, Goody brooded, fingering his moustache as all the pieces of the puzzle finally fell neatly in place. He had already envisioned what he wanted to do to Lil Slick AKA Sometimey, and that shit wasn't good. He pictured all the Goode Brothers who had gone to their graves at the hands of that cat and he shook quietly with fury.

It had been a long time since Goody had fallen off his game and let his guard down this way. Jewelz was the first bitch who had caught him snoozing in a minute. She had gotten straight into his heart and that shit really hurt him because she was everything he had ever wanted in a woman.

Sleeping on her was his bad, and he was gonna make her pay for playing him out. By the time Goody was through with her she was gonna wish she had never met him. Let alone deceived him and made him fall in love.

But that Sometimey muthafucka was a different story. That cat had crept up on his gang so smoove that Goody had never even seen him coming. But he saw that nigga now. He saw him as his true self. As *Lil Slick*. He was gonna crush that nigga's skull when he got his hands on him. He was gonna finish what Crazy Haz had started and straight-up take that lil nigga's head off!

CHAPTER 19

Watch How the Tables Turn

It was early evening and Slick was sitting at the bar in his living room waiting for Honore to show up. He had just worked out intensely and he was still wearing his damp clothes as he listened to some sounds over the in-ceiling speakers. He was in a reflective mood and he had some incense burning and a glass of Remy on the rocks in his hand.

Earlier he had done an hour of kickboxing and then left his plush condo and taken a thirty-minute jog around the neighborhood. When he came back he'd gotten down on his living room floor and pumped out two hundred quick sit-ups and two hundred deep push-ups. By the time he was done every muscle in his body was screaming and his clothes were soaked in sweat.

In addition to punishing his body for hours, Slick had also been mentally kicking himself up the ass for being so stupid. Jewelz was mad at him again. He had ducked out on their lunch date and no matter how many times he dialed her number or banged on her door, she igged his ass.

Slick knew he deserved her fury too, because for the first time in a minute he had slid off his game in a way that truly shamed him.

For most of his life he had prided himself on being bullshit proof, yet he had slipped up and invited his business into his bedroom, and not a damn thing had been going right for him ever since.

He took a big swig of the yak and winced as it burned its way down into his stomach. Common sense told him that he should have been drinking a glass of ice water because his muscles were on fire and in need of replenishing. But after the phone call he had just gotten he knew water wasn't gonna be strong enough to help him out.

Slick shook his head. Wild Man had been right about "Mister Perfect" taking a fall. But it wasn't on the job like his manz had predicted. Nah, Slick's stumbling block had come in the form of a female, which was how most stupid niggas got took down to the mat.

But he was grateful that his eyes were finally wide open now, and what fucked his head up the most was the knowledge that Honore wasn't even worth all that. Yeah, the girl had mad sexual swag, and she was cool for a delicious slice of ass every now and then, but that was about it.

She definitely wasn't the type of chick that Slick could see himself going long distance with. He realized now that she didn't even have the kind of intellectual curiosity it took to wanna travel the globe and learn new languages, explore new cultures, or build a solid empire from the foundation up.

But she had sounded real sweet and sexy a few minutes ago when she hit him on the cell and invited herself over.

"Hey baby!" she had gushed the moment he answered the phone. "Guess where I'm at? I'm right around the corner from your crib, bae! Ain't that some shit? Buzz me in when you hear the intercom. I wanna come up and holla at you real quick 'cause I miss you and I got a lil sumthin I wanna give you, 'kay?"

Slick had drained his shot glass and told her to come on up. He knew she was tryna get up under his balls and he wasn't impressed with her lil sugary act for one fuckin minute. By all rights he shoulda straight deaded her ass right out when they hooked up at the bowling alley, but since he hadn't actually come out and just told her to bounce, now was the time to speak those words out loud and dead that entire situation. Since she "just happened" to be in the neighborhood, he would "just happen" to let her know that whatever lil shit they'd once had going, it was now a flat-line.

Slick closed his eyes and silently thanked his mama. He had dreamt about her just last night. They had been walking together in some real tall grass and she had warned him to watch out for the snakes.

He thought about how his grandmother used to look up numbers in the Big Red Dream Book when he was a kid. She swore all dreams signified something important, and she musta been right because she used to hit the number left and right. Slick knew the dream he'd had about Kea wasn't just some random shit. He felt his mother and his grandmother both looking out for him beyond the grave. They were guiding him and warning him to get his shit together. And Slick was ready to listen to them and make the right move. The move that his mother would most definitely approve of.

Less than five minutes after he buzzed Honore into the building Slick heard the doorbell ring. He chuckled as he got up off his barstool. Miss Honore was out there waiting on deck. She claimed she had something she wanted to give him? Well, he had something he wanted to give her ass too.

The *boot.*

"Hey, baby!" Honore said, sounding all peppy and wearing a big smile when he opened the door.

"Yo, you got a key made or something? How did you get in downstairs without me buzzing you in?"

Honore shrugged. "A white man was on his way out so I hollered for him to hold the door and I came right on in. Anyway, I'm up here now."

She stepped inside his crib wearing some crisp, fashionable gear, and she took one look at his sweat-drenched t-shirt and frowned.

"Dagg!" she fanned her hand in front of her nose. "Boy what in the world you been doing up in here?"

"Working out," Slick said quietly, drilling her with his eyes.

Honore wrinkled her nose up and walked over to the sofa. "Ummm, you are fine as hell, Slick, but all that sweat don't smell cute I want you to know."

"Yo, whattup?" Slick said, igging that noise. "How you just happened to be sliding around in my hood today?"

Honore laughed. "What? You think you own this whole zip code? Man, please! I got plenty of people around here. I was on my way to check out one of my cousins but I decided to swing by here first."

"Oh yeah? So what you got to give me?"

"Uh-uh," Honore shook her head, then sat on the sofa in her cute lil skirt and crossed her legs real sexy-like. She grinned up at him and smirked.

"Go get yourself right first, son. You need a shower like right now, dude. I'ma hit ya lil bar over there and have me a glass of wine while I wait for you. Trust me, what I got will still be nice and fresh when you're done."

Slick opened his mouth to chop her up, but then he lifted his arm and caught a whiff of his pit. Yeah, she was right. His shit was hittin. He nodded and tossed back his drink, then he headed to the bathroom to get up in some water.

CHAPTER 20

Get it Poppin!

Jewelz had been driving around New York all day long. Right now the half-moon floating in the sky was a pale orange color as she sat slouched down in her whip on a semi-dark street in Manhattan. Her mind was in a serious tail-spin as she stared up at the windows of Slick's condo. She had been hot on the tail of her target, and it shocked the hell out of her when she realized she'd been led into Slick's neighborhood by some sort of cosmic coincidence.

The lights in his crib were on and blazing so she knew he was home. Or maybe he wasn't. She used to think she knew him like a book, but nothing he was doing these days made sense to her and Jewelz was too sick to try to figure him out. After he ditched on her like that the other day she had given up on him. She just didn't have the energy for his shady ass anymore. All she was tryna do now was save the last of her strength to plant the big ugly nigga she was going after.

For the longest time Jewelz had been in hunt-mode on the Internet where she was able to find out everything she needed to know about her target. And after all these years of hating him from a distance, she finally had him in her crosshairs.

Jewelz now knew his last name, she knew he had done a bid in an upstate prison, and she knew he had moved to Queens a while back and had registered as a sex offender. Jewelz also knew his mother was still alive and confined to a bed in a nursing home in the Boogie Down Bronx. And that's where she had started out today. Trailing behind Chimp Charlie as he made his weekly trip to visit his elderly mother.

Even though she still felt sicker than sick, Jewelz had laid low patiently while the rapist and child pimp had spent what was gonna be his last day with the woman who had brought his beastly ass into the world. And once Chimp Charlie's visit with his mother was finally over and he left the facility, Jewelz had trailed him all the way to Queens and waited as he drove into a gated underground garage.

It had taken Charlie over two hours to drive back out, and despite the heat of the day, Jewelz had sat in her car coughing and shivering with her entire body shuddering and spasming.

She had felt feverish and close to exhaustion as she slumped behind the wheel, but she had forced herself to stay awake and keep her eyes trained on that garage door because she was determined to see her plan through. Even if it killed her.

"Shit!" she had cursed when her target finally drove back out of the garage. To Jewelz's dismay Chimp Charlie had picked up some company. Someone was sitting beside him in the front passenger seat. Jewelz's heart sank. She needed to catch the old bastard alone, and it was too dark to tell if it was a man or a woman in his whip. But he had a rider with him for sure.

Jewelz trailed him a few cars back as Charlie drove all the way into Manhattan. When he finally turned onto a very familiar residential street and slowed down like he was looking for a space to park, she didn't know what the fuck was what.

"Why in the world is this nasty nigga coming around here?" she wondered out loud as she pulled into a spot about halfway down the block behind him. She was parked directly in front of a fire hydrant but wasn't no traffic cops out at this time of night so she didn't give a damn.

Jewelz sat there with her eyes glued on Chimp Charlie's whip trying to figure shit out. And when she finally saw the passenger door open and a person begin to climb out, she almost jumped for joy.

"Yeah," she muttered under her breath urging the figure to climb completely outta the car. "Get your ass on out and get gone so I can catch that old nasty perv by himself!"

Jewelz was real amped for a moment by the passenger's pending departure, but that lil burst of happiness died quicker than shit. Recognition crashed down on her as she realized exactly who had gotten outta the whip and was now strutting her ass across the street toward Slick's condo.

"Oh, *hell* no!" Jewelz shrieked. "What in the hell is *she* doing riding with *him?*"

Jewelz's eyes got big as she watched the chick step up on the curb. She knew damn well this bitch wasn't going up in that building to see Slick!

Chimp Charlie put on his signal and started pulling out of the parking space and for a moment Jewelz couldn't decide if she should follow him while she still had the energy to slump him, or if she should run up behind that piss-colored bitch and plant a hot one in the back of her head!

She hesitated, seething with indecision as an elderly white man exited the building's lobby and the chick ran real quick to catch the front door before it slammed closed.

Suddenly a light bulb went off in Jewelz's memory and she lurched forward in her seat, shocked as hell.

"Uh-uh," she shook her head trying to dismiss the vision that had just popped into her mind. Uh-*uh*, goddammit! Hell *no!*"

Something about the way that chick ran looked real familiar to her. Jewelz had seen this chick running before. She had *seen* her!

Jewelz's mind clicked and suddenly everything started adding up. *Pride, betrayal, envy, greed, lust, trickery,* and *revenge* were all deadly sins that had played a part in sending the Zip 'em up Crew tumbling down to their knees, but right now it was the deadly sin of *stupidity* that threatened to smash their skulls and spill their brains all over the chopping block!

So that's why the BBU said they had failed on two consecutive hits!

Jewelz took a deep breath and fanned her face. Her heart was pounding like a muthafucka and she started having palpitations. She needed to pull herself together and calm the fuck down. This was some crucial shit she was about to slide up on and she didn't wanna fuck it up. Jewelz knew she was at a crossroad. She had a critical decision to make, and all she could do was pray she choose the right path. Gripping her keys in her fist, she checked the nine-millimeter on her waist, then slid outta the car and jetted across the street.

She had no idea what the hell she was gonna do, but she had to find out whether she was just buggin or if the crazy shit she was thinking could really *really* be true!

$$$$$

While Jewelz had been consumed with stalking Chimp Charlie's ass like a hungry lioness on a piece of raw meat, she had no idea that there was a pack of wild animals sniffing behind her and nipping at her heels too.

Goody and his three gutter gun boyz were traveling in a low-key black Ford Taurus. Grieving over his dead brothers had him wracked with guilt, and nothing but payback was on his mind.

He had been tailing Jewelz like a bloodhound as she drove through the streets of New York. Finding out that she was down with that nigga Slick had been like stumbling on a goldmine. Goody and his pack didn't know exactly where she was headed, but it didn't matter because as soon as she stopped somewhere sweet, Goody was gonna line her ass up properly.

The mood in the car was tense, and conflicting thoughts raced through Handgun's head as his driver navigated through traffic.

That bitch thought she was smarter than me huh? Goody thought as he glared at the taillights on Jewelz's car and raged in silent shame. *She thought she was gonna take a nigga out and be my downfall?* He shook his head. *Bitch had me eating her pussy and all up in my feelings while she was plotting and scheming the whole fuckin time! I can hear Crazy Haz laughing at me down in hell right now! Jewelz almost rocked me right to sleep. She's thorough, though. Truly a bad bitch if I've ever seen one. I'm gonna love killing her.*

While Goody was running on emotions, the gunner team rolling in the car with him was making cold and calculated moves. Teebo was stuffing a burner down the side of his boot and putting extra ammo in his pocket. Spaz was in the backseat sliding on his black gloves and checking the clip of his gat to make sure it was fully loaded. He had stepped into Black Pearl's shoes to be one of Goody's best young gunnas, and he was ready to do whatever his big homey required of him.

"You want me to pull up beside her at the next light and let Spaz blow that bitch full of holes?" his boy Young Flip asked Goody.

Goody shook his head. "Nah, that's too easy. This shit is personal right here. That bitch gotta catch a bad one up close. She gotta know it's me. I'ma enjoy tearing her world the fuck apart. I put that on the hood, this bitch is gonna feel my pain."

"So how we gonna smash this hoe then, big bruh?" Spaz asked, leaning over the front seat.

"We ain't gonna smash her. At least not yet. We're gonna use this bitch to get next to the big homey. She's gonna lead us straight to the jackpot. Don't worry, she gotta stop sometime," Goody responded. "We just stay patient. We ain't in no rush and we ain't stopping until the bitch is in my grasp."

Young Flip stayed at least a car length behind Jewelz as much as possible. He could see that his boss had a calm rage brewing in him. He almost felt sorry for what was gonna happen when he caught up with the unlucky girl.

Goody plucked a Newport butt outta his window and kept his eyes glued on Jewelz's whip. Pretty soon she pulled up in a neighborhood that had some real nice apartment buildings.

"Ay, hurry up and get ready to pull over. She's slowing down and it looks like she's about to stop," Goody barked at Young Flip.

Just as he said that Jewelz pulled over to the right and parked her car about five spots ahead of them.

"Keep some cars between us," Handgun Goody instructed Young Flip. "I don't want that bitch to spot us. Spaz and Teebo, y'all hop out and follow her ass," Goody told his other two troops. "Make sure you know where she's going and don't do nothing to make her suspicious."

Without hesitation his two gunners jumped outta the ride and approached the building from the opposite side of the street. They paced themselves so that when Jewelz emerged from her car they could converge on her position. Spaz hit Goody up on the cell phone.

"She's getting out the car. Now she's crossing the street, coming to my side," Spaz whispered. "What you want me to do, boss?"

"Follow that ass! Make sure you see what floor she's going to," Goody directed him as he opened his car door and climbed out. "I'm coming in right behind you."

"Got you," Spaz said and then hung up.

Young Flip crossed the street behind Jewelz and nonchalantly followed her into the building as another resident was coming out. Jewelz walked straight into the elevator while Young Flip stopped to act as if he was checking a mailbox. A few moments later he let Spaz and Teebo inside the lobby too.

"Call Goody back," Young Flip told Spaz as he stared up at the electronic console. "Let him know the elevator just stopped on the twelfth floor."

"Cool," Goody said as Spaz spotted him at the door and let him in. "We'll go up there and wait for her ass."

"A'ight," Flip said. "So what's the plan? What we doing? All of us going up or what?"

"Nah, me and Spaz are gonna go up and check shit out," Goody said. "I want you and Teebo to stay down here and watch the elevator. Call me if anything starts looking funny."

Goody couldn't wait to get up on that bitch. His adrenaline was so spiked he decided to take the stairs up to the twelfth floor instead of waiting for the elevator, much to Spaz's dismay.

The two killers hit the staircase and Handgun ran up them bitches like he was a prime stallion. He welcomed the physical exertion so he could get his blood flowing and loosen up his tense muscles.

It's on now, Jewelz. You shoulda never made me fall in love with you, girl. I remember what I did to you twenty years ago and I'm sorry. That nigga Haz had me doing shit I'm gonna have nightmares about until I die. He gave me a taste of blood, but he also saved my life. I made the choice though, the choice to be more ruthless than that nigga could ever be. I woulda gave you the world if you had just stood by me. But you betrayed me and you took my brothers. So I'm gonna finish what I helped Haz start all those years ago. Bitch, you gotta die.

$$$$$

The new Go Hard Family track featuring Reem Raw was blaring loudly as Jewelz paused in the hallway outside of apartment 12D. Getting into Slick's crib was gonna be just as easy as getting into his building had been. All she had to do was use her key.

With her nine gripped tightly in her fist, she slid her key into the lock and slowly turned it until it clicked. Quietly, she eased the knob to the right and pushed the door open.

The first thing she noticed was that Slick was nowhere in sight. But somebody else was. The bitch that Jewelz had followed into the building was sitting on his sofa with her feet propped up on the coffee table. She was looking down at her phone as she sipped from a goblet of wine.

Jewelz froze for a split second as she checked the chick out. She had a red and black scarf tied around her forehead and she was dressed in a designer skirt and blouse that had to have set her back a good couple of yards.

Honore glanced up from her phone and looked shocked as hell when the door swung open and the trained killer walked inside.

"*Sssh!*" Jewelz said, showing the chick the bizzness end of her gat. Girlfriend took her feet down off the coffee table and opened her mouth to say something and Jewelz cocked her piece and aimed it dead at her forehead.

"Bitch I said, *ssshhh!*" she barked, knowing damn well the chick had heard her even with the music going strong. "And put that goddamn phone down!"

Jewelz stepped fully inside the apartment and stuck her foot out behind her and rode the door shut.

"Where's Slick?" she asked quietly.

The girl angled her head over her shoulder toward the bathroom and Jewelz heard the faint sound of water running in the shower.

Keeping her gun hand steady, Jewelz stuck her finger through the chain loop of Slick's house keys and fanned her hand under her nose.

"Honore," she said and then sneezed real hard. "Oh! Excuse me. I see you back in here stankin up the joint with that funky-ass perfume. You do remember me, don't you?"

The bitch had the nerve to smirk and put her hand on her hip.

"Yeah, I remember you," Honore said coolly. She reached for her goblet and took a sip of wine and then said, "I remember you needed your gun the last time we crossed paths too. I definitely remember that."

"Shut up and put the fuckin glass down," Jewelz snapped, motioning with her piece. She knew what she needed to do, and with Slick in the shower she might just have enough time to get it done.

"Yo, that's a bad-ass skirt you got on, ma," Jewelz said admiringly. "I bet that baby got a silk lining and real metal hooks on the side and the whole nine. Is it a Kate Spade?"

Honore laughed like *bitch please.* "Um, Chanel," she corrected smugly. "Kate Spade is for bird bitches like you."

"Cool, stand up and take it off," Jewelz ordered, fighting to keep her gun hand steady.

Honore bucked her eyes wide in surprise.

"You want me to take off my skirt in front of you?"

Jewelz sniffed and nodded. "Yep. And take that skank-looking blouse off too. Ga'head. Act like you up on stage hanging off one of them golden poles you used to ride. You know how to do it. Strip, baby. Strip."

Honore waved her hand. "I ain't about to—"

Jewelz crossed the room in three strides and the sound of the hammer cocking on her tool seemed like it was ten times louder than the music.

"Bitch, I *promise* you," she spit, trembling with fatigue and rage. "I fuckin *promise* you 'cause I ain't got a muthafuckin thing to lose! Fuck with me and your brains will be splattered all over that back wall. And if you think Slick can get out here in time to save you then your dumb ass better think again. Now strip, bitch! *Strip!*"

Reluctantly Honore stood up. She reached toward her throat and started unbuttoning her blouse. She slipped it off her shoulders and let it fall to the floor. She wore a cherry-red bra over her round breasts that looked expensive as hell and contrasted sharply with her smooth butterscotch skin, but Jewelz wasn't impressed in the least.

Jewelz brought her inner arm toward her nose and sneezed again. "Now get outta that skirt," she ordered.

A quick look of fear flashed across Honore's face.

"I ain't never heard of no stupid shit like this before! I shoulda known you was one of *them* types," Honore said with a cold sneer. "You a stud or something? Yeah, bitch I thought you looked kinda hard. I saw you checking out my ass the first night I met you. What? You wanna eat my pussy? Is that why you wanna see me na—"

Jewelz tightened her finger on the trigger ready to blast the bitch into the next room, but Honore's hands flew to her side as she hurried up and started zipping down her skirt.

With her eyes downcast she wriggled it past her curvy hips and stood before Jewelz in a pair of cherry-red silk panties that matched her bra.

With her head spinning, Jewelz's eyes swept over Honore from her neck to her toes. She examined every inch of the girl's exposed skin searching for that telltale sign.

"Turn around and let me see the back," Jewelz demanded.

"What???? C'mon, now!" Honore said, but that look of straight bizzness in Jewelz's eyes sent her turning around to face the wall.

Suddenly Jewelz felt another sneeze coming on. She did her best to hold it back but it ripped from her nose and sent a long spray of blood shooting out of her left nostril.

"Yuck!" Honore looked over her shoulder and twisted her lips as Jewelz picked up a throw pillow from the sofa and ran it across her nose.

"Turn your ass back around to that wall!" Jewelz sniffed and swallowed a mouthful of warm blood.

Ignoring her own suffering, she stepped closer and stared at Honore's slender back. She eyeballed the girl's trim waist and the way her firm round ass exploded in a pronounced question mark curve away from her body.

It was easy to see why Slick had feened so hard for her. Honore had a banging package, Jewelz had to admit. But hell, she used to have a prime frame on her too, especially before her illness had started eating the meat off her bones.

"Damn! Why you got your eyes all up my booty?" Honore snapped over her shoulder. "What? You want me to pull my panties down now so you can see what color my coochie hairs is—"

"Turn your ass back around!" Jewelz barked, disappointed as hell that her hunch had been so wrong. Honore's skin was smoother than a baby's ass. There were no stitches, no healing wound, and absolutely no sign of the bullet that Jewelz coulda sworn had spit from her gat and tagged the bitch somewhere on her body.

As disappointment washed over her Jewelz felt faint and her skin began to flush and sweat. She swallowed hard, gripping her keys and the gun.

"Um, can you step the fuck away from me please?" Honore asked with much attitude. "I need to put my clothes back on and I don't want your sick ass sneezing none of them nasty germs all over me."

"Oh, you think this is a game?" Jewelz barked. Tag or no tag, Honore owed her a fade. "Yeah, turn around bitch."

Honore must have been feeling the same way because as soon as she turned around she rocked Jewelz with a left hook. It was on and mothafucking poppin. The gun fell from Jewelz's hand and both of the project chicks started swinging for dear life. Honore kicked Jewelz hard between her legs and caught her with a clean right hook that flipped Jewelz right over the coffee table and dislodged her wig.

"Yeah, hoe!" Honore roared. "Come get this fucking work, sneezy! You had this ass-beating coming for a minute now. I ain't forgot about how you pressed that gun up against my head the night I first met you, bitch!"

Fueled up by rage and adrenaline, Jewelz slapped her wig back on crooked then pulled herself to her feet and smiled.

"Bitch you been begging me to see you for a minute now. Ok, now you got my attention," Jewelz said with narrowed eyes. "Let's get it."

Jewelz charged in and ducked a punch from Honore. With her keys still dangling from her finger, she hit Honore with a throat chop followed by a sharp uppercut. As sick as she was Jewelz was running on borrowed gas and she started digging into Honore's ass with everything she had in the tank.

Bitch! Bitch! Bitch!

Jewelz's training kicked in and she went into gunslinger mode. Honore was balled up on her knees trying her best to defend herself from the swift punches, high knees, key jabs, and snapping kicks that Jewelz was delivering.

"Where's all that shit you was just talking?" Jewelz spit with venom as sweat ran down her face. She spotted an opening and kicked Honore in the temple, snapping her head sharply to the side and flooring her flat. "Get the fuck up you thot-ass smut! I will *murder* your ass in up in this mothafucka!"

Honore was down but she wasn't out.

"Bitch you just jelly!" Honore sneered. She jumped up from the floor as Jewelz swayed on her feet, at the brink of exhaustion.

"You just mad 'cause Slick don't even wanna stick his dick up in your ugly ass! You mad 'cause every time that dumb nigga puckers up his lips you be tasting the crack of my ass!"

Jewelz blacked the fuck out. Her hands were trembling as she snatched her gun up off the floor. She was shaking like a leaf as she raised that bitch to squeeze a hot one off right in Honore's pretty face.

But instead of squeezing the trigger, she swung that shit. Hard. The gun cracked into Honore's skull with a sickening sound, and Jewelz stumbled forward, carried by the momentum. She shifted her weight and gripped the burner extra-tight so she could slam the bitch upside her head again, this time with a backhand stroke when—

Pop!

The barrel flashed orange and Honore slumped down and hit the deck again. Splayed out flat on the floor, she started screaming her fuckin head off, and when she realized she wasn't shot she scurried forward like a crab and tried to squeeze her shook ass under the couch.

On the other side of the wall, Slick was just rinsing the soap off his balls when the shower tile exploded behind him and a hot bullet whizzed past his ear.

A piece of ceramic tile skimmed the side of his face and cut a surgical line across his cheek as it passed by. Slick dropped down to his knees and protected his bloody face as the bullet exited the shower stall and clear glass flew everywhere. A hole opened up in his window as the bullet continued on its path.

"What the fuck!" he hollered as he jumped outta the enclosure and damn near impaled his foot on a shard of glass as he scrambled into his gym shorts.

Dripping wet, Slick charged outta the bathroom and ran into the living room. What he saw when he got there was enough to make his blood pressure shoot up off the charts.

"Slick!" Honore screamed from the top of her lungs. *"Help!* This crazy bitch tried to shoot me! She's got a *gun!"*

Time seemed to stand still, then rush into slow-mo for Jewelz. She heard buzzing noises in her ears and hot bile rose to the back of her throat as Slick ran up on her with beads of water all over his buff chest and a pair of wet gym shorts clinging to his body.

"Jewelz! What the fuck is you doing!?!"

"Slick I'm sor—"

"Gimme that shit!" Slick roared. He was on her in two seconds flat, twisting the heat out of her grip.

Jewelz had used up every ounce of her energy reserves fighting Honore, and now she was barely able to stand on her feet. She reached out for Slick's arm to steady herself, and the man of her dreams shook her hand off and glared at her with the fury of a ghetto beast.

"What the fuck is you doin?"

"Slick!" Honore interrupted as she cried out again. She pulled herself up to the couch then collapsed down on it and dramatically clutched a pillow to her chest. "Thank God you came out here to save me! This crazy bitch tried to *sh-sh-sh-shoot* me!" she wailed.

"I-I-I'm sorry, Slick…I thought…" Jewelz licked her lips as she tried to explain, but the buzzing noise in her head was making her dizzy and her right leg suddenly felt numb.

"What the hell is wrong with you!" Slick jerked her hard by her arm. "You almost fuckin shot me!!! What the fuck is you doing coming up in here popping off ya gat *in my house?"*

Jewelz swallowed hard and tried again. Her vision was blurry and the buzzing noise in her head was getting louder and louder, but somehow she had to make Slick see!

This bitch might not be the Queen of Diamonds like Jewelz had originally thought she was, but with Papa Duke dead she was damn sure the monkey with the red briefcase!

"Slick!" Jewelz cried out weakly as she prayed for God to open his eyes. "C-c-can't you see who she is?"

"This ain't about her!" Slick roared as a steady stream of blood dripped down his sliced cheek. "Right now I just see *you* goddammit! All of this over some kinda jealousy bullshit? Nah, fuck that Jewelz! I don't see nobody but *you!"*

"But Slick…she's the—" Jewelz muttered again, fighting to keep the blackness from swooping down over her. "Lil Slick this bitch is the—"

"Slick you *bleeding!"* Honore shrieked as she ran over and pressed her hand under his dripping cheek wound. "Oh my God! I can see way down to your white meat and look at all that fuckin blood! C'mon, bae. We gotta get you to the hospital. You need stitches for real, right fuckin now!"

Jewelz stared at the blood that she had spilled. The realization of what she coulda done to Slick when she fired her gun slammed into her like a wrecking ball.

"Slick…" she reached out to him, horrified at the thought that she could have killed the man she loved. "Oh my God…Slick…I'm so—"

"Gimme my fuckin keys!" he exploded as he grabbed her wrist and went to twist the keys off her fingers. "Give up my shit right fuckin *now!"*

Jewelz opened her hand and let the keys slip from her grasp. She was sweating like crazy and her lips moved slowly as she tried to tell Slick, to plead with him, as the music blared and Honore wailed that he was bleeding to death and they needed to get to the hospital.

"Yo, you gotta *go,"* Slick said, snatching Jewelz by the arm and hustling her toward the door.

The room was spinning in crazy circles and Jewelz was starting to sag at the knees. "Slick…"

"Get gone, Jewelz!" He pushed her. "Haul ass! We ain't having no fuckin conversations until you get your shit together!"

"But Slick…" Jewelz moaned one last time. Her heart was fluttering wildly in her chest and she felt a hot drop of blood trying to slip from her right nostril. She sniffed it back up and wiped at her nose with the back of her hand. "Just listen to me, Slick…"

"Hell nah! I ain't tryna hear shit you gotta say!" He shoved her toward the door and then opened it and pushed her out. "You coulda rocked me to sleep in there goddammit! Step the fuck off *and get the fuck outta here!"*

Shoved out into the hallway, Jewelz staggered against the wall as the door went *slam!*

Almost in a state of panic, Jewelz stumbled down the hall half-blind and sicker than a dying dog. She tripped over her feet near the incinerator and slammed against the wall, twisting her ankle and losing a shoe.

"*Oh God, oh God, oh God*," she whispered over and over as she fought against the blackness that was coming down on her. She tried her best to hold on to her senses long enough to get downstairs to her car where she could grab her cell phone and call for help.

I ain't gonna make it, she realized as a huge wave of unbearable weakness swept over her whole body. She needed a phone right away. She needed to dial 911 and call for an ambulance.

"Help!" she tried to scream, but the word came out as a mere whisper. *Somebody help me...*

Leaning against the wall for support, Jewelz dragged her way toward the elevator, praying to make it to the apartment that was on the other side of the hall. She would knock on the door. She would beg whoever answered for help...all she had to do was make it a few more steps and she'd be okay.

Jewelz stumbled helplessly with only the concrete wall to keep her up on her feet. *Just a few more steps...just a few more...*

Another wave of sickness rushed over her and it tossed her into a dark sea. She was almost at the end of the hall when suddenly she lost control of her bladder. Crying out in shame and fear, Jewelz staggered blindly around the corner. As blackness rushed down to cloak her, Jewelz's knees buckled and she collapsed into a pair of very familiar and very deadly arms.

"Hey, love," Handgun Goody said with a sickening grin as his brutal hands clamped down tightly on her wrists.

Jewelz looked up at him weak and confused.

"Help me," she muttered as her eyes rolled around in her head. "Help me..."

"Don't worry shorty, I got you," Goody said coldly as Spaz walked up behind her and dug his thick fingers deep into the back of her neck. "I got you, mami. Trust me. You're in Goode hands."

EMPIRE

STATE of MINE$!

(A Movie in a Book)

Episode 5

Wildin on Staten Island

A NOIRE & REEM RAW JOINT

There are eight million stories in the naked city of New York.

These five are all the way live.

"Shout out to my niggas on Staten,

them cats know how to make it happen,

You know they 'bout that action cause they wit the gun clappin!"

CHAPTER 1

Body Snatchers

Slick had slammed the front door in Jewelz's face hard enough to shake the whole damn building. And now, in a rage, he whirled around and smashed his fist hard into his living room wall.

"Yo!" he stared at Honore and demanded, ready to amp out on her ass. "What the fuck was that shit all about?"

Honore threw her hands up in the air.

"Fuck is you asking me for?" she riffed, standing there half-dressed and giving him the stupid eye. "That tore-down bitch just rolled up in here outta nowhere waving a gun around and acting all crazy!"

"Acting crazy for *what?*" Slick blasted on her with death rays blazing in his eyes. "What kinda business y'all got between y'all? What was all that beef about?"

"Hell if I know!" Honore bucked her eyes at him and barked right back. "That trick is the one who got up in here with a key! She stuck that shit in the lock and walked up in your joint like she be paying the rent or something. So *you* tell *me* what the hell she came here for!"

"There had to be a reason!" Slick said, storming into his bedroom so he could put on some sweats and a hoodie. "Jewelz didn't just come up in here wildin out for nothing!"

"She tried to *shoot* me!" Honore hollered. "Look at my damn head!" she demanded as Slick pulled some sweats over his shorts and finished getting dressed. She swiveled her neck. "You see this big-ass knot? Your bitch did that with her gun! She smacked me with it! You up in here asking me all kinds of stupid questions when *I'm* the one with the headache and *you* the one with your face sliced open! While you busy worrying about that dehydrated looking germ-ball you need to be tryna get yourself to the hospital and get your shit stitched up!"

"Fuck the hospital!" Slick barked as he walked in the kitchen and grabbed a clean dishtowel off the counter. He was fuming so hard as he pressed it to his bleeding wound that he couldn't even think straight.

A pulse beat hard in Slick's temple as he walked outta the kitchen and glanced around his living room. Them chicks had fucked his shit up. Mad items were everywhere. His coffee table had been knocked over and glass shards from a crystal lamp were scattered all over the floor. The bullet hole that was in the wall above the couch was a glaring visual reminder of just how close he had come to getting his melon split right in his own crib!

But remembering how his life had flashed before his eyes wasn't even what had Slick faded. Nah, it was that last look in Jewelz's eyes that had him all fucked up in the gut. That look of betrayal that she had hit him with when he told her to fly up outta his joint. That look of deep pain and even deeper love.

Slick! Can't you see who she is?

Slick's stomach clenched as he turned his back on Honore. Suddenly a hood alarm was ringing in his ear. Ringing louder than a po-po siren. Something didn't feel right. Something in the mix was off. Way the fuck off.

Slick trusted Jewelz with his life, without a doubt. He knew that on any day of the week she would take a bullet between the eyes for him just as he would for her. Popping up at his crib shooting off a strap wasn't exactly her style, but with this crazy-jealous-envy shit she had going on with Honore, anything was possible.

"Man, fade that tweakin hoe out ya mind, Slick!" Honore mouthed off behind him as she started putting her clothes back on. "That bitch got a real nice bumper on her so I know you probably smashing her unstable ass, but you need to change ya damn locks and tell her to kick rocks!"

"Yo, miss me with the feedback!" Slick chastised her as he walked over to the bar to pour himself another drink. "All that hate ain't a good look."

"Hate? I ain't a hater! I'm just not the one for all that extra disrespect shit, a'ight? I came here to give you some pussy tonight, not to get shot by one of your baldheaded low-budget jump-off bitches who don't know how to stay her ugly ass in her lane."

"Ay!" Slick whirled around. He nailed Honore to the wall in a cold, deadly glare. "Who the *fuck* is you disrespecting like that?" he demanded.

Slick shook his head like a bull as he abandoned the bar and stalked up on her ass like a lion. Ever since he'd met this bitch his shit had been falling off and sliding downhill. Every move he made, and every single thing he touched, had turned shitty with Honore up underneath him polluting up the fuckin game!

"Yo, you better watch ya fuckin mouth when you spittin about Jewelz, a'ight?"

Honore's hazel eyes got big like two moons. "Watch my mouth? You want *me* to watch *my* mouth?" She chuckled mirthlessly and let it all hang out.

"That burnt-out dusty duck of yours is the one rolling around here acting like she got a goddamn screw loose! Coming in here pointing a damn ratchet in my face and trying to shoot me! Look at your face! She coulda twisted your wig back real good for you in that bathroom, Slick! And you want *me* to watch *my* muthafuckin mouth?"

She smirked and flicked her hand. "Nigga, please! I don't know what you and that trick got going on, but if that's the type of bird you like to slum with then maybe you should be trying to get up in her drawers tonight instead of mines!"

Slick chuckled coldly. This bitch just didn't know what type of bomb he had been planning to drop down on her head tonight. She was standing up there testing his loyalty like he wasn't about that life.

"Yo, baby, if you asking me to choose between you and Jewelz then you can ga'head and fade away like a jump shot because that choice already been made. It ain't even a competition."

"*What?*" Honore shot back. She narrowed her eyes and spit back at him with much attitude. "I know you not stacking that bucket-head bitch up against me! Damn right there ain't no competition! I roll outta the bed after a rough night looking ten times better than she do on her *best* day! Yeah, you musta been running game when you told me you didn't have no special woman in ya life. Obviously that bitch must mean something special to you because you about to let her wreck this good thing you and me got going on!"

Slick couldn't believe this shit. Right about now everything in his world was looking brand new. He felt like he was just waking up from a long, drunken nap, and he couldn't believe he had been pussy-whipped and booty-blinded for so fucking long.

"C'mon, French Fry." Slick picked Honore's purse up off the floor and walked over to his front door. "It's time for you to get gone. Forever. C'mon, now. Skip to the Lou. Hit the Quan and do the Nae Nae up outta my damn crib!"

Slick opened his door wide as fuck, looking back and forth from Honore's shocked face to the long stretch of the empty hallway.

"Slick!" Honore pouted. "Nigga I know you ain't putting me outta ya crib!"

Slick grilled her coldly and held out her purse to her. He glanced down the hall again like, *ga'head and bounce baby,* and that's when it caught his eye.

A shoe.

In the middle of the hallway and turned over on its side.

Slick stuck his head out the door and peered at it closely. It sure nuff was a shoe. A chick's shoe.

Jewelz's shoe.

Dropping Honore's purse, Slick rushed into the hallway and snatched the shoe up with both hands. He was straightening up to a stand when he peeped the trail of wet droplets that were splattered all over the floor. He bent over and dipped his middle finger in one and his heart banged when he saw what it was.

Blood.

And that's when he heard thought he heard a faint cry.

Slickkkk...

He glanced up at Honore to see if she had heard anything but she was grilling him and the expression on her face never changed.

Slickkkk...

Da fuck? Was that Jewelz screaming for him? Or was his fuckin ears playing tricks on him?

He paused and listened hard, straining to see if the cries would come again.

Slickkkk...

In the absolute silence of the hallway Slick finally realized that it wasn't his ears he was hearing with. Nah, he was hearing with his *heart.* Jewelz needed him, goddammit! Her *heart* was calling him!

In an instant Slick took off running back to his apartment. He hit his front door with a bang. He was going for the blicky. Some ill shit was going down and he wasn't taking no chances.

"What's wrong?" Honore said giving him a worried look as he dashed back up in the apartment moving on a hundred. "Slick!" she called behind him as he rushed right past her. "Baby please tell me what's *wrong?*"

He didn't even see her. Moving silently Slick dashed into his bedroom and reached under the mattress and retrieved a loaded Glock. He jammed that shit down firmly in his waistband and he was beating feet out the door again when he snatched his phone off the clip and pressed Jewelz's number on speed dial.

Slick hit the hallway like a mad sprinter. He knew better than to mess around with the elevator. With Honore still hollering out behind him he busted through the 12th floor stairwell door gripping his heat in one hand and his phone in the other one as Jewelz's shit rang over and over again on the other end.

By the time Slick got down to the first floor her phone had gone to voicemail.

Shit! He cursed under his breath as he darted across the glamorous lobby and burst outta the front door of his condo.

The streets of his upscale neighborhood were quiet and deserted. All he saw when he hit the sidewalk was the fading taillights of a car moving off in the distance and turning the corner.

Slick stood there feeling helpless as fuck. Helpless and guilty too. He just couldn't believe this shit. This shit was insane and he just couldn't fuckin believe it! He was a veteran hitman and he had witnessed a lot of treacherous shit on his grind, but it didn't take a genius to figure out what had gone down outside of his apartment door.

Somebody had snatched Jewelz.

Somebody *got* her.

And as Slick's hood senses screamed out to him, he knew exactly who had gripped Jewelz too.

CHAPTER 2

Ultimatum

Goody gut-punched Jewelz so hard she swung backwards and collided into the frozen slab of beef that was hanging behind her in the industrial-sized freezer.

Hanging by her wrists, Jewelz gasped at the impact of the fierce blow. Raising her head she started coughing up so much blood that it dragged her out of her dazed state of semi-consciousness.

Handgun stood there glaring at her with madness in his eyes. They were in a meat-packing warehouse and the frigid temperature sent cloudy puffs of air exploding from both their parted lips. His brother Ice Pick had convinced him to stash Jewelz outta sight so they could use her as bait to lure Slick into a trap. Instead of outright killing her ass on the spot like he had wanted to do, they were gonna hold her hostage and make her lil fuck-boy steal that fitty-million dollar diamond Cucci had put them on to. If Slick wanted to keep this bitch breathing then he was gonna have to run down on that diamond and toss it off to the Goode Brothers Gang in order to get Jewelz back alive.

And if he fucked around and bucked...they'd put the hammer down on this hoe right in front of his bitch ass!

Goody had stripped Jewelz outta everything she had on, including her wig, and now she hung there naked and bald, swaying back and forth from two chains he had clamped around her wrists and then suspended from a meat hook in the ceiling.

She shivered as she bit back moans of agony. Her slender shoulders were on fire and coming outta their sockets. Both of her lips were busted and her right eye was swollen shut. The icy air burned her throat with each breath she took, and her nose had started bleeding again. Goose-bumps covered every inch of her bruised, exposed flesh, and her feet were so cold they were numb.

"Wake up, bitch!" Goody snarled. "You thought you was a slick lil broad, huh? You thought you was gonna lay low and take a thorough nigga like me out? I'm *Handgun Goody*, hoe! I'm certified in these muh'fuckin streets! You think them lil bitch-ass stick-up ants you be rolling with can fuck with me? *Really?*"

Goody's eyes dropped down to the faded scars on her stomach, evidence of his past handiwork and he smirked. "You thought you was gonna catch me sleepin and get you a little payback, huh?"

All Jewelz could do was moan. She already knew screaming was useless because not a soul would hear her as she swung back and forth deep in the back of the industrial freezer.

"See what I *shoulda* fuckin did that day is," Goody spit, ignoring the cold as he paced back and forth and glared at the scars on her belly. "I shoulda stabbed your ass in the heart instead of the stomach, bitch!"

Goody thought about how he had closed his eyes and thrust his knife so deeply into the little girl that the blade had passed clean through her body and hit the floor on the other side of her. He had to have torn up some guts, some kidneys, and some liver too. At the time, he had been too scared and too ashamed to look at what he was doing, but right now the evidence of his crimes was staring dead at him.

The fact that Jewelz had survived that type of violence and brutality and walked up in his life to make him re-live it swelled Goody's chest up with guilt and rage. He grunted furiously as he hauled off and footed her deep in her naked ass, serving her viciously with a powerful roundhouse kick.

Jewelz grimaced at the painful impact. Swinging silently from the hook she gazed coldly at Goody outta her one good eye. He expected her to cry and beg for mercy, but to his surprise her busted and bloody lips formed a big, scornful smile.

"Dirty Mike...is...that all you got?" Jewelz tapped into her gangsta reserves and mumbled through her pain. "Yeah, bitch-nigga...you shoulda finished the job when you had a chance..."

She licked a drop of blood from her top lip and sneered. "It don't matter what you do to me..." she continued boldly. "You're still a dead man," she promised him with all her heart. "You can kick me all you want to. You'll be kicking up dirt in hell with that sloppy-ass Haz soon enough."

Goody was infuriated by the conviction in her words, but he kept himself in check as he stared at her hanging there by her wrists, naked and unafraid. This bitch was beautiful and fearless. Even beaten down and facing certain death she was still defiant and spitting fire from her soul.

Deep down inside Goody admired the shit outta Jewelz. He probably shoulda accepted her request to be the first Goode Sister because she had the heart of a hunter. He couldn't help thinking that with a woman like her by his side the two of them together coulda turned New York City—nah, the whole damn Empire State, upside fuckin down.

But then he checked himself. All that bullshit Bonnie and Clyde shit mighta worked in a young boy's fantasy, but in reality Goody knew he was looking into the eyes of a woman that he had attempted to murder. He had played a major role in destroying her whole fuckin life, and judging by the way she had sniffed him out and infiltrated his inner click, she had never forgotten it. Or forgiven it either.

And why the fuck would she? The scars that he had left on her both physically and mentally were enough to make them bitter enemies all the way to the grave. No matter how much he was feeling her pain, or how deeply he had grown to love her, Goody knew they could never be together.

"Yo, I did what I had to do, Jewelz," he said grimly. Something in his voice made it sound like he was trying to convince himself more than he was trying to convince her. With his breath coming out in little clouds of smoke, Goody posted up to her face-to-face and tried to keep his tone even.

"None a' that shit that happened back then was personal for me, ma. You was just at the wrong place at the wrong time, darling. And so was I. Not for nothing, I didn't have no other choice. One of us had to go and it sure as fuck wasn't gonna be me."

Through frozen and shivering lips, Jewelz opened her mouth and spit a big glob of bloody phlegm down in Handgun Goody's face.

"*Pussy!*" she snarled as a tear of rage slid out of her swollen right eye. "Fuck the choices your bitch-ass didn't have! You stabbed up little *kids*, nigga! Innocent fuckin *kids*, you fuckin coward!"

"Bitch!" Goody shrieked. "And *you* got my brothers bodied! They all dead because of YOU!"

Goody wiped her bloody spit off his face with his sleeve and then he started throwing crazy wild punches at her. He pounded Jewelz's half-frozen flesh like he was a boxer training on a heavy bag. His clenched fists made hollow smacking noises in the sound-proof freezer as he cursed and spit in rage.

Chainsaw, Hammerhead, Razorblade...he grunted and groaned as he thought about his dead fam and lowered his head and pounded her over and over again.

Goody was boxing Jewelz hard enough to break her ribs and knock her fragile ass out when Ice Pick rushed in the door and hollered, "Yo! Yo! *Yo*, muthafucka! What the fuck is you doin!"

He hurried over to his brother and clenched Goody around the waist and slung him hard against the wall.

"Nigga hold the fuck up!" Ice Pick barked as he peeped Jewelz's slumped head and her limp, swinging body.

"Fuck is you tryna do, big bruh? Nigga keep ya paws to ya'self for a minute! We snatched this skin-headed bitch for a *reason*, 'member? Fuck all that personal shit y'all got going on. We tryna get that icy rock outta this deal! This bitch is already half-dead and we gotta make sure she keeps breathing until we get that hit in our pockets."

"True dat, bruh. True dat," Goody muttered, trying to pull his shit together as he wiped a stream of sweat from his face. He was even more pissed off with himself now for letting this bitch get him all emotional. For making him lose his fuckin head like that. But that's the crazy effect Jewelz had on him. She had been making him sweat since the moment she walked her fine self into his club.

Goody swallowed hard and nodded at his brother, letting him know his shit was straight. He wanted that nigga Slick bodied and he wanted that fifty million dollar diamond too. Jewelz was the ticket to him getting both. Yeah, he was still gonna kill the bitch for chumping him in the heart, but she would have to die another day. Not today.

"A'ight," he told Ice Pick as he walked calmly toward the freezer's door. "Cut that bitch down and get her outta here. Throw some clothes on her ass, patch her up, and give her something hot to drink."

"That's what's up then," Ice Pick nodded in approval. "We gotta stay using our heads on this one, bruh. Why don't you go get you some pussy or hit the gym and get you a lil workout in. Do something to put ya mind in chill mode while all this shit plays out. And don't worry about tryna catch that nigga Slick out there neither. We ain't gotta take the battle to that coward. Once that clown realizes we got our feet on this bitch's neck *he'll* come gunning for *us*."

Goody was almost at the door when he turned back around and addressed Jewelz coldly.

"You lucky this shit is business," he spit quietly, hardening his heart against the pure emotion that swelled there. "I'ma get that diamond and then I'ma pop Slick right in ya face. I'ma make that nigga beg for his life, and then after you watch me peel the skin off the back of his neck I'ma finish what I started with you years ago, baby girl. If you thought Crazy Haz was a mutha-fuckin animal, just wait till I get my hands on that fuckin diamond. That's when I'ma show you how I really get down."

CHAPTER 3

Reality Bites

Honore stood watching from the doorway as Slick busted outta his crib gripping his hammer, then jetted down the hall and disappeared into the stairwell. When she was sure he was gone she slammed the door closed and then stormed into his living room.

"Oh, so you wanna run off behind that ugly bitch?" she muttered as she ripped an expensive African portrait off the wall and flung it across the room.

The frame struck a ceramic vase and it shattered all over the place but Honore had no fucks to give. She wasn't used to getting played out and disrespected by *no* man. Or no bitch neither for that matter!

Seeing that orange heat burst outta the muzzle of Jewelz's gun had been a real close call and Honore's hands were still shaking. Jewelz had straight came up in Slick's crib and tried to bang on her, but on top of that she had almost *exposed* her!

"That heffa was looking for my bullet wound!" Honore said out loud. She reached back and patted her soft ass right on the tender spot. It was a good thing she had worn some regular panties instead of a thong. She woulda been busted! "Yeah, that bitch knew I got shot. She fuckin *knew!*"

Honore picked up her purse and got ready to head out of Slick's crib, but she stopped when she got to the door. Her whole reason for fucking with Slick in the first place was to get her hands on that diamond he'd stolen from her. Yeah, she had gotten in her feelings a lil bit and she'd fallen for his ass, but all that wasted time she had spent smiling in his face, all the lies she'd had to tell him and the pussy she had to give up…it looked like it was all gonna be for nothing. And that didn't sit well with the Queen of Diamonds at all.

Honore turned back around and dropped her purse on the couch. Without hesitation she strutted down the hall and straight into Slick's bedroom. She took a look around the large, stylishly furnished man-cave and decided to put in some work.

Somebody shoulda been paying her by the hour because Honore was a pro at this shit. She combed through every drawer at a feverish pace without even bothering to cover her tracks. *Fuck* Slick! That smoove chocolate dick-swinger could kiss her ass!

Honore was throwing wife-beaters, silk drawers, and designer socks everywhere as she searched for anything that could be valuable.

In one of the bottom drawers she found a chrome .38 pistol with the serial number scratched off. She left it in its place and kept her fingers roaming.

After searching three more drawers and still coming up empty, Honore bit her bottom lip and paused for a second.

Her gaze traveled over to the other side of the room.

She jetted over to the huge walk-in closet and opened it up wide. She was seriously impressed. It was filled with top-of-the line name brand threads that all the street niggas loved. Polo, Gucci, Versace, and Zegna were draped out lavishly. Slick had two rows of designer leather shoes and four rows of multi-colored sneakers ranging from Jordans and Lebrons, to Ferragamos and Balenciagas and Bruno Maglis.

Yeah, Honore nodded in appreciation. Slick's wardrobe game was super-strong but she wasn't there to boost none of his gear. She started tossing sneakers and shirts on the floor looking for anything unusual and out of the ordinary.

I know this nigga got something stashed in here and I hope like hell it's that sweet money and the red briefcase!

Honore ransacked through a couple of Fendi Zuccha suitcases and she tossed endless racks full of tailored three-piece suits around only to come up with nothing. When she stood back and looked at her handiwork the closet was a fucking mess. It looked like a tornado had came through and blew Slick's shit every which way but loose.

Standing in the aftermath of the retail storm that she had caused, Honore was about to give up and be out. She knew she didn't have a lot of time to linger because if Slick came back and caught her going through his shit they would probably have a shoot-out.

Sweaty and frustrated, Honore was about get herself together and dip on out until something funny caught her eye. In between the only two suits that were still left hanging up Honore saw a small black button protruding from a seam in the wall. It was barely noticeable, and if the clothes had still been on the hangers she would've never even seen it.

She reached out to push the button but then jerked her hand back real quick.

What the hell is this? I hope it ain't some type of dooms-day self-destruct thingy that's gonna blow the whole damn building up if I push it.

Honore's nature wouldn't let her just leave it alone though. She pushed the button and all of a sudden the whole damn wall lifted up and she stumbled backwards with her eyes bucked wide.

She had come up around street legends like Sly McFly and she'd seen plenty of elaborate stash spots, but nothing quite like this one.

She stared into the tucky room that was about twice the size as the walk-in closet. It held a desk that had two iMac computers on it, and their screens were showing different areas of the apartment, obviously streaming from hidden cameras.

There was also a wall that was lined with all types of battle gear ranging from machine guns, knives, binoculars, grenades, swords, ski masks, high-tech electronic equipment, and the type of mass-casualty weaponry and shit you only saw in the movies.

Honore's eyes got wide as fuck.

What the hell? Slick can't be no regular goddamn stick up kid! This nigga gotta be some type of war-weirdo or the chief of a fuckin S.W.A.T. team or something!

Honore stepped inside the secret room to take a closer look. She trailed her fingers across the desk and sifted through a few papers and books that Slick had laying around. Her greedy eyes were everywhere. She took it all in and the only article of clothing she saw was a Dickie's jumpsuit that was balled up in the corner with a bunch of splotchy stains on it that looked like dried up pigeon shit.

Honore sat down behind the desk and picked up a nicely framed photo of two smiling adults surrounded by a bunch of cute kids. The big guy in the photo had a handsome chocolate face and looked just like Slick. Honore figured that it had to be his father. She sat the picture down and continued to look all through Slick's business. She opened a drawer and found a stuffed manila envelope that had duct tape over the seal. She ripped the bottom open and dug out the contents, and when she saw what it was she wanted to throw the whole shit across the room.

What in the almighty fuck? Slick! You lying-ass bastard!

The envelope was filled with old pictures that must have been of Slick and his cousins or sisters and brothers when they were little. As Honore looked closer she recognized that bitch Jewelz as a child in some of the pictures as well.

She smirked.

Slick was a real sneaky and secretive-type nigga. Him and that trick went way back. No wonder she had a key to his crib. They had known each other since forever. Jewelz was obviously on his dick, but what type of freaky fuck-shit did them two have going on?

Honore shook her head. Niggas these days just couldn't be trusted. She stuffed the pictures back in the envelope and then opened up another drawer. This time she found a huge photo album. She flipped it open and saw a bunch of random people of all races. The only thing that linked them was the big red X that had been drawn over their faces.

Who are these people, Slick? And how are they connected to you?

Her mind flashed back to the Fulton Street jewelry store on the night the red briefcase was jacked. Slick and his crew had run up in the joint dressed in black and brandishing big guns, but they damn sure wasn't there to rob no daggone jewelry store!

Honore's mind replayed some of the deep pillow-talk conversations that her and Slick used to have. Slick had always played his game close and sounded so guarded and introspective. She racked her brain hard and forced herself to remember all the strange little details and characteristics that stood out about his convo.

She looked around the room one more time, her eyes fixated on all the guns, silencers, masks, and the fancy electronic equipment. She glanced back down at the X'd out faces in the photo album and suddenly the reality of the situation dropped on her head and hit her like a ton of bricks.

Everybody in this damn book must be dead! Slick and his gang are probably a bunch of gunslingers! They gotta be! Not just murderers, but real-life mothafuckin hit men!

$$$$$

Handgun Goody was sweating like a hooker at a mega church, from his head down to his toes. It was after hours and he was in Ray-Ray's Gym finishing up a hellacious workout. Back in the day when he had done his first bid on Rikers Island he had been as skinny as a light pole, but not anymore. There were cats behind those walls who could break your fuckin neck with just a few calculated moves. Goody had gotten into a couple of violent fights trying to earn his rep and prove he had heart, but they had usually ended with him getting fucked up.

And that's when he learned the value of pumping iron. He understood that if he was gonna survive in the joint then he had to get his weight up and sharpen every tool in his box in order to keep niggas off his ass. He had hooked up with a gang of thoroughbred niggas and started getting in shape. He learned to love the feeling of lifting heavy steel and pushing his body to its maximum capacity in order to forge a strong and muscular physique.

The niggas he was locked up with also taught him the value of being mentally strong. He'd devoured books like *The Art of War* and *Blood In My Eyes* and began to adopt different patterns of thinking. By the time he hit the streets again he had absorbed enough lessons from tried and true career criminals to become a well-rounded leader.

Goody had gotten on his grind and garnered the same ruthless rep of legendary stick-up kids like Crazy Haz, Killer Ben, and King Tut. Before long, Handgun Goody was a major player on the streets of New York City and Brooknam was his kingdom.

"Ay, boss," Ray-Ray poked his head outta the back room and called out. "I got a hot chickenhead coming through for you. Ice Pick already picked her out and paid her. His treat."

Handgun had been slamming the heavy weights up and down and throwing that solid iron all around, but that raging fuckin monster of fury was still riding on his back. A nice piece of pussy would be real chill right now, and when the hoe walked through the door he was visually stimulated and real pleased by what he saw.

"Get on the floor," he ordered her gruffly, his shit already bricking up. Mami had came to put in work, and when she took off her jacket and handed him a glove, all she had on her gorgeous body was a hot pink thong and a matching bra.

Goody ripped all that shit off. He slid the condom on, then threw her legs over his shoulder and got up in that pussy right there in the empty gym. There wasn't no kissing, no caressing, no licking, no sucking, or none of that other sweet shit he had done with Jewelz. This was some straight up fuck-fighting he was doing as he shoved his heavy package up in her and started pounding into her guts like she was a measly piece of meat.

His hands were hard and heavy as he squeezed her titties and pulled on her nipples. The hoe squealed and gasped as he thrust his meat into her as deep as he could, scraping his knees on the gym mats as he banged into her pussy so hard her weaved head damn near slid under a weight bench.

Goody handled the hoe like a ruffneck. He deep-drilled into her and gave that pussy a black eye. He pounded the shit outta her guts, popping his hips powerfully and smacking into her hot flesh like he had a piston in his lower back. But no matter what Goody did to her, no matter how cruelly he fucked her, he couldn't cum. For the life of him his nut just wouldn't fuckin rise, but his anger frustration damn sure did.

"You wanna stick it in my ass?" the hoe suggested after he flipped her over on her stomach for the third time and entered her bronco-buster style again.

"You take it up the ass?"

"Hell yeah," she shrugged. "You paid for it."

Instantly Goody's dick went soft and he pulled his meat outta her. He was disgusted as he stood up and looked down at her waiting patiently with her ass in the air.

"Yo get the fuck outta here!" he barked as he mushed her in the ass with his foot and stuffed his limp shit back in his shorts. "How the fuck a nigga supposed to nut when your nasty ass around here stanking the joint up like it's a goddamn fish market! Get outta here and go put some soap on your filthy ass!"

Goody left the naked hoe cowering on the floor as he stormed off and entered the men's locker room. He cut on the shower and stripped outta his clothes, then stood under the steaming water until he got his rage under control.

Wasn't nothing wrong with that girl's pussy, he went on and admitted to himself. Her shit was clean, she had a prime body, and she knew how to fuck.

She just wasn't who he wanted, that's all. She just wasn't Jewelz.

After showering and getting dressed Goody stepped outside the gym with a thick towel around his neck. He was feeling a lot more relaxed as he breathed in deeply and let the cool night air fill his lungs. He walked towards the parking lot located in the back of the building with his gym bag over his shoulder and a chrome pistol on his waist. His eyes were on mad alert for anything that looked unusual.

He had just reached his glistening black Mercedes coupe and clicked the unlock button on his key when he heard a voice boom from deep in the shadows of the lot.

"Well if it ain't the infamous *Hand-Job* Goody," a heavy voice growled from the cut. "I see you living it up and enjoying the fruits of your crimes, my nigga. Too bad you won't be enjoying that shit for much longer."

Goody whirled around and reached for the blicky on his waist.

"Don't do nothing stupid now nigga," Slick said as he slowly emerged from the shadows wearing a hoodie. His eyes narrowed dangerously as he faced the cat he wanted to slump more than he wanted to draw his next breath.

"Believe it, if I wanted to blow your hoe-ass head off you woulda been dead by now. Look at ya punk ass," Slick sneered coldly. "You still the same bum-fuck dope-fiend Dirty Mike you was back when you was crab-hopping on Big Haz's nuts! Only difference is, instead of riding stolen bikes you got you a nice shiny Benz now. And instead of slaughtering entire families, now Haz is the one dead and you next on deck for the grave, nigga!"

Realization slowly flooded Goody's eyes and he took his hand off his burner. He let the gym bag fall from his shoulder and started clapping his hands like he had just watched a good-ass movie and was giving it a standing ovation.

Clap. Clap. Clap. Clap.

"Now ain't this some shit," Goody smirked at the killer who had emerged outta the shadows. "It's Lil fuckin *Slick!* Goddamn, baby boy! You's a hard dude to catch up to!" Goody grinned broadly.

"Look at you," he beamed. "All grown up. Glad to see you still alive and well. But what can I do for you, son?"

"Cut the dumb shit," Slick spit as he lowered the hood from his head to let Goody get a good look at him.

"What happened, my nigga?" Goody stared at the bandage on Slick's cheek. "You cut ya'self shaving lil boy?"

"Don't worry about me. I know you snatched Jewelz, you wack-ass nigga! You better not a' done no idiot shit to her neither 'cause I will run straight through you, nigga! You know, the same way you and Haz ran through me and my fam."

"Ya know," Goody chuckled. For the moment he igged the tough talk, but he definitely filed it in his mental Rolodex under "M" for murder. Because that's what he was gonna do to Lil Slick Williams. Murder his ass! On the strength of his brothers's lives, Goody had to off the coward who stood in front of him! But not tonight. There would be plenty of time to make this nigga pay for his violations after he delivered that fuckin diamond.

"You got some heavy balls on you, Lil Slick. I gotta admit that shit. I mean, I don't know how you and Jewelz got up and walked away from ya mom's crib that day, but I have to admit I'm very impressed. And I see you've developed some other skills over the years too, huh?"

Slick nodded. "Skills? Yeah, I got plenty of those."

"Uh-huh. My lil nephew Trill—you know him, that slanga you chased down in the street and put in the hospital a while back? He told me you done turned into some kinda project ninja warrior playing the retarded wino role. You catch niggas sleepin cause they think you can't get right. And then you blast on 'em. Now that's real fuckin smoove, man."

Goody took a few steps toward Slick so he could look directly into the eyes of the young cub who, against all odds, had lived to become a full-grown lion.

"I bet you and Jewelz been waiting all these years to gimme a long dirt nap, am I right? Since you already did Haz and you bodied my lil brothers and some of my best soldiers too, I guess that means you gonna be gunnin for my throat next, huh?"

Slick chilled and held his tongue, letting the nigga talk himself out.

"Yeah, a'ight," Goody said, his deep voice cock-sure and arrogant, "I prolly do deserve the same treatment ya Unc Haz got but see, I'm not ready to go just yet, you feel me? I mean I got a whole lot to live for! I got a whole lot more pussy to fuck! Seriously, that bitch of yours is sweet as fuck, son! She got them big ol titties and a mean piece of ass on her, my nigga! I bet you *do* wanna get her back. And guess what?" Goody chuckled again. "I'ma let you have her back too. And I'ma make sure you get her back in real good condition, homey. All you gotta do is go get me a diamond and you can have Jewelz back whenever you want her."

"Get you a diamond?" Slick almost laughed at him. "Nigga, fuck is you talking about? Do I look like a fuckin ice burglar to you? Don't fuck with me, Goody! Fuck I look like—"

"No *muthafucka*!" Handgun Goody roared. "You best not fuck with *me!* What you look like? You look like the nigga who killed my brothers! You look like a nigga who wants his bitch back *alive!* You look like a nigga who's gonna do exactly what the fuck I tell him to do! You look like the nigga who's gonna get out there and steal me that fuckin fitty-million dollar Pink fuckin Lady diamond!"

Slick shook his head in disbelief. "Is you high, homey? *What* Pink Lady? I ain't in the jewelry game! How the fuck you expect me to steal a goddamn fifty million dollar diamond?"

Goody shrugged. "Ay, figure it out just like you figured out how to handle that five million dollar Fulton Street job you scored, bruh. I don't give a fuck how you do it. I just know the shit better get done!"

"I don't know shit about no five million dollar job—"

"*Play pussy!*" Goody barked, swelling all the way up. "Ga' head, mutha-fucka! Play pussy and see don't your bitch get fucked! I know your team ain't new to this shit! You think I got this far by sleeping on my homework? Fuck with me and you'll find Jewelz's bald fuckin head stuck on a pole at the top of that pigeon-shit roof of yours! I'll turn that whole fuckin building into a Friday the fuckin 13th movie! Fuck with me, nigga! I *want* you to fuck with me!"

Hot blood rushed through Slick's veins and he fought to keep himself from yanking his trigger and decapitating that nigga right there in the parking lot. He wanted Goody's head so bad he coulda ripped his neck in half, but instead he forced himself to keep his cool. Because somehow this nigga knew more than he was supposed to know. And in some ways he seemed to know more than Slick knew.

Figure it out just like you figured out how to handle that five million dollar Fulton Street job you scored!

Something told Slick he needed to ease up and walk this shit out. He needed to see where it led, and find out exactly which cards Goody was holding in his hand.

"Now that I got your attention lil nigga make sure you listen up," Goody said as he watched Slick fighting like hell to keep himself in check.

"That shiny rock I need you to yap for me is gonna be going up for auction at a new museum on Staten Island. Like I said, they call her the Pink Lady, and I wanna marry that hoe and make her all minez! You go get her for me and I'll give you Jewelz back in one piece. You try some funny-style shit and I'll finish what I started all them years ago. I'll slice that bitch up in strips and send her back to you one piece at a time. And after that you and me can go to war until one of us drops. Because by then won't none of this shit even matter."

Slick grilled Goody to the bone as the kingpin's murderous words hung in the air. He wanted to bite that nigga's face off. To devour him the way a snake swallows up a fuckin mouse. He could easily lick one off right now and stretch Goody out where he stood. But Jewelz's life was on the line, and one wrong move could get her zipped up.

Slick didn't mind going to war with the Goode Brothers Gang. And he didn't have a problem dying out here on the streets in a hail of bullets neither. But he wasn't about to leave Jewelz in the hands of a madman, and nothing in the world was gonna stand in the way of him finding her and keeping her alive.

"Yo, why the fuck should I trust you?" Slick barked. "How the fuck do I know Jewelz is cool? How I know she ain't already dead?"

Goody grinned. "You *don't* know, chump! You gotta take my word, nigga! Cause believe it, if she ain't dead now she damn sure will be if you fuck this shit up. Now you go get that diamond and bring it to my maintenance warehouse out on Staten Island, you got it? You dish that shit off properly and I'll toss you back ya cute lil hunny. But I'm telling you now, my nigga. Don't try no hero shit and don't fuckin be late, you feel me? You better not be two fuckin seconds late bringing me that pink bitch, or word to the life of my brothers, your hoe is dead!"

Slick couldn't do shit except stand there and watch helplessly as Goody hopped in his whip and started up his ride. That nigga was laughing loud as fuck as he punched the gas pedal and jetted outta the lot. Slick wanted to pull out his tool and Swiss cheese that nigga *and* his Mercedes full of holes.

But he didn't. Because he was a soldier and he had been given a mission to accomplish, and as far as he was concerned it was the most important mission of his entire life. Slick knew he couldn't fuck it up, but he also knew he couldn't go at it alone, neither.

Jewelz's life was in his hands, and right now there was only one gunslinger in the world that he could trust without a doubt to have his back on a hundred. And with the smell of Goody's exhaust fumes funking up the air, Slick pulled out his cell phone and called him.

CHAPTER 4

Life's on the Line

"Ay," Slick barked when his ace answered the phone. The bitter taste of rage burned in his throat and his whole body trembled with fury. "I got a crucial mission standing in front of me, yo," he said, his voice quiet and deadly. "It's a matter of life or death, and I'ma need some back up."

Whitey was all over that shit.

"Whattup, chief? Where's the static? What kinda reinforcements you need?"

"It's *Jewelz*," Slick blurted out, trying his best to choke back the fury that flooded his heart. "Me and her got into a lil dust-up and the Goode Brothers snatched her. She was rolling up outta my joint and they rained on her."

"You and Jewelz had static between y'all? Fuck for?"

"Man, she rushed up in my crib banging a burner! She almost fuckin shot me, but that shit don't even matter. Them bitch-ass Goode Brothers got her, Whitey. Them cowards got their paws on her and they gonna clip her off if I don't give 'em what they want."

"What the hell do you mean *they got her?*" Whitey demanded. "What the fuck is going on here!?! I thought we voted against going after those guys. Why would they wanna snatch Jewelz?"

"We were casing them," Slick admitted. "Lining them up. Them niggas musta got wise and peeped the plot, then got the drop on Jewelz. She came over to my crib making noise on my lil side piece and she messed around and popped a hammer off in the air. I told her to chill with that madness and to get the fuck—"

Slick hesitated, feeling guilty as hell as he remembered the look of pure pain in Jewelz's eyes, "She almost shot me and I told her to kick rocks, bruh. I put her the fuck outta my spot. But then when I looked out in the hallway a few minutes later I saw her shoe laying out there and there were drops of blood all over the floor and shit..."

"What?" Whiteys voice was full of pain. "You guys were casing those cats and they snatched her? Why in the world would Goody wanna get with Jewelz though?"

Slick could barely speak it. "He don't wanna get with her. He just wants to *use* her. So he can get at me. That nigga said he's gonna wet her up if I don't come up with some pink diamond ice he wants me to steal from a goddamn jewelry auction."

The surprise in Whitey's voice was deep as hell as he spit back at his man sharply, "Hold up! Does Handgun Goody want you to steal the *Pink Lady* diamond?"

"Yeah!" Slick frowned. "You know something about that shit, or what?"

"Um, nah," Whitey played it off, rubbing his hands together like his palms suddenly itched. "I mean, I don't know nothing more than what I heard them talking about on the news the other day. They just opened up a new branch of the Sotheby Museum right here on Staten Island. The Pink Lady is supposed to be one of those extremely rare jewels, and if I remember right, they say she's worth a pretty deep grip."

"She's batting at fifty mill and I gotta get my hands on her!" Slick spit. "Them Goode Brothers got Jewelz stashed outta sight somewhere and if they don't get that ice they're gonna off her. If I fail with this shit Jewelz is as good as gone."

"Fuck!" Whitey cursed out loud as his mind moved a million miles a minute. "Come on, Slick. This shit is impossible! What makes those guys think you can get away with stealing a high-profile piece of jewelry like that without getting hit up?"

"I don't know, but ay, man," Slick switched the flow up quietly. "Lemme ask you something. What the fuck was in that briefcase that night, my brother?"

"What briefcase?"

"That red jawn we snatched outta the jewelry store on Fulton Street. You know. The briefcase the BBU ordered us to stash in that locker in Midtown."

Slick couldn't see it, but on the other end of the line Whitey's eyes narrowed and glinted dangerously.

"Oh, *that* shit? Yeah, now I remember." The crafty white man shook his head. "I don't know what the fuck was in there, Slick. You told me to go make the drop and that's what I did. Why you asking?"

Slick's stomach clenched. "Because that nigga Goody was up on that Fulton Street hit, yo. He knew about it. Somebody got him thinking there was a five-million dollar diamond involved with it. Goody thinks I yanked that shit, and that's why he wants me to steal him another one. But this one is worth damn near ten times as much."

"Damn," Whitey said as he deliberately steered the convo in a different direction. "This could be problematic, my man. I just don't know if we have the kind of resources it takes to pull off something of that magnitude, Slick. I thought the Goode Brothers were primarily running things on the drug scene? What kind of dope-boy takes a sick woman hostage in exchange for a world-class diamond?"

"A sick woman?" Slick froze. "Fuck you talkin 'bout, son? Jewelz is *sick?* Sick from what?"

For a long moment Whitey went silent. And then he said slowly, "Man, Jewelz is sick, Slick. *Real* sick. She has *cancer*. You didn't know? She didn't tell you about it?"

Slick felt the universe shift. It felt like the whole Earth had suddenly flown off its axis and he was plummeting into a deep black hole.

"*Cancer?*" he whispered. His gut rose up in his throat and his knees got weak. "Stop fuckin with me, Whitey! You *serious?*"

"Yeah," Whitey said quietly. "I'm fucking serious."

Slick's mind went on rewind as he thought about the last couple of times he had seen Jewelz. Yeah, she had lost some weight and she looked kinda tired, but that's because she was fuckin around in the club with that nigga Goody all night long!

And that no-appetite thing she had going on...all that picking over her grub when they went out to eat...even though her eyes stayed red from puffing that sticky and she shoulda been starving...

Plus he remembered seeing the back of her head looking smooth as fuck under her scarf one day...Nah, that wasn't no donation to needy kids type a shit. Every strand of her hair had been gone.... He shoulda known something was up. He shoulda fuckin known!

Whitey drew in a deep breath. "Look, my friend," he said, "If I remember correctly the news report I saw said the Pink Lady diamond is coming into the country from Brazil and they're gonna auction it off at the Sotheby Museum on Staten Island."

"So?" Slick couldn't hardly track with his boy because he couldn't stop hearing the word *cancer* and seeing the back of Jewelz's bald head in his mind.

"So..." Whitey's voice trailed off as he tapped his finger on the table and calculated that shit out. He had been in on that secret meeting with Don Benny's crew during his son's bar mitzvah. It had been decided that they would block up the streets and cause a distraction, and then snatch the Pink Lady diamond just before the courier tried to deliver it to the Sotheby. But hearing this new shit coming out of Slick's mouth was like a godsend to Whitey. Why split the cut with Don Benny and a bunch of other idiots when he could let Slick steal that shit, dirt-nap him real quick, and then keep all the profits for himself?

"So," Whitey continued, "that means they gotta be flying the diamond into an airport somewhere close by, and then transporting it to the Sotheby Museum. I say we hit 'em as soon as the diamond is outta range of the airport, my friend. That's how we save Jewelz's life! We pick it off and hit that shit right after it leaves the airport, and *way* before it gets dropped off at the Sotheby."

"We hit *what*, nigga?" Slick growled impatiently.

"The *truck*, my dude," Whitey said. "We hit the fucking Brinks truck!"

$$$$$

Whitey walked through the doors of the neighborhood community center with his eyes on scan. There were colorful posters taped up everywhere to advertise the major Black Hair and Fashion Show that had just kicked off and was going strong.

In less than ten seconds his dick bricked up. He felt like a fat kid in a donut shop because some of the sexiest black women in the city were packed inside the joint. Just the scent of these gorgeous chocolate bunnies made Whitey wanna fuck. Tall, short, light-skinned, dark-skinned, tits and ass of all shapes and sizes were on display and they sported the most outrageous hairstyles and skimpiest outfits that he had ever seen.

The expensive business suit he wore looked real out of place in the midst of such flamboyance, but Whitey didn't give a fuck. He was all about scoping out a new ally who could potentially turn into a major threat: Honore.

With Slick about to run down on the Pink Lady diamond, Whitey didn't trust that bitch Honore as far as he could throw her. The meeting at the Jewish Center had been an eye-opening experience for him in more ways than one.

Seeing the same chick that they had kidnapped from the Brooklyn jewelry store standing there in Westchester getting down with Benny and Avi had been surprising as shit. But it told Whitey a couple of very important things: One, Slick was stupid as fuck and way off his game, and two, Honore hadn't been in that Fulton Street jewelry store studying for a biology test like she had claimed.

Hell no, she wasn't no student. The girl was a jewelry thief. A scheming get-money monkey. She had her sights set on living the champagne life, and Whitey would have put his last dollar on the fact that she was the one who had been dropping off the red briefcase that night, and not the old man whose face they had shattered.

As Whitey walked around the hair show he knew Honore was somewhere in the building right now because he had trailed her car and watched her and her friends come inside.

Whitey had a hunch that Noodles might have been hot on Honore's heels before he got dirt-napped too. Knowing his old friend, Noodles had probably been tracking her 24/7, which was probably why he was nosing around up in Westchester in the first place.

This new theory gave Whitey a lot of relief because it meant that more than likely Noodles hadn't been up there stalking *him* like he'd always believed.

The crowded building was packed out and Whitey walked through the noisy throngs of black women getting bumped and jostled by sharp elbows and soft asses. The music was rocking and there were vendors set up on both sides of the hallway selling fake hair and outlandish beauty items and delicious-smelling food.

Whitey's eagle eyes scanned from left to right like a wide-lens camera. Every now and then he stopped at the vendor tables to check out some of the items that were up for sale. He saw the type of silly shit that was popular in ghetto black culture like faux dreadlocks, nappy green pony-puffs, and spiky blonde Chinese hair weaves.

Whitey had just stopped at a booth and picked up a rainbow-colored curly Afro wig when somebody yanked hard on his sleeve.

"What the fuck are you doing?" a sexy young woman with a jet-black curly weave demanded as she dug her fingers deep into his bicep. "You can't be walking up in here looking all like that!"

Whitey frowned down at the pissed-off chocolate-skinned beauty. "Looking all like what?"

"Looking all *white!* You can't be coming up in here frontin like you tryna buy no damn weave!" She snatched the wig outta his hand then rolled her eyes and shoved him toward the door.

"Mothafucka you sticking out like a piece of lint on a black sweater, boy! Walk yo ass back outside and meet me in the parking lot."

Whitey was completely caught off guard. He had noticed the stylish chick when she got out of the car with Honore, but he had no clue who she was or what the fuck she was talking about.

For a second he thought she was sending him outside so she could set him up to get cooked, but that look of fear and annoyance on her face, and the way she was whispering, said otherwise. Something told him to roll with it, so he nodded at her then turned around and walked back outside.

A few minutes later Whitey was leaning coolly against his ride when the chick busted outta the doors and stormed toward the parking lot. She was switching her ass like a champ and moving super-fast as her feet clomped loudly across the concrete in a pair of bright pink high-heel boots.

Whitey couldn't help but stare. Her hips were working the hell outta her tight denim mini-skirt and her large, but pert titties bounced up and down under her fitted white tank top.

She spotted him standing there and flicked her hand toward his car. "Get in, stupid!" she demanded with her face all frowned up. "What you standing out here looking like a goddamn FBI billboard for? Are you tryna get me erased, asshole?"

She climbed in on the passenger side of his whip and slammed the door as she continued to bitch.

"Who told you to come looking for me? I told y'all dumb-asses that *I* would name the time and place! I said I would meet y'all after the hair show was over! Y'all alphabet boys think y'all can just show up anywhere and do whatever the hell you wanna do? Well, not with Cucci Momma, homey! Now before I say another damn word I wanna know w'sup with my damn reward money?"

Whitey was trapped off-guard, but he caught on fast as fuck. This girl thought he was a federal agent and she was ready to drop a dime! He chuckled coldly inside as he got ready to play the role. Just how stupid could this beautiful idiot be? He was about to find out!

"Listen, you contacted us, right?" Whitey said as he swelled up big with a white man's authority. "Then before we talk about any type of reward I need to know exactly what information you have that's relevant to this case."

"Uh-uh. This ain't the time or the place for me to be doing no more talking!" Cucci hissed. Her neck was on a swivel as she looked back and forth over her shoulder toward the community center like she was paranoid as hell.

"I already said enough and you putting me in a trick bag just by showing up here! I can't let nobody see me blabbing with you! Snitches get stiches *and* ditches, baby! That's why I said I was gonna meet y'all *after* the damn hair show! Niggas out here can smell a cop a mile away."

"If you want my help then *I* need to know everything *you* know," Whitey stated firmly. "The sooner you spit it out, the faster I can be out of here."

Cucci tossed her hair and smirked. "I already told y'all everything on the phone! I got some information on my cousin. They call her the Queen of Diamonds. Her real name is Honore Morales though, and she's the one who set our boss up to get robbed and killed so she could snatch his diamond and his money!"

The Queen of Diamonds???

Whitey couldn't fuckin believe it. He felt like he had just hit the jackpot and he was happy as shit that he had decided to track Honore's sweet ass today!

"So you suspect your cousin Honore is the Queen of Diamonds?" he clarified.

"That's what I just said, ain't it? She's the damn diamond diva! She's the *Queen!*"

Whitey fought to keep himself from laughing out loud as he thought about that failed hit on the beauty parlor in Queens. Honore was one greasy-ass chick! She had ass-fucked every last one of them! She was the monkey with the red briefcase and the Queen of Diamonds too!

Whitey found himself admiring Honore for her cunning and scheming ways. He couldn't believe how loose her cousin's lips were, though. Just hearing the word "diamonds" falling outta her big mouth was blissful to his ears. On the real, with friends like this beautiful ghetto princess Honore didn't need a single fuckin enemy!

"And you believe your cousin is not only stealing diamonds, but she's arranging murders too? Well, that's a very serious allegation you're making and I'm going to need you to tell me everything you know right away."

"*Sheeeiiit*," Cucci drawled and shook her head. "See now, y'all scum bags already tried to play me once already so I gotta have everything in writing this time. I ain't giving up none a' my info unless I'm assured on paper that I'ma get my reward money, ya dig?"

"In that case," Whitey answered agreeably, "you'll just need to come down to the office with me. I'll take your written statement and videotape your interview for the official record. If you'd just put on your seatbelt I can drive you over there and we can get the process started right now."

"Oh no the hell we can't!" Cucci bucked and slid closer to the door with her lip poked out. "Fuck outta here with that, Mister Man! I ain't going no damn where with you!"

Whitey gazed into her pretty face and then let his eyes drop down to her bulging cleavage. Those were some pretty chocolate titties she had on her and suddenly he had himself a craving.

"Okay, listen," he said with his tone softening. "How about you and I make a little deal, just between us?"

Cucci smirked as his eyeballs rolled hungrily over her nipples. "What kinda deal, white boy? If it ain't involving my reward money then I ain't wit' it!"

"Oh, there's a reward involved," Whitey said as he pushed the driver's seat back and unbuttoned his suit jacket. "The reward is going to be your freedom."

"My freedom?" The smirk dropped off Cucci's face and her glamorous eyes narrowed. "I ain't do shit to get locked up so how you figure?"

"The way I figure is, you said you called into our office, so that means we have your voice recorded where you admit to having information about a jewelry heist and a cold-blooded murder. That makes you an accomplice and a co-conspirator. On an obstruction of justice charge you'd be looking at the same lengthy prison sentence as whoever actually committed the crimes. That is, if you aren't actually the Queen yourself. But I suspect you are."

Fear was all over Cucci's mug. "Uh-uh! Hold up, Mister! Don't you start no funny shit with me! I didn't kill nobody and I didn't steal a goddamn thing, so keep my name out of it! I ain't the Queen of Diamonds so don't even play like that!"

Cucci lunged for her door handle but Whitey was much quicker on the cap. He clicked the lock button, trapping her inside.

He was calm as fuck as they eyed each other warily. Then he said, "You know, there's an easy way to prove whether you're the Queen or not. But I'm afraid I'll have to arrest you and take you in for fingerprinting. Let's see if you can convince a magistrate judge that I didn't just bag the mysterious diamond thief that everyone is after. Yeah, I'll have to take you in and let the judge decide. Unless we can come to some sort of other agreement. Right here and right now. Just between us."

Cucci sat there eyeing him like he was a snake. She could see how hard his dick was getting through the rising print in his pants leg. White men were some slimy mothafuckas when it came to black pussy! But she knew the drill because she had been caught in this position many times before. It was a trade-off game, and it wouldn't be the first time that she had gotten hooked like a fish while swimming out there in deep water. It was go hard or go down time, and Cucci Momma wasn't about to go down.

"How you want it?" she twisted her lips and asked dryly, cutting through the bullshit and going straight to the bottom line. She shifted her meaty ass toward him and lifted up the bottom hem of her skirt so he could hit it from the back. "You got a glove?"

Whitey grinned and reached out for her neck. He ran his fingers up over the glued-in tracks of her silky weave and cupped the back of her head.

"We don't need a glove," he said, eyeing her pretty lips. With a white man's authority he pulled her head down toward his crotch as he unbuckled his belt and freed his hard dick.

"That pretty little mouth of yours is going to do all the work, sweetie. First you're going to tell me everything you know about that diamond, and then you're going to give me a nice wet reward for hearing you out."

Cucci knew when she was beat. With her lip poked out she took his pale dick in her fist and started stroking that shit real hard. She was surprised he was holding so heavy for a white boy, but she still wasn't beat for that shit.

The white man moaned like he was digging her rhythm, and Cucci poked her lip out some more as she dug down in his silk drawers and got a handful of his balls. She squeezed and jacked and juggled until he started gasping and bucking his hips in the air.

"Lick it," he urged her as he palmed the back of her head and pushed her face down closer to his groin. "Suck that shit!"

"Hold up!" Cucci froze in place and cut her eyes up at him angrily. "Don't touch the fuckin hair, a'ight?"

Rolling her eyes and giving him big-time attitude, she opened her mouth and got to waxing his dick. The whole time she was bobbing up and down in his lap she was thinking to herself, "Bite this muthafucka, Cucci! Bite his pink-ass dick off!"

But of course she didn't bite him. She was mad, but she wasn't stupid. This federal mothafucka held all the cards in his hand and he had way too much dirt on her for her to be flexing. With her voice recording on the FBI hotline and his threat to make it look like she was the Queen of Diamonds....*sheiiit*...Cucci was ghetto-boojie and too damn prissy to even think about going to jail. So instead of acting up, she submitted to the madness and did exactly what was required of her. She sucked his dick meat down to the bone.

CHAPTER 5

The Grimy Niggas Live a Long Time

Slick was pretty sure that no criminal in the modern world had a mind that was more brilliant and calculating than his ace Whitey Reynolds. So when it came to getting his hands on that Pink Lady diamond Slick was glad to have his boy down on his team.

"Yeah, I'm rolling with you to the end, but we gotta go at this thing the right way," Whitey cautioned him as they plotted their next move.

They were laying low in a tucky spot that Slick had rented as a temporary office and they had the doors locked and the shades pulled down as they sorted shit out.

"We should run up on that museum and crush them guards as soon as they deliver the diamond," Slick said. "Or better yet, we can lay low outside that bitch and jump on whoever buys it as soon as they try to leave. Then we can toss it off to Goody and get Jewelz back."

Whitey shook his head. That shit was outta the question. Slick's plan was far too similar to what Honore and her posse were planning to do, and that meant they might fuck around and bump heads with the enemy by showing up at the same place at the same time. Hell no. Whitey wanted to beat Avi and Honore to the punch and get his hands on that diamond before they had a chance to get anywhere near it.

He shook his head again and spoke to Slick in a reasonable white man's tone. "Look partner, I don't care what Handgun Goody promised you, there's no way in hell those cats are just going to give Jewelz up," Whitey predicted. "Even if we do manage to steal that diamond and hand it over to them, you and I both know the deal. Nine times out of ten this shit ends badly, Slick. Especially when it's personal the way it is. A cat like Goody can't just take the damn diamond and walk away. He'll take the damn diamond and still murder Jewelz right there in front of you, just for the hell of it."

"Then them cowards are gonna have to murder me too!"

"And they will," Whitey said quietly. "If we fuck around and fail to play our cards the right way, they will."

"So what you got on your mind?"

"Here's the deal," Whitey explained. "Forget about hitting anybody anywhere near the Sotheby Museum. It's too risky. Dead that right outta your mind. But on the other hand, stealing a diamond off a Brink's truck can be a suicide mission too, unless you do it the right way. Believe me, if we played this shit out like amateurs and just rolled up and blasted on the truck all willy nilly we'd be setting ourselves up to get caught in a double-cross two different ways."

"How so?"

"Well, for one thing the drivers would sound the electronic alarm indicating that the truck had been robbed. That right there would trigger a nation-wide manhunt all by itself. But even if we did manage to lay low we'd never be able to sell the Pink Lady diamond. *Never.* Not even on the underground market. With almost fifty-million dollars on the line that thing would be on the radar of every fuckin security agency in the whole world, man. I mean, we could always cut it up and try to dish it off in smaller pieces, but the true value in a gemstone like that is in the beauty of the entire piece.

"Nah," Whitey shook his head and said firmly. "We can't just go at it like no amateurs. We have to find a way to hit the truck *and* take the diamond. Without anybody realizing we've done either one."

Slick threw his hands up in frustration. "Man, that shit sounds crazy. How the hell are we supposed to steal a truck and a fitty-million dollar rock without nobody noticing, nigga?"

Whitey shot him a crafty grin.

"We play a game, my friend. A game that's older than the hands of time. It's called a bait and switch. First we make sure the truck stays on its scheduled course. And then we make sure the Pink Lady gets picked up by the truck's couriers and delivered to the Sotheby auction on time."

As Slick pondered the details, Whitey sat back looking like an alley cat who had just licked out some real creamy pussy. With Slick's unknowing help, he was going to ass-fuck Honore and her crew until shit dripped outta that bitch's eyeballs!

And the fate of his boss Slick? Whitey grinned broadly and at the same time he chuckled coldly inside.

No witnesses, no worries.

Unfortunately, *half*-Slick wasn't gonna make it out of the Sotheby museum at all. Whitey was gonna put a hot one in the back of his homey's head and cancel Christmas for his slime as soon as the diamond was delivered.

Noting Whitey's confident smile, Slick stood up and took a deep breath, and then nodded at his boy skeptically.

"A'ight, cool. I don't care what kinda plan you come up with. I trust you, bruh. I know you gonna make sure this shit goes off real smooth. Only fuckin thing I'm worried about is getting Jewelz back. I gotta *get her* man, you feel me? So fuck that diamond! If I gotta roll up in that joint and blast my tools at all them niggas at the same time, then that's what I gotta do!"

"Suicide," Whitey said firmly, "is not the answer. The answer is to go in with a solid plan, boss. A solid fuckin plan."

$$$$$

Hymie Lovitz had gotten the pure shit scared out of him. The back of his drawers were brown and soupy as he stood trembling and sweating across from the two young men who lurked in the confines of his small, dim kitchen.

Both men were hulking and strong like schoolyard bullies. The fact that they had busted up in his house was scary enough, but the prehistoric killer-look glinting in the black man's eyes soaked the front of Hymie's trousers and sent a stream of hot piss trickling down his scrawny leg.

However, it was the white man, with his clear blue eyes and clean-cut smile that had the old man's heart galloping like a thoroughbred as his pacemaker kicked in and tried to slow that shit down.

"I-I-I'm finished with the jewelry business," Hymie explained breathlessly as he pointed at the countless packing boxes and stacks of newspaper that littered his small kitchen. He had been wrapping up his late wife's favorite china when the two thugs appeared out of nowhere, terrorizing him and his precious daughter. And what they were demanding that he do right now was utterly preposterous.

"I mean, I'd really like to help you, gentlemen," Hymie blabbered. "I really would! But I've already put a padlock on my shop and we're moving to Florida in a couple of days. Besides, this thing is beyond me. The Pink Lady is one of the world's most exquisite premier jewels. It would take a great deal of time and skill to replicate a diamond of that magnitude and quality, even once! Fabricating *two identical* copies would be nearly impossible to do by one old man in such a short period of—"

In a flash Whitey reached out and gripped the old man by his throat, strangling off his words. The man gurgled for air as Whitey's stony eyes slid over to the homely-looking female who lay sprawled halfway up against the refrigerator where he had knocked her mousy ass.

"Go get your fucking keys," Whitey said, his gaze slicing into the old man's daughter like his eyeballs were made of razor blades.

"We're gonna go to your shop right fucking now, and in the next forty-eight hours you're going to make me two diamonds, muthafucka. Two. In forty-*eight* hours. Not forty-nine. And unless you want me to wake that ugly bitch up and put some heat on her pale white ass, you'd better work hard and you better work fast."

$$$$$

It was the longest forty-eight hours of Slick's whole life.

Jewelz. Jewelz. Jewelz.

She was all he could think about. She was the only thing he cared about. She was all his heart could bear.

Slick paced the floor in the back room of the boarded-up jewelry store raging inside. He felt like shit for putting Jewelz outta his crib, and he was filled with the dark fury and certain knowledge that he was gonna flatline Handgun Goody. Yeah, Goody and every fuckin brother he had left, had to go. Jewelz had ran him some bullshit about how that grimy nigga loved her, and how he would never harm her, but Slick knew better than that and he was gonna cold slump that entire set!

Standing on his left, Whitey was amped and on edge too. He stood by edgy as fuck as the fabricator sat hunched over his worktable trying to save his and his daughter's lives.

The old jeweler wore magnifying glasses and had two bright spotlights shining down on a large but rough diamond as he carefully examined a 3D computer-generated replica of the Pink Lady diamond.

Hog-tied over in the corner was his daughter. She was bent forward over a chair with her dressed pulled up in the back and her drawers pulled down. Her stringy hair fell around her face, obscuring the mouth that was tightly bound and the eyes that bulged with fear.

From a small table right beside her, Whitey had aimed the open end of a blow-torch at the left cheek of her pale ass. Every thirty minutes an orange-blue flame shot from the tip and sent a tortured shriek flying from her mouth as it singed her tender flesh into blisters.

They had been locked away in the jewelry shop for over twelve hours now, and the old man had been working furiously the entire time. Whitey had promised to set them both free if he fabricated the diamonds to ultimate perfection, and the old man was working frantically because he was desperate for his child to live.

"Remember," Whitey reminded him. "Your daughter's ass is on the line," he said as another blast of heat hit her blackened skin and the smell of Kosher-fried tush rose into the air. Sweat dripped from the old man's chin and tears fell from his eyes at the sound of his child's pitiful cries.

"That's what I like to see," Whitey chuckled gleefully. "Cry, you son-of-a-bitch, because this whore's jiggly ass is literally on the line."

CHAPTER 6

Beast Mode

Almost forty-eight hours after the foursome had entered the Fulton Street jewelry shop, Whitey stood beside the workbench holding two brilliantly fabricated replicas of the Pink Lady diamond in the palms of his hands.

Studying the bright screen, he glanced at the computer-generated model of the replica and then back at a high-resolution picture of the original diamond that had been enlarged to five-hundred percent. To his amazement the stunning gemstones looked absolutely fuckin identical.

"Now that's what I'm talking about," Whitely nudged the exhausted jeweler proudly as the man sat with his craggly white head slumped down on his chest. "You put in some real quality work, old man," Whitey praised him.

"You're happy with it?" the exhausted jeweler muttered as his droopy eyes lit up with hope. "So now you'll stop hurting my daughter and let us go?"

Whitey nodded solemnly. "Of course I will. I gave you my word, didn't I?'

"Ay, we gotta hurry the fuck up," Slick told him, holding out two white satin jewelry bags as he motioned for Whitey to give up the jewels. He glanced at his watch. They were gonna have to move fast in order to intercept the Brinks truck and get to Goody's maintenance warehouse in time for the hand-off.

Slick swiped his hand roughly over his face. His eyes were bloodshot and blurry but his whole fuckin body was wired. He had been on a hunnid for forty-eight hours straight, but he wasn't tired and his game wasn't slippin neither. He was in assassin-mode. Focused as fuck and mission-ready. All he could think about was finding Jewelz and body-bagging Dirty Mike. That's the only thing in the whole fuckin world that he knew.

Minutes later it was time to roll. Slick had just tied the old Jewish man up and left him laying next to his moaning-ass daughter, and he was heading toward the front door of the jewelry shop when he heard the shots ring out behind him.

Pop! Pop!

Slick whirled around in time to catch sight of a flash of heat flying outta the muzzle of Whitey's burner. There was a brief pause, and then the elderly jeweler and his daughter both crumpled facedown with their wigs twisted completely back.

Slick stared at his manz, and Whitey just shrugged.

"No witnesses, no worries, chief,"

Slick took a deep breath and nodded. "A'ight. Let's pack these bitches up and get outta here," he said as Whitey nestled each diamond deeply into a satin-lined velvet box and then slid them both into the white silk bag.

Whitey stepped over the dead bodies and glanced at his watch. "Yeah, let's move. We have to catch that truck, my friend. That commuter flight is gonna be landing right on time and we can't afford to miss it. Once the airline signs that diamond over to the truck driver we've gotta run down on his ass and *go get* that shit, man."

Slick smirked and waved him off. "Fuck that diamond." He gave zero fucks about the money. "We gotta get to Staten Island and go get *Jewelz*."

CHAPTER 7

Run Down on 'Em

Cookie Townsend maneuvered the military-style armored vehicle expertly through the crowded parking lot of the busy strip mall. It was close to lunchtime and thoughts of some sweet white pussy and a strawberry milkshake were heavy on his mind.

Behind him on the other side of the bullet-proof partition, Lil Smitty, his messenger and road dawg, was chillin in the back compartment scribbling notes and logging in the cash pick-up they'd just gotten from a large supermarket.

They'd been driving all over Staten Island since 6am, and so far they'd made stops at a couple of banks, two hotels, a commuter airport, a Wal-Mart, and two supermarkets.

Cookie was locked in with his eyes sharp and focused as he drove. He was an ex-Marine who had been driving for Brinks for over ten years and he was damn good at what he did. He rubbed his protruding stomach as he eyed the row of restaurants and small shops in the strip mall and tried to decide which one to hit up for lunch.

Company policy prohibited drivers from leaving their vehicles under non-emergency conditions, but Cookie was a vet at this shit and he knew how to work around the rules.

For years he had played Brinks' game by the rulebook and he either brought his grub from home or starved his ass off on his twelve-hour shift. But then a couple of older cats had hipped him to the hustle and showed him how this shit was really done.

Spotting a small mom-and-pop joint that sold burgers and fries, Cookie exited the parking lot and drove around the corner. He pulled up in the alley behind the store and parked in front of an eighteen-wheeler that was being unloaded by two young white guys.

"Yo, what you want, homey?" Lil Smitty asked as he reached for the door handle.

Cookie shrugged. They had eaten from this joint many times in the past and the cheese fries were good as fuck.

"Yo just get me the usual, man. A double cheeseburger and some a' them cheese fries. I want my burger well-done, and make sure they put a whole lotta cheese on them fries and don't let them stingy bastards short you neither."

Cookie reached under his seat and whipped out his iPhone as Smitty got outta the armored truck and jetted through the back door of the restaurant. Getting caught with a phone on the job was a violation of the rules too, but Cookie wasn't worried about it. There were no cameras in his truck and after ten years of stellar performance wasn't nobody monitoring his moves or playing him close neither.

With Smitty gone for the food Cookie knew he had about ten good minutes to himself. He needed to get him one off real quick and ten minutes would be plenty of time.

He hit a FaceTime number on his favorite list and then leaned back in his seat as the phone rang and the connection was made.

A live image popped up on the screen and a hot Asian chick pressed her face close to the camera.

"Hey *Papa-san*," she purred. "You're late. You know I can't stand to be kept waiting..." She had short black hair and she looked like she was straight off the boat from Japan, but she purred in a sexy kitten voice that was straight outta west Philly.

She angled the camera and stepped back, and Cookie gasped at the sight of her flawless skin and flat ass, covered by a bright yellow corset.

The Asian hoe stepped deeper into the room and Cookie saw a skinny blonde chick with pale skin and big tits laying on a narrow cot that was covered with a red blanket. Her heels were up against her ass, and her legs were cocked open wide, and if Cookie squinted real hard he could see straight up into her pussy.

The blonde was wearing a similar corset as her friend, but hers was jet black. She was stretched out flat on her back playing with her pointy nipples, and it looked like her gigantic implants were about to explode at any minute.

Cookie was a regular to this shit. This was his normal timeslot and he paid for their services in advance every week like clockwork. Both chicks knew the drill, and since they also knew he didn't have much of a lunch break, they got right to work.

Cookie undid his belt and opened his pants. His dick was already half-hard from anticipation and the sounds of their practiced porno moans and slurps and groans was enough to get him the rest of the way there.

With his four-inch joint gripped in his hand, he sat back to watch the show. The blonde hoe spread her legs and started playing in her pussy, getting herself wet. The Asian chick smiled for the camera, then began licking all over the blonde chick's 40 DD's.

The sight of that darting tongue all over those erect pink nipples turned Cookie straight the fuck on. He jacked his dick and moaned, and his eyes got even bigger when the Asian chick slid between her partner's legs and started licking her shaved muff like a kitten at a bowl of sweet milk.

"Yeah..." Cookie muttered, sweat popping out on his nose as he squeezed his dick and his fist pumps became faster and more feverish. "Eat that pussy up! Eat that shit the fuck up!"

The girls were really moaning and performing for him now, and Cookie was so busy digging in his drawers and jacking his dick that he got the shit shocked outta him when his door was snatched open and Lil Smitty was standing there holding his lunch.

"Here, nasty!" Lil Smitty frowned as he pushed the bag of greasy smelling food at him. "Them fuckers charged extra for all that cheese man—"

Cookie got the shit shocked outta him again as without warning, Lil Smitty slumped to the ground. Suddenly Cookie felt the cold barrel of a .45 snub-nose jammed under his jaw.

"Give it up chicken-choker," a white dude barked as he reached across Cookie's body and slid the keys outta the ignition.

"Yo, yo, yo!" Cookie screeched, dropping the phone and throwing his hands up in the air as his dick went limp and he almost shit in his pants. He gulped against the cold metal that was pressing into his throat, knowing in his heart that his worst fuckin nightmare was about to come true.

"Yo, be easy, white boy," he said with his voice trembling. "Whatever you want outta this bitch you can have it. It's yours, homey. Just be easy, dammit. Be *easy!*"

Without a word the white dude smashed him hard across the temple with the butt of the gun. Cookie slumped over in pain and the dude yanked him outta the armored vehicle and tossed him on the ground right next to Lil Smitty.

Cookie looked up and saw a black dude wearing a ski-mask and holding a semi-automatic trained dead on him.

"Over there," the brother gestured. "Get your ass up under them fuckin bushes."

Cookie scrambled over to a bunch of prickly hedges and watched as dude reached down and dragged Lil Smitty's limp ass over there too.

"Come up out ya shit, bruh."

"W-w-what?" Cookie stammered, his eyeballs trained on the barrel of dude's banger.

"I said take off ya shit!" the guy spit impatiently as he kicked Lil Smitty in the face hard enough to wake his ass up. "Hurry up! Get all that shit off! Both of y'all!"

Cookie hurried up and stripped outta his uniform. He pulled his shit off down to his drawers, including his boots. Lil Smitty was dazed so he moved a lil bit slower, but he came up outta his gear too.

"Take off them drawers too," the white guy said quietly as he trained his gun on them.

Both men submitted meekly as they peeled off their drawers and held them out to the gunman.

"Ball yours up and stuff 'em in his mouth!" the white boy demanded of Cookie.

Cookie didn't even hesitate as he turned to his homeboy and crammed his drawers all down in his mouth.

"Your turn," dude directed Lil Smitty as he choked and gagged. "It's only right. Let your partner see what your ass tastes like too."

Less than sixty seconds later Cookie was naked on his hands and knees and hogtied the fuck up. He couldn't believe he'd just gotten jacked for his shit. He wracked his mind tryna come up with a good lie because there was no way in fuck he was gonna be able to explain this shit to his bosses or justify his failure to follow company procedures.

I got fuckin robbed! He thought in dismay. Suckers on this job got stuck for their load all the fuckin time, and every time he heard about it Cookie shook his head and wondered how in the hell the dumb-fuck driver had allowed somebody to get the drop on him and take his shit.

Well now he knew. Bent over with his hands and feet tied in knots and Lil Smitty's funky drawers crammed halfway down his throat, now he knew!

Seconds later Cookie's eyes got big as shit as the white boy walked up and loomed over him with his heat pointed dead at his grill. A silencer was on the tip and immediately Cookie's bowels went loose because he knew what time it was.

"Noooooo!" Cookie squeezed his eyes shut and screeched past his gag. *"Noooooo!"*

Whewt! Whewt!

Slick glanced over at Whitey as both security guards slumped over in the bushes, dead.

"Yeah, I got it," Slick told his manz before he could even open his mouth. "That's why you took off ya mask, huh? No witnesses, no worries, right? Now let's fuckin move."

CHAPTER 8

Time is Money

After checking to make sure the fifty million dollar Pink Lady diamond was safe and secure in the back of the Brinks truck, Slick and Whitey stripped down to their boxers and slid on the uniforms that they'd taken off the security guards. Slick's joint fit short and tight, but Whitey got the fat dude's gear and it fit him loose as fuck.

They tossed their backpacks in the truck and climbed inside. Riding in the armored Brinks truck felt like being inside of a miniature military tank. They were strapped up crazy and ready to go gun-for-gun.

Whitey took the wheel while Slick kept his eyes peeled for signs of static. After a few miles he realized that they weren't being followed, but his senses stayed on high alert because with Jewelz's life on the line there was very little room for error.

The plan was to slide Goody one of the fabricated diamonds so they could get Jewelz back. And once Slick was sure the woman he loved was safe, he was gonna make those Goode Brothers pay dearly.

"Yo, bruh." Slick's tone was cold as him and Whitey headed toward Handgun Goody's warehouse where the handoff was going down. "You can best believe I'm tryna get Jewelz back at all costs, but if something goes wrong out there or those bastards try some fuck-shit then I'm getting dumb and going Rambo on all them niggas! I'm going for that nigga Goody's *blood* even if it costs me my own. So if the bullets start flying then do what you gotta do and get low. I'm just telling you where my head is at."

"You can cool it with all that dumb talk, Slick," Whitey said sounding annoyed as he maneuvered the truck through traffic. "We're brothers, man. We've always been brothers. And that means we're gonna go up in there and get Jewelz out together. And after that all three of us are gonna get the hell outta there. *Alive.* I don't want you trying to go out on that hero shit, you hear me? But if those guys play games and fuck around with the fuck around, then we can *all* fuck around!"

Slick nodded. For a white boy Whitey was a bang or bleed-type down-ass rider. Slick felt real secure knowing his manz had his back no matter what type of flagrant shit sparked off.

And Jewelz...Slick shook his head. It was a shame that it had taken something crucial like this for him to finally admit how much pure love he had in his heart for that girl. But he had already come to terms with whatever the outcome was gonna be.

He was getting Jewelz out no matter what. After that, maybe he would live or maybe he would die. It didn't really matter to Slick as long as Jewelz got out safe. One thing he could be sure of, he knew his bro Whitey would look out for Jewelz if he fucked around and got cut down.

"Remember," Whitey said as they approached Goody's maintenance warehouse. They had taken the diamonds out of their satin bags and placed them directly into their tiny boxes. Whitey had one of the fake diamonds in his pocket while Slick had possession of the other two.

"Just keep the box with the real diamond in your right pocket," Whitey reminded Slick, "and stash the fake one in your left pocket. We're probably gonna be outnumbered and out-gunned when we get inside Goody's warehouse," Whitey admitted quietly, "but we won't be outsmarted. All we have to do is keep our heads cool and handle our business and we can be in and out of there in less than five minutes flat."

"Straight up," Slick said as he looked down the long driveway and spotted Handgun Goody posted up out front with two of his top street soldiers. "You just stay on point my G, and remember what the fuck I said. When it's time to do the hand-off I'll just slide them niggas that fake shit real easy like. Then once we have Jewelz safe and secure we can start going ham on those suckers."

"I got it. Don't worry. Everything is going to go down righteously," Whitey predicted with mad confidence.

Slick nodded. "Yeah, I hope you right, but I don't trust Handgun Goody. This shit is way past personal between us so I'm warning you right now. If them Goode Brothers show any signs of crossing us I'm letting off everything I got dead in Handgun's ass. Zip 'em up style."

$$$$$

Handgun Goody sat in style at a huge granite table surrounded by his team. The Brooklyn boss had rented out his favorite spot, Ruth's Chris restaurant so his team could eat a good lunch and get prepared.

Today was their final meet-up before Goody was gonna meet with Slick and retrieve the Pink Lady Diamond from his punk ass. In attendance were Handgun's two remaining brothers, along with Ice's bitch Cucci, and a five of his best shooters.

"Shit is about to get real," Goody said he pushed his plate away and drank from a glass of expensive wine. "If we do this shit right then we all get to ride the fuck off into the sunset, you copy? No more beating up the block on the daily just to get at a dollar."

Goody looked around the table and his crew was so transfixed that you could hear a pin drop. His presence and his message demanded all eyes and ears and attention be on him. But the gravity of the situation wasn't lost on the Goode Brothers Gang. They had taken some heavy losses and they'd been forced to paint the town red in order to maintain power on the streets of Brooklyn.

"I'm ready to roll out and wash my hands of all this shit anyway," Goody confessed. "I lost my baby brothers and a lot of good young hittas to this game. Everybody at this table has done some ill shit just to survive out here. Fuck it though, we made it this far and now we have a chance to make it even farther. Only a few more bodies have to be put in the dirt before we can get to this jackpot."

"I hear you, big homey," Cannonball said. "So let's get ready to go. Everything is all mapped out just like you instructed. The location is tight and the shooters know where they're supposed to be positioned. That bitch Jewelz is wrapped up and ready to be transported. All we need to know is when to start sparking at that nigga Slick."

Goody lit up a cigar and sat back in his seat. He looked up at the ceiling and exhaled as he contemplated the brutality he wanted to inflict upon Slick.

"I underestimated Slick a long time ago," Goody said as he gazed around at his crew. "That was a mistake that I won't make again 'cause he ain't just some punk-ass flunky off the street that you can just walk up on and wipe out. Slick's a smart, tactical shithead. He didn't survive this long by being one-dimensional, so ere'body better be bouncing on they fucking toes and expect him to have a trick up his sleeve."

"One thing is for sure though," Goody acknowledged as he leaned back in his seat. "After we get that diamond, neither him nor that bitch Jewelz is gonna live to see another day. Therefore, nobody make a fuckin move until you see me raise my left hand up high in the air. That's the signal. And once you see that, then you fly that nigga's roof back. I'll add half-a-million to the split for whoever hits him first."

The crew of killers at the table nodded their heads and stood up, ready to go. They all wanted that extra half milli and they would be itching to be the one to deliver the kill shot.

Cucci had sat beside Ice Pick quietly the whole time, hanging off every word of Handgun's speech. She knew her spot in the lineup was solidified and secure because she was the only one who could broker a deal with the underground trader once they had the diamond in their hands.

Standing up to follow the men out, she giggled inside with excitement. Now was her best chance to get one up on Honore and cash the fuck out. But Cucci wasn't nobody's fool. She knew how gooned-up these Brooklyn niggas really was, and in some ways Handgun Goody was more dangerous and cut-throat than Sly McFly was.

Cucci shivered inside. She knew a shit-storm could possibly be brewing, because if them two psychos ever clutched up then shit was gonna get ugly as fuck. But whatever. She was fiending in the pockets and it was too late to turn back now. Handgun had given them the green light to move forward, and like it or not, everybody in the joint was on "go" mode. But still…Cucci just couldn't shake the feeling that even though the stage was set for everything to go down nice and clean, somebody's dirty-ass blood was gonna get spilled.

$$$$$

"All right, just relax," Whitey said as he brought the armored vehicle to a stop. The old maintenance warehouse had two extra-wide double doors and Whitey parked several yards away. With a cool and calm glance at Slick, he cut the truck off and left the keys dangling from the ignition as he opened his door and climbed out.

Handgun Goody stood there dressed in the utmost finery and sporting a big grin.

"So glad you pussies could make it," Goody said with a chuckle as he watched Slick and Whitey exit the truck with their hammers hanging out.

"What's all the hardware for, gentlemen? I thought this was supposed to be a simple lil business transaction."

"Punk-ass bitch!" Slick spit. "Ain't never been no pussy in my blood! Ask ya dead brothers!"

"Damn, Lil Slick! Fuck wrong with you?" Goody said in a real cocky tone as he grinned broadly. "You ain't gonna say w'sup or ask me how I'm doing or nothin? Nigga you was raised by old folks! I know your granny taught you better than that. Where's your manners at son?"

Slick sneered. "Oh, you think this is a fuckin game, huh? You's a certified child-killing coward, muthafucka, so miss me with the small talk."

"Oh, I'ma miss ya ass, alright," Handgun said coldly as he dropped his grin and glared. "I'ma miss the fuck outta you because yo ass ain't even getting up in the building, nigga!"

"What?" Slick said, taking a step closer.

"Ay, you heard me, lil nigga!" Handgun barked as his soldiers cocked their shit. "Back the fuck up! Back your black ass the fuck *up!* Matter fact," Goody fumed, "go sit the fuck back in ya truck, bitch! You wanna get ya lil stank hoe back and conduct some bizz with me today? Then you stay ya ass out here and send the white boy in to handle the transaction!"

Slick scoffed and raised his heat high too. Ignoring the soldiers, he pointed his hammer straight at Handgun Goody's grill.

"Nah, I ain't staying nowhere, son. I'm coming inside and handling my own fuckin handle! Now where the fuck is Jewelz?"

"Nigga what I just say?" Handgun aimed his shit at Slick's dome too as they sighted on each other in a standoff.

"Yo, Yo, *YO!*" Whitey barked, his voice deep and commanding. "Neither one of y'all motherfuckers knows what the word "business" means! This isn't how it's done, gentlemen! All this shit-talking and gun-pointing isn't the way to get things accomplished in the modern world, okay? This type of thing will only get somebody deaded, and since I didn't come here to get killed today, Slick, I'm going to ask you to wait outside and let me go in there and get Jewelz."

"What?" Slick glared at his roady. "Man you buggin! Hell fuckin n—"

"Please. You have to trust me, man," Whitey said, palming the tip of Slick's gat and gently pushing the barrel toward the ground. He leaned in close to his manz and stared him deep in the eyes and whispered quietly, "You're too close to this one, boss. Too emotional. Let me handle it. I promise you I'll go in and bring Jewelz out safely. You can trust me, Slick. You know I'd never let you down."

Slick shook him off and aimed his shit at Goody again. "Nah, fuck this nigga! He must be smoking his own shit! The fuck I look like to you?"

"You want that bitch back or not?" Handgun demanded. "Wait till you see her. She ain't got much left in the tank anyway, so you might wanna speed this bullshit up."

"Yo, Slick, please just chill out here and watch my back," Whitey insisted as he took a couple of steps toward the door. "Make sure no clowns sneak in behind me and try to sleep walk me."

Slick paused for a long moment. Then he nodded reluctantly as his eyes narrowed dangerously.

"A'ight, man," he said. "Go in there and get my Jewelz back, fam. You make sure they handle my baby real gentle too 'cause you already know I'm ready to rock out."

"Ay, you two bitches can hug and kiss and whisper all that sweet shit later," Goody said, turning toward the door with his men bringing up the rear. "I wanna get my hands on that shiny get-rich come-up shit right now!"

Left outside to wait by himself, Slick fumed like a raging bull. His whole body felt like a coiled snake, ready to strike. All he could think about was Jewelz. Jewelz. *Jewelz*. Her mental state, her physical state, and the safety of her entire spiritual being.

"Lord help these simple niggas if they brought any harm to my woman," he paced and vowed, his heart full and swole. There was no doubt in Slick's mind that he was in love with Jewelz. He had fought against it hard and long, but he was finally ready to admit that she was his queen and his jewel, and right now his heart was bleeding for his closest and best friend in the whole fuckin world.

He prayed to God that she still cared about him because as soon as this shit was over with he was gonna beg for Jewelz's forgiveness and spend the rest of his life showering her with his love.

But if his baby walked outta that warehouse door with so much as a scratch on her there would be no restraining him. He'd spray that shit until every Goode Brother up in there had a hole in him and the filthy blood of their entire genealogy soaked into the ground.

No doubt about it, Slick thought as he strode around to the side of the raggedy building gripping his heat. If Jewelz didn't come up outta there in one fuckin piece then that's exactly what he was gonna do.

$$$$$

There was a certain dirty cop on Staten Island who walked a certain dirty beat. He met up with a certain dirty prostitute on a certain day of the week.

Patrolman Darren Wilson had a thing for dirty pussy. He was a funny-looking white boy from Missouri who was known for his hatred for black men. It looked like straight up racism to hood folks in the star-studded town of Staten Island, but in reality it stemmed from the fact that deep down inside, Officer Darren Wilson was secretly jealous of black men and he envied practically everything about them. He had studied black men closely, and there was something in their dominating physical structure and that natural athleticism in their DNA, that gave them a fearsome aura of power and stealth.

Officer Wilson didn't like that shit.

He was of the pale and frail sort, himself, and he had barely passed the rigors of the police academy. In fact, two of his stupid black classmates had cheated for him on the final exam, and when it was all over he had turned them both in and accused them of helping each other pass the test.

Today, Officer Darren Wilson was doing what he loved to do best while he was in uniform.

He was eating black pussy.

That was another thing that pissed Officer Wilson off about black men. They got to eat all the black pussy they wanted for free, while he had to give up his precious few dollars just to get him a taste.

"I'm telling you right fuckin now," the shapely young prostitute named Taquanoshia snapped as she put her foot up on the bumper of Officer Wilson's patrol car. They were parked in the area of the Ferry, behind an abandoned storage facility, right down the street from a maintenance warehouse.

Sucking her teeth, she lifted her skirt and spread her legs, and offered him her naked pussy. "This ain't no goddamn buffet, a'ight? I wanna get paid for real this time, and you gonna have to pay me extra 'cause yo ass be eatin too damn long!"

Officer Wilson's mouth was watering as she tooted her ass out and he prepared to attack her from the back. He took off his shoulder holster and unbuckled his belt, then he took his stiff pecker out and squeezed it in his fist.

This was the stuff of his fantasies, and he always made sure he hit Taquanoshia near the middle of her day, after she had already been with quite a few other tricks. He bent over and stuck his large nose between her booty cheeks and took a deep, long whiff. What would have knocked an ordinary man off his feet smelled like heaven to Officer Darren Wilson. Still digging with his nose, he started lapping her out, going back and forth between swirling his tongue deep into her pussy and tossin her salad. The whole time his lips were nibbling and sucking up as much of her juice as he could get. They were the same lips that he kissed his wife and kids with, but right now they were kissing that thang that Officer Wilson loved best. Pussy and ass!

Taquanoshia leaned over the warm hood of the squad car, bored as hell.

"Hurry up," she looked back over her shoulder and snapped. "Don't eat all the damn pussy up! Save some for the next damn trick!"

He rooted deeper and Taquanoshia fell forward on her elbows and yelped. Officer Darren Wilson's head was buried so far up her coochie it felt like she was giving birth. "I gotta fart," she grit her teeth and warned him. "So you better hurry the fuck up!"

Jerking his dick, Officer Wilson started lapping at her ass with a frenzy. He stiffened his tongue like a dagger and jabbed it in her pussy and then inserted it deeply into her asshole. His balls swelled up and his dick started jerking. He had to get his. He just had to! His tongue was moving a million miles a minute and he felt his nut rising. He moaned and slurped and humped and panted. He was almost there. He was *almost there*! And that's when he heard the blast go off.

$$$$$

Whitey stepped through the double bay doors of the large warehouse and blinked against the sudden vastness inside. He found himself in a large open workroom, the type of maintenance joint where big trucks were repaired, and used tires and equipment was stored.

There were about a dozen Hispanic mechanics dressed in coveralls busting truck tires and stripping down stolen cars. At least five or six more soldiers from the Goode Brothers Gang were posted up on point too, waiting for instructions from their chief capo.

Handgun's brother had backed up his ebony stretch Mercedes Benz SUV right into the middle of the bay, and as soon as Goody walked over and tapped on the hood all the doors flew wide open.

The first man out was Ice Pick Goody. He got outta the driver's seat and his younger brother Cannonball and two of his cousins climbed outta the back seat right after him.

Jewelz was pushed outta the back of the whip next. She was buck-naked and her eyes looked wild and weak. Two shiny pieces of silver duct tape were crisscrossed over her mouth and her hands were tied together in front of her with a piece of thick yellow rope.

She stood there unwilted under everybody's harsh gaze. Even bald, naked, and beaten, her bruised brown body was beautiful and dignified, and her magnificent breasts rose and fell with each labored breath.

"Jewelz," Whitey muttered under his breath as Handgun Goody motioned for Ice Pick to send her over.

"Hur'rup, goddammit," Goody spit, eyeing Jewelz's high, curvy ass with a sneer. "Give that stank bitch up and let's make this shit happen."

Whitey took a step forward as Jewelz staggered toward him slowly and painfully. She was battered but unbroken, and although the Goode Brothers had tried to humiliate her by parading her around in her nakedness, she held her head high and refused to cry.

Whitey met her at the halfway mark and Jewelz fell into his arms like dead meat. He caught her and supported her thin frame with ease. He peeled the thick tape gently from her mouth then looked down at her abused body and saw the torment that the Goode Brothers had put her through. He sighed deeply and his blue eyes teared up.

"Ah, shit!" he said as his voice broke with pain. "Oh damn, baby girl. *Shit!*"

Staring at all the bloody lumps and bruises that stood out on her naked flesh, Whitey shook his head in disbelief as he gazed into the eyes of the woman he loved. Suddenly deep pain and anger filled his heart and white-hot murder rushed through his mind.

"See there…look at what that punk-bitch got you into," Whitey whispered coldly in Jewelz's ear. "He was supposed to love you, but instead his sucka-ass walked you right into a trap! Why didn't you just choose me, Jewelz? I never would've allowed these scumbags to put their hands on you. Never! Why didn't you just let me love you?"

Whitey looked up at the Goode Brothers and sneered. "Stupid motherfuck-as! What the fuck did y'all *do* to her?"

"Nah, what the fuck did *you* do!" Cucci Momma hollered as she jumped outta the whip looking pissed and shocked at the same damn time.

"Fuck is *your* ass doing here?" she demanded, killing the whole transaction as she grilled the shit outta Whitey with the mad eye.

"You low-down cracka mothafucka, you! You lying-ass trick *bitch!* Mothafucka you made me suck your white-ass dick for *nothing!*" she screeched, jabbing her manicured finger at him as she killed him with her glare. "I sucked your pink shit down to the nub for *nothing!*"

Cucci's eyes were blazing as she put her hand on her hip and turned to her man.

"Shoot this mothafucka, Ice Pick! *Dead* his white ass! This mothafucka is FBI, y'all!" Cucci hollered at the team. "His alphabet ass is *F-B-fuckin-I!*"

$$$$$

A huge pile of empty gas cans were stacked up high and blocking the side entrance to the warehouse. Slick flung about twenty of them shits outta his way only to find that the swinging door was chained closed and secured with a big silver padlock.

The chain rattled a little bit as he pushed against the door, and a cool breeze escaped the crack as he pressed his face close and peered inside.

He squinted through the two-inch space and cursed under his breath when he saw Jewelz stumbling naked across the floor toward Whitey.

Jewelz! Slick bit down on his bottom lip, his heart hurting to the very core at the sight of her ravaged naked body and what they had done to her.

Even from this distance he could see that Jewelz had been fucked up. She looked like she was hanging on by some miraculous thread that Slick couldn't even fathom. His mind flashed back to that horrible day when Haz and Handgun had brutalized and slaughtered his fuckin family like they were just a bunch of stray dogs.

Jewelz looked vulnerable and weak just like that again right now, and something inside Slick snapped as he peered through that crack in the door. He made his decision right then and there.

Suddenly a brown-skinned chick jumped outta the back of Handgun's whip and more words were tossed back and forth. Slick could only make out a couple of phrases here and there, but it didn't matter what they were saying. Handgun Goody wasn't leaving up outta there alive no matter what kinda shit they was talking or how smooth this deal went down. Hell, nah. That nigga had to die, and he had to die *today!*

$$$$$

"Blast his ass!" Cucci hollered again as the Goode Brothers paused for a split second to ponder the repercussions of murking a Federal Officer. "Shoot him, goddammit!"

"None of y'all bitches better fucking move!" Whitey yelled as he yanked his burner out then spun Jewelz around and yoked his forearm tightly around her neck. Raising his hand high, he smashed the butt of his piece down hard against her temple, drawing blood as he dropped his mask and let his true colors show.

"Clap him!" Cucci screeched again. "Shoot him and get the fuckin diamond, y'all!"

"I said *don't none of y'all niggas fucking move,*" Whitey warned coldly as the Goode Brothers drew beads on him.

Huddled up close behind Jewelz and using her body as a human shield he barked, "Toss your fuckin burners down or I'll kill this bitch. I swear I'll blow her top clean the fuck off!"

Handgun Goody chuckled loudly. "Ga'head! Bust that bitch's melon, nigga! We'll wait. Fuck I care?"

"You care because you wanna get paid and Slick's sitting on the diamond outside in the truck, idiot," Whitey told him. "Who the fuck do you think is stupid enough to walk in here carrying a fifty-million dollar jewel?"

A look of hesitation crossed Goody's face and Whitey knew he had him.

"Uh-huh, mothafucka, that's right," Whitey nodded. "You told Slick to stay in the truck and he stayed there. *With* the fuckin diamond! Now, unless I walk outta that door with this stinking bitch all in one piece, Slick is taking off in that armored truck. And if he takes off then all y'all bitch-boys are ass-out and you won't be getting a goddamn thing!"

$$$$$

"*Whitey!"* Slick screamed as he peeped through the door crack and watched his manz yoke Jewelz up and smash the tool against her head. "Nigga what the fuck is you doing?" he shrieked, enraged and bewildered as fuck.

The sound of multiple gats cocking filled the air as the Goode Brothers and all their soldiers simultaneously aimed deadly heat at Whitey's dome.

Outside, Slick leaned away from the chained door and blew a chunk outta the padlock, shattering that shit. He twisted the shards of broken metal away and kicked the door open wide as sunlight flooded inside the large bay.

"Ay, dammit!" he screamed in disbelief as he charged into the warehouse with his muzzle sighted on the center of Whitey's forehead. "Whitey what the *fuck* are you doing? Nigga you hit her! I saw you fuckin hit her!"

With every gun in the joint trained dead on him, Whitey was sweating from head to toe. "Fuck this bitch, Slick! Tell these muthafuckas I ain't no federal agent!"

"Nigga I don't know *who* the fuck you are!" Slick spit. "I know you better take ya fuckin hands off her and give these idiots they diamond!"

Whitey's eyes darted crazily. "I ain't got it! Stop bullshitting, Slick! These dumb fucks think I'm the FBI! Go in your right pocket and give that shit up!"

"Yo," Slick said, staring into his homey's wild blue eyes. Whitey looked like a trapped rat, and suddenly Slick understood the role reversal and the game that was being played. The wrong muthafucka was holding Jewelz hostage, and this shit wasn't gonna be nothing nice. "Nigga maybe you *is* FBI," Slick said slowly. "Maybe you tryna set all of us up!"

"Haa-haaa!" Handgun yelled in amusement. "Look at the fuckin irony here, now would ya! Homeboy vs. Homeboy! This shit is better than Jerry Springer! This goes to show you that you can't trust nobody Lil Slick."

"Oh I see what you tryna do," Whitey sneered at Slick. He dug the muzzle of the gun even deeper into Jewelz's bloody head as she slumped limply in his arms. "You tryna save this bitch and get these guys to flatline me at the same time!"

Slick cocked the hammer back and spoke in a voice colder than ice. "Give up the diamond you pussy-ass nigga, and gimme my woman."

"Your woman?" Whitey laughed. "I been sticking my dick in this bitch for months! While you was running around crying over that old woman I clipped off and a bunch of shitty pigeons, *I'm* the one who was taking care of her and making her feel good! And what did I get in return? I got shitted on! This bitch couldn't even love me because you were always in the way!"

"Damn, Jewelz!" Goody sounded off with an evil chuckle. "You was suckin my dick like that and fuckin this white boy too? You's a smut-ass hoe!"

"Ay, Goody," Whitey said. He kept his gun jammed on Jewelz and his eyes on Slick as he directed his attention to the druglord. "Slick ran through your whole family. It was all him. Allow me to put this sucker down for a nap, and then you and I can discuss a very lucrative business venture. I have a few top-notch connects that I can put together to help you get your diamond outta the country."

"Don't believe him!" Cucci yelled. "This pale-face fuck is 5-0 y'all! I'm telling y'all he's the damn enemy!"

"I ain't no fucking pig!" Whitey snapped.

"Yes you is!" Cucci pointed her manicured finger at him. "You locked me in your damn car and made me suck your dick! You tried to beat me outta my reward money too!"

"Bitch shut up!" Goody yelled over his shoulder. "We can kill two birds with one stone right here and right now! Listen up, white boy. You wanna live? Then ga'head and rock Slick *and* Jewelz to sleep and prove you ain't no cop! Then maybe, just maybe after I get that diamond I'll lend an ear to the lil side-deal you tryna cut and let you walk outta here alive."

Whitey and Slick were locked in a Mexican standoff with a dying hostage between them. Both men were top-shot gunslingers, and Jewelz's fate was gonna come down to who was smarter, who was quicker, and who wanted that shit more.

"Put your strap down, Slick," Whitey commanded. He tightened his grip on Jewelz's neck and pressed the gun deeper into her temple. "Lay that hammer right down on the floor or I'll spray this hoe's DNA all over ya face."

"Bro, why the fuck are you doing this?" Slick pleaded. "That's *Jewelz* you over there pawing up, man! She's one of *us*. Why you switching up on me?"

"Cause he's a cop!" Cucci screamed. "He's a goddamn cop!!!"

"Put ya shit down!" Whitey shrieked. "Or watch this bitch die!"

Slick stared into that snake-nigga's blue eyes. The calm, all-American demeanor that was Whitey's trademark was completely gone. He had absolutely no chill left and he looked like he coulda shot up a movie theater or an elementary school without blinking an eye.

"A'ight you bitch-made pussy," Slick finally conceded. He hated to do it but he had no choice. It had come down to either him or Jewelz, and the choice was easy. He had looked into Jewelz's eyes and seen real fear. She was beaten and broken, but she wasn't ready to die yet.

"Enough with all the soap opera shit!" Goody spit. His patience with the dumb shit had evaporated. "Handle ya handle, white boy, or we gone start ripping all three of y'all the fuck up."

There wasn't even a question in Slick's mind about what he had to do. If he didn't do it then him and Jewelz would both be corpses in just a matter of seconds. He squatted down slowly to put his ratchet on the floor.

"Just fuckin relax Whitey," Slick said calmly, fixing him in his gaze and knowing full well he was about to get shot. "You ain't even gotta do this shit slime..."

Slick was in a full squat when he went to put the gun down, but instead of dropping it he dove forward and lunged flat toward the ground, raising his ratchet and aiming it at Whitey before his stomach even hit the concrete.

The unmistakable crack of a sniper rifle split the air from up above, quickly followed by rapid machine gun fire.

"*Jewelz!!!*" Slick yelled as he looked up from the ground and saw Whitey's head explode behind her and his brains shoot skyward like a gushing water fountain.

It seemed to take all day for Whitey's brain gore to rise up toward the ceiling. And when gravity caught it and it finally rained back down toward the ground, it splashed all over Jewelz and she screamed and dropped down to her knees.

Whitey's body hit the deck like all his batteries had been knocked out. The sniper rifle had gone silent, but the machine gun was still spitting rapidly from someplace up high, and Handgun and his brothers were ducking and diving to escape the unknown shooter as they scrambled to take cover behind their stretch SUV.

Time seemed to go into extra-slow Matrix-mode as Slick jumped up and ran toward Jewelz. His eyes shot up toward the ceiling of the warehouse and he had a brief flashback to his Special Ops days.

What he saw up there fucked him right up. It was a shooter. And he was on the move. To Slick's surprise, the shooter was poppin off with a purpose, keeping the Goode Brothers running while at the same time covering his ass on the ground.

As Slick aimed his hammer and started firing, dude came scurrying down outta the rafters and took up a position on a high ledge right above the bay doors. With deadly precision he started picking Goody's boys off with his submachine gun like they were a bunch of sitting ducks.

Slick peered up at the ledge real quick and he couldn't believe what the fuck he was seeing.

Wild Man!

His bruh was on it! Goody's crew was ducking and scrambling as they caught countless hot shells from the Zip 'em up gunslinger and started hitting the ground like hijacked airplanes.

Maintenance workers and mechanics were running wild and screaming like bitches as they dove behind big trucks and slid up under cars hoping to avoid a stray bullet.

Leaping over one of his fallen dun-duns, Ice Pick Goody jumped behind the wheel of the stretch-SUV and gunned the gas pedal to the max. Cannonball tried to hop in on the passenger side but he only managed to get one leg in the whip. Handgun caught the handle of the back door just as his brother peeled off and busted that fine automobile straight through the double bay doors.

The force of the impact shook Cannonball loose from the SUV. It sent him sailing violently through the air toward a pile of twisted steel and rusted metal. He landed face up, right on a sharp metal spike. It impaled him from the back. Clean through the neck. He was dead before he could draw another breath.

The impact also tore Handgun Goody's hands free from the door handle and sent him crashing down to the hard concrete. He landed face-first and quickly scrambled to his feet to try and catch up with the whip, and that's when Slick drew a bead on that muthafucka.

Goody was beating feet toward the shattered bay door, desperate to catch up with Ice Pick and escape the hot bursts of fire that Wild Man was laying down, when Slick squinted his gun-eye and squeezed one off.

Pop!

His first round took out Goody's knee. The gangsta screeched like a bitch as his joint exploded outward, from the back to the front, and he went down hard on his ass.

Goody rolled over clutching his leg and howling. A look of pure rage was in his eyes as he tried to pull himself up. Slick's next shot was just as accurate and it tore into Goody's gut and burrowed clean through his lower back.

That nigga forgot all about his knee as he clutched his stomach, grimacing and grunting in pain as hot blood seeped through his fingers.

"How you like getting gut-ripped?" Slick walked over and breathed heat down on him. "That's where you stabbed all of us kids at, ain't it?"

His next couple of shots came in rapid succession as Slick went to war on Dirty Mike, AKA Handgun Goody. He tic-tac-toed that screaming nigga, blasting him once in each shoulder, then in his other knee, and then finally he aimed his tool at the center of his enemy's dome.

The scent of death was in the air and it smelled delicious to Slick. He was about to send Goody straight to hell and he couldn't help but crack a smile. This coward was the last one alive out of those who'd been responsible for the murder of his parents and siblings. The circle of vengeance was about to be complete, and Slick knew that pulling the trigger was gonna give him the ultimate satisfaction.

It's over, Momma Kia. It's over, Big Slick. Samira, Sameek, Samille, Samir II. I love y'all, fam. This shit is finally over. Now everybody can rest in peace.

The pain of losing his entire family and being forced to grow up alone on the streets of Crooklyn would never go away. But Slick could take pride in knowing that the last nigga on his list was about to be maggot food.

"I shoulda erased you a long time ago," Slick spit as he stared into Handgun's fearful eyes as the kingpin wriggled and gasped and bled all over the floor.

And then Slick lowered his gun.

"But unfortunately your dirty ass ain't mine to kill."

Slick walked over to Jewelz and crouched down beside her. Soft cries escaped her bruised lips and Whitey's blood and gore dripped from her bald head.

Slick pulled out his knife and cut the rope away from her wrists in one smooth stroke. Then he gathered her in his arms and turned her naked body around until she was sitting with her back against his chest, facing Handgun

Goody.

"Here," Slick said, placing his gat between her trembling hands as he helped her find the grip.

"Get yours, baby. Do his bitch ass any kinda way you wanna do him. Finish this shit up for once and for all so our family can finally sleep easy, baby. Finish his ass!"

Jewelz was so weak she could barely hold her head up. Her naked breasts heaved and her whole body trembled as she leaned back against Slick's chest and allowed him to support her weight.

She was exhausted as all hell, but what she lacked in strength she made up for in commitment. Slowly, she curled her finger around the trigger. A look of pure hatred flowed from her eyes and set fire to Handgun Goody's soon-to-be departed soul.

"Jewelz," Goody moaned, raising up on one elbow as his eyes begged her for mercy. "You know I luh you, girl," he gasped in desperation. "Don't do this shit. You ain't gotta do this. Please, baby. I wasn't really gonna hurt you. I swear on my mother I wasn't. Just hold the fuck up baby and let's talk about it..."

Jewelz's hands were steady as fuck as she tightened the pressure on her index finger. Handgun Goody's lil fake love didn't sway her one damn bit. Her lifelong need for vengeance and retribution was stronger than her cancer. It was stronger than all the pimps and all the tricks, and all the rapes she had endured. It was stronger than the beatings, stronger than her damaged spirit, and it was stronger than her humanity too.

There wasn't an ounce of mercy in Jewelz's heart as she squinted through her good eye and squeezed that trigger. Without a shred of remorse she jerked her finger and planted a heat round dead in the middle of Handgun Goody's forehead.

Pop!

And in that instant, it was over. The weight of Jewelz's tortured past collided in the air with Goody's criminal soul, and both spiraled down to the pits of hell where they belonged.

"You got him, baby," Slick whispered in her ear and caught the burner as it fell from her weak grip. "You whacked his bitch-ass. Now it's over."

All Jewelz could do was nod weakly. Her insides felt all busted up and a tear slid from the corner of her eye.

Yes. It was finally over. All of it.

CHAPTER 9

The Smooth Getaway

Officer Darren Wilson paused with his nose deep between the hoe's butt cheeks. His mouth was wide open and ass juice was dripping from his chin.

"Did you hear that?"

"Nope," Taquanoshia smirked as she leaned her elbows on the hood of his patrol car and tooted her ass up higher. "I ain't hear shit because it was one of them SBD's."

"SBD's?"

"Yeah," she giggled. "My fart was the Silent But Deadly type."

Officer Wilson was still gripping his dick. He listened for a few more seconds and then got back to licking that pussy and tryna get excited again so he could get the nut he was about to pay for.

But suddenly a series of staccato pops sounded off in the air. They were coming from the other end of the alley where the maintenance shop was located, and they were followed by several more blasts.

Officer Wilson froze again. This time he knew for sure that it wasn't no fart he was dealing with. Those were gun-shots, and they were coming from somewhere up the street.

Rising up out of his crouch, he pushed his favorite dish away and took off running down towards the other end of the long pathway where the shots had come from. He looked comical as hell tryna stuff his dick back inside his pants and buckle his belt and put on his shoulder holster at the same time.

"Get outta here!" he hollered back to Taquanoshia. "Get gone! I'll find you tomorrow and we can do it again!"

"Shit!" Taquanoshia stomped her feet and cursed as she watched him haul ass down the extra-long alley, screaming into his walkie-talkie for backup. Her pussy was sore as hell and she was late for her next trick. "You stingy lil-dick

bastard, you! I knew your cheap ass wasn't gonna fuckin pay me!"

$$$$$

Slick was still holding Jewelz in his arms when Wild Man walked up carrying a backpack. He had a sniper rifle over one shoulder and his sub-machinegun was slung over the other one.

"Sup, son." He nodded toward the daylight that was streaming in through the entrance of the maintenance shop where the Mercedes SUV had just torn the doors off the hinges and disappeared from view.

"I got most of them Goode Brother bitches but one of them maggots got away."

Inhaling the fumes from the whip's burnt rubber, Slick nodded back. *Ice Pick*. That lil bitch had peeled out and left his brothers to run or gun.

"Yeah, he got away for now," Slick grunted, knowing that one day he would hunt Ice Pick Goody down and finish the job. "For now."

Suddenly Wild Man froze and turned his head like he was listening closely. "Yo, you hear that shit? Sirens. The pigs are about to be here in a minute and Jewelz looks like she needs to get to a hospital. Let's roll, man."

"Nah." Slick shook his head as he gathered Jewelz closer in his arms and gently rocked her back and forth. "You go 'head. I ain't leaving her."

"Sup with the Brinks uniforms?" Wild Man asked, eyeing Whitey's dead body. "Fuck was y'all gunslingers doing?"

"We ran down on the drivers and stole a forty-seven million dollar diamond for Goody," Slick muttered. "They call it the Pink Lady."

Wild Man's eyes got big. "Damn! That fuckin diamond is in high demand! Y'all was gunnin for that shit too?"

Slick nodded. "I had to do it to get Jewelz back. We was supposed to be delivering that shit to a museum in twenty minutes so we can keep the Feds off our asses but..."

"Go," Jewelz whispered as she pushed Slick away and tried to break free of his clinging arms. "Get outta here. Go do what you gotta do..."

Slick hesitated as the sound of sirens grew closer and the mechanics and maintenance men began emerging outta their hiding places now that the bullets were no longer flying.

He shook his head again. "I ain't leaving you here, Jewelz. Fuck that! I *can't* leave you."

"Don't be stupid," Jewelz gasped, pulling away from him with the last bit of her strength. "This is the murder game, Slick! Don't be acting like no fuckin rookie. Get gone," she dismissed him. "Fuck outta here!"

"A'ight," he said reluctantly. "I'll meet you at the hospital, okay?" He paused to kiss her on her chin. "You're gonna be all right, Jewelz. I swear every fuckin thing I'm doing is for *us*, baby. For me and for you. Go to the hospital. I'ma handle this shit and meet you there as soon as I can."

Slick kissed Jewelz again and then looked up at Wild Man. "Yo, take off your shirt and put on Whitey's."

Wild Man stripped outta his clean shirt and Slick draped it over Jewelz and covered her nakedness. In an instant Wild Man pulled Whitey's shirt off of his dead corpse and put that shit on, blood and all.

Slick hated to leave Jewelz, but she was a gunslinger and he knew she would survive.

"I'll see you in a few," he promised her as he backed away, leading Wild Man toward the armored Brinks truck that was parked outside. The sirens were getting louder and there was no time to lose.

"I'ma go make this move so me and you can be set for the rest of our lives, baby. But I swear to God I'll be at that hospital as soon as I can. I promise you, Jewelz. Wait for me there, okay? I swear to God..." Slick stared into her eyes and let every ounce of his love show.

"If you don't never believe nothing else I say, please believe this. I *promise* you, Jewelz. If you gimme one more chance I'll be there for you forever. Word is life, ma."

$$$$$

That buff Chinese monster came outta nowhere!!! Cucci Momma thought as she hauled ass down the streets of Staten Island wearing a designer skirt and heels.

In the confusion of smoking gats and flying bullets there had been one thing on her mind and one thing only: Get that fuckin diamond and get the fuck up outta there!

Cucci was the mistress of forked tongues and it was a good thing she knew a lie when she heard one. Wasn't no way in hell a white FBI mothafucka would leave a hood nigga outside holding a fifty-million dollar jewel! No fuckin way!

With her senses on high alert Cucci had pounced on the white FBI dude almost as soon as his dead body hit the ground. While Ice Pick and his dumb fuckers were busy ducking and shooting and trying not to get ripped, Cucci had risked her life by going for the rock!

Ignoring the blood and brain goo that was all over the corpse, she had straddled the white boy's body like she was about to ride his pale lil dick to town. But instead of giving him some more of that good shit he had gotten in his car outside of the hair show, Cucci had attacked all his fuckin pockets, rifling through them shits until she found what she was searching for.

It was in his pants, pushed down deep in the right front pocket. Quick as hell she had snatched that shit out and shoved it way down in her bra and wedged it between her fat titties. With guns popping off in all directions, Cucci had low-crawled toward the side of the warehouse and hugged the wall. Instincts told her to get far, far away from Goody and his crew, so she jetted blindly, going deeper into the warehouse.

She was crawling on her hands and knees with her skirt hiked up over her hips when an old Puerto Rican maintenance man dressed in coveralls spotted her.

"*Senorita! Aqui!*" he hollered.

A sub-machine gun was spitting hot lead and Cucci didn't know what the hell to do. She froze helplessly as the grease monkey mechanic snatched her by the arm and practically dragged her through a grimy kitchen and out of a propped-open side door.

Her and dude had taken off running down the long alley in opposite directions, and now, walking furiously fast, Cucci was making her way toward a big crowd of people who were heading toward the Staten Island Ferry.

It took her a moment to realize that she had lost her damn purse back there in the warehouse, but she wasn't giving a single damn. She knew if she could make it across the river to Manhattan then she could lay low for a minute and figure out her next move.

Switching her bouncy ass without even meaning to, Cucci moved as fast as she could in her high heels and mid-thigh skirt. Every few seconds she stole a glance over her shoulder to make sure that the Chinese cat with the sub-machine gun wasn't sneaking up behind her. The last time she had seen him was that day he yoked Honore up at the job, and he had shocked the pure shit outta her when he jumped down from the ceiling and started spraying them niggas like roaches with his rat-a-tat-tat toolie.

Cucci was nearing the end of the alley when she peeked back over her shoulder one more time. And that's when she saw the cop. He was beating feet down the alley, fumbling with his pants and coming straight at her.

"Hey you! Stop right fucking there!"

Cucci took off running like fuck in her silver high heels.

She pumped her knees until they damn near hit her chest as she jetted like a pack of wild pit bulls was nipping at her ass.

"Stop right now or I'll shoot! I swear to God I'll shoot you, you stupid black *bitch!*"

Cucci was in pure panic mode as she scurried around the corner and down a busy street. The first store she came to was a bakery and she ducked inside. Hiding behind a fat old man she peered out the glass and watched the cop rush by. His head turned left and right as he scanned the crowd searching for her.

Cucci's heart pounded in her chest as she ducked deeper into the store. She hid the best way she could, using the white people who were crowded in the joint as a shield. She was breathing real hard and their uppity white asses was staring at her all funny as she pushed past knocking the hell outta them, but Cucci didn't give a fuck. The smell of warm cake slid up her nose and then the front door opened a gust of cool air swept into the store and touched her legs. She looked down at herself and cursed.

Shit!

No wonder these snooty-ass white people were grilling her so hard. She looked like a goddamn grease monkey! Her pale pink stockings were ripped and covered in black gunk from crawling all over the floor of the maintenance warehouse. Oil stains covered her pink and gray plaid Dior skirt and the front of her gray silk shirt too.

Cucci pushed her way back outside again and froze in the doorway. She crooked her neck and scanned up and down the street, and since the coast seemed clear she blended back into the milling crowd once again.

Get it together Cucci Momma! she amped herself up. She was almost there. All she had to do was make it to the corner, cross the street, and then go one more block until she was at the Ferry. She would get a ticket real quick and then run and hide in the bathroom until it was time for the next boat to leave. And when it pulled out into that water she was gonna jump on that bitch and lock herself in a bathroom until they hit the Manhattan side of the New York Harbor.

With her plan firming up in her head, Cucci had just hit the corner and jetted across the street, and that's when she heard the unmistakable "bleep-bleep-bleep" of a police siren rolling up behind her.

Shit! Wasn't no need to look over her shoulder because Cucci knew what time it was. With panic rising up in her throat she broke the fuck out once again.

She kicked off her designer heels and darted through the crowd as she dug for the tiny jewelry box that was wedged between her titties.

Cucci got that shit out as she ran, and without breaking her stride she pried the box open and snatched the gorgeous pink gemstone out, then stuck it in her mouth and tossed the box over her shoulder.

"Hey you!" Somebody yelled out behind her with firm authority. "Stop right there! Stop goddammit and give it up!"

Damn! The cop had some back-up po-po rolling with him now, and although Cucci glanced over her shoulder real quick, she never broke her stride. It was on and popping as she ran like a track star. Fuck the stupid shit. She wasn't giving up shit! Them mothafuckas was gonna have to *catch* her!

Cucci ran like crazy down the walkway of the pier. She did her best to stay parallel to the shoreline and she knocked people outta her way left and right as the sound of rushing footsteps closed in behind her.

Cucci ran fast as fuck, but the men behind her were even faster. Sheer desperation set in when she realized she wasn't gonna make it. Them bastards were so far up her ass and so hot on her neck that she could already smell their stankin baloney breath.

Suddenly two of them leaped forward and tackled her from behind. Cucci yelped as she was slammed into the pavement so hard the air left her lungs and the pink diamond went flying straight outta her mouth!

Crawling for it, she stuffed that shit back between her lips and slid it under her tongue and clenched her jaws tight.

The first cop jerked her arm behind her back and chicken winged that shit up to her neck as he scrambled to get the cuffs on her. Cucci twisted and turned and donkey-kicked backward and caught him flush in his soft little nuts. He grunted and reached for his dick, and Cucci came up off the ground running like she was a prime racehorse.

She beat feet in her designer skirt like she was running for her life. Her eyes searched for an escape route, but desperation gripped her when she saw there was no place left to run except straight into the filthy-ass freezing cold river.

Cucci Momma Jones wasn't nobody's punk. She was a real down bitch, and desperate times called for desperate measures. So with a fitty-million-dollar diamond tucked under her tongue and no other escape in sight, Cucci said fuck it and took the plunge.

$$$$$

Open your mouth...breathe, dammit! Open your mouth, open your mouth, open your mouth, open your mouth!

Cucci was straight outta the projects and she couldn't swim a lick. Trapped in a cold, watery grave she held her breath and kicked her feet and flailed her arms all around. She could hear them po-po pigs screaming at her and telling her to open her mouth and breathe, but the water was cold as fuck and she was drowning!

Open your mouth, open your mouth, open your mouth, bitch open your muthafuckin mouth and breathe!

Cucci's eyes were squeezed shut, her cheeks were puffed out like a blow fish, and her lungs felt like they were gonna burst. Stubbornly she arched her back and started sinking. She was getting weaker and her body was starving for air. She wanted to breathe! She wanted to *live!* She wanted to be *rich!* She wanted that fuckin *diamond!*

All her oxygen was just about gone and Cucci Momma was at the end of her rope when she felt hands grasping at her and dragging her up through the icy water. Gratitude rushed over her as she kicked her feet frantically and anticipated that first sweet sip of air.

Her heart was banging louder than everything else in the whole goddamn universe. Her face finally broke through the water and Cucci opened her greedy lips preparing to suck in that precious hit of life-sustaining oxygen. But before she could inhale it the stupid-ass cop snatched her by the back of her shirt and smacked the living shit outta her.

"Stand up you dumb bitch!" he hollered as Cucci coughed and choked and snotted water all through her nose. She pressed down with her feet and to her surprise they were in shallow water that was barely up to her neck. The red-faced cop was mad as hell.

"Fuck is wrong with you? Making me jump in here and get my shit wet! Your ass wanna drink this shit?" He palmed the back of her head and smacked her face right back down into the water again and pushed her head under so deep that her feet rose up behind her.

Cucci really panicked this time. This mothafucka was tryna drown her! Icy river water rushed straight up her goddamn nose. Gasping for air with her face pressed damn near down to the bottom and her eyeballs bulging outta their sockets, Cucci heard trumpets and she saw stars. White lightening struck deep in her brain and she fought like a lion to suck in a gulp of cool precious air.

She bucked hard against the cop, arching her back as she clawed toward the surface, but he gripped her neck and held her down firmly.

Feeling death coming for her, Cucci opened her mouth big and wide, letting a cold rush of river water in. And that's when the beautiful pink diamond slipped past her lips, became one with the river, and floated right away.

CHAPTER 10

Get Right or Get Left

While her cousin Cucci damn-near drowned in the cold waters off the New York Harbor, Honore was riding an exciting wave of high hopes.

Benny the Don had provided two commercial vans for their use today, and they were heading out to put in some work. A young cat named Quest and three more of Sly McFly's gunners were riding in the second van. Honore, Avi, Sly McFly, and Chimp Charlie were riding point in the front van and taking the lead.

The time had finally arrived for the big payday. They rode in silence and each of them were well aware that this once-in-a-lifetime hit would determine whether they would spend the rest of their natural lives relaxing in the lap of luxury or whether they'd all grow old making little rocks outta big rocks in the state pen.

"Y'all mothafuckas better wake up and look alive back there!" Sly said from the front seat as he sipped on a cold one he held gripped between his thighs. "It ain't no turning back now, my niggas! If you having second thoughts just slide ya damn door open and roll yo ass out in the street while the rest of us keep it moving. Other than that, everybody best be on they toes. Avi, I'm about to make your scary ass a rich muthafucka, baby!"

"Fuck you," Avi said playfully. "Without me your team would still be peddling shitty little ice chips all around the city. Scary people don't last in this game. The smart ones do. And I'm one of the smart ones, Mister McFly."

The group shared a nervous but good chuckle that was definitely needed. In the back of all their minds was some deep-seated fear, but they hid that shit behind faces of stone cold bravery. There were no guarantees in this business and danger was a big part of everything they did. After a while it became just as much about the rush as it was about the cash.

"So what happened to your friend?" Honore asked Avi. "That white boy.

He didn't look like the type who digs getting dished off."

"I don't know," Avi said as a troubled look crossed his face. "I didn't ditch him. That fucking demon just never showed up this morning. Thank God."

"Good," Honore said with a smirk. "There was something about his eyes that gave me the creeps any damn way. I swear I seen his ass somewhere before."

"He really was a creep," Avi admitted. "And a cold-blooded killer too. I never wanted him involved, you know. He muscled his way in on me and threatened my sons. I don't know why he didn't show up today, but I sure don't miss him."

"I feel ya," Honore responded. "We had some asshole who called himself muscling in on our piece of the action too but—"

"But guess the fuck what?" Sly laughed as he cut Honore off. "We sent that slant-eyed chink on a wild goose chase. He's heading to the Sotheby to hook up with us after the auction. The greedy cat-killing sucka! No free wontons over this way, playa! Fuck 'em and feed 'em beans!"

"Yup," Honore giggled. "By the time his stupid ass realizes we ain't showing up the auction will be over and we'll be ghost. We'll be way outta the country and laughing all the way to some foreign bank!"

"Damn, right! *To the bank!*" Sly McFly lifted his cold brew in the air and toasted from the front seat.

"Yes," Avi said, grinning and visibly relaxing. "To the bank."

CHAPTER 11

The Price of Betrayal

With Wild Man posted up behind the wheel of the Brinks truck Slick was riding shotgun and fuming fuckin mad.

Whitey? Whitey! Whitey!!!!

"That backstabbing crab-ass snake!" Slick spit as they sped down the streets of Staten Island. His guilt and remorse over Jewelz was a real close match to his shock and disbelief over Whitey's deception and betrayal.

That white nigga had straight up played him. The sight of his former bro putting Jewelz in a head-lock and pistol-whipping the shit outta her had truly fucked Slick up. That shit seemed unreal. Like he had dreamt the whole thing up.

Puttin his filthy fuckin paws on my lady?

This shit was inconceivable. Him and Whitey went way back! Whitey was the one who had gotten him outta the Devil's Asshole and turned him on to the murder game! The two of them had fought mad battles together, side-by-fuckin-side, and if it wasn't for Whitey's good-looking-out then Slick woulda still been locked up in the dungeon of a cold military jail.

"Damn! How the *fuck* did that bitch nigga catch me sleepin like that? How in the *fuck* did he catch me so blinded? He was lining me up the whole fuckin time! He was the one who killed my birds and murked old lady Maddie Taylor in my building!"

"Yo, that pussy was a straight *rat!*" Wild Man spit bitterly as him and Slick filled each other in on everything that had been going down. Wild Man had stripped Whitey's dead body down to his silk drawers, and for the second time that day the blue Brink's monkey suit was being worn by someone other than the owner.

Slick shook his head. "He was a back-biting *bitch!* But yo, how the fuck did you end up at that warehouse today, yo? What made you just show up outta nowhere strapped up like that? You had the scoop on Whitey's fake ass too or what?"

Wild Man snorted as he whipped the wheel and handled the heavy armored truck like it was a luxury Maybach.

"Fuck yeah I peeped him! He was a turn-coat! A slimeball! I got up on his hustle not too long after Noodles got murked," Wild Man said. "Noodles took a hidden camera with him up to Westchester, bruh. I got my cousin to download the film so I could see what he went up there looking for. I wanted to tell you what I saw right away but you was on some other shit..."

"What was on that camera?" Slick demanded.

Wild Man steered the truck around a sharp corner and shook his head in disgust.

"Yo, *every* fuckin thing was on there, son! *Everything.* Noodles had the goods on that grimy scab Whitey *and* on ya shawty Honore! Did you know that thot was the Queen of Diamonds and the Monkey with the Red Briefcase too?"

"Say word nigga?" Slick said as he grimaced. "Bruh how the fuck could I lack so hard on that shit? I swear I slept like a corpse on that bitch. I slept like I was dead!"

"That's why you shoulda fuckin listened to me!" Wild Man bitched. "You was on one and couldn't nobody tell you shit, fam! Honore and Whitey was under the sheets together. The two of them were scheming up on that diamond too, yo! Them rodents was getting down dirty together and gunning for it, son. I knew something was shitty as soon as I watched the film because there was no way Whitey shoulda even been around that bitch and her click. None!

"So I stuck a tracker up Whitey's ass. I started hounding that cat, following him around. Trust me, wasn't no crew-love *never* in that shady white boy's heart! What I saw on that film proved it. And that's why I knocked his roof backwards and zipped him up."

Slick grunted and slowly shook his head, feeling like a true chump. "Noodles knew, man. He fuckin knew. My ass been on some eyes-wide-shut shit, homey. Blind as a bat to the facts. And I can't even front," he admitted shamefully. "Jewelz tried to put me on to Honore too, but I wasn't tryna hear it. That chick was gassing me the whole time, yo. But one day I'ma deal with that scheming slut. On God, I am. I put that on everything I love."

"*Fuck* her!" Wild Man said waving him off. He wasn't about to admit that he had gotten caught up in Honore's powerful pussy trap too. Shit, Slick wasn't the only one who had taken a nosedive between that bitch's legs. Wild Man had murdered the cat that Honore had sent to kill him, and yet he still woulda got deep up in them guts again if given the opportunity.

Wild Man shrugged. "Now ain't the time to be worrying about that smut! We got a lot more work to put in, baby. Goody's gang ain't the only ones tryna get they hands on that ice. Honore and her click are breathing all over that Pink Lady diamond. They planning to yap that shit too. They're gonna gun for it after it gets sold at the Sotheby museum. They prolly heading there to get in position right now."

Slick's eyebrow went up. "So what, they tryna rush the auction spot?"

Wild Man nodded. "Hell yeah. Honore is one of the biggest diamond thieves in New York and she's running with a thugged-out old head who's backing her up and orchestrating all her moves. They gonna wait until that shine gets sold to a buyer at the auction and then they gonna pounce on 'em and snatch that shit up."

"Word?" Slick's eyes narrowed. "Well I got some hot shit for both of them rats. Yo," he patted his pants, "I got a fitty million dollar diamond chillin in my front pocket and I gotta stay on schedule cause I ain't tryna raise no alarms."

"What? You got the diamond *on you,* homey?" Wild Man's eyes got big. "How the fuck could that be possible? Yo, how the *fuck* did you get your hands on that shit?"

"It's a long story," Slick said grinning. "And I'ma definitely hook you up and tear you off for saving Jewelz's life. But first we gotta get this shit to the Sotheby's if I'ma keep the Feds off my ass. You said Honore and them are gonna run down on the museum right after the auction, word?"

Wild Man nodded.

"A'ight, say dat. We gonna make sure a diamond gets delivered and fuckin let 'em."

"No the fuck we not!" Wild Man bucked. "We ain't giving that jump-off shit! Nah, man. We can't let that type of paper get away from us. Fuck you mean?"

Slick laughed bitterly. "Here's the deal, son. The diamond that Whitey was about to dish off to Handgun Goody was a *clone,* my nigga. It was a *fake.*

"Whitey put the pressure on the Jew who owned the Fulton Street store and forced him to make two copies of the Pink Lady diamond. One was supposed to go to Goody so he could give up Jewelz. We were gonna deliver the other one to the Sotheby museum so them cats wouldn't sound no alarms, dig?"

Wild Man nodded and started grinning his ass off. "That's how you finesse 'em, bruh! Y'all cats was pulling a bait-and-switch hustle so you could keep the real diamond in ya pocket, huh?"

"Damn straight," Slick said, rubbing his hands together as his mind clicked full speed and his brain started to whir. With the fog of Honore's pussy lifted from his head he was the leader of the pack again. He was back in his rightful place as the brains of the operation and he was ready to strike hard.

"Goddamn." Wild Man laughed. "Whitey was a dirty bitch but dude was a genius, too."

"Yeah he was. So fall back and keep ya cool, my nigga," Slick told his ace as he gripped his heat. It was time to rock out 'cause there was 'bout to be some wildin on Staten Island.

"I got this shit, fam. Believe that."

CHAPTER 12

Not Without Incident

They were cruising in the Brinks truck just three blocks over from Sotheby's and it was looking like they were gonna arrive right on time to make their delivery. But as Wild Man drove around the corner on a one-way side street, Slick knew the sight that greeted them had the potential to fuck up all their plans.

Up ahead, two over-sized commercial concrete trucks had suddenly stopped in the middle of the narrow street, completely blocking their path.

"Fuckin traffic jam," Wild Man muttered, but Slick shook his head as his eyes went on scan.

"Nah," he said quietly as he peered into the side-view mirror and checked out the crowd of bumper-to-bumper cars packed in behind them. "This ain't no fuckin traffic jam. It's just a *jam,* my G. Somebody's tryna jam us up."

Slick turned around in his seat and quickly slid open the little window that separated the back compartment of the armored truck from the front. With the ease of an athlete he angled his body and climbed through. Then he snatched his gat outta his waistband and scrambled over to the back window. He looked out just in time to peep two dark-colored vans pulling up close enough behind them to prevent Wild Man from putting the armored truck in reverse and backing out of the street.

One van had the logo of a popular florist shop on the side, and the other one was covered in a colorful mural from a bakery.

"Ay, we got some company, bruh," Slick said loudly as he stuck his gun back in his pants.

He peered out the back window again and made his decision. "Yo, I'm about to open up this door, homey. If they bust up in here you keep your head down and ya fuckin hands up high, but don't let them take you outta this truck.

I'ma do the same damn thing but if you hear shots poppin off then you know all bets are off."

Slick had barely gotten his words out when the Brinks truck was surrounded by four masked assailants brandishing automatic weapons. He frowned as he peered at them through the window but he damn sure respected their hustle. It took a lotta balls to roll up and jam an armored truck in broad daylight, but the risk was an acceptable one because the Pink Lady diamond was worth a whole lot of doe.

Up front, Wild Man cut the engine but kept the keys in the ignition.

"Listen up goddammit!" a booming voice sounded instructions from outside. "You got five seconds to open that door or I'll *blow* that bitch open! You know what we want, so give it up! I'm spraying armor-piercing bullets muthafucka, so if you wanna die over some shit that don't even belong to you then fuck around and be my guest!"

"Ay!" Wild Man hissed from the front seat. "That's them! Yo, my nigga that's *them!*"

"Who?" Slick said quickly. "Who the fuck is *them?*"

"That bitch Honore and the cats she's rolling with! That's Sly McFly barking orders out there!"

Slick peered out the window again and saw a woman sitting in the front seat of the bakery van. He couldn't make out her face all that good but it damn sure looked like it was Honore sitting there watching the action go down.

Bitch! Slick muttered under his breath. Just the sight of her sent a bolt of rage through the pit of his stomach. He wanted that trick-hoe's head and he wanted it bad.

He gripped his heat tight in his hand. The gangsta warrior in him wanted to gun it out even against the odds, but the trained assassin in him knew now wasn't the right time. So quick as shit he emptied the contents of his pockets.

Slick took the jewelry box from his right pocket and slipped the real Pink Lady diamond out of its case, then he pushed the naked jewel back down deep in his pocket again.

Quick as shit he did a switcheroo and placed the fake fabricated diamond inside the jewelry box and arranged it on top of the satin cushion and snapped the box closed tight.

Gripping the jewelry box in his left hand, he cocked his strap just in case shit got crazy.

The tall man outside yelled, "Open the door, muthafucka or I'ma blast the shit outta that bitch!"

"Okay, okay!" Slick shrieked forcing fear into his voice. If he wanted to live he was gonna have to move fast. Brinks trucks were supposed to be bulletproof, but armor-piercing rounds would smash through the thick metal and through his head too.

"Don't shoot me!" Slick hollered loudly. "Please! I'll open the door and toss it out! Please don't shoot me, sir! I'm just doing my fucking job!"

"Stop stalling!" Sly shouted back. He licked a couple of harmless shots at the bottom edge of the door, and then he moved over to the driver's door. He aimed his strap through the window as Wild Man dove face-down across the front seat and threw his arms over his head, concealing his mug. He had grimy history with Sly McFly, and he knew for a fact that if that bastard recognized him he would shoot through the glass and plant one right in his melon.

"I'm not gonna repeat my muthafuckin self!" Sly warned for the last time. "You try some super-hero shit and I'ma dump a whole clip right into this fuckin window!"

Slick quickly undid the latch on the back door. With his cap pulled down low, he tossed the jewelry box outta the truck and then yanked the door shut and locked it again.

"Take it!" he screamed in a terrified voice. "Just take it and leave us alone!"

Two members of the stick-up crew scrambled to retrieve the small jewelry box, and then along with the old head who was aiming his ratchet at the back of Wild Man's skull through the window, they wasted no time in making their retreat.

But before they could get in their vans and jet, the sounds of sirens started wailing and Slick knew that meant trouble for all of them.

"Move out!" Sly McFly screamed into his cell phone. "Thirty seconds, you bitches! We got thirty seconds to clear the fuck out so let's *go!*"

The two concrete trucks up ahead got to rolling and pulled off toward the intersection, and Sly McFly's set scattered like roaches as they rushed back to their vans. The sirens were getting louder as the police began to close in, and both of Sly's vans hit reverse with their tires screeching and backed off quickly down the street.

"Ayo, *Slick!*" Wild Man yelled from the front seat. The concrete trucks were gone and now two police cars were speeding the wrong way down the one-way street and coming right at them. "Here come the pigs, yo! They right up on us!"

"Get outta the damn truck!" Slick yelled. "Act like you got stabbed!" he spit over his shoulder, and two seconds later him and Wild Man were both hopping outta the armored truck looking panicked as fuck. The officers jumped outta their patrol cars too, and when Slick saw their weapons drawn he acted swiftly.

"Officer! Officer! We need help!" Slick pointed at Wild Man and making sure the pigs saw he was Asian. "Call an ambulance! We just got ambushed! Two vans and two concrete trucks! They stabbed my partner and stole our whole fuckin load!"

He let Wild Man go and pointed up the street and down the street at the same time. "The vans went that way and the concrete trucks headed that way!"

The officer took one look at Whitey's gory blood that was splattered all over Wild Man's shirt, and he got ready to say something when suddenly two explosions went off on opposite ends of the block.

Boom! Boom!

The earth seemed to shake under their feet and people started screaming off in the distance.

"Stay with him!" the young white cop shouted as he pointed to Wild Man. "We gotta check that out! I'll put out a call for the paramedics and they'll be on the way!"

Slick nodded as the cops split into pairs again and took off in their cruisers in opposite directions with their lights flashing and their sirens blaring.

The cruisers weren't even off the block good when the two Zip 'em up gunslingers dove back in the Brinks truck to retrieve their backpacks.

Unit 201, come in. There seems to be a problem on your route. Copy with your location if you hear me.

The staticky two-way radio was steady squelching with a message from Brinks' base operations, but Slick and Wild Man ignored that shit as they grabbed their bags and took off walking quickly down the sidewalk.

With the fifty million dollar Pink Lady diamond nestled safely in Slick's front pocket, they beat feet and kept their heads low and strode smoothly away from the scene of the crime.

CHAPTER 13

Play Ya Cards Right

Sly McFly was in the front seat of the bakery van barking orders into his cell phone when the explosives went off in the distance.

"What the fuck?" Sly screwed up his face as Chimp Charlie gripped the steering wheel and pushed the van down the busy Staten Island streets. "They set the goddamn bombs off too early!" he bitched. "Stupid idiots! They ain't even give us enough time to get away!"

The heat was on, and although they had pulled off the Brinks heist and they had the Pink Lady diamond safely in their possession, 5-0 was hot on their asses and it was time to sky up.

Honore turned around and climbed over her seat, and now she sat on the second row bench seat beside Avi. Both of them glanced around nervously as Chimp Charlie drove with precision and full concentration. They rode in silence as they listened to the sirens getting closer and closer and sweated AK-47 bullets.

"Them muthafuckas are closing in!" Quest's voice crackled through Sly's speakerphone as he rode a block or so up ahead of them in the other van. "Them bombs is drawing every cop right to our location! We about to get caught up in the drag-net!"

Quest was one of Sly's coolest niggas in the trenches, but right now his voice was so high it sounded like he had some bitch in him.

"Just get yo ass to the tucky spot nigga and stay off my line!" Sly spit into his phone. He couldn't believe that young nigga was in panic mode and wearing his ear out on the other end. But moments later Sly heard gunshots and screams and suddenly the phone went silent.

"Shit!" Sly cursed. "Yo, Charlie," he urged his boy. "You gotta get us the fuck outta here man! The pigs are crawling around everywhere and I think they just hit Quest and his crew!"

Chimp Charlie nodded. He made a quick left down a side street and then a sharp right turn dead into heavy traffic. The street was clogged tight but Charlie didn't appear shook. In fact, under the circumstances he was doing a damn good job of keeping his cool. But the sirens were starting to become deafening and the traffic up ahead was at a standstill as people flooded the streets tryna find out what the hell had blown up.

"Hey, Sly," Honore whispered from the backseat like the Feds had wire-tapped the van and might overhear her. "Pass that diamond back here real quick so Avi can take a look at it. Let him check it out while you and Charlie focus on getting us the fuck outta this goddamn borough."

Sly reached inside his jacket pocket and passed Honore the small, well-designed container that held the Pink Lady diamond.

When Honore opened the box and saw what was inside she damn near fainted. That shit was blinging like BLING fuckin *BLAHW!*

None of the stories she'd read about the precious stone did it a damn bit of justice. It was the most beautiful thing she had ever laid her deceitful little eyes on. It was more stunning than she coulda ever imagined, and even Avi's mouth was hanging open as he marveled at the masterfully crafted multi-million dollar prize.

"Oh my fucking God!" Avi said, dazed and taken aback. "This is really fucking *it!* The one and only Pink Lady! Can you believe it, Honore? Can you believe it?"

"It's gorgeous," Honore responded in glee. "This is the one y'all! This baby right here is a mothafuckin game changer! It's so pretty it hurts my eyes. I ain't never in life seen anything so flawless."

"Yes," Avi said eagerly. "We've gotten our hands on the most exquisite jewel on the market right now. In my professional opinion we're going to be wealthy beyond our wildest imaginations."

"Are you sure?" Honore pressed her hand to her chest and asked breathlessly. "Are you really, really sure?"

Avi beamed as he nodded. "I'm sure. I mean, I'm as sure as I can be with only an examination with the naked eye, but I've been in this business for a long time and I'd bet my life on it."

"Is that right?" Honore asked, seizing the moment. As Avi nodded again she yanked her pistol outta her purse and planted a slug dead in his heart at point-blank range.

Whewpt!

The silencer on the tip muffled the sound as Avi pitched forward and banged his face into the back of Sly's headrest. He was dead before he even knew what hit him.

Sly whirled around in his seat, startled by the impact and the muffled sound of the gunshot.

"Honore! What the fuck type shit you on? You crazy bitch!"

"Oh shut up Mister Mack," Honore shot back as she passed the diamond over the seat and back to him. "He already gave us his professional opinion and now that's one less money split we gotta worry about. Don't act like you wasn't gonna off his ass later on down the line anyway, Sly. We ain't never trusted this bastard for real like that."

"Yeah, I was gonna dirt-nap the idiot," Sly spit and pocketed the diamond with his lips tight. "But not right here and not right now, you fuckin airhead dummy! We need Avi's connections to get that shit outta the country and sell it, remember?"

Honore waved her hand. "No we don't. Avi ain't the only shiesty motha-fucka out there who wanna make some money, Sly! I already found us somebody else who can trade underground for us and he's way cheaper."

"That's all you worried about is who's cheaper? Goddammit!" Sly spit, biting back his rage. "Baby girl your greedy ass just fucked us up big time!"

While Sly and Honore were arguing back and forth over the dead connect, Chimp Charlie made a turn onto a main street and his heart almost jumped outta his fat chest.

A police check-point and roadblock had been set up right up ahead. Traffic was being merged into one jam-packed lane. The street was crawling with po-po's out the ass and they were walking back and forth and in between cars, shining their flashlights in windows and picking out random vehicles to search.

Chimp Charlie finally lost his cool.

"*Awwww, fuckkkk meeeee*!" he squealed as a cop looked dead at him. The cop pointed his nightstick and motioned for Charlie to pull over and be searched. Escapism jumped into Charlie's heart but he was jammed in tight. With traffic held up in front of him, and a line of cars packing in behind him, there was no place to run.

"This shit is *over,* y'all!" Charlie yelped, sweat popping out all over his ape-looking nose. "These fuckin pigs wanna search us and we fucked, baby, fucked!"

"Charlie shut yo bitch-ass up!" Sly barked, ready to slap the shit outta him. "It ain't over till it's *over* goddammit, so take off ya pink panties, bitch! Gangstas like us don't fold under pressure nigga, so you better tighten yo spine up!"

"*You* shut the fuck up, Sly!" Charlie barked, dissing his boss for the first time in his life. "Y'all muthafuckas got me driving around with a dead body and a hot-ass diamond in the van and I'm about to go to jail!"

Three cops were approaching them now and despite his brave barking Sly could see that they were in a very sticky situation. Staten Island's finest were heavy on the scene and it looked like they were squeezing down with a serious purpose.

SHIT! SHIT! SHIT!

Sly glanced over at Charlie and got madder than a sum bitch. He had never seen his friend drenched in so much hot stankin sweat in his life. He didn't even know his partner had this level of bitch living inside of him. Judging by the way Charlie's hands were shaking on the steering wheel Sly knew for sure that they would never make it through the cop's search or past the NYPD barricade.

"*Shit,* goddammit!" Charlie cried out as he sat there shitting bricks. The cops were still searching the car directly ahead of them and they were doing a real thorough job. "Them bastards are coming for us next! What we gonna do when they get here, Sly? I can't go back to jail, goddammit! I can't go back to the joint!"

Sly McFly stared at the uniformed police officers who were now less than five minutes away from busting them in the middle of the biggest heist in the whole fuckin world!

"Well what the hell *are* we gonna do, Sly?" Honore piped in. Her voice quivered as she glanced over at Avi's dead body as he lay bleeding all over the seat beside her.

Suddenly she regretted clapping him so hastily. "Come on, old man!" she hollered at Sly. *Think,* goddammit! You the damn boss! There's gotta be some way outta this mess!"

Sly sat there silently as his nimble mind raced all around the track and kept coming up the same results.

Abso-fuckin-lutley *nothing.*

The cops were finishing up at the car in front of them and Charlie was babbling and losing all control.

Sly turned his head and hit his man with a bitter cold look of disgust.

Coward!

And that's when the shit really hit the fuckin fan.

"I just *can't*, man!" Charlie hollered as he looked at Sly with a pair of panicked eyes that resembled a gutter rat caught in a trap. "I'm telling you I can't go to fuckin jail! I'm a convicted pedophile, man! A *short eyes!* Them muthafuckas'll kill me in the joint! Man, fuck you *and* that stupid diamond, Sly!"

"Charlie, *noooo*!!!" Sly roared but it was too late.

Chimp Charlie, one of Sly's oldest and most trusted friends, flung open the van door and made a run for it. Sly watched in horror as the cop right ahead of him looked up and saw Charlie running wildly through traffic.

"Freeze, nigger!" the cop shouted as he yanked out his heat and gave chase. "Freeze, I said, goddammit!"

Suddenly it dawned on Sly that Charlie's bitchery mighta been a great big blessing in disguise because right now all the attention was on the fleeing black man instead of the fake bakery van. He had just put his hand on the door latch and was getting ready to jump out when Honore yelled, "Sly! Where you going? You not leaving me here by myself, are you?"

Sly turned over his shoulder toward Honore and shook his head sadly. A strange look entered his eyes as he reached out and gently stroked the side of her face.

"You look just like your momma," he whispered. "You dumb as shit, but you beautiful, just like she was."

Sly turned back around and hit the door handle. "You on ya own, now baby girl!" he hollered as he pushed his door open and jumped outta the van. "It's time to sink or swim, my darling! And I taught you how to *swim!*"

"*Slyyyy!*" Honore wailed as she lunged over the seat to grab the back of his jacket and missed. "Don't you fuckin *leave* me! You said you loved *meeeee!* You supposed to be my godfather!!!! *Slyyyyyyy!!!!*"

Dressed in his dapper blue suit, Sly strode off with a mean pep in his step and ducked quickly behind a garbage truck that was parked at the curb. He never even looked back as a bunch of cops swarmed on the bakery van and yanked Honore out and threw her on the ground.

The rest of the cops were so focused on catching Chimp Charlie that they didn't even notice one of the slickest masterminds in the Empire State as he slipped right out of their dragnet and beat feet deeply into the crowd.

But the cracking sound of gunshots splitting the air almost froze Sly McFly in his tracks. Onlookers and pedestrians ducked down and started screaming like crazy. It took everything Sly had in him not to turn around because he knew Chimp Charlie had just met his fate and Honore would soon be meeting hers too.

As Sly pushed his way through the sidewalk crowd he noticed a bum slumped over in a wheelchair just up ahead. The handicapped man was parked in a doorway of a liquor store, and he looked like he was sleeping one off.

Without hesitating Sly rushed up behind him and smooth picked him up. Lifting him high in the air, he tossed his drunk ass right outta the wheelchair.

"Hey!" the homeless bum yelled as his bony ass cracked on the pavement. "What the hell are you doing, dude?"

Sly McFly ignored him as he plopped down in the dirty chair and started wheeling himself furiously down the street. He kept his head low as he jetted in the opposite direction of the cops and the dragnet. He was halfway to the corner when he heard Honore scream loudly and cry out in pain. His heart quaked with love and he couldn't help but look back with sorrow and worry in his eyes. But when he saw the legion of cops who were surrounding her and swinging their billy clubs high in the air, he dropped his head back down and kept right on rolling.

CHAPTER 14

Get Low

Still dressed in their security uniforms, Slick and Wild Man had played it smooth and cool as they walked away from the stolen Brinks truck. Experienced professionals, they hadn't given so much as a backward glance toward the scene of their crime as they moved swiftly down the streets of Staten Island.

Fifteen minutes later they came upon a strip-mall shopping plaza and headed around towards the back of the stores. They ducked behind the loading dock of a large grocery joint, and then they finally paused to catch their breaths.

"Yo, I think we good man," Wild Man said, looking around as he breathed heavily. "Ain't nobody on us, so what's the next move?"

Slick shrugged and took off his backpack. "The next move is for us to split up and be out, bruh. I'ma change clothes and go up to the hospital and find Jewelz and snatch her up. And after that I'm catching a flight. I'm getting Jewelz the fuck outta here, yo. She's sick man, so I'ma take her overseas somewhere and get her right. I gotta get her the best medical treatment that money can buy so we can live the rest of our lives somewhere chill. *Together.*"

"Word? It's like that? Where you taking her? The Bahamas?"

"Nah," Slick shook his head. "Prolly somewhere further. Maybe Europe. But check it, you need to fade out and keep your head low too, slime. Shit is hot. The last thing you wanna do is come up on somebody's fuckin radar, you feel me?"

"Ay, I'm good, man. Ain't nobody checkin for me. Besides, I'm Asian and we all look alike, remember?"

Wild Man laughed at that shit but Slick didn't.

Instead, he looked square in his manz eyes with mad love and respect.

"Yo, I owe you," Slick acknowledged straight up. "You came through righteously for Jewelz and you saved her life. I'll never forget that. You looked out for me too, man, when I never even expected you to care. Me and Jewelz both owe you forever, homey. That's word. From the heart."

"You know how we get down," Wild Man shrugged the love off. "Besides, y'all woulda done the same thing for me too. But check it," he said looking around as his eyes went on scan. "This shit ain't over yet. That diamond you yanked just elevated our criminal hustle to a whole different level. We gotta be super on-point with everything we do from here on out because we're on our own. No more BBU, no more zippin 'em up. Fuck it, if this was our last hoorah then I'm glad we went out with a bang." He shook his head. "I just wish Noodles coulda been here to roll out with us, man."

"He *is* here, man," Slick said, glancing up at the clear blue sky. "Noodles is still down with the crew man, and he's gonna always be with us."

"Yeah," Wild Man said, blinking hard like he was about to choke up.

"But I was real wrong about something," Slick said quietly. "I accused you of getting Noodles smoked and I kicked you off the crew. And yet and still you showed up to help me and Jewelz at that warehouse anyway. I was dead wrong for that, slime, and I apologize."

Wild Man accepted Slick's apology with a dap, then he nodded as he reached into his backpack and started pulling out his gear. He slipped outta the blood-stained security shirt and slid on a white button-down jacket with the words "Foo Man Chu's Delivery" embroidered over the pocket in bold black letters.

He reached back inside his bag again and retrieved a folded white hat made of thin paper that was commonly worn by short order cooks. He set the hat on his head and paused for a moment as he watched Slick strip outta his security guard gear too.

His ace pulled a dingy t-shirt shirt on, and then quick as shit he snatched a raggedy, peasy-haired wig outta his backpack and yanked that shit down on his head. Then right before Wild Man's eyes a look of stupidity washed over Slick's cunning face. He slumped forward at the shoulders, and then shuffling his feet in his bird shit-stained boots, he opened his pocket-watch and went straight into Sometimey mode.

"Yo, you still got that diamond, son!" Wild Man hollered as his day-one turned away and started limp-walking toward the street. "Whassup with my fuckin cut?"

Slick looked over his slumped shoulder and shot his partner-in-crime a sly grin.

"C'mon, now. I owe you my life, son. I owe you *Jewelz's* life. You just gonna have to trust a muthafucka," Slick said as he headed toward the hospital so he could be by the side of the woman he loved. "Nigga you gonna have to trust and believe."

$$$$$

Slick got to the hospital as fast as he could. His heart was beating fast and he was moving on a thousand, but he took off his bird cap and stopped at a vendor in the lobby and bought every long-stemmed white lily the man had on his cart. He even picked out a nice Hallmark card with a sweet poem written inside of it.

Slick made his way through the packed emergency room and headed straight over to the front desk clerk. Every inch of his spirit ached for Jewelz, and just knowing she had gone through all that trauma with Goody and was fighting cancer on top of it left Slick with a feeling of utter guilt in his bones.

He just couldn't get around the fact that Jewelz coulda got ended today and it was all his fault. He put the blame for all the shit that happened squarely on his own shoulders because he was the one who had sent Jewelz out there to risk her life for a mission that in hindsight wasn't even worth it.

Slick was directed upstairs to the intensive care unit where he slipped a few hundred bucks to the receptionist so he could bypass all the drama. A million thoughts ran through his mind as he walked into the room where Jewelz lay sleeping. He peered down into her face and damn near wept.

Jewelz looked run over. She had a little oxygen port in her nose, and all kinds of tubes and shit were sticking outta her arms. As Slick stood there staring down at her he could see that even in her sleep she was in very deep pain.

"Hey tough girl," Slick whispered to her softly. "It's ya dude Slick. I told you I would come back for you, and I'm here. I'm here and I'ma stay right by your side until you're ready to get outta here and come home with me, ya heard?"

Jewelz's eyes fluttered for a moment and then they slowly opened up. Slick took her hand in his then bent forward and kissed her forehead. Jewelz moaned. They had doped her up on some good shit and she struggled to see him through her grogginess. When she realized who was standing there holding her hand, all the energy in the room changed.

"Get...get the fuck away from me," Jewelz muttered in a weak voice as she pulled her hand out of his grasp. "I don't want you in here. I don't need you no more."

"Hold up, slow down baby," Slick said, his own emotions running wild too. "Please don't talk like that. You been through a lot and I just wanna comfort you, that's all. Look, I'm sorry for how all of this got twisted and tangled up. I'm sorry I hurt you, Jewelz. I was on some next level bullshit and I got caught looking stupid as shit. Forget what popped off at my crib. Fuck the gun, the bullet, and please forget all the stupid shit I said to you. I didn't mean none of it and I'm sorry. Just let me just be here for you baby. That's all I wanna do for the rest of my life is be here for you."

"Nah," Jewelz said as she shook her head and started coughing. Slick grabbed a cup of water off her night table and tried to get her to sit up and drink some, but she wasn't beat for that shit. She pushed him and the cup away.

"Just get away from me, Slick. You turned your back on me. You pushed me outta your house. I don't need your love and I don't want your pity. Handgun is dead, Noodles is dead, Whitey is dead, and the Zip 'em Up Crew is dead too! I ain't got no more rap for you, Slick. I tried to give you everything I had in my heart and it was never good enough. Anything that me and you mighta ever had together is dead and over with. It's done."

Jewelz's words came outta her mouth softly, but they cut Slick deeper than any knife he'd ever faced. He started to deny it, but as doped up as she was, he could tell Jewelz meant every single word she said. And what made it even worse was that everything she was saying was true. When she had been tryna give him her love he didn't even want it. How much more could she have done? How many more ways could she have shown him just how deep she cared?

Slick felt his blood growing cold in his veins. And as he looked into the eyes of his oldest friend and she stared back at him with undisguised wrath, Slick knew it was a dub. It was a wrap. The love train had pulled outta the station and Jewelz was finally done. But he still had to try.

"C'mon, Jewelz," Slick pleaded as a tear slipped from his eye and rolled down his face without him even realizing it. "Gimme another chance, baby. Please."

The chief gunslinger was practically on his knees. He was lower than he had ever been in his life, and he was willing to beg and plead all night long if it meant Jewelz would let him back into her heart again.

"Look, baby," he said softly, "I get it. I swear I do. There's no excuse for the type of fuck-shit that I put you through. I've got no defense. I placed everything and everybody else in front of you. I let cheap bullshit come between us, and I was dead-ass wrong for that. But I love you, Jewelz. I love you with my whole fuckin heart, and I can make it up to you. I swear on my mother, I can. You my rider and you always have been. I owe you everything, Jewelz. Everything. Don't leave me here alone, love. You're all I have left in this whole fuckin world. Please don't leave me here alone."

"You'll be just fine Samir," Jewelz said dryly. "Save them tears for the next dumb bitch 'cause I'm all the way cool on you. Matter fact, I need you to leave. Get on outta here before I tell the nurse to call security. There's no reason for me and you to ever be in the same room again, Slick. Not even at my funeral."

Jewelz reached for the emergency call button and clicked it for assistance.

Slick wanted to wait for security and then tear shit up, but he decided to respect Jewelz's wishes and just fade out.

With his heart ripping apart at the seams, he walked outta Jewelz's room and headed downstairs toward the hospital exit in stunned silence. Tears streamed freely down his face as Slick dropped the lilies and the card in the trash on his way out the door.

He felt like shit but he was getting exactly what he deserved and he knew it. He'd been so hell-bent on revenge and blinded by lust that he had lost the only woman in the world that he truly loved. In his stupid attempt to safeguard his heart and protect himself from the bittersweet trials of love, the scared little boy in him had tried to win at a grown-man's game and he'd failed.

If you ain't loving you ain't living, baby!

Slick heard his father's deep voice in his ear and there was no doubt that Big Slick had been right. Slick had misused his cards and played himself right off the board. Like a dumb-ass pup, he had made his bed hard and lumpy, and now he had no other choice but to lay in that shit.

$$$$$

Out on the Rock, Honore Morales, aka Prisoner 104579, stepped into the intake tank with a fresh murder charge over her head and a brand new jumpsuit.

Just like all the other inner-city criminals, she was unshackled and told to strip down to her birthday suit. A fat white female guard ordered her to stick out her tongue and bend over and spread those beautiful cheeks apart. Honore had done that shit plenty of times before, but this time there was no dick waiting for her, and a probing latex-covered finger was about to become her new man.

The intake cell was dirty as fuck. Strands of hair and caked-up mildew and grime were all over the place and the dank aroma mingled with the faint odor of musk and stale piss.

Two other inmates were already sitting on the bench waiting to get processed, and Honore sat down between them. On the outside Honore looked fearless just like every other inmate, but inside her head was whirling with questions and anxiety.

"If you wanna take a shower you can do so," the guard said as she handed Honore a bar of generic soap and some shower shoes. "You'll be taken up to see the nurse in a few. Fold your street clothes up and leave them on the bench next to you."

Honore wasn't even thinking about stepping foot in that grime-filled shower. She stared at the shoes she'd been given. They were flimsier than the flip-flops you got at the damn Chinese nail salon.

Shaking her head, she flashed back to that last look that had been on Sly McFly's face right before he jumped outta the van and left her behind so the pigs could get her. With Avi's body slumped over and blood flowing everywhere, she was lucky them cops didn't Mike Brown her ass right then and there on the spot.

Instead, they had ripped her from the van and slammed her on the ground like she was a grown-ass nigga. They swung their billy clubs down on her like maniacs as she screamed and begged for mercy, and the only reason they had stopped is because peeps on the streets started wildin and filming the assault with their cell phone cameras. Honore's back and shoulder were sore as shit, and the side of her face was bruised and swollen from smacking the concrete, but she knew she was lucky to be alive, especially since they had swiss-cheesed Chimp Charlie like he had just murdered a baby.

And it was all his own fault too. That fat idiot had panicked like a goddamn coward! If he hadn't'a jumped outta the van and ran they all coulda gotten away!

Honore was gritting her teeth and rocking back and forth when the prisoner sitting on her left patted her on her shoulder.

"Hey, w'sup light-skin," the disheveled older woman whispered as she nudged Honore with her elbow "Baby girl please tell me you snuck some percs or some mollies or something up in here. I'll pay you, but I'm itching real bad and I need something to calm me down."

"Back the fuck away from me!" Honore snapped at the fiend. "I don't give a fuck about your habit or whatever kinda fix you need. Just don't put your nasty hands on me no more!"

"Well damn!" the woman twisted her lips and recoiled with an attitude. She leaned away from Honore and snarled, "You ain't have to come at me all disrespectful like that! All you had to fucking say was no. You young bitches think 'cause you got a little perfume on and ya nails are done up that you better than somebody. But you sitting up in here witcha lip poked out like a fucking punk though. Suck it up! I bet that lip wasn't all over the floor when you was out there on the streets doing whatever the hell landed you in here right next to me!"

Without a word Honore slapped the fiend so hard her head bounced off the wall and she fell straight to the floor. Honore jumped all over her old ass with a quickness. She had heard mad stories about crazy dyke bitches in the joint and she started wildin on the smoker with right and left hooks for days.

But not because she thought the chick wanted to fuck her, and not because the older woman was talking shit neither. Honore had pounced because the bitch was right!

It seemed like just minutes ago she had been about to pull off the jewelry heist of the century, and now she was holed up in a damp and dirty cell that she might not ever get out of.

Honore was on autopilot as she kept on chipping up the loud-mouthed fiend. The lady was old enough to be her mother, but when she looked down into her face all Honore saw was a bunch of people who had done her wrong!

She saw Sly, Cucci, Slick, Wild Man and everybody else in her life who had played her out, and she kept right on punching.

The lady tried to fight back but she was too dope-sick and way too light in the ass to deal with Honore's fire. The intake guard sitting at the desk heard the commotion but she turned her head and kept right on texting her boyfriend. It was almost time for her break and didn't feel like filling out no incident report, so she just tuned out the noise and let them fight.

Finally the other chick in the cell stood up and walked over to Honore as she was pounding away on the poor woman.

"I'm not trying to get in ya business," the heavy-set chick said calmly. "I know ol' auntie here was outta line, but I think she's had enough. Plus I heard you in here for a body. You prolly got a lotta steam on ya chest and I know you stressed out, but this ain't the way to start off. Now, if you done already gave up hopes of getting outta here one day, then keep doing you, boo. But if you got other plans, then this ain't the way to go. Just like you fighting this chick all tough, you gonna need to fight your charges even harder."

Honore looked up at the chick with tears of rage in her eyes. She looked back down at the fragile woman she was beating on and got up off her. Honore sat back down on the bench and soaked up the wise jailhouse words.

Ol' girl was right. She needed to pull herself together until she could find herself a way the hell up outta there and get her some payback. Beating up fiends wasn't the answer. Honore forced herself to think about the bigger picture. She had a lil money in the stash for a lawyer and she needed to get prepared. Shit, this was jail, not fuckin prison! She hadn't been convicted of a damn thing yet! It was time to put her thinking cap on because it wasn't over till it was over!

CHAPTER 15

You Do Dirt You Get Dirty

For six long weeks Sly McFly had been laying low in one of his plush and comfortable tucky spots waiting for shit to cool down. With the police-shooting death of Chimp Charlie and the arrest of Honore, his front-line support structure had collapsed all around him but it hadn't slowed him down not one fuckin bit.

Sitting back in the cut and sipping on top-shelf liquor and eating sardines and Ritz crackers, he had watched the news reports about the infamous Pink Lady diamond with a bitter taste of vengeance in his mouth.

"Stupid muthafuckas!" he spit at the television reporters as they pinned the entire Brinks truck robbery and murders on him and Chimp Charlie. "Me and Charlie ain't steal no Brinks truck and we didn't shoot no damn naked security guards neither!"

The hunt was still on hot and heavy for the stolen diamond, which was why Sly was sitting on that shit like a hen on an egg. With Avi dead he had been forced to make a connection with a cat from Paris who knew some underground diamond traders. They were eager to get their hands on the rock he was holding and promised they could get him a good price for it.

All Sly McFly had to do was get his ass on a plane to France this afternoon and hook up with his connect and he would be swimming in cream for the rest of his life.

Sly glanced at the fine attire that was laid out on his plush king-sized bed. The old-lady bloomers, the padded bra, the carefully brushed wig, the plain church dress, the coffee-colored stockings, and the white half-slip, were all about to serve a serious purpose.

"A man's gotta do what a man's gotta do," Sly muttered under his breath as he walked into the bathroom and stripped down naked. He stood in front of the full-length mirror staring into his own hazel eyes. Satisfied by what he saw in himself, he picked up a small baggie from the edge of the sink. With steady hands he dropped the key to his future into the baggie, and then he carefully sealed it.

Next, he dug two fingers deep into an open jar of Vaseline and scooped out a big glob. Smearing the petroleum jelly all over the plastic baggie, Sly McFly bent over and made like a mule as he took a deep breath and stuck the Pink Lady diamond straight up his ass.

$$$$$

Prisoner 104579 sat in the dayroom of Rosie Singer's Women's Facility on Rikers Island eating a pack of saltine crackers and watching Breaking News on Channel Seven at Six.

"In stunning and dramatic fashion, suspected murderer and jewelry mastermind Sylvester Mack Morales, also known as Sly McFly, was gunned down at La Guardia airport today while attempting to board an international flight to France...

Sylvester Mack *Morales?* Honore sat up straight. Sly ain't never told her that his last name was Morales too!

Mr. Morales triggered the suspicions of TSA personnel when he refused to submit to a body cavity search, prompting a violent confrontation that ended with his detainment.

According to TSA officials, security personnel were forced to open fire on the suspect when he became combative and lunged for their weapons. Early reports indicate that the infamous Pink Lady diamond that was stolen from a Brinks truck earlier this month was found on Mr. Morales's body. Arrangements are being made to return the gemstone, valued by experts at more than forty-seven million dollars, over to officials at the new Sotheby Museum on Staten Island. More details to come at eleven...

Honore jumped up from her chair. He had it! Sly had almost gotten away with the Pink Lady diamond! Here she was rotting away in a stankin jail cell and that old bastard had been planning to sneak up outta the country with that sparkling jewel stuck up his ass and then let her go down the tubes for stealing it! He was actually gonna shit on her and let her take the rap!

"You old rat-ass turncoat!" Honore put her hands over her queasy stomach as she shrieked up at the television. The face of her lifelong mentor and guru stared down at her from the screen and she was glad as fuck that he was dead. "That's what you get for leaving me by myself, you stank old bastard!" she screamed. "That's what the *fuck* you get!"

$$$$$

Cucci Momma Jones was all lavender sass and glittering finery as she strutted her stuff through the doors of the New York Diamond and Jewelry Exchange. She was dressed in a slim-fitting lavender dress and sleek purple stiletto pumps, and her thick, wavy hair hung past her shoulders looking just like ebony butter.

The news about Sly McFly getting popped at La Guardia airport was buzzing on the airwaves all over the city, and as Cucci walked toward her desk and greeted her co-workers she could barely hold back her smile.

The last few weeks had been rough as fuck, but just like a lucky black cat Cucci had landed on her feet and came out on top. The massacre in the Goode Brothers maintenance warehouse had been enough to wreck her last nerve. That white FBI mothafucka had gotten his top blown off, but where in the fuck that fine Asian nigga had come from with his machine-gun blicky popping off mega bullets, was anybody's guess. Cucci had recognized him as the dude who had yoked up Honore at the job, and he had jumped down outta the damn ceiling laying everybody down!

Cucci had been lucky to escape with her life, but the cops who had yanked her outta the river and arrested her at the Staten Island Ferry had tried to fuck her sideways. They'd taken her down to the station house and put some work in on her ass as they questioned her to death and tried to make her spill the beans about the shoot-out in the warehouse and the secret heist of the Pink Lady diamond.

"*What* fuckin diamond?" Cucci had stood up in that jailhouse and screamed on them over and over again as they tried to connect the dead bodies in the warehouse to the stolen diamond and then pin the whole shit on her. "Do you see me with any goddamn diamond? If I stole a diamond then where's that shit at then? Huh? Where the fuck is it at?"

Of course she knew exactly where that shit was! It was way down at the bottom of that nasty green river! But since the cops didn't *find* nothing on her, they didn't *have* nothing on her, and without any evidence of a crime being committed specifically by her, they had no choice but to let her go.

At first Cucci had been puzzled as fuck about a few aspects of the Pink Lady heist, but after watching the news reports it only took her a quick minute to figure out what had actually gone down. Ice Pick was still out there somewhere on the run, but as soon as she heard that Honore had gotten locked up and was being charged with robbery and murder, she hurried up and used that shit to her advantage.

"Mr. Goldberg," Cucci had pleaded with the CEO of the New York Diamond and Jewelry Exchange when she was called in front of the big bosses the morning after they released her from questioning. "I swear to God I don't know what possessed my cousin to do such a terrible thing. But if I had to guess I'd say it was greed. Greed and stupidity! Two horrible traits!

"But I can assure you that I had no clue about what that silly girl was planning on doing! In fact, she had me suspicious with her shadiness too, and I'm the one who called the FBI hotline and asked them to investigate her! I really hate that people had to die behind the greed that my cousin Honore carries in her heart, but I'm happy the cops finally got to her and took her off the street. My job means so much to me that I wouldn't risk it for nobody. Especially somebody as coldblooded as Honore."

Cucci had walked outta that meeting feeling like she shoulda won an academy award. She had bullshitted her bosses so good that not only had she kept her job, she had gotten a promotion to Honore's old position, and now *she* was the bad bitch who traveled all over New York City going from jewelry store to jewelry store stealing discounted stones to be sold underground as crushed ice. *She* was now the leader of the Crushed Ice Clique. *She* was now the Queen of fuckin Diamonds, and *she* planned to reign over her queendom and sit up on her throne for many more years to come!

Hell yeah, Cucci thought as she gathered around her co-workers in the employee lounge and listened to all the clear people act all happy to hear that the Pink Lady diamond had been recovered.

"I heard they found it stuck up his rear-end!" one of the older white ladies giggled like she had never heard of such craziness in her whole life. "I mean that guy actually had an asshole full of money!"

Cucci smiled politely at the old woman but she wasn't impressed in the least. These basic white mothafuckas might be blinded by the news, but Cucci damn sure wasn't.

Because if she had had *one* Pink Lady diamond in her mouth, and Sly McFly had had *another* Pink Lady diamond up his ass, then how many more Pink Lady diamonds were out there floating around?

Just knowing that there were probably multiple stones in existence told Cucci that somebody real cold and slick had been two steps ahead of them the whole damn game.

And that slick-ass somebody probably had him a Pink Lady diamond too. A *real* one. And that meant that Handgun Goody, Ice Pick, Cannonball and all the rest of them cut-throat gangstas had gotten shitted on and played out, and screwed right up the ass too!

Cucci laughed hard as shit as she left the employee lounge and made her way downstairs to the diamond vault. Somebody had gotten away clean with the *real* fuckin diamond and she wasn't even mad about that shit. She couldn't be. She respected the hustle too much to be a hater. It tickled the shit outta her to think that some slick nigga had beat these rich white mothafuckas at their own damn game. There was no doubt in her mind that the real Pink Lady diamond was probably somewhere in Venezuela or the South of fuckin France by now. Getting cut up like a mothafucka!

Six Months Later

Prisoner #104579 had beads of sweat dripping from her body even though she was shivering inside and felt a cold chill deep down in her bones. Her legs were gapped wide open on a hospital gurney. Her ankles were strapped to the foot stirrups and one of her wrists was handcuffed to the bedrail.

She had tried to slip out of confinement twice and was considered a security risk so the room was guarded up. With a murder sentence of two dimes and a nickel hanging around her neck, she was on her way upstate and she had given up hope. She had turned into a real hell-raiser behind bars; stealing shit, starting fights, selling contraband, and shaking down other prisoners for their commissary rations.

And now she was here.

Contractions cut through her body at regular intervals and she felt like every muscle fiber she possessed was being torn in half.

Another massive wave of pain hit her and she grit her teeth and strained, but no matter how hard she grunted and bore down and pushed, the mass that was bulging between her legs refused to budge.

"Get this shit outta me," she pleaded under her breath to no one in particular. "Oh God, please get this shit outta me!"

The pain that radiated within her womb was so intense that she wasn't sure if she could stay conscious for much longer. But she refused to succumb to the agony and give the people standing around watching the satisfaction of seeing her break down.

She took a series of shallow breaths as she glanced around the room at the two ass-ugly female guards who were posted up nearby. She glared at them and then looked at the fat prison doctor who was standing between her legs urging her to keep pushing.

Suddenly reality slapped her in the face and this shit wasn't about Prisoner 104579 being a problem child no more.

It was about Honore Morales and the fact that she was about to have herself a brand new baby girl. And not only was she bringing a new life into this world, she had pushed away everybody who had ever loved her, so she was doing it all alone with no family to help her get through it.

A violent burst of pain smacked the shit outta her and she opened her mouth and screamed at the top of her lungs.

"Ahhhhhhhhhhhhh!!!!!! Ahhhhhhhhhhhhh!!!!!!"

"Inmate Morales, pay attention!" the doctor said sharply. "Stop screaming and listen! I need you to breathe deeply and bear down. Push as hard as you can!"

As Honore pushed and strained, various scenes from her life flashed through her mind. All the money, the ballers, the diamonds, the sex, the clothes, the scheming and the outrageous lies... all of that shit had been for nothing. She had chased all that materialism because she had wanted to be the queen of a life that had landed her right where she was at. In jail!

Determined to make her get-money dreams come true, Honore had gotten burned by the game every which way she turned. And then when shit got real out there, the one man she had trusted above all others, the notorious *Sly McFly* had turned his fuckin back on her and left her hanging out to dry.

As rage filled her heart Honore balled up her fists and clenched her teeth and pushed so hard that she damn near blacked out. To her surprise she felt a huge wave of pressure building down there and then something big and warm shot outta her coochie with a whoosh!

Honore's eyes flew open. The pain had disappeared and she couldn't believe that the bloody, screaming little beauty queen the doctor was holding up had actually came out of her body. The baby was perfectly formed. She had all her fingers and toes and she also had a head full of jet-black hair. Her tiny lips trembled as she cried, and when she opened her eyes Honore saw her own hazel eyes reflected back at her.

Completely mesmerized and in awe of the beautiful creature that she had just produced, Honore cuddled her squalling child against her breasts as the doctor sucked out her nose and mouth and cut the umbilical cord.

Suddenly the loneliness was no more. With the gift of this child Honore was finally complete. She could give a fuck less about Sly, Cucci, Aunt Frita, or Slick. The only thing that mattered to her was the slippery little bundle that was nestling up against her breast as unconditional love and affection flooded her soul and damn near consumed her heart.

"My baby," Honore whispered into the infant's ear as she cradled her in her free arm. "You're really here now. Mommy's baby! Thank the lord! Oh God, I love you so much!"

Love at first sight was the best way to describe what Honore was feeling. After all those months of being locked down in a dull gray jail, she was finally seeing vibrant colors again and it felt so good.

In that moment she had forgotten all about the jail sentence she was serving. In her mind she wasn't chained to no prison gurney with her legs wide open, she was in paradise, holding tightly to her most prized possession. But all that joy and elation came to an abrupt end when the nurse suddenly reached out and took the baby from her arms.

"It's time for her to go now," she said.

"Wait," Honore said, reaching out with wild, wide eyes. "What are you doing? Where are you taking her? You gonna give her right back, right?"

"I'm sorry, Morales," the nurse said quietly as she shook her head. "It's time to get you cleaned up and get the child ready to be processed out of the facility."

"Outta the facility? Uh-uh, bitch!" Honore spit. "She ain't going *nowhere!* Gimme back my goddamn baby!"

Her maternal instincts kicked into overdrive. Instead of sorrow she felt anger and rage. She wanted her goddamn baby! She didn't care about hell or high water, jail or no jail, all she wanted was her child!

Honore struggled to sit up on the gurney as she strained against her handcuff. She couldn't close her legs because her ankles were strapped down. "She's mine! I pushed her outta *my* ass! Gimme back my fucking daughter, bitch!" she demanded.

"Sorry," the nurse told her. "A prison cell is no place for a newborn child, and that's where you'll be living for a long, long time."

"Bitch!" Honore lashed out and tried to smack the nurse with her free hand. She missed and started bucking up and down uncontrollably on the stretcher. "I want my *babyyyy!* Don't take my fuckin *babyyyyyy!!*"

Fighting like a wild animal Honore thrashed and shook and raged against the world. Ignoring the blood seeping from between her legs she screeched and snarled and snapped her teeth trying to bite the shit outta the nurse as the guards rushed over to immobilize her.

"Where y'all taking her?" Honore sobbed pitifully. "Where the fuck are y'all taking my baby? Please! Just tell me where she's going!"

The prison nurse had witnessed these types of violent outbursts many times before and she went on about her business silently, displaying zero emotion. All the paperwork had already been approved by the department of social services and signed by a judge, and after recording the infant's weight, height, and vital signs, she dressed the newborn and wrapped her in a warm blanket. Ignoring the chaos, she held the infant tightly in her arms as she stepped out of the room with the sounds of the mother's screams echoing off the walls behind her.

Standing under the bright lights of the hallway, the nurse approached a well-dressed young black man who stood anxiously nearby with his attorney. With a small smile playing on her lips, the nurse placed the precious bundle of joy into his waiting arms before turning away to head back into the delivery room. Before she entered she paused with her hand on the doorknob as she listened to the nutcase who had just given birth shrieking out the most horrible obscenities and threats that one could imagine.

"Trust me, you're better off without her, lil baby," the nurse muttered under her breath as she looked over her shoulder and watched the new father cuddling his baby with tears in his eyes. "Thank God you got you a good daddy because your jailbird momma is crazy as shit."

EMPIRE STATE OF MINE$!

A few years later...

The elegant wedding chapel was packed all the way out. The bride was brown and beautiful in her off-the-shoulder lacy white dress complete with an elegant satin train that flowed behind her like she was a royal princess.

The groom looked diesel and handsome in his white tuxedo, and standing beside him, dressed in black, his best man looked damn good too.

Seated halfway back in the pews and on the groom's side of the aisle was a beautiful young woman. Her waist-length natural hair was twisted in jet-black coils. Her brown eyes were serene as she looked toward the front of the church and listened to the binding words of matrimony as they fell from the minister's mouth.

"...To have and to hold, to honor and to cherish, from this day forward until death do you part?"

The beautiful woman sitting in the pews smiled inside. They had history together, her and the groom did. Watching him standing up there holding onto his bride made her heart ache for all the things that she had missed out on, and for all the things that she would never have.

She had been surprised to get the wedding invitation and the only reason she had come is because her and the groom used to be real cool. They had cared about each other back in the day. And even after all the crazy shit that had happened in their lives, she still cared about him now.

She watched the groom's hands tremble as he held his ring out to his gorgeous bride. The cute chocolate sista couldn't stop grinning as the man she was marrying slid the symbol of his loyalty onto her finger.

The beautiful chick couldn't actually see the ring from where she was sitting, but she knew without a doubt that it was straight up top-shelf finery and that its diamonds were some of the best that money could buy.

The preacher said a few more words and then the vows were completed. When it came time to seal the nuptials the groom raised the bride's veil and kissed her full lips. The room erupted in clapping and laughter as the new couple turned around to face their family and friends as one.

Somehow, the beautiful young lady found herself leaving the pew and joining the long line of guests who were waiting to congratulate the new couple. When it was her turn to greet them the beautiful chick smiled at the bride and shook her hand, and then she stepped over to the new husband and looked deeply into his eyes.

"Never in a million years did I think you would do some crazy shit like this."

The groom bust out laughing and swept her up in his strong arms and planted kisses all over her cheek.

"Jewelz! Goddamn, baby! It's been a long time, lil sister! I didn't know if you was gonna come, but I'm glad you made it."

Jewelz punched him lightly on the arm. "Stop playing, Wild Man. You? Getting cuffed?" She rolled her eyes and smiled. "Shit, I had to come see this for myself, homeboy."

Mindful of his bride, Jewelz squeezed Wild Man's hand tightly and was preparing to move on when she felt somebody tugging at the back of her dress.

She turned around and looked down and saw the flower girl of the wedding. She was a gorgeous little four-year-old and she was offering Jewelz a single long-stemmed white lily and a folded piece of a napkin.

"This is for you," the little girl said shyly. Her pretty hazel eyes were big and round in her cinnamon-brown face, and suddenly Jewelz's breath caught in the back of her throat.

"Thank you," she whispered as she accepted both items from the little girl and quickly turned away. Rage burned through her damn blood. She had made a big mistake coming here. A big fuckin mistake!

With her head held down she gripped the lily in her fist and pushed through the crowd of happy people like all hell was scorching the back of her neck. Jewelz didn't stop and she didn't look up until she got to the church door, and then she burst out into the sunshine and allowed the tears to spill freely from her eyes.

$$$$$

Back in her high-rise hotel room in midtown Manhattan, Jewelz sipped from a glass of wine and stared down at the crumpled napkin in her hand. The words that had been written on it in black ink stared right back at her.

Although her past had been totally fucked up, Jewelz had done a lot with her life over the last five years. After claiming victory over cancer and triumphing once again, she had become reflective about the world around her and her purpose in the universe. It took a lot of time and self-discovery for her to not only let go of what had been done to her, but to also come to terms with the harm that she had done to others as well.

Jewelz thought a lot about her mother during that time, and she grieved for the woman she had never known in a way that she had never even thought was possible. Her mother might not'a been able to give her much during their brief time together, but she had made damn sure that her baby girl would always have her own dreams. And Jewelz had decided that there was no time like the present to start dreaming as big as she possibly could.

So she had gone back to school and gotten her GED, and then enrolled in community college where she graduated with an associate degree in computer science. She had a lot of lost time to make up for, so she figured why stop there? She had applied to NYU, and when she got accepted she majored in counseling so she could help other young girls who were scarred from living a life of pure hell just like hers had been.

Thanks to her days of rolling with the Zip 'em up Crew, Jewelz had stacked plenty of money in her safe and she didn't need no regular nine-to-five. After thinking it over, she had decided to start her life all over again and keep it brand new.

Refusing to look back, Jewelz had moved out of the city and taken a job upstate as a youth counselor for victims of sexual trafficking. Five days a week she shared her testimony of struggle and triumph with vulnerable girls in the Empire State whose young bodies had been tricked out and their tender minds victimized, just like hers had been.

Taking a big sip from her wineglass, Jewelz stared down at the napkin she held in her hand. Twice she had balled that shit up and tossed it in the hotel garbage can. And twice she had changed her mind and dug it right back out again.

It took her a good minute, but she had finally unfolded the napkin and read what was written on it. She read the simple words over and over again, and when it was all said and done she had decided to go.

Old habits died hard, and the next afternoon she left Manhattan and drove through the old Brooklyn neighborhood with her eyes on scan. The streets were still the streets. Static could pop off at anytime so Jewelz stayed strapped.

She pulled into Brooklyn's Canarsie pier and drove toward the ocean. Moments later she spotted him in the last row of the parking lot leaning against the bumper of his freshly waxed SUV. He looked like a boss in his Balmain outfit and kicks. Immediately her blood got heated and her lip poked out. Wearing her bitch face, Jewelz pulled into a spot about five cars away from him and then cut off her engine and stepped out looking stacked and sexy in her Brunella Cucinelli hip hugging summer dress that was straight from Neiman's.

Cancer had slowed her roll but it hadn't stopped her show. With her head on straight and a clean bill of health, once again her frame was curved and banging and her hair was long and thick.

Jewelz looked over at him and her heart thudded in her chest. It had been five long years since the last time she'd seen him and he definitely looked older and wiser and finer than ever before.

"Jewelz." He flashed her that handsome crooked smile and said her name like it was a melody in a song that he had practiced singing every day.

"What?" she blurted out, her eyes cutting into him coldly as the memory of his betrayal rushed up in her throat.

The last time they were together she had cursed him out in a hospital room on Staten Island, just a few hours after she had zipped up Handgun Goody. Slick had walked into her intensive care room and cried real tears for the first time since that long ago day at his family's funeral.

Clutching Jewelz's hand he had begged for her forgiveness. He had told her just how wrong he had been, and promised that he would spend the rest of his life making it up to her.

But Jewelz wasn't trying to hear none of that shit. She had been so beaten down and sick and outta her mind with rage and grief that she had cursed him out and threatened to have the nurses call the cops on him.

And now, Slick's intense brown eyes stayed steady on her as they both stood there remembering the past. The passion in his gaze ate her up from head to toe like he was a starving man looking at an all-you-can-eat buffet. And then finally he spoke.

"What's good, Miss Lady?"

His voice was smooth and sure, and all Jewelz could do was nod in response. About a year after she had cursed him out in that hospital room she had started receiving all kinds of stuff in the mail.

Expensive stuff. Jewelry, designer clothes, books, and even airline tickets to some of the faraway places that she had always dreamed of seeing. Slick had never put his name on none of it, but he didn't have to. The packages came from an address in Switzerland, and they were full of all the fancy shit that she had fantasized about having when they were kids.

About six months after that his letters had started coming in the mail and they had really fucked her up. The handwritten notes had laid her heart wide open because they were filled with all the love that she had always wanted from him. The love she had always dreamed that he would give her from the heart.

"I wasn't sure if you were gonna show up today," Slick finally said, breaking the silence. "I really appreciate you for giving me this chance."

"Oh, really?" Jewelz snapped. "Giving you a chance for what?"

Outta all the foul shit that had happened in her life, the one thing that had hurt her above all else was the look on Slick's face the day he told her to get the fuck outta his crib. Jewelz had cried rivers of tears over the memory of the bitter words he had spoken to her that day, and even after five long years she still wasn't over that shit.

Slick accepted her outburst without reacting. He knew what she was going through and he stood by patiently. Giving her a chance to work it out in her own way. Then finally he took a step forward and answered her.

"I want a chance to make shit *right*, Jewelz. A chance to show and prove what you mean to me, and what I've always had in my heart for you. I swear to God I never meant to hurt you. I was fighting real hard against my feelings all those years, and if I had just been honest with myself that night on Fulton Street I never woulda—"

"Nigga, *please!*" Jewelz smirked and crossed her arms over her breasts. "You can sing that bullshit song to somebody else because my shit is straight! I *survived*, Slick! It's been five damn years, baby! Yeah, you shit on me over that lying bitch, but I took all your lil punches, rolled wit'em, and got right back up on my feet!"

He nodded quietly. "I know. You've always been strong like that, Jewelz."

"Damn right. Because I always *had* to be!"

"But you don't anymore," he said. "I'm here for you now. I've been trying to be here for you for the last five years! You were right that time when you said people change. *I* changed! I didn't come back here for Wild Man, baby. I came back to this country for *you!* I came back to get you, Jewelz. So I can make all your dreams come true. I came back to take you with me to the place you always wanted to be! I came back so I could tell you right to your face that the only woman I ever wanna be with in this whole fuckin world is *you!*"

Jewelz smirked and shook her head. "Nope. I'm not feeling none of what you're saying. It's too much, Slick. And it's too late."

"Nah," he said calmly. "It ain't never too late. When Wild Man told me you were coming to his wedding all I could think about was seeing you. Like I told you in all them letters I wrote, I was wrong as hell about everything back then. And you were right. I *did* wrong and you did right. I shoulda listened to you, Jewelz. I shoulda believed you and trusted your word the way you always trusted mine. I get that now. And I'm sorry, baby. All those years I was scared to let you get too close to me, and for the past five years the only thing I could think about was what in the world I could do to get myself closer to you."

Jewelz shook her head and smirked. "You really expect me to just trust you now, Slick? You think I'm that damn stupid? It sounds like you're the one who's living in the past now!"

His eyes stayed strong and steady on hers as he walked up on her and took her in his arms. He pulled her rigid body close to his hard chest and laid his cheek down on the top of her head.

"I know I hurt you, baby," he said quietly. "And I apologize. But I can make it up to you, Jewelz. *Let* me make it up to you. Let me be that dude you need me to be. That dude you used to share your dreams with in the back of the closet and way up under the bed. That dude you know you can trust and lean on. I swear to God I'll never let you down again. I swear on my *mother*. On *our* mother. I'm gonna make sure you dream forever baby. And that's word."

Jewelz pulled away from him. She stared down at the ground as the tears fell from her eyes. So much had happened between them. There was so much fuckin shit. So much pain, so much anger… and there was still so much…love.

Jewelz was caught up in her feelings. She had been loving on this nigga since before she could spell her own damn name. Lil Slick was the only man she had ever truly cared about. He was the only man her tender heart had ever ached for. But still. He had done her wrong and the pain… Oh, the mothafucking *pain!*

Slick reached out and pulled her close again, and this time she pressed her face to his chest and allowed herself to inhale his familiar scent. He smelled just like a Thunder Cats cartoon and those buttery grits his mother used to cook in the projects on Saturday mornings.

Slick lifted her chin with his finger and Jewelz sighed as she stared up at him. That cut on his cheek was now just a faded memory. His warm lips found hers and he kissed her with the need of a hungry man. His tongue was strong and probing. It found her need and ignited it into a raging flame.

"I love you, Jewelz," Slick murmured. "I been loving you ever since I was a tyke, girl. And I'ma *always* love you. I promise you that won't nothing in the world ever come between us again. You got my whole heart, baby. Believe that.

My whole fuckin heart."

Jewelz didn't answer. Instead, she pulled away from him again and looked out at the waves as they lapped back and forth against the pier. This world was stranger than a muthafucka, she thought as she followed the path of the frothy water with her eyes. It was crazy how the same water that washed out to sea was the same damn water that eventually came right back home to kiss the shores.

And what was even crazier was how nobody had to tell that water to come back home. It came home because it was supposed to. Because it was *meant* to.

"Let me ask you something," she gazed at Slick with a burning look and said, "Did you really kill that baby who was in the car with Hammerhead Goody that night?"

Slick stared at her with something unreadable in his eyes. And then he finally opened his mouth and said quietly, "No. I didn't. Did you smoke Handgun Goody's mother that night?"

Jewelz smirked. "I already told you. I gave that old lady exactly what she deserved."

"Yeah? And what was that?"

"A hug. I gave her a hug."

Ignoring Slick's look of surprise, Jewelz walked over to his whip and peered into the open window of the backseat. The gorgeous little girl with the hazel eyes sat there playing with a chocolate-skinned doll baby who had a huge head and two long thick braids.

Jewelz smiled.

"Hi, Ma-Ma. You're the pretty little angel who gave me that beautiful flower yesterday, right?"

The child nodded and grinned, and the distinctive features staring back at Jewelz hit her like a brick.

Suddenly it felt like a butcher knife was twisting in her gut. She glanced over at Slick, then looked back down at the little girl. Those hazel eyes on her were a cold reminder of all the shit that had gone bad between them. They were a reminder of all the pain, all the betrayal, all the heartache, and all the grief. Those eyes were a reminder of the love that had been stolen from her, and of every single good thing in life that she had missed out on.

But there was such brightness in those eyes. Such pure damn innocence that Jewelz found herself smiling and she couldn't tear her gaze away. Maybe she could dream again. Maybe she didn't have to miss out on anything after all. Maybe everything that she had ever wanted, she could still have it. Hell, it was all right here. Waiting just for her.

Jewelz grinned down at the little girl and leaned in closer to the window.

"Do you like the ocean?"

The child nodded again and suddenly the color of her eyes seemed so sweet and beautiful.

"You wanna walk down to the shore with me and put your feet in some of those pretty white waves?"

The little girl gave her another shy nod and Jewelz opened the car door and unbuckled her from the car seat.

"I like your cute purple dress," Jewelz complimented her as she held out her hand and helped the little girl get outta the car. She reached out and touched the pink and purple bows that held the child's curly ponytails in place.

"What's your name, Ma-Ma?" Jewelz asked softly as the two of them walked past Slick holding hands and swinging their arms back and forth.

The child with the pretty eyes grinned real wide as she looked up at her. "My name is Diamond Ruby Emerald Amethyst Moonstone Sapphire Williams," the little girl said proudly. "But my Daddy calls me Jewelz."

Diamond

Ruby

Emerald

Amethyst

Moonstone

Sapphire

ALWAYS Follow Your DREAMS!

One Love, Noire & Reem Raw

THE END

#BookBinge #ESOM

Ready for another dope Noire serial novel?

Go to Amazon and Check out

G-Spot 2: The Seven Deadly Sins

A Serial Novel Told in 7 Parts

Pride

Betrayal

Greed

Envy

Lust

Trickery

Revenge

Revenge: The Alternate Ending

www.ingramcontent.com/pod-product-compliance
Lightning Source LLC
Chambersburg PA
CBHW081138020726
47504CB00009B/1912
* 9 7 8 0 9 8 3 0 9 3 6 9 5 *